DESULTAMAR

Thomas Snook

DESULTAMAR

RED RABBIT RISES
PUBLISHING

A publication of Red Rabbit Rises Publishing
Inverness, Scotland, United Kingdom

First published in Great Britain in 2022
by Red Rabbit Rises.

Printed and bound by IngramSpark
ISBN: 978-1-913667-04-7

"Desultamar" available in a range of formats. For this
and other titles, please visit www.redrabbitrises.com

RED RABBIT RISES
PUBLISHING

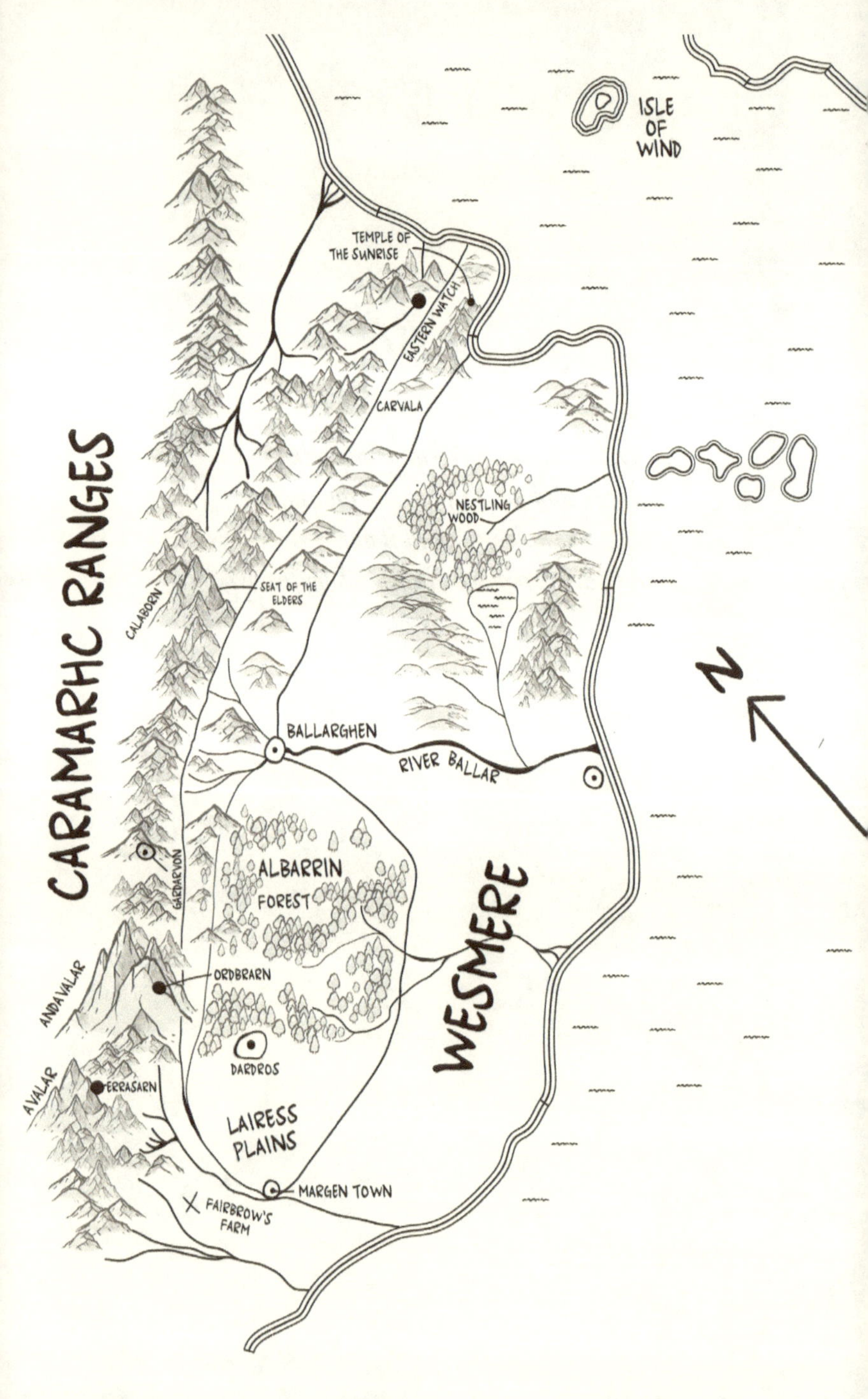

CARAMARHC RANGES
ISLE OF WIND
TEMPLE OF THE SUNRISE
EASTERN WATCH
CARVALA
NESTLING WOOD
CALABORN
SEAT OF THE ELDERS
BALLARGHEN
RIVER BALLAR
GARDARVON
ALBARRIN FOREST
WESMERE
ANDAVALAR
ORDBRARN
AVALAR
ERRASARN
DARDROS
LAIRESS PLAINS
MARGEN TOWN
FAIRBROW'S FARM
N

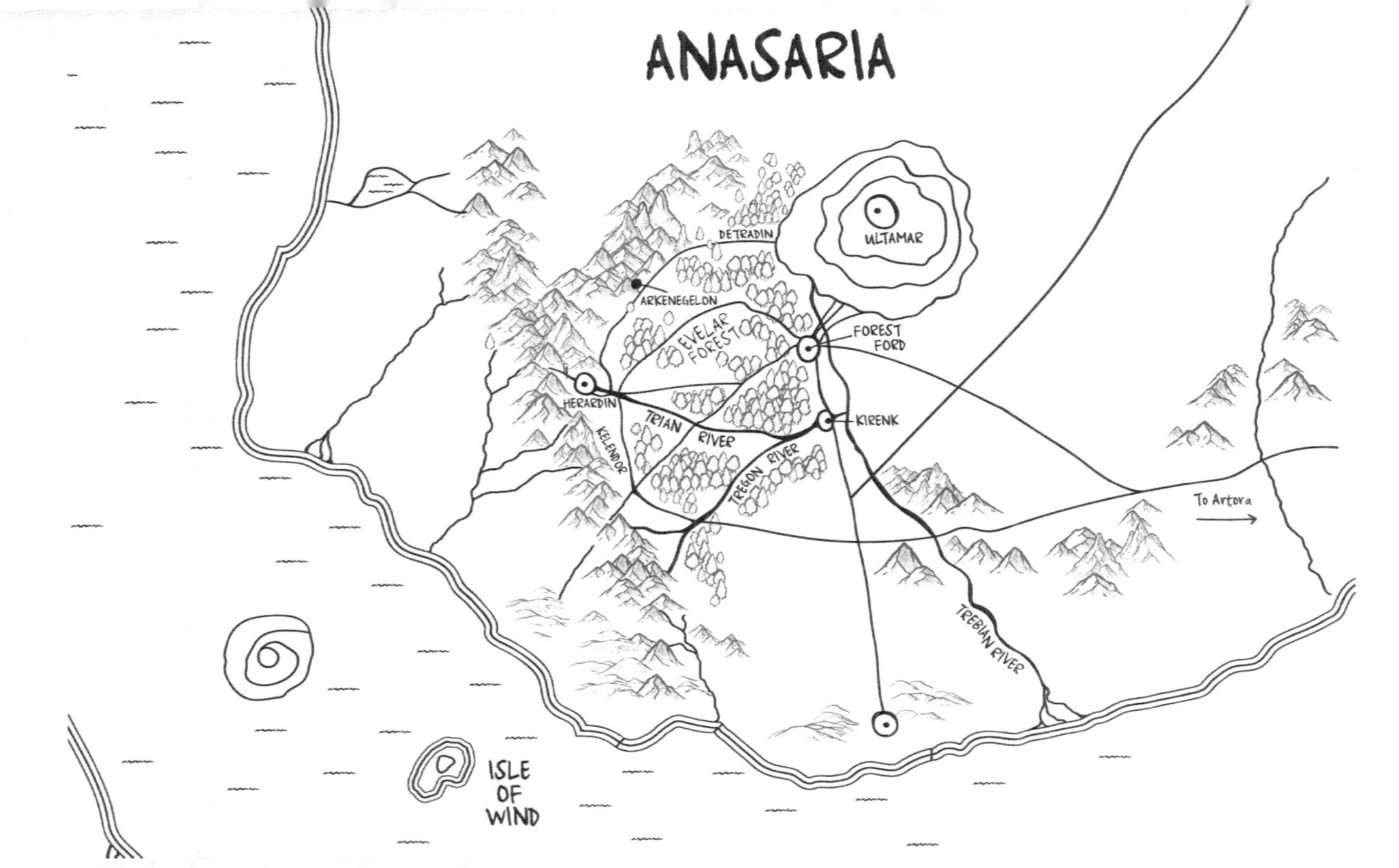

ANASARIA
ULTAMAR
DETRADIN
ARKENEGELON
EVELAR FOREST
FOREST FORD
HERARDIN
KIRENK
KELENDOR
TRIAN RIVER
TREGON RIVER
TREBIAN RIVER
To Artova
ISLE OF WIND

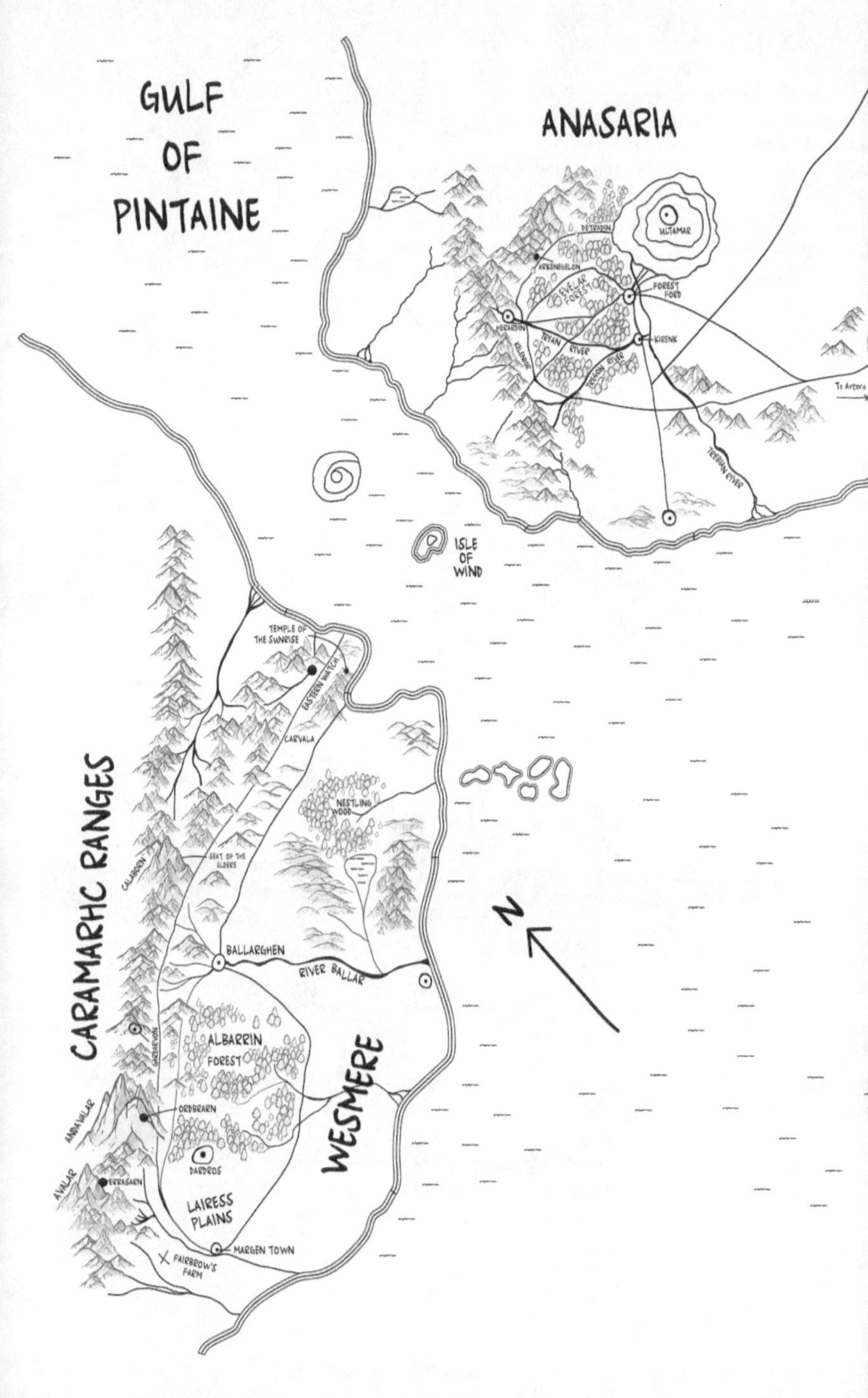

GULF OF PINTAINE
ANASARIA
ULTAMAR
DETRADIN
ARKENBELON
EVELAR FOREST
FOREST FORD
HERARDIN
KELENSIS
TRIAN RIVER
KIRENK
TEESIAN RIVER
TEESIAN RIVER
To Artoria
ISLE OF WIND
TEMPLE OF THE SUNRISE
EASTERN WATCH
CARVALA
CARAMARHC RANGES
NESTLING WOOD
SEAT OF THE ELDERS
CALARDON
BALLARGHEN
RIVER BALLAR
WESMERE
ALBARRIN FOREST
GRENAVON
ORDBRARN
ANDAVALAR
DARDROS
AVALAR
ERRASAEN
LAIRESS PLAINS
MARGEN TOWN
FAIRBROW'S FARM
N

CHAPTER ONE

King Darion's Stone

A familiar figure on horseback crested the hill ahead of them silhouetted against the light of the setting sun. Rowan and Hyrn broke into a run. A flock of frightened birds clambered noisily from the road's edge and settled in a nearby stand of trees. The Rider sat silently watching as the two brothers approached. They stopped before reaching him, puffing and panting.

"It's good to see you, Careil," said Rowan breathlessly.

"Good evening, my friends," replied the Rider.

"We have strange news," said Hyrn. His breath was catching in his throat as he spoke.

Careil read anxiety in their faces as the boys trudged up the last of the hill and stopped next to the large horse. Behind his horse were tethered two smaller horses.

"Be that as it may," he said, "you are late, and your parents are worried. Your tale can wait until you are home and fed. You shall ride. I guessed you'd be tired."

He laughed. "But Erras is impatient with having to lead your horses. You may have to try and keep up."

Careil patted the horse's neck and Erras snorted softly. Rowan walked to one of the other horses, Blade, and hooking his bag on the saddle, climbed up. Hyrn stood there facing the fading shape of the mountains with a faraway look in his eyes. He suddenly looked up at Careil and smiled.

"Yes, let's hurry. I'm starving," he said.

Once Hyrn had mounted, Careil turned Erras back the way they had come. He muttered a few quiet words and Erras lifted his head and the great warhorse broke into a run. The two boys followed quickly behind. As the light disappeared and darkness fell, they rode off westward leaving the stillness of the night behind.

"We had travelled further than ever before, into parts of the mountains we had never seen." The firelight caught Rowan's face as he spoke, leaving his features in shadow.

They had waited until after dinner and now Rowan began to tell their story. Hyrn, Careil, and the boys' parents, Meralie and Baraman, had got themselves comfortable. They sat around the fire listening, warming themselves, as the wind began to become restless, and grow stronger, blowing down from the slopes of the mountains to the north.

Rowan continued, and the events of the day unfolded.

The two boys had been walking uphill through a heavily wooded area for some time, when they came to the end of a rise and found themselves overlooking a valley. The valley was strange. Steep hillsides disappeared into a sea of mist stretching across to the ridge on the other side and along the valley, until it stopped where the sides of the valley almost met. To the left of the valley the mass of Mount Andavalar rose in a succession of sheer ridges. To the right sat the smaller peak of Mount Avalar. The bottom of the valley was completely obscured by the mist. The woods from which they had emerged thinned out, leaving the odd tree scattered down the hillside below them. What lay beneath the mist was a mystery, and Hyrn was somewhat reluctant when Rowan suggested that they go down and explore.

"What if we can't find our way out again?" Hyrn said, worriedly.

"Don't worry," said Rowan as encouragingly as possible, "one end of the valley lies to the west and one to the east, so we can get our bearings from the sun."

"There doesn't seem to be any sun down there," said Hyrn.

Hyrn finally agreed, and they carefully made their way down towards the veil of mist, silent except for the labouring of their breath.

The slope was sparsely vegetated at first, but as they made their way down, they moved amongst ferns that became gradually thicker. The border of the mist was not as abrupt as it had appeared from the top of the ridge. It began light at first, and grew gradually heavier and became a thick fog, until they could see only a few yards in front of them. The ferns gave way to brambles, which slowed their downward progress, and they were repeatedly unable to pick their way amongst them and had to move along the hillside until they found another way through. Occasionally they were even forced to go back and find another path.

"It's going to be hard to find our way back through these," said Hyrn suddenly, as if he had wanted to speak for a long time and had only just found the courage.

"Stop worrying will you," said Rowan and they fell into silence again.

It wasn't long before the ground began to level out and they heard the sound of running water. They began to make their way towards it. As they did so, the brambles and ferns disappeared almost completely. The sound grew louder as they went, and shortly they came upon its source. There before them, flowing swiftly into the fog, was a river. The ground at its banks was covered only with grass and a few small shrubs, as if all the natural vegetation had been cleared and a long-neglected lawn planted.

The river ran westward, and almost impulsively Rowan and Hyrn started walking upstream, the fog opening before them and closing as quickly behind.

"Look!" said Hyrn suddenly.

Rowan looked to where Hyrn pointed ahead of them. It was a stone bridge. As they approached, they could see that it was skilfully constructed. Moss now grew on the almost smooth stonework, and weeds sprouted from the cracks between the stones. There was an iron gate at the entrance to the bridge, slightly ajar and covered in rust. The gate was supported by two square stone columns. As the two boys drew closer, they could see that the columns were both carven with the same image, two mountain peaks one on the right large and the one on the left smaller and between them an oval shape with a star.

"What does it mean?" asked Hyrn, a look of awe on his face.

"The two peaks are the mountains between which this valley lies, I suppose," began Rowan. "The larger, you know, Andavalar, to the north-west, and the smaller to the south-west is Mount Avalar," he paused, "and it looks like an egg between them with a star shining through it. I wonder what it means."

"I wonder," said Hyrn, as if he were about to repeat Rowan's words, "who built it and..." he hesitated, "and if they still live around here?"

"From the look of these weeds, and the rust on this gate, I doubt that anyone has been here for ages," said Rowan.

The opposite bank was not visible through the mist.

Letting his curiosity get the better of him, Rowan added, "Come on let's see what's on the other side."

It seemed Hyrn was curious as well, and he said almost boldly, "Yes let's."

Rowan went through the gates first. They were open just widely enough for them to walk through, but if open fully, they would have allowed five horses abreast. Hyrn followed closely behind Rowan as they traversed the bridge, the sound of their footsteps on the stone muffled by its mossy covering. As they crossed the last of the large flagstones that paved the bridge, they saw that a stone roadway led away before them and then met another wider one. The roadway was overgrown through years of disuse. Grass encroached along its edges.

When they came to where the ways met, they saw that large moss-covered statues stood along what appeared to be a main thoroughfare. The statues depicted regal looking men crowned and richly dressed, green with moss and stained from the moisture over the years. Rowan and Hyrn stood silently at the junction looking about them, when suddenly, through the mist, where the road led eastwards, there was a flash and then an eerie glow. The light was welcome in the gloom and it spread a warmth as if it was beckoning to them. They moved towards the light, silent, not thinking, just curious as to what was drawing them. Then, as quickly as it had appeared, it was extinguished. They continued in the direction that the light had been, as if it was still drawing them. Rowan was slightly ahead of Hyrn when suddenly he froze.

A face appeared out of the mist, and eyes of great age held him. As Hyrn reached where Rowan had stopped, he gripped Rowan's arm in shock, and before the impulse to turn and run overcame him, the figure spoke.

"Greetings, little friends. I am Devarnia."

A woman stood before them clothed in a grey robe.

She appeared old though an air of youthful vitality surrounded her. A feeling of goodness flowed from her. Her voice was high and lilting, but solemn.

She spoke again. "Welcome to the mountain kingdom of Errasarn, the realm of King Darion of old. Come, we have much to discuss."

With that, she smiled, turned and headed up the roadway into the mist.

Rowan paused and cleared his throat, pleased with the effect his story was having on the others. The wind had become fierce, howling through the trees around the farmhouse. A storm was brewing over the mountains. The deep rumbling of thunder could be heard, and flashes of lightning lit up the sky. Rowan looked about at the faces, making sure they were sufficiently in suspense, and then continued, and the five drifted back into the misty valley.

Rowan and Hyrn hesitated, exchanging glances. Then, in silent agreement, they hurried after the woman. They walked a few paces behind her as she followed the roadway along its unerring course. Without realising it at first, their attention concentrated on the figure in front, walls loomed up on either side sloping upwards until they were higher than the three figure's heads. The height of the walls increased until they levelled off and each met a pillar. An arch that formed the entrance to a dark tunnel joined the pillars. As they entered the tunnel, Rowan and Hyrn saw that it ended in a gloom of light not too far ahead. It was dank inside the tunnel and when they broke out into the direct light at the other end, it felt good to breathe clean air again.

They had emerged into a courtyard, its stonework overgrown. A fountain stood in the middle, silent, a large tree at each corner. The ground around was thick with mulch from years of unswept leaves. Columns stood in two rows down the sides of the courtyard, hiding shadowed verandas behind a tangle of vines. At the far end they could see, through statues and overgrown shrubberies and up a few broad steps, a shadowed portico, and beyond a pair of large wooden doors, the entrance to the heart of the castle.

The woman led them across to the left side of the courtyard and between two columns. They came into a dark veranda. A row of stone benches and tables stretched into the gloom. They crossed the veranda and passed under an arch leading into the north wing of the castle.

They walked a short way down a dark, dusty corridor before the woman stopped at a wooden door on the left. From beneath her robe, she produced a large ornate key, which she fitted in the lock. The key turned easily and with a push, the door creaked open.

The room they entered was dark and cold. The sound of running water came from one side. The woman reached into her robes again and suddenly the room was bathed in light. The same warm glow that had led them to the woman, emanated from a smooth Stone about the size and shape of a goose egg.

The room was clean and sparsely furnished; a small bed to one side, a table and two benches in the middle and, against the wall, a basin with water flowing from the mouth of a stone lion. The woman beckoned for them to sit down on one of the benches at the stone table. They did so, and she sat on the other across from them. She placed the Stone in a small hollow in the centre of the table. The three of them sat there in silence, their faces glowing in the strange light. Rowan and Hyrn sat in wonder. The woman stared into the Stone as if drinking from it with her eyes, then looked up at them and began to speak.

"Before you sits one of the great wonders of our world, Ilah, one of the Twin Stones of Angil. Long has it been lost. Much sorrow has been caused by that loss. Here, in this valley, has it lain hidden until now. One of creation's great gifts, formed far off, high in the Angilanian Mountains, with its twin Ivah. They were given to King Eriallen of Anasaria, a land far to the east, to help stop the spread of evil throughout the lands.

"But how did it get here?" Rowan's voice sounded small in the dimness of the room.

"It was brought here by Prince Darion of Anasaria," said Devarnia. "He, like Ilah, was a twin, younger than his brother by a few minutes and therefore, his brother, Keridan, was heir to the throne. Darion was jealous of his brother's birthright. So, he stole one of the Stones of Angil from the Tower of the Stones, high in the fortress of Abessair, and taking those loyal to him he fled to become a king in his own right. He disappeared from Anasaria. Much sorrow followed and after ten generations the line of King Abess declined and Anasaria fell into evil. Long have I sought Ilah, and I grow tired, my young friends. I have waited for you. For it is up to you to return Ilah and Ivah to Abessair and free Anasaria.

Rowan half rose as if to protest but Hyrn reached out and grabbed his arm.

"Why us?" he said to the woman. "And how did you know we would come here?"

The woman smiled. "There is much I know and much I can only guess, but Ilah has been my purpose now for over a hundred years. It has been foretold that the Stones would be reunited and that two would come that would carry the light. To them hope would be entrusted. I cannot take it," she continued. "It is not mine to carry and my time on this world is given to another duty. You are the ones that have been given this task."

Rowan and Hyrn looked at each other sceptically. Hyrn shrugged. They both looked at Devarnia.

"You still haven't told us how Ilah got here," said Rowan.

"There is much I still have to tell you. I suppose I can begin there. Listen well," she said, "for when you leave here you must remember. It is important.

It took a long time to uncover the trail of Prince Darion, for he was long gone before the Keepers became aware that Ilah had been—"

"Who are the Keepers?" Hyrn asked

"Me and my kind," said Devarnia. "We are here to balance the powers of good and evil, to preserve this world by strengthening the power of good. Too much has turned to evil.

I was appointed by my fellow Keepers to find Ilah and help reunite the Twin Stones so that they could be returned. It was an important task and I have devoted all my worldly energies to it."

The Keeper studied the two boys before her, their faces glowing in the light of the Stone, and then continued. "Darion had fled to the west, for to go east or south was to go into evil and to go north was to head towards the Power in the East, and the finders of the Stones, the Angilanians. Therefore, the west was the only way open to him. He passed through the Evelar Forest, crossed the mountains, and came into the coastal regions of Anasaria. He then realised that he must build ships to cross the sea and escape. He travelled to the forested hills that nestled beneath the end of the Anasarian Mountains, overlooking the sea. As he crossed the hills and neared the coast, he came upon an evil army. They were Drargs from the mountains and they were preparing an assault on a large gateway that led beneath the sea; The Realm of the Underdwellers.

Darion, seeing the danger at hand, marshalled his men. The troops of his household were for the most part skilled warriors, having trained with the Abessairian army. They attacked the Drargs before they knew they were upon them, and the Underdwellers seeing that the Drargs were under attack released their army upon them. The Drargs were quickly defeated and on the battlefield, Prince Darion met the king of the Underdwellers, King Mergam. King Mergam was so grateful for the aid in releasing the gates of his kingdom that he allowed Darion and his party to travel across the sea through his realm. And so it was, that Darion came into Wesmere through the West Door. He then travelled along the coast and came through the pass between the end of the Caramarhc and the Spire. He travelled along the length of the Caramarhc Ranges until he saw the two peaks and the valley between and decided to set up his kingdom. The kingdom lasted for four hundred years and then died out. Why? I do not know. I must tell you, Darion had been gone for over three hundred years before we Keepers became aware. We thought this part of the world safe with the Twin Stones at Abessair. The war in the east takes up much of our time."

"Where is the other Stone?" Hyrn asked, his face filled with both fear and wonderment.

"The last king of Anasaria, Bharain, when he was exiled by the Seven Dark Lords, took the Stone with him," replied Devarnia. "In his wisdom he left it in safe keeping with the King of the Underdwellers. I have seen it and it cries with loss for its twin. King Bharain is known to have entered Wesmere, but he disappeared. I have found no trace of him. However, on finding Ilah I have used its power of seeking. The Sword of Acclimoss, King Bharain's sword, lies at Gardarvon, high in the mountains. It is here that you must go first. For I believe it is here you will find the clue to the fate of Bharain.

Rowan, still disbelieving it all, spoke up. "Why did you not use the other Stone to find this sword or even to find this Stone?"

The Keeper smiled and replied, "Ivah's powers are different to Ilah's. Ilah means 'seeker' and Ivah means 'see-er'. Ivah cannot be used to find things that are lost, only to foresee the future. It was Ivah that told me of you, that you were our hope and I can see now that it is true. If only Darion had taken Ivah, Ilah could have been used to bring the Stones together. This was either fate, or else Darion knew that Ilah could be used to find him. Besides, Rowan, Ilah was hidden here in darkness. No Stone would have been able to uncover her without light." She looked at Rowan. "I can see that you still need convincing. Hyrn, look into the Stone and call out 'Ivah'."

Hyrn looked at her and she smiled reassuringly and nodded. Hyrn did as she said, staring into the Stone, and softly, he called, "Ivah. Ivah."

The Stone in front of them began to glow and as Hyrn stared, he began to see pictures, faint at first and then becoming clearer. There was a battle raging although no fighting could be seen. People were rushing past in battle dress.

Two men stopped and one said, "The Stone of Angil is glowing. Maybe it is the miracle for which we have waited." He approached the Stone and looked into it. "Whoever you are that contacts Ivah, help us. We are under attack again. I don't know how long we can hold out. Days? Weeks? Months? The Lords of Ultamar send fresh troops every day. The Underrealm cannot fall. Please help us!"

Hyrn looked up from the Stone bewildered and Ilah went dark again. "That was incredible." He paused, lost for words. "I would never have imagined that something like that was possible. It is hard to believe, but what you say must somehow be true. We…" He looked at Rowan who nodded. "We will help if we can."

"The situation grows desperate," said Devarnia. "The Underdwellers are under attack. If the Underrealm falls to Ultamar, the way will be open to the invasion of Wesmere and Ivah will fall to the Dark Lords. You must begin as soon as possible. There is no time to lose."

The Keeper looked at the two boys. She thought how young and unprepared they were. Her ancient heart ached for them, but the prophecy was clear.

"But where shall we go?" asked Hyrn.

Devarnia paused as if deep in thought and then shook herself from her reverie.

"Gardarvon is your first goal," she said. "You must find the Sword of Acclimoss. Look for any assistance along the way. Come, we can talk further while I show you the way out of this valley and back to familiar paths."

With that, the Keeper rose to her feet and, holding out the softly glowing Stone before her, led Rowan and Hyrn out of the room, leaving it cold and dusty behind them.

CHAPTER TWO

The Journey Begins

The morning dawned wet and cloudy, yet Hyrn saw that it held the promise of fine weather. He sat on a wooden stool at the foot of his bed looking out of the window towards the mountains. He had not slept well. The excitement over what had finally been decided was too much for him. They had all stayed up for hours discussing the significance of what Devarnia had told him and Rowan, and although doubts and anxieties had been aired, it was agreed by all that the two of them must start out at once. Careil was to accompany them to the city of Ballarghen, by way of Gardarvon, and there accept the King's Council's decision on the next course of action. Meralie and Baraman would remain to keep the farm running with help from their neighbours. Hyrn thought again about this and it brought a lump to his throat. He had thought that his mother and father would be coming along, and he had voiced that wish, but the practical argument of the need to keep the farm running had won out.

Well, at least they had Careil...and the Stone. He picked it up from where he had placed it on the little table next to him, still wrapped in the piece of velvety cloth. He unwrapped it and looked at it. It was dull grey and felt cold and smooth in his hands. He still found it hard to believe that if he called it by name it would begin to glow and would speak to him. He considered doing just that but remembered Dervarnia's words before they parted, when she had handed the Stone to him to carry.

"Do not treat Ilah foolishly. It has great power and must be used with care and purpose."

She had then told them to stay true to their hearts and reminded them to take comfort in the help of others along the way. A noise from behind him startled him from his thoughts. Rowan was stretching in his bed against the opposite wall. He looked at Hyrn, and Hyrn looked guiltily down at the Stone in his hands.

"Morning Hyrn," said Rowan.

"Morning Row," said Hyrn softly, not looking at him.

He picked up the piece of cloth and carefully wrapped the Stone in it. Rowan continued looking at him.

"I see you can't help being curious," he said.

"I was just—" began Hyrn.

Rowan laughed. "It's alright little brother. I understand." He pulled himself into a sitting position. "I think we'd best start getting organised. There's a lot to do."

"Yes" said Hyrn, placing the wrapped Stone back on the table. "I wonder if the others are up."

Baraman and Meralie had only just risen when Hyrn went out into the kitchen. They both ambled about the room still shaking off sleep, preparing breakfast.

"Morning, son," said Baraman. "Finally up, eh?"

"I've been up for ages," replied Hyrn with feigned indignation. "I didn't sleep very well. I was thinking about… well… what we have to do."

"Don't worry about it Hyrn," said Meralie. "You'll have the best advisers in Wesmere to take over when you reach Ballarghen. They'll know what to do."

"I hope so," said Hyrn. "It may not be that easy."

"Well for the time being we'd best concentrate on getting you all ready," put in Baraman, "and that starts with a good breakfast," he added smiling.

"Yes," said Hyrn. "I couldn't agree more."

Baraman turned and winked to his wife and she smiled in return, but a trace of a frown briefly crossed her face.

Outside, Careil was feeding and watering his horse in preparation for the journey. Hyrn went and stood in the doorway that looked onto the yard. He watched the easy way that Cariel handled his horse Erras. The horse responded to his unspoken commands, moving back and forth, as Careil attended to him. Careil left Erras to his breakfast and walked towards the house. As he did, he saw Hyrn.

"Why so gloomy?" he asked, taking note of Hyrn's pensive expression.

"I'm alright," Hyrn replied. "…it's just that it's all a bit sudden. I mean we don't know what we are getting into. Yesterday it was all exciting, like a story, but now we have to leave everything behind. I guess it's all a bit scary."

Careil smiled. "No one was prepared for this. We were all taken by surprise, but this task has been given to you and Rowan. You just have to give it your best, and I will be there to help you in whatever way I can. I know you would have liked your parents to come with us, but they must stay here and keep the farm running. You wouldn't want to come back to a rundown farm, would you?"

"I suppose not," replied Hyrn. "It's just that I've never been away from home for very long before."

"You'll be alright," said Careil reassuringly. "It will all be over before you know it and you'll be back home and telling your parents all about your adventures."

He placed his hand on Hyrn's shoulder and steered him back into the kitchen.

"Come on, let's get some breakfast," he said cheerily. "I think we're going to need it."

"Good idea," said Hyrn, though his face still bore a worried expression.

After breakfast, the preparation for the journey began. Packs were made up to carry Rowan and Hyrn's equipment and provisions. Careil already had his travelling pack but gratefully accepted food for the journey. Rowan and Hyrn also packed ample food to last them until they reached Ballarghen. Their packs were put on the two horses Blade and Marly. They were farm horses, but had become the two boy's own horses. The two horses knew that they were destined for a journey. They were skittish in anticipation, making the job of loading them and putting on their gear just that bit more difficult.

The morning was wearing on by the time the three were finished packing and had loaded their gear onto the horses. The day had become fine and sunny, although clouds still congregated around the peaks of the Caramarhc. Hyrn looked up at the familiar view. He knew that the mountains would not be far away on the journey east to Ballarghen but the aspect would change as they left the farm behind. He walked a short way across the near field towards the mountains. He stopped still, looking at the heights and turning his thoughts over in his head. He put his hand in his pocket and felt the Stone where he had stowed it inside his jacket. It felt strangely warm, even through the tough fabric. Hyrn undid the buttons of the jacket and slowly took the Stone out, still wrapped in the cloth. He unwrapped the Stone. As he did, light burst from it.

"What is your need, Child of Light?" said a voice.

Hyrn looked about him startled and then back at the Stone. Ilah had spoken to him. "You are troubled," Ilah's voice spilled again from the heart of the Stone. Its tone was reassuring, and it filled Hyrn with wonder.

"I am worried Ilah, worried that I will never see this farm again," Hyrn's voice was trembling as he spoke.

"You worry needlessly, Hyrn. All that is dear to you will remain close to your heart, you will find that time, and distance, will not make you forget your home and your family. Indeed, in times of need, that memory will be a light in the darkness. You will be reunited with those you love, perhaps when least expected. Go now Hyrn, and even though you look forward, let what you leave behind make your road easier."

Hyrn started to reply, but as quickly as the light had erupted from the Stone, it was extinguished. Hyrn smiled and put Ilah carefully back inside his jacket. He turned his back on the mountains and walked back to the farmhouse.

As he turned the corner, he saw everyone gathered in the yard. They turned to look at him.

"We thought you'd changed your mind and run off," said Rowan.

"No," said Hyrn. "I'm ready to go." He walked up to his mother and hugged her.

"Farewell, Ma. Take care," he said.

"I will Hyrn," said Meralie, kissing his forehead, "if you do the same."

"Yes, I will," he promised.

Baraman came up and hugged Hyrn.

"All the best son," he said, and smiled, "and try to keep out of mischief."

Rowan came up and hugged his mother and father. "We'll be alright, and I'll keep an eye on Hyrn."

Hyrn started to protest but was cut short by Careil. "Come on, we better make a start before we lose any more of the day."

Careil shook Baraman's hand, and then Meralie's, and said, "I will send word of our progress with other Riders that may venture this way. Don't worry about these two, I am sure they will be fine, and I think they will learn a lot from this experience."

"Yes, I'm sure you're right," said Baraman. "Farewell for now, Careil."

The three of them mounted their horses and with shouts of farewell rode through the yard and down to the gate. Hyrn looked back to the diminishing shape of his parents and waved. The pair waved back and then walked back inside. The three went out through the gate and turned northward up the track to the main road that linked the Lairess Plains with Ballarghen, the royal seat of the Kingdom of Wesmere.

The first day's journey was a pleasant one. The three had ridden along the main road north towards the main mass of the mountains. The road then swung around to the northeast and entered a wide valley between the mountains on the north and a smaller mass to the south. Alongside the road ran a small river, the Caldara, which flowed back towards the Lairess Plains, the same river that ran through Margen Town, the town that serviced the Lairess. It flowed down to meet the Lairess River and then down to the sea. The Caldara had formed the valley floor over countless years and had created a flat area over which the riders now travelled. Along the way, they passed through scattered small settlements. The few that saw them as they rode through, recognised the apparel of the King's Rider and waved or called out in greeting.

By late afternoon, the southern ridge of the hills began to fall away, and the company could see that they had gradually started to climb into the mountains. They came to a point where the river they had been following turned away from the road and they could see further up where it passed through a smaller, steeper valley that led up to its headwaters in the heights of the Caramarhc. To their left, the valley passed between the southern flank of the looming Mount Andavalar and a smaller peak to the west.

The sun was getting lower and their shadows were starting to lengthen in front of as they climbed higher up the southern feet of Mount Andavalar. The hills were now behind them, leaving the road higher above on the flanks of the mountains. Across the plain to the east, they could see what appeared to be a circular walled city. Even from this distance they could see that it was in ruins.

"What's that down there Careil?" asked Rowan.

"You surprise me Rowan," replied Careil. "Don't you remember your history? That is Dardros, the Fortress of Challenge.

"The fortress of the traitor, Ruglan," said Hyrn. "Didn't he fight against King Tridan?"

"He did," said Careil. "But did you also know that he was his brother?"

"His brother!" exclaimed Hyrn. "Why would he fight his brother?"

"I could think of a few good reasons," laughed Rowan.

Hyrn glared at him. Rowan glared back, and retorted, "Well, at least I knew he was his brother."

"Come," said Careil. "We'll make camp for the night, and after we've eaten, I'll tell you the story of what became known as the Battle of the Princes."

They were wrapped in their blankets. The fire spread a circle of light that lit their faces and held back the dark of the night. They had camped amongst tall fir trees not far from one of the small streams that fed the Caldara. Above them, through the haze of smoke, a multitude of stars lay scattered across the sky. Occasionally a wisp of cloud extinguished a patch of stars, but they burst back into life as it passed. They had eaten well on the food provided by the farm for the first part of their journey.

Careil observed Hyrn and Rowan for a while, watched them settle into their sleeping gear. They argued idly with each other as they did so, but eventually they settled down and looked to him expectantly. The nearby stream babbled in the darkness. He collected his thoughts and then began.

"Well," he said. "It was like this. A long time ago, long before the wild, dangerous days preceding the Battle of Everlasting Peace, there reigned a powerful king in Wesmere. He was King Avarrin. He was wise, and kind, and the land flourished. He had reigned for almost fifty years before his wife Queen Halana finally gave birth to a child, a son. All of Wesmere rejoiced at the news of the birth of an heir to the throne…"

And Careil told of how Avarrin loved his son, Ruglan, and even when another son, Tridan, was born he still favoured Ruglan. As the two boys grew, Ruglan became wilful and proud, whilst Tridan remained humble and caring. As the brothers became men, Ruglan began to covet his father's kingship. As he schemed against his father, Avarrin became aware that his son sought to usurp him, and he named Tridan his heir. Ruglan fled to the forest of Albarrin and built a fortress where he dwelt, seemingly in peace, but he was gathering an army. When Avarrin died, and Tridan became King, Ruglan unleashed his forces and the two brothers went to war. Tridan, though, was just and wise, as a king should be, and the people of Wesmere rallied to him. The challenge of Ruglan was put down, but Ruglan escaped and spent the rest of his days hidden in the Albarrin Forest with the broken and desperate remains of his army."

"Some say that they still haunt the forest to this day," finished Careil.

Rowan and Hyrn, despite their tiredness, had listened intently to the story.

"Big brothers are nothing but trouble," said Hyrn sleepily.

"But surely Ruglan should have still been King," said Rowan. "Tridan wasn't…"

Careil spoke calmly. "The lesson is, that being a king is about being worthy. Ruglan may have become King, but his pride and arrogance would have made him less a leader, and more a tyrant. It is an important lesson. A leader is followed, whereas a tyrant is resented and feared.

Now it is time for sleep."

And with that Careil nestled into his sleeping gear. In the light of the glowing embers of the fire, and with the faint smoke trailing up into the starlit, moonless sky, he watched as Hyrn and Rowan slowly gave up awareness for sleep, and he fell asleep himself.

"The sun's late," Hyrn said, yawning.

"It's not late, sleepy-head," said Careil as he toiled over the fire preparing breakfast. "There are storms out to the east. The sun has only just risen above the clouds. The storms are heading north so we should have a nice clear day."

"Oh," said Hyrn, and looking around added, "Where's Rowan?"

"He's gone down to the stream to wash himself before breakfast," replied Careil. "It might be an idea if you joined him."

"Alright," said Hyrn.

He wandered off in the direction of the nearby stream. He found Rowan kneeling by the stream, apparently drying his hair.

"Is the water cold?" he asked Rowan.

Rowan turned to him, raising his finger to his mouth in a silencing gesture. "Shhh!" he hissed.

Hyrn crouched down next to him and whispered, "What is it?"

"I don't know," Rowan whispered back. "I thought I saw something over on the other side of the stream."

He pointed to an area on the opposite bank where trees and bushes overhung the water.

"What sort of something?" said Hyrn softly, eyes wide.

"Well...," said Rowan, "...like...eyes in the bushes."

"Eyes?" began Hyrn, "but—"

Just then, he spied movement across the stream. The bushes trembled and for a fleeting moment, he saw a weathered face emerge and then disappear. He turned to Rowan mouth agape.

"See?" whispered Rowan. "I told you."

Slowly, and almost imperceptibly, a murmuring grew around them. The boys looked about trying to locate the source of the sound. All of a sudden, dropping from trees and stepping from behind bushes, figures clad in dappled brown appeared, all looking at them intently. Before they had a chance to react, one of the people came closer to them.

"Who are you?" he said in a deep, strong voice.

"We're friends," said Rowan, trying to sound reassuring.

"You are plains people, but you have the mountains in your eyes," said the man. "It is well. We have been at peace for centuries and we wish you well. Where are you headed, friends?"

"Well..." Rowan's voice wavered and then became steady. "We go to Gardarvon." Hyrn gasped.

Rowan turned to him. "What's wrong?"

Hyrn's face reddened. "We're not supposed to say that."

"Don't be silly," said Rowan. "It isn't a secret. It's the truth."

"But.., but...," said Hyrn.

"Enough of this!" said the man sternly. "Hear me! My name is Duburinga and we are the Caramar. 'Gardarvon,' you say. Well we may be able to help you with, or try to dissuade you from, such a journey."

"What do you mean dissuade us?" asked Rowan.

"Well," replied Duburinga, "Gardarvon is a place we know well and treat warily. It is a place strongly entwined with our history."

"What should we do?" whispered Hyrn to Rowan.

"We should take them to Careil," answered Rowan.

Rowan addressed Duburinga. "Come if you will," he said. "We will take you to Careil, our friend and a King's Rider."

Careil looked up as he heard a murmur travelling through the forest. Rowan and Hyrn emerged from the bushes at the edge of the clearing and following them, to his surprise, were a group of Caramar warriors. Careil sprang to his feet.

"Welcome," he said. "Long live the Treaty of Everlasting Peace and the friendship of Wesmere and the Caramar."

"Greetings, Rider," said the warrior. "I am Duburinga of the Caramar. Welcome to our homeland."

"I beg forgiveness for welcoming you in your own land," said Careil quickly. "I only meant to convey our friendship to the Caramar."

"It is alright, friend," said Duburinga. "Well met. Your young companions tell us that you are headed to Gardarvon."

"Yes," said Careil. "We have a most pressing mission given to Rowan and Hyrn by Dervarnia, a Keeper."

"We know of one," said Duburinga. "She has travelled through these mountains and amongst my people for many years searching for something. Our people have not heard from her for many years."

"She is the one that entrusted Rowan and Hyrn with this mission," said Careil.

"She also spoke of Darion," said Duburinga. "Did she discover his fate?"

"Yes, she did," blurted Hyrn. "And she said that the Sword of Acclimoss, King Bharain's sword, is at Gardarvon."

"Ah, yes. It is said, she spoke of Bharain and wished to learn his fate," said Duburinga. "So once again our fate is tied with Gardarvon. It is well that we are here. We may be able to help you, and perhaps have an opportunity to confront the ghosts of Gardarvon."

"We will be glad of your guidance," said Careil.

Rowan spoke out. "We have to have breakfast first." He then added, "Would you like to join us?"

"No," said Duburinga. "Many thanks, but we have eaten our morning meal after sun-up. We must, in any case, be on the move and send reports ahead. This will enable the word of your journey to spread and allow you sure passage through the great Caramarhc."

In uttering the mountains' name, he placed his hands across his eyes and then continued, "Mighty Caramarhc help us to find your true paths and lead us to our goal, Gardarvon. Hail friends, I will meet you on the path you have been following before the day gets much older."

With this, he signalled his companions with a small flick of his hand, and they all melted silently into the surrounding bushes and disappeared.

"Right then," said Careil, still looking toward where Duburinga had disappeared. "Let's get you two fed, get packed up, and be on our way."

Duburinga walked with them all the rest of that day as they made their way northeast and further into the mountains. None of the other Caramar reappeared, although Duburinga assured them that there were many in the surrounding countryside and that others had gone on ahead to prepare a welcome for them. They had stayed on the main road most of the day but had left the road when it dropped down towards Wesmere. They now followed a road that led into the mountains which had become narrower as it passed through a great forest, the trees forming a green canopy overhead.

As the sun began to go down behind them, Duburinga guided them onto a smaller trail that ran north into the forest. After a while, the trail narrowed further. The three were forced to dismount and lead their horses. The path took many twists and turns through thick forest that brushed at their faces and made the horses have to force their way through as they were led with their heads down. Then the path straightened and began to widen. A narrow cleft in a wall of rock opened in front of them, and the path passed through. The rockface on the sides of the cleft had been carved with images. Once through the cleft, the area opened out into a small circular gorge. Houses, and a few larger buildings, were clustered on the far side of the gorge towards a steep cliff face. A large cave yawned at the base of the cliff. To the right a waterfall cascaded down the gorge wall into a small lake that fed a stream which flowed down the side of the gorge and then disappeared into a crevice near to where Rowan, Hyrn and Careil stood.

"Welcome to Ordbrarn," said Duburinga. "Now that you are here you can never leave!"

Rowan and Hyrn looked at him, startled.

Duburinga laughed, "At least until you have sampled our hospitality."

The two boys let out an audible sigh of relief.

"Thank you," said Rowan, nudging Hyrn in the back. "We are honoured."

"Yes," said Hyrn. "Um... we are."

That night, they gathered at the mouth of the great cave of Ordbrarn. The rock of the cave mouth had been fashioned into an ornate archway. In front of the entrance, within a large circular stone hearth, a roaring fire burned, lighting up the cliff face. The people of Ordbrarn had gathered and were eating and drinking in groups seated around the fire. Rowan, Hyrn and Careil sat with Duburinga and other warriors. They ate some type of poultry, with mushrooms and roasted tubers. They washed this down with a wildberry drink that Rowan and Hyrn both agreed was by far the best drink that they had ever tasted.

After everyone had eaten, an impromptu dance started up to the music of wooden pipes. The two boys were soon whisked off, much to their chagrin, by a group of young girls. The girls took turns at making them look foolish as they whirled and stumbled about, bringing uproarious laughter from the adults. Careil was still laughing when Hyrn and then Rowan made their way breathlessly back towards him.

"Great dancing," said Careil, wiping tears of laughter from his eyes.

"Very funny," replied Rowan. "My legs are too tired to dance."

"My legs are too tired to stand," said Hyrn, flopping himself down beside Careil.

"Then you'd best rest them, my friends," Duburinga said, rising to his feet. "Tomorrow we cross the pass from Andavalar to the main mass of the mountains and then we climb up the old paths to Gardarvon. We should get there by nightfall, if all goes well."

The rest of them got to their feet and Duburinga led them to a stone house nearby. As they went, a few of the girls waved to Rowan and Hyrn, stifling laughs.

"Why do I get the impression that we've been the evening's entertainment?" said Rowan gruffly.

"Don't worry," laughed Careil. "I doubt you'll be asked for an encore."

Rowan glared. "Well at least we're not short of a comedian."

The stone house was smaller than the others, and when they entered, they saw that it was a single room. The room was furnished with beds at each end and a basin in the middle next to a small hearth where a fire burned.

Duburinga gestured around. "This is our guest lodge for any visitors. Although, this is the first time for many years that any but other Caramar have stayed here. Your gear is all here. You will be awoken in the morning. In the meantime, have a good night's sleep."

"Thank you," replied Careil. "Your hospitality honours us."

Duburinga wished them goodnight and left for his own dwelling, closing the wooden door as he left.

"Right!" Careil turned to Rowan and Hyrn. "Bed!"

There were no arguments from the two boys as they sleepily prepared for bed.

Hyrn soon lay in bed almost ready for sleep.

"Careil," he said, "how will we find Acclimoss when we get to Gardarvon if it has been there all this time?"

"We'll worry about that when we get there," said Careil. "I think we may need the help of the Stone. But for now, get some sleep."

"Alright," said Hyrn, as he settled into his blankets, yawning. "Goodnight then."

That night Hyrn dreamed that he was in a cold dark place and that he was searching for something but couldn't remember what it was. Suddenly, a bright light broke into the darkness, calling his name.

"Hyrn. Hyrn. Hyrn..."

"Hyrn!" Rowan was shaking him.

He opened his eyes. Rowan stood next to him half-dressed. Behind him stood Careil and two Caramar carrying torches.

"Time to get up," said Rowan.

"What? Already?" yawned Hyrn.

"They have something they want us to see. So, get up and get dressed," said Rowan.

When they were ready, the Caramar led them outside and towards the cliff face to one side of the cave mouth. A few other Caramar moved in the same direction. As they got closer to the cliff, they saw that there was a stairway hugging the rock face leading up into the pre-dawn gloom. They began to climb, and the stairs slowly curved round a spur on one side of the cliff. The stairs then turned back on themselves and led onto a path that ran along a ledge high above the cave. They followed the path and came to a platform that was ringed by a natural stone balcony which looked out over Ordbrarn.

As they faced out from the balcony, they could see that the sky was beginning to lighten. They began to see the shapes of the houses below them and beyond that, the rock walls that surrounded Ordbrarn. As it became lighter, they could see the forest beyond the walls falling away into the gloom.

The clouds, scattered low in the sky, were painted orange. Then the sun began to brighten the horizon and as it slowly came into view, they could see that it was rising far away above the plains of Wesmere. The view was breathtaking in its immensity. To the northeast, the bulk of the Caramarhc glowed orange on its peaks, fading to grey at its feet. Below them to the south, they could see the edge of the Albarrin Forest. The details of the plains began to come into focus; the low hills, the end of the Willmara Valley where the city of Ballarghen nestled.

Suddenly, as the disc of the sun began to show itself, a long low chant began around them. It was a sound that Rowan and Hyrn had heard before from far off, on the wind, when they had camped in the mountains, though they didn't know what it was. The Caramar were welcoming the dawn. The chant rose to a crescendo and echoed around the mountains as the sun climbed further above the horizon. When the disc of the sun was visible, the chant dropped and stopped abruptly.

"Thus, we welcome the day as we have done for generations."

Duburinga stood to one side of them. They had not noticed him among the Caramar in the darkness.

"It looks like it will be a fine one," he said. "Let us make the most of it. We go to Gardarvon."

"Gardarvon," agreed Careil.

"Come," said Duburinga.

He led them back down the steps and they returned to their quarters to prepare to continue their journey. He told them that breakfast would soon be prepared and left them.

They ate breakfast at the same stone circle where they had sat the night before. The sun had begun to pierce the forest that surrounded Ordbrarn as they finally prepared to leave. Duburinga spent some time speaking to those leaders that were to remain. He spoke to others that seemed close to him. Others of the Caramar said goodbye to husbands, wives, and children and joined the travelling party. Some had left long before, scouting the mountain pass since dawn. Rowan, Hyrn and Careil thanked the people of Ordbrarn for their hospitality and said goodbye. The party moved out towards the entrance to Ordbrarn. The three horses were waiting near the rock cleft. Hyrn took Marly's reins and followed Duburinga, Careil, and Rowan down the narrow passage.

As he did, he looked back. The rays of the morning sun lit the cliff face behind them. Shafts of light had just pierced the darkness of the cave at the base of the cliff. Hyrn saw that the cave walls glistened like gold. The whole of the village seemed to glow. He saw the figures of the people of Ordbrarn waving, silhouetted against the glow of the sun. A light in the dark. He remembered his dream. He was leaving the light for who knew what ahead. He shivered. Then he faced forward again and straightened his back. The Sword of Acclimoss lay ahead, in Gardarvon.

CHAPTER THREE

Gardarvon

They travelled through dense forest for a while, but it soon began to thin out. Eventually they reached a path that led onto the main trail. The trail led northeast and the sun rose in the sky to their right as the morning wore on. Three Caramar scouts returned to report that the pass from Andavalar to the bulk of the Caramarhc was safe. The trail began to curve to the north and to widen out as the forest opened out to reveal the pass. Mount Andavalar was joined to the rest of the Mountains by a narrow ridge whose eastern flank fell away, steep and rocky, down to the foothills below. The western flank formed a forested slope. The trail led to the beginning of the pass, which was flanked by two large pine trees. They moved down towards the two trees where other Caramar waited to help them. As they passed between the trees, Hyrn saw that two crumbling pillars stood beyond. A Caramar stood by each pillar, as if guarding the pass.

Duburinga spoke. "Things are not as they once were. Once this pass was a thriving road between us and our fellow Caramar in the east. Now this pass is seldom used. We are not united as we once were. Gardarvon was once our fortress in the west, a stronghold to link the west with our people in the east. Now its emptiness divides us. We only venture across the pass occasionally to see our people and to visit the Seat of the Elders."

He paused and looked across to the mountains across the pass. "We Caramar have begun to feel that something is changing. The mountains are beginning to stir, to shake off an old wound. The time has come for us to be bold. We have sent messengers to the Seat of the Elders. We are going to reclaim Gardarvon."

A cheer went up amongst the gathered Caramar.

"Come friends," said Duburinga. "Your journey has become our journey. We will help you find what you seek."

The path along the top of the ridge looked treacherous from a distance, but as they passed onto it they could see that it was quite wide. An overgrown low wall ran along each side. Rowan, Hyrn and Careil had dismounted and led their horses. The Caramar helped them over parts of the path that were eroded, or stood guard where sections of the eastern wall had crumbled and collapsed down the cliff face. As they crossed the stonework, they could clearly see the great river on the plains to the east. To the west, across the top of the trees, they could see the northern lands beyond a spur of the mountains. As they approached the other side of the pass, the ridge began to widen out into a plateau. The path veered away from the cliff and across a broad meadow fringed on the western side by trees that continued on to the mountainside ahead. To the right of where the path met the mountain, a large waterfall cascaded down the mountainside. Its waters flowed across the northeast corner of the plateau, and plunged over the cliff. The path itself seemed to come to a dead end against the mountainside.

When they reached the point where the path ended, they could see that another pathway led to the west to where the trees met the steep slope of the mountains. The Caramar led them down this path, which eventually ended at the beginning of a large stairway. The stairway was broad with wide stone steps. They could see some way ahead until it curved around and out of sight. Rowan and Hyrn were relieved when it was suggested that they stop and rest, and have some food. They let their horses graze nearby, and sat down on the grass to eat.

After they had eaten, Hyrn lay back in the grass. During lunch they had been told that Gardarvon lay high on a plateau at the top of the stairway which zig-zagged its way up the mountain slope. They were nearly there.

Careil called him. They were off again. They packed up their things, rounded up their horses, and began to climb the steps.

The broad steps were carved from the stone of the mountainside. Blocks of stone had been used to build a parapet along the outside edge of the stairway. The stairs led north at first and climbed slowly up the steep mountainside. As the road where they had crossed the ridge dropped away behind them, Rowan and Hyrn could see that they were now perched high up above the foothills that fell down the northwest flank of the mountain. To the southwest back across the ridge below and beyond towered Mount Andavalar. They were both glad of the parapet along the side of the stairway.

After they had climbed for a while, the stairway turned sharply back round to the south. The wall that had been on their left, curved back around and ended against the rock-face which now formed the left hand-side of the stairs. The parapet now began on the right side of the stairway. As they climbed to the south, the steps they had traversed fell away below them. Rowan looked up. The mountainside towered above them. There were more steps above, all the way up, he realised. Not only was that an even greater height, but it seemed a long way. The sun had now passed overhead and was starting to get lower in the sky. He hoped that they got to Gardarvon before night fell. He didn't like the idea of spending a night on the mountainside... or climbing the stairs in the dark. It was not long, however, before the stairs turned back towards the north. As the afternoon passed, the stairway continued to climb winding back and forth up the mountainside.

Duburinga said to Careil, "We will make the ruins of Gardarvon well before sunset. Something that has been hidden for so long, will be hard to find though. We may have to continue to search in the morning."

"We will search for as long as it takes," said Careil.

"We also will not give up," replied Duburinga. "If the sword you seek is in Gardarvon it will be found."

The rock-hewn steps turned south once again, and as they continued climbing they could see that the mountainside levelled out ahead. The stairway curved towards the mountain and ended at a large, stone wall. Two stone pillars stood at a break in the wall where the stairway led onto a roadway. Duburinga led them through the gateway, and as they passed between the pillars, the plateau opened out in front of them. Crouching above the plateau rose the city of Gardarvon. The city dominated the open expanse before them.

The city looked like an out-cropping of the final peak of the central mountains which climbed to the east. The plateau itself was not overly large. The wall they had passed through ran around its edge. The wall curved around to their left to meet the high walls of the city on the north. To their right, the wall met an archway that joined it to the great wall of the city. The centre of the city was enclosed within a stone wall, four stories high, that curved around to meet a cliff face that formed the eastern end of the plateau. The entrance to the city was a ramp that led to a gate halfway up the wall. The area between the outer wall of the plateau and the wall of the city, was flat and open. Here and there were the ruins of small buildings. Amongst the buildings, the ground was overgrown with shrubs, small trees, and long grass. This area was once the farms of Gardarvon, now growing wild. The roadway they were on led straight to the entrance of the city. They followed it, silently, in awe of the looming city. The roadway was mostly clear of vegetation except for the grasses that encroached upon it. As they drew nearer to the ramp, they could see buildings through the open gateway. They left the horses at the foot of the ramp in the care of one of the younger Caramar.

Careil turned to Rowan and Hyrn. "Do you have any clue as to where we must start looking?"

"No," said Rowan.

Hyrn shook his head. "Dervarnia only told us that Ilah said the Sword of Acclimoss was at Gardarvon, and that we must find it."

"It won't be an easy task," said Careil. "We don't know where to start." He looked up at the walls of the city and then looked down one way and then the other to where the ends of the wall curved back around to the east. "We may need Ilah's help."

"Let us enter the city first," said Duburinga.

The other Caramar agreed, anxious to see the city their ancestors built, that had been visited by only a few of them in generations.

"Yes," said Careil.

He looked at Hyrn and Rowan. They looked at each other.

"Come on," said Rowan to Hyrn.

Hyrn hesitated. He felt the warmth of Ilah inside his shirt. He put his hand against the outside of his vest. Ilah. They must ask it for help. He hoped that this was a time of need and that Ilah would help them. The others had begun to move up the large stone ramp. He shouldered his pack and followed.

At the top of the ramp, they passed through the large gateway. Large stone gates had been flung wide, their edges worn and broken. As they passed under the wall, the city opened before them. The gateway was at street level. Paved streets led onto an open plaza in the centre of the city. The buildings were all one or two stories high, and all built of the same grey stone. A street ran from the gateway, and they walked down it towards a plaza. The streets were littered with debris and the buildings were empty and silent. They walked past the entrances to stairways that led below street level. Drenga of the Caramar spoke.

"I know much of Gardarvon," she said. "I have studied it, as have others, to keep our history alive. If I can help, please ask. The city you see is only part of Gardarvon. Much of it is under our feet. I fear that if anything is hidden here, it will be below." A troubled look came over her face. "That is where our people were imprisoned by the Northerners. The stone we loved became our prison where we were kept as slaves. It is time to reclaim what is ours and remove the stains of the past."

They reached the centre of the city and stopped. The sun had sunk further in the west and although they were still in sunlight, it would soon drop below the level of the city wall. Hyrn put down his pack and looked at Careil.

"I will call Ilah," he said.

Careil nodded. Hyrn put his hand under his vest and inside his shirt. He felt the cloth wrapping and grasped the hard Stone. The Caramar gathered around. They had heard of the Stone that he carried. He pulled out the bundle and undid it. He took Ilah in his hands and looked into it. It was dull and grey but still warm.

He called it, "Ilah, Ilah."

At first, nothing happened. Then the Stone began to lighten and then glow. Finally, Ilah shone brightly and spoke. "The thing that you seek is close at hand. I have seen it. Now, the Sword of Acclimoss is in darkness, enclosed in stone. There are times when the light pierces that darkness. From afar, I could not tell where it was. It was Gardarvon. I could see that much, but where, I do not know. It is in darkness now. I cannot see it."

Hyrn sighed. He looked around at the disappointment on the faces of the small group. The sun began to drop behind the wall until the spot where they stood was in shadow. Ilah still glowed brightly.

"The setting sun against the city walls!" Ilah suddenly spoke. "Hurry! That is what I have seen."

Hyrn grasped Ilah firmly.

Careil looked back the way they had come.

"Come on!" he said. "Back to the gateway."

They all began to move back down the roadway. The Caramar broke into a trot and Rowan and Hyrn were forced to keep pace. They finally reached the gateway and went through onto the ramp. They went back down and began to study the walls. They broke into two groups; Careil and Duburinga, in one group of Caramar, and Rowan, Hyrn and Drenga in the other. They began to move around the walls in opposite directions.

Hyrn held Ilah in front of himself. Ilah spoke again. "Acclimoss lies in a stone room. The light shines through a small space in the wall. It was bright but it is beginning to fade."

As the sun set below the edge of the plateau a shadow moved slowly up the wall of the city. Careil looked up, searching frantically.

"There!" he suddenly shouted, pointing.

They all looked to the spot where he was pointing near the line of the shadow. Hyrn could just make out a row of small dark slots that stretched around the wall.

"What are they?" he asked.

Drenga of the Caramar spoke. "They are below the level of the street. They must allow air to flow through the lower levels. They seem to be on the second under-story... but which one is the one we seek." She looked at Hyrn who in turn looked at Ilah.

"Ilah," Hyrn said imploringly, "which slot is the one?"

The light within Ilah had begun to fade. The Stone spoke faintly. "I can see no more. The room is now almost in darkness." With that, Ilah went silent and its light was extinguished. Hyrn held Ilah in his hand, still staring into it. Then as it became dark, he wrapped it carefully and placed it back inside his shirt.

"Well," said Careil resignedly, "it looks like we have to search the entire length of the inside of the wall at that level."

Drenga and the other Caramar moved off to inform the other group.

"Come on, Hyrn," continued Careil. "Let's get back up into the city."

When they reunited inside the city, it was almost dark. They debated whether to search straight away or to continue in the morning. There was a sense of urgency among them. Finally, it was agreed that they should have a quick meal and some would prepare camp whilst the others searched by torchlight. Some of the Caramar had already begun to clean out a street level dwelling near the city wall.

They ate their meal inside one of the stone dwellings. It was one of many adjoining dwellings that were carved from the same outcropping of native rock. They sat on stone benches at stone tables that were also carved from the same rock. As they finished eating, some of the Caramar, Drenga among them, began to move outside to prepare the way to the understoreys. Hyrn felt tired, and ate quietly. He thought of the search ahead underground. He remembered his dream of a cold, dark place. He shivered. Well at least he wouldn't be alone down there.

After they had eaten, they packed up and put on warm clothes against the chill of the mountain air. They went out into the street. There the Caramar had gathered wood to use for torches. Across the other side of the street, a torch burned, lighting the entrance to a stairway that led down below ground. Rowan, Hyrn and Careil were given torches made by wrapping cloth soaked in oil tightly around the end of stout pieces of wood. Duburinga led them to the top of the stairway. They could see that torches had been lit at the bottom of the stairs. They were led down until they stood in a dusty corridor with an arched ceiling, which led to the left and right. To the left, another corridor crossed theirs. One end of this bisecting corridor led west to the city wall, the other led east into the heart of the city. In the north-south corridor, in which they now stood, torches had been lit in both directions and placed in brackets in the wall. Despite the torches, it was still dim and the passages disappeared into darkness further down. Drenga approached them down the right hand corridor.

"The way seems clear," she said. "I will lead you down to the northern end of the city wall and Duburinga is to lead another party down to the southern end."

"We will locate each vent in turn and work our way around the wall," said Duburinga. "There is a passageway that follows the curve of the wall. We will meet in the middle or we will send a message if we find anything. Good luck."

Rowan, Hyrn, Careil, and several Caramar accompanied Drenga, while Duburinga and the rest of the Caramar disappeared behind them. As they worked their way down the corridor, they approached the last mounted torch. Drenga and another Caramar lit torches from it.

"Keep yours for when these burn low," she said. "We have not enough for more than two at one time."

They moved down the corridor surrounded by a band of light, the light of the last torch diminishing in the dark behind and the darkness being pushed back ahead. Every so often, they crossed an intersecting passage and a slight breeze, cool and musty, hit them from the direction of the wall. After a while, the passage ended in a T-junction. They turned left and proceeded silently except for the muffled echoes of their footsteps on the stone floor. Hyrn could see doorways with huge stone doors on each side of the passage. Most of these doors were closed, but some were open as if the inhabitants had left in a hurry. It was impossible to see inside the open rooms, but an unpleasant smell emanated from them. Every so often, a passage opened to their left, but they continued moving straight ahead, westward towards the outer wall.

Eventually, the passage began to curve slightly and Drenga halted.

"The right hand wall of this passage runs parallel to the outer wall," she said. "The vent system is located along this wall. Some vents will be inside the rooms along this side of the passage but the main vents are located opposite the east-west passages and have their own alcoves. We will have to check each one."

They came to the first of the doorways on the right hand side of the passage. The stone door was ajar and Drenga stepped forward and pushed it open fully. The light from her torch lit the room. There were two beds in the room, one against the far wall, and one on the left hand wall. In the middle of the room was a stone table and seats. Against the right hand wall were shelves and a long workbench. Everything was dusty and there were piles of what looked like rotted cloth on the beds. There were a few dusty utensils on the shelves and bench. They could plainly see the dark strip of the vent above the bed on the far wall. There was nothing else in the room.

The next door was closed tight and it took a bit of effort to open it. The room smelt dank but the light revealed that the room was very similar to the previous room, simply furnished and long abandoned. The party broke up into two groups so that they could cover the rooms quicker. As they worked their way along, they found each room fairly similar in appearance and state of disuse. Occasionally there were different humble possessions within, a stone knife or a simple ornament.

Hyrn was lagging behind the second group led by Drenga. Careil and Rowan were up ahead in the first group. He was beginning to get bored and a little disheartened. They had looked in about twenty rooms with little of interest to show for it. Hyrn was peering into the rooms on the left hand side of the passage. The light from Drenga's torch ahead illuminated them a little but they looked fairly similar to the ones they were inspecting. He glanced briefly into one room but Drenga was peering into a room ahead on the other side of the passage and so Hyrn could see very little. Out of the corner of his eye, Hyrn caught a glint of light. It seemed to glow briefly as two points of light, like a pair of yellow eyes. The hair stood up on the back of his neck and his heart skipped a beat. He thought that he must have been mistaken. He was tempted to take another look, but the feeling in his stomach told him not to, and as his breathing grew rapid, he turned to hurry and catch up with the others, but his legs felt like they had turned to stone. He tried to cry out but his voice deserted him. He could see the light of the torch getting further away.

All of a sudden, a rough, hairy hand grabbed him around the mouth from behind. Strong arms lifted him from the floor. Rough breath blasted in his ear and a harsh voice growled at him. As he was lifted, he saw another of the creatures. The yellow eyes were unmistakable. The face was roughly human but hairy, as was the creature's naked upper body and its ears were large and roughly pointed. The look on the creature's face was malicious and cunning. Hyrn was frozen with fear. He felt that at any moment he would be killed. Instead, the creature holding him and the other, both looked in the direction of the fading torchlight, and then turned and ran into the darkness in the opposite direction.

Rowan looked back to where Hyrn had been a moment before. Where had he got to? He wandered back along the darkening passage.

"Hyrn!" he called.

There was no answer.

"Hyrn this is no time to be playing games," he said sternly.

Rowan passed an open door on the inner wall of the passage. He stopped and went back to the door and stepped just inside. There was a strange, slightly disturbing smell. There was not enough light to see anything.

He backed out of the room and called out to Drenga, "Drenga I can't find Hyrn…and something doesn't feel right."

Drenga turned from where she was exiting a room on the outer wall and jogged back towards Rowan, the passage lightening as she approached.

"What's wrong Rowan?" she asked.

"Hyrn's gone," said Rowan a tone of worry in his voice. "He might just be hiding or something stupid like that… but this room smells funny and something feels strange."

Drenga held her torch aloft and passed through the doorway. Rowan followed her into the room. Once inside the room the smell was even stronger. Drenga let out an audible gasp.

"What is it?" said Rowan but as he looked past Drenga, he could see that someone or something had been in this room.

Bones and feathers lay strewn on the floor. There was a rough pile of cloths that had been used as bedding. There were various pieces of broken furniture and various sized containers, caskets and trunks all roughly broken open and discarded.

"Cave Drargs," hissed Drenga.

"Drargs?" exclaimed Rowan, his thoughts tumbling.

But Drargs weren't real. They were just from stories. People got lost in the mountains and were attacked by Drargs. Just stories to frighten small children and make sure they didn't wander off.

"Drargs… they're not real," he said.

Drenga turned her head and looked at Rowan quizzically, then half smiled.

"Unfortunately my young friend they are very real," she said, "and, although they don't hunt these mountains in the numbers they once did, they are still a curse to travellers and those not prepared. We did not expect that they would be here."

She motioned Rowan to move away from the doorway and began to examine the ground, a fierce look of concentration on her face.

"There were two of them," she said. "They have been using this room for a number of days." She moved through the doorway still peering at the floor. A look of worry came over her face.

"One of them picked up Hyrn and then they both ran off in that direction," Drenga said, pointing back down the passageway into the darkness.

She then let out a shrill whistle. Two Caramar came running down the passageway towards them closely followed by the rest of the party. Careil approached with a bewildered look on his face.

Drenga spoke quickly to the Caramar. "Young Hyrn has been taken by

Drargs. We must pursue them. They will be moving quickly."

She pointed to the marks in the dust leading off into the dark. The two Caramar instantly broke into a run, one carrying a torch that illuminated the passage as they went.

She addressed Careil and the remainder of the Caramar. "We will go the other way, in case they double back. Rowan, I suggest you stick close to Careil. We don't want anyone getting lost."

Hyrn was being held roughly, the breath being pushed out of his chest. The Drargs were moving quickly, disappearing deeper into the dark maze of tunnels. They seemed to be beyond the area where the party had entered and were now moving further away from the outer wall. The creatures must be able to see in the dark as Hyrn could see very little. The one carrying him smelled terrible. He occasionally shifted Hyrn's weight, but still held him firmly making it hard to breathe. As they ran, Hyrn was jolted up and down. His chest felt like a weight was being pushed into him, hard against his ribs, but strangely warm.

Warm? Of course! 'Ilah', he thought.

Hyrn's left arm was pinned, but his right was only held lightly by the tip of the creature's long fingers, the claw-like nails scraping against his upper arm. He wondered if he could reach the Stone and extract it from inside his tunic and what would happen when he did? What if they just took Ilah? Could he risk it? What if he ended up dead anyway? Then they would just take it off his dead body. Maybe after they had eaten him? A sharp wave of fear went through him. He had to try. He was being carried further and further away, and what if no-one had noticed he was missing. This was it.

He moved his right arm slightly and felt the Drargs clawed fingers brush along his arm as he moved. He could do it. He summoned all his courage and counted to three. He pulled his right arm free and quickly thrust his hand into his tunic. The Drarg noticed the movement and tried to tighten his grip. This just turned Hyrn slightly as the Drarg no longer had Hyrn's right arm but closed its grip tighter around his chest. This movement actually pushed Ilah closer to Hyrn's hand and with a last effort Hyrn thrust his hand deeper. He felt the soft cloth and the warm hardness of Ilah within. He gripped Ilah tightly and pulled the Stone from within his tunic. As he did so the cloth fell from around Ilah and there was pandemonium.

Bright, warm light burst from Ilah. The Drarg holding Hyrn let go and shielded its eyes. Hyrn fell to the ground with a thud. Both Drargs screeched as the sudden burst of light burned into eyes made for dark places.

Ilah, spoke in a loud commanding voice. "Begone, foul creatures! Leave this place and crawl back to the darkness from which you came!"

Whether the Drargs understood or not, the effect was the same. They ran stumbling and moaning, off into the dark passage. Hyrn was left lying on the passage floor, still clutching Ilah.

"Fear not Hyrn. They are gone," said the Stone. "You must find your way back now. I will show a little light to guide your feet."

With that, Ilah's light dimmed leaving a glow that softly lit the passage. Hyrn walked back the way they had come. He was not exactly sure which way to go. He tried just walking in the general direction of the outer wall but soon came to a junction that led both left and right. He chose left and continued until he came to another junction and then went right. He had no idea of how far he had been carried and only a vague idea of direction. He was beginning to feel very lost and alone. Ilah's light had dimmed slightly and Hyrn began to fear that he would be left in the dark.

"Forgive me," said Ilah. "I must rest. Trust in those you hold dear." And with that Ilah's light was extinguished and Hyrn was left in darkness.

Hyrn felt his way to the passage wall. He walked slowly along, feeling the wall as he went. He could still see the light of Ilah on his eyes, but slowly, this disappeared as well. He trudged on until the wall came to an end in open space. He could feel a slight breeze that came from his right but couldn't tell which way the passage went. He tried to walk straight ahead into space to see if the passage continued ahead but soon came across a wall blocking his way. He wondered whether to go to the right in the direction of the breeze, or continue to the left as he had before. He suddenly felt very tired. He just needed a little rest and time to think. He sank down against the wall and sat on the floor. He wrapped Ilah in the cloth and placed the Stone back inside his tunic. He closed his eyes.

He awoke with a start. He must have dozed off. Something had woken him. He listened. He heard it again. A cry. He suddenly felt afraid. What if it was the Drargs coming to get him again. He was all alone in the dark without even Ilah to help. The cry came again. This time more distinct.

It was someone calling his name. "Hyrn! Hyrn!"

Hyrn quickly got to his feet. He took a moment to try to work out where the sound came from. He began to feel his way along the wall again. He came to another cross passage. He could hear the voices but it was difficult to tell which way they came from. He decided to keep going the way he had been going, and felt his way across the dark passage. He touched the wall on the other side and continued on. He stopped and listened. The voices seemed to have become more distant. He began to panic. What if he was going the wrong way? He decided to make his way to the next cross passage, and turn right. He continued feeling his way along the wall, expecting any moment to reach the passage, but this section of wall seemed to go on a lot further than previously, unless his mind was playing tricks on him.

He was just about to stop to listen out for voices, when something strange happened. The wall along which he had been dragging his hand seemed to give way. He felt around the place where he had rested his hand. Sure enough a small square piece of the wall moved when he pressed it. He pushed it a bit harder. It moved in almost to his knuckles until he let go and it slid back into place. He pushed it again this time even further and suddenly the piece of stone stopped with a loud click. He started to reach into the hole again when the whole section of wall in front of him moved aside under his weight and he fell forward into empty space and crashed to the ground.

Ilah dug into his ribs and he rolled onto his back and reached inside his shirt and pulled out the Stone. Ilah must have regained some of its strength, as when he removed it from its cloth the Stone burst into light. He looked up at the walls and ceiling of a passageway but unlike the plain and austere passages he had seen elsewhere in Gardarvon these were ornately carved and decorated. He stood up. He was just inside the doorway of a passage that seemed to go on for quite a way. He walked down the passage for a while until the passage came to an end at a large ornate wall. The wall depicted what looked like Caramar people, but not dressed in their normal warrior garb. These Caramar wore long robes and held various objects. At the right hand side of the wall was a circular decoration that protruded from the wall. By its position this looked almost like a door handle. Hyrn put his hand on the circle and pushed. Nothing happened. He gripped the edges of the circle and tried to twist it to the right. It wouldn't move. He then twisted it to the left and as he did so the circle turned and clicked and the wall pivoted to show a doorway.

Hyrn took a deep breath.

Ilah spoke. "Go forward, young friend."

Hyrn stepped through the doorway, and as he did so, Ilah's light illuminated a large circular room. There was a sunken floor in the middle of the chamber with terraced steps leading down from an outer wall completely lined with shelves, except for four doorways, including the one he had just entered through. The shelves were filled with books, along with a variety of strange objects, and there was one section which was covered with regularly sized rectangular objects. The area in the centre of the room was covered in benches, and tables and chairs, but instead of the usual plain furniture these were highly ornate. Hyrn walked down the steps and across the floor. One of the benches and several of the tables had some of the rectangular objects on them along with dusty and disintegrating books. He went over and carefully picked one of the objects up. They were stone tablets with strange characters carved intricately into them. And then it struck Hyrn. They were books of some sort, made of stone to stand against the ravages of time. He put down the tablet and walked towards one of the shelves with differently shaped objects. He noticed that the doorway opposite from the door he had come in had a pile of something against it. Curious, he walked up the steps to investigate. It looked like a large roll of old cloth placed against the door. He leant down to feel it and it rolled over towards him to reveal a skeleton dressed in hooded robe. Hyrn let out a shout. He raced back across the room and through the doorway and stood panting. As he did he heard voices and noticed the doorway at the other end of the passage showing light.

Without thinking he yelled out, "Hello!"

He loped up to the doorway and poked his head around the corner. There, walking down the passageway towards him, were Rowan, Cariel, Drenga, Duburinga and several other Caramar. Rowan raced up to him and without thinking grabbed him in a hug.

"We thought we'd never see you again," Rowan said and then releasing him said sternly "Don't ever go wandering off again."

Hyrn began to protest, "I didn't"

Rowan cut him off, "It's alright. I'm just glad you're safe."

Careil and the Caramar had gathered around him where he stood in front of the doorway looking at the passage he had found.

"I'm glad you are safe," said Careil. "You gave us quite a scare," and then added, "What is this place?"

"I found it accidentally," said Hyrn. "I was walking in the dark, feeling the wall and I found a hole and it opened this door."

Careil looked at Hyrn's hand where he still held Ilah, now almost dark.

"Oh. Ilah had to rest so I walked in the dark for a while," said Hyrn.

"Yes," said Duburinga, "you led us quite a merry chase. We found where you and the Drargs parted company. You must have walked for hours."

"Drargs?" said Hyrn. "Is that what they were? But I thought—"

"So did I.," chipped in Rowan, "but apparently they are real, and you were kidnapped by them."

"It is just as well you got away," said Duburinga. "Drargs have a liking for human flesh when they can get it. However, those two seemed to have left in quite a hurry. Something must have scared them."

"It was Ilah," said Hyrn. "I managed to get it out, and they ran away screaming when Ilah lit up and yelled at them."

"Ah!" said Duburinga. "The light and power of the Stone would have been more than enough to terrify them. They must have felt that all their nightmares had come to get them. A Stone of power wielded by a great warrior."

The Caramar warrior laughed, "That would have been good to see. Now what is this place?"

He held up his torch and walked through the doorway. He began examining the walls and let out a gasp. He began to mumble to himself. Then Drenga was by his side.

"It can't be." she almost whispered.

She began to walk down the corridor, Duburinga by her side. The others all followed with Hyrn in front. The group came to the large stone door. Drenga turned to Hyrn.

"Did you open this?" she asked

"Yes," said Hyrn meekly.

"Good," said Drenga. "Then the room may have been secure."

The two Caramar walked through the doorway with the others close behind.

Rowan gasped. The Caramar all stood awestruck.

Duburinga spoke. "It survived. I cannot believe it. All these years."

He turned to Hyrn. "You have found something that the Caramar thought destroyed long ago. This is the Great Room of Scholars. Here all the history of Gardarvon was kept, along with a great deal of the knowledge of the Caramar. It is only rivalled by the Library at the Seat of the Elders, and even then, there were things here that were nowhere else. It has remained hidden here all this time. The scholars protected it well."

Hyrn looked at Duburinga. "There is a body over by that door," he said, pointing across the room.

✴

Hyrn woke up. For a moment he couldn't work out where he was. A stone slab loomed above him. Then he remembered; The Great Room of Scholars. He had slept under a large stone table. The Caramar had brought down their packs, and he and Rowan had gone to sleep, exhausted, under a table in the middle of the room. Rowan was no longer there, and his gear had been packed up.

Hyrn crawled out from under the table, and stood and stretched. He looked around. Light came from the ceiling above, illuminating the room. Sunlight, yet how it came through was hard to see. There didn't appear to be windows, just a series of holes. It must somehow be reflected from the outside. The Caramar were spread around the room, ardently inspecting various items. Duburinga was by the far door with Careil and Drenga. The body was no longer there. Behind one of the other doors in a corridor similar to the one he had first entered by, they had found a dozen more bodies. They were all laid out and covered. The body by the door had been the last to die with no one to lay him to rest. He had apparently died keeping watch at the door.

Hyrn walked over to the door.

"Good morning," he said.

Careil turned to him. "Good morning Hyrn. I hope you are rested. You had quite an adventure last night."

"I feel much better. I'm hungry though," said Hyrn.

"We will have some lunch soon," said Careil. "I'm afraid you slept through breakfast. It is nearly midday. Pack your bedding up. We have much to do."

"I will," said Hyrn. "Have you had any luck with the door?"

They had been unable to open the door the night before, after they had moved the body.

Duburinga spoke. "I'm afraid not. The scholars obviously used some powerful knowledge to secure the door. They must have taken turns to secure it until the last one died on duty. I believe they had been under attack. The Northerners must have found this entrance but were unable to get through. We have been unable to determine how it was done."

Just then one of the Caramar called out, "I have found something!"

Duburinga and Careil walked over to where the Caramar held a stone tablet.

"This speaks of Bharain," he said.

"What does it say, Doriga?" asked Duburinga.

"It speaks of how he came to Gardarvon," he began. "He was exhausted and sick from his journey. The people cared for him, and he spoke of his quest for Darion and the Stone of Angil. They made him as comfortable as possible in a room on the Western wall but he died after a few weeks. The Gardarvons decided to lay him to rest in the room and seal it up as a tomb." Doriga paused. "…It doesn't say where. Just that it was on the western wall."

"However," said Duburinga, "we have been looking for a room with a door but we now know to look for a sealed room. I have a feeling that the skills of the people of Gardarvon may make the seal hard to find, but there will be a wall where a room would normally be. We must let the others know."

Careil turned to Hyrn. "You should go and join Rowan."

Hyrn looked around. Rowan was nowhere to be seen.

"He is out searching the western wall with several Caramar," said Careil.

"They will need this information. Take some food. You can eat on the way."

Hyrn, accompanied by Doriga, found Rowan and the others starting another sweep at the northern end of the wall. Here the light came from shafts hidden in the corridor ceiling. Doriga told the others of the stone tablet and what Duburinga had said, and they set out. There were eight rooms evenly spaced along each section of the wall and then there was a space at the end of each dissecting corridor to allow airflow directly through the vents in the outer wall. They crossed each corridor and began checking to make sure that each section had no gaps in the doorways. They continued on until they came to the most western part of the wall. There was a wide part of the wall at the end of a corridor that had no vents.

"What about this wall here?" asked Hyrn.

"This is where the entry ramp to the city lies," said one of the Caramar. "There are no vents here."

When they began looking at the next section, the doorways began a little further down, and as they counted them, it was clear that there were only seven rooms in the section. They hurried back to the beginning of the section. There was just a blank corner wall that formed the end of the section that butted onto the alcove that marked the location of the large entry ramp outside. They inspected both sections of the wall but couldn't see any traces of where a doorway may have been. As they inspected the last section they noticed faint markings on the wall. It looked as if there had been words carved into the wall but these had been rubbed off.

"Inform Duburinga," said Doriga to one of the Caramar.

The warrior turned and sprinted back up the corridor and out of sight around the bend.

Duburinga soon arrived with Drenga and Careil and one other Caramar. Drenga and Duburinga inspected the end wall where the markings had been.

"Yes," said Drenga. "There is writing here but it has been erased. If this is where Bharain's tomb is then it is likely that there would have been an inscription. The Caramar may have erased it when they were being invaded, to hide it and ensure that the invaders did not raid the tomb."

She walked around the corner and looked at the other section of wall. "It is difficult to see any signs that this wall has been altered," she said, and turned to the other Caramar who had accompanied them. "Greina, perhaps you can find something."

The Caramar, Greina, approached the wall. He pushed his palms against it and began softly chanting.

"Greina is one of our most gifted stonesmiths," said Drenga. "He may be able to read the stone and see if it has been altered.

Greina continued to run his palms across the wall. As he ran his hand across, he stopped and concentrated. He reached into his cloak, pulled out a small white stone, and marked the wall. He then ran his hand up and down the wall marking a vertical line as he went. Once he reached a certain height he stopped and ran his hand horizontally to the left and then to the right. As he moved his hand right he began to trace a horizontal line. Again he stopped and ran his hand down the wall and then traced another vertical line. When he had finished he had drawn a doorway on the wall. He turned around looking drained and pale.

"Such skill," he said. "The stones feel almost as if they had always been together. I wonder if the stone that was used was originally carved from this piece of rock, or whether they had skills that we no longer possess. It will take a while to remove this. I will need any of us who have skill in stonework."

"You will have them," said Duburinga. "Any of us not needed here will return to the Great Room to see if we can have any more luck with the southern door. Hyrn I would be grateful if you could join us. We may need the power of Ilah, if the Stone has had time to gain back its energy."

"Alright," said Hyrn. "But I don't know whether Ilah can help at all."

Hyrn stood before the closed door at the southern side of the Room of Scholars. Rowan had stayed behind to watch progress on the tomb wall. Hyrn took Ilah from inside his vest and unwrapped the Stone carefully.

He called softly, "Ilah, Ilah."

The Stone began to glow. "What do you need, Child of Light."

"We need to open this door. There is something keeping it closed," said Hyrn.

Ilah began to glow more brightly. "There is much power here. The lives of many have gone into keeping out anger and evil intent."

Ilah began to hum. The humming began to get higher in pitch. It sounded almost like singing. As it got louder the door began to vibrate. Hyrn felt like blocking his ears. The noise was becoming difficult to bear. All of a sudden there was a loud click and the noise stopped. Ilah went silent and stopped glowing.

"Thank you, Ilah," said Hyrn.

He wrapped the Stone, put it back in his vest, and stepped aside. Duburinga went to the door and grasped the handle. He pulled and the door swung slowly open. He stepped through. Hyrn, Drenga and Careil followed. The scene was one of chaos. There were large chunks of stone scattered everywhere. The stonework was pitted and scarred. A large bar of iron lay on the floor. The end was bent and twisted.

Duburinga spoke. "They must have tried everything to break through. Only the power of the Scholars prevented them. They must have given up. It is just as well. Eventually they would have succeeded and the sacrifice of the Scholars would have been for nothing."

He walked down the corridor towards the far end. The door had been closed. He pulled it open easily, and they walked through. They were in one of the main corridors.

"This looks like the central thoroughfare," said Duburinga "We must be quite close to where we first came down."

He looked at the outside of the door. There were no signs of forced entry.

"Somehow the Northerners found this doorway," he continued. "Treachery or torture may have played a part. Someone has resealed the door. Perhaps the Northerners tired of trying to find out what was behind the door. Maybe they weren't looking for the Great Room. The stories of those who survived Gardarvon don't mention this attack. Perhaps they weren't aware of what the Scholars endured. It was always assumed that the room was destroyed or looted along with the rest of the city. We now know the bravery the Scholars showed. Their story can now be told. They must be given a proper memorial service. We will have their bodies taken up into the burial ground in the mountains behind Gardarvon. We will send word out to all the Caramar. The heart of Gardarvon has survived. People can now return and we can restore Gardarvon to its former glory. The sacrifice of the Scholars will not have been in vain."

Duburinga sighed, a steely look in his eyes, "Come, we have much to do. Let us see how the stonesmiths are going. Drenga, return to the Great Room and see if there is anything else we can find out. We will need to send a report to the Seat of the Elders. We will go down this way. The tomb should lie at the end of this thoroughfare if my bearings are correct."

With that he turned and headed down the passage.

After they had walked a short way they could see the end of the corridor in the gloomy light and as they approached they could hear the sounds of voices. When they came to the end of the corridor they could see that progress had been made. A large but shallow square recess had now been made in the top half of the doorway that Greina had drawn.

Greina turned to Duburinga, "We have broken the seal. It was difficult but the old ways are still remembered. The doorway has been blocked by two stones. We are removing the top one. That should allow us entry to the room."

Drenga stood at one of the large stone tables in the centre of the room. She had been looking at the stone tablets stacked there, most of which were blank. The others seemed to have been used for practicing writing. She leaned against the table as she peered at one of the tablets. She felt something, just a passing pulse of power. She ran her hand along the edge of the table. There it was again. She continued to feel along the stone surface of the table.

Back at the tomb, work was progressing well. As Rowan and Hyrn watched on, the stone block was steadily moving back into the wall, creating a deeper and deeper recess. The Caramar took it in turns at working the large stone, softly chanting and pushing their hands against it.

After what seemed an eternity Greina spoke. "It is almost done. This should be the last push."

He braced himself and placed his hands against the stone. The stone moved slightly, gave a shudder and fell through with a crash and a puff of dust, leaving a large square hole halfway up the doorway.

He turned to Duburinga. "Who should go through first?"

Duburinga turned to Rowan and Hyrn. "You have been given this quest. You should enter first."

Hyrn gulped and looked at Rowan.

Rowan shrugged. "I will go in first. Hyrn you come in next. We may need Ilah."

With that he vaulted up into the hole and climbed through. Hyrn hesitated, and then stepped closer. He grabbed the ledge, pulled himself up, and then scrambled through and down onto the block of stone that had landed just inside. He saw the dim figure of Rowan standing there. He jumped down to the floor and stood next to Rowan. Careil followed along with Duburinga, Greina, Doriga and the rest of the Caramar.

The room was dimly lit. A faint light came from the vents in the outer wall and light came in through the hole where they had entered. Duburinga took a torch from his pack and deftly lit it. The contents of the room were instantly revealed. In the middle of the room stood a stone bed supporting a long stone box with a stone lid, a coffin. Rowan and Hyrn approached the coffin and Hyrn could see that the lid was carved with the same writing he had seen elsewhere in Ordbrarn and Gardarvon.

Duburinga came and stood beside them. He read the inscription. 'Here lies King Bharain of Anasaria. From faraway he came seeking a lost Stone but here he died in the winter of 885.'

"That is in the old calendar," said Duburinga. "It is about twenty years before the war between Wesmere and the Northerners. Almost three hundred years ago. Come, we will have to remove the lid. Greina, can you help."

Duburinga handed his torch to Careil. Greina stepped forward and grasped the end of the stone lid while Duburinga stood at the other end and placed his palms against the lid. As Greina pulled at the lid, Duburinga pushed it. With a loud grating the stone lid began to slide. As the end began to come free, other Caramar took up positions on either side to take the weight. The stone continued to slide free until the Caramar held it completely and gently carried it and placed it against the side wall.

Duburinga motioned for Rowan and Hyrn to come forward. A slight sickly smell came from the coffin. Rowan and Hyrn moved closer with Careil behind them. The boys peered over the stone lip of the coffin. Hyrn gasped. Lying there was the body of a tall man richly dressed with a tarnished breastplate and chain mail. Inside his hood was just a skull, the hollow eyes staring up. His arms were crossed over his chest and grasped in his bony hands was the ornate hilt of a large sword glittering in the torchlight. The sword lay down the length of the body to just below the knees.

"The Sword of Acclimoss," whispered Rowan. He turned to Careil standing behind him. "What do we do now?"

"We must take the Sword. It belongs in Anasaria," said Careil.

Careil handed the torch back to Duburinga. He stepped forward and bowed his head towards the body. He grasped the bony hand and tried to pry the fingers from the hilt. A puzzled look came over his face. He tried again. The fingers would not move. He turned to the boys.

"You must try," he said.

Hyrn plucked up courage and reached his hand out. He felt the cold hardness of the bony fingers and almost cried out but he grasped tighter and tried to move them. It felt as if the bones were stuck onto the hilt of the sword. No matter how hard he tried they would not move.

Rowan stepped forward.

"Let me try, Hyrn," he said softly.

Hyrn withdrew his hand. He could still feel the coldness of the bone on his flesh. Rowan reached out his hand and touched the bony fingers. As he did so the dead king's hands let go of the hilt of the sword. Rowan's mouth gaped with shock and surprise, but he grasped the hilt of the sword and it lifted easily from the body. As he pulled it clear, he raised the tip of the sword into the air. The sword was heavy but he felt as if it was made for his hand. He thought for a moment that he saw a faint glow of light shimmer up the blade. A breath of air blew in through the vents in the outside wall. Everyone stood and stared at him. Hyrn, standing beside him, reached inside his vest and pulled out Ilah.

The cloth fell away and light burst forth from the Stone.

Ilah spoke. "The Sword of Acclimoss is free, the sword of the kings of Anasaria. Bharain has kept it well but now it must return to free Anasaria."

The group assembled around Rowan and Hyrn let out a cheer. Hyrn looked over at the body of King Bharain. The fingers were now entwined, his hands crossed across his chest as if in sleep. A cold shiver ran down Hyrn's spine but the warmth of the Stone in his hand quickly chased it away.

For a moment everyone was silent, then, Duburinga spoke. "If there is nothing else that you require from the tomb we must close it up."

Careil stepped over and examined the coffin. Lying alongside the body clasped at its waist was a long scabbard. He undid the buckle and it came away easily and the belt slid from around the body. He pulled it free and turned and handed it to Rowan.

"You will need this," he said. "You were obviously meant to carry the Sword. It is a bit long to wear at your waist. I will modify it so that you can wear it across your back. Hold it for now."

Rowan took the scabbard and gently slid the sword into it. He turned towards the coffin and bowed his head.

"Thank you," he said. "I will take care of it until it can be returned to where it belongs."

Hyrn bowed his head too and then straightened. Wrapping Ilah, he stood and watched as the Caramar lifted the stone lid and slid it back into place. The group one by one exited the room, leaving only Greina and the stonesmiths to begin to repair the wall.

As the group assembled back in the corridor, they heard the sound of running footsteps coming towards them. Drenga appeared from down the corridor. She arrived next to Duburinga, breathless.

"It is here," she said. "We have found it."

⁎

Far off in the central heights of the Caramarhc in the centre of a chamber at the heart of The Seat of the Elders, a large, red glassy stone resting atop a pedestal of rock, began to sing. After hundreds of years the Gragenstone had been found.

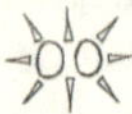

Back in the Great Room of Scholars the company gathered around one of the large stone tables. In the centre was a red crystal. It seemed to capture the light and hold it inside.

"What is it?" asked Hyrn.

"It is the Gragenstone," said Drenga. "It is also called the blood of the Sagenstone, the great Stone of wisdom that sits at the centre of the Seat of the Elders."

"What does it do?" asked Hyrn.

"Its powers are many," said Drenga. "It is a direct link to the Sagenstone. It was used by Gardarvon to communicate directly with the Elders in the Great Hall. But its importance was far greater for Gardarvon. Its power was used in the building and shaping of Gardarvon. It is the key to many of the secret places of Gardarvon. It was thought lost when the Northerners invaded and it hasn't been heard of since then. The scholars kept it hidden here enclosed in stone."

Drenga showed them a compartment in one of the legs of the stone table, and said, "The scholars probably didn't dare to risk using it in case its power brought the attention of the invaders. They were not just protecting the Great Room but also the Stone itself. If we are to restore Gardarvon, its power will be vital. Unfortunately, I do not know how to wield it. We will need to awaken it. If there is not the knowledge here, we may need to wait until someone can be sent from the Seat of the Elders. I dare not try. Its power is beyond me."

"There are none from Ordbrarn or these regions that have that skill," said Duburinga. "We will act with caution. It has waited for over two hundred years. It can wait a little longer." He looked at it reverently. "It is a great day for the Caramar..." he turned to Rowan, Hyrn and Careil, "and your quest has led us to it. We will be forever grateful. But now we must help you on your way. You must continue your quest. We are happy that we could play a part. Whatever you need we will provide."

Careil reached out and took his hand.

"We are grateful for the aid you have given," he said. "We must now head to Ballarghen and report to the King and his Council. We will travel back towards Ordbrarn and take the King's Road that runs east of the Albarrin Forest. This will take us at least two days, perhaps three. Some of the roads through the mountain valleys are quite treacherous at times."

Duburinga studied him for a moment as if weighing up his words.

"There is another way," he said, "although it hasn't been used for many years and is generally only travelled by foot. Horses travelled on it in old times. It may be passable."

"I know of no other way," said Careil. "The King's Riders know of many paths that others do not travel but none from this part of the mountains. The terrain is too steep."

"You will not know of it," said Duburinga. "It is a path known only to the Caramar. Even the Northerners did not discover it. It is just as well, else Wesmere would have been in greater peril. The Northerners would have had a direct and secret route to Ballarghen and could have mounted a surprise attack on the capital. We kept the secret well. As I have said though, it is not used and it may be difficult and possibly dangerous at times. It will get you to Ballarghen in less than a day."

Careil looked at Rowan and Hyrn in turn and then to Duburinga.

"Can you guarantee that it is safe?" he asked.

"I will travel with you myself, along with several of my warriors," said Duburinga. "We will do everything in our power to ensure your safety."

Careil looked at Rowan and Hyrn again.

Rowan shrugged and said, "Why not, if it saves us two days."

Hyrn nodded his head in agreement but a thought of plummeting to his death flashed through his head. He smiled grimly to hide this thought from the others.

"Very well then," said Duburinga. "It will start to get dark soon. We will eat well tonight and get a good night's sleep. We head off for Ballarghen at first light."

CHAPTER FOUR

Ballarghen

As the last echoes of the Caramar's dawn greeting chant reverberated around the stone walls of Gardarvon, Rowan, Hyrn and Careil waited at the foot of the entrance ramp with their horses. Soon Duburinga and five other Caramar walked through the gateway and down the ramp. Drenga, Doriga, Greina and the others were to stay behind and continue the job of reawakening Gardarvon. Some Caramar had left to travel eastwards to take news to the Seat of the Elders. The travellers had farewelled the remaining Caramar before dawn and had been presented with their horses by Arienga, one of the youngest of the Caramar at Gardarvon. She had kept them well looked after. The horses were well rested and were a little skittish as they were saddled up.

Arienga, who had only recently finished her warrior training, had asked Duburinga if she could accompany them on the road to Ballarghen. After some thought, he had agreed. Arienga had never been far from Ordbrarn and the surrounding area and this was a great opportunity for her to see more of the world and broaden her experience. And as she had obviously established some rapport with the horses, it was felt that she would be able to assist with bringing them through the secret route to Wesmere.

Careil and the boys took the reins of their horses. Duburinga had suggested that they not ride, as the path may become treacherous, and the horses would need to conserve their strength for the descent down the secret trail. Duburinga signalled and two of the Caramar jogged down the path that led through a large stone arch and along the southern wall of Gardarvon. They disappeared from view, as the path followed the curve of the wall. Duburinga then led off and the others fell in behind. As they moved off Hyrn looked back towards the gateway to Gardarvon.

One stage of their journey was over and now they were off to Ballarghen where the King's Council awaited. Hopefully they would be able to work out what needed to be done and maybe they would be able to go home soon. So much had happened in the few days since they had left home. It felt like a lifetime. He thought about the path ahead. The first thing was to get to Ballarghen. That may be hard enough. He looked again at the entrance to Gardarvon. Would he ever see it again? What would it be like now that the Caramar had returned? He imagined a thriving city full of people. That would be something to see. With that he turned away and concentrated on the path ahead. The party passed through the archway, Duburinga leading, then Careil, Rowan and himself, with Arienga and the other Caramar bringing up the rear.

The path ran between the southern wall of Gardarvon on the left, and the wall that edged the plateau on the right. As the wall on the left curved away, the path veered away to the east to follow it. The wall that ringed the plateau ended here in an outcropping of rock that rose up and formed a natural wall on their right, creating a gorge that the path ran through. It was quite dim in the gorge as the sun was still not high enough in the sky to penetrate. Soon the smooth wall of Gardarvon on the left gave way to a natural rockface. After they had travelled some way, the sound of flowing water could be heard ahead. The path veered gently around to the right. As they followed it, they saw further on, the two Caramar who had gone ahead, waiting at a stone bridge.

The entrance to the bridge was flanked by two large pillars. As they approached Hyrn could see that the bridge spanned a narrow chasm. Water cascaded down the cliff to the left and rushed boiling through the chasm and out through a gash in the rockface on the right.

"This is the same watercourse that we saw at the foot of the steps that we climbed to Gardarvon," said Duburinga. "It runs down to the waterfall near where we stopped to eat. Here it is called the Gardwater."

He spoke to one of the Caramar waiting at the bridge and then turned and continued, "The bridge is safe, although the parapet wall is a bit unstable. We will need to stay to the middle as we cross."

He addressed Careil. "The three of you and the horses will go first. One of us will help each of you guide your horse. It is a good test of how the horses will handle the path ahead. Arienga, you will help Rowan. Boriega, you stay with Hyrn. I will assist Careil at the front."

He looked again at Careil. "I am sure that a King's Rider doesn't need my help with his mount but I will be there to ensure that there is nothing in the stone that may cause trouble, and Erras will set an example for the other horses."

Careil bowed his head in response and they set off. The closer they got to the bridge the louder the water became. The first two Caramar stood alongside the pillars and ensured that they were guided onto the centre of the bridge. They would bring up the rear. As the other two horses entered the bridge the Caramar, Boriega took hold of one side of the reins of Hyrn's horse, and signalled with his head for Hyrn to follow with a wink of reassurance as they started off. As they passed between the pillars Hyrn could feel the vibrations from the force of the water. The sound now was overwhelming. He could feel spray from the water on his face and the stone of the bridge was glistening with water, although the surface of the stone was such that it was not slippery. Boriega was holding the reins firmly and concentrating on keeping to the centre of the bridge.

Hyrn could see ahead of him that Careil and Duburinga had traversed the bridge and had exited between two pillars on the other side. Rowan and Arienga were almost to the other side. The wet air in the chasm seemed to be pushing across the bridge following the flow of water. Hyrn could see that the wall to the right was crumbling and in one place almost non-existent. Through the gap he could see the water rushing through the chasm below and down to the large vee shaped gash in the rockface. He could almost imagine he was being sucked down through that gash, swirling and crashing against the unforgiving rocks. He shook his head and concentrated on the back of Boriega. He could feel his hand gripping the reins tightly despite the dampness. Before he knew it they were passing through the pillars and were back on the path. The other Caramar followed and the party resumed as before. With a signal from Duburinga, Boriega and Arienga went ahead to scout the path.

The path continued through the gorge and veered again, this time slightly to the left and gradually disappeared around the bend. The cliff to the left remained as sheer as ever but the rockface on the right was broken up and at times dropped further back from the path. In these areas small trees and bushes grew, breaking up the monotony of the rocky surroundings. Hyrn noticed that it had become lighter as the sun rose a little higher and the gorge became wider. They came to an area of bushes and trees to the right of the path surrounded by outcroppings of rock. Duburinga stopped abruptly and waited. As if from nowhere, Arienga and Boriega appeared from amongst the foliage.

"The way is open," said Boriega.

Duburinga signalled and they followed towards the row of bushes. At first it was difficult to see a way through. It was only when they were right up against the bushes that Hyrn could see that there was a path that led behind a row of bushes and then curved around behind others that stood just a little further back. The foliage was thick and they had to push branches aside. They were careful to keep the horses' heads low. The path wound back and forth irregularly until it opened out on a small clearing surrounded by a wall of rock. There didn't seem to be any way through.

Duburinga approached the rock. He ran his hand along it until he found the right spot. He held his hand there and softly chanted. An almost imperceptible hum arose from the rock and slowly a large section slid to one side with a slight grating sound. As it did, Hyrn could see an open vista on the other side that stretched far to the horizon. Duburinga walked through and stood on a rock platform surrounded by a low wall that seemed to hang in the air. One of the other Caramar went and stood alongside him. The party then formed up as they had to cross the bridge. Duburinga led Careil and Erras to the left and out of view. Rowan and Arienga followed with Blade, and then Boriega led Hyrn and Marly through the gap in the rockwall. The other Caramar stood on the platform and guided them away from the low wall.

As they turned to the left Hyrn could see that a long wide stairway led downwards partly cut into the cliff-face. To the right of the stairway the cliff fell steeply and Hyrn could see forest and then open land stretching away into the distance. Boriega held the reins steady and walked to the outside of the stairway, whilst Hyrn stayed on the inside under the overhang of the cliff. The surface of the stairs was weathered and broken in places but loose pieces had been pushed to the edges by the Caramar to ensure steady footing for the horses. Hyrn looked back and saw that one of the Caramar bringing up the rear stood with his hand against the rock. He heard the grating noise as the rock closed behind them. No wonder no-one had ever found this path. They would need to know where it was and how to open the rock. Here they were walking where probably no other but Caramar had walked.

As they progressed, vines and creepers formed a roof over the stairway and hung over the side down to the top of the low wall on their right. Hyrn could see that the vines overhead had been trained so that they intertwined to form the roof. This provided shelter but would also serve to hide the stairway so that it couldn't be seen from below. After a while the stairway veered to the left and they entered a stone tunnel. It was dim in the tunnel but Hyrn could see that there was daylight ahead. As they emerged the stairway continued as it had before. Hyrn noticed that ahead of him Rowan and Arienga were deep in conversation.

"It must be exciting to train as a warrior," said Rowan.

Arienga looked at him.

"It is exciting but it is a lot of hard work," she said. "It must be much more exciting for you to be chosen for this quest."

"I don't know that we were chosen," replied Rowan. "We were just in the wrong place at the wrong time."

"Nothing important happens by accident," said Arienga. "Fate has chosen you and Hyrn for this."

"It does seem strange that all this is happening to us but—"

As Rowan spoke his feet suddenly went out from under him. The stone on which he stood crumbled and the edge of the stairway collapsed and he plummeted. Below him stretched the mountainside and far below that a boulder strewn, wooded hillside and certain death. As he fell Arienga, dived and reached out her hand and grabbed his left wrist. Her other hand held tightly to the reins of Rowan's horse, Blade. Rowan's weight dragged Arienga closer to the edge of the hole in the stairway. Blade began to move forward.

Arienga looked quickly at Blade and loudly commanded, "Stop Blade!"

The horse hesitated but the pull on the reins was still telling him to move forward. Arienga looked deeply at the horse and then repeated the command. Blade stood firm. By this time, Boriega had dashed down the stairway and lay down alongside Arienga. He reached down and grabbed Rowan's shoulder. As he tried to pull Rowan up, Hyrn grabbed Blade's halter and pulled him backwards. This dragged Arienga, still clutching Rowan's arm, away from the edge. As they pulled him up, the Sword of Acclimoss caught on the rockface and the scabbard was twisted around so that the hilt of the sword began to point downwards.

Hyrn cried out "The Sword!"

As he said this the sword began to slip from its scabbard and dangle precariously. With horror Hyrn saw the sword clear the scabbard. As it began to fall Rowan's right hand shot out and grasped the hilt. Boriega and Arienga lifted Rowan up and away from the edge. He lay on the stone trembling and panting. The Sword of Acclimoss was firmly grasped to his chest.

Careil and Duburinga had made their way back up the stairway in the short time that the incident had taken. After they had made sure that Rowan was alright, and had moved the party down the stairway away from the danger, Duburinga addressed Arienga.

"Why were you not on the outside of the path?' he demanded sternly. "It is your duty as warrior and guide to face danger first. Your training would have enabled you to feel the weakness in the rock."

Before the shamefaced Arienga had a chance to answer Rowan spoke up. "It is my fault, Duburinga. I asked Arienga to let me walk there so that I had a better view."

Duburinga looked at Rowan and then to Arienga.

"Be that as it may," he said and addressing Arienga, continued sharply. "Your training should have directed you to counsel Rowan against this. It is just as well that no harm came to him." He looked at Rowan. "...apart from a few scrapes and bruises." "Come," he continued, "the morning wears on."

He addressed all the Caramar. "Take care. Watch the edges. They are unstable and in need of repair. They have not been maintained as they should have been. Perhaps if..." he paused, "when Gardarvon is restored these mountain ways will be returned to their former condition."

With that he turned and moved to take up his position at the front of the party.

Arienga walked to where Rowan was now on his feet dusting himself off.

"Thank you Rowan," she said with a smile, "but Duburinga is right I should have warned you from taking the outside of the path."

"It's my fault," said Rowan. "I should have been more careful, but there's no harm done."

Arienga took Blade's reins and moved to the outside of the path. Rowan took up his position on the inside and the party continued their journey downwards.

After some time Duburinga called a halt and spoke to them all. "The path now continues into the mountain. The passage is low at first but will open out. We will not emerge until we meet the path of the Gardwater again. We will then pass through the secret gateway and out into Wesmere."

They entered the entrance to the passage into the mountain. The horses were forced to bow their heads below the low ceiling. The passage was also narrow in places and the party was forced to travel in single file. Hyrn noticed that the rock walls gave off a dull light. It helped illuminate the path but it was still fairly dim, and it was necessary to tread carefully so as not to stumble. After what seemed like an age, the passage began to widen and become higher until they broke out into a large cavern. The walls here too gave off the same light and Hyrn could see some distance into the gloom, although it was still hard to judge how large the cavern was. He could hear the faint sound of water rushing somewhere ahead.

They made their way across the cavern and as they did Hyrn could see that another much larger passage began on the other side. The party entered this passage. The stone floor sloped gently downwards. As they made their way through, the sound of water grew louder. Hyrn also noticed that it was growing lighter as they went. Eventually they emerged into another cavern smaller than the first. The sight and sound struck Hyrn with awe. The cavern was filled with dappled, shimmering light. The sound of cascading water came from the opposite end, where a curtain of water separated the cavern from the sunlight outside.

Duburinga spoke in a voice full of reverence. "Behold the Carabrarn. The Crystal Gate, entrance to the Caramarhc. Few outsiders have ever seen this side of the gate. It was well defended in the past, and its natural hidden position has kept it secret when our people were unable to post sentries here."

When Hyrn looked carefully, he could see that there were doorways in the rockface at each side of the waterfall that must have been the sentry posts. He could not see any way through the cascade of water without getting very wet.

"How do we get through?" he asked in a voice louder than he intended.

His words echoed off the walls.

Duburinga smiled. "There is a path just past the guardhouse at one side that allows access," he said. "Come, I will lead you."

He moved towards the doorway to the right of the waterfall and as they approached Hyrn saw that there was a half tunnel cut into the rockface parallel with the waterfall. They walked through this, the cascade of water on one side and the face of the rock on the other. The wall of water ended abruptly and the path switched back so that they passed around the end of the curtain of water. The turn was quite tight and the horses were splashed with water. Hyrn could hear Erras snorting in indignation. They were now on the other side of the waterfall. The passage continued a short way and then they emerged into the open air and the brightness of the summer sun.

A large pool of water stretched in front of them. The waterfall crashed noisily into the pool sending ripples outwards. Where they had emerged from the passage a large wall of rock jutted out obscuring the far end of the pool. Duburinga led them to the rock wall. He stopped, and then laying his right hand on the rock began murmuring something in a deep singsong voice. A doorway slowly opened in the rock and Duburinga motioned for them to pass through. They came out into a glade of trees that grew right up to the water's edge. Hyrn could see that the pool continued for a little way and then narrowed into a rapidly flowing channel that disappeared around a bend disappearing into a heavily forested area ahead. The sun was high in the sky. Hyrn heard a dull thud from behind him and turned to see what it was. One of the Caramar had closed the doorway behind them.

"We will stop briefly to have a midday meal, and then continue on," said Duburinga.

After they had eaten, they packed up and readied themselves to continue on.

"The Gardwater joins with other streams to form the River Ballar below Ballarghen," said Duburinga. "We will travel away from the course of the Gardwater and travel southwards and meet up with the King's Road a few miles outside the city."

With that he led them into the forest and along an overgrown path. The path was hard to discern at first and had obviously not been used for some time. At times they were forced to abandon the path where trees had fallen or where new trees and bushes had sprung up. The ground they had been travelling over had gradually risen until the path crested a ridge and they could see that the land sloped downwards to the east. The forest grew sparser ahead of them and into the distance they could see rolling farmland. They continued on, and after a while, as the woodland became a scattering of trees, they joined a track heading northeast. This path was obviously more heavily used. The packed dirt surface was rutted with wheel tracks and hoof marks. They travelled much more easily and it wasn't long before they reached a crossroads where the track intercepted a large paved road, the King's Road.

They entered the King's Road and the horses' hooves clattered on the paved surface as they started towards Ballarghen. They had not travelled far along this road before they saw a man on horseback coming towards them.

Careil moved ahead of Duburinga.

As the Rider approached, Careil called out to him, "Bregal, well met."

The Rider pulled up, a look of astonishment on his face.

"Careil," he said. "We have had no word from you for days. There has been no news of your party travelling on this road."

He glanced at the others and surprise passed across his face again.

"Caramar warriors!" he exclaimed. "What strange times are these that Caramar travel down from the mountains unannounced? Had we known we would have sent a party to greet you."

Careil laughed. "It is alright, Bregal. We have newly come from Gardarvon and before that from the Lairess. We have news that we must bring before the King and Council."

"Gardarvon?" said Bregal with puzzlement on his face. "Even stranger still. Dark names from the past on a bright summer's afternoon on the King's Road."

Careil laughed again. "All will be explained, Bregal. Until then let me introduce you to everyone."

Bregal dismounted and Careil introduced him to each of the party. With this done Duburinga spoke on behalf of the Caramar.

"You honour us with your greetings and goodwill," he said solemnly.

Bregal bowed in response.

"We welcome you as honoured guests," he said.

The Rider then mounted his horse and said, "I will go on ahead and announce your imminent arrival, and your desire for an audience with the King and the Council."

He waved his hand, wheeled his horse around and sped off with a clatter of hooves.

The sun was getting lower in the afternoon sky by the time they reached the outskirts of Ballarghen. They had passed numerous farmsteads along the way, but now they increasingly passed houses and commercial buildings. They came to a large stone bridge that passed across the river and into the main part of the city. As they moved across and into the city, the King's Way became a street lined with buildings, some two or three stories high. The people of the city turned to look at them as they passed. Many stopped and stared at the procession, a King's Rider, two boys, and a band of Caramar warriors, all travel worn and with determined looks on their faces. The street became busier as the word spread, and more people came to watch them pass. After a while four horsemen rode up in formation. They were clothed in brightly coloured uniforms and carried long lances.

"King's Guards," said Careil.

One of the horsemen dismounted and approached them.

"Greetings, Rider Careil," he said, and then addressed the rest of the party. "I am Captain Argil of the King's Guards. We are here to escort you to your lodgings within the castle. You will have time to freshen up while an audience with the King's Council is arranged."

He remounted and the four guards took up positions, two at the front and two at the rear. Captain Argil signalled and the party moved off. The guards motioned the people who now lined the streets to move back as they went. They came to a large square with a fountain in the middle. Many people milled about the square. Market stalls and shopfronts lined the outer edges all decorated with garlands, flags and brightly painted signs. There were entertainers of all sorts, jugglers, musicians. The smell of all kinds of food wafted through the air. The city of Ballarghen was a lively, colourful place and Hyrn and Rowan looked about with wonder. They had never been anywhere bigger than Margen Town near their parent's farm, but that was a mere village compared to this. The guards led them diagonally across the corner of the square, and then turned left into a wider street that led gently up a hill towards the gates of a large walled citadel that rose above the city.

Hyrn looked around the room that had been assigned to him and Rowan. It felt good to be clean again after travelling for so long. The room had access to bathing facilities, heated water and soap. Their clothes had been laundered and returned to them. They had also been brought food, a delicious hot stew, and mugs of warm milk and honey. Night had fallen. He moved over to the window and looked out across the city. Lamps burned in the streets and in the windows of houses. He had never seen such a display of lights before.

The members of the King's Council were being summoned. They would meet with them later that evening. Hyrn was tired but he doubted that he would have been able to sleep with all that was going on. Careil had been in to see them, and had now gone down into the city to see his family. It was strange that he had never thought about Careil's family. He had only seen him alone, apart from Erras. Erras had been stabled at the King's Rider's station just outside the citadel. Blade and Marly had been granted the privilege of being stabled there too, so as to be close to Erras in the strange city. They too had never been anywhere as big and noisy as Ballarghen.

Rowan was lying on his bed with his eyes shut. Hyrn wasn't sure if he was asleep or not. It was the first time that he and Rowan had been alone for any length of time since they had left home.

"Rowan!" Hyrn called softly so as not to wake him if he was asleep.

"What?" Rowan answered with a tinge of annoyance in his voice.

"What do you think will happen at the Council?" Hyrn asked quietly.

Rowan opened his eyes and turned his head towards Hyrn. "They'll probably decide that the army can take it from here and we'll be sent home," he said, sounding a little disappointed.

"But what about Ilah and the Sword?" asked Hyrn. "They can't just take them can they? What if they decide it's just a story and just put them in a museum or something?"

Rowan's face took on a more serious look.

"Look Hyrn," he said, "when they see Ilah it will show them we're not just making this up. Ilah is real and powerful. They'll have to take notice."

Hyrn looked over to where Ilah lay on his bed wrapped in the cloth. He turned back towards Rowan.

"What about the Sword?" he said.

The Sword of Acclimoss was propped against the head of Rowan's bed.

"I don't know," said Rowan. "I don't really like the idea of handing it over to anyone else. You heard what Careil said. He thought that I was meant to carry it."

He looked worried but then shrugged and said with an almost dismissive tone, "Maybe it should go to the King though."

He sat up on the edge of the bed and picked up the Sword. It felt good in his hand. He laid it across his knees and looked at the hilt. It was carved with strange symbols that he didn't recognise. At each end of the guard was an oval shape. He wondered when it had been made and how many kings had held it, fought with it, killed with it. He shivered. Perhaps he was not the right person to be carrying such a weapon. He was just a farm boy. He knew nothing about fighting. The last few days were like a dream. Stones, and swords, and Drargs, and... Arienga.

That thought brought a smile to his face and then he thought. What about the Caramar? Would they just go home now? They were staying somewhere else in the castle. No doubt being given special treatment as honoured guests. He and Hyrn were just Wesmerian farm boys from the Lairess Plains.

"Why were you smiling?"

Hyrn's voice interrupted his thoughts.

"No reason," replied Rowan defensively.

"I know why," said Hyrn." I saw you talking to Arienga, and you couldn't take your eyes off her when the Caramar went to their rooms."

Rowan reddened slightly.

"Shut up Hyrn," he said, and picking up a pillow, lobbed it at Hyrn.

Just then there was a knock at the door.

"Come in," said Hyrn.

The door opened and Careil stepped in. He looked at the pillow on the floor, and then at Rowan and Hyrn.

"I hope you aren't disrespecting King Almar's hospitality," he said in a mock tone of reproach.

The King's Rider then abruptly became serious and said, "Pick that up and let's get going. The King and his Council are gathering in the Council chamber."

"So you are coming too, Careil?" asked Hyrn. "I was thinking we would have to face them alone."

"Nothing like that," said Careil and added, with a short laugh, "They will need a reliable witness."

Rowan climbed to his feet holding the Sword.

"Bring the Sword and the Stone," said Careil.

He turned towards the door. Hyrn scooped up Ilah and put the Stone inside his now clean vest, and he and Rowan followed Careil through the door.

As the doors opened, Hyrn's heart skipped a beat. The chamber they entered was luxurious. A massive table dominated the room. Around this table sat well dressed and ostentatiously adorned men. The Caramar were seated together. At the head of the table, on a large chair, sat the King.

Hyrn's heart started to pound in his chest. He felt out of place. They were just going to laugh at him. But he felt the warmth of Ilah in his vest. Hyrn looked at Careil. Careil bowed his head to the King. Hyrn and Rowan followed his example. King Almar beckoned to them and gestured for them to sit in chairs to his left. Hyrn, Rowan and Careil walked down towards the King. Hyrn could feel the eyes of the seated Council members upon him. The three of them took their seats. Hyrn felt that the chair was too big for him as he settled himself into it.

"Welcome," said King Almar.

Rowan glanced down the table and his eyes met those of Arienga. She quickly looked away and concentrated on the King.

"This is indeed an unusual occasion," the King continued. "We are pleased to welcome our friends and allies from the Caramar. It has been many years since we have been honoured by their presence in Wesmere. It is not clear what part they play here but Duburinga has asked that their counsel be kept until other stories have been told."

Duburinga rose and spoke, "King Almar, we thank you for your hospitality and your kind words."

He bowed towards the King and then resumed his seat.

Almar continued, looking towards Careil, "Rider Careil, you have requested an audience with this Council. Please explain what we are all doing here."

Careil rose to his feet. "Your Majesty, Esteemed Councillors…" he started.

The King waved his hand dismissively and said impatiently, "Please get to the point, Rider."

Careil began again, "I was on patrol in the Lairess Plains. As I was passing the farm of Meralie and Baraman Fairbrow, Baraman was waiting at the front looking troubled and glancing anxiously down the road. He told me that his sons, Rowan and Hyrn, had not returned from a trip into the mountains. They had been expecting them earlier that afternoon. It was about an hour before sunset so I offered to look for them.

I rode towards the mountains and came across them as the sun was setting. They were still quite a distance from home. After getting them home, Rowan told us all a very strange story. With the Council's permission, I think it best if Rowan and Hyrn tell you the next part of the story."

The King nodded his agreement, and nervously Rowan and Hyrn got to their feet. Rowan began the story as he had back at the farm, leaving out any embellishments, as the Council sat and listened with serious faces. Occasionally, Hyrn would nod his head in agreement but he was too afraid to correct Rowan or add anything. When Rowan had told the story, Careil stood and motioned Rowan and Hyrn to resume their seats.

"We needed to come to Ballarghen," he said, "but the boys had been charged to go to Gardarvon and seek out the Sword of Acclimoss. We were aided in this by the Caramar."

He turned to Duburinga and the rest of the Caramar warriors.

"I will not go into detail about the events within the lands of the Caramar," he said. "I will leave it to Duburinga to speak of this as he sees fit. Suffice to say that the quest for the Sword was successful. Rowan, if you would, please."

Rowan stood nervously. He bent and lifted the sword a little clumsily from where it leant against his chair. He drew the sword smoothly from its scabbard and placed it on the table.

"This is the Sword of Acclimoss, the sword of the Kings of Anasaria," said Careil. "As Rowan has told, it must be returned to Anasaria. They seek the Council's advice and assistance in realising this, and also in reuniting the Twin Stones of Angil and returning them to their rightful place in the fortress of Abessair."

There were a few muttered words at this declaration. Councillor Drey spoke up. He represented the parts of Wesmere that bordered the eastern coast.

"Our fishing boats have braved the treacherous Eastern Sea," he said with arrogance and disdain. They have reported sighting the rocky, fog-shrouded coast of Ansaria…"

"It's called Anasaria!" Hyrn's voice sounded loud and intrusive, as he blurted out the words.

The Councillor gave Hyrn a contemptuous look.

"Even so," he continued, "there is nowhere to land."

"We were told that we must pass through the Realm of the Underdwellers!" blurted out Hyrn.

A general hubbub of voices arose around the table. A tall skinny councillor rose to his feet, a smirk on his face.

"This is absurd. The Realm of the Underdwellers is a myth, a stupid old legend," he scoffed, seemingly ignoring Hyrn and speaking directly to the King. "And what is this of talking Stones. I see a fine sword but must we believe all this nonsense of Stones, and Keepers, and Dark Lords."

There was a general murmuring amongst the Council as others put voice to their disbelief. The King had a concerned look upon his face and made as if to speak.

Hyrn could feel anger building inside him, and then he felt Ilah become hot inside his vest. He hesitated but then resolutely drew Ilah out and held it out in front of him.

Ilah spoke and all eyes turned to the Stone shining in Hyrn's outstretched hands, "Hail to you King Almar, and to the people of Wesmere."

The skinny councillor stood with his mouth agape and then dropped back into his seat.

Ilah continued, "They have spoken truly. Anasaria needs your help. The Sword of Acclimoss must return to Anasaria. I must be reunited with my twin and be returned to Abessair to free the people of Anasaria from the thrall of evil. King Darion passed through the Realm of the Underdwellers six hundred years ago and Bharain three hundred years ago. The way must be tried again. There are parts of Anasaria that can be reached by sea. If you travel south and then west you would find a safe harbour."

Hyrn held the Stone bright and hot in his hand and was filled with hope as Ilah implored the Council further, "Great evil has taken over Anasaria. Abessair is under the rule of the Dark Lords and has become Ultamar. The Abessairian army are under an evil curse and are being used to enslave the people of Anasaria. I implore you to aid Rowan and Hyrn. Their fate is entwined with mine."

And with that Ilah went silent and faded into darkness.

Duburinga rose and said, "With your permission I will speak."

Almar nodded.

"The quest for the Sword and for Bharain's resting place has set the Caramar on a new course. It has reawakened our spirit," Duburinga's voice was stern and strident as he spoke. "Gardarvon has been reclaimed and things thought lost have been found. These two young men have been sent for a reason. Something is changing that we don't quite understand."

He turned and looked at the Councillors around the table. "The Realm of the Underdwellers is known among the Caramar. The entrance is known to lie in the east of the Caramarhc. The Elders will know more. Word has been sent that this knowledge is sought."

"For our part," he motioned to the Caramar seated around him, "our fate is tied to these two and, whatever is decided, we will do all we can to ensure that their quest is fulfilled."

Duburinga sat down again. He looked at Rowan and Hyrn and nodded his head, a reassuring look on his face.

King Almar was silent for a few moments and then spoke. "We have much to consider. I suggest that we break for tonight and resume in the morning. Our guests are welcome to our hospitality while the Council considers these matters. If we need further information, we will call for you. Rider Careil, I will expect you to be on call to report further, if necessary."

Duburinga bowed his head in respect at the King's wishes. Rowan and Hyrn looked at each other, and then at Careil, a little bewildered. Careil just shook his head slightly with a look of warning in his eyes to stifle any complaints. The King rose to his feet and everyone else rose too. The King turned, and two guards appeared and escorted him through a velvet curtain in the back wall of the chamber.

Once the King had left, the councillors began to leave too. The Caramar quickly moved out through a doorway on the other side of the chamber. Rowan glanced over and saw Arienga disappearing through the doorway. Careil came over to Rowan and Hyrn.

"Come on you two," he said. "You need to get some sleep."

Hyrn looked up at Careil and said, "Does this mean we won't be able to hear what they're saying about us? They are going to decide without us?"

"It is necessary," said Careil, trying to sound reassuring, "The Council needs to be able to deliberate without interference. The Councillors need to be able to speak their minds. They have heard much that they must discuss and decide upon. This may have consequences that we haven't considered that could affect the lives of many in Wesmere."

"Unless they decide to do nothing," said Rowan.

"Then we will just go ourselves," said Hyrn. "From what Duburinga said at least we will have some Caramar warriors to help us… and they know where the Realm of the Underdwellers is."

"We will see. We will see," said Careil. "If I can, I will also help you. I promised your mother and father that I would look after you, but the King may have other ideas. Come on now. It is time for bed. I will take you back to your room and then I will go home. It will be good to sleep in my own bed, even if it is just for one night."

With that he turned and led the way out of the Council chamber with Rowan and Hyrn behind him, both quiet and deep in thought.

CHAPTER FIVE

The Halestone

Rowan and Hyrn ate breakfast in a small dining room on the floor below their bedroom. One of the staff had directed them downstairs to where an assortment of food awaited them. They were alone in the room and ate mostly in silence. At one point Hyrn started to complain about how unfair it was that they were not included in the deliberations of the Council, but Rowan just looked at him and shrugged, and Hyrn went back to eating. A page came and saw them as they were finishing. He told them that the King had requested they remain in their room until they were summoned.

Rowan lay on his bed staring at the ceiling. Hyrn was leaning on the window sill looking out across the city. There had been no word from the Council and the morning was wearing on. The boys were bored. They could not even go and explore. They were getting increasingly worried by the lack of any news. A noise from the corridor brought Hyrn out of his reverie.

"What was that?" he said, turning to face Rowan.

Rowan sat up. A soft but insistent knocking sounded at the door. Hyrn dashed to the door and opened it. Careil moved quickly into the room. He was slightly out of breath and had a worried look on his face.

"Grab your things," he said abruptly.

"What's going on?" asked Rowan, getting to his feet.

"The Council is not letting you go any further," replied Careil. "You are being sent home, and they intend to keep the Sword and Ilah."

"No," said Hyrn shaking his head.

"They can't," said Rowan, with a note of desperation in his voice.

The Rider studied each of the boys in turn. His face bore a look of determination.

"I am risking much but after all I have seen I cannot let this happen," he said.

"What...?" began Hyrn.

"There is no time for questions," said Careil insistently. "We must go now!"

Rowan grasped the Sword of Acclimoss and picked up his bag. He pulled his shoes on and stood ready. Hyrn, Ilah already safely inside his vest, grabbed his bag, and the two boys fell in behind Careil. Careil went to the door and listened, then furtively stuck his head out and motioned for the boys to follow. There was no need for him to tell them to be quiet, as they silently followed closely behind. Careil turned left and hurried down the corridor. He turned into a small alcove that led into a narrow stairway that took them down to near where the boys had eaten breakfast.

At the bottom, they turned quickly into a narrow corridor that led towards the outer wall of the Citadel. They came to a low door at the end of the corridor. The door was locked but Careil pulled a small bunch of ornate keys from his pocket, selected one, and quickly unlocked the door. The door was stiff and opened with what seemed like a loud creak in the silence. Sunlight came through the open door. Careil ducked through, quickly looked around, and then motioned the boys through. He turned and locked the door behind them.

They were in a narrow alleyway, deserted and cluttered with rubbish and broken barrels and items of furniture. They moved diagonally across the alley to a small archway. They passed into a stone building divided into stalls. There was a strong smell of horses and hay, and the soft sounds of horses at rest. A short, old man stood holding the reins of Erras.

"He is ready, Careil," he said. "I will ensure that the boy's horses are looked after. I will arrange for my son to move them to our place outside the city. If need be, he will make sure they are returned to their home."

"Thank you, Bardon," replied Careil. "Make sure you hurry from here. I do not want you to suffer any punishment on my behalf."

Bardon laughed softly and his eyes sparkled. "There is little they can do to an old man like me, and you have always been good to me, young Rider, and treated Erras well."

He handed Careil the reins and reached up and gripped his shoulder.

"Take care, Careil," said Bardon. "I hope to see you again, hopefully not too soon. And goodbye young men," he said to Rowan and Hyrn. "I hear that great things are in your future."

Careil smiled at him. "Goodbye, Bardon," he said.

The boys both smiled and nodded to Bardon. With that Careil led Erras and the boys between two stalls and through an archway that led out into another alleyway. They crossed quickly and passed through a doorway that led into another stable, this one empty. Careil pulled a cloak from his saddle bags and draped it over his Rider's apparel. They continued through the stable and out into a broader pathway. They passed a couple of townspeople but they didn't take much notice of the party as they went about their business. After a while they turned into a narrow alley between two houses which abruptly ended at a large stone wall.

Hyrn had a sudden thought that they were trapped. The distant sound of raised voices and clamour arose behind them. Careil signalled to the right and Hyrn saw that there was a narrow way that ran between the rear of the house and the wall. They filed through the narrow path which was just wide enough to allow Erras through. They came to a pile of rubble and Hyrn saw that there was an arched door in the wall. The door was not locked but took a bit of effort from Careil before it burst open.

They hurried through and came out on a slope that led down from the wall towards the river. There were bushes and small trees covering the slope and these afforded some shelter from observation from the wall above. Careil pushed the door closed with some difficulty. He then grabbed a sturdy log and planted it against the door at an angle.

"Not many know of this door," he said, "but just in case."

"Where are we going?" blurted Hyrn.

"We will talk once we are away from the city," said Careil.

The two boys followed him down the slope and towards the river. They turned left and Careil led them into the shallows at the edge of the river. The opposite shore was heavily wooded and appeared deserted. They travelled upstream, and after a while, they turned a bend, where the river flowed round a spur of the hill on which the city sat. They were now blocked from view from the city. They left the shallows and continued along the bank through a wooded area. The forest became thicker as they moved further away from the city.

They had travelled for some time, when they came upon a forested ridge that blocked their path and continued out into the river down to their right. Careil turned left and they continued along a barely discernible path that followed the base of the ridge westwards. As they left the river behind them, Careil began scanning the woods that led up the slope to the ridge above. Eventually he seemed to find what he was looking for and they turned into the forest. After a difficult climb through the trees, they came out into an open area that led up into a narrow gorge that continued northward up towards the spine of the ridge. They continued up the gorge and finally they could see that it led up to a pass that crossed the top of the ridge. Careil led Erras to a small level grassed area at the right of the gorge and let the horse graze.

"We'll rest here and have something to eat while I fill you in on what has occurred," said the Rider.

Rowan and Hyrn were both hungry. They had had no food since breakfast and the afternoon was wearing on.

"I'm starving," said Rowan.

"Me too," agreed Hyrn.

They sat on the grass, eating the food that Bardon had provided. They could see back down the gorge, and across the top of the forest, the shape of the city of Ballarghen to the south.

This will keep us going until we can get over this ridge and into the lands of the Caramar," said Careil. "We can then risk a fire tonight and have a cooked meal. We are too exposed here to light a fire. The smoke may well be seen by the troops that will be out looking for us."

"Won't they know where we are anyway?" asked Hyrn.

"This part of Wesmere is little known to many, even amongst the King's Riders," said Careil. "They will be expecting us to try and cross one of the bridges downstream. The lesser paths into the Caramarhc are seldom visited."

"Where are we going?" asked Rowan. "And won't they know that you would have gone to the stables to get Erras?"

"I will begin with that," said Careil. "Last night, after I left you, I thought long and hard about how the Council was proceeding. I thought it may be prudent to make plans in case things went badly. I asked Bardon to move Erras from the Riders' stable when no one was around, and to prepare him for a journey at short notice. The stables that we went to are little used and then only by merchants and travellers. They are also close to a place I discovered many years ago while I was in training. I occasionally used it to sneak out of the city and travel into these lands and up into the mountains."

"While I was not allowed into the Council," he continued, "I received an update from a friend, that the Council, under the direction of the King, was considering taking the Stone and the Sword. They then planned to decide how they could use them to best serve the interests of Wesmere. I was also told to expect a message. I received it just before I came to your room."

Careil pulled a small piece of parchment from his pocket and showed it to Rowan and Hyrn. On it was a symbol that showed a mountain peak with rays shining from it.

"What does it mean?" asked Hyrn.

"It is a Caramar symbol," said Careil. "It is the symbol of the Seat of the Elders."

"The Seat of the Elders!" exclaimed Hyrn. "Is that where we're going?"

"The message came from Duburinga," said Careil. "He sent it to me when the Caramar left the Council."

"They left?" said Rowan, getting to his feet. "Where did they go?"

"They are leaving Ballarghen the way we came," answered Careil. "They will not risk coming this way. I believe they will meet up with us by another route. The King will assume we will go the same way and probably try to follow them. Rest assured though that the Caramar will soon lose anyone that tries to follow their trail. And yes, Hyrn we are going to the Seat of The Elders."

Hyrn looked at him in wonder.

"The Seat of the Elders," he said. "I would never have believed that we would see that." He paused and looked at Careil with a concerned look on his face, "but won't you be in trouble with the King?"

"I have made my decision," Careil replied. "I have discussed this with Duburinga and it is clear that this is beyond any loyalty I have to the King and Council. This is part of something bigger than I could have ever imagined. I believe that I was meant to help you with the task you have been given. I will accept any punishment that arises from my actions, but I will do all I can to make sure that your quest is not caught up in the petty politics of Wesmere. My path is your path and I will do all I can to help and protect you."

Rowan stood looking at Careil as he sat beside Hyrn. Without knowing why Rowan pulled the Sword of Acclimoss from its sheath on his back and raised it above his head. The Sword was heavy but he spoke in a voice that was strange but unfaltering.

"Careil, King's Rider," he said, "You are now the guardian and protector of the carriers of the Sword and Stone of Anasaria."

Careil looked at Rowan and a slight smile was on his face but he became serious as he said, "I will guard and protect the bearers of the Sword and the Stone, and will give my all to see the Sword and the Stone returned to their rightful place."

Hyrn felt Ilah become hot against his chest. He stood and removed the Stone from under his vest and as he unwrapped it, Ilah burst with light bathing them all in its glow and then went dark again.

"W-what just happened?" stammered Hyrn.

"I'm not sure," said Careil. "But I think that Ilah has shown that we are bound together. Now I think that we should get moving. That light may have drawn unwanted attention."

After an arduous climb, they crested the ridge and passed over into the fringe lands between Wesmere and the lands of the Caramar.

Far below, a lone man on horseback rode slowly through the forest. He followed the trail of a man, a horse, and two boys, and he pondered the meaning of a bright flash of light to the north.

Rowan awoke abruptly. Morning light slanted through the trees. The fire was out and Careil and Hyrn were nowhere to be seen. He sat up. Erras was grazing at the edge of the clearing. Rowan got up and stretched.

Just then, Careil and Hyrn appeared from amongst the trees, accompanied by two Caramar warriors.

"Good. You are awake. Rowan, this is Carunda and Delanga," said Careil, pointing to the two warriors in turn.

He explained that they had entered the camp at first light and had taken them to the rest of their group at a nearby camp. He had taken Hyrn to show them Ilah.

"They now know of our visit to Gardarvon and what occurred there," he continued. "Carunda and Delanga are going to escort us part of the way into the mountains, and then we will meet with other Caramar. They are keen to see the Sword first."

Rowan went to his pack. He unwrapped the sword, drew it from its scabbard and lifted it into the air. The morning sunlight flashed off the surface of the blade.

"This is the Sword of Acclimoss," said Rowan.

The two Caramar approached and looked at the blade with awe.

"It is beautiful," said Delanga, and she continued. "Bharain and his quest are well remembered in The Seat of the Elders, although no record has been found as to his resting place. It must have been kept secret."

"We never would have found it without the aid of the Caramar," said Rowan. "We are grateful to you for your help."

Delanga smiled. "We are happy to help and will be glad to escort you to The Seat of the Elders." She turned to Careil. "The road into the mountains is safe for now but there have been reports of sightings of Mountain Drargs. It is unusual. The Drargs usually keep to the north-eastern regions of the Caramarhc."

"It is probably best that we get moving as soon as possible," said Careil.

After following barely visible paths through heavily wooded areas for most of the morning, they eventually emerged onto a stone roadway that led northward and upwards towards the central peaks of the mountains. To the east, the land sloped steeply away down to a river far below.

"That's the Tarnflow," said Careil. "The same river we followed when we left Ballarghen. It is fed by a large lake high in the mountains. I have never been this far upriver before. I believe that there is a bridge that crosses the headwaters."

He turned to Carunda beside him.

"That is true," said Carunda. "The Bridge of Mist. The bridge is where the main road crosses the river gorge below Thundering Falls. It can be treacherous after winter, but it is safe now."

Hyrn stood looking back down the roadway. "Where does this road go?" he asked.

"There is a watchtower that looks out over the river below, and out across Wesmere," said Delanga. It is not usually occupied these days, although it is kept in good condition and new warriors are often taken there as part of their training."

"I'd like to see the view," said Hyrn. "But—"

"Perhaps another time," said Delanga. We should continue on and get across the bridge and to shelter before nightfall."

Just as he was turning back to join them, Hyrn thought he saw movement in the trees on the verge of the road behind them. He swung back around and peered down the road. All was still. He shook his head. "You're seeing things," he thought, and with that, he turned back and joined the rest of the party as they began the trek up the roadway towards the sunlit peaks of the central Caramarhc.

After a brief pause for lunch they moved quickly on. As the afternoon wore on they could see that the road was heading towards a towering cliff. The mountainside rose sheer ahead of them. The river valley to the right of the road had now become a steep gorge and a low stone wall followed the roadway preventing travellers from plunging over the precipice. They also noticed that a low rumbling noise could be heard and it became louder as they continued on. As they drew closer to the cliff ahead, the rumbling became louder still. The air began to feel moist and there was a smell of dampness all around. As they moved up over a crest in the road, a large waterfall came into view at the head of the gorge. Water thundered over a channel at the top of the cliff, down into the gorge. Soon they could see ahead that a long stone bridge crossed the gorge to their right. The waterfall passed behind the bridge down into the mist. The bridge was far enough away from the cliff that the cascading water poured through the gap between without hitting it, but clouds of mist rose all around.

Just then, Hyrn saw movement across the chasm. It looked like small figures were scrambling up the side of the gorge.

Suddenly, Carunda called out loudly. "Drargs!"

Everything immediately descended into chaos. Heads appeared above the parapet wall. Sharp, angular faces with rows of pointed teeth. Careil pushed Rowan and Hyrn behind Erras. He quickly unlatched a long bundle in his saddle pack and drew out a long sword. Hyrn had never seen Careil wear a sword but the way that he swung it around he seemed to know how to use it. Delanga had a bow in her hand and was unleashing arrows at the heads as they appeared above the wall. Carunda wielded a short sword and a heavy cudgel. He jumped up on the wall and began swiping at the Drargs.

"To the bridge!" he cried.

"Take Erras!" yelled Careil.

Hyrn grabbed Erras's reins. He clambered up into the saddle. He turned to help Rowan up but Rowan was standing facing the wall. The Sword of Acclimoss was in his hands. His face looked strange; frightened, but determined.

"Rowan. Come on!" shouted Hyrn.

Rowan looked at him.

"Just ride towards the bridge!" he said loudly, almost angrily.

Hyrn pushed his heels into Erras's sides and Erras began trotting up the roadway towards the bridge. Rowan followed behind with Careil alongside and slightly behind him. The two Caramar warriors worked their way along the wall, striking out at Drargs as they went. There was a lull in the Drargs appearing and Careil urged them on. Hyrn pushed Erras and the horse broke away. The rest of the party followed, on guard against further attacks. Hyrn looked back towards them. He noticed Rowan with the sword raised above his head. He looked like a different person.

As they approached the bridge a group of about seven or eight Drargs jumped the wall behind them and began to lope after them their clawed hands raised, ready to attack. Hyrn could see that there were Drargs climbing the gorge wall on the other side but there were none on the bridge. Hyrn looked behind again and could see that the Drargs were gaining on them, although just then, one caught an arrow in the chest and collapsed heavily, spraying blood. Hyrn gripped the reins, terror beginning to grow within him. He reached the bridge and turned Erras onto the stonework.

As he did, he saw behind them, a figure on horseback come galloping up the road gaining rapidly on the Drargs. Hyrn slowed down and watched as the rider rode into the Drargs, running down two, and slashing at others as he rode amongst them. He wheeled his horse and attacked, bringing down two of the remaining three Drargs. The last of Delanga's arrows brought the remaining one down and the rider rode up the roadway towards them.

As he approached Careil called out in recognition with a puzzled look on his face. "Bregal. How..?"

"No questions now," called the Rider, who Hyrn recognized as the Rider they had met on the road as they approached Ballarghen.

"Across the bridge!" shouted Delanga.

"Take Rowan!" called Careil to Bregal.

Bregal rode alongside Rowan and pulled him up behind him, ducking his head to avoid being beheaded by the sword in Rowan's hand. Delanga and Carunda dashed ahead as Careil leapt up behind Hyrn and the two horses broke into a gallop.

The Bridge of Mist and Thundering Falls were well named. Clouds of spray floated in the air. The waterfall thundered to their left. The stones of the bridge were wet but the horses trod surely. Careil and Bregal pulled ahead of the two Caramar, but at that moment Drargs began to climb onto the bridge ahead of them. Hyrn looked around and saw that Drargs were also coming onto the bridge behind them. Halfway along the bridge a small tower stood on the parapet, looking away down the gorge. They rode past the tower and as the Caramar reached it, Carunda peeled off through the arched doorway and into the tower. Almost immediately there was a loud trumpeting noise. It echoed down the gorge and along the cliff walls to their left.

Careil spoke in to Hyrn's ear. "Hold on tight," and then he cried loudly, "Run Erras!"

The horse put on a spurt of speed and Bregal's horse beside them also broke into a full gallop. The two horses thundered along the bridge. The Drargs ahead who had been loping towards them, now hesitated at the sight of the two horses charging at them. Hyrn saw the blade of Careil's sword poised beside him. He looked over and saw Bregal and Rowan also brandishing their swords. His eyes met Rowan's. Rowan's face was fierce. He raised the Sword of Acclimoss.

Then they were upon the Drargs blocking the bridge. Some dived out of the way. Others stood their ground and were run down or fell beneath the slash of steel. One clawed hand reached out and grabbed at Hyrn's leg but Careil's sword came scything down severing the arm. Then they were through. The horses continued across the bridge and came to a halt on the roadway. Careil told Hyrn to get down and Bregal lifted Rowan down beside him. There was a small alcove in the cliff to the left of the roadway.

"Stay here!" commanded Careil. "We need to help the Caramar."

Hyrn moved into the alcove and Rowan stood beside him. As Careil and Bregal wheeled their horses and charged back onto the bridge, Hyrn could see the two Caramar still making their way across. They were deftly running along the parapet of the bridge. The pursuing Drargs were gaining on them and the remainder of the Drargs they had ridden through were starting to move towards the Caramar. Carunda reached them swinging his cudgel and slashing with his sword. Delanga now also wielded a short sword and struck out as she followed.

As the two horses closed on the fray Carunda broke through and then turned and attacked, urging Delanga on. As the horses reached them a large Drarg knocked the sword from Delanga's hand and with another Drarg grabbed the Caramar slashing at her with their clawed hands. Bregal broke through and hacked the large Drarg across its neck sending it sprawling. Carunda reached Delanga and clubbed the other Drarg just as it bit into Delanga's shoulder. Careil charged among the rest of the Drargs slashing some, as others were trampled beneath Erras's hooves. Carunda lifted Delanga and turned back towards the boys, carrying her limp blood-covered body. Bregal had joined Careil attacking the Drargs, trying to allow Carunda time to get across the bridge. At that moment there came the sound of another horn blaring from nearby and there was a rushing sound as figures came storming down the roadway. Hyrn saw the flash of arrows and then twenty or so Caramar warriors charged past them.

Two of the Caramar stopped to help Carunda with Delanga's limp body. They carefully carried her off of the bridge and lay her down next to where Hyrn and Rowan waited. There was a large jagged wound across her shoulder that was bleeding heavily. Her clothes were drenched in blood, her eyes were closed and her face was pale. Carunda had removed his jacket and was tying it tightly around the wound trying to stop the flow of blood. Delanga's eyes opened and she moaned with pain.

On the bridge, the sound of fighting continued briefly, and then ceased. The sounds of feet and horses came towards them. Careil and Bregal dismounted and walked towards them followed by some of the Caramar. Hyrn saw that other Caramar were dragging the bodies of dead Drargs off of the bridge and laying them at the side of the road. Careil knelt next to Delanga and examined her bandaged shoulder.

"The bleeding has slowed but I fear the wound is deep," he said.

One of the Caramar spoke. "We have no healers nearby. We need to take her further into the mountains. We can reach aid by morning."

"I don't know that she can survive that long," replied Careil.

"You have to help her," said Carunda, in a quiet, desperate voice, looking at Careil.

Delanga opened her eyes.

"The Stone…" she moaned.

Her eyes strayed to Hyrn and flickered briefly, then closed. Hyrn, whose eyes had been locked on Delanga, looked around taking a moment to register.

"Ilah," he whispered.

Hyrn felt Ilah beneath his vest then reached inside and pulled the Stone out. He removed the dark cloth and spoke in a low voice. "Ilah. Ilah. Please help Delanga. She's hurt. Can you heal her?"

Ilah began to glow with a light that was not as bright as usual. "I am sorry, Hyrn. I do not possess the power of healing."

Hyrn looked at Rowan desperately. Rowan shrugged uncomfortably.

Ilah spoke again. "There is one who wields the power of healing not too far. Along this road a way and then up into a gully that opens towards the setting sun. That is your best hope. Hurry!"

Ilah went dull and Hyrn rewrapped the Stone and replaced it inside his vest. Careil sprang to his feet.

"We will need a litter to carry her on," he said.

One of the Caramar named Gebarana, spoke to the others gathered around. "Break branches from those trees along the road. Bring them here and bind them together."

Careil went over to Erras and pulled a blanket from his pack.

"Use this," he said.

In a short time, the Caramar had fashioned a stretcher and placed it alongside Delanga. Carefully, they lifted her on to it. She let out a soft moan. Six Caramar gently lifted the stretcher and they set out along the road as quickly as they dared. Rowan, Hyrn, Carunda, Gebarana and some of the other Caramar followed. Careil and Bregal brought up the rear, leading their horses. The remainder of the Caramar remained behind busily clearing up the remains of the battle.

The road continued along the cliff face and as they rounded a spur the view opened into a broad vale. The road continued across the open spaces towards a ridge to the east. Above the ridge a great mountain peak rose. Calaborn the highest peak of the Caramarhc, and where lay the Seat of the Elders.

"There is a gully to the north of the road on the other side of that ridge," said Carunda. "It opens out onto the western flank of Mount Calaborn."

At the rear of the procession Careil turned to Bregal.

"Well met indeed, old friend," he said. "How were you able to find us?"

Bregal laughed softly.

"You are not the only one who knows how to leave the city secretly," he said. "I remember when we were in training, wondering where a certain cadet

Rider disappeared to. I followed you one day and thought I had lost you. I just managed to see the rear of your horse disappear around the corner of a house and then saw you leave through that doorway. Yesterday, once I heard you had gone along with these two," he gestured to Rowan and Hyrn, "I knew how you had left. The door was blocked but I went out another way but soon picked up your trail. After that it wasn't hard to track you. You weren't exactly covering your tracks. I came upon your camp late last night but held back to see what you were up to. When you joined the Caramar this morning I followed at a distance. It was all a bit baffling, considering the King was very keen to find you and the boys, and here you were heading up into the Caramarhc with two Caramar warriors, after the group of Caramar you arrived in Ballarghen with had left down the King's Road."

Careil studied Bregal's face for a moment. "What do you intend to do?" he asked anxiously.

Bregal paused with a slight puzzled smile on his face.

"I'm not sure yet," he eventually replied. "I haven't quite worked out what is going on here. With the Drargs and this strange Stone I'm not sure what to think."

Careil looked at Bregal again as if to judge whether he should trust him.

"Bregal," he said "I will try to explain and I hope that I can trust you. We have been friends and fellow Riders for many years. If at the end you wish to stand in my way…Well, we will see."

As they travelled through the vale, Hyrn noticed scattered farm buildings. Occasionally, they saw people who stopped and looked at the strange party as they passed by. The sun was beginning to get lower in the sky as they trudged up the road that led up the eastern ridge. When they finally reached the top of the ridge they saw that the road continued on towards the southern flank of Mount Calaborn. A little way ahead a wooded valley led off north of the road. They left the road and Gebarana led them up the valley which gently rose and met a ridge that ran westerly down from the lower flank of the mountain. A path ran up the valley towards the ridge. The group continued on as fast as they were able and climbed the ridge and followed the path as it disappeared down into a gorge between trees dappled in the westering light.

Gebarana moved ahead of the party again and led them along the path. Careil and Erras moved alongside her. As the path led down into the gorge they moved beneath the canopy of trees. Apart from a slice of view along the path they could not see the rest of the gully. The path moved gently downwards and then swung round to the east. The Caramar carrying Delanga adjusted their holds to keep the stretcher as level as possible. Eventually the party broke out from under the trees and ahead of them a vista opened. The path continued down to the bottom of the gorge and between large boulders that were scattered across the sides of the gorge and along the narrow gorge floor. As the path levelled out at the bottom it petered out and they saw that a small watercourse ran along the floor of the gorge.

"There doesn't seem to be anyone here," said Hyrn.

They made their way down and then halted. The stretcher bearers lowered Delanga onto the grass near the water's edge. The stream tinkled softly and a slight breeze blew up the gorge from the west where the sun was getting lower still in the sky. The party scanned the gorge walls but couldn't see any obvious signs of habitation.

Hyrn was about to ask whether he should speak to Ilah again when out of the corner of his eye he caught a brief flash of green up towards the head of the gorge.

"What was that?" he asked. "I saw green light up there."

He pointed eastwards to where a broken cliff face made up the head of the gorge. The others looked up to where he pointed and then suddenly another green flash of light came from the base of the cliff.

"Come," said Gebarana. "There is something there."

The Caramar lifted Delanga again. No sound issued from her at this sudden movement. Hyrn looked at her face. She was pale and her eyes were closed.

"Please be alright," murmured Hyrn. "We're almost there."

As the party drew closer to the head of the gorge, they could see that there was a stone dwelling built against the base of the cliff on the right of the stream. Water flowed down the cliff alongside to join the stream. The dwelling had a wooden door with a small window on either side. From the window closest to the waterfall, green light flashed as the light of the setting sun played across the front of the house. Suddenly the door of the house sprang open, and an old man, followed closely by an equally old woman, came out quickly, traversed the two stone front steps and moved towards them.

Without a word they headed straight for the supine form of Delanga.

The man turned to Gebarana and spoke in a strong deep voice. "Quickly, bring her inside."

Hyrn and Rowan followed as Delanga was carried along the path, up the stairs and through the open door. When Hyrn entered he saw that they had laid Delanga on a small bed in one corner of the room. The house had one large room at the front and a doorway that led further back into the cliff. The room was tidy with sparse but sturdy furniture; a table and chairs, a fireplace and benches along one wall. The benches held an array of bottles and jars filled with coloured powders and liquids. Everywhere green light flickered. A strong shaft of sunlight burst through one of the windows and the whole room lit up with a bright green glow. It made Hyrn feel happy and full of life. Then he saw the source of the green glow. On a small dresser level with the window sill stood a green crystal.

The woman walked over and picked up the crystal. Her face was bathed in green light. She went and knelt alongside the bed where Delanga lay. She gently pulled off the bandage from Delanga's shoulder and placed the crystal on the evil looking wound. Delanga didn't move. The crystal began to pulse and as it did the woman softly hummed. This continued for a while and then the woman began to softly shake her head. The light of the Stone began to flicker.

Suddenly, the woman stopped shaking her head and, still kneeling, turned to look directly at Hyrn.

"The Stone, child," she said in a strong but soft voice. "Bring it here."

"But…" Hyrn began.

But as he spoke he felt Ilah grow warm inside his vest. He stepped over to where the woman knelt and withdrew Ilah.

"Place the Stone above the Halestone," the woman said.

Hyrn reached out and held Ilah above where the green stone flickered upon Delanga's shoulder. Ilah burst into life. A beam of light shone from Ilah onto the green Stone and it began to glow brighter and brighter. Green light began to flow out of it and it seemed to Hyrn that it poured into the jagged wound across the Caramar's shoulder. Ilah too seemed to glow green so strong was the light. Hyrn began to feel light-headed. He felt as if every happy thought he had ever had was filling his head. He felt as if he could do anything.

And then he felt nothing at all, and everything went black.

Hyrn was floating above a green meadow in the sunlight. The scent of flowers drifted on the warm air. Butterflies flitted amongst the grass, and the hum of insects and the sounds of birds filled his ears. He heard soft laughter and he turned his head and saw a young girl of about his age walking towards him. She called out to him and held her hand up towards where he floated. She had a smile on her face. She looked familiar but he couldn't remember where he had seen her before.

"Come on Hyrn," she said, with a soft, musical laugh in her voice. "You can't float up there forever. There are things to be done."

Hyrn felt as if she was right but thought he would like to stay longer and breathe in the warm air. The girl laughed again.

"Come on Hyrn," she insisted.

A thought came into Hyrn's head, that if he floated higher she wouldn't be able to reach him. He smiled to himself and then tried to push upwards. He thought he may have moved a little higher and then noticed that the girl looked a little sad.

"Hyrn," she said and smiled at him again. "Why don't you come with me? I have lots to show you."

Hyrn began to think that he should get further away and then noticed that the girl began to look worried. He felt a breath of cold air and looked over to the edge of the meadow and noticed that a dark forest grew there. There was something about those trees that Hyrn didn't like. He began to feel a little frightened. The girl stood beneath him, now stretching out her hand. Her eyes were filled with tears but she still managed to smile at him. He suddenly felt that all he wanted to do was to get down. He stretched towards the girl's hand but he couldn't quite reach. He felt as if something was trying to pull him away. He looked over at the forest and black shapes seemed to be gathering under the eaves. He thought he could hear voices, harsh voices, calling to him. He turned back to the girl and tried with all his will to reach her hand. He was almost there but he felt like he was being pulled apart.

"Please, Hyrn," the girl said pleadingly.

And, with a final strain, he reached out and the girl grasped his fingers in her soft warm hand and he fell to the ground.

He awoke on a soft bed in a small room. Candlelight flickered against the ceiling. The old woman sat in a chair next to him holding his hand. He realized that she was the young girl in his dream.

"Welcome back Hyrn," she said softly. "I am Merana."

"What happened?" asked Hyrn groggily.

He abruptly sat up.

"Delanga!" he pleaded. "How..?"

"Peace child," said Merana soothingly, gently pushing Hyrn back down. "Delanga is in a deep sleep. She was close to death but we managed to bring her back. I am sorry that I had to use your help, but without it Delanga would have died. If you had not arrived here when you did she would also have died. I felt the power of the Stone you carry."

Hyrn suddenly grabbed at his chest with a look of worry but he felt Ilah nestled there and sighed with relief.

"It is a remarkable and powerful force of good that you have there," said

Merana. "The Halestone has great powers of healing but was not strong enough. Ilah gave her strength and together they brought Delanga back. That can sometimes be a dangerous journey and I fear that you were too close. While you were within the power of the Halestone you were safe but the battle between life and death was close by.

She paused and looked at Hyrn with concern and then said softly, "It is night now. I will bring you something to eat and then I think you must sleep. Your brother and your protector are anxious to see you. They are waiting outside. I will let them in, but you must rest."

Merana arose and moved towards the door. She hesitated then turned to face him again.

"I meant what I told you," she said. "There is much to be done and I do have much to show you, but that can wait."

She smiled and then turned away, opened the door and disappeared from view. Hyrn heard her voice and then Rowan burst through the door followed closely by Careil.

"What happened to you?" asked Rowan. "Everything happened so fast. The green light and then you fell to the floor. I thought you were dead."

"I'm fine," said Hyrn. "I'm not really sure what happened. The green Stone, the Halestone, took over my mind, I think."

"It was amazing," said Rowan. "It felt like soaking in a warm bath. Everyone was feeling refreshed and all our aches and pains and scratches and bruises are gone. Merana and Pharla are healers, and the wielders of the Halestone. They are very old but they continue to heal those who come to them." He paused and looked at Hyrn. "I'm so glad you are alright."

"As am I," cut in Careil. "Merana has told us that you must rest. Rowan can stay with you while you eat and then you need to sleep. Rowan will sleep with the rest of us in the main room. Delanga has been moved to the room next door to you. The rest of the Caramar, apart from Carunda and Gebarana, have left. Carunda insisted on staying with Delanga at least until the healers see how she has responded to their healing. We will see what tomorrow brings."

Careil looked down at Hyrn with worry on his face. His training and experience as a King's Rider may not have prepared him enough for all this, but the truth of their mission seemed clear.

"Goodnight Hyrn," he said with a smile, and then looked at Rowan. "Not too many questions Rowan, and then straight out when he has eaten."

Rowan nodded, and with that Careil left the room. When the two boys were alone Hyrn tried to tell Rowan what he had dreamt but it didn't sound right. It hadn't felt like a dream. They started to talk about the Drarg attack but then Merana and the old man, Pharla, knocked and entered. Pharla carried a tray with two steaming bowls of stew, two bread rolls and two cups of a clear fragrant liquid.

"Enough of dark stories," said Merana. "They can wait for the light of day."

She moved around to the other side of the bed and plumped up Hyrn's pillows so that he could sit up. She rested her hand on his forehead. Her hand was warm and soft like in the dream. Pharla rested the tray in Hyrn's lap and then put a hand above Merana's.   He closed his eyes then sighed. "He is strong, Merana. He has fared well."

"Yes," said Merana, as they both moved away from the bed and towards the door. "But will he be strong enough for what is to come? He is not ready. He understands little of what he is a part of. If only Devarnia had had more time."

"The Keepers do what they must," said Pharla.

"You know Devarnia?" blurted out Rowan

"Yes," replied Pharla, "but that can wait until tomorrow. For now, eat and talk of bright things. Rowan, when you are both finished eating, please bring the tray and things out with you. Hyrn, settle down to sleep once Rowan has left. We will check on you when we extinguish the candles. But for now goodnight."

They left the room, closing the door behind them. The two boys ate mostly in silence and then something occurred to Hyrn.

"That's strange. She remembered what she said in my dream, when she was a girl," he said wonderingly.

"There is definitely something strange here," said Rowan. "Good, but strange."

After Rowan had said goodnight and left, Hyrn snuggled down in bed. Thoughts whirled around his head and then tumbled into sleep.

When Hyrn awoke dim light was coming into the room from a small window behind his bed. He had a vague feeling that he had dreamt but the memory eluded him and faded away. He felt well rested and hungry. He lay in bed, warm and cosy, and thought about getting up. As he lay there he realised there were voices coming from somewhere else in the house. They were too faint to hear what was being said, or who was speaking. Hyrn sat up and started to get out of bed. As he did there came a knock on the door.

"Come in," he said.

The door opened and Merana came in followed closely by Rowan.

"How are you?" asked the healer.

She walked over and placed her hand on Hyrn's forehead.

"I feel fine," Hyrn replied. "I am hungry though."

"That is good," said Merana. "There is breakfast in the front room. Get dressed and join the others. Most have already eaten."

"How is Delanga?" asked Hyrn.

"She is still sleeping deeply and still has a way to go. Time will tell."

With that she turned and left the room leaving the two boys alone.

"You'll never guess who is here," said Rowan.

Hyrn looked at Rowan quizzically. "Well?"

"See for yourself," said Rowan.

Hyrn gave him a dirty look and then hurried and got dressed. The two boys left the room and Hyrn followed Rowan down a narrow hallway and into the room that they had first entered the day before. The room was dimly lit by the muted morning light coming in through the front windows, Hyrn saw that the Halestone sat back below the window, dark now. Pharla, Careil, Carunda and Gebarana were seated at the table, deep in conversation with Duburinga and Boriega.

As Rowan and Hyrn approached the table, Duburinga rose and greeted Hyrn heartily.

"Hyrn!" he exclaimed. "It is good to see that you have recovered from your ordeal yesterday."

"I'm fine," said Hyrn. "How are you all?"

"Well enough," replied Duburinga. "I am glad that the Stone was able to help Delanga. It is strange that the Drargs were in large numbers this close to Calaborn. You were unlucky to be caught up in the attack. Although…" he trailed off and looked at Pharla.

Pharla returned his gaze then looked at Careil. Careil nodded and Pharla faced Hyrn.

"Hyrn," he began. "The Drargs are on the move throughout the mountains. It is a strange coincidence that this is happening when a Stone of power has been found and is being carried through the Caramarhc. We think they may be drawn by the Stone and that you and Ilah may have been the target of the attack. The Stone may be drawing them even if they don't know what it is. Remember what happened in Gardarvon with the cave Drargs. If it is not the Stone, then something very powerful is happening. I wish we knew where Devarnia is. She would be able to shed some light on this, no doubt."

Rowan spoke. "She said that she was going to stay in Errasarn and find out what happened to King Darion."

"That is certainly a mystery," said Pharla pensively. He paused as if deep in thought then broke out of his reverie. "Hyrn you haven't eaten. Sit down and eat while we discuss the next part of your journey."

Hyrn moved to the table and seated himself. There were a variety of foods and he suddenly realised how hungry he was. He began to help himself and then realised Rowan wasn't sitting down. Rowan was walking towards the door.

"I'm just going to see how Bregal is doing with the horses," he said.

Hyrn wondered why Rowan would volunteer to help with the horses, and then it dawned on him. If Duburinga and Boriega were here, then a certain young Caramar warrior was quite possibly also here. The door closed as Rowan went outside.

Arienga was holding the reins of Bregal's horse, Marran, while Bregal brushed her coat, as Rowan stepped down from the cottage doorway. He barely noticed walking down the front path and then crossing the grass towards them. Before Rowan had a chance to call out to Arienga, Bregal spoke.

"Rowan. Where's your sword? I'd better watch my neck," Bregal laughed.

Rowan began to redden but Arienga spoke and looked straight at Rowan.

"I heard what happened. How you fought," she paused. "I didn't know you had it in you."

Rowan felt umbrage at this.

"Why? Because I'm just a stupid farm boy?" he retorted.

Arienga looked taken aback at this, and then quietly answered, "No. Because you're young and untrained."

"I'm sixteen," retorted Rowan "How old are you?

I'm seventeen," answered Arienga.

"Well I'll be seventeen in autumn," said Rowan.

Bregal interrupted. "Arienga, please take care of Marran. I'm going to find out where we're going next."

As he walked off he gave Rowan a derisive smile.

Rowan walked over to Arienga and, as he did, she took Marran's reins and began to walk further down the gorge towards where Erras grazed.

"Wait," said Rowan. "Can't we talk?"

"You can talk," said Arienga.

Rowan hurried after and pulled alongside her as she led the horse. They neared Erras and she dropped Marran's reins and left her to graze. Arienga turned towards him and looked at him briefly then spoke.

"Well? What did you want to say?"

"I didn't get to see you when we were in Ballarghen," said Rowan quietly.

"We were taken away as guests of the King and put in special guest rooms," said Arienga. "It was almost like we were being kept prisoner. I would much have preferred to be allowed to move around the castle."

She paused, "Why did you want to see me?" she asked.

"I just wanted to talk. I don't know anything about you," Rowan began. "I thought—"

Arienga interrupted. "Why do you want to know about me?"

Rowan paused and began again. "I don't get to talk to girls much. There are girls at the Town School but most of them are younger than me, and I was never much good at talking to girls anyway."

Rowan felt like he was rambling but Arienga spoke again.

"I am a Caramar warrior you know," she said almost sternly, but her eyes betrayed a smile.

"I know you're a Caramar warrior," said Rowan. "That's what makes you so interesting. You've done things, seen places. All I've ever done is work on my parents' farm and go to a boring school."

"I've had to work hard," said Arienga, with almost a hint of resentment. "It is an honour to be accepted for training as a warrior and my mother and father were proud, but I sometimes have thought of the other things I could do." she paused and then spoke in a sincere tone. "But I'm here and this is one of the most interesting and exciting things that has happened in Ordbrarn, or even the whole of the Caramarhc, in a long time," she paused and looked at Rowan, "and I get to meet a Wesmerian boy who wields an ancient sword."

Rowan looked at her and his tense expression turned to a hesitant smile. Arienga's face also broke into a smile.

"Come on," she said. "Tell me about what happened when you left Ballarghen. Your journey was a lot more exciting than mine. It was good to see more of the mountains. I have never been this far to the east, but not much happened."

"Alright," said Rowan and, as he began to recount their escape from Ballarghen, the two of them walked down towards the stream, as the light from the rising sun, hidden by the mountain peak behind them, began to light the foothills far beyond the end of the gorge, away to the south and west.

⚬

As Hyrn ate, Duburinga recounted the Caramar's journey from Ballarghen. They had returned up the stairway near Gardarvon after losing the King's

Guard in the forest off the King's Road, and then followed the road east along the southern flank of the Caramarhc towards the Bridge of Mists and the Seat of the Elders. They had found a few faint but unusual signs of Drarg activity. They had received word, late the night before, that there had been a Drarg attack on the Bridge. They had travelled through the night and met with a squad of warriors. They conveyed as much as they could. The Drargs had either all been killed, or there were more, but they had fled. They were waiting until morning to continue the search.

When they had heard that Careil, Rowan and Hyrn were with a party of Caramar carrying a wounded warrior, Duburinga, Boriega and Arienga left the rest of their party and travelled swiftly ahead in time to greet the morning sun as it rose far to the east behind the mass of Mount Calaborn. They had arrived at the cottage and Careil had explained to Duburinga and Boriega what had occurred since they had left Ballarghen.

After Duburinga had finished speaking and Hyrn had finished eating, Pharla spoke. "Come now Hyrn. Merana wishes to speak to you."

Merana walked through the door at that moment and beckoned Hyrn over to the window. Two chairs stood in the corner, in front of where the Halestone stood glistening, dark green, silhouetted against the glow of the morning light outside the window. She beckoned for Hyrn to sit. Once they were seated Merana spoke.

"Hyrn, what I am about to say to you is important," she said softly, but insistently. "You can tell your brother, or even Careil if you must, but this is important to you, and you, above all, must keep it inside. You are part of something that perhaps you could never imagine. Your fate is tied up, not just in great events that affect your land and ours and Anasaria, but in a battle that is waged right across this world. Ivah told Devarnia that there were two who were to unite the Twin Stones and bring them to Anasaria."

"Where do you know Devarnia from?" asked Hyrn.

"From here," replied Merana.

"Here? When?" Hyrn asked, astounded.

"Devarnia was in these parts almost eighty years ago," said Merana. "That was when we first met and we saw her about ten years later. But she has not returned since.

"But you..." began Hyrn. "You're not old enough. You would have to be..." he trailed off.

"I am one hundred and thirty-eight years old," said Merana.

"How?" asked Hyrn.

Merana gestured towards the Stone in front of them and said, "The Halestone is a powerful healer. We are kept strong and well in its presence.

We still grow old but the Stone helps keep us alive and keeps our bodies strong."

"But you must listen, Hyrn," she continued imploringly. "The world was formed in chaos. The forces of good and evil were birthed in the act of creating a place where life could flourish. Perhaps they are meant to balance, but here on this world those forces do battle, and we are caught up in that battle whether we understand it or not.

The Stone you carry was formed of the essence of the power of good. It is a powerful being but there are many manifestations of power. The Halestone before you is also one, and the great Sagenstone at the Seat of the Elders is another. There are equally forms of evil that have been forged within this world.

Ivah's vision of the future is imperfect as are all things. Your destiny is tied to the Stones and in some way with the throne of Anasaria, but there is much danger. Things are stirring within the Caramarhc that I don't understand. I feel in my bones the heart of the mountains waking up and shaking off a long sleep, a sleep filled with restlessness and nightmares. Your meeting with Devarnia. The things that she told you."

"How did you know about that?" asked Hyrn.

"That is easy," said Merana. "Your brother and Careil have told me of what occurred in that forsaken valley."

"Why do you call it that?" asked Hyrn.

"You have lived at the feet of the Caramarhc. Has it ever struck you that you have never seen the Caramar? That part of the mountains is shunned by our people. No settlement has been able to thrive there for centuries. Ordbrarn is an outpost within what sometimes seems hostile territory. I don't believe that it is coincidence that Darion's kingdom fell and that part of the Caramarhc is tainted. There is evil at work there and I don't know what it could be. Devarnia is powerful and strong though. The Keepers are not easily daunted. My hope is that she will find an answer to this mystery.

She looked deeply at Hyrn. "Child," she said. "I don't know how your fate is tied to that of the Caramar, but somehow events here are tied to your quest." She paused. "You are destined, I feel, to go beyond Wesmere, beyond the Caramarhc, to Anasaria. It is clear that this is beyond those on this side of the sea. Great evil is not understood in your land. In Anasaria evil walks in the open air. Anasaria is a land enslaved by beings steeped in evil. The Lords of Ultamar have reigned in Anasaria for over two hundred years. All the beauty has been dulled and trampled by their forces. But there is hope. The Stone you carry and its twin are powerful forces individually, but together they are as they were made, an immense power beyond any in this part of the world. If your quest is fulfilled Hyrn it will help push back a tide that would eventually engulf all the lands including ours.

The Dark Lords of Ultamar are just an outpost of the forces of evil that wage war in the east. Ultamar stands within lands that were felt safe. If this evil can be defeated, this part of the world can be cleansed, and those who defend good in the east can rest easy that they do not have to fight on two fronts."

Merana's voice had become strident but she spoke more softly now. "Hyrn, no one can make you and Rowan undertake this quest and in the end you need to decide. Your party goes on to Calaborn, to the Seat of the Elders. There you will hear the advice of our most knowledgeable thinkers and scholars. The power of the Sagenstone abides there and it helps to guide the Elders and imbues them with wisdom. It may help you to decide what you must do. If you decide to go on we will send word to your Mother and Father. We are not aware what the Wesmerian Council may convey to them, but we will ensure that they hear the true story. If you decide not to go on, the Elders will try to work out a way to continue the quest and you will have a Caramar escort back to your home.

It is difficult to know what fate has in store. Some things though are beyond our control and destiny plays its hand. Events somehow conspired to lead you here to this house, and to me."

Hyrn shifted uneasily in his chair. The others had left their seats and were tidying up and getting gear ready for the road. He thought of what lay ahead, what he was a part of. He couldn't give up now. Anasaria seemed far off. He thought of what lay there. A land ruled by evil. A land he was supposed to, maybe, help free. But when he thought of it, it seemed that it was there where his future lay. He couldn't imagine going back to the farm now. He thought of his mother and father and felt a pang of pain. He would be back there soon enough to see them. He couldn't quite envisage how far he had to go, but he had to go.

Merana spoke. "You are troubled Hyrn. You don't need to decide just yet. Calaborn is not much further and your decision can wait until then."

"I've already decided," Hyrn said fervently. "I don't know about Rowan. I want him to come too and bear The Sword of Acclimoss back to Anasaria, but I have to go. I feel it. I felt it ever since Devarnia handed me Ilah and asked me to carry it."

Hyrn paused. It didn't feel right calling the Stone 'it'.

"Carry her," he corrected.

Merana smiled. "Why do you call Ilah 'her'?" she asked.

"I don't know," replied Hyrn. "It just feels right."

Merana laughed lightly. "You lighten my heart, child," she said. "I can keep hope that there is much good in the world and people of good heart. You have a special bond with Ilah and that means much in all this. I am not sure why you are connected to Ilah but I feel that your destinies are somehow intertwined. But, come. You must get ready to go. Why don't you go and see where that brother of yours has got to."

She gave a knowing smile and Hyrn remembered that Rowan had gone outside, presumably to see Arienga.

He smiled slightly himself, then looked at Merana. "Thank you Merana, for everything," he said.

"You have done much yourself, Hyrn," she said.

And with that she rose from her chair and Hyrn got to his feet too and turned towards the door to go outside and look for Rowan.

Hyrn spied Rowan and Arienga walking up the gully towards him. As they drew near Arienga greeted him. "Hello Hyrn. I'm glad that you're alright."

"Hello and thanks," said Hyrn. He was getting tired of people worrying about how he was but he smiled and said to Rowan, "We're leaving soon so we'd better get ready."

"I'm already packed," said Rowan, as he continued to walk past Hyrn towards the door of the cottage with a contented smile on his face.

CHAPTER SIX

The Seat of the Elders

The Caramar, Duburinga, Boriega, Gebarana and Arienga, led the way up a narrow path that climbed up the southern wall of the gorge, and up to the flank of Mount Calaborn. Carunda had stayed behind with Delanga to help with her care. It was rough going at first, but after an hour or so the small rocky path joined a wider one that skirted the southern flank of the mountain. The path slowly rose as they continued eastward and, after a brief stop at midday to eat, the path began to bend around to the north and become steeper. The peak of the mountain rose ahead of them and then to their left as the afternoon wore on. As the eastern flank of the mountain came into view they could see ahead and high above them a glistening white mass on the side of the mountain that matched the snow-capped peak of the mountain's summit high above.

"There lies the Seat of the Elders," said Boriega.

Hyrn looked with wonder at the city perched high above, balanced almost precariously on the mountainside. The path they were on began to widen and became a wide roadway as they travelled further up the flank of the mountain towards the city. As they came closer to the city they moved higher and higher up the mountain. Hyrn found that he was getting tired and it felt harder and harder to breathe properly. Duburinga halted the party and let them rest.

"The air this high in the mountain is harder to breathe for those unaccustomed," he said. "Careil, Bregal, there is a place nearby where you can leave your horses. The heights are hard on them and horses are not permitted within the city."

They began to see various signs of habitation as they continued on. Stone buildings skirted the road on the left under the steep slopes of the mountain's flank. They came across barracks for warriors, guard posts and simple dwellings all carved from the grey stone of the mountain. Duburinga halted at one of these barracks and spoke to the guard on duty. He beckoned and Careil and Bregal led their horses forward.

"Your horses will be well looked after here, and Arienga can stay and tend them if you wish," said Duburinga.

Arienga stood a little way back next to Rowan, a look of surprise and consternation on her face. She made as if to protest, but Bregal spoke.

"I'm sure the horses will be fine with your people here," he said. "And it would be a shame for Arienga not to see the Seat of the Elders, so close at hand."

Duburinga gave Arienga a searching look. She stood stoically and unmoving, as if holding her breath.

"Very well," said the Caramar leader. "Arienga. Remember your protocols when we enter the city."

He glanced at Rowan and then looked back at Arienga.

"Remember that you are a warrior," he said sternly, "and you are expected to act like one."

Arienga let out a sigh of relief but kept her face composed.

"Yes, Duburinga," she said and moved away from Rowan without looking at him, and formed up with the rest of the Caramar warriors.

Careil and Bregal had removed the packs from the horses, and then Erras and Marran were led into the barracks by two Caramar. Duburinga farewelled the guard and the party continued up the roadway.

The city was magnificent. The stone of the roadway and the various buildings had moved from the grey of the rock and slowly became paler until, as they had approached the city it was replaced by bright white stone, and the buildings were replaced by ornamental pillars and sculptures. This culminated in a large ornately carved archway that marked the entrance to the Seat of the Elders. Guard posts were situated in the pillars of the arch and the guards had appeared and sounded a challenge. The guards were dressed in a pale cloth that blended with the stone of the arch. Duburinga had approached with the other Caramar and had spoken for a short while, gesturing occasionally to the Wesmerians. One of the guards blew a short low note on a stone instrument he held. A group of four Caramar, also dressed in the same pale fashion, came forward and guided the party into the city, two in front and two taking up the rear, as the travellers moved through the arch.

As they moved through the city, Rowan and Hyrn stared in wonder at the sights around them. Everywhere the white stone of the city shone bright.

They admired the intricate sculptures and fountains, pallisades and hidden parks of mountain shrubs, hardy trees and manicured lawns, and amidst the wonder were the people dressed in white and pale tones, but in fashions the boys had never seen before; long flowing robes, in various cloths, begemmed stone jewellery and headdresses. The people all seemed calm and happy and were often deep in conversation. They looked at the Wesmerians and greeted them as they passed by. Rowan and Hyrn began to feel as if they were in a dream. The whole feeling of the city was one of peace, tranquillity and wisdom.

The local Caramar led them up terraced pathways, climbing higher up into the city where a great domed building stood. As they wound their way up through the city they grew closer to this building.

Duburinga turned to Rowan and Hyrn and said reverently "That is the Hall of the Elders. We are expected, and the Elders are eager to speak to the two of you."

Rowan and Hyrn looked at each other and Rowan spoke. "I guess we knew that they would be interested in Ilah and …the Sword."

He had almost said 'my' sword.

"Indeed," said Duburinga. "The Elders know of your journey through the Caramarhc and especially what occurred in Gardarvon. They are very interested in the Stone and the story of Bharain's sword."

They finally came to a broad straight roadway lined with columns that ran up to the large magnificent building. The Hall of the Elders stood against the cliff that towered above and up towards the peak of the mountain. They climbed up several terraced steps and between great columns that formed a portico that framed two large stone doors. Guards stood at either side of the doorway holding tall lances. As they approached, the doors swung inwards and a white-bearded man wearing long white flowing robes appeared and greeted them.

"Welcome," he said. "I am Faranalga, of the Elders of the Caramar. Please enter."

He turned, and the party followed him through the great doors. They traversed a small anteroom and then passed through a second set of doors into a large open expanse crowned by the great dome high above. The Hall was circular and there were doorways at regular intervals around the outside. In the centre of the Hall was a large jagged sculpture which stood atop a stone table. At first Hyrn wondered what it was but then realised that it was a model of the Caramarhc Ranges. Faranalga led them to the left of the great hall and as they passed the statue they could see large doors opposite where they had entered. The doors were intricately carved with the symbol that Careil had shown Rowan and Hyrn after they had left Ballarghen, the symbol of The Seat of the Elders. Two guards stood there, one either side of the doors.

Faranalga led them through an arched doorway into an alcove where a single door stood. Here a single guard stood in front of the door. Faranalga said something to her in a low voice and she opened the door and stood aside. They followed Faranalga through the door and into a large round room where circular terraced steps led down to a round flat floor with a low circular platform in the centre. Through high windows in the far wall they could see the late afternoon sky. On the steps, spread out around the central podium, about forty or fifty men and women sat all dressed in similar white robes. Faranalga led them down to a spot at floor level and gestured for them to sit. When they were seated Faranalga stepped up onto the platform and spoke.

"Welcome to the Chamber of the Elder Council and to the Seat of the Elders," he said in a strident but cheerful voice. "On behalf of the Caramar we invite you to speak to us and to hear our counsel. There is much that troubles us, but also much that lightens our hearts. We have had word from Gardarvon. Already there are scholars and some of our number, along with warriors, farmers and builders on their way there to begin the process of bringing it back to life. There is still a wound that festers there but something is happening that speaks to us of a long overdue healing. The discovery of the Gragenstone has given us all joy and hope."

His face darkened a little. "We are also getting reports of Drarg activities. The Drargs have long mostly stayed in the north eastern arm of the Caramarhc in the areas around the Pinnacles and the Spire, but they are on the move. There are reports of Drargs moving westward down the northern flank of the mountains. We are also told that there are numbers moving through the northern plains. We have no idea why, but the fact that this is happening now when a Stone of power has been found, cannot be coincidence.

I will ask Duburinga to speak for the Caramar, and then, if our Wesmerian guests would be so kind, we ask that you tell your story. Some we already know, but we desire to hear the full story."

He beckoned for Duburinga to step forward and the Caramar warrior rose to his feet and took the place of Faranalga on the dais. Faranalga sat alongside the rest of the guests and looked at Hyrn and Rowan with a smile of warmth on his face. Duburinga began in his calm matter of fact way to recount the story starting with the encounter with Careil, Rowan and Hyrn on the roadway below Mt Andavalar, what to Hyrn seemed like an age ago.

"We were on a scouting patrol near the roadway beneath Mount Andavalar," he began. "We had not intended to travel that far west of Ordbrarn but somehow we kept to that westward track. We had camped at night in the lands above the Dark Forest that the Wesmerians call 'Albarrin'. Early the next morning we came upon a Wesmerian boy washing himself in one of the pools that is fed by springs from the mountain. He was soon joined by another boy and it is thus we met Rowan and Hyrn and they brought us to Careil."

Duburinga then recounted the journey to Ordbrarn and on to Gardarvon. As he spoke, occasionally an Elder would stand and ask a question to clarify what was being said, or to ask a question that related to the events or else was concerned with things that may have been observed on the journey. There seemed a lot of interest in the behaviour of the Wesmerian Council, and it seemed to Hyrn that the Caramar Elders did not trust the Wesmerians, or felt that they behaved foolishly and without understanding.

After Duburinga had recounted the end of their journey the sky through the windows was darkening towards evening. Faranalga spoke to Careil and asked that he speak. Careil spoke in turn covering the events before they had met the Caramar and after they had left Ballarghen and, as he did, he continually looked to Rowan and Hyrn. As Hyrn heard Careil's recounting he felt almost as if he was listening to a story about someone else. The Elders seemed particularly interested in Merana and Pharla, and the Halestone. Lastly Faranalga asked Rowan and Hyrn to speak.

"We are interested to know of Devarnia and about the quest that she has given you. We are also keen to see the Stone and the Sword."

When Rowan and Hyrn got up to speak they stood nervously together on the dais.

Rowan spoke.

"You have heard from Careil about what Devarnia told us," he said. "I don't know what else to say."

An Elder rose to her feet. "How was Devarnia?" she asked. "Was she anxious or troubled?"

Hyrn looked at Rowan. "I don't know," he said.

He thought back to that time deep in the misty valley in the dark and dusty halls of Errasarn.

"She seemed very tired," he said finally.

"She was glad to pass the Stone on to us," said Rowan, "It was almost as if it was too heavy for her to carry and she needed us to take it on its way."

"Why did she not accompany you?" asked Faranalga.

"She said she needed to find out what happened to King Darion's people," said Rowan. "It was almost as if she thought something terrible had happened."

Another Elder rose to her feet. "Is it possible that the fate of Errasarn is tied to something evil that has haunted the Caramarhc for centuries? I fear that perhaps King Darion brought some evil with him from Anasaria, but I cannot see how that would be possible if he had the Stone with him. It may have been that Darion encountered something in that valley."

Faranalga nodded his head and stared at the floor as if deep in thought then lifted his gaze toward Rowan and Hyrn.

"If you would allow us, we are interested to see Ilah and the Sword of Acclimoss," he said solemnly.

Rowan and Hyrn exchanged glances, then Rowan reached behind his shoulder and drew the Sword and held it out in front of him. Hyrn brought out Ilah and unwrapped the Stone holding it in his hand.

"Can we speak with the Stone?" asked the woman who had spoken earlier.

"Ilah speaks only when she wants to," replied Hyrn.

He brought the Stone up in front of his face and called softly, "Ilah, Ilah."

The Stone remained dull and silent. Hyrn looked up and then shrugged.

Faranalga spoke. "That is sufficient. We know that such Stones are not to be trifled with. Thank you, Rowan and Hyrn. I think that now we should show you to your lodgings and then you may join us for our evening meal."

They sat in a dining room that adjoined the Hall of the Elders. The room was large enough to seat all of the Elders and their guests, and, although the room was full, the sound of conversation was muted.

Faranalga was speaking to the Wesmerians about the Elders. "The Elders are chosen by the Sagenstone. Any of the Caramar, when they come of age, may stand before the Stone and open their hearts and minds to its power. If they are chosen, the Sagenstone will speak to them words sacred to the Caramar and known only to the Elders, words that can be spoken only once before the Elders within the inner sanctum of this hall."

Faranalga spoke directly to Careil. "If you have no objections I would like to bring Rowan and Hyrn before the Sagenstone. They need to decide which path they take next. The Sagenstone may help them to make a wise choice."

Careil looked to Rowan and Hyrn. They both looked expectantly at him but said nothing.

"I will not object if they wish to accompany you," said Careil.

Faranalga looked to the two boys and Hyrn quickly spoke. "We will go with you. Won't we Row."

"Yes," replied Rowan.

Faranalga approached the doorway in the western wall of the great domed chamber, which they had seen earlier. The guards stood aside and Faranalga approached the large ornate doors and placed his palms against them. He uttered a low, almost inaudible chant in a singsong voice. There was a slight clicking sound and the doors opened to reveal a dark arched entrance. The Caramar Elder led them through a wide tunnel roughly hewn out of the rock, and through into a chamber that glowed with a vivid red light. The chamber was round and carved with a smooth surface all except for the centre where the floor was the roughness of the native rock. Stone benches carved from the rock of the chamber formed a circle in the centre of the chamber, and in the heart of the circle, on a natural pedestal, stood a large red Stone the size of a man's head but shaped like a mountain peak. The Stone glowed red but Hyrn could see that deep within its heart was a dark stain like a black tongue of fire.

"The Sagenstone has stood here for millenia, since long before our cities were built." Faranalga gestured to the walls of the hall with a sweep of his arm and continued, "This hall was carved out of the rock of the mountain that surrounded the cavern in which the Stone dwelt. Hundreds of years ago a stain grew in the heart of the Stone. The darkness that you see at the heart of the Stone coincides with a sickness that affects our people. We were once a powerful and prosperous kingdom. The Caramarhc rang with our industry and the power of the Sagenstone guided and nourished us. When the stain began to grow, we became lesser. The Caramar in the West began to become restless and things began to go awry. At this time the Sagenstone shed a part of itself and some of our people took what was named the Gragenstone, to the West and built the city of Gardarvon.

The city prospered for a while, but war came and the Caramar in the West were enslaved, while those of our people in the East, continued to fight the Northerners, and, together with the Wesmerians, we overthrew the invaders and so began the Everlasting Peace.

But we were greatly weakened. The war with the Northerners was not a battle waged with weapons of power but with steel, and flesh and bones. Evil exists even within the hearts of common people, and in some more strongly than others. The city of Gardarvon was abandoned before the war had ended, the enslaved Caramar there had long perished and the Gragenstone was lost and for a while passed out of knowledge. When we regained our strength it had long been assumed that the Stone had been stolen by the Northerners and taken to their stronghold, Karsted, deep within the Northern lands. Little was remembered about Gardarvon and records were left unread and ignored within our libraries."

Faranalga turned to Hyrn. "Your deeds, however fortuitous, have done us a great service, Hyrn. You and your brother have set off a chain of events that we don't yet understand. The Stone and Sword you carry have been sent to the Caramar for a reason, we believe. It has taken centuries for this purpose to be realised but the time has come for things to change. Come, Hyrn and Rowan, and look upon the Sagenstone."

Faranalga walked to the centre of the hall and crossed the rough native rock surrounding the great Stone. He beckoned for the two boys to stand either side of him. They stood thus, drinking in the red glow of the Stone. Hyrn felt Ilah grow warm and then almost hot against his chest. He felt as if the Stone was almost vibrating. Hyrn reached in and withdrew the Stone. It indeed felt hot in his hand and glowed brightly as he held it out in front of him. Faranalga looked at the Stone as Hyrn held it and as he did so the Sagenstone began to also glow brighter. The red of the large Stone was like a bright fire but they could see in its centre the dark stain and as they watched, transfixed the dark stain began to dance.

Hyrn stared at the dark stain. There was something about it he didn't like, something wrong, something evil. He felt almost like it watched him with malice and evil intent. He wanted to look away but he felt it drawing him towards the Stone. Hyrn fought against it. Faranalga stood seemingly frozen. On the other side of the Elder, Rowan looked as if he were struggling. Then with a strangled cry he reached above his shoulder and grasped the hilt of the Sword of Acclimoss and drew it swiftly in one sweeping action. He appeared as if he intended to attack the Sagenstone.

It was at that moment that the Stone in Hyrn's outstretched hand, Ilah, formed high up in the far off Angilanian Mountains, burst into brilliant light. A beam of blinding light shot forth from the Stone and burrowed into the Sagenstone and clashed with the dark stain. Hyrn felt the power of the Stone, felt the effort. Ilah was wrestling with the dark stain which began to struggle, to fight, as if for its life. The darkness began to diminish and then pushed back against the white light struggling for dominance. Ilah began to hum and the hum grew into a whine that began to grow higher and higher in pitch until it sounded almost like a scream. The white light poured from Ilah and as it did the darkness at the centre of the Sagenstone began to lose the battle, and started to fade, wriggling and then wavering as it fought and then with a sudden surge Ilah exploded with heat, and light, and sound and then went dark.

Faranalga, Rowan and Hyrn stood shaken and temporarily blinded from the brightness of Ilah. Hyrn's hand felt as if it was burning. He placed Ilah back inside his vest. As the three of them recovered they looked at the Sagenstone in front of them. The Stone stood, glowing more dully now, but as they looked into it, they saw with amazement and wonder that the dark stain had disappeared. The Sagenstone was healed. Faranalga stood and then raised his hands to his face, tears welled in his eyes and rolled down his cheeks. He made as if to speak but then just shook his head and wept softly.

Hyrn looked over at Rowan. The sword hung loosely in his brother's hands, the point touching the floor. Rowan was looking at the Sagenstone as if transfixed. Hyrn turned his head and peered into the Stone. A warmth seemed to spread from the top of his head and then he felt as if a voice spoke to him, a voice soft but deep.

"Welcome Child of Light. I have waited for you for many years. I thank you for bringing Ilah to me. You have healed me and in doing so have helped to heal the Caramarhc and its people. A great evil lies to the West, but I can't discern what it is. It is hidden from me but the time is drawing near. Your fate and that of your brother has fulfilled a part in our history, but this is just a part of your journey. You have been asked whether you should continue on your quest but your mind is already telling you that what you should do, and what you wish to do, are the same thing. Go to Anasaria. You feel deeply that this is where your path lies and I feel that destiny awaits you there. Go now. Perhaps when you come of age you would test yourself to become an Elder. You are of the mountains, but no, you are much more. Tread carefully Hyrn, and trust in yourself and your brother. You have strong hands around you to help you on your way, but it is the two of you that are central to this quest."

Far away, deep beneath the mountains, in the warren of tunnels and caves that wormed their way under the foundations of Errasarn, the long deserted kingdom of King Darion, something dark and evil stirred.

CHAPTER SEVEN

The Stained

The next day the boys were allowed to sleep in, but they rose early to see the sunrise. Their apartment, in one of the large buildings just down from the dome of the great hall, looked east over the city and away over the southeastern ridge of the mountains and out to the distant sea, and Anasaria beyond the horizon. As they stood on the small balcony adjoining their rooms, they could see everywhere Caramar facing east as the sky began to lighten. The morning was cool up here in the mountains but the sky was clear apart from a low band of cloud far to the south. The day would be bright and sunny and the prospect of a day spent resting and seeing the sights of the city seemed like a haven amidst the turmoil and exertion of their journey.

Faranalga and the rest of the Elders had given them a day to consider their decision before they would hear their answer. After the events in the chamber the boys had once more come before the Elders. The news of the healing of the Sagenstone had been discussed and then the journey ahead and Anasaria. The boys were eager to tell them their decision but they had been urged not to be hasty, but to consider while they enjoyed the sights of the city. They would hear from them that evening.

As the first sliver of the sun peeped above the horizon the familiar chanting began. Here in the city on the side of the great Mount Calaborn the voices of many Caramar were lifted. The stone of the city echoed and vibrated with the sound. The very construction of the city seemed to be designed to amplify the sound. Rowan and Hyrn were held transfixed in awe. The great chant rose into a crescendo as the disk of the sun appeared and climbed above the horizon, and then abruptly the sound ceased.

Breakfast was brought to them in their apartment and after they had eaten they decided they would have a look around the city. They went to look for

Careil. He and Bregal had rooms in the same building. They went down the stairway from their apartment into a courtyard with a fountain in the centre, Careil and Bregal were seated on a bench alongside the fountain, deep in conversation. They looked up as the boys approached.

"Good morning," said Careil. "I thought you two would have taken the opportunity to have a sleep-in."

"No," said Rowan. "We didn't want to waste the morning. We thought we could have a look around the city."

"That's fine," said Careil. "The Elders have said that you are free to do what you like today. Just try not to get up to any mischief."

"We won't," said Hyrn quickly.

"I don't think you will need your sword," said Bregal, eyeing the hilt of the sword poking above Rowan's shoulder.

"I didn't want to leave it in our room," said Rowan. "I have to look after it and I would be worried about it all the time if I left it."

"Alright," said Careil. "Just remember that it is a weapon and should be treated accordingly. I am sure that there are people though who would be interested in seeing the Sword, as well as Ilah. Just be sure to be polite but don't be too cavalier with them. Remember what you are carrying, and how important they are."

"Of course we will," said Hyrn, feeling somewhat like he was being treated like a little child.

"Be back in time for the evening meal," said Careil. "Faranalga has asked that we dine with them again. Until then you will need to make do."

"We have brought some of the food from breakfast to eat later," said Rowan.

"We will see you later then," said Careil, and added as the boys turned to go "And don't get lost."

The boys glanced back, both with a look of umbrage on their faces but didn't answer. They made their way through the large archway that led from the courtyard, out into the sunlit street.

Arienga stood before the doors carved with the symbol of the Seat of the Elders that led to the chamber containing the Sagenstone. Beside her was one of the Elders, Aliana.

"Are you sure you wish to do this?" asked Aliana.

"Yes," replied Arienga.

The elderly woman continued. "It is unusual for those trained as warriors to put themselves forward to be accepted into the ranks of the Elders. It has happened before. We have had over the centuries some warriors who have been accepted. We have also had Elders who have become warriors. The Sagenstone will decide if you are worthy."

Aliana approached the doorway and, as Faranalga had, placed her hands against the door and chanted softly. The doors opened and they walked through the doorway and onwards into the cavern beyond. They crossed the floor and passed between the stone benches and stood before the Stone.

Aliana, as if reciting a mantra, said, "Stone of wisdom, a child of the mountains, come of age, stands before you to be tested. Her name is Arienga."

She turned to the young warrior. "Look into the Stone and try to clear your mind."

Arienga faced the Stone and looked deep into its depth. The Sagenstone glowed red and clear. Arienga felt a warmth spread from the top of her head and she heard a voice in her mind.

"Greetings Warrior," said the voice. "You come to be tested. You believe that the life of a warrior may not be your path. You think that perhaps the path of wisdom is your calling, and that you may become an Elder. You question your path because it is hard, but all paths are difficult."

In her mind, Arienga saw flashes of herself seated writing, and reading from large books, speaking to other Elders dressed like her in long flowing robes, but in each vision dark shapes moved in the background and she saw herself distracted by the shapes. People were talking to her but she wasn't listening and kept looking away. The people in her vision became annoyed and spoke harshly to her but she couldn't concentrate on what they were saying.

Faranalga stood before her speaking, but a dark shape swooped down towards him. From beneath her robes she drew a bright sword and slashed at the air as the dark shape approached. Abruptly the vision disappeared.

The Sagenstone spoke to her powerfully, "You cannot escape the warrior in you, Arienga. The life of a scholar is not for you. Dark times are ahead and you are caught up in them. Your destiny lies alongside that of others who tread a dangerous path. They have need of you Arienga, and although you are young, your strength and skill are needed. I see that there is much that may lie in store, adventures and great events, and there is one who looms large, but nothing is clear. You have things that you must do. You must travel far yet. Go with them and stay true to your heart. The warrior in you will keep you strong and true but what is in your heart will guide you and speak to you when things seem darkest. Go now warrior and trust in your strength."

With that, the connection with the Stone was broken and Arienga felt almost as if she had just woken from a dream. She turned to Aliana and the Elder smiled.

"Do you have your answer?" asked Aliana. "Did the Sagenstone speak the sacred words to you?"

"No," replied Arienga. "I know now that I am a warrior and that is what I must be."

She paused and looked deep in thought, then shook her head as if to shake herself out of a trance.

"I have to speak to Duburinga," she said.

Arienga turned quickly and moved towards the arched tunnel that led from the cavern. She stopped abruptly and turned to Aliana.

"Thank you, Elder, Aliana," she said and then turned again and rushed out of the cavern.

Aliana turned to the Sagenstone and smiled.

"What did you tell her?" she said, shaking her head softly.

As they walked through the city Rowan and Hyrn were greeted by everyone they met. People were fascinated by them, and were eager to hear their story. They were interested to see the Stone and the Sword that they had heard about. After a while the two boys began to get tired of the constant attention. They longed to just walk around and see the sights without having to stop and tell the same story, or to answer more questions. They were walking along an empty street that ran southward, the mass of Mount Calaborn rose to their right.

Just then Rowan grabbed Hyrn's arm. "Quick, down here."

Hyrn followed his brother into a narrow alley that ran between two buildings. They crouched down behind a stone water cistern that stood against one of the buildings and peeped out. Two Caramar all dressed in white came walking past talking animatedly. They passed the mouth of the alley and kept walking, unaware that the boys were there.

"That was close," said Rowan. "I couldn't stand having to go through that again. The people are nice and friendly here but I need a rest from them."

"Me too," agreed Hyrn.

They stood up and looked around. At the other end of the alley they could see a gate that led up on to a hillside that sloped up towards the peak of the mountain.

"Let's go that way," said Rowan.

They walked up the alley. There were no windows overlooking the alley, just high blank walls built from the same white stone. The sky above was still blue but a slight breeze had picked up to break the stillness of the morning. When they came to the end of the alley they saw that a laneway ran behind the buildings separating them from the hillside beyond. A low wooden fence formed a boundary, with a gate directly opposite the end of the alley. They could see that beyond the fence, a path ran up the hillside, disappearing amongst shrubs and stunted trees.

"Come on," said Rowan. "I bet we could get a good view of the city from up the hill."

Hyrn didn't reply but followed as Rowan opened the gate and walked through. They followed the path up the hillside, winding back and forth. The vegetation hid them from the city below, and as they made their way higher, the path began to get quite steep and rocky in places. They reached a crest in the hill and saw that beyond, the land grew steeper. High above, the mountainside became sheer cliffs towering up to the snow covered peak. The path turned to the left along the top of the crest of the hill and then led across a wide meadow that ended at another hillside much steeper than the one they had just climbed. The meadow was bordered on the south by a stand of dark fir trees. They could hear water running somewhere amongst the grass of the meadow. As they followed the path it dipped down lower and then forded a stream. The stream was not deep but flowed swiftly. The boys came to the stream and looked across the water.

"I don't want to walk through that," said Hyrn.

"Let's go upstream a bit and see if there is somewhere else we can cross," said Rowan.

They walked along the bank of the stream. The grass was high in places but they were able to navigate their way along. They travelled towards the stand of trees, the tops of which were still visible from down in the gully formed by the stream. As they walked further, the stream broadened out and they could see that a small lake stretched towards where the trees stood. The lake had been hidden from view by the grass of the meadow. A little way ahead a small wooden pier jutted out into the water. The wood looked quite worn but it seemed stable enough. The boys walked out onto the pier and Rowan sat down at the end, his feet dangling just above the water. Hyrn sat down alongside him and they both looked out across the water to where the trees stood, beneath the imposing heights of Calaborn. The breeze had picked up and large white clouds were scurrying across the sky from the south. Rowan pulled food from his pack and passed some to Hyrn.

Neither of them said anything for a while, as they ate and looked out across the water. Then Hyrn spoke in a quiet voice.

"I am going to Anasaria, Row," he said. "I don't know why, but I know that I must. I can feel it. Everyone keeps telling me to take my time and think it over, but I don't need to. I have already decided. I am taking Ilah to Anasaria."

His voice became softer still. "You'll come too, won't you Row?"

Rowan looked at his younger brother. This all seemed hard and dangerous.

"Of course I'm coming," he said. "I feel the same. I must carry The Sword of Acclimoss back to where it belongs."

"And besides," he added. I can't let you just wander off getting yourself into all kinds of trouble."

Hyrn looked taken aback, and swiped at Rowan's arm. Rowan went to grab him, but Hyrn leapt to his feet and ran down the short pier, and then stopped abruptly. A ragged figure stood there.

His features were hidden beneath a cowl. He was clothed in a loose tattered cloak, a dark, mottled brown in colour. His arms were by his side and a dark wooden cudgel hung loosely in his right hand. Hyrn noticed that the sky had darkened quickly. The clouds had become heavier and were blocking the sun. The wind had picked up and the air felt heavy with the threat of rain. The man's ragged clothes were being buffeted by the wind. Rowan was now on his feet and came up behind Hyrn.

"Who are you?" demanded Rowan.

The figure raised his free hand and pointed a gnarled finger at them.

He spoke in a harsh gravelly voice. "There is no hope for you. They know you come, and they will be waiting."

The man laughed with a rasping croak and spoke again. "Can't you feel it? The time of the Mocker is near and none will stand in his way."

He laughed again and lowered his left hand. At the same time, he raised the cudgel. As he did so, Rowan drew the Sword of Acclimoss and held it before him, pushing Hyrn behind him.

"Leave us alone, old man," demanded Rowan.

The old man laughed again. "Old swords from bones and dust," he said mockingly.

At that moment Hyrn noticed that among the trees beyond the water, other figures were moving, making their way to where they stood. Large droplets of rain began to fall. Hyrn could hear them hitting the surface of the water behind him. A feeling like ice grew in his stomach. He had a sudden thought and fumbled inside his vest and brought forth Ilah. A bolt of lightning flashed across the sky and thunder crashed all around them. He held the Stone out in front of him but Ilah remained dark and silent.

The man laughed again, this time with a higher almost maniacal cackle.

"Your Stone will not help you. It has felt the power of the Mocker and has failed the test."

Hyrn stood frozen. The rain was heavier now. Rowan and the ragged man faced each other. The rest of the figures began to get closer. There were too many of them to fight. If only Careil was here, but he wasn't expecting to see them until evening. The man raised his arm, and Rowan held his sword ready. Lightning flashed again, and the answering thunder seemed to Hyrn to sound their doom.

Arienga ran through the streets. She had spoken to Duburinga of what the Sagenstone had told her. He had listened and then gave her his answer. If the Elders decided that the Caramar would continue on this quest, she was free to go. The condition was that she follow her training, remember her protocols, and behave as a warrior should. She felt light and happy as she ran through the streets. She wanted to let Rowan and Hyrn know that if they chose to go on, and the Elders sent Caramar, she could go with them.

Where had they got to? She hadn't been able to find them anywhere. People had seen them, but not for a while. Where would two boys go in a strange city like this? They were not accustomed to cities, they only knew the open lands of Wesmere…That was it. They would go… She turned back the way she had come and ran towards the southwest of the city. There was only one piece of open country near the city. She ran past an alley and then stopped as she spied the green of a hillside, and at the end of the alley an open gate. She sprinted down the alley, through the gate and onto the path that led up the hillside.

The figures drew closer now. Rowan took a step back pushing Hyrn behind him, and further along the pier towards the lake.

"Stay away!" shouted Rowan. "Or I will run you through."

The man laughed again. His laugh grew into a screech of rage. He raised his club above his head, and still screeching, charged at Rowan and Hyrn. As he did, with a sharp 'Thwuck!' an arrow pierced his head, and he collapsed to the ground, his cry dying as he fell.

Rowan and Hyrn looked up, startled, and charging up the gully towards them came Arienga. Her bow was raised and already another arrow was notched and drawn. She let the arrow fly and the nearest of the approaching figures fell to the ground clutching an arrow that sprouted from their chest. She reached the entrance to the pier and drew a short sword. Rowan and Hyrn met her and she handed the sword to Hyrn. He pushed Ilah back inside his vest and stood holding the sword, his hands shaking. Arienga notched another arrow, and the three stood facing the remaining attackers. They had halted now and seemed wary.

"The first to take a step closer dies!" shouted Arienga threateningly.

One of the figures, taller than the rest, let out a shout and charged. An arrow struck him in the throat and he stumbled and then collapsed. The others began to mumble, and some turned and began to move back towards the trees.

"Go! All of you!" shouted Arienga, and the rest turned and began to lope away back the way they had come.

Arienga turned to Rowan and Hyrn. "Come on," she said. "Let's get back to the city."

"Who were those people?" asked Hyrn as they fell in behind Arienga and headed down the river towards the ford. The rain fell steadily now, soaking them and turning the path muddy as they went.

"They are the Stained," said Arienga.

"Why are they called the Stained?" asked Rowan. "And where do they come from?"

"They are Caramar," said Arienga, "but Caramar who have been touched by evil. I don't know all the history but supposedly they have something to do with the stain that is…or was, in the heart of the Sagenstone. You don't generally see many of them, and when you do, they are usually alone and wandering the mountains. People feel sorry for them and try to help them, but they don't want help and they tend to get up to some sort of mischief or other. I have never heard of them attacking people like that or being in such a large group. We must ask the Elders when we return."

"Will Faranalga know?" asked Hyrn.

"Faranalga is no longer First Voice," said Arienga.

"What does that mean?" asked Rowan.

"The Elders take turns in leading Elder Gatherings," replied Arienga. "Aliana is First Voice as of this morning. We can ask her."

With that Arienga fell silent and strode ahead back towards the city. Rowan tried to get alongside her and engage her in conversation, but Arienga remained facing fixedly ahead as she walked steadfastly forward, a look of concentration and determination on her face. Only a short time before, all she had been thinking was that she would be able to join in an adventure. It had all seemed like it would be exciting, but she now realised that this was serious. The words of the Sagenstone now became clear. This was a dark and dangerous situation. She glanced back at Rowan and Hyrn. They both looked shaken and had worried looks on their faces. She remembered what Rowan had said the previous morning. They were just farm boys. Even if they carried the Sword and a Stone of power, they were untrained and unprepared for what lay ahead. She needed to help them; to protect them.

Rowan had a sword but he didn't know how to fight. A sense of determination grew in her. He may not like it but she must teach him how to fight if she could. He had Careil and Bregal, but she would do all she could to make sure that if he needed to fight, he would be ready. She set her jaw as they crested the hill and headed down towards the city, through the pouring rain.

When the three arrived back in the streets of the city, wet and tired, they headed for the Hall of the Elders. Rowan and Hyrn stopped by the apartments but Careil and Bregal were nowhere to be seen. Arienga sent them on towards the Hall and went to find Duburinga, to give her report. When the two boys arrived at the great doors they were stopped by the guards.

"We need to speak to the Elders," said Rowan sternly.

The guard pulled a lever and a great booming sounded from within. A short time later the doors opened and a young man dressed in the robes of an Elder but with a grey sash appeared.

"I am Novice Yarga," he said. "Please come with me."

He re-entered the hall and the boys followed him. He turned to the left and continued through an archway into a small area furnished with low couches and armchairs.

"We will wait here until the Elders are ready," said Yarga. "A Gathering is in progress. There is much being discussed concerning you and your quest. If there is anything you would like to ask, I will do my best."

"Where is Careil?" asked Rowan.

Yarga laughed lightly.

"That is an easy one," he said. He and his fellow Rider are guests at the Gathering."

"Why can't we go in?" asked Hyrn.

"I believe that the Elders do not wish to influence your decision," replied Yarga. "What is being discussed is about the fate of the quest, whether you decide to continue, or whether you decide to return home."

"We have already decided," said Rowan. "We are both going to try to get to Anasaria and do what Devarnia asked us to do."

Yarga laughed again. "I wish decisions were made that quickly here. We are accustomed to lengthy debate and weighing all options."

The Novice Elder paused and looked at the two boys dripping water onto the floor and shivering.

"Oh, forgive me, your clothes are wet," he said hurriedly. "I will get a fire started and you can dry yourselves while we wait."

The two boys were standing in front of a roaring fire when Arienga and Duburinga entered the room. The Caramar came over and Duburinga spoke.

"Arienga has told me what happened outside the city. You were very lucky. We were unaware that there was any danger. Strange things are happening around you. From now on you will be guarded at all times. I have spoken to the City Guard and they will provide guards, if needed, but for now Arienga, Boriega, Gebarana and I will watch you. Please do not go wandering off anywhere. The Elders will speak to you soon."

As if on cue, an Elder entered the room.

"I am Aliana," she said. "Please tell me what took place today."

Rowan, Hyrn and Arienga related what had happened. Aliana listened carefully, with an increasingly worried look on her face. When they had finished Aliana addressed their questions about the people that had attacked them.

"The Stained are Caramar that have been touched by evil. They first appeared at the time the darkness began to grow in the heart of the Sagenstone. They appear to have been corrupted by whatever affected the Stone. They usually shun the rest of the Caramar, and despite our ministrations, we have been unable to help them, and indeed they do not want to be helped. They do not seem to have any purpose in their lives apart from creating trouble wherever they go. It does not seem to be coordinated or premeditated, it just seems to be within their nature. When we have tried to heal them they have become violent and bestial. We have tried to treat them well but mostly they just want to be left alone, to live away from us and wander aimlessly from place to place. I have never heard of such an attack as you witnessed today.

We will think on this some more, but it appears that the presence of Ilah is creating a disturbance. The Gathering has agreed that the Stone must move on. As to the Mocker. We have heard of this, but it is a creature of legend. Our scholars will see what they can find out about it.

Tonight, whatever you have decided, the Caramar have agreed that they will help to fulfill the quest. Careil will accompany you whether you go on or return home, and Bregal has said that he will go wherever he is needed. Indeed Bregal is now convinced that the quest is beyond his loyalties to the

Wesmerian Council, and that Careil had no choice but to defy them.

For now, you may join us for our evening meal and then we will meet in the Council Hall."

Rowan and Hyrn stood atop the dais in the centre of the Elder Council.

Aliana asked them formally to state their intentions. "Do you wish to continue your quest? To seek out the Realm of the Underdwellers, to travel to Anasaria, to unite the Twin Stones of Angil, to return the Stones and the Sword of Acclimoss to Abessair and to free the Anasarians from the tyranny of the seven Dark Lords?"

Hyrn felt small under the gaze of the Gathering of the Elders. He felt their eyes upon him and Rowan, but deep inside he knew what he must do, if only he could speak it out loud. He felt a slight warmth within his clothing. Ilah. Aliana had explained to them at dinner that Ilah must have been severely weakened by the battle to defeat the evil within the Sagenstone. Hyrn had felt nothing until now. But he heard almost a whisper in his head.

"Tell them, Stonebearer."

Hyrn tensed with surprise. What was that? What did it mean? Was it Ilah speaking? Confusion filled his thoughts. He had heard a voice in his head. It sounded almost like the voice of the Sagenstone... or like Ilah. He dismissed it and took a breath.

Hyrn drew Ilah from within his vest and removed the cloth that covered the Stone. Beside him Rowan drew Acclimoss.

The two brothers looked at each other and then both said together, "We will go to Anasaria."

The Stone in Hyrn's hand flashed brightly, but briefly, its light reflecting along the blade of the Sword. A murmur of wonder travelled around the chamber and then Aliana spoke.

"It is decided," she said loudly. "Behold the children of destiny. The quest to free Anasaria goes forth. I now name the party that will accompany them."

With that Aliana listed Careil and Bregal, the four Caramar that had brought them to the Seat of the Elders; Duburinga, Boriega, Gebarana and Arienga, two of the City Guard; Terrana and Margana, and then lastly she named herself and the Novice Elder, Yarga.

CHAPTER EIGHT

Forgotten Paths

Two large stone pillars loomed out of the fog. The edges of the pillars were rough and broken. The party gathered on a small courtyard to the east of the city. This area seemed older than the rest of the city. Broken stone lay strewn across the paved ground. The fog still persisted and it was difficult to see very far beyond the area they all stood in. The air was cool and damp and the light of the sun was dim and diffused. Beyond the two pillars, the fog stretched out obscuring the descent into the valley below and on into the eastern regions of the Caramarhc. Their voices were muffled as they readied themselves to begin the journey.

They had awoken that morning to a blanket of white fog that had swallowed the Seat of the Elders. The light of the rising sun weakly illuminated the fog. After an early breakfast Rowan and Hyrn had stowed their gear in their packs and gone down into the courtyard to meet with Careil and Bregal. The two Riders were waiting for them, ready to take them down towards the eastern entrance to the city. This entrance was less used, with most traffic to and from the city using the southern gate. The people of the town had come out to see them off, but with the fog they did not get much of a chance to see them. The four Caramar from the west had fallen in behind them without being noticed. Hyrn had looked behind them and saw dim figures through the mist. Once they arrived at the eastern gate the figures had materialised into Duburinga, Arienga, Boriega and Gebarana.

The two members of the City Guard, Terrana and Margana, were waiting for them at the gate, speaking to the guards who were on duty. Terrana told them that Aliana and Yarga were already outside the city, waiting for them at the beginning of the old eastern road. He explained that this road was little used and had fallen into disrepair. Caramar that wished to travel east usually took the main road to the south which was the same road that they had travelled on at the Bridge of Mists and beyond. The main road ran eastwards and took a route south of the steep sided narrow ridge of Mount Carvala. They would be taking a more direct route, to the north of this mountain through areas only sparsely inhabited.

They followed a terraced roadway down from the gate, and eventually came to the wide paved area alongside the two pillars that marked the beginning of the old East Road. Presently, they heard the muffled sound of horse's hooves and out of the fog appeared two Caramar leading Erras and Marran. Bregal and Careil met the Caramar and took the reins from them, thanking them. Hyrn walked over and patted Erras's neck. It felt good to have the horses back with them. He had got used to having the great horse with them, and having Marran join them, helped to make up for the fact that they had had to leave their own horses back in Ballarghen. Erras snorted softly as Hyrn rubbed his neck.

"I think he is eager to get started," said Careil.

Just then Aliana spoke. "Here we are at the start of the next stage of this great quest. We are beyond the city walls now, and, although I still carry the authority of the Elders throughout these mountains, outside the city I defer to the training of the warriors. Therefore I ask that Duburinga lead us along with his three warriors. With your leave Careil and Bregal, I ask that you assist in this. Although this is the Caramarhc, your knowledge of the ways of the wild are invaluable."

Careil and Bregal both nodded assent and Bregal said formally, "We are honoured to work with Duburinga and his people."

"So," said Aliana, "let us begin."

Duburinga and Boriega moved towards the two pillars. Careil fell in behind them and signalled for Rowan and Hyrn to move. Next came Terrana and Margana, followed by Aliana and Yarga, and bringing up the rear were Arienga and Gebarana. As they approached the pillars Hyrn could see that there were broad steps that led down from them. The middle of the steps had been cleared of debris, but the sides were piled with broken bits of stone and the edges of the steps were chipped and broken in places.

"Why is this place so old and broken?" asked Hyrn.

"This place has seen much war," answered Aliana. "In the war with the Northerners, this area, now known as the Battle Vales, was the main route for the Northerners to attack Wesmere. It is through this pass that the Wesmerians drove the retreating Northerners before them, and just to the north, at the Pass of Vigilance, the Northerners surrendered. The Seat of the Elders was attacked but managed to hold off the Northerners. The Northerners sought to lay siege to the city but the Southern gate is protected by deep gorges and steep cliffs. Also paths from the city lead up to the mountain and our people are able to seek refuge there. We were relieved by more Caramar from the West and eventually a force of Caramar from the Eastern Watch came to our aid and drove the Northerners off.

"Why haven't you repaired all this?" asked Rowan.

Aliana considered this and then answered, "At first we had more pressing concerns. Caramar society was severly damaged. Our people were dispersed and we had lost contact with vast areas of the Caramarhc. When the time came to think about this area, it was felt that it should be left as a reminder of the suffering of the Caramar, so that the people of the Seat of the Elders, and indeed all Caramar, would remember that evil can touch us even here, high in our mountain home."

Aliana fell silent. The roadway levelled out and headed east. The party travelled amongst ruined stone buildings that appeared out of the fog, crumbling and overgrown with vegetation. In places, large trees grew within what once were houses and places of business. The roadway sloped gently downwards as they travelled, and the fog became less thick the further they descended. Eventually they came out into clearer air and the fog became a layer of cloud above them. They could now see that the road continued eastwards towards a tall peak that jutted up steep and sheer, like a giant axe head towering up towards the sky; Mount Carvala. The area around them was heavily forested with few signs of habitation, old or new. The road levelled out and followed the line of a long ridge to their right that led eastward towards the mountain ahead.

They stopped at midday to eat and rest, in a place where the land fell away to the north. The sky was now clear and blue, and the sun shone above them. A long valley stretched below them running eastwards and then widening out and dividing up where the Northeastern Caramarhc divided from the main mass of the mountains. Where the mountains divided a great haze sat over the abyss and beyond that the land opened out into a large plain hemmed in by the mountains and stretching down towards the sea. Through this plain a great river ran, finally opening out into marshlands before it found the sea.

Margana pointed the haze out to Rowan, Hyrn and Careil, who sat looking out across the valley.

"There are the mists created by the Falls of Sorrow," she said. "Northward across the falls lies the northeastern mountains leading to the Pinnacles and the Spire. In ancient times they were an important part of the Caramar but after the war they were overrun by Drargs and we had not the power to drive the evil beings out."

She pointed directly across the valley to a large gap between a small peak and the rest of the northeastern ridge.

"That is the Pass of Vigilance," she continued. "There paths lead down into the lands of the Northerners. There is a watchtower there, but after the war had been ended for a few years, the Wesmerians and the Caramar no longer felt the need, or the desire, to look out over the lands of our former enemies. The whole area is overrun with Drargs now. One day we hope that we will take back control of that land all the way to the Spire. For the time being, we are honoured to be part of your quest. We head east now to the Eastern Watch and beyond."

Over the next two days they travelled east along the mountain ridges. The roadway was overgrown and almost non-existent in places. Time and neglect had destroyed what was once a major thoroughfare of the Caramarhc. Mount Carvala grew as they travelled from the west along its northern flank, until it towered above them, and then slipped by as they continued east. Near the end of the second day of their trek, the roadway joined with the main highway, north of the smaller peak of Mount Garva. This road was in better condition; well used and kept in a good state of repair.

On the third day, as they traveled along the road where it crossed the northern flank of Mount Garva, a troop of Caramar approached from the east. They greeted Aliana and spoke with the other Caramar. They were Caramar from the Eastern Watch, the fortress at the eastern end of the Caramarhc that looked out over the sea. They were to escort them the rest of the way.

The Eastern Watch was a large stone fortress that stood astride a river that flowed through a sloping valley. This valley formed a divide between the forked ridges at the eastern end of the southeastern branch of the Caramarhc. It overlooked a succession of large hills that tumbled down to the sea. As they approached the fortress they could see on the most eastern point of the southeastern ridge, a large tower.

"What is that tower?" Hyrn asked Margana.

"That is the Temple of the Sunrise," said Margana. "It is a most sacred place to the Caramar. There the Priests of the Sun pay homage to the lifegiver the Sun. I have heard that long ago a great Stone stood atop that tower, The Stone of the Sun."

"What happened to it?" asked Hyrn.

"It is said, that a group of Priests took the Stone to seek for the place where the sun rises first on this world. None know where they went or what became of them. It is also said, that when they return, the Caramar will be whole again. It has supposedly been many hundreds of years since the Stone was taken."

Margana fell silent and they continued down the road into the valley towards the great fortress.

They met that night in the great stone keep of the fortress of the Eastern Watch. There were around a hundred warriors stationed in the fortress and most of them seemed to be gathered around them.

Aliana addressed them all. "Fellow Caramar and members of the quest, tomorrow we continue on to seek the entrance to the Realm of the Underdwellers. It has been many years since any have trodden that path, but if our knowledge serves us well, we will find the entrance and enter that realm. We hope that the way will be clear, but no-one has had any dealings with the Underdwellers for more than two hundred years. The account of Devarnia tells us that the Underdwellers are still there, but mostly at the eastern entrance where their realm enters into Anasaria. We hear that they wage war against the Ultamarians. The passage to Anasaria will be a difficult one, but we must help the Stone and Sword bearers to find their way there. It is felt that we may be of help to the Underdwellers in their war. Fifty of the warriors stationed here in this fortress will accompany us."

A murmur rose among those listening.

Aliana continued, "Long have the Caramar dreamt of regaining our past. So much evil has been thrown upon us and grown amongst us. We know now that the path to our redemption is to fight against the evil that threatens the world. If the quest for Anasaria can help to defeat a great evil, then our path is clearer. Much is changing even now and destiny has come upon us. It is these times that we have waited for. Let us go on with hope and defiance to restore the power of good in our world."

All those Caramar gathered roared their approval. Hyrn felt his heart swell in his chest and felt Ilah stir. He withdrew the Stone. Ilah had shown no signs of life since the brief flash of light in the Hall of the Elders. Hyrn had worried that the Stone had lost its power, just as the Stained man had said. But as he raised Ilah above his head the Stone burst into life. Brilliant light shone out illuminating the great stone walls around them. All those there looked toward Hyrn.

The Stone shone brighter still and one word issued from within its depths and, though they knew not what it meant, all there took heart and felt uplifted.

"Desultamar!" cried Ilah.

They awoke to a grey and wet morning. They had slept on cots made up in the large hall that adjoined the keep. The sound of the greeting of the sunrise awoke Hyrn, and he sat up. Rowan stirred beside him. Careil and Bregal were only recently awake and were packing their gear. The Caramar were nowhere to be seen. They were obviously all outside greeting the sun as it rose behind the blanket of clouds and rain that shrouded the fortress of the Eastern Watch. After they were up, the Caramar returned. Food was laid upon the tables in the centre of the hall and they were invited to breakfast. As they ate they were joined by the rest of their fellow travellers.

Aliana told them that scouts had travelled down into the foothills to prepare the way. The warriors that were to join them were provisioned and ready to leave. They also carried food for the two horses. They were to begin south of where the waters of the river discharged from undeneath the fortress and flowed swiftly down through the hills towards the sea.

Below the eastern wall of the fortress, the river poured down a large sluice and cascaded into a steep gorge. The water roared beside them as they followed a path down to the hills below. The area was dominated by large outcrops of rock, steep drops and a scattering of pockets of forest. As they descended, the pathway wove its way through gullies and down hillsides. On a promontory overlooking the path stood a watchtower crumbling and abandoned. They passed beneath it and, as they did, they broke from amongst a stand of trees and stood looking over the hills to the foggy sea beyond. The grey skies had begun to break up and patches of sunlight were playing across the landscape below them.

The path they were following, became a trail as they continued and then petered out in the midst of a clearing, leaving several smaller trails leading off in several directions. They halted and one of the Caramar leaders from the Eastern Watch, Harla, came and addressed them.

"The paths here lead in many directions and mostly to dead ends," she said. "There is known to be a path through to the Underdwellers but we do not usually go beyond here. This area is protected by steep cliffs and treacherous slopes. We will find a way through. I have sent warriors ahead to seek a path. We can wait here and take provisions until we have word back from the scouts."

They broke out food and drink and sat themselves around the clearing. Hyrn sat himself down on a fallen log and looked out through the treetops to the sea which was visible beyond. Curtains of fog hung languidly above the water. Rowan was seated over near Arienga. Hyrn watched them for a while. Rowan was trying to talk to Arienga, but she seemed more intent on what Boriega and Duburinga were talking about. She appeared to be actively ignoring Rowan. Arienga had barely spoken to the two of them since they had left the Seat of the Elders and she had mostly stayed close to Duburinga, often deep in conversation. As Hyrn watched, Arienga suddenly leapt to her feet and stood in front of Rowan.

Arienga gathered her strength as she looked down at Rowan.

"Stand up, farm boy!" she said sternly.

Her stomach twisted as she spoke but she knew what she had to do. Rowan looked up at her with hurt and bewilderment on his face.

"I said 'stand up'!" she said more forcefully still.

Rowan rose to his feet. His hands were clenched at his side. He didn't know what to think. His face flushed red with embarrassment and indignation. He looked over to his pack where his sword lay in its sheath. Arienga's eyes darted towards the sword and then back to Rowan.

"You won't need your sword," she said. "But you will need to fight."

With this she launched herself at Rowan, grappled him around his torso and threw him to the ground. She stood upright then turned and walked down the hill towards the trees. Rowan leapt to his feet and took off after her. Arienga broke into a jog and disappeared into the woods. Rowan followed. He broke through the trees into a small glade. Arienga stood at the other side waiting.

"What did you do that for?" complained Rowan angrily.

"I need to train you," said Arienga, quickly. "I asked Duburinga for permission, and he said that I could as long as I was serious. I had to show him that I was committed to training you."

"Training me?" said Rowan. "Training me to do what?"

Arienga became stern.

"To fight," she said. "And possibly to kill."

She looked at him sternly and continued, "This isn't a game Rowan. This is dangerous. You have a powerful weapon and you don't know how to use it. I am going to help you."

"Help me? How are you…?" started Rowan.

Arienga stared at him and planted her hand on her hips.

"I am going to attack you," she stated. "Prepare to defend yourself."

With that, she quickly stooped and grabbed a stick from the ground and ran towards Rowan. Rowan paused, then scrambled to his left and grabbed a small branch and raised it in front of him. As he did Arienga brought her stick down and broke the top of the branch off, knocking it from Rowan's hands. Before he knew it she held the point of the stick at his throat.

"You're dead," she said. "You'll have to try harder than that."

"I wasn't ready," protested Rowan.

"You will be," said Arienga, allowing the hint of a smile to cross her face.

"Is this how it's going to be?" asked Rowan, a hint of pained resignation in his voice.

"I'm afraid so," said Arienga.

"Alright," said Rowan. "Does this mean that you'll at least talk to me?"

"I think that you'll wish that I didn't talk to you after a while," she said. "Now, take up your weapon and prepare to defend yourself."

Rowan looked at her and sighed. He then bent down and picked up the now shorter branch. He held it loosely in front of him. Arienga just looked at him and shook her head. She had a lot of work to do.

Rowan picked himself up off the ground again. Arienga stood over him and he tried to launch himself at her but she merely moved out of the way and he sprawled onto the ground. He went to get up again, but Arienga suddenly motioned him to be silent. She moved quickly through the trees down to where the other side of the gorge could be seen. Rowan came up behind her, trying to be as quiet as possible. She pointed through the trees across the chasm to the far ridge. At first Rowan couldn't see anything and then he discerned dark figures moving swiftly westward up the ridge through the trees.

"Drargs," whispered Arienga. "Come on, we have to warn the others."

Just then, one of the Caramar from the Eastern Watch appeared before them. Arienga nodded to signify that they had seen the Drargs.

The Caramar approached and spoke in a low voice. "There are hundreds of them moving up towards the fortress. Go back to the others. Runners have been sent to warn the Watch. Thirty of our number are returning to help them out. The others of us will continue on and reinforcements will join us when they can. Come now we must get further down, as quietly and invisibly as possible."

Arienga and Rowan joined the others in the clearing and quickly stowed their gear. Caramar warriors led them down one of the paths that led from the clearing. They stayed on one of the more southerly paths where there were more trees to shield them from sight. After a while, the path became a rocky trail. The path here was more difficult. Careil and Bregal led their horses carefully as they descended. The trail wove between trees and stone outcrops and eventually stopped in an open space, completely surrounded by natural stone walls. They gathered there unsure what to do next; the twelve who had left The Seat of the Elders and about fifteen of the remaining Caramar. A short time later four more Caramar entered the clearing. One of them came over to speak to Aliana and Duburinga. It was Harla.

"The Drargs are distant from here," she said. "The rest of our number are tracking them and the Eastern Watch have been warned. If the Drargs attack the fortress they will regret it. I and these three will head back to the Eastern Watch and will return with reinforcements, and a report when we may. For now, we have been unable to find the path down to the coast. It is believed that there is a gateway in this place, there is no other way through. None of us have kept the knowledge of how to identify and unlock the entrance."

Aliana spoke. "The key to that power is not of the Caramarhc but beyond, to the east. We will need to seek the help of the Angilanian Stone."

She turned to Hyrn nearby. "Hyrn, we need Ilah's help to find the way."

Hyrn came over to Aliana. He withdrew Ilah from his vest and uncovered her. Ilah had not shown any signs of life since the episode with the Sagenstone, apart from the brief flash in the Hall of the Elders, and then last night with the strange cry at the fortress.

He held the Stone in front of him.

"Ilah," he called softly. "We need to find the way through to the Underdwellers."

The Stone began to glow softly and then spoke. "Take me over to the wall, child."

Hyrn walked over to the rock wall at the edge of the clearing.

"Walk along the wall," said Ilah. "There is a place where a path is hidden."

Hyrn walked along the rockface, holding the Stone in front of him.

When he reached the northeast corner Ilah spoke again. "Here, child. Hold me near the rock."

Hyrn did so and Ilah began to chant softly. The chant sounded like a low song, sung by many voices. The rock began to hum and then a scraping noise began.

Slowly, a large section of the rock moved aside revealing a wide dark passage lit by an archway of light further into the rock. Holding Ilah before him, Hyrn walked forward and entered the passage. The floor was dusty and cobwebs hung from the ceiling. As Hyrn approached the other end, he saw the fog enshrouded sea framed by the stone archway. He walked out into the light and onto a broad stone platform. To the left was a steep drop. Ahead, a stairway led downward hugging the cliff face to the right, heading down to an area of dark boulders far below. Beyond the boulders was the sea. He felt the breeze coming up from the sea and smelt the salty tang in the air.

He turned around and Aliana and Rowan were behind him. The rest of the party began to make their way through.

"Let the warriors go ahead to make sure the way is safe, then we will walk down in single file," said Aliana. "Duburinga and Boriega will guard Hyrn and Rowan and Arienga and Gebarana can help the Riders with their horses.

She smiled at Hyrn. "Thank you, Hyrn. We Caramar have not seen this sight for generations. Let us tread carefully but with joy."

"Thank you Ilah," he whispered and placed the Stone back in his vest.

CHAPTER NINE

The Realm of the Underdwellers

The stairway was worn and treacherous in places, but they made it down without any mishaps. Erras and Marran were led calmly down with them. At the bottom, they found themselves on a stone pathway that led between high boulders of dark stone. They followed the path and it wound amongst the boulders and eventually petered out to a patch of sand surrounded by tall, black stones with gaps between leading in different directions. It was decided that they should split up and follow different paths to find a way through. Rowan and Hyrn followed Careil and Duburinga and a group of other Caramar. They found that the paths wound their way between more boulders, often crossing over allowing them to meet up with each other. As they made their way through, they began to hear the sound of waves crashing.

Eventually, the paths met up again in another area of sand. This time only one path led onwards. Aliana and Yarga took the lead, with Terrana and Margana behind them. Rowan and Hyrn followed closely. They walked through a narrow ravine formed by the dark stone. At the end of the ravine they could see a high cliff above an expanse of sand. The sound of the sea was now much louder. They traversed the last of the ravine and came out into a small inlet enclosing a sandy beach guarded on either side by dark steep cliffs that continued out into the water like two massive horns pointing out to sea. Waves crashed against the horns of rock, but the inlet was sheltered from the power of the sea.

Rowan and Hyrn followed Aliana down to the water's edge.

At their feet, the sea washed gently against a beach of black sand. As they lifted their eyes, they saw an islet of black rock jutting out of the water. Beyond where the horns of rocks stood, a wall of fog descended. As Hyrn's eyes adjusted to the light on the open beach, he realised that part of the blackness of the island of rock, was the mouth of a cave. The cave entrance was in the form of a rough arch in the black rock. As the waves flowed around either side of the islet, they lessened in height and power, and then became smaller wavelets that flowed gently towards them across the expanse of water with barely a murmur.

"That must be it," said Hyrn, pointing towards the islet. "The entrance to the Realm of the Underdwellers."

He looked at the water and then said, "But how do we get across."

Careil holding the reins of Erras came up beside Hyrn.

"It looks shallow," he said. "There is a rock platform in front of the cave entrance. It is only a short walk. I am more concerned about whether the horses can get into the cave. Still, from what Devarnia said, it is clear that Darion came through with horses."

He patted Erras and the horse snorted as if impatient to make the attempt. By now, they were all gathered on the beach. Aliana turned her back to the sea and faced them all.

She lifted her arms and spoke. "Caramar and Wesmerians, we have found the way through to the Underdwellers and Anasaria. We hope to make the passage through to Anasaria, but in doing so we leave our lands behind. If any are not ready to do so they may speak now."

Everyone remained silent, looking determinedly at Aliana.

She smiled and continued, "We will have to get our feet wet, but I am sure that there are greater hardships ahead. Come."

And with that, she turned and walked into the water, towards the yawning mouth of the cave. Everyone followed, and the water proved to be barely up to their calves. Hyrn was glad that it was summer. He hated to think what it would be like in the depths of winter.

The crossing was short and they soon stood before the cave entrance. At this distance they could now see that a short stairway carved from the black rock climbed from the water up to the lip of the cave. Two warriors went ahead. They took torches from their packs and lit them from a small tinderbox. They then walked up the stairs and passed over the lip of the entrance and then began to descend down into the cave. They disappeared from view but the light of their torches could still be seen dancing on the roof of the cave.

One of the warriors reappeared and addressed them. "There is a stairway down and then the cave opens out and continues downward. The floor is flat and sandy and there is a drainage channel that leads off to one side. All is dry at present."

He then turned to Careil and Bregal and said, "The passage is large enough for your horses."

They made their way up the stairs and then down into the cave. The two Caramar with torches moved ahead. Some of the others lit torches and distributed them as the rest of the party moved along. At first the walls and ceiling were lit by torchlight, but gradually the passage grew higher and wider, until the light illuminated only the floor, which steadily turned from sand to dark rock. The echo of their footfalls now became more muted, until they faded as the passage opened out further into a wide tunnel.

They had seen no signs of civilisation as they walked, mostly in silence, with just a smattering of muted conversation. After walking for some considerable time, the rock floor suddenly became a stone pathway. The leading Caramar called back to those following. As they approached, they saw a large stone archway that led through a high stone wall. The path led beyond into the darkness. The rock ceiling stretched high into the dimness above. The stone of the arch was largely unadorned, apart from symbols that were carved at its apex.

"I don't know these symbols," said Careil.

"They are ancient forms of the Common Speech," said Aliana. "The concepts are a little obscure but they basically signify 'people of the light in the dark'. They mean, I believe, the Underdwellers. This is the boundary of their realm, but there seems to be no-one to greet us."

She walked up and stood before the archway and said stridently, "Underwellers we seek entrance to your land. We will hold ourselves accountable to you as we pass through and we will bring ourselves before you and accept your judgement on us if we do you ill."

She turned and said, "Let us now enter, and take care to respect that we are entering into land that is sacred to others. We should seek a place to rest for the night soon."

With that, two torch bearers came alongside her. They passed through the arch and the others moved to follow. As they moved beyond the arch Hyrn could see that there were stone buildings on the inside of the wall, stretching away into the darkness on either side. No signs of life, no light or sound issued from them. All that could be heard in the silence, was the sound of their feet upon the stone road and the steady clip clop of the horses' hooves. As they travelled along the roadway, more stone buildings appeared in the torchlight. Ahead, Hyrn noticed that he could discern a dim glow.

Just at that moment, the earth seemed to shake. A tremor went through the ground and all there felt a sudden fear and sense of danger. Further tremors shivered through the rock. They all faced back the way they had come, as if something was coming up behind them.

Yarga cried out, "The Caramarhc is in pain."

At that instance, Hyrn felt Ilah burning against his skin. He quickly pulled the stone out and Ilah glowed brilliantly, lighting up huge expanses of the chamber.

Ilah cried out in anguish, "Devarnia! No! The Mocker!"

Everyone was looking around wildly.

Aliana spoke. "Something is happening in our mountains. Battle has been joined between the forces of good and evil. This being, the Mocker it must be…"

She faltered, staring at the ground. She looked up, an expression of comprehension dawning on her face.

"Errasarn," she gasped. "The fall of Darion's realm. What Devarnia is seeking is something that is a legendary evil but must be no legend. Ah! The stain on the Sagenstone. The evil in the mountains. This creature must be hidden there and Devarnia has uncovered it…or else?" she paused. "Ilah and the battle within the Sagenstone. Ilah has awoken it, and Devarnia is there."

Some of the Caramar looked as if they wanted to go back. To help. To fight.

Aliana stopped them with a calm voice. "We are too far away. There is nothing we can do. Stand and wait. Devarnia possesses great power beyond anything we possess, except perhaps Ilah. We have made a vow to accompany this quest. We cannot abandon it."

Ilah spoke in low tones. "They battle. They are on the feet of Mount Avalar. It is night now but I see the fire and light of their attacks. They seem evenly matched. But… No! Devarnia. She is struck and has fallen. The light has gone… No! Devarnia has struck back and the Mocker stumbles. It is dark again. I can see no more."

Hyrn had stood transfixed looking into the Stone as Ilah spoke. He had seen flashes of light amid darkness and then nothing. He looked around dartingly and, as he did, Ilah went dark and silent. His eyes sought out Aliana.

"I do not know, Hyrn," she said. "I can feel that the rock no longer cries out. I feel that the pain of the Caramar, the darkness in our hearts is lifting. We should stop here now and eat and make camp and prepare for what may come."

They settled down that night as best they could amongst the abandoned buildings. They made a fire from a small store of firewood they had discovered alongside one of the stone houses. Rowan had gone off with Arienga to train and had returned groaning and sore. He had lain down and gone straight to sleep.

Hyrn lay awake, worried about the fate of Devarnia. He had seen the battle through Ilah. He had felt the presence of that evil thing, The Mocker. What was it? Was it dead? And was…? He recalled when he and Rowan met her. She seemed so strong, almost like a Stone of power. He remembered her eyes when she had first appeared out of the mist. Those eyes full of the power of good. Smiling but powerful eyes.

Hyrn woke with a start. He didn't remember falling asleep. The Caramar were on their feet all looking westward towards their home. He felt it. Something had changed. The Caramar were smiling, or else standing with a look of wonder on their faces. It felt as if there was a sense of relief all around, as if a great worry had disappeared.

✳

Throughout their mountains, the Caramar stirred from their sleep, or at their posts, as a weight lifted from their hearts. The next day dawned bright and fresh in the midsummer sun, and they greeted it with joy and with a renewed sense of hope.

✳

Within the abandoned Underdweller town, they awoke that same morning, lighthearted and prepared for the day ahead. The fire had burned down in the night but the faint glow from the east diffused the darkness. They had spoken briefly of their hopes and fears, but they were still no wiser. They had eventually settled down for the night, exhausted and, other than the Caramar who had taken turns standing guard, slept peacefully. They gathered up their things after a quick breakfast and assembled ready for the day's journey

They moved off along the stone roadway. This time Duburinga and Gebarana scouted ahead, their torches shrinking ahead of them. The glow they had seen the previous day, steadily grew brighter as they continued on. They began to notice that the roadway that had followed the gradual downward slope of the passage, began to descend more steeply as the cavern plunged further into the bedrock. There had been no buildings since they had moved beyond where they had spent the night.

As the light before them had become sufficient that they no longer needed to carry torches, Duburinga and Gebarana came jogging back down the roadway towards them. Duburinga came before Aliana. He breathed deeply but steadily from the exertion but spoke clearly.

"There is a great lake ahead. The roadway passes to the right," he said. "There is a great cavern beyond. The very rock glows and lights the lake. As we grew closer, we saw from afar a force of people, some mounted, heading this way. They will not be far behind us."

They continued on down the sloping roadway, and as the light became brighter still, they could see the lake ahead. Some distance down the roadway, as it curved to the right to skirt the lake, they could see a group of people approaching. Aliana called for a halt. Some of the Eastern Watch began to form up defensively ahead of them. Aliana called them back and asked them to stand ready, but at peace.

They waited as the group grew nearer, until they could discern individuals amongst them and could see that in the van rode two soldiers, armoured and helmed, and riding what at first appeared to be horses. As they approached, their mounts proved to be beasts of a kind that Hyrn had never seen before. The animals were heavy coated, almost like cows but longer and with bowed backs. Their eyes were large and almost shone in the lamplight. The two mounted and armoured soldiers led a group of about twenty, more lightly armoured soldiers. The troop came to a halt in front of them. The two soldiers dismounted and removed their helmets. They walked up and stood before Aliana who had moved to position herself ahead of the others. Yarga stood at her right elbow and Careil, Rowan and Hyrn moved up behind them.

One of the soldiers spoke. His voice was stern but calm.

"We felt a great disturbance," he said. "We have been sent to seek out an answer. The west is left unguarded, and considered safe, but here we find intruders in our realm. Speak. Tell us why you are here and why the earth shakes as you approach."

Aliana raised her hand palm outwards.

"Peace," she said. "I am Aliana, Elder of the Caramar, the people of the Caramarhc Mountains, the land that lies to the west. We seek entry to your realm. We come here with these two Wesmerian boys on an urgent quest."

She motioned to Rowan and Hyrn and they moved forward and stood to her left.

"We seek Anasaria," continued Aliana. "The Keeper, Devarnia, has charged these two to bring the Stone Ilah and the Sword of Acclimoss back to that land, to unite the Twin Stones of Angil, and to free the people of Anasaria. We also seek to aid the Underdwellers in their fight against evil."

"I am Droom," said the Underdweller. "Captain of the West and Guardian of the Light in the Dark."

He looked at Aliana and continued in his stern voice. "These words bring joy and wonder to my heart. You speak of hope long awaited, but these matters are beyond my duties. I have been charged to keep guard in the west. The Western Gate is long abandoned. We have not the people or the resources to populate this region any longer. Our western defences are now a small portion of our forces. All those remaining in the rest of our realm are now gathered in the City of the Vortex beneath the Great Circle of Sky and the Isle of Wind. We have only come to investigate the shaking and pain in the rock. Is this of your doing?"

"We also felt the pain in the rock, but it comes from far off," replied Aliana. "We were within your realm when this occurred. There was a battle far in the west of the Caramarhc. Devarnia herself fought an evil being called the Mocker."

There were audible gasps and mutterings amongst the assembled Underdwellers.

"We know of the Mocker, but only in legend," said Droom. "It is an evil in the dark. We speak of using the light to pierce the darkness, and in the darkness, it is visions of such evil as the spectre of the Mocker, that give shape to our fears. How did the Keeper fare?"

"We don't know." All eyes turned to Hyrn as he spoke. "Ilah saw the battle but it all went dark."

"We felt a change through the rock," continued Aliana. "An evil that has been troubling us for centuries has gone. I believe the Mocker to be dead, or else it has fled from our mountains."

Droom directed his gaze to Hyrn. "I would be interested in seeing the Stone," he said. "I saw its twin many years ago. Bharain's trust meant much to us. We were charged to keep Ivah safe and not to use it except in times of dire need. We know that the Keeper Devarnia saw the Stone long ago. We were also given a mission to seek her with the Stone from time to time. We have been told that if we were ever unable to find her for any great span of time, we were to seek out the Keepers and report that she had failed. I do not know if she has been contacted recently."

"We spoke to Ivah," Rowan said. "Devarnia asked us to call Ivah through Ilah. There was a battle going on. They wanted help."

"There has been a war at the Eastern Gates for many years," explained Captain Droom. "We are assailed by Ultamarians, Artorans and Drargs. We have managed to keep our realm secure, but recently the fighting has become more intense. Most of our strength is now in the East. The Central regions are populated by the young and elderly, the sick and injured. We still have farmers, builders and artisans here, what strength we can spare. These days, even they need to take up arms."

"How do you farm down here?" asked Hyrn.

Droom laughed. "We will show you if you like. If you will come with us to the City of the Vortex we will provide lodgings for you. We will send word to King Darlam of you and your quest. You come at a very auspicious time in our calendar and it would gladden our hearts to share it with you."

"We would be honoured," said Aliana. "More of our warriors are charged to follow and rejoin us. They had returned to strengthen our eastern fortress against an attack by a large force of Drargs."

"We would welcome them," said Droom. "Any help in our war is sorely needed, and trained warriors would be a great boon to us. We will forsake riding so that we may speak further as we travel. Elder Aliana, it would be a great honour if you and your fellow Elder, and these two boys," he added, motioning to Rowan and Hyrn, "would walk with me."

The two strange steeds were taken by two of the Underdwellers. Rowan and Hyrn, with Aliana and Yarga, joined Droom and the other armoured soldier as they continued down the roadway towards the shimmering lake. Careil and Bregal took an immediate interest in the two beasts that the Underwellers had ridden.

"They are called charigas," said the soldier leading one of the beasts. "They come from the Isle of Wind originally. Great herds used to inhabit the slopes of the island. They are sure of foot and hardy. They are not as numerous as they once were. The war has taken a great toll on them, as it has on our people."

Droom spoke to Aliana of the war that raged to the east. They had steadfastly defended their realm for centuries. It was believed amongst the Underdwellers that the power of the Stone helped them to remain strong.

"Do you use Ivah as a weapon?" asked Rowan.

"No," answered Droom. "Ivah is kept hidden and covered at most times but his power is felt amongst our people. We have long waited for the time promised to us by Bharain when the Twin Stone would return to end the war and bring us peace. It is hard for me to believe that this time could be at hand. You say that Ilah contacted Ivah. Have you tried again to make a connection?"

"We were told only to use Ilah in times of need," said Hyrn. "Ilah has had to help us out a few times. She did battle with the evil in the Sagenstone."

Hyrn wasn't sure why he said this, but he felt safe with the Underdwellers.

"I would like to see Ilah," said Droom again. "If only to compare the Stones. I have only seen Ivah briefly but the sight lifted my heart and stays with me even now. We are the holders of the light against the dark, and it is in the Stone that I have seen the true embodiment of what that means. But

I do not ask frivolously and I do not ask you to treat a Stone of power as a mere bauble to be displayed and stared at."

"And what of Bharain's sword?" he then asked, addressing Rowan. "That must be a fine ancient blade. Do you know how to wield it?"

"I am learning still," said Rowan. He glanced back to where Arienga walked further down the procession. "I still need training."

"I trust that you have a skilled trainer," said Droom.

Rowan felt the bruises on his body.

"Yes, I do," he said stiffly.

The lake passed by on their left as they traversed the large cavern. The rock walls and ceiling glittered all around them and the light was almost as bright as that of the daylight. The roadway began to curve gradually around the lake as they continued on. Further ahead they could discern buildings clustered around the shoreline of the lake. They began to notice too, that a breeze blew towards them fresh and clear. This breeze grew to a steady wind as they approached the end of the lake, and beyond they could now see the outskirts of a city. The roadway passed between large buildings ahead of them. Before the buildings an arched entrance marked the beginning of the city. They could see guards standing there, and beyond the arch, they could see that there were people milling about as if they were waiting for them.

They approached the gateway and the guards stood to attention and raised their right hands outwards in a gesture for them to halt.

Droom walked to them and said in a clear voice, "I am Droom, Captain of the West, and Guardian of the Light in the Dark. I return to bring guests to the City and to send news of great importance to the King."

The guards dropped their hands and one said, "Enter Captain. Welcome awaits you and your guests."

They entered the city. Ahead of them people crowded the roadway. The crowd parted as they approached. Hyrn noticed that the people were mostly old or very young. They all had fascinated looks on their faces. They were silent, apart from the odd murmuring.

One small boy all of a sudden cried out, "Desultamar!"

Hyrn turned to him with surprise. This was the same word that Ilah had cried out back at the fortress. He felt Ilah stir against his chest. He gingerly pulled the Stone out and uncovered it.

Ilah burst into light and spoke clearly and loudly. "The time of our destiny is at hand. The Stones and the Sword seek the path to Anasaria. Desultamar!"

Hyrn held Ilah before him as they walked.

The people of the city cried out, "The Stone, the Stone!" and chanted,

"Des-ul-tamar Des-ul-tamar!"

Hyrn looked at Droom and said in wonder, "What does it mean? What is that word?"

Droom smiled broadly and the light of Ilah shone in his face as he replied, "It is a cry of hope and defiance in the face of evil. It is the battle-cry of those who fight the Ultamarians. It comes from the rebels who still remain in Anasaria, battling the evil of Ultamar. We have taken it up as well, as we defy them in protecting our realm. It means 'Destroy Ultamar!'"

The chant echoed through the city, and seemed magnified. They felt the wind in their faces as they continued towards the centre of the city and they could see that ahead the city was brightly lit as if a great lamp was suspended above it. More people came out from their houses to look in wonder as the procession walked on with Hyrn at the head, holding the still glowing Ilah in his hand.

They approached the centre of the city, and as they did, they could hear the sound of the wind. The buildings gave way to a great open space bathed in light. In the centre of this open space, stood a rotunda of stone pillars with a pedestal at its centre. Above the open space the roof of the cavern rose up steeply. As they crossed towards the centre of the plaza, they could see that a great cone rose high above them like a giant chimney, and at its heart, high above, they could see an immense opening that encircled an expanse of open sky. All around them the wind rushed and grabbed at their clothing.

"Behold!" called Droom. "The Great Circle of Sky and the entrance to the Isle of Wind."

The vast cone above them was festooned with ropes that hung from the heights down to the edges of the cavern on either side of the large central plaza. High above, platforms rose or descended, suspended on this vast web of ropes.

The group gathered around, looking up at the immensity of the gaping chasm above.

Yarga spoke almost timidly from beside Rowan. "Do you climb up there?" He breathed nervously as he peered upwards.

"Our people conquered the Isle of Wind almost a thousand years ago, when we first settled this realm," said Droom. "It is the source of much of our needs. We farm the slopes and fish the seas. We plant and reap forests."

"Isn't it dangerous?" asked Yarga.

"Yes it has its dangers," said Droom. "But the knowledge and skills required are passed down from generation to generation. None command the climb who have not been trained in the ways of their craft."

Just then, they noticed that a group of people were walking quickly across the plaza towards them. A middle aged man dressed in elaborate robes, led the way. The rest of the group followed closely behind. They also were robed, but more plainly.

The group arrived before them and the leader spoke breathlessly, but in a condescending voice.

"Droom, Droom," he sneered. "It is not for a soldier to show our guests around our city."

"Artisan Carlum," said Droom. "I—" he began.

"Mayor! Mayor!" demanded the man.

"My apologies, Mayor!" said Droom coolly. "As Captain of the West, I am responsible for who enters this realm."

"This is my city," blustered the Mayor. "It is my responsibility to host official engagements."

Aliana stepped out from where she stood behind Droom.

"Mayor Carlum," she said calmly, "Captain Droom has escorted us into your city and shown us great trust. I am Aliana, Elder of the Caramar. Droom has undertaken to alert the King of our quest. We are determined to aid in your fight, and to gain entry to Anasaria."

"I have just had word that you have entered the city," said the Mayor fawningly. "We are honoured to welcome you."

"Your spies travel quickly," muttered Droom under his breath.

"What is that, Droom?" enquired the Mayor. "My cousin, the King, will hear of any accusations against me."

Droom looked at the Mayor defiantly. "I would be happy to report my views directly to the King. It is he who appointed me Captain of the West. I would happily give up my post and go into battle rather than deal with the likes of you."

Droom turned to Aliana and the rest of the gathering. "I will send a full report to the King," he said. "Enjoy the hospitality of the city until word returns from the east. If I, or any of my troops, can be of any service, please let me know."

He bowed his head to them and with a signal he strode back towards the roadway. His soldiers fell in behind him, with the two charigas plodding along beside them.

The travellers stood before the Mayor and his welcoming party. They eyed each other for a moment before the Mayor spoke.

"Come, come," said the Mayor, in a cheerful but patronising tone. "You must be hungry. You must come and dine with us. I am dying to hear all about your quest. Come Elder Aliana, you will walk with me."

He moved forward and locked his arm with hers, and turning his back on the rest of them, he began walking back across the plaza. The rest of his group followed, leaving the others standing behind. Hyrn looked at Rowan and then at Careil behind him.

Careil looked bemused. "I think we're supposed to follow."

One of the Mayor's people came back towards them and beckoned to Rowan and Hyrn.

"The Mayor would like you also to walk with him," he said tonelessly. "It is a great privilege but the Mayor has heard about the Stone and the Sword."

Rowan and Hyrn both looked at Careil.

"Go, go. We are amongst friends here," said Careil.

"I think," he added, under his breath.

Rowan and Hyrn shouldered their packs and trailed behind the man as he hurried to catch up with Mayor Carlum and Aliana. The rest of them gathered their things and moved to follow. Above them clouds scudded across the disc of blue sky, lit by the sun as it moved towards the west.

The building they entered was more ornate and larger than others they had seen. They had crossed the plaza and entered the eastern part of the city. A promontory in the rock, stood above the surrounding buildings, overlooking their rooftops to the plaza beyond. Atop this promontory, stood the Mayor's official residence. They had climbed a grand stairway and entered. Aliana and the two boys had been rushed off ahead. The rest of them stood in a large foyer. The two horses, Erras and Marran, had been taken to a chariga stable nearby. The foyer was brightly lit with many lamps burning all around.

Bregal turned to Careil and Duburinga. "I don't like this," he said, gruffly. "We are supposed to be in a war. Not attending fancy dinners."

"There is not much we can do until we hear that the King consents to our passage through this land," said Careil. "We may as well be good guests until then."

Duburinga spoke. "A stop here will allow us to hear news from the Caramarhc. Harla, and the rest of the Caramar from the Eastern Watch assigned to this quest, should be able to rejoin us and report on the Drargs, and hopefully what has occurred in the mountains since last night."

"I still don't like it," said Bregal. "And I don't much like their Mayor."

Hyrn sat next to Rowan alongside the Mayor who had taken up his position at the head of a long table. The table stood in the middle of a lavishly decorated room. Aliana sat across from them on the other side of the Mayor. Two attendants stood at either side of the Mayor, just behind his large and intricately carved chair. The Mayor was speaking about his chair.

"All my design," he was saying. "Of course, I didn't carve it all myself but I made sure that my vision was followed exactly."

Hyrn and Rowan exchanged furtive glances. This all seemed so out of place amid the drama and danger that had followed them since they had left the farm, what seemed to them a lifetime ago.

Aliana had waited for the Mayor to pause, and spoke. "Mayor Carlum. We have come here on a preordained quest. Those of our party are bound to this quest. I trust that they will dine with us."

"Come, come," replied the Mayor. "They will be looked after and well fed. I'm sure that we don't need common soldiers to eat with us here in my dining room. This is reserved for special guests."

He looked at them as he said this, smiling obsequiously.

"It is our custom to treat all guests equally," continued Aliana.

"But soldiers are so boring," said Mayor Carlum. "They are all so very serious and prone to exaggeration and obsession. I am sure that the war is going well, and now that you are here, the war will no doubt soon be over."

"Your war is just a small part of the greater war that rages beyond your borders," said Aliana. "And what of my fellow Elder, Novice Yarga."

"A novice," said the Mayor, dismissively. "Why, I have many around here. Their time will come perhaps, but in the meantime, we must be the ones to show the way."

Hyrn felt uncomfortable as large plates of food were placed before them. He wondered what was happening to Careil and the others. He and Rowan ate politely as the Mayor continued to regale them with stories about his doings, and his connection with the King and other important figures. A sudden commotion broke this tirade. Two door attendants were bundled out the way as a tall, thin, severe looking man hurried into the room, closely followed by two Underdweller soldiers, along with Duburinga, Yarga, Careil, and Harla from the Eastern Watch.

"Your Excellency, Your Excellency!" exclaimed the thin man. "I have tried to tell these people that you must not be disturbed when you are entertaining, but these soldiers have ignored my protestations."

Harla and Duburinga continued down the opposite side of the table, flanked by the two Underdweller soldiers, and stood before Aliana.

"Elder," said Harla. She seemed tired but spoke clearly. "The Drargs attacked the fortress. They were aggressive and unrelenting but uncoordinated. We engaged with them. Many of their number were killed and we lost seven warriors. The Drargs ceased their attack and escaped to the southwest. We trailed them for a while but they struck southwards down the southern flank of the mountains towards the great marshes and Wesmere."

The Mayor sprang to his feet. "Show some respect!" he bellowed. "How dare you barge in here uninvited?"

His attention was suddenly diverted as, at that moment, the two attendants at the door were again pushed aside as the doors swung inwards. Captain Droom, his lieutenant and a contingent of soldiers burst into the room and marched up behind where Rowan and Hyrn sat.

Droom spoke in a loud and commanding voice.

"Mayor Carlum, I invoke my power as commander of the King's forces in the West," he stated. "Events demand that we stand ready. Our destiny is at hand. I place myself, and the people of this city, at the disposal of the Westerners and their quest. I await the word of the King, and I will stand before his judgement. Your petty grovellings have no place in this dire time. You show no respect for those who are not just guests, but a boon in our battle against the forces of evil."

The Mayor's face reddened with fury as he spat out, "How dare you! How dare you! The King will hear of this. You dare to come before me with this lack of respect. You, a common soldier. Men!"

He motioned to his two attendants, and cried, "Have this rabble shown to the door."

The two attendants behind the Mayor looked at him, and then looked into the resolute face of Droom, Captain of the West, Guardian of the Light in the Dark, as he stood surrounded by his stony-faced soldiers. They both stepped back, shaking their heads with a look of submission on their faces.

"Insubordination!" cried the Mayor. "Captain Droom, I order you to remove yourself and your soldiers from my palace!"

"It's 'Captain' now is it?" said Droom, calmly. He then announced sternly, "Mayor Carlum, I am assuming authority in this matter, on behalf of the King. I defer to the judgement of the holders of the Stone and the Sword and all those that accompany their quest. I will do all in my power to ensure that they are all treated with the respect they deserve. You are welcome to stay here in your 'palace'. I am sure that the people of this city would prefer you do just that. I invite our guests to accompany me to lodgings on the Grand Plaza. We have much of importance to discuss, and I would like to show them the wonders of our city and, if they wish, the Isle of Wind."

Rowan and Hyrn looked at each other and immediately started to get up. They paused as Aliana spoke.

"Mayor Carlum we must return to the other members of our quest," said the Elder in a measured tone. "While we appreciate your hospitality, I will defer to the decision of Captain Droom. This is a matter of great import and urgency, and I think that the Captain is in the best position to guide us here."

She stood up and bowed her head slightly to the Mayor. He sat there red-faced but silent. She motioned to Rowan and Hyrn, but they were already up and taking up their packs. Rowan took up the sword that hung from the back of his chair and draped it over his shoulder, twinging with the pain from one of his training injuries.

"I know about soldiers," he said looking at Mayor Carlum. "You don't want to mess with them."

Rowan stepped up and stood in front of Droom with Hyrn just behind him. Aliana and the others on her side of the table, began to walk towards the door. Droom signalled to his men who parted into two ranks, and then he and his lieutenant led Rowan and Hyrn toward the door, with the two rows of soldiers forming up behind them as they passed between their ranks.

As they neared the door, Mayor Carlum leapt to his feet and shouted angrily, "The King will hear of this. You mark my words. You will soon be at the front line facing Drargs. We will have a new Captain of the West. One who understands his proper place!"

Droom looked briefly back at Carlum, as he passed through the door and said forcefully, "I would rather face a thousand Drargs than listen to your endless prattling."

They were given rooms in a series of low houses that faced the great plaza. The open expanse stood bathed in the light from the great chasm in the ceiling above. The Underdwellers had erected tables and benches on the edge of the plaza, and they had eaten frugally but well. Some of the people had assembled around them, eager to speak with the visitors from the west. Rowan and Hyrn were particularly of interest. Word had spread about the Sword and the Stone and the children of destiny who carried them. An elderly man approached. Droom's lieutenant, who Rowan and Hyrn had learnt was named Gorum, introduced the man as Murralum, Master of the Ropes, and Gatekeeper of the Great Circle of Sky. Gorum explained that his position was one of great importance, and one much honoured by the Underdwellers for generations.

Murralum addressed the two boys and the rest of their party gathered nearby, "If you are able, while you are here, I would be proud to show you the ropes, and take you up to see the Isle of Wind."

Rowan and Hyrn were both eager to go as soon as possible, but deferred to Aliana when she said that it was important that they meet to discuss recent events, and to determine what action needed to be taken.

Rowan, Hyrn, Careil, Bregal, Duburinga, Boriega, Aliana, Yarga, Margana and Harla were seated with Droom and Gorum at a large, black stone table in a small hall on a street behind the houses that faced the plaza.

Harla gave a full report of the attack on the fortress of the Eastern Watch, and their journey back. Word had been sent to the Seat of the Elders of the attack, and the threat to Wesmere from an army of Drargs crossing their borders. They too, had felt the disturbance in the west, and the passing of evil from the mountains. All thirty Caramar warriors had returned with her.

Aliana thanked her for her report, and then briefly told Droom and Gorum of the details of Rowan and Hyrn's quest, and the support of the Caramar. Careil spoke of his and Bregal's position and events in Wesmere. It was then Droom's turn to explain the situation in the city and elsewhere in their land.

"Carlum was sent here by his cousin the King to take up the position of Mayor," began Droom. "The activities of the city that aren't associated with the defence of the realm, largely run themselves, without any help from the Mayor."

He said the word 'Mayor' with a clear tone of derision in his voice.

"I believe," he continued, "that he was causing problems for the King, and taking up time and resources that were needed for the war. The situation in the east has continued to drain our resources, and a parasite like Carlum is a burden that we can ill afford near our eastern defences. But he is of little concern here. As I have said, word has been sent to the King. We should hear back within two days. There is battle to be joined in the east and we would welcome your help and to see the Stones and the Sword of Anasaria reunited. In the meantime, I invite you to enjoy our hospitality and, for those of you who are willing to take up Master Murralum's invitation, to ride the ropes up to the heights to see the sun set over the centre of our realm high up on the Isle of Wind."

Rowan and Hyrn stood with Careil, Duburinga, Aliana and Arienga, watching the descent of a large wooden platform. This platform was suspended on thick ropes as it descended from the heights above. There was a soft creaking and then a thud as it came to rest on the ground at the northern edge of the plaza. Yarga had walked some of the way with them but had said that he had to attend to his journal. He had hastily retreated as their transport had made its way from high above their heads.

At the rail that enclosed the platform, stood Murralum smiling. Two young Underdwellers handled the winches at either end. Once down, Murralum opened a gate in the railing and welcomed them aboard. They stepped up onto the wooden deck, as Captain Droom approached and stepped up behind them. The wind gusted around them but the structure remained steady as it began to rise off the ground.

"You are about to see something that few from beyond our realm have ever seen," said Murralum.

The platform rose higher, suspended in open space. To either side of them they could see that other members of their party were being similarly taken up. As they continued upward, the curving roof grew nearer until they met it where the walls of the great chimney rose sheerly up towards the massive opening to the sky above. As the platform passed this wall they could see great iron rings where the ropes passed through guiding them steadily upwards. The circle of light below began to grow smaller, as the circle of sky above grew larger. All around were more structures, platforms, cages, and loads of various shapes, large and small, either stationary or moving up and down. Platforms coming down were laden with goods in barrels, crates or bags while those going up tended to be empty, apart from the people operating them. The cages and smaller loads travelled unaccompanied.

Hyrn held on to the railing. Although the wooden platform was sturdy and travelled smoothly and steadily, the wind rushed around them, and he could sense the expanse of space below them. It felt as if the wind was trying to pull him over the edge. He could see every now and then that there were alcoves and walkways in the rock wall. Most of these seemed to be empty, apart from one that he saw a little way around from them, where people appeared to be digging away at the rock and loading whatever they were digging into small carts.

"What are they digging for?" Hyrn asked Murralum.

"They are mining ore," answered Murralum. "The rock here contains many metals; iron, copper, even gold. It is not large quantities but it is useful to us especially for making tools and weapons. Long ago, these were found easily below, but now, this area, although more difficult to mine, is one of our richest sources of metal."

"Gold?" breathed Hyrn.

Murralum smiled. "Not much. It is used mainly for decoration and has one other use that will become clear to you soon enough."

Hyrn was baffled by this but didn't pursue it further. After rising a little higher he could see great blankets of green hanging above them. As they got closer he could see that they were massive tangles of vines that draped down the walls from above. They reached the vines and Hyrn could see that the iron rings held the platform ropes away from the vines and it was apparent that the vines were kept pruned to stop them impeding the platform's progress. They continued higher and higher until above them could be seen two large crane arms that protruded out. These cranes supported the ropes that were raising them up. They neared these winches, and as they did, a large stone alcove appeared with vines curtained on either side. The platform docked level with the lip of the alcove. The two Underdwellers who had been operating the machinery, secured the ropes and then moved over to open a gate in the railing alongside the dock. They pushed out a wooden panel that bridged the small gap between the wooden deck and the stone lip of the dock. They then signalled for them all to walk across and into the alcove.

After they had all crossed they could see that the space was quite large. To their right a stone stairway led upwards, shielded from the chasm below by the curtain of vines.

"Please follow me," said Murralum. "It is not far to the top, even for an old pair of legs like mine."

Murralum led the way and they walked up the stone stairway, their footsteps on the stone muffled by the vines alongside them. After they had gone a little way along, they came to another alcove where other Caramar were gathered waiting for them. They too followed Murralum as the stairway continued upwards.

"The others are on another dock further down," said Droom. "We will meet them at the top."

As Murralum had promised, the climb was not a long one. The stairway swung into the rockface away from the vines and continued through a short tunnel, where a patch of daylight could be seen ahead. They came out of the tunnel and into an immensity of sky and open air that was almost dizzying after their time below ground. Hyrn felt the wind buffeting him and the sunshine on his face.

They had come out onto a semicircle of paved ground surrounded by an arc of low stone wall. Below them, a broad expanse of lawn bathed in sunlight sloped down to a forested area, and beyond that a patchwork of fields continued down to the glittering sea. Further out the sea disappeared in a wall of fog.

"Welcome to the Isle of Wind," said Murralum in a strong voice. He stood there with his arms wide encompassing the vista before them, a look of pride and reverence on his face.

A path led away to their right and followed the curve of the crater, rising higher up the slope as they followed it around. They came to another paved area where the rest of the party waited and then continued on, travelling higher still. Eventually, they came to the highest point of the crater rim and they could see that a paved walkway, bordered on either side by a stone wall, ran around the top of the crater. To the east, a ridge led away from the crater and to a rocky point in the distance that formed the highest point of the island. The wind gusted all around them as they stood in the open, in the sunlight, with a broad expanse of blue sky above them. Ahead of them a large platform stood straddling the inner wall. A large circular disc was mounted atop this platform, covered in a dark canvas. Far across the crater, on the opposite side, stood another platform. This platform was taller than the one on their side but held a similar circular object. Some men were on the platform and were untying the canvas as they approached.

Murralum spoke. "You are just in time, Hyrn, to see another of our uses for gold."

The men undraped the large disc and revealed a great circle of shining gold. Hyrn looked in wonder at this spectacle.

"The disc is being cleaned ready for tomorrow," said Murralum.

"What happens tomorrow?" asked Hyrn.

"Ah," said Murralum. "You shall see. You shall see."

"Tomorrow is Midsummer's Day," said Aliana.

"Why, so it is," said Murralum mischieviously.

He continued, "Come now let's leave the gold-crafters to their work."

They walked further around until they stood on the southern side of the crater, halfway between the two platforms. There was a gap in the outer wall where a stone stairway led down between two short square pillars. They walked down the stairway, which widened as they descended, ending in a paved courtyard. Beyond the courtyard was a lawned area which surrounded a pavilion built from tall narrow stone columns. They crossed the courtyard and the lawn, and walked between the pillars. The pavilion was open on the southern side looking down at an expanse of lawn surrounded by trees. The lawn was golden in the afternoon sun. The trees to the west threw long shadows, while the trees on the eastern edge stood bathed in the golden light. Within the pavilion, tables and chairs were laid out, and atop the tables was arrayed a magnificent feast.

"This is the Garden of the Southern Wind," said Droom. "We have laid out a banquet in your honour. Please, people of the West. Join us, and enjoy the hospitality of the heart of our realm."

Rowan and Hyrn sat on the lawn with full stomachs and looked out across the gardens. It felt good to be in the open air with grass beneath them. The others either remained seated at the table, deep in conversation, or spread out around the garden enjoying the air and sunshine. The breeze had picked up from the south but it was still warm and carried the smell of the grass and trees and the slight scent of the sea far below. The danger and worry of their quest seemed far away.

"I wonder whether Ma and Pa know what is going on yet?" asked Hyrn.

"The Caramar probably should have got there by now," replied Rowan. "I just hope that the King hasn't sent soldiers to arrest them after we ran away from Ballarghen."

"I keep getting the feeling that something is wrong, ever since what happened last night," said Hyrn.

"The Caramar will sort things out. I'm sure that even the King's Guard won't have a chance against Caramar warriors," said Rowan.

"It's not the King I'm worried about," said Hyrn. "There's something else, something worse, some kind of danger."

"You worry too much," said Rowan. "They're probably more worried about us."

Rowan looked away distractedly. Hyrn looked to where Rowan's gaze had been drawn, and saw Arienga down towards the trees at the edge of the lawns.

"You can go and talk to her," said Hyrn. "I'm just going to lie in the sun for a while."

Rowan got to his feet and walked down the gentle slope towards Arienga. Hyrn lay back and closed his eyes. The sun was warm on his face and the wind felt soothing as it ruffled his hair. He thought he may have dozed off and was dreaming. He heard a voice in his head.

"They are strong, child. They have their part to play in this, as do you. Worry not. They are in good hands but their strength is needed. Things are moving in the world and none can sit and let them go past. We all must strive to prevail over evil."

Hyrn sat up with a start. He felt his clothing. Ilah was tucked safely away and he hadn't felt her stir. He must have been dreaming…but those words were strangely comforting.

Just then Careil walked up from behind him. He stopped beside Hyrn and looked down at him.

"Come on Hyrn," said Careil. "We need to get back down to the City before dark. Where's Rowan?"

"He's down there with Arienga," said Hyrn, pointing as he got to his feet.

Careil looked down the lawn to where Hyrn pointed. Rowan and Arienga were walking back towards them, Rowan listening as Arienga spoke. Arienga seemed to be demonstrating something to Rowan. She held her arm out and then brought it down and across. Rowan copied her and Arienga nodded.

Careil studied them with a thoughtful look on his face.

"She might make a fighter out of him yet," he said, then added. "If we have time."

He turned and headed back towards the others. Hyrn looked at Rowan and Arienga briefly and then followed Careil.

The trip back down on the suspended platform was much quicker than the one going up. The circle of sky above was reddening towards sunset by the time they came to rest on the floor of the great cavern. They went to bed early that night. They were all exhausted. Rowan and Arienga had gone off to train, but this time Duburinga had gone with them to see if progress was being made. By the time Rowan returned, Hyrn was in bed and almost asleep. When Rowan came into the room, Hyrn told him dozingly about the dream he'd had up on the Isle of Wind.

"It could have just been a dream," said Rowan, "but I think you should take notice. They'll be alright. Now we should get some sleep. We have to be up early in the morning."

"Why?" asked Hyrn.

"I don't know," replied Rowan. "The Underdwellers have something planned. Something to do with Midsummer's Day."

"I wonder what…?" began Hyrn but he didn't finish his question before he had fallen asleep.

Rowan looked at Hyrn sleeping. He was beginning to realise the danger they were heading towards but he wasn't sure that Hyrn understood yet. Still, given that a young warrior like Arienga showed such power and skill, being surrounded by Caramar warriors gave him great comfort.

He smiled at the thought of Arienga as he got ready for bed, but winced with pain as he removed his clothes. She was certainly different from any girl he had ever met. Pretty, he thought, but dangerous. With that he got into bed and extinguished the lamp that stood on the nightstand between him and Hyrn.

CHAPTER TEN

The Power of the Light in the Dark

It was still dark the next morning when they were awoken by a knocking on their door. They dressed by lamplight and stepped out into the corridor outside their room. Others were also up and heading towards the front door. They walked out onto the stone paving of the central plaza. Although it was still dark, they could see that many people were gathering in the centre of the plaza, around the structure that stood there. Hyrn had given little thought to this circle of pillars when they had walked through the plaza the previous day. Droom came up to meet them and escorted them through the crowd until they stood at the front directly facing the rotunda. The sky above was beginning to lighten with the promise of dawn.

Hyrn noticed that there were many people at the front of the crowd holding swords and shields. He looked between the pillars and saw that steps went up to a pedestal on top of which was a large pointed object. He couldn't quite make out what it was but it almost seemed to flicker with light. Droom motioned to Rowan to step forward and Hyrn saw that Rowan carried the Sword of Acclimoss. He hadn't noticed Rowan get it from where it had hung on a hook beside his bed. Rowan stood beside Droom and drew the Sword. The sky above began to lighten more and the murmuring of talk amongst the gathered crowd died down.

Droom spoke in a loud clear voice. "Stand ready soldiers and swordsmiths."

All around swords were drawn by Underdwellers and Caramar alike. They all raised their swords and shields and Rowan held his sword aloft, its tip pointing up towards the lightening sky above. There was absolute silence, almost as if everyone was holding their breath. Hyrn realised that there was no wind, as if the great chasm above was also holding its breath. Everyone gazed upwards and Hyrn looked up too. At that moment he saw a beam of light pierce the darkness, bouncing from the western to the eastern rim of the crater, and then down the western face of the great chimney.

Instantly the beam of light hit something large and circular, which burst into life as the beam reflected off and lit the object in the centre of the circle of pillars before them. Dazzling yellow light burst out from what Hyrn could now see was a giant crystal. At that moment all the Caramar began their chant to greet the morning sun. The circle of swords and shields and the faces of those gathered were bathed in the shimmering light. The metal of their weapons flashed. The facets of the crystal bounced light all around the cavern illuminating the plaza and the buildings of the city. Amongst the chanting of the Caramar, Hyrn could hear the Underdwellers reciting something in low voices. Hyrn stood mesmerised, with his hand outstretched, and he realised that he held Ilah, although he didn't remember taking the Stone out. Ilah instead of her usual glow seemed to almost reflect the light from the crystal. The voices of the Caramar and the Underdwellers rose to a crescendo, and then the light from the crystal began to wane as the beam of light moved on and then abruptly ceased.

Hyrn felt energised. He felt as if his body had been filled with fire. The people around him were all looking at each other with a look of wonder on their faces. Beside Hyrn, Rowan lowered the Sword of Acclimoss. Captain Droom lowered his sword and looked around at those Caramar and Wesmerians standing nearby. He turned to Aliana.

"The Sun Crystal, with the Lake of Light, is at the heart of our belief in the Light in the Dark," he said. "It absorbs sunlight and reflects its power, increased by the power within. There are times in the year when the sun shines directly upon the crystal. But the crystal gives its most power when the rising sun of midsummer shines upon it.

It was discovered in a cave facing towards where the sun rises. It was found to magnify the power of the sun, but its power was dispersed if it was in sunlight all the time. It was brought down here into the Underrealm and only bathed in sun at those times of the year when the sun shone from above. It took many years to realise that it grew weaker year by year. We sought out the cave where it was found and it was discovered that the sun only shone directly into the cave at sunrise on Midsummer's Day. We built the Sundiscs to bring the midsummer sunrise into our realm. It is the time of the year when our strength is renewed. We have found that our weapons when bathed in this light are powerful against the power of evil that besieges us. Our newly forged weapons are brought here and imbued with the light of the Crystal and then shipped to the front."

"How did the Caramar all know to draw their weapons?" asked Hyrn.

"I spoke to Aliana last night," replied Droom. "She explained that the

Caramar welcome the rising sun. So I invited her to ask the Caramar to unite our rituals together."

Hyrn turned to Rowan. "But how did you know?"

"I didn't," said Rowan. "Duburinga just advised me last night to bring my sword when we got up in the morning."

"It is a day of celebration," said Droom. "Feel free to take part. There will be much rejoicing and merrymaking all day. While we await a message from the King, you should all take the opportunity to revel in our most joyful day. The city is much emptier than it was in the past and many of the people are defending our eastern border, but we keep the tradition alive while we are here."

"We are honoured," said Aliana.

The crowd had begun to break up. People were talking happily and moving off to prepare for the day. Harla moved off to talk to the Caramar of the Eastern Watch. Across the dispersing circle of people, Hyrn saw a group of richly dressed Underdwellers who had previously been hidden behind the rotunda. Mayor Carlum and his attendants had been present at the ceremony and were now quickly heading off, back to the eastern half of the city. No doubt straight back to the Mayor's palace, thought Hyrn. Just to his right, he noticed Arienga. She stood before Duburinga, holding herself in a stiff upright posture.

She addressed Duburinga in a formal tone, "Duburinga I ask to be allowed a break from my duties."

It was the first time Hyrn thought he had seen Duburinga smile.

"Warrior, you have earned a break," said the older warrior. "Go. Enjoy your free time." He suddenly looked a little grimmer. "War will be before us soon enough."

Arienga nodded solemnly and then losing her stiff composure, but trying to contain her excitement, said, "Thank you, Duburinga. I won't forget my protocols."

She bowed slightly, then turned quickly towards Rowan and Hyrn.

Droom broke in. "Throughout the city, bakers and cooks will just be beginning to prepare breakfast and food for the day's festivities. You will all be welcome wherever you go."

Hyrn realised he was still holding Ilah. The Stone still felt warm. He replaced Ilah in her place under his vest. As he did, Arienga approached him and looped her arm through his. She then grabbed Rowan's arm. Rowan hoisted the now sheathed sword over his shoulder and they walked off, Arienga with one of the brothers on each arm, to enjoy Midsummer's Day.

Later that day they sat on stone benches on the western side of the city. They looked out over the shimmering lake. Many of the city's people were also gathered on the shore of the lake. The young and the braver of the older citizens were taking an afternoon swim in the waters. It had been explained by a family of Underwdwellers, an elderly couple with their three grandchildren, that the water of the lake, especially on Midsummer's Day, gave strength to those that swam in it.

They had travelled through the lamplit streets of the city finding food to eat. During the morning, pavilions and stalls had been erected in the central plaza to bathe in the light from the Great Circle of Sky. Food stalls, performers, mainly children with occasionally older people, performing more traditional songs and dances, and everywhere happiness and celebration. Arienga had led Rowan and Hyrn on a frenzied chase throught the city, delighting in everything. Hyrn was amazed by her enthusiasm but supposed that she didn't often get much of a chance to escape her duties. They had finally come to rest here on the shore of the lake.

"It looks nice in the water," said Hyrn, suddenly.

He didn't know why he said it. He was watching a group of young Underdwellers splashing around in the shallows.

"You should go for a swim," said Arienga.

"Yeah. Go on," urged Rowan.

"No," said Hyrn. "I was just thinking how cool and refereshing it looks."

In his head Hyrn felt a push. An image of him in the water holding Ilah sprang into his mind.

"Take me to the water."

The voice was clear in his head. He felt a tremor from the Stone beneath his vest. It was Ilah. That voice. It was Ilah speaking to him inside his head. He reached down and took off his boots. He stood up and took off his jacket and laid it on the bench. He took Ilah out from inside his vest, still wrapped in the cloth, and laid her on top of his jacket. He removed his vest and undershirt. He unwrapped Ilah and took her in his hands and walked bare-chested down towards the water. Arienga and Rowan watched him with puzzlement on their faces. Hyrn did not speak. He moved almost in a trance down to where the water lapped against the shore.

The water was warm. It was shallow near the edge but the bottom sloped gently downwards as he moved away from the shore. The water was up to his waist. He could feel the warmth of the water making his skin tingle. It slowly began to feel as if the warmth was seeping into his bones. He went a little deeper still holding Ilah above the water.

"Immerse me in the water," came the voice in his head.

He held Ilah in front of him as he faced out into the lake. The surface of the lake shimmered with soft pink light. He then lowered his hands immersing Ilah in the warm water. At first the Stone lay dark just beneath the surface of the clear water. Then a pink glow like that of the rock above the lake began to grow in the heart of the Stone. He heard murmuring, and glancing around, realised that the people gathered in the water and around the shore were watching him. He turned back to look down at Ilah and saw that the Stone was glowing brightly now. It was almost as if the light reflecting on the surface of the lake was being drawn into the Stone and then radiated outwards. Hyrn felt Ilah becoming warmer and as he watched she grew brighter and brighter until the water all around glowed with the light. Then mixing with the pink light he could see the colour of Ilah's own brightness. The two colours swirled together until they became a dazzling brightness that Hyrn found difficult to look at directly.

"Lift me out," said Ilah in his head.

Hyrn lifted Ilah out of the water and bright light erupted all around him. He held Ilah above his head to shield his eyes from the light and the brightness shone out across the lake and back towards the city making it as bright as daylight.

People called out, "The Stone. The Stone."

And one voice cried, "The light in the dark. The power of the Stone is with us. Ilah, the Stone of Angil is amongst us. The time of our delivery is at hand."

Hyrn had turned around and was heading back towards the shore holding the Stone aloft. The people gathered around as he emerged from the water, a look of wonder on their faces.

Someone said, "Look at the water!"

Hyrn turned and could see that the water seemed to glow brighter than before. It still had the same pink hue but tempered by the purer white light of Ilah.

Ilah spoke. "The power of the Lake of Light is very great. The earth all around sings with the spirit of good. Be blessed all those who keep the light in the dark."

Ilah glowed brightly for a few moments more and then dimmed and went dark. The people all around were reaching out and touching Hyrn and clasping his arms with smiles on their faces.

An elderly woman grasped Hyrn's wrist gently and said, "Thank you, Child of Light. You bring hope and joy to our hearts."

The people parted and began to walk back to their groups talking happily. Hyrn made his way over to where Rowan and Arienga waited. They both sat with their mouths open staring at Hyrn with bewilderment on their faces. Finally, Rowan spoke.

"What happened?" he asked.

"I'm not sure," said Hyrn. "Ilah seemed to be drawing power from the lake but then it was like she then gave some of her own power back."

"You must speak to Aliana and Yarga," said Arienga. "They may know what this means."

Hyrn wrapped Ilah and then began to get dressed. His trousers, which had been wet when he emerged from the lake, now seemed quite dry. He shook his head. Strange things were going on. He felt that he didn't really understand the power of the Stone he carried. He knew Ilah was powerful, but what was her purpose? What was she capable of? And what would happen when the Twin Stones were reunited after six hundred years? He supposed they would find out soon enough. But she had spoken to him in his mind.

That night they ate again at tables outside their accommodation, but this time they were surrounded by the sound and colour of Midsummer celebrations. Hyrn was seated next to Yarga. The novice Elder had a large book in front of him and was writing in it. When Hyrn asked him what he was writing, he explained that he was keeping a journal so that it could be added to the store of knowledge kept at the Seat of the Elders. He asked Hyrn for a description of the Isle of Wind so that he could add this to what Aliana had told him.

"Why did you not come with us to see for yourself?" asked Hyrn.

Yarga looked embarrassed and replied meekly, "I couldn't go up in that thing, up into the air."

"Why not?" asked Hyrn.

"Well," said Yarga, "I am afraid of heights."

Hyrn suppressed a laugh, and then said seriously, "But you are a Caramar. You live in the mountains. You're up high all the time."

"Yes," said Yarga. "But with stone under my feet and away from anywhere where I could fall. I have never left the city before. When I was a child, other children wanted to become warriors. Even though they tested themselves with the Sagenstone many of them hoped that they would be rejected and could train to be warriors. All I ever wanted was to be an Elder. I studied whenever I could and offered my services at the Great Hall. When I was chosen it was the happiest day of my life. I felt safe then until… Well, until Aliana and the other Elders insisted that I accompany your quest. They felt that it would be important to me and I could aid Aliana and keep a record of the quest. Going up with you yesterday was too much though. I couldn't do it."

"It's alright," said Hyrn. "We are all afraid of something."

"What are you—?" began Yarga.

But just at that moment, there was a clamour to their left, where the roadway that led to the east entered the plaza. A pair of soldiers mounted on charigas rode into the plaza and headed towards them. They halted and swiftly dismounted. They marched past the table where Hyrn and Yarga sat, and over to the next table where Captain Droom sat next to Aliana and Careil. Droom saw them approach and rose to his feet. The two soldiers stopped before him and raised their arms in salute.

"Captain Droom," said one of the soldiers. "We were told by the guards at the Eastern Gate that you would be here. We bring word from the King."

A small group had assembled in the same small hall they had met in the day before. Rowan and Hyrn, along with Duburinga, Careil, Aliana and Harla, represented the quest.. Droom, with Gorum on his left, sat at the head of the table. The soldier who had addressed him in the plaza sat to his right.

"Speak freely," said Droom. "What news from the King?"

The soldier spoke. "The King asks that the members of the quest continue eastwards and says that they are welcome in this realm. He asks that they come before him and tell their tale in full. He welcomes the Stone of Angil and the Sword of Acclimoss. He also asks that you accompany them, Captain."

Captain Droom nodded in acceptance and the soldier drew in a deep breath and continued, "There is also much to report about the situation at the front. In the last two days there has been a concerted attack on our eastern defences. It is said that a large force of Artorans have joined the Ultamarian and Drarg forces. Our defences were holding but the situation is dire. The King asks that you make haste and that any forces that can be spared from the Western troop be dispatched to the front with great urgency."

Preparations were made to leave immediately. It was felt that any delay could risk dire consequences. Rowan and Hyrn heard that they would march until midnight, rest and then rise early. Arienga had joined them outside their lodging, where all around Caramar and Wesmerians prepared for the next part of their quest.

Rowan complained, "We've been up since before dawn. How are we going to be able to walk for that long?"

Arienga looked at him sternly. "We focus on the importance of the trust placed in us. We have a duty and we carry it out."

Rowan looked slightly wounded. "I'm only saying I'm tired."

"You need to rest when you are able, and continue on when you must," said Arienga, and then looked directly at Rowan questioningly.

"Yes. I understand and I will try," he said formally.

Arienga smiled at this. "Good," she said. "It will give me a chance to teach you more techniques and tactics."

"Great," said Rowan, sarcastically but with a slight smile on his face.

Hyrn spoke. "Come on you two. We're moving off."

All around people were shouldering their packs and weapons. Careil and Bregal approached from further around the plaza, leading Erras and Marran. Arienga turned around and walked up to the Riders as they neared. She patted the two horses' necks in turn as they stopped either side of her.

"Would you like to ride?" asked Bregal. "I haven't seen you ride."

"I have had some riding training," replied Arienga. "But horses are rare around Ordbran and Caramar warriors generally prefer to travel on foot. This allows us quick access to all terrains in the mountains."

"Well, you are welcome to," said Bregal.

"I would prefer to stay on my feet," said Arienga. "I am happy to lead her when you are not riding."

"You may lead her now," said Bregal. "There is little need to ride when most of our force will be on foot. If we are needed for scouting duties then we can ride. I think though that the Underdwellers have that under control."

At the head of their march rode Droom and Gorum riding charigas. Several soldiers riding charigas surrounded them. Men of the Western troop were forming up throughout the train of people. Hyrn looked back as they began to move off, following directly behind a group of Underdweller soldiers. Hyrn thought to himself that they didn't look much older than him. Although, Arienga was only three years older than him, and she was scary. He looked back and saw that the end of the train of people stretched back quite a way along the edge of the plaza. In all, almost three hundred, mostly soldiers, moved eastwards, closer towards their goal, Anasaria.

The cavern had closed in around them as they marched. They moved beyond the city and passed scattered buildings that grew fewer and then disappeared. The buildings had been mostly deserted, as their inhabitants were still in the city for the festival, or were long gone away to the war in the east. They camped for the night in a broad area to the right of the road that featured intricate carving in its rock walls. Hyrn was exhausted. They had paused earlier for a brief rest and some quick nourishment, and had then quickly continued on.

Hyrn settled down in his blanket and laid his head on his pack. All around him others too settled down to sleep. A fire burned nearby, illuminating the carvings and throwing them into relief, flickering as the shadows danced around. Against the wall, Hyrn could see the silhouettes of Arienga and Rowan fencing, their shadows merging and moving with the carven images. Hyrn watched them, and before he knew, was fast asleep.

"IVAH! IVAH!"

Hyrn struggled out of his blanket and leapt to his feet. His chest was burning and bright light burst out from under his clothing.

"IVAH! IVAH!" Ilah cried.

Hyrn pulled the Stone from his vest. Hot white light poured out, swirling and flashing.

"Evil hands are on my Brother! The darkness! It burns all around him. They are…. He is gone. Hidden from my sight."

All around people roused from their sleep looking with bewilderment towards Hyrn as the Stone of Angil coruscated in his clasping hands. Aliana was on her feet and rushed to stand beside Hyrn.

"What has happened, See-er?" she asked.

"Oath-takers and corrupted ones have seized my brother!" cried the Stone in answer. "They have locked him in darkness. I heard his cries and saw him while the light remained. You must help him."

Ilah let out a piercing cry, the light flashing from within and then dissapating as the cry faded, and the Stone went dark. Droom had quickly approached. Gorum was at his shoulder and Droom turned to him and spoke stiffly.

"Gorum, ride to the Eastern Gate with all speed. Take what riders you need. Send word that we are hurrying on our way with what force we have. Send riders back with a report of the situation at the front as soon as possible. I will travel on foot with the rest. Take my mount."

Gorum raised his arm in salute and said, "Captain, we will bring word within the day if we can."

He turned on his heel and called to men now standing, or crouching packing up their bedding and gear.

Droom spoke in a loud voice so that all could hear. "It is still two hours before dawn. You have all had little sleep but we must push forward. It will take a day and a night to reach the Eastern Gate. I fear evil has entered our realm in force for the first time. We must march."

Nearby Bregal was saddling Marron. He finished preparing his mount and then hoisted himself onto her back.

"I will ride with Gorum," he said. "If the Captain permits," he added.

"You are welcome, Rider," answered Droom.

"We shall test ourselves against the riders of the Underrealm," he said boldly. "Won't we Marron," he addded patting the great mare's neck.

The horse snorted and stamped her hoof in answer. The Rider raised his hand in farewell and then turned the horse and trotted off to where Gorum was marshalling the riders. Droom's chariga had been assigned to one of the soldiers. Bregal joined the group and spoke briefly to Gorum. The soldier clasped his arm with a gauntleted hand and then turned and lifted his hand and motioned forward. The mounted group broke into a canter and then into a gallop and disappeared quickly into the darkness.

They trudged along unerringly. Rowan looked just ahead to where Hyrn strode beside Droom. Hyrn had said little as they started out and now walked, his gaze fixed ahead, keeping up with the tall captain as he led the marchers through the stone tunnel. The light of torches burnt throughout the procession. Rowan felt that something had changed with Hyrn. He seemed almost in a trance. He looked like something was pushing at his back driving him on. Rowan jogged up to where Hyrn was walking and tried to speak to him.

"Hyrn," he said. "You're acting weird. What's going on?"

"Hyrn looked at him, puzzled, and said, "The Oathbreakers. Evil has come."

"What does that mean?" asked Rowan.

Droom replied. "The Oathbreakers are the Artorans. Artora is a small land to the south-east of Anasaria. It is walled by steep mountains that enclose its northern borders and surrounded by sea. Long ago the Artorans were defeated in battle by Eriallen of Anasaria. He brought their army to the brink of defeat at the entrance to Artora. He carried the sword that you now have at your shoulder and he wore Ilah and Ivah on his brow. The Artorans surrendered and swore an oath that they would remain at peace with Anasaria while the Twin Stones remained at Abessair. That oath was honoured until Bharain was sent into exile and the once fair Abessair became Ultamar. The Artorans then entered Anasaria and swore allegiance to the Dark Lords, but they have their own interests. Their ancient grudge against Anasaria has led them to take any chance to inflict pain on the forces of good. They have at their heart a priesthood of dark Sorcerers who delight in inflicting pain on the bodies and minds of any that don't bow before them."

"They are in league with the corrupted ones," said Hyrn angrily, beside him.

Rowan looked at Hyrn bewildered, and then to Droom.

"The corrupted ones are the Ultamarians. The army of Abessair, possessed by evil and serving the will of the Dark Lords," said Droom.

But Rowan's attention was fixed on Hyrn.

"Hyrn. Hyrn!" he almost shouted, grabbing his arm.

"What? What?" said Hyrn, with a dazed expression on his face.

He shook his head and looked at Rowan.

"Rowan," he pleaded. "We have to get to Ivah. They have taken him. Ilah is crying out for him."

"We will!" said Rowan determinedly. "We said we would unite the Stones, and we will!"

Outside, the sun shone from directly above. Deep within the dark stone tunnels of the Underrealm they stopped and rested briefly. They ate and drank quickly and with purpose. They were soon on their feet again and moving. Droom led them again, and, untiring beside him, strode Hyrn with the same haunted, fixed expression on his face.

As the afternoon wore on towards evening the clatter of hooves came to them rolling down the walls of the cavern. Ahead of them, two riders appeared out of the gloom into the light of their torches. Gorum, soldier of the Light in the Dark and Bregal, King's Rider of Wesmere pulled their mounts up before them. Gorum leapt down and saluted Droom.

"Captain, there has been an attack on the Underrealm," he said. The Stone, Ivah, has been taken and the attackers have escaped. There is great evil at work. There was a massive push by the forces that attacked the gate, and while this was drawing our forces, a band of Artoran Sorcerers aided by Ultamarian soldiers entered the Underrealm. They wielded a Stone of great darkness and evil. None could stand before it. The Stone they carried seemed to draw them to where Ivah was hidden. Those who stood guard over the Stone were slain and the protections around the Stone were defeated. They quickly escaped and the attackers at the gate have withdrawn their forces to the head of the valley. The attack was obviously designed for one purpose; to capture the Stone, Ivah."

Beside Droom, Hyrn cried out, "Where have they taken Ivah?"

Gorum looked at Hyrn and then to Droom. Droom nodded, encouraging him to answer.

"They withdrew through the ranks of the attackers," answered Gorum. "Rangers have been sent out to try to discover where they have gone but none had returned by the time we left."

Hyrn shook his head. "We must hurry," he said, plaintively.

Droom addressed Gorum. "Rest your mounts and bring up the rear. We will continue marching until evening. We will rest for a few hours and then continue on. What is the King's strategy?"

"The King only says that he awaits the counsel of the Westerners before we act decisively," replied Gorum. "He anticipates the arrival of the wielders of the Stone and the Sword."

The marchers were exhausted. They had been roused after what seemed to Rowan, a very brief sleep, and continued onwards. The cavern remained roughly straight and uniform as they marched on. Buildings began to appear at the road's edge, some lit by torchlight but others dark and silent. They were either long empty or people were still asleep, thought Rowan.

Before they had slept, Arienga had asked Rowan to bring the Sword to a brief training session. The dire events engulfing them seemed to draw it naturally to his hands. The training that Arienga had given him seemed to make more sense when he held the ancient blade.

Rowan sensed the Sword's power at his shoulder as he trudged on, the shape of Hyrn's back drawing him forward, while the proud Caramar warrior, Arienga, marched beside him. Rowan felt her presence and it gave him strength, and he felt within him a drive to prove that he was worthy of the belief that she showed in him.

A few hours later a group of mounted soldiers met them and took up the vanguard, leading them ever on, as the outskirts of the city grew around them. Although it was hours before dawn, people began to be seen milling along the roadway. There were many worried and frightened faces amongst them. Before long they began to see troops of soldiers patrolling the city's streets. The buildings began to get larger and closer together. The road that they had travelled had now become a major thoroughfare. As dawn approached the sounds of the city grew louder. There was a sense of anticipation and fervour in the air. As they continued along the roadway the city's streets began to steepen slightly and they were slowly drawn upwards and, as they were, the light began to grow around them.

A stern soldier marched towards them followed by a phalanx of soldiers. The escort of soldiers in their van parted, and the incoming soldiers approached and came to a halt in front of Droom.

"Captain Droom," said the stern looking soldier.

"Captain Arum," answered Droom.

"Welcome back, Droom," said the soldier, a weary smile on his face. "We need you old friend, and those you bring are a miracle in dark times. I knew there was a reason that the King sent you to the west."

"How goes the war?" asked Droom.

Arum looked grim. "We have been under fierce attack from Drargs and Ultamarians for a few days. Then two days ago Artoran soldiers accompanied by Sorcerers joined the fight. There was an onslaught upon our defences. That was when a band of Artoran Sorcerers broke through wielding a dark Stone that burned any that stood in the way. Things looked grave as the battle intensified but as the Sorcerers fled with the Stone the attackers all withdrew up the valley. We believe they were covering the retreat of those who took the Stone. The King seeks your counsel and an audience with the Westerners."

Droom looked to Rowan, Hyrn, Aliana and Careil. They all nodded their assent except Hyrn who was staring fixedly to the east.

"We must hurry," said Hyrn desperately.

"Lead us to the King," said Droom.

As they came closer to the eastern portion of the city the light became brighter and as they drew near to the outer defences bright orange light burst through a large opening that spanned the width of the cavern in a great mouth. The teeth of the mouth were great stone battlements and a defensive wall with a large gateway in the centre, barred and heavily guarded.

As they marched, the Caramar present broke into the familiar chant and the Underdwellers began their litany as the rising sun pierced the darkness of the Underrealm.

At either side of the large gateway, stood twin guard towers. Arum led the party to a doorway at the base of the right-hand tower. As they got closer they could see that the gates were scarred and pitted at their edges. Large scorch marks were evident on the gates and the flagstones leading up to them.

"These gates were breached for the first time, just two nights ago," said Arum, gravely. "It is the only time that the forces of evil have entered the Underrealm."

He turned to Droom. "If you could bring the representatives of the Westerners," he said. "We will go up and see the King. There is lodging and food for you all. Barracks have been prepared for Caramar and Underdwellers, if indeed there is time for rest. We also have stables available for the horses and charigas. From among the ranks Gorum and Bregal approached leading their mounts."

"And these two will need extra," continued Arum. "You must have ridden like the wind."

Beside Rowan, Erras shook his mane and snorted indignantly.

Arum smiled up at the great horse. "There is plenty for you too."

Aliana, Yarga, Duburinga, Careil, Rowan and Hyrn followed Arum through the heavy door and into a small torchlit courtyard. A spiral staircase wound up the wall and passed through a wooden platform that formed the ceiling above. They ascended this stairs and passed though the opening and into a large circular room peopled by a dozen soldiers who stood looking out through arrow slits in the wall. One turned and saluted. Arum then signalled for them to follow him as he led them across to where the stairway continued higher up into the tower. They came up through another opening and out into a room similar to the one below. Armed men stood around the edges of the room. In the centre of the room was a large table. A tall man clad in armour stood bent over peering at a large map. Beside him a short, slightly paunchy, balding man was gesticulating at the map and speaking sternly. As the party entered the two men turned and faced them.

As they approached the two men, Hyrn rushed forward and spoke desperately to the tall man. "Your Majesty, we must rescue Ivah. Ilah is crying out in pain."

The man turned to the shorter man, who looked up at him and then at Hyrn.

"I don't think Captain Cram would relish the kingship in these times," said the shorter man. "That is my unfortunate responsibility. Of course, the Captain is free to challenge for the right to be King."

"Captain?" he asked, looking to the taller man.

The tall soldier shook his head with a wry smile on his face.

"I thought not," said the King. "No-one has challenged in over a hundred years. My family have borne the burden of protecting the realm for all those years. My father passed the duty on to me. I am Darlam, King of the Underdwellers."

"I am sorry, Your Majesty," said Hyrn red-faced.

King Darlam smiled. "It is quite all right," he said. "I know I don't look the regal type, but I do my best."

He turned to the rest of the party and said sternly. "These are dark times. This is a council of war. I invite you to tell what you must and to speak your minds freely."

Aliana stepped forward. "King Darlam forgive my bluntness," she said. "The Stone, Ivah, must be recovered at all costs. It can not be allowed to fall into the hands of the Dark Lords."

"Ah," said the King. "It is just what we have been discussing. Our spies in the hills say that the Artorans passed amidst the retreating attackers and were lost to sight near the head of the valley. The attacking army now forms a wedge blocking the way out of the valley and up to the pass through into Anasaria. The only way that we can see to get through without a long trek around is a direct assault on the forces of evil that besiege us. We believe that if we can forge a path, a small raiding party could break through and pursue the Artorans and Ultamarians who have the Stone."

"We have to go with them," said Rowan.

The King turned and looked at him. "The quest must be allowed to continue," he said. "But only a small group must go. Anasaria is hostile territory. We have no hope of challenging the Ultamarian army. The key will be stealth rather than force of arms. I suggest that the Wesmerians and a few Caramar go and I will send some of my most skilled warriors."

They spent the next hour discussing tactics while Aliana and Careil filled the King in on details of the quest. Word had been sent to the rest of the Caramar and the commanders of the Underdweller army to prepare for battle. The King had told them that he would lead the assault with his Captains.

Droom and Gorum were assigned to accompany the party that would try to get through. Rowan, Hyrn, Careil, Bregal, Aliana, Yarga, Duburinga, Harla, Boriega, Gebarana, Arienga, Terrana, Margana, and two Rangers of the Underdwellers would make up the rest of the party. The party would be behind the main assault. The assault would attempt to drive a wedge through the forces of evil while Rangers would attack their flanks from the hills.

"I don't hold out much hope that we can break through," said Darlam. "But that is our only chance. If things go badly you must retreat and we will try to get through another way. Rowan and Hyrn must be protected. The quest must find a way, but we cannot send them into the hands of the evil ones."

They assembled at the great iron-bound stone gates. The signs of the attack on the gates were more evident in the bright light of day. Rowan and Hyrn were to ride with Careil and Bregal, while Aliana and Yarga would ride with Droom and Gorum. The Caramar warriors and the Rangers would accompany them on foot.

Amid the bustle of the amassing armies, Hyrn came to his senses. He felt exhausted. He sat astride Erras with Careil. Beside them were Rowan and Bregal, riding Marran.

Hyrn called to Rowan hoarsely. "It's too much. I don't know if I can keep feeling this."

Rowan turned to Hyrn with a worried look on his face. "It's alright little brother," he said. "We're all here to help."

Hyrn interrupted him. "It wasn't so bad when Ilah was flashing and burning. Now it is like an angry, frightened voice in my head. I feel like I want to explode."

"Everyone is doing all they can to get Ivah back," said Rowan. "The Stone was given to you for a reason. I'll do all I can to help, Hyrn."

At that moment the great gates began to rumble open. The King, flanked by his two tall Captains, Arum and Cram, the three mounted on large charigas, waited as the morning light began to stream through the gates. The light glistened on their armour. Flags fluttered at their sides.

When the gates came to rest the King turned his mount around and faced the gathered army. "We are the Keepers of the Light in the Dark," he said stridently. "We are strengthened by the people of the mountains and people of the plains, from the west. We march now, to show the forces of evil that we are not cowed. If they strike us, we will strike back. The people of Anasaria and the powers in the east are counting on us. For the first time in centuries, we march into open battle as a challenge to those who seek to extinguish the light. The Stone, Ivah, has been stolen. The quest to unite the Stones must continue. That is what we strive for and we will fight gloriously and without fear. Ours is the fight for good in this world."

King Darlam turned his chariga around and then raised his hand and motioned them forward. They moved off and the gathered army began to move in behind them, filing through the gates. Groups of Underdweller soldiers were interspersed with small groups of Caramar warriors. The Underdwellers were armour-clad while the Caramar went into battle unarmoured but resolute, and lethal. After the troops that would form the frontal assault had moved through the gate, Careil and Bregal, with Rowan and Hyrn, moved in behind them. They were led by the two Underdweller Rangers assigned to the quest, Jorunum and Turum.

As they came through the gates, Hyrn could see that the ground rose upwards towards where the valley opened out before them. More fortifications had been built further up this rise. Large stone walls stretched across the valley with watchtowers at intervals. The walls were destroyed in places and several of the towers were crumbling. A large gateway stood at the centre of the wall. The gates no longer stood and the guard towers at either side were in ruins. The army were traversing the open expanse and forming up behind the stone walls. Everywhere there was the detritus of war, left behind when the attackers had retreated up the valley. The King rode up towards the open gateway. He paused and at his signal war horns sounded from their midst. The Underdwellers began to chant. They beat their swords against their shields and the sound echoed across the valley.

"To war!" cried the King.

And all around the chant went up. "To war! To war!"

And with that the army began to move forward. Many soldiers filed through the broken gates behind the King and his Captains while others passed through breaches along the wall. When the armies had passed through the outer defences and had formed up into ranks, the war horns were sounded again, echoing up the valley, and the army began to move forward. The Drargs and Ultamarians were difficult to see where they had encamped at the head of the valley, but soon the answering horns blared and the clamour of many feet and voices could be heard as they answered the call to battle and began to move down the valley towards the oncoming army.

As the evil army began to move towards them, it became clear that the Underdwellers and Caramar soldiers were greatly outnumbered. With King Darlam at their head, they marched resolutely forward, undaunted, and with stern faces. The rising ground levelled out as the valley widened, but the main body of the army kept to the centre. They came to a point where the ground began to fall away forming a great bowl in the valley floor. The opposing forces were beginning to pour down the far side of this bowl. The army halted behind the King. Two columns of soldiers, the front ranks carrying long lances, formed up alongside Darlam and his guard. Behind these columns rode Rowan and Hyrn and the rest of the quest, with Jorunum and Turum ahead of them. Two more columns formed up on either side of them, the outer columns made up of archers, so that they were now surrounded by a great wedge of soldiers. Behind them were more soldiers, protecting the rear of the formation.

Rowan sat behind Bregal. His heart was beating hard in his chest. The scene before them was surreal. A dark blanket of soldiers was now flooding the valley ahead of them forming a barrier to the head of the valley beyond. He began to hear more clearly their harsh cries, and could now distinguish individual figures; the dark hairy Drargs and the brown uniformed Ultamarians, some helmeted and wearing dark breastplates over their brown tunics.

Captain Cram yelled a command and the lancers brought their lances down. The archers raised their bows.

In a clear voice, King Darlam roared, "Desultamar!" and all around the army moved forward down into the field of battle.

As they closed on the enemy the archers let loose waves of arrows and many of the dark figures fell as they began to rush towards them. Most Ultamarians were armed with sword and shield but there were a few archers amongst them and some arrows were loosed upon the army but most were deflected by the shields of the Underdwellers. The Drargs carried only crude knives but preferred to use claw and tooth to fight and kill.

The columns of archers fell back and the two columns alongside the quest fanned out as the opposing armies closed and with a resounding crash the great wedge of soldiers met the oncoming wall of evil fury. The lancers drove through the wall and the swords of Underdwellers and Caramar formed a wall around the questers, fighting furiously as the Drargs and Ultamarians pushed in around them. The sound of battle was all around.

Rowan felt trapped. They were protected on all sides as they pushed through the forces barring their way. The archers continued to loose arrows from behind aiming ahead and to the sides of the great wedge. As they entered into the midst of the throng, the soldiers behind began to join the fight as the Drargs and Ultamarians closed around them. Rowan felt the urge to draw his sword and fight but there were no enemy fighters close enough to where he sat surrounded by defenders. Beside him strode Arienga. Her sword was in her hand and just for a brief moment she looked at Rowan. The look on her face was one of grim determination.

The ground beneath their feet began to slope upwards as they reached the other side of the bowl, and soon they were up and onto level ground. It seemed that they might make it through but then Rowan looked ahead over the level ground and saw that the army they fought still stretched further up the valley, though more dispersed than those at the front of the attack. The soldiers around them were exacting a heavy toll on the Drargs and Ultamarians but Rowan could see that many Underdwellers were falling around them. The Caramar were more agile and were better able to evade the attackers and strike out without losing stride. As they moved further up the valley they seemed to be making better progress, although behind them the sounds of battle were still fierce. It was hard to see, amid the chaos, what was happening ahead but the flags of the King still flew high above the battle.

Then all of a sudden they were halted. Rowan could see that the soldiers around them were being pushed back. Evil fighters were closing in around them and there was a great roar of cries from the sides of the valleys and dark figures could be seen streaming down from either side of them. More enemy troops were pouring in from the hillsides above the valley. They were trapped. Captain Arum had turned about and began to call for a retreat but as he did he was struck down by a blow from an Ultamarian soldier. The battle clashed around them. In front of them a wall of Drargs crashed into their troops. They were cut off from the King's party. Caramar and Underdweller fighters formed ranks around them but they were sore pressed. A wedge of Drargs led by a tall Ultamarian, drove through the defenders straight towards where Droom rode with Aliana. Droom pulled around to meet the attack, and as he did, a knife flashed through the air past him at the exact moment that the Ultamarian raised his sword and struck at him. Droom met the blow and parried it. He swung his sword back towards the Ultamarian. The enemy soldier ducked and attempted to bring his sword up, but Droom brought his sword down in answer and the Ultamarian was forced back. As they fought, the battle closed in around the party of the quest. Arienga stood facing outwards, as above her Rowan drew the Sword of Acclimoss.

"ENOUGH!" boomed Ilah, and the cry resounded all around.

Hyrn held the ancient Stone of power above his head. A dazzingly bright explosion of pink light burst from the Stone in a great wall that scythed across the battlefield. The light reminded Rowan of the light that reflected on the great lake deep within the Realm of the Underdwellers. The blinding light exploded out across the entire valley, washed up against the surrounding slopes and then dispersed. All around, Drargs and Ultamarians had been cast to the ground and lay sprawled still clutching their weapons. The army led by King Darlam still stood, unharmed by the blast, resolute, and in wonderment.

CHAPTER ELEVEN

Anasaria

Hyrn still clutched Ilah in his outstretched hand. The Stone was now dark but still felt hot. It seemed as if a great weight had been lifted from his mind. All was silent for a moment, and then the sounds from around him came to his ears. Wounded soldiers cried out in pain, and then from behind him came a piercing cry.

"Aliana!"

It was the voice of Yarga.

Hyrn turned from where he sat behind Careil on Erras's back. Amidst the throng of soldiers, Aliana lay on the ground. Her white robes were stained red with blood. From her side protruded the handle of a crude dagger. The knife that had flashed through the air had found its mark. Yarga knelt beside her. Aliana looked up at him desperately. She attempted to speak, but a look of pain crossed her face. Hyrn had already dismounted, and quickly moved to kneel beside Yarga, his thoughts in a whirl.

"Aliana," said Hyrn tearfully. "We must get you help. Maybe the Stone—"

"Hush, child," said the Elder. "Much good has been done here today. The Stone cannot help me now. Be at peace, and stay true to your quest."

She then turned her face towards Yarga and reached out and grasped his arm. His face was stricken with horror and streaked with tears.

"You must take my place, Yarga," she said fitfully.

"Elder. I am only a Novice. I can't...You will be alright," said Yarga, his voice breaking.

Aliana smiled. "I am old and my body is ready. This wound cannot be healed. You must listen to me."

She grimaced with pain and then looked directly into Yarga's eyes and spoke with a clear voice.

"Yarga, I bestow the mantle of Elder upon you," she said. "The wisdom of the Sagenstone is within you. Use this wisdom to guide you and keep you strong. Protect and guide the quest as you are able, and return to tell the story of the quest to the Council of Elders."

She reached up to her throat and from beneath her robes pulled a small, red crystal attached to a chain around her neck.

"Elder, Yarga," she began. "I wish that you could have had your bestowal in the Chamber of the Sagenstone, as befits a new Elder. There you would have received the fruit of the Sagenstone left by an Elder that had passed beyond. This is now yours."

She tried to pull the chain over her head but the effort was too much.

"Take it, Yarga," she said, her face contorting with pain.

Tears streamed down Yarga's face as he leant over and gently pulled the chain over Aliana's head.

"Put it on," she said with effort.

Yarga placed the chain over his head, and as he did, the crystal briefly flashed.

Aliana looked at him and smiled.

"Be brave, Elder," she said. "There are great things ahead for you."

She looked at Hyrn where he knelt beside Yarga.

"Child of Light," she said and her eyes shone through the pain. "You are here when you are needed. I am happy to go, now that I know that there is hope in the world."

King Darlam had dismounted and now knelt beside them.

"We will get you help," he said.

"Peace, Keeper of the Light," said Aliana, glancing up at him. "There is no help for me now. Your realm is free but there is still much that needs to be done."

The King looked helplessly at Yarga and Hyrn.

Yarga spoke and his voice was solemn but strong. He held the crystal in his hand. "Peace to you, Elder, Aliana," he said. "Your name will be remembered and there will be joy in the hearts of all those who hear it."

Duburinga and Harla came and knelt at the Elder's feet. Aliana's eyes had closed but she opened them and looked at the two warriors.

"Harla, Duburinga," she said, with pride in her trembling voice. "You are the East and the West of the Caramarhc. Stay strong and guide the Caramar in this quest. Even should your paths divide, the strength of the mountains will burn in you."

Aliana closed her eyes and then they fluttered briefly open. She feebly gripped the hand of the King, beside her. "King Darlam, I ask only that you return me and all my fallen people to our mountains, that we may rest there where our hearts belong."

"It shall be done," said the King, bowing his head to her.

Aliana smiled weakly and released her grasp and her hand fell to her side. Her eyelids fluttered briefly, and then closed, and Aliana, Elder of the Caramar, passed beyond, to where the power of evil could not follow.

The members of the quest were all gathered around Aliana, when there began to be shouts of panic from the battlefield.

"They are not dead! They still live!"

From just behind them the tall soldier that had fought Droom rose to his feet. His face shone. He shook his head, and all those around looked at him bewildered. His uniform, once brown, now glowed white, and his breastplate and helm shone silver and bright. The sword in his hand glistened as if newly forged. The soldiers gathered around, raised their swords. Hyrn, in shock, rose to his feet and stood next to Rowan. Rowan had turned from where Aliana lay, and faced the glowing apparition. The Sword of Acclimoss was still in Rowan's hand. Its point rested on the ground. Hyrn still clutched Ilah in his hand. The soldier stumbled towards them and the Underdweller and Caramar soldiers closed on him, almost hesitantly, with some confusion. But the soldier fell to his knees and bowed his head to the ground, directly towards Rowan and Hyrn. He laid the hilt of his sword towards the two boys.

"The Sword of Acclimoss and the Stone of Angil have returned!" he cried. "We are saved! We are free! We have been enslaved for centuries under their spell. We are yours to command."

Across the battlefield, the remaining Ultamarians all began to rise. Their uniforms and armour shone bright. The Stone in Hyrn's hand began to glow softly. He raised it in the air, without knowing why, and stepped out from amongst the throng of soldiers. Besides him Rowan moved forward, trance-like, and raised the Sword of Acclimoss. The blade flashed briefly and all around the once Ultamarians, the soldiers of Abessair and Anasaria, long under the spell of the Dark Lords of Ultamar, fell to their knees in praise at their release from torment.

"Soldiers of Anasaria!" called Yarga. He had risen and stood beside Hyrn. "The quest to unite the Stones must continue. You are bound again with the Stones of Angil. You must join in the fight. Anasaria must be free."

The Abessairians rose to their feet and then, as one, raised their swords and cried. "Anasaria."

The Stone in Hyrn's hand went dark again and he fell to his knees drained and exhausted. Rowan stood alongside him, his sword still held aloft. Arienga came and stood beside Rowan. She gently grasped the hand that held his raised sword, and lowered it to the ground.

"The battle is over," she said simply.

Rowan turned and looked into her face, and he saw that it was wet with tears.

Across the battlefield, the dead were being recovered and carried back down the valley with honour. One of the bodies was that of Captain Arum. Aliana's body was covered and placed on a litter. Six Caramar warriors lifted the litter and, with a guard of Underdweller soldiers, carried the Elder down towards the gateway of the Realm of the Underdwellers, westwards, towards home.

Rowan and Careil knelt beside Hyrn. He was still dazed and in a catatonic state. Bregal stood beside them, eyeing the tall Abessairian soldier who stood facing them.

Rowan looked up. "What does he want?" he asked.

Bregal glanced at the Abessairian, and then answered matter of factly, "I think he wants you to tell him what to do."

"Perhaps you could get him and the rest of them to help clean up this mess," suggested Bregal.

Rowan stood. "Help us carry our dead and bury yours here." For even the dead Ultamarians were cleansed. "The Drargs you can throw in the sea for all I care."

"What sea?" asked the Abessairian.

"Just leave them," growled Bregal. "They will serve as a warning that this valley is dangerous."

"Leave them," said Rowan tiredly.

The soldier turned and signalled to the white and silver clad soldiers gathered behind him. "Honour the dead," he called. "We have much to repay."

The remaining members of the quest stood before King Darlam. Rowan supported Hyrn, who seemingly dozed beside him. Yarga faced the King.

"Our hearts lie with Aliana, but our path is clear," he said solemnly. "We must retrieve Ivah."

"We will send our scouts ahead of you," said Darlam. "Remember though, that beyond this valley the enemy still awaits. You also must decide what becomes of the soldiers of Anasaria. It is too soon to attempt to enter Anasaria in force."

The tall Abessairian soldier stepped forward. His white uniform and armor had become soiled with blood and grime. "I am General Ferian, loyal to the crown of Anasaria. We know the land of Anasaria. We can help you find your way. All of us are willing to return to fight against the Dark Lords."

"Your time will come I think," said Darlam. "But I would still counsel for a small force to try to recapture the other Stone."

The party were skirting the heavily forested foothills of the mountains that formed a great wall guarding the land of Anasaria's western boundary. The Artorans and Ultamarians that had stolen Ivah, had followed the road that crossed the narrow plain that lay directly between the hills surrounding the entrance to the Underrealm and the mountains. But that was Drarg territory and too dangerous for the questers to risk, so they had followed hidden paths, escorted by Rangers, and had crossed into these foothills. They hoped to make up some time on their quarry. The paths they were following were a quicker route into the mountains and these were lands patrolled by Underdweller Rangers. Parties of enemy soldiers had been known to disappear here, so the road across the plain was safer for the enemy force that carried Ivah.

The sun was beginning to set and they had decided to stop for the night and then in the morning attempt to make their way up the paths that led back to the road that would take them over the mountains and down into Anasaria.

They had travelled in a daze. The march to the Eastern Gate, and the events of the day, and then the loss of Aliana, had left them drained. Hyrn had ridden half asleep on Erras's back, as Careil led the horse along the often narrow pathways. The rest of the party were exhausted too, apart from the four Abessairians that now accompanied them. General Ferian and three of his soldiers had joined them and were eager to return to Anasaria and to aid in the quest. Ferian's knowledge of Anasaria was deemed as being an invaluable help to them, and once they joined the main road they would need his guidance.

"The pass has become known as the Pass of Exile," said Ferian. "Although before Darion and Bharain took this road out of Anasaria, it was called the Pass of the Setting Sun. Once we are through this pass, the land of Anasaria will open out before us, and you will see for the first time the once great fortress Abessair, the now dark and evil Ultamar, where abide the seven Dark Lords."

He addressed the leaders of the party, Yarga, Careil, Duburinga, Harla and

Droom. They sat around the fire, their faces lit by its glow as their shadows danced behind them. The rest of the party were either standing watch, or were huddled in their blankets, asleep or dozing fitfully.

"The force that took the Stone," continued Ferian, "was led by one of my Captains, Bardan. He is a brutal and committed soldier. I used him for the most difficult tasks."

Ferian took in a gulp of air and then paused to steady himself. "The Artorans were led by a high ranking Sorcerer. He carried a dark Stone. The Artorans are largely a mystery to us but they pay homage to the Dark Lords and are much in their favour. They are sadistic and fanatical and glory in cruelly inflicting pain on any that stand in their way. The Artorans have been enemies of Anasaria since the building of Abessair. Anasaria is not evil. It is ruled by evil. Artora too, is ruled by evil, but we don't know whether their people defy them. No Anasarian has been into Artora. Even when Eriellan defeated the Artorans, they swore allegiance at the entrance to their land and then retreated, only returning when the Dark Lords seized control of Anasaria."

"My knowledge is not up to that of my fellow Elders," said Yarga. He paused and stared into the fire, tears glistening in his eyes, and then continued steadily. "But I have never heard of this type of Stone. Its power is possibly beyond all we carry, except perhaps Ilah."

He lowered his voice. "I would rather that the Stone and the bearer were not put to the test just yet."

Ferian glanced towards where the others rested or slept, and nodded in agreement.

Hyrn was too agitated to sleep. He had been aroused from his daze and had been given something to eat and drink. This helped him return to reality and the events of the day played over and over in his mind.

Beside him Rowan slept. There had been no training that night. After the battle and the death of Aliana, and with the rigours of the previous days, he and Arienga were in no mood for it. Arienga was on guard duty and had headed back down the path to take up her post. The Sword of Acclimoss lay beside Rowan and his hand rested on its hilt as he slept.

At Rowan and Hyrn's feet, facing away from them, crouched one of the Abessairian soldiers, Garan. He had not let the two boys out of his sight since they had left the valley. General Ferian had ordered him to guard the wielders of the Stone and the Sword, and he had not relented in his duty.

Hyrn studied the back of Garan and thought about what Ilah had been able to do. The Ultamarians were the soldiers of Abessair but they were under some sort of evil curse. Ilah had freed them and now they were going to lead them into Anasaria. Hyrn wondered who they were and how they came to be Ultamarians.

"Garan!" Hyrn called softly.

The soldier still in a crouch turned on his haunches and then knelt, facing Hyrn.

"What can I do to assist you, Stonebearer?" he asked.

"Well, for a start, could you please just call me Hyrn?" asked Hyrn and then quickly followed with. "And how long were you an Ultamarian?"

"It is a hard history to tell, Hyrn," answered Garan. "I feel as I did when I was taken. The Ultamarians are any of the soldiers, or sometimes the people of Anasaria, that are forced into the service of the Dark Lords. They are the soldiers that were in the army of Abessair or have since been forced into service. Some have been that way for hundreds of years and others have been recruited from amongst the people of Anasaria more recently, and twisted to the service of Ultamar."

He paused and looked directly at Hyrn. "You don't know what this means to us soldiers that were in that valley. Ilah has washed the evil out of us and returned us to who we were before."

He shook his head as if to wake himself, and continued, "Ferian and I were soldiers when Bharain went into exile and we were imprisoned by the evil of the Dark Lords. I was young, just out of cadetship, when Bharain fled and took the remaining Twin Stone. Those close to Ultamar came under the influence of the Dark Lords first. It took some years before the whole Abessairian army was under their thrall. We were weak. The army had been in decline, along with the kingship, since Prince Darion exiled himself and took the Stone you hold with him. I had seen over thirty summers when the area where I was stationed came under their power. I have been imprisoned by that evil for over two hundred and fifty years."

"But that means that you are nearly three hundred years old," said Hyrn. "How is that possible?"

"The Dark Lords wield a power of evil." Garan replied. "None know what it is, but it gives them the power of control and immortality. Its power keeps them, and those who serve them, frozen in time. It is a nightmare."

"But doesn't that mean you will die now?" asked Hyrn.

"Aye," said Garan. "As all those that live should."

Hyrn settled back in his blankets. "Thank you, Garan," he said.

Garan laughed softly and said sincerely. "I am the one who needs to give thanks, Hyrn."

"What resistance are we likely to see?" Harla addressed Ferian.

As they talked, the full moon began to peek above the mountains that rose in a great wall above them, blocking the horizon to the east. They had now come to the crux of their dilemma; how to enter Anasaria through the continuously guarded, narrow pass that was the only possible way through, without abandoning their pressing pursuit and seeking a long way around the mountains.

"The western and southern areas are lightly garrisoned," the General replied. "Most of our defences are in the north and the east since the Power in the East took an interest in this region. There are some staging posts for attacks on the Underrealm but they were mostly emptied to carry out the attack led by the Artorans. That was a happy twist of fate, as it meant that more of our soldiers were freed by the Stone of Angil. There is a guardpost just below the pass and another at the foot of the mountains. We need to get past these. There is no other way through."

Ferian stood up, his large frame lit by the firelight. "I have an idea that may help us get past these posts. Look at me. My uniform is stained by our labours on the battlefield. If I and my men stain our uniforms, we will appear as Ultamarians. I am a General in the Abessairian army and was a General in the service of Ultamar. If the Ultamarians believe I am one of them, I can lead you into Anasaria."

Careil looked up at Ferian. "But you will be accompanied by all of us."

"Yes," said Ferian and then continued almost sheepishly, but grimly. "You will be my prisoners."

The road that led up to the pass through the mountains was deserted. It was only as they began to crest the hill that they saw any signs of life. Small groups of houses, and individual dwellings, appeared amongst the hills at either side of the road.

Ferian walked beside the grim and tired-looking Yarga.

The General smirked looking up at the signs of habitation, and spoke to the new Elder. "These are Anasarians. Many fled up here to try to escape the evil of Ultamar. They were a constant source of trouble for us and we tried to subdue them. They were stubborn and used their mountain location to harry us and cause us pain, but they now make my heart light. The spirit of Anasaria lives and these people here are a sign that goodness still inhabits the hearts of our people."

The big General rested his hand on Yarga's shoulder. "All is not lost. We are free and all of Anasaria will be free."

The tone of Ferian's voice became more solemn as he said, "We should get ready to enter Anasaria."

"The plan is a good one," said Yarga. "I just hope that the Ultamarians don't sense the change in you. We also have the Stone. I suggest that we enclose it, so that its power is not felt by the guards."

Hyrn's hands were bound close to his chest. Under his vest a bulky weight protruded, hidden behind his bound hands. The Stone of Angil lay nestled within the heavy iron gauntlet that was previously worn on the hand of Captain Droom. The ropes around Hyrn's wrists were bound loosely but the rope that linked him to Erras's saddle was taut. All around, the rest of the party were bound together. Their weapons were hidden from sight, but within easy reach if needed. The road was passing through a narrow gap between the hills on either side. The hillsides were forested with large conifers growing closely together. It was dark beneath the trees and little sunlight penetrated through the dense branches. Ahead of them two squat towers stood at either side of the road. General Ferian marched defiantly ahead of them. Garan and Carlan, one of the other Abessairians, marched either side of Rowan and Hyrn, who rode atop Marran and Erras. The other Anasarian, Captain Kerian, brought up the rear. The sun was moving towards midday.

As they approached the towers, two soldiers who had been lazing on the bank of the roadside, rose to their feet and, calling out towards the towers, drew their swords and took up positions blocking the roadway.

Ferian did not hesitate. "Move aside you fools!" he bellowed. "Ultamar calls!"

The two soldiers sheathed their weapons and stood aside at attention. Ferian marched between them leading the others behind him. As they neared the two towers a group of soldiers bustled out of the right hand tower, led by a tall stocky soldier who was busy fastening a sword-belt around his waist. He swiftly approached them and raised his hand in salute.

"General, I thought you would have still been off fighting the Earthworms," he said contemptuously.

"Captain Karklan," said Ferian dismissively. "I see that you have left this post poorly guarded. Ultamar will hear of this in my report. Your incompetence does not go unnoticed."

"Come now, General," said Karklan with a sneer. His men stood behind him looking nervously towards the formidable figure of General Ferian. "Surely you don't believe that our Lords care about this forsaken backwater."

"Are you not aware," interrupted Ferian, forcefully, "that there has been a breach of our defences? A group of our soldiers led by some Artoran traitors have stolen something that the Dark Lords greatly desired. We had hoped that they had been stopped at this post."

Karklan visibly blanched.

"They were here last night but moved on before dawn. Captain Bardan commanded the Ultamarians," he said quickly, with a note of fear in his voice, and then continued more evenly. "I assure you, General. There was nothing to suggest that they were doing anything in defiance of Ultamar. Captain Bardan himself spoke of his pride in serving Ultamar."

"How long?" growled Ferian.

"Less than half a day," replied Karklan.

"Move your men south into the foothills," ordered Ferian, pointing back down they way they had come. "Spread them out, and keep a watch out for Artorans. We believe they are secretly conspiring to attack Ultamar using their sorcery. This latest theft is proof of their treachery."

"What did they take?" asked the Ultamarian Captain, almost greedily.

"It is none of your concern, Captain," said Ferian sternly. "You have your orders."

With that Ferian signalled his men to move forward and pulled on the rope that linked his chain of prisoners together. Garan and Carlan yelled orders at the people bound together between them. The procession moved on as Karklan started giving his men desperate instructions. As Hyrn passed by, the evil Captain seemed to shudder and quickly turned and looked directly at him. The Ultamarian lifted his nose up and almost seemed to sniff the air with a look of disgust on his face. Hyrn was gripped by fear. He felt the malice emanating from the Ultamarian. Karklan turned fully and confronted Garan.

"Who are these scum, soldier?" he asked.

Garan looked at Karklan with a look of submission but with a barely hidden smirk on his face and said, "Don't know, sir. I'm just an ignorant soldier. No-one tells me anything."

Captain Karklan looked ready to angrily retort. Hyrn could feel his heart beating hard in his chest against the iron gauntlet. It seemed so loud that he was sure that it would give him away.

The Ultamarian Captain's eyes alighted on Hyrn, but at that moment General Ferian turned and roared back down the line, "Captain! You have your orders!"

Red-faced and quietly fuming, Karklan turned and stormed off, his men trailing in his wake. He hurried to prepare to march his men southwards, towards where Ferian knew the Rangers, Caramar and soldiers of the Underdwellers, and the freed Abessairians, were now scouting, ready to take any Ultamarians by surprise.

They passed between the two towers. Small barrack rooms adjoined them on the other side. A small corral stood alongside. Four horses grazed within. One lifted its head and whinnied softly at the sight of the horses carrying Rowan and Hyrn. The road now followed an incline down the mountainside. The roadway was clear ahead of them as far as they could see, until the road took a bend and disappeared from view. The thick forest still lined the road and continued on, blocking their view of what lay beyond. They could smell the fresh pine scent in the air as the breeze ruffled the trees, their branches creaking and groaning softly.

They continued down the road and as they rounded the bend the towers disappeared from sight. As the end of the procession moved out of sight of the towers, Ferian turned and spoke.

"Welcome to Anasaria," he said proudly. "Our hope is renewed. We will get to the second guard post in a couple of hours. I suggest we get closer and then stop to have something to eat away from the road amongst the trees. It may be wise to keep your ropes on until then in case any troops come up from below.

They sat in a small glade amidst towering trees. Finally, free of the ropes Hyrn had taken the chance to walk around and get the stiffness from his limbs. He now sat on a log beside Careil, eating. Yarga came and sat beside them.

"How are you Hyrn?" asked the young Elder.

"I'm alright I guess, just a little tired," answered Hyrn.

He thought for a brief moment and then asked the Elder. "What happened back there, on the battlefield? I didn't think Ilah could do that."

"I'm not sure," replied Yarga. "The power of Ilah is unfamiliar to me. I think maybe Ilah absorbed the power that resides in the Lake of Light. That power was released along with Ilah's own power. No evil there could stand against it. The Drargs are beings of evil and were killed outright, but the Ultamarians are under an evil spell. It seems that spell was broken and they were cleansed, becoming the Abessairians they once were. Our hope is that when Ilah and Ivah are reunited and returned to Ultamar, Abessair will be restored and the Ultamarians and Anasarians will be freed."

"What if Ivah is taken to the Dark Lords?" asked Careil. "Can they destroy it?"

"I don't know," answered Yarga. "If only..." his voice caught but he composed himself and continued. "I wish that Aliana was here. I fear that I am not up to this challenge."

Careil rested his hand on Yarga's shoulder.

"Aliana trusted you enough to bring you along and she put her faith in you," he said. "You are now an Elder and we will trust in your wisdom."

"I will try to repay that trust," Yarga said glumly.

He turned to Hyrn and said, "It is told that the Stones will be reunited and we must believe that it is so. We will find Ivah."

Hyrn looked at the Elder and forced a smile but in the pit of his stomach he felt a dread, and the Stone under his vest filled his mind with a deep sadness.

"We must keep moving," said Hyrn.

As they neared the lower reaches of the mountains, the road that had curved back and forth, straightened out, and a vista opened before them. Across the tops of the trees, they could see forest stretching out in front of them off into the distance. The sun was getting lower in the sky, hidden now by the mountains behind them. The land of Anasaria lay before them still bathed in sunlight. Directly ahead of them, across the expanse of forest and hills, stood a steep-sided plateau. Atop that plateau, silhouetted against the distant horizon, stood a vast towering fortress, its many towers pointed defiantly at the sky. The eyes of the questers beheld the dark fortress of Ultamar, strong and brooding, dominating the land at its feet.

They made their way down the steep roadway. They were all bound together again, apart from the four Abessairians, led by General Ferian. At the bottom of the road stood two more guard towers. These were taller and seemed to be well kept. As they approached they could see that there was a hive of activity. Two mounted Ultamarians rode out to meet them, stopping in front of the tall General.

"General Ferian," one said. "This is a strange sight after what has happened here."

"What do you mean?" demanded Ferian.

"A party of soldiers, led by Captain Bardan and accompanied by Artorans, passed through here earlier today," replied the soldier. "There was some dispute amongst them about a package they were carrying. We tried to hold them here to determine what was going on but the Captain insisted that they were on a mission to Ultamar that could not wait. This caused some anger amongst the Artorans who insisted that their masters were the ones who had ordered the mission. Bardan said it was possible that they were being pursued by the enemies of Ultamar, and here you are with Underdweller prisoners."

He eyed Droom and Gorum and then looked down the line.

"And what appear to be strangers," he continued. "What is going on here?"

Ferian looked resolutely up at the soldier. "Are you in the habit of questioning your Generals?" he said fiercely.

"No, General," said the soldier. "I am trying to do my duty protecting the border but something does not seem right here."

"I answer to the Dark Lords," said the General. "These prisoners are headed for the dungeons of Ultamar. The Dark Lords are very interested in speaking with them."

He emphasised the word 'speaking' as he spoke and then laughed darkly. "I suggest you do not keep us waiting."

"General, if you will allow me to send word to the nearest command post while you wait here," said the soldier hesitantly.

"We have no time for that!" exclaimed Ferian. "There is treachery at hand. The Artorans are not to be trusted. Bardan needs to keep on his guard. Do you know which way the party went?"

"We have stayed at our posts as ordered, but this all seems suspicious," replied the soldier. "We have seen no activity since the Artorans came through here four days ago heading west, and now we have two unusual parties heading east passing through in one day."

General Ferian drew himself up then leaning towards the soldier, spoke almost conspiratorially. "We believe we have knowledge that will help the Dark Lords finally wipe out the resistance. Say nothing of this but know that you will be remembered if you play your part. For now, we must pass through and make haste to Ultamar."

"It is usual practice for us to search any prisoners," said the soldier desperately.

Ferian laughed.

"I do not think that would be wise," he said. "Our Lords may be displeased to know that their prisoners had been ransacked by a border guard."

"As you wish, General," said the soldier.

He looked with contempt at the prisoners before him. "I just hope they are made to suffer," he continued, coldly.

"Oh, they are already suffering," said Ferian. "They will feel the full power of Ultamar. Now stand aside."

He pulled on the rope and bellowed, "Move, you filthy scum!"

The two soldiers moved their horses aside and the party moved between them. The eyes of the Ultamarians bored into them. Hyrn kept his head down unwilling to look at them, and silently hoping that they could not see the bundle beneath his clothes. More soldiers stood alongside the guard towers, but at a command from the General, they moved aside and let the party pass through.

The road continued on as the ground levelled out but the forest still lay thick on either side. There followed a long sweeping curve, but they were still in sight of the towers for quite a distance before the trees finally hid them from view. They remained as they were until they could get a reasonable distance from the border post, and then they stopped.

"We will have to leave the road," said Ferian. "There was no other way through into Anasaria but we can now follow more secluded paths."

Some of the party had begun to remove the ropes and then froze as the sound of horses travelling quickly came from behind, and before they knew it, three riders came galloping round the bend and were pulling up alongside them. The riders were the two mounted soldiers, and leading them, Captain Karklan. Their swords were drawn and they moved to surround the party. Karklan faced General Ferian, his horse was thick with sweat and obviously suffering.

"What is the meaning of this?" demanded Ferian.

"This is all wrong!" snarled Karklan. "You smell wrong!"

He brandished his sword towards the General's face.

"I believe that you are up to something," he said menacingly. "There is a stink of virtuousness about you, and something is here. Something dangerous and yet you accuse Bardan of treachery. No. Bardan is loyal to the Dark Lords. It is you who are a traitor!"

Karklan moved forward, his sword levelled at the General. Ferian went for the sword at his waist but there was a sudden flash of movement alongside Karklan, and the Ultamarian Captain's head was lifted away from his body and thudded on the side of the road. The two Ultamarian soldiers spurred their horses forward as Karklan's sword fell from his hand and his body toppled from his horse. Several arrows pierced their bodies and one of them fell from the saddle while the other slumped forward. Their horses came to a stop. Captain Droom sat astride his chariga alongside Karklan's horse, a bloody sword in his hand. Behind him, the remainder of the soldiers, warriors, Rangers and Riders brandished weapons.

"We have to get off the road," said Ferian quickly.

They dragged the bodies of the Ultamarians well into the forest and left them in a hollow covered with branches. They then split into two groups, one on either side of the road, and headed into the forest. They were to follow in line with the road, with the main groups deeper in the forest, while Caramar warriors and the two Rangers scouted the roadside and the forest ahead using their wilderness skills to remain hidden. The Ultamarian's horses were led along with them, two with the group led by General Ferian. Careil led the two horses while Hyrn rode Erras. The other horse was led by Bregal, with Rowan riding Marran in the group led by Kerian. Gorum, Duburinga and Arienga accompanied Kerian while Droom, Harla and Yarga accompanied General Ferian. Garan still guarded Hyrn, and Carlan watched over Rowan.

It was difficult going within the forest. The ground was thick with pine needles and the trees grew densely in places. They had been travelling for a couple of hours since the clash with the Ultamarians. Gebarana, Margana and Turum were scouting ahead of General Ferian's group, moving stealthily through the trees to the south of the road. The sounds of the forest were all around them; woodland birds, and the noises of the wind moving through the trees. Almost indiscernibly, other strange sounds came to them through the forest. Movement like the sound of small animals came to their trained ears. The three secreted themselves and waited.

Up ahead, between the trees, they saw three figures moving quietly across their path, heading towards the road. The two Caramar and the Ranger began to move from cover to cover tracking them. The strangers were moving towards the roadside. The three figures went behind a thicket and then didn't reappear on the other side. Turum signalled that he was going to move around behind them. He moved from tree to tree quietly but when he was able to see beyond the thicket the strangers were nowhere to be seen. He saw movement behind him and turned with his bow up and aimed. A man dressed in shades of green and brown stood before him. He had a crossbow pointed at the Ranger's head.

"Who are you?" demanded the man.

"I might ask you the same question," said Turum.

"Put down your bow," the stranger ordered.

From either side of Turum the other two appeared. One was dressed like the man with the crossbow. The other's clothes were shabby and grey. They both had arrows trained on the Ranger. Suddenly the two Caramar appeared on either side with their bows trained on the two new arrivals.

"Drop your weapons," said Gebarana.

The first man laughed almost as if he was enjoying himself.

"It looks like we have a stand-off," he said. "You are not Ultamarians, or Drargs, or Artorans. You don't appear evil but you don't belong here."

At that moment the group led by General Ferian appeared a short distance away. The stranger with the crossbow swung around.

He aimed his weapon at the figure of Ferian and hissed, "Ultamarians."

"No!" cried Turum. "Don't shoot! He is an Abessairian."

The stranger looked quickly at Turum with a puzzled look on his face. "There are no Abessairians," and then looking back at the General said with hatred in his voice. "It is General Ferian!"

"It is Ferian," said Turum, "but he is no longer under the spell of Ultamar."

General Ferian saw the scene ahead and moved closer, then halted. Captain Droom rode up and stopped beside the General.

"An Underdweller!" said the stranger with amazement, his crossbow still pointed at Ferian.

Turum said desperately, "You are obviously not friends of Ultamar."

The shabbily dressed stranger said in a bitter tone, "Curse them and curse the name of Ferian! Shoot him!"

Gebarana, who had an arrow drawn and aimed at him, realised that the speaker was just a young boy. Droom, fully armoured, rode forward and placed himself between Ferian and the crossbow.

He spoke forcefully. "We follow a sacred quest; to free Anasaria and release the army of Abessair. The General here is free as a result of our quest. If you are enemies of Ultamar we are both on the same side. If not, we have fighters all around you and you will not escape. Lower your weapons and we can talk."

"Don't listen to them!" hissed the boy. He still had his bow pointed at Turum but his aim wavered.

"Peace, Wren," said the first stranger in a strained voice, as Harla appeared suddenly beside him, with a short sword pressed to his throat.

"I think you need to talk to us," said the Caramar warrior.

He lowered his crossbow resignedly, and said with exasperation, "Who are you people?"

Harla motioned for Gebarana and Margana to lower their weapons.

She spoke threateningly to the man whose throat rested at the tip of her blade.

"Tell these two to stand down," she said, motioning to the other two strangers.

"Wren, Biren-So, drop your weapons," he said calmly.

The boy and the man slackened their bow-strings and lowered their bows. Turum with a sigh of relief lowered his too and Harla withdrew her sword and sheathed it.

From behind Ferian and Droom, Yarga stepped forward and walked up to where the newcomers stood.

He spoke clearly and with a note of authority in his voice. "I am Yarga, Elder of the Caramar, bearer of the wisdom of the Sagenstone." He reached down and pulled the small crystal still on his chain from beneath his gown.

"Our quest is foretold and is central to the fate of Anasaria. In my mind I believe that you are friends. The Stone has told us to seek help along the way wherever it can be found. Will you help us?"

The stranger turned and faced Yarga. "I am Jarta Den, a…" he began.

Ferian interrupted. "A Quigling," he said with a note of exasperation in his voice.

"Yes. A Quigling," said Jarta Den.

"We have heard of the Quiglings," said Droom. "You help the Anasarians to resist Ultamar but none of our spies have ever seen any of you and none could tell where you came from."

"The Ultamarians curse your name," said Ferian. "It is impossible to ever find you. To my knowledge only two have ever been captured but they escaped before they could be taken to Ultamar. They killed all of their guards except one who they used to send a message to the Dark Lords."

Hyrn had ridden up with Garan at his side and had stopped next to Droom.

"What was the message?" he asked.

Ferian answered, "We never quite understood, but the Dark Lords seemed angry about it. I delivered the message myself. The message said, 'We know who you are. We remember Guran-Badur. We remember the rats that escaped and we will never rest until your bones are dragged back and thrown into the pit, where they will rot with the rest of your kind.'"

Jarta-Den laughed. "I hope they think on those words and that they gnaw at their evil minds every waking moment."

"But what does it mean?" asked Hyrn.

Jarta Den looked at Hyrn with a puzzled look on his face. "I see your youngsters like to ask questions too," he said. "This one here," he motioned with his head towards Wren, "is always asking 'why?' and 'how?' and 'when?'. But the answer to that is a long one and perhaps for another time. I and Biren-So are Quiglings. We are here to cause as much trouble for Ultamar as we can. We were sent by the Keepers and the Angilanians to help when it was discovered that Anasaria was in danger.

We Quiglings are trouble-makers by nature. We are not much for standing at attention and marching in lines. This is much more our kind of fight and we have history with the Dark Lords that goes back centuries. The young fellow is Wren, an Anasarian."

Yarga spoke. "We are in need of haste. We are following a party of Ultamarians and Artorans who…"

"Artorans?" said Jarta-Den quizzically. "We saw a group of Artorans travelling south on the main road a couple of hours ago. Some of their number were wounded but we are too few to confront them. We were heading back up the road to see if we could find out who attacked them."

"Were there any Ultamarians with them?" asked Ferian.

Jarta-Den looked at Ferian with a suspicious expression, but answered, "No, we saw no Ultamarians."

"Were they carrying anything?" asked Hyrn

"Not that we could see," replied the Quigling. "What would they be carrying?"

Just then Terrana and Jorunum came through the trees and stopped. They looked at the strangers and then Terrana looked at Harla.

"What have you to report?" asked Harla.

"There is a crossroad ahead," said Terrana. "There is evidence of a battle and several dead Artorans and Ultamarians. There are signs that the party argued and have split up and gone in different directions on the roads that run north and south of the junction. There is no sign of the Stone."

"How far is this junction?" asked Harla.

"It is only a short distance from here," interjected Jarta-Den. "We will accompany you and perhaps on the way you will tell us what is going on."

"One of the Twin Stones!" Jarta-Den exclaimed in disbelief.

He walked beside Yarga as they moved through the edges of the forest trailing the road.

The Quigling turned his head and looked at Hyrn who rode not far behind.

"And this boy has the Stone now?" he asked.

"Yes," said Yarga. "And his brother carries the Sword of Acclimoss."

Jarta-Den shook his head, bewildered. "Where is his brother?"

"Not far," said Yarga. "We will meet up with the rest of the quest soon. We are chasing a party of Ultamarians and Artorans. They have stolen the other Stone, Ivah, which King Bharain left with the Underdwellers. We must retrieve it."

As Yarga said these words, he could see ahead that the trees thinned out and beyond them the rest of the party were gathered where the road down from the Pass of Exile was crossed by another road.

As they emerged from the forest, they saw a scene of chaos and carnage. Bodies lay strewn across the road. There was blood everywhere and the roadway and surrounds were scorched and scarred. Bregal and Kerian were down on the ground examining the bodies.

Bregal looked up as the rest of the party approached.

"Looks like they weren't getting along so well," he said.

Hyrn had alighted from Erras and came closer.

"Is there any sign of Ivah?" he said.

"I think," replied Kerian, rising to his feet, "that is what they were fighting about. It looks like the survivors split up and went their separate ways."

"Which of them took the Stone, I wonder," said Yarga, "and why would the other not pursue them if it meant so much?"

"Maybe they are seeking reinforcements," suggested Ferian.

"Something is not right here," said Jarta-Den.

Kerian suddenly noticed the Quigling standing beside Ferian.

"Where did he come from?" he asked.

"That is a long story," said Jarta-Den. "But I think I arrived just where I was supposed to be."

"We finally caught ourselves a Quigling," said Ferian.

Jarta-Den looked sternly at Ferian.

"That's not in the least amusing," he said wryly. "We chose to approach your scouts, and we chose to not fight. I could have shot you. We are used to fighting Ultamarians."

Kerian stepped forward with his fist clenched at his sides.

"We are not Ultamarians!" he said angrily. "We are soldiers of Abessair."

Jarta-Den stared at Kerian. "My people have been fighting those that inhabit Ultamar for centuries. Forgive me if I treat you with mistrust."

"And I have been under the yoke of Ultamar for over three lifetimes," said Kerian, bitterly. "I believe that my hatred of them is the equal of yours."

Jarta-Den attempted to speak, but Ferian cut in. "We were cleansed by the Stone of Angil but we have stained our uniforms to appear as Ultamarians."

Jarta-Den looked at Ferian and said humbly, "As your prisoner, I ask for proof of your claims. Let us see the Stone."

Yarga spoke emphatically. "Do not ask idly of Ilah. There is much we don't understand of her power but there is much we have witnessed."

As Yarga spoke, the young Anasarian, Wren, attempted to stand beside Hyrn. The bulk of Garan moved to block his way.

Wren poked his head around Garan.

"Is it true that you have one of the Stones?" he whispered to Hyrn, a little too loudly.

Yarga turned from addressing Jarta-Den and spoke to the boy. "It is true, but Hyrn knows best what the Stone wishes."

"I don't!" said Hyrn angrily. "I don't know what she wants, or what's going to happen, or what I am supposed to do. It just happens."

Wren, still peering around Garan, seemed oblivious to Hyrn's outburst, and asked innocently. "Can I see it?"

Hyrn looked at the young Anasarian. He felt the eyes of the adults upon him, but saw the look of wonder in Wren's eyes.

Hyrn looked up at Garan and said, "Don't follow us, please."

He stepped around Garan and grabbed Wren by the arm. "Come with me," he said conspiratorially.

Garan restrained his impulse to follow and looked on helplessly as Hyrn led Wren a little way down the south road and crossed into the trees. Ferian stepped up and laid his hand on Garan's shoulder as the two boys disappeared.

Yarga turned to Jarta-Den and said, "You trust your companion, I hope."

"He can be prone to exaggeration but his heart is true," Jarta-Den said in answer.

Rowan and Arienga came into sight of the scene at the crossroads from beyond a bend in the road to the north. They walked up and Arienga approached Harla.

"The remaining Ultamarians have gone north and have gone beyond a sharp curve in the road but not too quickly," she said. "There are trails of blood, so it appears that some of them are wounded. There are also trails of gore that glows. It felt wrong and to be avoided. Duburinga has gone with Boriega to higher ground at the west of the road to get a view ahead."

Hyrn and Wren walked a little way into the trees before Hyrn stopped and turned to Wren.

"Why are you here?" he asked.

"I am fighting against Ultamar," said Wren proudly.

"Where are your parents?" asked Hyrn.

Wren's face became downcast. "My mother died a long time ago. I lived with my father in the Evelar Forest. They came and took him away to the dungeons of Ultamar. They said he was a rebel. He was just trying to survive and look after me. So, I became a rebel," he said proudly. "I was lucky enough to meet up with the Quiglings."

Wren stopped and looked at Hyrn.

"Hey, I thought you were going to show me the Stone," he said.

Hyrn let out a short laugh and said with a smile. "Alright but I don't think she is very strong at the moment."

Hyrn reached in and grasped the Stone. He brought her out still wrapped in the cloth. Hyrn unwrapped the Stone and held her in his hand.

Wren stepped closer and spoke hesitantly and almost reverently.

"Can I touch it?" he asked.

"Her," said Hyrn.

"Her. Can I touch her?" asked Wren.

"Yes," replied Hyrn.

Wren reached out and lay the tips of the fingers of his right hand on the Stone.

"She's warm," he said.

"Can I hold her?" he asked hopefully.

Hyrn hesitated. It felt right.

He shrugged and answered, "Alright, but don't drop her."

He gently placed Ilah in Wren's hand. The Anasarian boy had a look of ecstasy on his face.

"She is very warm and she's humming," he said.

Hyrn looked surprised at this.

"Humming?" he asked.

"Yes," said Wren with the Stone held before him.

Ilah began to glow. Softly at first and then brightening.

Ilah spoke. "I am home. Anasaria! You are still free, child. It gives me joy that you and others of my people have survived, but you have all suffered long enough. What you desire most will be realised if Anasaria can be free."

"What should I do?" asked Wren in a whisper as he stared at the Stone.

"That is easy," replied the Stone. "You were drawn to me for a purpose. Help Hyrn! Help him find Ivah! Help us free your people!"

The two Caramar had returned at speed to the crossroad.

"A mounted company of Ultamarians is coming towards us from the north," said Duburinga, catching his breath.

"They will have heard no news from the front and perhaps even suspect treachery," said Ferian.

"They will meet up with the group that may have the Stone," said Careil.

"That's the strange thing," said Boriega. "The ones we were tracking left the road and headed west towards the mountains."

"The mounted troops are an hour or so away," said Duburinga.

He turned to Yarga and said, "Elder we must remove the traces of this battle. We do not want the Ultamarian soldiers to discover more than they need to."

The young Elder was taken aback.

"Warrior," he said, "I of course trust your judgement in this. But we need to work out where the Stone has been taken and recapture it."

Harla approached from the roadside.

"There is no evidence of the Stone or any indication which group took the Stone," she said. "We are losing time and it will be getting dark soon. We will need to split up and pursue both parties. I suggest that we clear up quickly and then move into the forest for the night. We can work out who is to go which way and then be ready to move at dawn. The road is not safe. We will need to keep to the trees. The Ultamarians have already left the road but the Artorans still travel in the open. Both groups are carrying wounded so they will be slowed down. We must hope that they too stop for the night and that we can make up ground on them tomorrow."

At that moment, Hyrn and Wren appeared from the trees at the road's edge. They walked side by side, quiet but both with an intent look on their faces. As they approached, Wren walked towards Jarta-Den.

He said simply but forthrightly. "We have to help them!"

Jarta-Den studied the face of the young Anasarian. He had been looking after this boy for almost a year since his father had been imprisoned. Wren was young, but brave and determined, and true.

The Quigling looked at Yarga. "You have our trust and support," he said. "Desultamar!"

Jarta-Den looked startledly to his left where Wren and Hyrn both stood with their fists raised in the air and a look of defiance on their faces.

"We'll make them pay!" said the Quigling, roughly.

Duburinga and Jorunum crouched at the roadside each hidden behind low bushes that sprouted there away from the darkness under the trees. Jorunum signalled to Duburinga as he saw the outriders of the mounted soldiers come round the bend. Duburinga needed no signal, as the sound of horses' hooves and the clank of bridle, armour and weapons echoed down the roadway.

As the two watched on, a formation of what Duburinga estimated to be about sixty mounted soldiers came into view and approached the junction. When they reached it, the lead riders split up, half turned left and faced east where the road down from the Pass of Exile continued into the forest, while the rest halted with their horses facing south down towards where the Artorans had gone. The rest of the company thundered past, turning their horses west towards the Pass that led to the Underrealm. The riders standing guard at the southern and eastern roads then turned their horses and spurred them on to follow the rest of the company. As they passed the spot where the remains of the battle had taken place, one slowed for a moment and looked around with a puzzled expression.

The sun was now setting, and beyond the mountains where the soldiers headed, the sky was reddening. At the junction the light was fading and the signs of the battle that were left were difficult to discern. The rider stared out towards where the members of the quest had disappeared into the forest and then shook his head still looking puzzled. But he then faced west and spurred his horse on into a gallop to catch up with the rest of the Ultamarians. Duburinga and Jorunum exchanged glances and then melted back into the forest towards where the members of the quest were camped for the night, planning the next stage of the quest to free Anasaria.

The mounted Ultamarians stopped to get a brief report from the guards at the border post and then thundered off up the roadway towards the guard post at the top of the pass. When they reached the top of the pass, they received a sketchy report of what had happened. Captain Karklan had not returned. The Captain that led the soldiers, Evlan, called a halt for the night. In the morning, they would head to the frontier with the Underrealm to see how their army fared. The Lords of Ultamar were awaiting news from the front.

CHAPTER TWELVE

The Castle Herardin

Hyrn stood looking over to where Rowan was packing his gear and talking to Arienga. Rain had fallen during the night, sweeping up from the south and drenching Anasaria. The forest had afforded them some protection but they had stretched canvas sheets between the trees to try to keep dry. They had not lit a fire, and the damp and darkness and the weight of decision, had left the quest with a sense of foreboding. Water still dripped from the trees towering above them, but the rain had now stopped. Sunlight could be seen beginning to light the tops of the trees high above them but the forest where they stood was still gloomy.

There had been a brief but decisive discussion. The main point of argument had been Rowan and Hyrn. They had both been present while the debate took place and in the end had acceded to the opinion that one of them must be present in each party. The quest was to divide into the two groups which had formed after the encounter with Captain Karklan. The party accompanying Rowan was to include Biren-So. He and Kerian would lead this party south to follow the Artorans. The party with Hyrn would head north and would be joined by Jarta-Den and Wren.

Wren stood alongside Hyrn and was saying something as Hyrn stared at Rowan, contemplating the fact that he and his brother would be parting and heading in different directions, towards who knew what.

"Hyrn. Hyrn!"

Hyrn broke out of his reverie and looked at Wren.

"Sorry, what were you saying?" he asked.

"Stones!" said Wren with an exasperated tone. "Haven't you been listening to me at all?"

Hyrn looked apologetic and said, "Sorry," and then paused looking at Wren and asked, "Why did you say that?"

"Say what?" asked Wren, confused.

"You said 'Stones'," said Hyrn.

"Oh," responded Wren. "That's just something people say. It's kind of not supposed to be said like that. It's supposed to be something you say to give thanks for things or to ask for help. You know. To call on the Stones."

He looked at Hyrn and in a tone of reverence said, "And you have one of the Stones."

Wren shook his head softly and beamed and then continued. "But adults say it when they're angry or frustrated. I remember my Mother used to say it when I was small and getting into trouble."

He paused for a moment looking towards Hyrn but not directly at his face. His eyes became misty.

"Imagine if she could have known that I would see Ilah with my own eyes and even hold her in my hands," he said softly.

Hyrn rested his hand on Wren's shoulder.

"She probably would have told you to be careful not to drop Ilah or you might break her," he said.

Wren gave a short, hesitant laugh.

"Anyway, what were you saying?" asked Hyrn.

Wren paused and then said, "Oh. I was asking if you were going to be riding your horse."

"It's not my horse. It's Careil's," said Hyrn. "But I want to walk now. I've had enough of being trapped on the back of a horse for a while."

"Come on," continued Hyrn. "You'd better get packed up. I have to talk to Rowan."

Wren nodded and headed back to where they had slept. The awning they had slept beneath was now being folded to be packed on one of the charigas. Hyrn turned and walked across to where Rowan was now shouldering his pack. Arienga had gone to report to Duburinga.

Rowan turned towards him and Hyrn felt his throat catch. Hyrn walked up to Rowan and without thinking threw his arms around his brother. Hyrn's hand brushed the sheath that held the Sword of Acclimoss. It made him somehow feel that his brother was safe. Hyrn felt the Stone at his chest glow with warmth. It was going to be alright.

Hyrn let go of Rowan, but Rowan grasped him by the shoulders.

"Don't get in to any trouble," he said.

"Me?" said Hyrn indignantly. "I'm not the one who nearly fell off a cliff?"

Rowan released his grasp and looked at his younger brother defiantly and countered. "Yes, but who got captured by Cave Drargs?"

Hyrn smirked.

"Take care, Row," he said, and he punched Rowan half-heartedly on the arm.

Rowan looked like he was preparing to retaliate but instead leaned down and embraced Hyrn.

"I owe you one," he said, "and I'll make sure to give it to you when we're back together. Go on now. Hopefully we'll find the other Stone soon and then…" he trailed off. "I'm not really sure what happens then."

"I'm sure that once the Stones are together we'll know what to do," said Hyrn.

He turned his head and looked at the others. "I think we're moving out now. I'll see you soon Rowan," he said.

"See you little brother," said Rowan.

Hyrn felt like he should object to being called 'little' but didn't have the heart. Instead he walked off and headed over to where Careil and Yarga were waiting, with a weight in his chest that wasn't caused by Ilah.

There had been no further sign of the mounted soldiers. The group led by Kerian and Biren-So had headed south through the forest eager to make up as much time on the Artorans as they could. Bregal and Gorum had ridden ahead to scout southward along the road while Duburinga and Arienga scouted the roadside ahead of them. Rowan had been allowed to ride the horse that had belonged to the Ultamarian soldier. He called the horse Arrow, in reference to the fate of his last rider. Hyrn watched as they disappeared into the forest. Rowan gave him a wave and then was hidden from view behind the trees.

Hyrn sighed and then shouldered his pack, and the group led by Ferian and Jarta-Den headed towards the forest's edge. They reached the road and then travelled quickly along it until they passed the ridge of hills that Duburinga and Boriega had climbed the previous day. Once they were past the ridge, they left the road and moved into the forest on the western side of the road. They made their way northeast moving away from the flanks of the tall peak of Mount Kelendor that dominated the western ranges, heading towards the mountains to the east that formed a wall dividing Anasaria from the open country to the north.

The party of Ultamarians had left the road further north, but Ferian advised that they should get off the road as quickly as possible in case any more patrols were about. The General told them that the Ultamarians were probably heading for the old road that skirted the mountains. The road was not used any more this far west, but they would have to cross the valley that lay between the western and eastern parts of the Anasarian mountains.

There was an Ultamarian outpost guarding the pass between Anasaria and the northern plains. Beyond, the road led to Ultamar and Ultamarian patrols. These mountains were also inhabited by Drargs so they would need to be vigilant.

The ground steadily rose as they travelled, and some of the terrain was difficult; heavily forested and broken by rocky outcrops and sheer cliffs. It was thought that the direction they were heading in should cross the path of the Ultamarians. After a few hours of steady going Careil and Droom rode back to report that they had found evidence that the Ultamarians had come through ahead of them, heading directly north. The rest of the party were soon led to where the trail could be seen trampled through the undergrowth. They then changed direction following the path of the Ultamarians, determined now that they were finally in direct pursuit of the enemy.

Hyrn walked beside Wren. Just behind him strode Garan; ever vigilant, ensuring that the holder of the Stone was not in any danger. Hyrn had been telling Wren about their journey and the events that had taken place. Wren was particularly enthralled by the story of the battle in the valley and the freeing of the Abessairians.

Wren spoke to Garan. "Whereabouts did you come from, before you were an Ultamarian?" he asked.

"The Quigling was right," said Garan gruffly. "You do ask a lot of questions?"

The Abessairian soldier thought for a moment as if it was difficult to remember and then answered. "It was a long time ago but I was from a small village out on the southern plains near the Trebian River. My people were farmers but I always wanted to join the army."

"My family are farmers," piped up Hyrn. "I always thought it was dull and often hard work. I think it would be nice right now to be back on the farm, even if I had lots of chores to do. It seems so far away now, like another lifetime."

"I'd like to see your farm," said Wren.

"Hopefully one day you can," Hyrn answered.

Just then Harla and Margana came into view ahead and rushed up to where Yarga walked beside General Ferian.

Harla spoke urgently. "There are Drargs ahead. They have picked up the trail of the Ultamarians and are following them."

"How many?" asked Ferian.

"About a dozen," answered Harla.

"They must not be allowed to meet up with the Ultamarians," said Jarta-Den. "I propose that we send people ahead to hunt the Drargs down."

The Ultamarian troop led by Captain Evlan had ridden down the pass and had swiftly crossed the plain that led up towards the hills that surrounded the valley of the Underdwellers. As they rode through the foothills, the Captain felt an air of danger and signalled his soldiers to halt. He felt that they were being watched. He scanned the hillsides but could see no signs of movement. As they continued on, the sense of foreboding grew. There seemed to be almost a wind creeping alongside them, sweeping through the forested slopes on either side.

They finally came to the pass that led down into the valley. Something was not right. There was normally the raucous noise of an army encampment. There was just silence except for the sound of the wind. They continued on down the valley cautiously. Evlan began to notice that there were seemingly burnt bodies of Drargs scattered about. He halted and surveyed the scene. He then began to be worried. But before he or his soldiers could react, Rangers, Caramar and Abessairians swept down out of the hills on either side and from behind them. Looking at the grim faces of the enemy surrounding him, Evlan drew his sword and, brandishing it, spurred his horse into the fray.

The large Drarg loped behind his pack. The smell of the soldiers was strong on the ground; blood and gore and corruption. He could also smell the scent of his pack ahead of him, drawing him on. They were hunting and he felt the lust of pursuit in his chest and thoughts of ripping and tearing burned in his mind. A slight noise from beside him caught his attention but before he had a chance to react he was wrenched violently into the bushes at the side of the trail.

One of the Drargs just ahead looked back towards his companion and, not seeing him, slowed to investigate, and was suddenly lifted through the air and thrown to the ground with a knife being driven through his throat. By the time the fifth Drarg had disappeared, the largest of them, who led the pack doggedly along the trail, sensed something in the air. He halted and looked around noticing that some of the pack were missing. An arrow pierced his neck and as he fell he saw his pack falling around him sprouting arrows, and figures appearing from the bushes and finishing off the rest.

By the time Hyrn and the rest of the party arrived at the scene of the ambush, the bodies of the Drargs had been cleared from the path. Jarta-Den stood on the path to meet them, wiping his hands with some leaves.

"We may now have attracted some unwanted attention," he said blithely. "We may now become the hunted."

"The Ultamarians should reach the road soon," said General Ferian. "We will have to travel more openly if we are to follow. The road above hugs the side of the mountains in places; cliffs above and cliffs below. The road is the only way through. If we are to be hunted, they cannot come upon us unawares. We'll know they are coming, but we will have nowhere to hide."

"They may wish they had decided to stay away," said Harla, appearing from the bushes beside the trail.

"Let's just hope that there are not too many of them," grumbled Jarta-Den.

"Ilah will protect us," piped up Wren.

Hyrn looked at the young Anasarian.

"I'm not sure if Ilah is ready for that," he said.

The road emerged abruptly from between the trees. The sun was disappearing as it started to sink behind the mountains. The road looked desolate. It ran alongside a great cliff face and then disappeared around a bend further ahead. The forested hillside they had climbed followed the roadway to the right and then fell away where the bend in the road lay. The roadway was broken and littered with fallen rocks. Weeds grew in places where the road was cracked. Gebarana and Turum sprinted back from around the bend up ahead.

Turum arrived first and spoke. "The road is clear ahead, The Ultamarians are not in sight. The road follows more bends and we cannot see much further ahead."

Gebarana joined in. "There is a dead Ultamarian ahead. They have abandoned him and continued on. The body is covered in burns and oozes the glowing liquid that we have seen. The Artorans used dark power upon him."

Yarga spoke up with a tone of warning. "None must touch the body! The power of evil will still lurk in the flesh. Any who comes in contact may absorb that power. If the others of their party are also afflicted they may be driven to greater evil."

Careil looked at Yarga. "How do you know?" he asked.

"I'm not sure," said the Elder. "It is as if it comes from the Sagenstone."

Yarga unconsciously reached for the crystal at his chest, and added. "You must trust me on this."

The body was scarred and blackened. Hyrn looked quickly away. He could feel the wrongness emanating from the corpse. Wren beside him had a look of hatred on his face. He moved a few paces closer, and only after a hissed warning from Hyrn did he fall back in step. The party moved past and then left the grisly sight behind them.

The road looked ancient. It was well built of the black stone of the mountains, but it had long been left to deteriorate and fall into disrepair. In places, they could see the forests of Anasaria stretching out to the east and beyond to where, like a threat, loomed the fortress of Ultamar, standing massive and dark atop its plateau. In other places the forest came up to the roadside hemming them in against the steep side of the mountains. Occasionally the road would plunge into chasms bored into the mountainside so that the party were travelling through gorges. Everywhere there were signs of once great stoneworks; buildings, walls and towers all built of the same black stone, now abandoned and decaying.

"Who built all this?" asked Hyrn a little too loudly. His voice echoing down along the gorge they were following as the light began to fade towards a gloomy sunset.

"These are the remains of the old kingdom," said Ferian. "They were built by the Anasarians when they first settled this land and built Abessair. They moved west as part of the Great Migrations that followed the onslaught of Evil. Some went further to the Underrealm and beyond but King Abess established his realm here and began building the the fortress that became Abessair. He created a haven for peoples seeking refuge from war and hatred. After Abess's death the work was carried on by his son, King Eriallen. They built defences against the Drargs and patrolled them, keeping Anasaria as a bastion of good in the west. The Angilanians sent an envoy and gave the Twin Stones to the King. It was then that the ancient sword of Abess was remade and became the Sword of Acclimoss. That was the height of this kingdom. It was not long, though, before the Anasarians found they were under attack from the Sorcerers of Artora. It took many years to defeat the Artorans before Eriallen and the army of Abessair finally drove them from this land."

The tall General looked around wistfully and continued, "When Prince Darion fled with Ilah the kingdom declined. These defences were abandoned and only the mountain pass was left garrisoned. The castle at the pass, Castle Herardin, is a dark and dangerous place now. It is where we stationed the worst of our soldiers…" he paused, "'their' soldiers," he corrected himself.

"I'm not sure whether the Ultamarians we are pursuing will want to make themselves known to the garrison. Bardan has not been amongst the dead. I think the Captain may have his own ends in mind."

The bulk of the mountains began to veer away from the left of the road, and the terrain began to open out to the north. Forest grew on either side of the road as it continued on eastwards towards the Bridge. The bridge crossed the valley that led up to the pass that separated the western and eastern parts of the mountains. A castle guarded the bridge and the road beneath. That road ran down from the head of the pass towards Anasaria, following the river that fell down the mountainside into the Evelar Forest. The river, the Trian, flowed southward through the forest and met up with the Tregon River deep in the forest below. The road leading from the pass continued downward as far as the main road and joined it near where it crossed the Trian.

As they travelled east the road they were on began to slope downwards. At one point the trees thinned and they could see some distance ahead to where the road continued down through a heavily forested area and onwards to where a dark shape could be seen, ominous in the gathering dusk, guarding the bridge across the pass; the Castle Herardin.

"Perhaps we should stop soon and make camp for the night," suggested Careil.

Ferian stood looking towards the distant castle.

"I think we will need to use the cover of darkness to get past the castle," he said. "It will be almost impossible to avoid being seen in daylight. The guards at the pass are ever vigilant. I just wonder whether our quarry have already braved the pass."

They continued on down the road. Night had fallen and a blanket of high cloud now covered the sky. A growing feeling of dread came upon them as they approached closer to Herardin. Already weary from the day's travel it seemed as if the weight of the castle bore down upon them as they drew nearer.

Gebarana and Turum appeared from ahead where they, Harla, and Jarta-Den were following the trail.

Turum addressed Ferian and Yarga where they had stopped just ahead of Hyrn and the rest of the party.

"We cannot tell where the Ultamarians have gone," said the Ranger. "There were many tracks as we neared the castle. The road here is patrolled heavily and their trail is confused. The moon will rise soon and we may be able to pick up the trail but it will also help the eyes of the guards."

Just then from behind them back up the road a snarling, blood-chilling howl split the air.

"Drargs!" said Droom. "They have picked up our trail."

"We have to get off the road," said Ferian quickly. "We don't want to get caught between the castle and a pack of Drargs. If, as you say, the trail is confused maybe we can use it to our advantage. Let's move. Careil and Droom if you ride ahead and warn Harla and Jarta-Den, we can meet up with them and leave the road where the paths lead down to the lower stories of the castle beneath the bridge."

They dashed down the road with Droom and Careil galloping ahead. Wren and Hyrn rode one of the two horses captured from the Ultamarians. With Garan riding the other beside them they cantered ahead of the rest of the group. Wren gripped tightly to Hyrn with a pale terrified look on his face.

"Don't worry, boy," said Garan reassuringly. "We will protect you."

"I'm not worried about the Ultamarians or the Drargs," said Wren, "but do I have to ride on this horse? It's dangerous."

Hyrn, who had ridden horses since before he could walk, laughed.

"It's alright Wren," he said reassuringly. "You're safer up here. She's a good strong horse. She won't let you fall." And then to distract the Anasarian, added, "What shall we call her?"

"I-I don't know," said Wren hesitantly.

He was silent for a moment and then said in a soft voice, "Can we call her, Merralyn?"

"Why Merralyn?" asked Hyrn.

"Merralyn was my mother's name," said Wren.

"Merralyn it is," said Hyrn reaching forward and patting the horse's neck. "Come on Merralyn. Let's catch up to Careil and the others."

He urged the horse forward and she broke into a gallop. Beside them Garan's horse kept pace and they raced down the roadway towards the castle.

As the last of the party left the road, far to the east, a gibbous moon, its light suffused by the cloud cover, rose above the dark ominous shape of the fortress of Ultamar. Apart from the light of the moon, all was dark. The hillside they now picked their way down was steep and rocky with stunted trees growing in places. At the bottom of the hillside, a small gully ran parallel to the road down towards the river. They could see no trace of the Ultamarians. They had not come this way. Ahead, looming above them, was the dark mass of the evil Herardin. Its sheer stone walls rose high above the bridge it crouched over, and then thrust down to the bottom of the river valley. Strange sounds could be heard from the castle. Raucous laughter and shouting, and screams and anguished cries.

"What are those noises?" asked Hyrn in almost a whisper to Garan.

"The Ultamarians enjoying themselves," said Garan, darkly. "They have prisoners here. This place is renowned as a place of torture and torment."

Hyrn shuddered with the thought, as they continued downwards.

At the end of the gully was a wide open space that led down to the roadway that ran alongside the river as it grumbled and crashed down its narrow course. Both the road and the river emerged from a large stone archway at the base of the castle. The party halted behind a group of boulders that sat where the left slope of the gully ended.

"There will be guards posted at the other side of the arch guarding the pass." whispered Ferian. "We need to work out a way to get across the river. It is narrow here but deep and treacherous. There will also be guards up on the bridge at either side of the castle."

Just then they noticed a low moaning noise coming from somewhere in the direction of the castle.

"What is that?" said Careil.

"It sounds like someone in pain," said Yarga with a hint of fear and anguish in his voice.

Harla signalled to Gebarana.

"We will investigate," she said.

Before anyone could reply, the two crept out from behind the boulders and disappeared down the slope quickly blending in with their surroundings. The two Caramar warriors approached the castle walls towards where the moans came from. As they drew near they could just make out in the dim light, a figure hanging on the castle wall, high above the ground. It was difficult to see who the figure was but they appeared to be hanging by their wrists. Harla signalled to Gebarana that he was to stay below while she climbed up. She removed her bow and quiver and the short sword at her waist and rested them on the ground.

The walls were made up of blocks of stone roughly hewn, allowing the Caramar to grasp and carefully make her way up the wall. As Harla climbed she glanced up and could see that the figure appeared to be an old man dressed in a tattered hessian robe.

The man continued to moan but Harla called up to him. "Quiet. Help is at hand."

The man's voice came as a defiant snarl. "I will not tell you anything. The Stones will come. You will pay. Take my life. I, I…" his voice broke and the man began to sob.

Harla by now had come up close to the man.

She said simply, "Desultamar."

The man's sobs became louder and almost hysterical. Harla, still gripping the wall with her right hand, reached out her left arm and gently placed her hand over the man's mouth.

She said quietly, "Hush. We are here to help. I am Harla, of the Caramar. Who are you?"

The man had quietened down now but looked at Harla with confusion and suspicion.

He stared into her eyes and said, "Neferelon, of the Order of the Stones."

"Neferelon, we are here to help you. I must unbind you," said Harla, softly.

"I will fall!" said Neferelon a little too loudly and then softly. "I will fall."

Harla looked up. The man was suspended by his wrists by a long rope that stretched far above, running through rings that held the rope vertical and close to the wall. She looked down towards where Gebarana waited. She was about to signal her fellow warrior to climb up, but his face appeared out of the darkness, lit by the pale moonlight.

"Gebarana, hold the rope above the next ring," said Harla in a low whisper, pointing upwards. "You will have to take the weight of Neferelon here when I cut the rope."

She turned her head to the old man. "Neferelon if you can try to hold on to the wall when I cut the rope it will make Gebarana's job easier."

"What are you going to do," said Neferelon with fear in his voice.

"We are going to get you down safely," said Gebarana with a knowing look at Harla.

The two Caramar climbed upwards from their positions on either side of the old man. The warriors, protectors of the Caramarhc, born to the stone of their mountain home and highly trained, were in their element on the stone wall. They reached the first ring and Gebarana stopped and grasped the ring with his right hand, his left hand and his feet securely holding to the stonework. Harla continued upwards, using the next two rings as hand-holds as she went, but avoiding using the rope, unwilling to test its weight-bearing capacity until it was absolutely necessary. She reached a stretch of rope above the third ring and released her grip with her right hand and drew a knife from a sheath at her waist.

Harla called a muted whistle down the wall. She placed the knife against the rope and felt the tension go out of it. She drew her razor sharp knife rapidly back and forward three times and the rope severed. She inwardly tensed as the bottom half of the rope dropped and fell down the wall.

When Gebarana heard Harla's signal he started straining holding the ring with his left hand and taking the weight on the rope above the ring with his right, his foot holds firmly planted.

"Hold on," he said to Neferelon, below him.

He noticed that weight lessen as Neferelon strained to hold on. Suddenly he felt the full strain as the rope above was severed. He waited momentarily. He strained as he waited, as the weight of the rope added to his burden and then, as the severed end of the rope fell around him, he released his grip on the ring and thrust that hand upwards, twisting it around and grasping the rope. Simultaneously, he used all the force in his legs to throw himself sideways and as he did he momentarily released the grip of his other hand and spun it around and grabbed the rope again. The rope fell towards the ring as Neferelon's weight pulled it down but it was arrested by Gebarana's sideways momentum and, as the Caramar began to fall, the weight of his body halted the rope's progress.

Gebarana now hung suspended just above the old man, swinging back and forth. The ring above them creaked ominously. Neferelon mewled softly with pain as the jolt on the rope cut into his already bloody wrists. Gebarana began to move hand over hand quickly down the rope. Above him Harla scrambled down the stonework. Gebarana moved down the rope as quickly as possible but the swarthy warrior's body was heavier than the old man's and Neferelon began to be pulled up towards the ring. Gebarana began to let the rope glide slowly through his hands as he slid downwards. As he did, Neferelon was gently lowered to the ground. Gebarana allowed the braking on the rope to equalise their descent and as his feet hit the ground he released the rope and caught the old man before he collapsed. Harla arrived on the ground simultaneously and helped Gebarana hold Neferelon upright.

As the two Caramar supported the old man and started to slowly walk up the slope towards the gully a great commotion erupted from the bridge high above them. Harla and Gebarana both looked in that direction and as they did Ferian, Jarta-Den, Turum and Margana rushed up to them and began to pass them towards the road where it passed under the darkened arch.

"The Drargs have arrived at the castle. We must take out the lower guards," said Ferian quickly as they passed. "The others will follow with the horses."

Harla and Gebarana halted and the rest of the party came down the path.

Garan quickly explained, "There is a small bridge across the river further up the pass. It is our only chance."

The four Ultamarian guards stood at their posts, two on either side of the river. They were bored and just waiting for the hours to pass until they were relieved. The sudden clamour from above brought them to attention. Something was going on and they were eager to be a part but their duty was to hold their position. They waited alert. One of the guards on the eastern side of the river heard a noise. He turned his head and as he did a sword was driven through his side.

He let out a, "Humph."

The Ultamarian near him turned, and faced someone he knew; a General. He looked confused, and said, "General Ferian?"

But before he had a chance to continue, the large General smashed a fist into his face.

On the opposite side of the river the two guards fell to the ground, as Turum and Margana released a quick succession of arrows. From behind them they heard the rest of the party approaching. Hyrn and Wren were now on foot. Slumped on the back of Merralyn was Neferelon.

"The General and Jarta-Den vaulted the river," said Turum as the others approached. "They will meet us at the other side of the bridge. We must hurry."

The bridge was a small stone path that arched over the narrow river gorge. They crossed in single file. Droom and Careil were further behind watching for any signs of pursuit. Once the others had crossed Droom rode onto the bridge followed by Careil. Careil looked back and just down the roadway where the black castle stood he saw figures emerging from the doorway alongside the guard post. The bodies of the guards had been dumped in the river, but the Ultamarians were immediately aware that the guards were no longer at their posts. From their midst a brazen horn was sounded. Careil quickly crossed the bridge and joined the others who had assembled on the path that led up the other side of the valley to the old road.

Jarta-Den and Ferian came into view from down the pass. Ferian carried a large burden on his shoulder. As he approached Careil could see that it was the body of an Ultamarian. Jarta-Den was arguing with the General.

"Why didn't you just kill him?" asked the Quigling.

"We need information," said the General gruffly.

"Well don't expect me to carry him," said Jarta-Den fiercely.

Ferian ignored him and spoke to Garan who led his horse alongside Hyrn and Wren. "Garan, bind this man and tie him to the horse," he said. "Then take the two boys and keep them safe."

The General turned to Careil, Harla and Droom and said hastily. "The old man and the Elder must also be guarded. The rest of us must hold off the Ultamarians while the others get to safety."

"Where will they go?" asked Careil.

"I suggest up the pass and into the hills," said Ferian "We cannot go back to the road. There is nowhere to hide there."

Careil, Margana and Garan escorted Hyrn, Wren and Yarga up the valley away from the castle. Hyrn and Wren now rode Erras while Careil led the newly named Merralyn carrying Neferelon. Garan led the other horse with the unconscious body of the Ultamarian guard draped over the saddle. Margana trailed behind keeping watch to the rear. Behind them the sound of fighting began as the Ultamarians attacked. From amongst the tumult the howls of Drargs could be heard. It filled Hyrn with dread but he just kept coaxing Erras forward.

The great horse seemed to be confused about leaving battle behind but Careil said softly., "Retreat now, Erras."

The walls of the mountain pass were steep and heavily forested and they could see no easy way up the hillside. The pass began to bend around to the east and after a while they were out of sight of the castle.

Careil addressed Garan, "There does not seem any easy way up this hillside."

Neferelon stirred on the back of Merralyn. He looked around him, dazedly taking in his surroundings."What is happening?" he asked with fear in his voice. "Where are you taking me?"

Yarga turned from where he walked just behind Erras.

"Peace," he said. "We are people of the Stones."

Harla had reported to Yarga what the old man had said. Yarga dropped back until he was level with the old man. He pulled from beneath his robes the crystal from the Sagenstone.

"I am Yarga, Elder of the Caramar," he said."I follow the wisdom of the Sagenstone."

"How is this possible?" asked Neferelon, eyeing the Stone as it glowed softly in Yarga's hand.

Yarga studied the old man and then, making up his mind, said, "We carry, Ilah. The Stone of Angil has returned to Anasaria."

The old man broke into sobs. "This is just another torment of Ultamar," he said in an anguished voice.

"No," said Yarga firmly. "The young boy ahead, Hyrn, is the child of prophecy. He carries Ilah. Devarnia of the Keepers retrieved the Stone from the ruins of Darion's realm in the west of the Caramarhc ranges. We are pursuing a group of Ultamarians who may have the other Stone, Ivah."

"This is all too much," said Neferelon, tearily.

"If we can find somewhere safe, we will tell you all," said Yarga.

Neferelon looked at Yarga with a pained expression and then said finally. "I know of a place where you will be safe. They do not know of it. There is a path up into the mountains not far from here. I will lead you. I have almost given up on hope. I have questioned my faith. But I will choose hope. I place myself in your hands."

At that moment, from behind them, a high clear note of a war horn sounded; not the harsh horn of the Ultamarians. As they escaped further up the pass, the sound lifted their hearts.

They battled grimly. They still held the bridge. The narrowness of the span meant that the attackers could only come across in ones and twos, to be easily picked off. Ferian and Jarta-Den had barred the door at the base of the castle on the eastern side of the river but it would not hold for long. Some of the Ultamarians and Drargs had leapt across the river. Droom and Gebarana skirted the river taking care of those that crossed; some falling with arrows piercing their bodies before they were able to reach the other side.

At the bridge, the bulk of General Ferian blocked the eastern end. His great sword hacked at any Ultamarian or Drarg that came near. Harla, Jarta-Den and Turum stood beside the General, loosing arrows. Suddenly a black arrow pierced Ferian's shoulder just beside his breastplate. He grimaced in pain but kept fighting. Blood began to show on the sleeve of his tunic. The throng of attackers now pushed across the bridge as the General began to weaken. The attack was relentless and more dark figures were coming up the pass towards the bridge. The defenders were tiring. They couldn't hold out much longer.

Then, a horn sounded from down the roadway beyond the castle. The sound of many horses could be heard galloping up the pass towards them. Some of the attackers turned back to confront whomever came up the pass. From underneath the dark archway a group of riders came two abreast and, as they rode through, those holding the bridge saw that there were many of them. The newcomers attacked the Drargs and Ultamarians relentlessly. Some turned to defend against any that came from the castle, while the others poured up the roadway crashing into the evil throng.

The Ultamarians fought grimly, but the Drargs suddenly turned and fled westwards into the hills that met the western end of the Bridge of Herardin. The dominant Drarg felt the desire to stay and kill all the enemies but he felt that pull again, stronger now. There was a painful power nearby that needed to be destroyed but something else dragged his will away. He and all his kind were being called to somewhere faraway by one who would dominate all, and the promise of boundless slaughter was irresistible.

Jarta-Den eased past Ferian and with his sword scything through the air took over the defence of the Bridge. The General stumbled back and Harla helped him to the ground. She then brought up her bow but, realising her quiver was empty, shouldered it and drew her short sword. Turum sprinted down the river to where his Captain and Gebarana were still beset by the Ultamarians on the eastern bank.

By now the riders had decimated the Ultamarians and were approaching those that were attempting to cross the bridge. After a short skirmish Jarta-Den and Harla had taken care of the few Ultamarians left on the bridge, The bodies of the attackers littered the ground or else had fallen into the swift flowing river and been swept downstream.

The lead rider stopped at the western end of the bridge and Jarta-Den, smiling broadly despite his exhaustion, said fiercely, "Desultamar!"

"Desultamar, Jarta-Den," said the rider.

"Coora-Jen," said Jarta-Den. "Your timing is perfect. How do you and your squad happen to be here?"

"We have an encampment downriver," said the rider. "Our scouts reported the sounds of Drargs on the hunt and we thought there may be someone in trouble. As we neared Herardin we heard an Ultamarian war horn and rode hard to see what was going on. There are more of our fighters on the way on foot."

Just then General Ferian rose to his feet clumsily.

Coora-Jen cried out, "Behind you!" as he raised his bow.

Jarta-Den looked around and then quickly back at the rider.

"No!" he shouted.

"It's an Ultamarian," said Coora-Jen. "General Ferian," he hissed.

"He's on our side," said Jarta-Den, quickly.

General Ferian walked unsteadily towards the bridge but Harla stepped in his way.

"I don't think it wise to attempt the bridge," said the Caramar. "We need to tend your wound."

The mounted Quigling shook his head. "I think I need an explanation," he said. "But first we must secure the castle. There must be more Ultamarians still inside."

"And prisoners too, I warrant," said Jarta-Den.

Coora-Jen called to the riders behind him. "Some of you cross here and ride up to the main road. The rest go back up to the western gate and secure that entrance. I want no Ultamarians to escape to send word to Ultamar."

He turned to Jarta-Den. "It was useful of you to draw so many of their troops out of the castle," he said.

Jarta-Den frowned but then smiled. "Glad we could help," he said.

Jarta-Den's expression then became stern. He fixed Coora-Jen's gaze.

"We are pursuing a party of Ultamarians. I will tell you about our purpose once we have dealt with those Ultamarians at the castle. I don't think we need to worry about the Drargs at the moment."

Coora-Jen called to the riders that were crossing the narrow bridge in single file. "Look for any signs of…?"

He turned to Jarta-Den.

"How many?" he asked.

"I would estimate about eight to ten, some wounded," said the other Quigling.

"About ten Ultamarians that may have passed through," called Coora-Jen to his comrades. "Look for any signs of a party that size and any blood trails."

The five riders that were filing across the bridge all raised their left arms in unison and then, as they reached the other side, each in turn spurred their horses forward.

After the riders had crossed the bridge Harla started to cross to where Jarta-Den stood beside the mounted Coora-Jen. Droom rode up the pass with Turum and Gebarana trailing behind. Harla turned and saw that Gebarana nursed a bloody wound on his forearm. She continued across and spoke to the two Quiglings.

"My duty lies with the Elder Yarga and the Stonebearer," she said. "We must catch up with them and then decide our next move. Ferian cannot travel and I must see how badly wounded my fellow warrior, Gebarana, is. I ask that you care for Ferian. Remember he is an Abessairian and crucial to our cause."

"Jarta-Den," she said, turning to the Quigling. "You must look for signs of those Ultamarians we pursue. We will seek to meet you on the road as soon as we can recover Hyrn and the others."

Harla, Turum, and Gebarana, now with his arm swathed in a quickly applied bandage, made their way up the pass, following the trail of the main party. The night was getting deeper as they followed the trail of Hyrn, Wren, Careil, Yarga, Garan, the old man, Neferelon, and an unconscious Ultamarian, the clearly defined tracks of three horses intermingled with the footprints of those on foot. Before long the trail led into rocky ground where traces disappeared into the darkness, difficult to follow, except to trained trackers like two Caramar warriors and a Ranger of the Underdwellers. They followed the signs up into a copse of trees that sat at the base of a glen that led up towards the mountains. As they passed under the trees, even the light of the moon deserted them, and the three came to a halt.

"We cannot go any further tonight without possibly losing their path," said

Turum.

"I agree," said Harla. "Let's get some sleep and wait for daybreak."

And as the moon moved towards the west the three lay amongst the leaf litter beneath the trees and slept.

They had travelled up a very circuitous path. At times the hillside broke into tree-covered ridges and between each of these were narrow gullys. Each gully they passed through took them further up the hill. They entered into one final gully that seemed to lead nowhere. Neferelon led them towards a stone cliff-face dimly lit by the shrouded moon. At the base of the cliff was a tall stone boulder.

Neferelon atop Merralyn spoke. "Help me down from here."

Careil approached the old man mounted on the mare. He reached up and grasped the old man and helped him from the saddle. Careil steadied Neferelon as the old man swayed. Neferelon straightened up and moved towards the large boulder with Careil supporting him as he walked. Hyrn and the others moved up behind Neferelon. Garan led the horse carrying the still unconcious Ultamarian.

Neferelon turned to Garan and lucidly and clearly said, "Blindfold him."

"He's still out," said Garan.

"Ultamar must not know our secrets," said Neferelon levelly.

Garan pulled a knife from his belt and moving alongside the horse's flank cut a strip of the edge of the saddle-blanket. He turned towards the head of the Ultamarian, prostrate across the saddle, and tightly tied the strip around his eyes, tying it off at the back of his head.

"Prisoner secure," said Garan formally.

The old man placed his hand upon the rock and began to mutter quietly. The skin at his wrist was bloody and raw. He stopped and waited peering up at the sheer rock above them. He placed his hand on the rock again and started his low mutter again.

Hyrn stood just behind Neferelon and watched as the old man performed his ritual.

A voice in Hyrn's head said. "Help him. Place your hand on the rock."

Hyrn moved forward. He stretched out his right hand and laid his hand on the rock. Words flowed into his head and without knowing why or what he was saying, Hyrn began speaking strange words in a low voice. As he continued the old man's chanting became stronger. And a grinding, rasping noise came from the base of the boulder. Slowly the stone began to move aside and, as it did, revealed behind it was a natural stone archway that led into darkness.

Neferelon raised himself up as the rock slid aside. He grasped Hyrn's shoulder and looked upon his face. Hyrn saw that the old man's eyes were brimming with tears but he felt that a sense of wisdom lay beyond the tears.

"I truly believe you carry the Stone," said Neferelon. "Do not reveal it here. Follow me."

Neferelon then strode forward resolutely and the others followed. The old man disappeared into the dark archway. Hyrn walked just behind him and, as he entered, the moonlight lit just the entrance, and then all beyond was pitch black.

"Run your hand along one of the walls as you go," said Neferelon from futher ahead. "The floor is quite level."

Careil had entered behind Hyrn leading Erras. The horse's head just cleared the roof.

"Shouldn't we strike a light?" asked the Rider.

"No light," said Neferelon from deeper in the tunnel. "Not much further."

Hyrn walked with his hand on the right hand wall. He could hear the others following behind, stumbling and bumping into each other. The tunnel swung around sharply to the right and Hyrn's hand lost contact with the wall. He blindly groped until he felt the wall again. A little further on he nearly walked into the wall as the tunnel turned sharply to the left and then he felt the wall straighten up. Then the darkness was broken by a slight glow all around him. The light grew brighter and as his eyes adjusted Hyrn saw that Neferelon stood with his hand against the wall. Ahead a doorway had opened at the end of a short tunnel revealing a brightly lit cavern. Neferelon beckoned for them to follow and strode ahead.

As Hyrn passed through the doorway he saw that there was a large room roughly furnished. Braziers in the walls gave off light. A large chair faced towards a fire burning in a hearth. A great stone chimney in the rockface drew the smoke of the fire upwards. As Neferelon walked into the chamber, Hyrn was startled when from behind the chair a figure, also robed, rose to her feet. The young woman looked shocked to see them. She looked at the old man.

"Neferelon what is the meaning of this?" she demanded, and then added. "We thought you were dead."

"Infiron, listen," said Neferelon a little sheepishly. "These people freed me. I have been held prisoner in Herardin for weeks. They are people of the Stones."

"How do you know?" said the woman fiercely. "Why did you bring them here? How do you know that they are not spies for the Ultamarians?"

The woman barely caught her breath, but Neferelon spoke as soon as he had a chance.

"They carry Stones with them," he said desperately. "They do not seem evil."

"That is what spies would be like and you have led them to one of our most secret places." the woman growled.

Hyrn stepped forward and faced the woman.

"Please," he said. "I am Hyrn from Wesmere. I have been sent to unite the Stones of Angil and help free Anasaria."

"Ha!" said the woman. "The Stones have been lost for centuries. How do you hope to find them?"

Hyrn reached into his vest and pulled out Ilah. He unwrapped the Stone and held her out for the woman to see.

"This is Ilah," said Hyrn simply.

The Stone in his hand began to glow and then spoke. "The child speaks truly, Infiron. I am Ilah from the Angilanian Mountains, the twin of my brother, Ivah."

Infiron stood with her mouth agape and then dropped to her knees. Beside Hyrn, Neferelon stood with the light of Ilah illuminating his face, his eyes wide with wonder and awe.

The old Priest spoke. "We are here, Infiron, at the time we have prepared for, for generations. The time of the Stones."

"It can't be. It can't be," said Infiron, still kneeling, her eyes shining.

Careil stepped forward. He had left Erras with the other two horses in the tunnel with Margana. Yarga, Garan and Wren stood behind him.

"Who are you?" asked the Rider. "And what is this place?"

The young woman rose to her feet and wiped her eyes.

"I am Infiron," she said, "and you have met Neferelon. We are Priests of the Order of the Stones. We have kept the faith and prepared for the return of the Twin Stones. This place is one of our sanctuaries. It was named Detrasarn long ago. It was once part of a network of hidden bastions that the Abessairians built as defences against the Drarg hordes."

Garan moved from behind Careil and the woman blanched.

"An Ultamarian," she squeaked.

"I am Garan, of the army of Abessair," said the soldier. "I was freed by the Stone. We are all tired and hungry, and Neferelon here is wounded. Can we talk later?"

Infiron gaped at him and then, gathering herself, said, "Of course. Neferelon, come and sit. I will fetch others."

She turned and walked towards a stone archway. As she did, Margana entered hurriedly from behind them.

"He's waking up," said the Caramar.

Garan looked at her and turned quickly and followed her back out into the tunnel. On the back of the horse the Ultamarian was beginning to struggle with his bonds. They had been quickly tied and were in danger of coming loose. Garan strode up and began fastening the ropes more tightly. He made sure that the cloth was still secure across the prisoner's eyes. He then lifted him off the horse and lay him on the ground.

"I hope the General knows what he's doing," he said. "This man could prove dangerous."

Infiron returned with three more of the Order. One of them carefully carried a bowl of water. He knelt before Neferelon, now seated in the chair facing the fire. From within his robes he produced a small bottle. The bottle gave off a soft glow. He opened it and poured a little of its contents into the bowl. He recapped the bottle and placed it back inside his robes. He dipped a white cloth in the water and then gently taking one of Neferelon's hands he began to clean the wounds on the old man's wrists.

Infiron introduced the new arrivals.

"These are Gerton and Mergon," she said, gesturing to the two standing alongside her.

"And that is Drivian," she said, pointing to the man kneeling in front of Neferelon's chair.

Yarga stepped forward. "I am Yarga, Elder of the Caramar. I share the wisdom of the Sagenstone."

He stood resolute as he faced the three robed figures. "You must aid us in our quest. If what I understand is true, this is why you are here. The Stones must be united and Anasaria must be freed."

CHAPTER THIRTEEN

The Road to Artora

Rowan walked beside Arrow holding the horse's reins as they followed Kerian through the forested terrain that skirted the road. The road continued in a southeastward direction, taking a long arc as it turned further towards the south. The land began to rise and the road ran between forested hills. It then slowly descended into a tree covered valley that led down from the spur of the mountains to the west and fell away to the east. Arienga and Duburinga were ahead with Jorunum, scouting the road. Behind Rowan strode Carlan, ever watchful, intent on the safety of the Swordbearer. Ahead of them rode Bregal and Gorum, deep in conversation, though Rowan could not hear what they were saying. At the front of the party strode Kerian and Biren-So. Terrana and Boriega were out of sight amongst the trees behind them, protecting their rear.

Beyond the trees, they could see down to where a river ran through the valley below them. Trees blocked their view of the road as it wound down the hillside, until it came into view where it emerged from amongst the trees and crossed a large bridge. Out of the trees Duburinga and Arienga appeared and approached Captain Kerian.

"There are guards on the bridge ahead," said Duburinga.

"How many?" asked Kerian.

"There are six in sight at this end and four at the other," said Duburinga.

"That is more than usual," said Biren-So.

"They seem very agitated," said Arienga. "They are patrolling the bridge constantly."

"The Artorans, perhaps?" said Bregal, from behind them.

Biren-So thought for a moment and then said, "The Artorans may have attacked the guards. We passed this way two days ago and the bridge was unguarded."

"How well armed are these guards?" said Gorum.

"If they have sent for reinforcements, they will be well armed," said Biren-So. "I would counsel that we head east down the valley and seek a crossing further downriver. There are farms in the lower valley. We have friends amongst the Anasarians but the Ultamarians are ever vigilant and patrol constantly, looking for any signs of rebellion."

Rowan had halted Arrow alongside Bregal and Gorum who were still mounted. At his shoulder stood Carlan.

"I know this valley," said the tall Abessairian soldier. "My people, my family are from the lands down the valley along the Tregon River."

He looked wistful and said softly, "They will all be long dead."

They made their way through the trees and headed east away from the road. As they moved off, a mounted Ultamarian stood at the head of the bridge facing north, looking back up the road. As he scanned the valley he caught a flash of movement up towards where the road began its descent down towards the river. He raised his hand and signalled towards the other guards at the northern end of the bridge.

"There is something moving in the forest up there," he said. "Three of you mount up and follow me."

Moving away from the road made the going tougher, especially with the horses and Gorum's chariga. Although the Underdwellers didn't officially name their mounts, as they belonged to no-one, Rowan had taken to calling the chariga, Stubborn. The trees closed in at times and Bregal and Gorum had dismounted and led their mounts under the low branches. They continued downwards following the course of the river that occasionally came into view below them. As they made their way down, the ground became more level and the trees began to thin out. They came to the edge of a copse and saw that beyond were fields of grain, vineyards, and orchards. Hedges lined the fields. There was no path through and they were forced to turn southwards down towards the river along the narrow corridor between the trees and the tall hedge.

They came to a place where the hedge on their left ended and a dirt path led up from the farmlands below and then turned the way they were facing, south down towards the river. They turned to the left and followed the path eastwards, the hedges continuing on either side. They were not far down the path when Terrana and Boriega ran up from behind them.

"We are being followed," said Boriega. "We must get off this path."

The party moved quickly ahead. Carlan and Rowan rode Arrow, escorted ahead by Bregal and Gorum. They reached a point where the hedges ceased and the land opened out into open fields. They struck out northwards. They crossed an area of undulating fields where stands of trees crowned small hills, and nestled in hollows and dales. The riders had ridden into a small wood and waited for those on foot to catch up.

The others came between the trees. Only Duburinga and Arienga were absent. Then appearing swiftly between the trees, the two Caramar came to a halt.

"There are four mounted Ultamarians coming down the path," said Duburinga, panting. "They may well pick up our trail. We must either hide or be prepared to fight."

Carlan spoke. "If my memory serves me well there used to be a village not far from here beyond these woods."

"There is a small village further down from here," said Biren-So. "Beyond there is a place in the river where goods are sometimes ferried across. We should head there. We must make haste to cross the river and get back up to the road if we are to have any hope of catching up with the Artorans. I counsel that we continue on."

Some of the party looked to Rowan.

He felt a little uncomfortable, but said in a steady voice, "We must pursue the Stone as quickly as possible."

They made their way quickly through the trees. The woodland descended a gentle slope that became steeper and then levelled out as the trees opened out into an expanse of small walled fields. Ahead, across the fields, they saw a cluster of buildings nestling at the end of a grassy, tree-lined laneway, which looped around near to where they stood. The small village ahead stood overlooking the course of the river. They scouted the edge of the forest southwards towards where the laneway came closest to the outer wall of the fields. A small path entered to their right and continued through a gate and across the field towards the village.

As they paused at the gate Bregal spoke. "Gorum and I will stay here and guard our trail. Look after Rowan."

The two riders broke away and rode back towards where they had exited the trees. Biren-So led them forward. Kerian followed with Rowan close behind riding Arrow, flanked by Carlan and Arienga. Terrana and Jorunum walked behind Rowan. Duburinga and Boriega watched from the gateway as Bregal and Gorum disappeared into the trees and then, closing the gate behind them, jogged down the path to join the others. There was a gateway in the wall on the opposite side of the field that led between the trees. The party filed through into the laneway. Duburinga closed the gate behind them.

A breeze blew down the valley from the west as they turned down the lane and headed towards the village. The sun was moving towards late afternoon behind them, and as they walked the light threw their shadows onto the ground ahead of them, intermingled with the shadows of the trees that stood on either side.

As they approached the village, everything seemed strangely quiet. The walls that had followed the road, partially hidden by the trees, came to an end where the village began. The laneway became a street lined with wooden and stone buildings. The buildings were all silent. Smoke wafted from some chimneys. A dog barked from somewhere ahead of them. Biren-So walked ahead of the group. They moved in silence; the mood of the quiet village weighing on them.

From around them Biren-So sensed that there were eyes following their progress. Arienga sensed it too and caught Rowan's sleeve.

"We are being watched," she whispered to Rowan. "Stay alert."

The Caramar all moved up and surrounded Rowan. All of a sudden there was a rush of noise as figures armed with sticks and farm implements burst into the road ahead of them and blocked the road behind them.

Biren-So raised his hand in the air and said in a low but strong voice, "Desultamar."

There seemed to be some consternation amongst the villagers. Biren-So moved forwards towards the group that was blocking the road.

He spoke a little more loudly. "I am Biren-So, of the Quiglings. I have been in these parts before and some of you may know me. Last time I was here things were a bit livelier, and a little more welcoming. What is happening here?"

A large man stepped forward. "I know you," he said gruffly. "But who are these others?"

"Gerardian!" exclaimed Biren-So. "Have you learned to brew a decent ale yet?"

"Finest in the valley," said the man.

"There are Ultamarians following us," said the Quigling.

"They're all over the place at the moment," said Gerardian. "This morning they came up along the other side of the river from Fort Kirenk."

The villager paused and looked around at the gathered party. "Who are all these…?"

He stiffened and said angrily, "You travel with Ultamarians?"

Biren-So sighed and said with frustration, "They really need to wash their uniforms. They are Abessairians."

Gerardian looked puzzled but Kerian stepped forward. There was much muttering amongst the gathered mob.

"I am Captain Kerian, loyal to the throne of Abessair and the Twin Stones of Angil," he said. "I and some of my comrades have been freed. We stand now against the evil of Ultamar."

"Let us discuss this away from the road," suggested Biren-So. "You may keep us under guard until we have made our acquaintances. But be warned, most of these people here," he gestured behind himself, "are highly trained fighters and have a sworn duty to protect what we are escorting."

Bregal and Gorum watched from the side of the trail as the four heavily armed, mounted Ultamarians made their way down to the eaves of the forest and then turned down towards where Rowan and the others had gone. As soon as they had passed by, the two riders looked at each other and nodded and then turned and cut back through the forest and then as soon as the terrain allowed crashed through the forest ahead of the Ultamarians out into the open and galloped along where the fringes of the woods followed the walled farmland down towards the river. The Ultamarian Captain let out a cry and spurred his horse forward. His three companions urged their mounts forward behind their Captain. The evil soldiers sensed the prey ahead and fixed their intent upon them. The two riders ahead did not belong here and they would be made to suffer. With a piercing whoop the evil Captain called his men to the chase. Bregal and Gorum thundered past the gate in the path, with the four Ultamarians in pursuit.

The front room of the inn in the centre of the village was rustic but spacious. The horse, Arrow, had been led to the stable that abutted the inn. Rowan was surrounded by the members of the party. Arienga stood alongside him. The party was in turn surrounded by the Anasarian villagers. Gerardien stood facing Biren-So. The people were murmuring and on edge. Biren-So was trying to be heard.

"People," he said, "we are here to help you. In turn we need your help. We must cross the river."

"Why should we help you?" said one villager.

"How do we know you are not with them?" said another.

Rowan stood there amonst his protectors, beginning to feel annoyed. These people didn't seem to understand that they were there to help them. He moved to stand next to where Biren-So confronted the crowd. Arienga grabbed his arm. He stopped and looked at her. Arienga saw the determination on his face and released his arm resignedly.

Rowan stepped forward. He reached up to his shoulder and grasped the hilt of his sword. There was a clamour amongst the crowd as people began to brandish weapons. In one swift movement, just as Arienga had taught him, he drew forth the Sword of Acclimoss and held it aloft.

Before anyone had the chance to react, he shouted loudly, "Behold the Sword of Acclimoss, the sword of the Kings of Anasaria! We are here to free you and defeat the evil of Ultamar!"

The gathered people fell into silence. Some fell to their knees and others dropped the improvised weapons they were carrying. Some stood resolutely with looks of bewilderment or awe, or disbelief and watchfulness on their faces.

"You must help us," said Rowan determindedly.

A villager who knelt just behind Gerardien cried out, "The sword of the King! The sword of the King!"

Gerardien raised his hand for silence, and said, "How do we know this is indeed the Sword of Acclimoss?"

Rowan looked at him and spoke solemnly. "This sword lay in the tomb of King Bharain. His hand released it into mine."

"No King would release his sword." An elderly man, still holding a short axe, stepped forward. "This can't be. Even in death such power is not easily relinquished."

Duburinga spoke from behind Rowan. His voice was strident and clear. "I witnessed Rowan removed the sword from the body of King Bharain. Your long dead King clasped the sword tightly until Rowan grasped it. It came easily to his hand."

"But he is not from Anasaria, and Bharain had no heirs," said another man over towards the door. "He cannot be allowed to wield the sword!"

There was low grumbling and muttering amongst the gathering.

Without them noticing, a figure had walked through the door that led from the street.

"But wield it he does," said the figure.

Bregal stood in the doorway.

"And I suggest you get used to it," he continued, "as you're soon to have a few Ultamarian soldiers on horseback come riding through here, chasing a crazy Underdweller on his ridiculous mount."

The street was deserted. All was quiet apart from the sound of the wind. Distantly they heard the sound of hooves. The sound grew steadily louder and then, from around the bend, came Gorum, riding fast but starting to slow as his chariga tired. He galloped closer and, as he did, those watching saw first one, and then three other Ultamarian soldiers, ride into view. Gorum approached and then rode past the watchers, with the Ultamarians closing on him from behind. As soon as he was through, a hay cart careered across the road, blocking the path of the dark riders. The Captain pulled his horse up and his three men pulled up alongside him.

"Get this piece of garbage out of my way!" shouted the Ultamarian captain.

A tall and lanky Anasarian stepped out into the street

"I'll have you know that this piece of garbage is my best cart," he said.

The soldier stared in disbelief at the farmer blocking his path.

"Kill this piece of scum," he said to the soldier to his right flank.

The soldier urged his horse forward but suddenly other Anasarians began pouring into the street, wielding their assortment of weapons. The rider paused.

"What is the meaning of this?" screamed the Captain.

He thrust his pointed finger towards the defiant farmer.

"I said, 'Kill him'," he roared at the soldier who still hesitated uncertainly.

The soldier began to move his horse forward towards the lanky farmer, and as he did, several arrows pierced his body and he slumped from his horse and onto the ground, his right foot still caught in his stirrup.

The Ultamarian Captain looked around uneasily and saw that behind them more Anasarians had appeared filling the street and blocking any escape. Biren-So strode out onto the street with Kerian beside him. They halted facing the mounted soldiers. The Ultamarian was bewildered. A fellow Captain of the army of Ultamar stood alongside a Quigling rebel.

"Lay down your arms," said Kerian, "or die."

From either side, people who didn't belong came into view. Some had bows drawn and others wielded swords. The Ultamarian felt his anger grow inside him and then felt something else. Over to the left, just behind some of these strangers, stood a boy wielding a sword. The soldier sat astride his horse, and felt something twist and burn inside him. He felt ill.

That sword. Something about that sword.

He almost remembered something from long ago. That wasn't real though. All that was important was serving the Dark Lords. An image of Ultamar came into his mind, seen from the forests beneath the plateau. The black fortress flashed for an instant in his mind's eye and then seemed to glow brightly, its white walls shining in the sunlight. He shook his head and tried to concentrate on what Kerian was saying. His head began to spin. His sword arm went limp and the sword clattered onto the street. He fell into a daze and slumped forward in the saddle.

Back in the front room of the inn, the three Ultamarian soldiers were huddled in a corner, bound and gagged. There had been many calls to kill them, and worse, but Biren-So had called for calm. He had noticed the dark Captain staring at Rowan as he had held aloft the ancient sword, out in the street. The Quigling was cautioning the Anasarians that more soldiers may be coming their way.

"Get these three locked away somewhere," said Biren-So. "If this village is searched they must not be found."

"What are we to do with them then?" asked Gerardien.

Kerian spoke. "If they attempt to escape you must kill them, but remember that, like me, they are Abessairians under the spell of the Dark Lords. That spell can be broken. Nevertheless, any true Abessairian soldier would expect to be killed rather than do the bidding of evil. I know that when I swore to protect Anasaria centuries ago, I would have been prepared to die at the hands of the Underdwellers or the Anasarians, rather than wage an evil war against them.If we are to defeat Ultamar, we must be prepared to fight and to kill Ultamarian soldiers. We must do so in the knowledge that we are freeing them and preventing them from breaking their oath. But the quest to unite the Stones and the Sword hopes to ultimately free Anasaria and release the entire Abessairian army from their enslavement. When that happens, if these three are still alive, they too will be free."

Carlan stood watching Rowan standing beside Arienga. The pair were both looking down at the Ultamarians. The Captain was awake again and glanced up at Rowan with a look of fear and confusion on his face. The Sword of Acclimoss was now back in its sheath on Rowan's back. The hilt of the sword still protruded above Rowan's shoulder.

Carlan looked at Rowan.

"He fears the Sword," he said.

Rowan stared at the Ultamarian Captain. The soldier turned his face, the gag still secure across his mouth, and looked directly into Rowan's eyes. The Ultamarian looked defiant for a moment but Rowan unconsciously raised his hand and placed it on the hilt of the sword. The soldier began to look agitated and shrunk back towards his fellows. The other two just struggled with their bonds with anger and loathing on their faces.

The Captain's head was spinning. The face of his King came into his mind. No, not his King. His allegiance was to the Dark Lords. The Kings of Anasaria had been just little whiners and dogs, that had used the people of Anasaria in defiance of the beautiful power of evil…or…?

His mind recalled for an instant, a pavilion on the plateau and a vision of a King clad in shimmering armour with a sword, that sword, clasped in his hand. He knelt before the King and swore… No. The Dark Lords ruled in Anasaria and Ultamar was … Abessair. The name rebounded within his mind and he felt himself spinning into darkness again.

Arienga reached out and pulled Rowan's hand from his sword hilt.

"Do not draw your sword unless you mean to use it," she said firmly.

Within the Realm of the Underdwellers, a group of Ultamarians were being led, bound together, through the city that surrounded the Eastern Gate. They were guarded by Caramar, Underdwellers and Abessairians. The party was led by the King. They marched beyond the outskirts of the city and headed along the road that led down to the City of the Vortex.

They had entered a marshy area and plunged between tall reeds. Rowan and the others followed a band of Anasarians down a narrow path, the reeds brushing the horses' flanks. The ground was soft but still allowed them to wind their way through, heading to where the river looped out towards the southern side of the valley. They tried to be as silent as possible. The day was now turning to night as the sun set towards the head of the river valley, and up further beyond the Anasarian Mountains. A blanket of cloud was moving up from the southwest and the sun was obscured, further dimming the daylight.

Gerardien appeared from between the reeds ahead, accompanied by Duburinga.

"There is a barge just ahead that will take you across the river," said Gerardien. "I ask only one thing. Send help soon. We have been waiting all our lives to be free of the tyranny of Ultamar."

Geradien, Innkeeper and fighter in the war against Ultamar, continued, "I only wish that I was coming with you. But the knowledge that the King's sword and the Stones are in Anasaria gives us hope. We will spread the word amongst those loyal to Abessair. We will prepare to fight but we are not soldiers."

An Anasarian woman standing alongside Rowan spoke. She had helped escort them down towards the river, wielding an axe handle menancingly. "Take care Sword carrier," she said.

She placed her hand on Rowan's arm as he stood holding Arrow's reins. As she did her face lit up and she faced eastwards towards where Ultamar was hidden beyond the ridge that edged the valley.

She smiled and said, "The light is returning."

As she spoke, a beam of sunlight broke out from beneath the blanket of cloud as the sun neared the horizon out to the west beyond the head of the valley. The party were bathed momentarily in golden light.

The Anasarian woman laughed. "The power of good is strong," she said. "We will defeat the evil ones. Stay strong Rowan. We need you and your brother to succeed. Your quest has been our quest for all our lives. Our hope is being rewarded."

With that, they continued on down to the edge of the river. Reeds grew out into the water around a peninsula where the river curved sharply around. A wide barge was moored amongst the reeds on one side. They approached, and a man leapt down from the barge onto the bank.

"I am Avarian," he said. "We can get loaded up, but it is best that we don't cross the river until after sunset. I fear that it will not be a dark night. The moon will rise soon, although this cloud will help. We will need to cross as soon as the sun sets."

The barge was steady as it made its way diagonally across the bend in the river to a point, near the end of the short cliffs, where the river straightened out. As they came closer the land began to be suffused by the dim light of the moon that began to rise beyond the plateau of Ultamar. They could see now that they were headed towards a place where the side of the valley was covered by trees. Avarian brought them alongside a small dock, in a place where the trees overhung the water, and secured the barge to a mooring post.Duburinga and Jorunum leapt down first and moved off into the trees to scout the area. Kerian, Biren-So, Bregal and Gorum led the three horses and the chariga down from the barge and onto the bank and then stopped amongst the trees. Rowan followed, flanked by Carlan and Arienga. Boriega and Terrana disembarked last and immediately turned to watch out across the river the way they had come. The river now shone in the soft moonlight.

Avarian approached Biren-So and spoke. "The lanes that lead up towards the troop road to the fort have been quiet most of the day. However, there has been much movement of soldiers along the road itself. If you are to get back to the road to Artora, you will need to cross the fort road as quickly as possible. If you make your way up through the forests and orchards on the southern flank of the valley, you can then move to the south and west diagonally across the ridgetop and down through the trees on the other side. You will then meet the Artoran road out on the Plain of the Winds."

The Anasarian looked at Rowan. "I am heading back across the river to help plan our strategy," he said. "We will do all we can to rally against Ultamar.

Our thoughts will be with you Rowan, and with your brother, Hyrn."

Avarian raised a clenched fist in salute and said stridently, "Desultamar!"

With that he turned and strode back down towards the river. Rowan watched as the man untied the barge and pushed it out onto the river. Rowan's gaze slipped across the glimmering water beyond the river out across the ridgetop and up to the dark shape of the mountains.

'Hyrn', he thought. I wonder where he is and if he is safe?

At that moment, Hyrn was fleeing up the pass away from the Castle Herardin and the battle that raged there.

All was quiet in the dim moonlight as they crept up the lane that ran up to meet the road that ran along the slopes high above the river. They kept close to the hedges as they approached. Duburinga and Boriega scouted ahead to where the hedges met the trees that lined the road. As he peered from cover Duburinga saw the shape of a lone rider coming down the road travelling east from where the bridge crossed the river. The mounted figure moved between patches of moonlight and the dappled shadows of the trees lining the road. Duburinga turned to Boriega.

"We cannot allow any word of the disappearance of the Ultamarians to get back to the soldiers at the fort," he said. "The villagers will be in peril if there is a search party sent out."

Boriega nodded and he and Duburinga flitted out from cover and took up positions. They had their bows ready and took aim. As the rider came closer they drew back their bowstrings.

As they prepared to fire, Duburinga spoke quietly to Boriega. "Stand down."

The rider continued towards them and then slowed as he approached the lane. His brown and green mottled clothing resembled that of Biren-So who was crouching with the others along the hedge waiting for the two Caramar to report. Duburinga leapt into the roadway in front of the rider simultaneously raising his bow and pointing a drawn arrow directly at him. The rider reached for the sword hanging at his waist and then as he lay his hand on the hilt paused with a puzzled look on his face.

"Who are you?" said the Quigling from atop his horse.

Duburinga looked at the rider and said firmly, "Remove your hand from your sword!"

The rider looked at the poised figure of the Caramar warrior in front of him. He released his grip on the hilt of his sword and raised his hand outwards in a sign of peace.

"I am Herra-Yen of the Quiglings," he said. "I fight against the evil of Ultamar. I sense that you are not evil."

Biren-So burst from between the trees and the rider let out a cry.

"Biren-So!" he said. "I heard that you were travelling north?"

"We were, but we are tracking Artorans," said Biren-So. "Have you any news from up at the bridge?"

"It's funny you should ask that," said Herra-Yen. "This horse belonged to an Ultamarian soldier. I took it from him, after I removed him from it. He had all sorts of interesting things to say when he was at the point of a sword."

"What is happening?" asked Duburinga who had replaced his arrow and hung his bow on his shoulder.

The other Quigling replied. "There was a disturbance at the bridge last night. Artorans apparently wielding some sort of dark power. They burst across, forcing the Ultamarians out of the way and killing any who dared to try to stop them. More Ultamarians came up this morning. Interestingly this soldier was reporting back to Fort Kirenk, so that a message can be sent to Ultamar. Some of the few soldiers remaining at the fort were sent to the bridge. Most of the soldiers stationed there had been sent to the front to attack the Underdwellers many days ago. There are only a handful of Ultamarians left at the fort and they are waiting for word from the bridge. They will still be waiting…"

He paused. A group of people had filed out from amongst the trees at the edge of the road.

"Who are your companions, Biren-So?" he asked with surprise in his voice.

"I will make introductions directly, but first where are you headed?" Biren-So demanded.

Herra-Yen said, quickly, "Oh, yes. I was on my way to the fort to see what was happening. There are some more rebels in the hills just above the fort. I was sent out to skirt the road with two others. They are on foot escorting our prisoner. They are not far behind."

A boy stepped forward. The hilt of a large sword jutted above his shoulder. "Where are the Artorans?" he asked.

Herra-Yen looked at the boy.

"And who might you be then?" he asked.

"I am Rowan of Wesmere." Rowan felt strange introducing himself formally, but continued. "We need to catch up to the Artorans and recover the Stone they may carry."

"What Stone is that?" asked the mounted Quigling.

Biren-So spoke up. "There is a chance it is the Stone held by the Underdwellers these past two hundred years or so."

"Ivah?" said the other Quigling with a puzzled look on his face

"There is more," said Biren-So. "I will explain quickly but know that Rowan here carries the Sword of Acclimoss, and the other Twin Stone, Ilah, is also back in Anasaria, being carried by Rowan's younger brother, Hyrn."

"What!?" exclaimed Herra-Yen.

"Come," said Biren-So, "I will let you know all the details and then we must continue on. If there are any more of our people around we must seek their help."

By the time Biren-So had introduced everyone and finished explaining the situation, Herra-Yen's companions had come into view with a figure bound and hobbling between them.

Biren-So spoke to Herra-Yen. "I think you should send one of your companions across the river to let the Anasarians know that the fort is lightly guarded. It may be their opportunity to strike a blow. Kirenk has been a source of torment and fear for them and no doubt some of their people are being held there."

"Both of them should go," said Herra-Yen. "But may I suggest that you send riders ahead to catch up with the Artorans. There are rebels stationed out on the plains amongst the Anasarian farms. They may be able to assist in slowing the Artoranas down."

He looked at the Ultamarian as the other rebels came to a halt, holding up either side of the prisoner. "I will take care of the baggage," he said.

Herra-Yen had ridden off down the road, with the bound Ultamarian trussed across the haunches of his own horse. The two other Quiglings had run off down the lane towards the river. They knew the location of the signal lamp that would alert Avarian that someone other than an Ultamarian needed passage across the river. Biren-So led the party up a hillside where rows of fruit trees grew, and then through into a woodland. The terrain was not too difficult with the light of the moon providing enough light for the party to pick their way between the trees.

Bregal and Gorum had ridden at speed up through the woodland and disappeared. They rode up towards the ridge and beyond to descend down to the plains below and back towards the road to Artora. They sped out through the night heading south. They reached the road, turning eastwards, and continued with speed closing the gap between themselves and the Artorans.

Duburinga had advised a halt for the night, once they had crossed the ridge.

"We must regain our strength to be able to continue the pursuit," said the Caramar. "Our hopes now lay with Bregal and Gorum. If they can slow the Artorans, we stand a chance of catching them."

The others assented and they set up camp amongst the trees that covered the hillside that led down towards the eastern plains of Anasaria.

Arienga took the opportunity to give Rowan some training.

"You must always be prepared to draw your sword, but…" began Arienga, taking up a stance across from him.

"…must never draw it unless you are prepared to use it," finished Rowan.

Arienga looked at him and said evenly. "Draw your sword and be prepared to use it."

Rowan reached for the hilt of his sword as Arienga's blade flashed from its sheath.

Rowan drew Acclimoss but said hesitantly. "I can't use it for real."

"Attack me," demanded the Caramar warrior. "Don't worry," she added. "I can defend myself."

Rowan launched himself at Arienga bringing his sword downwards towards her head. Arienga's sword was already up, blocking his blow and pushing his sword sideways. Rowan spun around away from her and slashed his sword at her midriff. Arienga's sword was down and ready and then she flung his sword back with her blade, almost wrenching it from his hands. He retreated and readied himself for another attack.

This continued for a while. Rowan was having no luck breaking through Arienga's defence. She blocked every attack but Rowan saw with a tiny bit of satisfaction that Arienga was beginning to exert some effort.

"Enough," said Duburinga from behind Rowan. "You both need to get some rest. Arienga you are on watch before dawn."

Duburinga turned and walked back towards the encampment. Rowan and Arienga started to follow, both out of breath from their exertions, although Arienga seemed to be recovering better. She turned to Rowan as they walked.

"That was good Rowan," she said. "I had to fight hard to repel your attacks."

Rowan thought for a moment and then said, "But I didn't want to kill you. If you were evil, I would fight harder."

"You will come across opponents much stronger and more aggressive than me," said Arienga. "And I could have killed you many times."

Rowan looked chagrined, but Arienga smiled at him.

"You are doing well, Rowan," she said. "And for now you have me and the others looking out for you. We just have to keep your training up."

"I'll never be as good as you," said Rowan.

Arienga shrugged and said, "No, but then I would have no reason to train you."

Rowan looked at her and she smiled again, and then what she was saying dawned on him.

He said quickly, "I definitely need more training."

Back down in the valley, Avarian navigated his barge across the river again. A number of small boats crossed with him. They transported a large group of Anasarians accompanied by the two Quiglings. The force amassed on the southern bank, and then, brandishing their weapons, headed eastwards down the valley towards the lightly guarded Ultamarian fort.

Rowan awoke early. Some of the others were still asleep but a few were awake and preparing for the day. The hillside they were on was still grey with the predawn light. Rowan noticed that the Caramar and the Underweller, Jorunum, were the ones that were awake. Kerian, Biren-So and Carlan were still asleep. Carlan stirred beside Rowan and quickly came awake, throwing his blanket off and launching himself to his feet. He stood in front of Rowan looking at him with groggy eyes for a moment and then said, "What is going on, Rowan?"

Rowan looked over to where the Caramar and Jorunum were moving out through the trees.

"They are off to greet the dawn," he said to the Abessairian. "I might join them and you can too, if you wish."

Carlan followed Rowan through the trees. They came out onto a rocky promontory that looked out over the grey land below. The others stood facing the lightening horizon. As the sun broke the horizon the chanting began. The disk of the sun rose and its light pierced the morning gloom but as it rose it began to disappear behind a layer of cloud. The land was lit with a crimson glow that painted the underside of the cloud layer that stretched towards them. The plains of Anasaria stretched out before them. In the middle distance they could see the ribbon of the great river. Near to where the road met the river Rowan noticed a large column of smoke. The sun cleared the horizon and then disappeared behind the clouds. The chanting ceased.

"What is that smoke?" asked Rowan, pointing.

Duburinga looked out to where Rowan pointed.

"Something is happening," he said. "It must be a large blaze to make that much smoke."

"It is a signal fire," said Carlan. "The rebels are being called to arms."

When they returned to the campsite Biren-So and Kerian were up and packing gear in the dim early morning light. They had a quick breakfast and prepared to make their way down the hill towards the road. Caramar scouted out ahead of them, and the others followed, Rowan leading Arrow who was loaded with gear. Jorunum and Terrana brought up the rear. The column of smoke came into view between the trees but was now beginning to dissipate. They made their way down the hillside, and after a while, the trees began to become sparser and the ground levelled out.

As the sun rose higher behind the blanket of cloud, they heard the sound of horses approaching. They hid themselves amongst the trees and waited. Three riders rode through the trees. As they drew near Biren-So leapt out from his hiding place. The riders pulled up in front of him.

"Biren-So," said the lead rider. "We were told that you were on your way back towards the road, although we have been riding back and forth for an hour trying to find you."

"Well, you have found us now, Dooren-Ga," said Biren-So. "What news of Gorum and Bregal."

"They were intercepted on the road by a troop of rebels and have reported to our men stationed closer to the river," said the mounted Quigling. "We have roused the country all around and set a signal fire. We have heard that the garrison at Fort Kirenk is no longer a threat. I fear, though, that the large garrison at the fortress above Forest Ford will soon become aware that something is afoot. Word will soon get back to Ultamar that there is trouble. We must prepare now for all-out war."

Biren-So interrupted. "Where are Gorum and Bregal?"

"Ah, yes," said Dooren-Ga. "They and a troop of our best riders rode off not long after sunrise. They are going to try and attack the Artorans before they cross the bridge at Roaring Gorge."

"That is foolhardy at best," said Kerian from behind Biren-So. "The Artorans wield a dark power that we do not understand."

"They are aware of that," said Dooren-Ga. "But if the Artorans leave the road beyond the bridge and get into the wilds we may never catch them. They at least intend to slow them down. We will escort you back down to the road, and if we make good time, we may be able to hear news of them before the day grows too old."

The riders raced down country lanes and across fields, keeping as close to the road as they dared. They left messages with any friends that they passed along the way. Many had seen the signal and were preparing, but weren't sure for what.

The message was short and to the point. "War is coming, let Ultamar tremble."

At any opportunity they tried to get a glimpse of the road to see if there were any signs of the Artorans. It was well into the morning, when one of their number mounted a hill that commanded a view of the road. A group of dark figures, numbering about twenty, were moving down the road. They were travelling slowly and some of their number seemed to be injured. The rider's path was clear now, quickly to the bridge. They rode on. The farmland gave way to rocky slopes and gullies. They were heading towards Roaring Gorge, where the River Trebian passed noisily through a steep narrow gorge. It was here that an ancient stone bridge carried the road high above the tumult of the river below.

A man, dressed in the garb of a King's Rider of Wesmere sat astride a tired but resolute mare. Alongside him was an armoured soldier, protector of the Light in the Dark, mounted on a dour chariga from the slopes of the Isle of Wind. They stood at the entrance to a bridge that hunkered above the churning waters of the river. They faced back up the road to where it ran between steep cliffs and then disappeared around a bend. Above them, the sky had become grey with the threat of rain. They waited, still, and with grim determination upon their faces.

After a while a dark mass moved around the bend. The mass distilled into a group of figures all similarly dressed in dark robes. They moved slowly but determinedly forward. As they neared, several of them spied the two riders on the bridge. They paused and then a group of them broke away from the main party and moved quickly towards the two riders.

The riders did not move or utter a sound.

As the dark figures approached, one of them moved ahead of the others. From his robe he pulled a dark, velvet Stone and held it in front of himself. He spoke in a harsh, rasping high pitched voice.

"Stand aside vermin, or die!" he said loudly but casually.

The riders remained silent and stared at the figure. Their faces did not betray that they had heard.

The robed figure raised his hand, and the Stone that he held high, began to glow with a bright purple light. The figure paused with a puzzled look on his face and looked quickly around up to his left and right where the cliffs lined the road. Suddenly large boulders, smaller rocks, and stones came cascading down the cliffside directly towards where the dark figure stood. At the same time, several riders rode out to where half of the dark figures had been left behind further back up the road. The rider's weapons were drawn and they attacked without mercy.

The two riders on the bridge spurred their mounts into action. The figure with the Stone was only momentarily distracted. He raced forward towards the two riders as large boulders crashed into his companions behind him. There was a blinding flash of purple light and one of the riders was flung from his mount. The other rider shielded his eyes but was stunned by the blast.

The figure with the Stone looked around quickly and then cried out, "Bragga, Carak with me!"

He raced ahead towards the bridge. Two of the other Artorans broke away from where several of their kin were lying in the road, and joined the wielder of the Stone. The taller of the two, wore on his back a small iron casket. They skirted around the two riders, one dazed and the other prostrate on the road, and entered the bridge. Free from their wounded companions they sped across the bridge.

Gorum's senses began to return. He glanced down at the figure of Bregal lying on the roadway at the entrance to the bridge. Marran stood, her head bowed down facing her fallen comrade. Gorum looked around, sighed heavily, and then drew himself up and turned his chariga and sped across the bridge in pursuit of the dark figures. Several riders skirted the rubble where Artorans lay buried or injured by fallen rocks and rode onto the bridge. One rider stopped, dismounted and knelt beside Bregal. The others rode on to catch up with Gorum.

As Gorum grew closer to the fleeing Artorans, the Sorcerer leading them turned as he continued to run, and launched blasts of purple light behind him back down the bridge. Gorum veered back and forth to avoid the blasts. The Artoran paused in his flight and raised the Stone high. The Stone began to pulse with brilliant light that increased in intensity. Halfway across the bridge the chariga that Gorum rode dug his hooves in and came to a grinding halt. Gorum shouted and cursed at his mount but the chariga remained standing.

"No wonder Rowan calls you 'Stubborn'," shouted Gorum angrily.

The rebel riders caught up with Gorum and then rode past. Ahead the Artorans had continued their flight and, completing the crossing, had now stopped on the road on the other side. In plain view of the riders, the Artorans stood defiantly. The rebels rode on but slowed hesitantly as the Artorans just stood in the centre of the roadway. The Artoran Sorcerer laughed harshly, and then, raising his hand holding the evil Stone, swung it backwards and forwards blasting the stone of the cliffs and slopes that lined the road. A cascade of boulders, trees and soil came crashing down and filled the end of the bridge. The riders pulled up, and as the Artorans disappeared behind a wall of rubble, they saw the Sorcerer laughing, his face contorted and contemptuous. The riders looked on helplessly and then all about them droplets of rain began to fall.

CHAPTER FOURTEEN

The Towers of Arkenegelon

Hyrn awoke late in the morning after a much needed sleep. They had forestalled any conversation until the morning. They ate a breakfast mainly of food from their packs, but supplemented with some nuts and berries that the Priests had provided. There was some commotion not long after. Careil and Margana had taken the horses down to the cave entrance and outside to graze in the gully. They had been quickly confronted by the sight of Harla, Gebarana and Turum who sprang from behind boulders as soon as they had walked out into the open air. Careil now led the three new arrivals into the chamber. Margana had stayed behind to watch the horses.

After introductions were made, Infiron invited them to sit. They gathered various mismatched chairs and sat around the fire. Firstly, Harla spoke of what had occurred at Herardin, after the others had fled up the valley of the pass. Yarga then began to briefly tell the members of the Order the tale of the quest. Careil and Hyrn were sometimes needed to add details of the events before they had met Yarga. The Elder skipped over much of the detail, mindful that time was pressing. He concentrated on telling of events that related to Ilah and Ivah and then some of what had occurred since they had entered Anasaria. When he had finally finished, Yarga made a plea to Infiron and her companions.

"We must get back down to the road and find the trail of the Ultamarians," said Yarga. "They must not be allowed to reach Ultamar if they have the other Stone."

Infiron rose to her feet.

"We will do all we can," she said. "We are Priests of the Order of the Stones. We are the remnants of those who tended the Stones before Bharain left. We gathered others to our cause and have kept faith. Over generations we have studied and revered the Stones. We held to the teachings of prophecy that the Stones would return to Anasaria and this land would be freed from evil.

We are privileged to be here when the prophecy is being fulfilled. This is our destiny and our purpose."

Infiron paused and Drivian rose and addressed them. "There are tunnels and pathways through these mountains that lead back down to the road further north. Some parts will be too difficult for horses though."

Careil spoke. "We must meet up with Ferian and the others. Hyrn, I fear I must leave you for a while. I will ride down to the Castle and see how things fare there. I will leave the other two horses here. If the others are now following the trail I will catch up with them and tell them what has occurred and where you are headed."

The Rider looked at Infiron and asked, "Are there any landmarks that will tell us where on the road you will come out?"

The Priest smiled and her eyes sparkled.

"Yes!" she said. "The Towers of Arkenegelon! When they come into view from the road, we will endeavour to meet you there."

Wren whistled softly through his teeth and said in awe, "The Towers of Arkenegelon. I used to look up at them from far away, there up on their mountainside. They were always there facing Ultamar like they were watching them. They always seemed so far away, but seeing them up close. Wow!"

"What are these towers?" asked Yarga.

Harla added, "Are they occupied?"

One of the other Priests, Gerton, spoke. "They are bastions of the might of old Anasaria. They were built high up on the mountain in view of the Angilanian Mountains. It is said that they were used to communicate with the Power in the East. They are long abandoned and none that I know of have entered them for countless years. The road is dangerous."

Garan cut in. "The Ultamarians shun the towers as a place of the enemy. They keep watch though, to ensure that no-one is able to enter and use them as a base or a sanctuary. The road will be guarded."

Careil rose to his feet. "Hopefully if all has gone well at Herardin we can ride in force and surprise any Ultamarians who guard the road," he said, then paused. "Speaking of Ultamarians. What are we to do with our new friend," he said, gesturing to the entrance.

"Fear not," said Infiron. "We will guard the Ultamarian. Ferian will have enough prisoners at Herardin to question."

"I suggest you keep him securely bound and not take any chances," said Garan.

"We have somewhere where he can be kept where he will not be able to cause any trouble," said Infiron.

"I will help you to take him there before we leave," said Garan.

"We must leave soon," said Yarga.

Hyrn stood in the entrance way just outside the chamber. He had packed his gear, now almost out of habit, as soon as he had arisen in the morning, so he was ready to go. He had farewelled Careil, and the Rider had taken Erras and ridden back down the gully and disappeared from sight. Hyrn felt strange as Careil rode off. He felt a little bit vulnerable without the Rider but remembered that Captain Garan of the Abessairian army was not far away and had sworn to protect him. In his head he spoke with Ilah dreamily.

"You can change him back," said Hyrn as he stood in the dim passage looking down.

The Ultamarian lay on the cave floor at Hyrn's feet, struggling with his bonds.

"I do not have that power alone." The voice of Ilah spoke distantly in Hyrn's head. "I need other's strength. I am far from home. The strength of the Angilanian Mountains cannot help me. I held the strength of the Lake of Light. It lies where its power emanates from the earth. That made me strong enough. There is one thing this far from Angilania that holds the strength of my home; my brother. Find him, Hyrn."

Garan came up from behind Hyrn, waking him from his trance.

"Come, Stonebearer," he said. "It is best you stay away from him. He is dangerous. I will take him now."

Garan pulled the evil soldier to his feet. The Ultamarians legs were bound so Garan hefted him over his shoulder and headed back into the cavern. The Ultamarian fought against his bonds at first, and then went limp as Garan crossed to the archway where Infiron and the others waited. Hyrn followed behind him. Neferelon sat in the chair by the fire, his legs covered with a blanket. His hands rested in his lap. His wrists were bandaged in clean white linen. They took turns farewelling him.

Harla stood beside his chair and, leaning down to the old Priest, said, "The climb was worth it to see you here safe."

"Thank you, Harla," said Neferelon. "You, and your comrade."

Hyrn approached to say goodbye.

Neferelon smiled at him and said, "Child of prophecy. I am honoured to have lived to see you. When your quest is fulfilled I hope to see you again."

"Goodbye," said Hyrn. "I hope you get better soon."

Once they were all together, Infiron led them through the archway and down a dimly lit passageway. The sides of the passage were straight but were roughly hewn. Dark doorways lined the passageway. As they approached one of these, Infiron halted and beckoned to Garan. The Abessairian walked up to the doorway, with the Ultamarian over his shoulder. Hyrn followed behind as Garan walked through the doorway.

A torch burned in a bracket on the wall. The room was narrow but long. Halfway down its length the stone floor became a mesh of iron bars. At the closest edge was a small square grid with an iron ring attached. Gerton moved past Hyrn and Garan and bent down and lifted the ring with some effort.

"Take him down and then unbind him," said Gerton. "He cannot escape from here. The walls are solid rock and too sheer to climb. This cage lid is secure and too high to reach, except with the ladder."

Gerton gestured to the open square at the top of the cell. Garan walked up and peered down into the opening and saw the top of the ladder. He bent down and lay the Ultamarian on the floor. He then turned and placed his right foot into the opening and on to the top rung of the ladder. When he had descended the ladder enough that he was through the trapdoor to his waist, he grasped the Ultamarian and dragged him towards the edge. Garan descended further, pulling the Ultamarian onto his shoulder as his bulk cleared the opening. The Ultamarian was knocked against the cage opening as Garan struggled down the ladder.

Hyrn came close to the edge and looked down. It was dark down below where the torchlight did not reach.

"I can't see," said a voice in his head.

Down below Garan had reached the bottom and was beginning to untie the prisoner lying on the cell floor. He left the gag and blindfold on and began to untie his hands and feet. From above a dim glow illuminated the cell. Garan undid the knots but left the ropes still lashed around the Ulatamarian's hands and feet. He would be able to free himself eventually. Garan left him lying on the floor and turned back to the ladder. He mounted the ladder and began to climb.

Hyrn, looking from above, watched as Garan mounted the ladder. Hyrn, with shock, saw the Ultamarian launch himself to his feet, loosening his bonds as he moved. He stumbled across the floor, tearing his blindfold off and quickly threw himself at the Abessairian.

Garan caught unawares, and thrown against the ladder, was unable to turn. The Ultamarian reached up to Garan's belt and, from the sheath that hung there, pulled out Garan's knife. The evil soldier pulled his arm back ready to strike, when a flash of blinding light threw him to the ground, clutching his eyes and moaning. As he fell, the knife clattered to the ground.

Garan turned and leapt down from the ladder. He quickly grabbed the knife and then scrambled up the ladder. He climbed out through the trapdoor. The Priest, Gerton, grasped the top of the ladder and fed it up out of the cell. Once it was clear. Garan slammed down the cage door. Gerton walked over to the wall and hung the ladder horizontally on hooks in the wall. He then walked back producing a padlock from within his robes. He bent down and fastened it to the cage door. Below the Ultamarian screamed with rage and pain.

"He will be secure here," said Gerton.

The group headed to the door. Wren had been standing behind Hyrn and slipped past him and looked down into the cell. Hatred flashed in his eyes but he turned back with a look of satisfaction.

"That's where they all belong," he said defiantly. "They can suffer like my father suffers."

They had passed through passages and caverns, some smaller, some larger than the one they had stayed in. They met other Priests of the Order along the way; their numbers seemed few though. At times they came out into the open air. Tunnels came out into small gardens or courtyards snuggled amongst steep hills. At one point they came to an open area where the hills formed a large bowl. Clouds obscured the sun and there was a sombre feel in the air that promised rain.

The area was a large courtyard with columns, statues and sculptures, all formed of the same black stone. The stone was weathered but the courtyard stood as it had for centuries. No weeds grew and it looked as if it had been well tended. They passed amongst the ancient stonework, the faces of the statues staring down at them. In the centre was a large statue, more weathered than the rest.

"Is that King Abess?" asked Wren loudly so that the Priests ahead could hear.

Mergon turned to him and said, "You know your history, Wren."

Wren spoke shyly. "My Father taught me when I was growing up."

"It is well that the history of Anasaria is being passed on," said the Priest.

As they filed past the statue, Wren looked up in awe. The party passed among the monuments and crossed to where another tunnel opened on the opposite side. They filed through the tunnel entrance and into the darkness.

After they had gone in a little way, Hyrn noticed that the walls were beginning to glow. Infiron and Drivian had their palms held against the rock walls and were softly humming. After a few moments, the tunnel was glowing brightly and Infiron, removing her hand from the wall beckoned them to follow.

"The power in the rock is strong here," she said as the party followed her onwards. "We will soon start to go down to the road and will enter more open territory. We will need to be on our guard as Ultamarian patrols sometimes come into this region closer to the road. And there is always the threat of Drargs."

Careil had ridden down through the succession of gullies and back down the pass towards Castle Herardin. All was quiet until he rounded the bend and the castle came into view. There was much activity around the castle. As he rode closer, he could see that there were Quigling soldiers milling about. Several of the rebel soldiers rode out to block his path.

"I am Careil, Rider of Wesmere," said Careil, as he pulled Erras up before them. "Harla has reported the events here last night after we fled with the Stonebearer. I must speak with the other members of the quest, or at least know where they have gone."

"The others of your party have gone east down the road," said one of the Quiglings, "except for General Ferian. He is wounded but still lives. We have patched him up as best we could. Coora-Jen leads here and he can answer your questions. Follow us."

The riders turned and started towards the castle. Careil followed them as they passed down the valley and across the small bridge. As they approached the castle, Careil saw that there were an assortment of bedraggled figures sitting around or lying down on the grass in the morning sun. Some were eating cups of steaming soup and slabs of bread. The prisoners of Herardin had been freed.

"We had to let this lot out," said one of the riders motioning with his head. "We needed their cells for our own prisoners."

They neared the castle and a tall Quigling walked up to meet them. He stopped before Careil.

"I am Coora-Jen," he said.

"Careil," said the Rider. "I must see Ferian and then ride east."

"I will take you to see the General," said the Quigling, "but you must tell me about the fate of the Stone."

"Agreed," said Careil.

In one of the upper chambers on the southern face of the western tower, lay General Ferian. Coora-Jen led Careil through the door. Ferian lay on a large bed. Light came through a window above him. On a chair rested his armour. His stained uniform hung over the back of the chair. The General slept fitfully muttering something in a low voice.

"He keeps saying the same things," said Coora-Jen. "Something about an old man, and swans."

"Swans?" said Careil, puzzled.

Careil approached the bed and moved around to the left hand side, opposite to where Ferian's shoulder was heavily bandaged. He reached out and softly shook the sleeping soldier.

"Ferian, Ferian," said the Rider. "It is Careil."

The General's eyes fluttered open and he looked at Careil glazedly.

He then seemed to recognise Careil and said to him imploringly. "Where is the old man?"

"He is safe," answered Careil.

"You must take me to him," said Ferian.

He seemed to become more lucid and tried to sit up in bed. He winced in pain but faced Careil.

He glanced up briefly to where Coora-Jen stood behind Careil and then spoke fervently. "There is a story within Ultamar, although the Dark Lords do not speak it openly. Before Bharain fled Anasaria he removed the remaining Stone from the Chamber of the Stones, atop the great tower that Eriallen added to the Fortress Abessair, the Tower of the Stones. It is said that Bharain left the empty chamber unlocked with the key still in the door.

When the Dark Lords entered Abessair, triumphant, they quickly took stock of their new possession, and one place drew their attention."

They were able to enter the Tower without any resistance, and as they climbed and approached the Chamber atop the tower, they saw ahead a great white swan fly in through an open window. As they traversed the top of the stairs, and up onto the landing that led to the chamber door, they witnessed the swan pull a golden key from the closed door with the attached gold chain and, looping it over her head, take flight and head towards the window, the key dangling below her graceful neck.

The foremost of the evil Lords launched himself forwards towards the swan. The white swan, the light of the westering sun making her glow as it shone through the open window, swerved gracefully up and away from the evil grasp and dove towards the shaft of sunlight and followed it up and through the window, out into the open air, off towards where the mountains stood dark against the glow of the sunset.

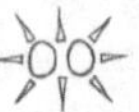

"The Dark Lords sometimes commanded that our patrols in the mountains keep an eye out for swans," continued Ferian. "I suspect that they did not know that the soldiers stationed at Ultamar knew the story."

"What does this have to do with the old man?" asked Careil.

The wounded General took in a breath and said, "We captured an Anasarian who was a Priest of the Order of the Stones. He wore the same robes as the old man. He told us, eventually," Ferian paused and looked grim, but continued, "that he was part of this Order. They hid mostly in the mountains but sometimes ventured forward to preach the message of the Stones and try to restore hope to the people.

Of course Ultamar could not allow this preaching to be tolerated. The Ultamarians that interrogated him never brought him to Ultamar alive. But they were able to get from him the story of a hidden lake in the mountains that was home to a flock of swans. They never found out exactly where it was and we were unable to find anything more about it or to discover its location. The others of the Order that we captured were all prepared to die rather than speak of the lake. If the old man knows where this lake is it may be important in returning the Stones to Abessair, and to their home in the Chamber of the Stones."

"The old man is called Neferelon," said Careil. "The place where he is is hidden, I could take you there, but I must travel east along the road to meet up with Hyrn and the rest of the Quest."

"How am I to find it without you?" asked Ferian.

"I will give you directions but you will have to find it alone," said Careil.

Coora-Jen spoke from behind Careil. "Oh, he won't have to find it alone," he said. "There is a young Priest of the Order just downstairs. I'm sure he is eager to get back, although he won't really say where that is."

General Ferian looked thoughtful and then said, "I need to get cleaned up."

Careil spoke with Coora-Jen as they walked down the stairway in the western tower and out onto the bridge. He told the Quigling all that had taken place since they had fled with Hyrn. They walked along the bridge, as it passed beneath the darkness of the castle, and came out at the eastern end into dull daylight. Clouds moved northwards across the sky. A rebel soldier was holding the reins of Erras, having brought the horse up from the river valley below. Careil mounted his horse and bidding farewell to the Quigling, rode off down the road, eastwards towards the towers that the Priest had described. The dark shape of Ultamar seemed to float ahead to his right, across the darkening forests of Anasaria, as the sky became gloomier and the smell of rain began to be sensed upon the air.

General Ferian rose to his feet and stepped out of the cramped tub. He felt as if the dirt of centuries had been washed from him. He looked to where his uniform lay on the bed, still damp, but white. He tested the bandage that wrapped his shoulder. It was damp but he had managed to keep it mostly dry. He dressed slowly and painfully. The movement in his left shoulder and arm was still hampered by his wound. Coora-Jen had asked for a volunteer and a young Quigling, intrigued by the hope of Abessair, was now cleaning the breastplate that was beginning to shine as it did when Anasaria was still free. Once Ferian was dressed he asked the Quigling to let Coora-Jen know that he was ready.

The young Priest waited in a small room on the ground floor of the western tower. He had been told that his help was needed. He knew from his few years in the Order to be aware of the tricks and deceits of the enemy. At the moment, he was not sure he could trust anyone. He had decided, against the advice of Infiron and the others, to try and find Neferelon. The day before, he had been discovered by an Ultamarian patrol and dragged to the castle. He had been thrown in a dirty cell. They had promised him torture and pain, but instead he found himself amongst Quiglings and various freed rebels. The Ultamarians had reportedly been thrown into the cells beneath the castle.

This all seemed like just the sort of trick that the enemy would use against the Order. He was being treated well. He was fed and clean and was free to leave. But that was just what they would want him to do, to leave, and lead them back to the Order. He was not that stupid. This was all too good to be true.

"Trion," he said to himself, "don't tell them anything. Just wait. They will reveal their evil intent soon enough. But what then? No doubt torture and…" he shuddered.

There was a knock on the door.

Clever. Pretend that he can decide if they can enter his cell or not. Oh well.

"Come in," said Trion with forced levity.

The door opened and the vision that filled the doorway was too much. Not even the most twisted mind could expect him to accept this. This was an almost legendary figure. An Abessairian officer.

The vision of white and gleaming silver walked into the room, almost hesitantly. He was a massive, imposing figure. He could probably tear Trion apart with his bare hands, except he seemed to be injured. He held his left arm clenched against his body. Trion tried to shake off what seemed like an enchantment, and stood defiantly.

"I am a Priest of the Order of the Stones," he said.

He tried to sound strong but his voice quavered as he spoke.

He continued, "I will die before I tell you anything."

The tall soldier in the doorway shrugged and then winced. He looked at the young Priest, and turning, seemed to be almost ready to leave but then turned back and looked at him indifferently.

"I am a soldier of Abessair, sworn to protect Anasaria," he said. "Ilah and Ivah have returned to Anasaria. The Sword of Acclimoss is worn once again in defiance of evil. The children of prophecy have come but they need your help. If you are not willing to help me, then I will need to find someone else."

The soldier turned back towards the doorway, walked through it, and closed the door behind him.

Trion's thoughts tumbled. 'The children of prophecy'? How do the Ultamarians know about that? That was something that came from Ivah, from Bharain; secret knowledge known only to the Order.

"Wait!" shouted Trion.

He moved towards the door but it quickly opened again and the large, glowingly garbed soldier walked back in.

"I have many things I must tell you," said Ferian. "Then you can decide if you want to help me." He shrugged nonchalantly, and then wished he hadn't, but continued grimly, "Or I could just kill you now." The General began to laugh. but then, with a pained expression on his face, said, "I really need your help and the liberation of Anasaria may depend upon it."

Trion gasped as he saw that the white tunic of the soldier had a patch of blood on one shoulder. He rushed to help as the Abessairian seemed to falter as he leaned against the doorframe.

"I will help you," said the young Priest. "But you must carry no weapon until I know that what you say is true."

"Good enough," said the General.

He stood upright and undid his sword-belt and then thrust his sheathed sword at the young Priest's chest.

"You can carry this for me," he said with a look of pain on his face.

Hyrn gasped as they were led into a large, brightly lit chamber. The whole space was filled with an immense assortment of artefacts. Statues, furniture, tapestries, paintings, chests, and ornaments were everywhere. He looked around in awe. They moved through the chamber. The members of the quest looked around in wonder at the assortment of objects. Some were magnificent works of crafting, ornate and beautiful, while others were plain but sturdy and rustic. They all seemed to give off a feeling of age. They looked like an assembled army slumbering waiting for the day that they would be called to battle.

"What is all this?" he asked finally.

Infiron stood with a look of pride and wonder on her face.

"These are the heirlooms of Abessair and of the Towers of Arkenegelon," she said. "They still fill me with amazement even after seeing them many times before."

"How did they get here?" asked Wren, equally awestruck.

"Ah!" said Infiron. "It was a mighty labour, but one that the Order undertook with great pride and purpose. We were tasked to do this by King Bharain. He hoped to keep the heritage of Anasaria alive until the Stones could be reunited and return to free our land."

"But how did Bharain know?" asked Hyrn. "Devarnia only found out about the prophecy from Ivah."

"You forget, Stonebearer, that the King carried Ivah," replied Infiron. "He was told the same prophecy by the Stone and he passed it onto the Priesthood within Abessair. They tended and protected the Stone. Many within Anasaria believe that Bharain was a coward and that he fled in fear of the Dark Lords, but he knew that the Stone must be protected and that he must seek out Ilah and that only the two Stones together could restore the power of Abessair.

The Dark Lords were beginning to gain influence within sections of the army outside Abessair. They presented themselves as an alternative to the weakness of the Kingship, and a way to make Abessair strong again. We suspected that they were using some dark force to bring soldiers under their power. Bharain came to the Chamber of the Stones to seek guidance from Ivah. He was told by the Stone that he must leave Anasaria and seek sanctuary. He was also told that two children would one day re-unite Ivah with his twin and would return to free Anasaria. The story was passed onto us and the hope of 'the children of prophecy' has lived in our hearts and been passed down through the Order for generations."

Hyrn thought with wonder how strange it was that it was he and Rowan that had been talked about for generations

Hyrn concentrated as Infiron continued, "Bharain asked that we take whatever we could from Abessair and hide it here until the time that the prophecy was fulfilled. There were still members of our Order at the Towers and it was decided that the artifacts of the old Kingdom still at the Towers should be removed to prevent them being ransacked. We were barely able to complete our task before Bharain went into exile and the Dark Lords took possession of Abessair and turned it into the evil of Ultamar."

Infiron paused and looked at Hyrn. "And here you are but only with Ilah. I am not sure if Ivah knew that this dark turn of events would take place. Prophecy is a difficult thing and not all can be foreseen. Our hope is that Ivah will be recovered and the Stones will be reunited. We have waited too long, to fail at the last turn."

Hyrn looked defiant. "We will recover Ivah," he said. "We must find the Ultamarians who entered the Underrealm, or we must hope that my brother can recover Ivah from the Artorans, if that is where the Stone has gone."

"We have only one regret," said Infiron. "In our rush to leave Abessair as the Dark Lords approached, we left something precious behind. The key to the Chamber of the Stones was left in the door. The Chamber was left unsecured. Without the key we cannot return the Stones to their rightful place."

Yarga spoke up from behind Hyrn. "We don't have the Stones yet. We must get back to the road and find the Ultamarians."

"Yes," said Infiron. "We must beware of any enemies that may be in the areas close to the road."

As they spoke Hyrn felt himself distracted. He wandered to his left amongst the trove surrounding them. Wren looked quickly around and then followed him. Garan was facing in the opposite direction looking at the objects with wonderment. He had been at Abessair only once and the splendour of the place was now sparked in his memory. Hyrn disappeared behind a statue of a lion, with Wren close behind.

"Where are you going?" hissed Wren quietly.

Hyrn didn't answer. He weaved his way between the gathered objects. He headed in as straight a line as the objects would allow him, at times having to squeeze between some. When he eventually stopped, he stood before a low cabinet. Atop the cabinet was a hook-shaped object that looked as if it was made of iron. The large hook was half the length of Hyrn's forearm. Within Hyrn's mind came the urge to pick the object up. He needed this. He reached out and grasped it. The hook felt heavy in his hand. Still in a trance, Hyrn opened his tunic and thrust the object inside. It nestled against the cloth covered Stone.

"What are you doing?" whispered Wren from behind Hyrn.

Hyrn awoke from his trance. "What? What do you mean?"

"You can't just take that," said Wren, still talking quietly.

"Take what?" asked Hyrn.

He suddenly felt the weight of the object under his vest and began to realise. But then within his mind Ilah assured him that everything was as it should be.

"Come on," said Hyrn to Wren. "We've got to get moving."

"But…?" began Wren as Hyrn began to walk back towards the others.

Wren shook his head and then with a shrug of his shoulders and a confused look on his face moved to catch up with Hyrn. All of a sudden a large figure appeared in front of Hyrn.

"What are you doing?" said Garan, gruffly. "Don't go wandering off!"

"It's alright," said Hyrn lightly. "We were just looking around. Weren't we, Wren?"

Wren, catching up with Hyrn, said quickly, "Yes. Just looking around."

They followed Garan back to the others who were beginning to make their way down the path that wound through the massive collection of artefacts. They fell in behind them. Yarga was still deep in conversation with Infiron, and neither had seemed to notice that the two boys had disappeared. However, Harla, walking just ahead of Garan, looked at Hyrn quizzically but appeared to pass no judgement. As they approached the other side of the chamber Hyrn saw that there was a hefty wooden door bound with iron.

"Beyond here is a series of traps and false passages that protect the entrance," said Infiron loudly enough that all could hear. "Follow the members of the Order closely and tread only where they tread. We will soon emerge out into the open and can make our way down to the road."

They followed a narrow path that wound through narrow gorges and then into a woodland and finally through an area of large boulders.

Infiron paused and spoke to Yarga. "The road lies just beyond. I suggest that you send your skilled warriors ahead to scout the road, to ensure that we are not caught unawares."

Yarga looked to Harla hesitantly. The Caramar warrior bowed her head towards him.

"We will scout ahead, Elder," she said.

Yarga looked relieved and a little embarrassed. Harla signalled to Gebarana and the two Caramar moved quickly off. Turum joined up behind them and the three disappeared between two large boulders. Above them, darkening clouds rolled across the sky. The smell of coming rain hung in the air.

Suddenly, from somewhere far off, a jagged sense of something disturbing rent the air. Hyrn felt an immediate sense of uneasiness and fear.

Ilah spoke within his mind. "The evil force has been used against us."

'Rowan!' thought Hyrn immediately. He felt Ilah stir and had removed the Stone without thinking.

"Your brother is not there," said the Stone. "The Artorans have been attacked and they are retaliating. The holder of the dark Stone is fleeing."

Yarga and Infiron had moved over as Ilah spoke but the Stone went dark and Hyrn replaced it.

"We need to find the Ultamarians and establish whether they have Ivah," said Yarga. "If not, the Stone may be slipping from our grasp."

"I wonder where Rowan is?" said Hyrn.

"Your brother is travelling towards where the fight took place," said Ilah in his mind. "It will take time for him to get there, but he has decided to ride ahead with some other riders."

Hyrn took this in while dismissing the voice in his head and was then distracted, as at that moment, Harla returned and reported to Yarga and Infiron.

"There are signs that riders have been going back and forth along the road," she said. "Gebarana and Turum are waiting by the road in case they reappear. I fear that they have not been able to locate the Ultamarians. There is no sign of any enemies about."

"Let's move down to the road then," said Infiron. "If we go a little further east you will be able to see the Towers of Arkenegelon. We can wait there to speak with the riders if they come back."

As they made their way eastwards down the road, the rain began to fall, lightly at first and then getting heavier. Gerton had returned to Detrasarn, but Mergon and Drivian still accompanied Infiron as she led them up the road. After a while the ridge of the mountains fell behind them and there, through the falling rain, stark against the lighter sky to the north, three dark fingers of stone pointed upwards towards the sky.

"Behold—" said Infiron.

But before she had time to finish, the thunder of hooves was heard approaching from the east. A large group of riders came into view. They were clad in the raiment of Quiglings. Harla and Margana moved into position ahead of the group to face the riders as they drew their horses up.

"Jarta-Den," said Harla.

The Quigling sat astride a horse amongst his comrades.

"Well met, Harla," he said. "I see that the Stonebearer is safe."

"Have you heard any report from Careil?" asked Harla.

"I have not seen him since he left Herardin last night," said Jarta-Den. "Did he not accompany Hyrn?"

"He rode back to the castle to meet up with you and report on our whereabouts," said Harla.

"I left with Captain Droom and several riders at first-light this morning to continue to search for the Ultamarians," said Jarta-Den. "Careil had not arrived when we left. Droom is searching for our quarry back towards Herardin. He is to return within the hour. Perhaps he has met with Careil."

The Quigling paused. "But we have more pressing concerns. A large party of Ultamarians is coming up the road from the east, we suspect they are relief soldiers sent from Ultamar to relieve the garrison at the Castle. They have come across the Detradin causeway. The Stonebearer must be hidden and it is best that you seek shelter. This storm will only get worse."

"What about up there," said a voice from behind Harla.

Wren stood, water dripping from his wet hair, pointing, with wonder in his eyes, up at the three towers standing resolutely on the hillside through the pouring rain.

"It is as good a place as any," said Jarta-Den. "There have been no sign of patrols on the road to the towers. You will need to be wary of any Drargs that may be about. Although, they tend to steer clear of the Towers themselves. We are preparing a reception for the Ultamarians at Herardin, but we will continue our search, and keep an eye out for Careil. We will report when we are able."

Hyrn stood beside Wren looking up at the Towers of Arkenegelon. Something in him yearned to see the Towers, something almost irresistible.

"Onwards to the Towers of Arkenegelon!" he cried.

They stood in the alcove of the doorway of the central tower which stood a little to the east of the other two. This tower was larger than the others. It looked almost as if the other two towers stood in attendance of the larger tower, which stood lower on the hillside, but at its height still rose just above its attendants.

In front of them was a large stone door. The alcove sheltered them partially from the pounding rain, but thunder was rolling across the sky from the south and there were flashes of lightning which lit up the gloomy late afternoon sky, throwing the tall shadows of the towers across the hillside. Even the brightness of the sky to the north had now paled as the storm rolled across the northern vales and on, to the Drarg infested mountains that ran out to the wilds, eastwards towards Angil and the war in the east.

Infiron stood in front of the door and pulled a large stone key from within her robes. The key had a round handle but its shaft was straight and square. The Priest pushed the square end of the key into a matching square hole in the door. She did not turn the key but removed her hand and placed it on the stone door above the keyhole. She began to chant softly and Yarga beside her looked on in fascination as the key turned. Hyrn peering around Yarga saw that the square keyhole turned with the key but the stone around it did not seem to move. Hyrn could not see how this was achieved but as he watched he felt Ilah humming softly against his chest. Suddenly with a loud echoing crack the door began to open. Infiron turned slightly and beckoned them all inside, out of the pouring rain.

It was dark inside. Even the light of the gloomy daylight outside did not reach far. But it was quiet after the noise of the storm outside. Hyrn heard Infiron move to his right and scrabble about. There was a striking sound and light glared in the darkness as Infiron struck a flame and then applied it to a torch. Drivian then brought forth another torch and lit it from the one in Infiron's hand. The torches lit a small area around them showing a dusty stone floor. A sudden flash of lightning from the doorway behind them gave a brief glimpse of a much larger space, empty apart from a structure in the centre.

"There are more torches around the walls," said Drivian.

He moved further to the left, illuminating the stone walls as he went and then stopped before another torch mounted in the wall. He reached up and lit it from the one in his hand. Infiron moved around the chamber in the opposite direction. At various places around the wall, doorways stood leading to rooms beyond. Hyrn could now see that the structure in the centre was a large circular hearth. Logs and kindling were stacked in the centre of the circle. As Drivian, Mergon and Infiron completed lighting the circle of torches around the walls, they approached the fireplace and thrust their torches into the stack of wood. They stooped, holding their torches in concentration, and the wood burst into flames. The rest of the party; Hyrn, Wren, Garan, Yarga, Harla, Margana, Turum and Gebarana, gathered in their wet clothes around the welcome heat of the fire.

They had eaten a satisfying meal of what provisions they had, as they dried off. Above them the smoke of the fire was drawn up into the dark chasm that led up to the heights of the tower. A narrow stone stairway spiralled around the circular wall and disappeared up into the darkness. Yarga was intrigued with the towers and their history and questioned Infiron incessantly, but gently. The young Elder and the Priest both spoke in awe of the power that lay in the stone, and the works of the powers that fought for good in the world. Hyrn listened intently but continued to feel uneasy, as if something was nagging at his mind. His interest was piqued when Infiron spoke of the chamber at the top of the tower and the last stairway that led upwards and out onto a platform that held a device that was used as a signal beacon. Infiron was unsure of the details, as this was from the old kingdom, and hadn't been used since before the time that Darion had fled Anasaria.

With the mention of Darion, Yarga spoke to Infiron and Drivian regarding Errasarn and the Keeper Devarnia. Neither Priest had any recollection of reading anything about Devarnia passing through Anasaria. They had read accounts of contact with the Angilanians that mentioned the Keepers as part of the forces that battled in the east, but not in much detail. When Yarga spoke of the battle with the Mocker, Infiron's face became puzzled.

"The Mocker is a story told in Anasaria," she said, "but it is not generally considered to be a real creature. It is a creature of folklore; a cautionary tale told to children. I don't think that any believe in it."

"It was thought so too by the Caramar," said Yarga, "but Ilah saw the creature battle with Devarnia."

"That is evil news indeed," said Infiron. "But I don't recall any factual accounts of such a creature."

"Trion would know if there were," suggested Drivian.

"Who is Trion?" asked Yarga.

"A young Priest of our Order," replied Infiron. She paused and a frown creased her brow. "He is headstrong and eager to learn but he does not follow direction well. He has read more of the books in our library than any other that I know. His head is full of facts, and history and tales."

"I would love to talk to him," said Yarga. "I don't remember seeing him in Detrasarn."

Infiron sighed. "Unfortunately, he went out in search of Neferelon a few days ago and we have not heard from him. He was warned against such a deed. We fear that he has met with trouble."

As the evening wore on, they made preparations for sleep. Harla insisted that even within the protection of the tower, the Caramar warriors would keep watch. Infiron assured Harla that none could defeat the door without the key that she held, and even with the key, they would need to know the incantation to make the lock work. Harla eventually gave in and agreed that an unbroken night's sleep was welcome.

Hyrn had placed his blankets over to one side of the chamber. Wren lay beside him and they had settled down a little away from the others and near to where the stairs began to climb around the tower wall. Hyrn felt wide awake. Wren was trying to speak to him in whispered tones but his mind kept drifting off, distracted. He lay on his back, looking up into the darkness above. The flickering light of the fire occasionally illuminated the walls higher up and showed the upper sections of the stairs.

"Hyrn, where are we going tomorrow?"

The whispered question brought Hyrn out of his reverie. Wren looked at him expectantly in the glow of the firelight.

"I don't know," said Hyrn in a hushed voice. "I guess we wait to hear from Jarta-Den and …"

He almost said 'Careil' and began to worry but the voice in his head soothed him and diverted his attention back up towards the top of the tower. Hyrn looked over to where the rest of the party were lying around the fire. There seemed to be no movement from any of them. Garan also seemed to be sleeping a little away from them, his unceasing vigilance giving way to a much needed rest within the protection of the ancient tower.

Hyrn fixed Wren with a serious expression.

"Be very quiet and follow me," whispered Hyrn, forcefully.

"What—?" began Wren in a low hiss, but Hyrn shushed him raising his finger to his lips in warning.

Wren sighed quietly and wriggled out of his blanket as Hyrn, already up, crouched low and made his way towards the stairway.

Wren thought about trying to talk Hyrn out of this, but he followed reluctantly behind as Hyrn mounted the first step and then began to creep slowly up the stairs. The stairs were not wide and had no rail but the two boys kept close to the wall. A noise from near the fire brought them to a halt. They stood motionless as Yarga grumbled in his sleep and then settled down again. They continued slowly up the stairs, the glow of the dying fire getting further below them as they climbed. As they circled the tower wall higher and higher, Wren began to feel sick with the thought of the fall below them but resolutely followed Hyrn up to the top of the stairway until, eventually, they came out onto a wide stone platform.

It was pitch black up here but Hyrn pulled Ilah from within his vest and the Stone glowed with a dim light that lit their surroundings. The chamber was furnished plainly with a table and some chairs. The ceiling was quite low and to their right a wooden staircase ran up to a trapdoor in the ceiling.

"Come on," said Hyrn.

"What are you doing?" asked Wren desperately.

"Just come on," replied Hyrn.

Hyrn felt a sense of excitement as he headed across the chamber towards the staircase. As he climbed, holding Ilah above him, with his other hand he pulled the iron hook from where it rested heavily against his ribs. He stopped just beneath the trapdoor. By the light of the Stone, he inserted the arm of the hook into a hole in the centre of the trapdoor. Ilah began to hum. There was a rasping creak that reverberated around the small chamber. Hyrn pushed upwards and the trapdoor moved up and away, and clattered against stone. The sky appeared above him. The air was cold and fresh. Overhead the cloud was breaking up. The light of the rising moon could be seen trying to break through, but lightning still flashed in the sky as the storm moved away northward.

Hyrn climbed up the last of the stairs and out onto the parapet of the tower. The strong wind buffeted him and he shivered as the cold air surrounded him. Wren appeared behind him, but Hyrn did not look around. If he had, he would have seen the look of worry on the Anasarian's face in the moonlight. Instead, he knelt down and pulled the iron hook from the open trapdoor where it lay beside the dark hole they had exited. Just behind Hyrn, in the centre of the parapet, was a strangely shaped sculpture. He rose to his feet and turned to face the looming shape. Wren moved up beside him.

It appeared to be a man but one whose features had been melted. It held out a misshapen arm pointing to the east, away from where the boys stood. Its other hand was by its side grasping at nothing.

"Ugly!" said Wren.

Hyrn ignored him.

What resembled the right arm of the statue hung downwards but was reaching towards the east. The right hand of the statue had its palm outwards. Hyrn took the iron hook and placed it in the hand of the statue. As he did, the stone hand grasped the iron hook and the hand turned downwards. At the same time, Hyrn felt Ilah begin to vibrate in his hand and saw that the Stone glowed more brightly. By the light of the Stone he saw that a small niche had opened in the back of the malformed man. Without giving any thought to what he was doing, Hyrn held Ilah forward and slotted the Stone into the niche.

The effect was immediate and stunning.

The statue began to change shape. From its distorted form it steadily metamorphosed into a tall beautifully carved figure. The features of the statue glowed with a pale greenish golden light. Its outstretched arm turned into a perfectly formed one. Its outstretched hand suddenly erupted in a dazzling beam of light that shot out eastwards into the night.

Hyrn stood dumbstruck.

Several things happened at once.

As Hyrn stood, rooted to the spot, the statue turned its head towards him peering over its right shoulder. Its eyes glowed with the greenish light, but tinged with sparks of gold. Then the statue spoke, and its voice was clear and loud.

"Who are you?" said the figure, its gaze strong and intent.

Hyrn's mouth gaped open. Wren was already turning to run, when Infiron burst from the trapdoor and in two bounds reached out and wrenched the hook from the statue's hand.

Instantly the beam of light was extinguished and the dark of the night returned. The statue regained its former stance and then melted into its original misshapen form.

Infiron turned to the two boys.

"What have you done?" she said furiously, but her voice held a tinge of fear.

High in their sanctuary atop the central tower of the Fortress of Ultamar, the seven Dark Lords sat around a large roughly hewn oval table. The table held the remnants of a ghastly meal. The room was dim. The only light came from torches burning dully in iron brackets around the walls. The room seemed as if it was bathed in blood. The room reeked of acrid smoke and decay. The hoods of the seven figures hid their cruel disfigured faces. They spoke in rasping, bitter tones.

The Dark Lords were troubled. There had still been no word from General Ferian at the front and no recent news had been received of the campaign to capture the Angilanian Stone. There had been news which had just come in, of signal fires out amongst the Anasarian rats out on the Plain of the Winds. Something was going on.

The large windows on the northern side of the circular chamber lit up from time to time with flashes of lightning piercing the dimness of the dark chamber.

All of a sudden, a startlingly bright beam of light exploded across the sky from the northwest and travelled north of the fortress and away to the east. It held in the sky for a few moments. The Dark Lords scrambled to their feet, and then abruptly the light vanished.

One of the evil Lords, Preskatchion, stood before the window closest to the source of the beam of light. "The Towers!" he screeched.

Then he raised his voice and screamed, "General Gardwan!"

CHAPTER FIFTEEN

The Sword of the King

They rode at pace down the road following the gentle slope of the terrain, down towards the river and onwards to Artora. Rowan had decided that they could not wait to hear news from Bregal and Gorum. He had insisted that he would ride alone if necessary, but instead he was surrounded by Quiglings on horseback. Behind him, holding on tightly, was Arienga. Beside him, to his right, rode Carlan, with Duburinga riding behind them competently, but seeming a little out of place, atop a fierce looking horse. Some of the Quiglings they had met that morning, had stayed behind with Kerian, Jorunum, Terrana and Boriega. The Quiglings had relinquished two horses for Carlan and Duburinga and another for Biren-So who was now ahead, scouting the road with Dooren-Ga.

Rowan felt a sense of dread. The sky above was beginning to darken. The air itself felt tense. Why had he let Bregal and Gorum go ahead without joining them? Something burned inside him that he could not name. As he had watched that signal fire out on the plain, something had sparked in him that he hadn't noticed at first, but had slowly become a feeling of determination. Despite the warnings of caution from Duburinga and Carlan amongst others, he had insisted on the need to join the pursuit. The others had acquiesced to Rowan as the bearer of the Sword, and as one of the two brothers that had been charged with this quest. A party had been formed, and the others were to follow, and to rouse the forces of resistance against Ultamar.

Just behind Duburinga, a young Quigling rode. Despite the seriousness of the situation, this Quigling could not hide his enthusiasm. He had continuously been bantering about the prospect of fighting against the forces of evil. It seemed like almost an adventure to him. One of the older Quiglings rode up alongside him and looked at his young comrade with disapproval.

"Grengal!" he said sternly. "Remember our purpose. Do not get caught up in childish thoughts of swordplay. We meet the old enemy and we take revenge by ensuring that justice is served. This is serious."

"I know, I know, Charen-Ba," said Grengal lightly. "But we are strong and we are finally moving openly."

"We are only moving openly because we have no choice," said the older Quigling. "The time for open war is not yet upon us."

Charen-Ba spurred his horse forward and moved past Rowan and his protectors. Grengal also moved forward past Duburinga and then slowed to ride to the left of Rowan and Arienga. He did not address Rowan but looked instead at Arienga. He switched his vision between watching the road ahead and the odd glance at Rowan, but the rest of his attention was directed towards Arienga.

He fixed the Caramar warrior with his gaze and said nonchalantly, "So do you often chase Artorans?"

Arienga, still holding on to Rowan, looked sideways at the Quigling with amazement on her face and replied, "Is that the best you can do?"

"Hey, we're riding down a road towards possible death," responded Grengal, with feigned indignation. "I for one am happy to die. I just want to make sure that I'm with experienced fighters."

"If we stopped for just a moment I could show you what fighting really looks like," said Arienga.

The last word was almost ripped out of her mouth as Rowan suddenly spurred Arrow forward and away from the Quigling. Arienga, almost losing her grasp, turned back quickly towards Rowan in front of her.

"What is it Rowan?" she said concernedly. "Can you see something?"

Rowan did not speak, but Arienga felt that he had tensed up. She felt the sword at his back dig into her.

"Rowan? What is it?" asked Arienga urgently.

Rowan responded gruffly. "It's nothing. I just need to concentrate without someone talking like a fool."

Arienga was confused for a second and then responded curtly, "I'd like to know who you think is the fool that you have to listen to."

Rowan stared forward and said contemptuously, "That idiot you were talking to."

Many things flashed through Arienga's head. This boy. This boy who she was trying to help. He wanted to tell her who she could talk to. She felt furious at the thought that he could be so ungrateful and angry…and jealous!

Without thinking, Arienga retorted, "He's just trying to be friendly."

"And I suppose you had to be friendly too?" said Rowan.

Taken aback, Arienga replied, "I challenged him to a fight."

Rowan stewed momentarily and then retorted, "I'm sure he would have loved that."

Arienga felt herself getting angry but refrained from replying. She thought how ridiculous it was.

They rode in silence for a while.

Rowan felt angry and annoyed and was trying to justify to himself why. They had serious business to deal with and Arienga was…was…

At that moment, the riders ahead pulled their mounts up. Rowan could see that they were on the outskirts of a small village. A group of people were blocking the roadway ahead. The two Quiglings, Biren-So and Dooren-Ga had dismounted and were talking to the gathering ahead. Rowan pushed Arrow towards the discussion, and as he did so, Biren-So turned back and signalled to him to come forward. Rowan rode through the Quiglings and stopped Arrow beside Biren-So. He felt that the eyes of all those gathered were upon him. He absent-mindedly helped Arienga to dismount and then did so himself.

Biren-So spoke to Rowan. "These are Anasarians from around here. They have heard that war is afoot and they have heard that the Sword of Acclimoss has returned to Anasaria. They are eager to challenge Ultamar but they want to know if what they hear is true, and that this is not just another trick of the Ultamarians."

Rowan was about to answer but Biren-So continued, "There is something else. There is an old woman here that says she must speak to you. She says it is vital that you hear what she has to say."

Rowan said nothing but he moved forward and stood before the gathering of Anasarians blocking the roadway. He felt the weight of their gaze. The mumbling amongst the crowd ceased and they looked towards him expectantly. Rowan ignored the sword on his back. For some reason he felt that he needed to speak to these people and make them understand. He looked around at their faces; faces filled with doubt and hope. There also seemed to be desperation in them, and a simmering anger that reflected their defiance in the face of oppression. They were on edge, and poised for something, even if they were not sure what it was.

Rowan steeled himself and began. "People, we come here to free Anasaria. My brother and I were charged with this duty; to unite the Twin Stones and to return the Sword. We want to help free Anasaria from the chains of Ultamar."

Rowan paused and looked around. The Anasarians were beginning to become even more worked up. They were murmuring and chattering amongst themselves. One word seemed to stand out, 'sword'. He felt the weight of at his back. He felt the desire to draw the Sword and hold it aloft for all those gathered to see, but he resisted. The words of Arienga played in his mind. "Do not draw your sword unless you are prepared to use it." He became resolute in what he must do.

"The Sword is here but I will not draw it until it is needed," said Rowan.

He undid the harness that secured the Sword and taking it by his sheath held it out in front of him with the tip pointing downwards and the hilt above displayed for the Anasarians to see.

"This is the Sword of Acclimoss!" he said loudly. "It is here to reclaim Abessair from the Dark Lords and to release Anasaria from them."

The crowd were now watching intently and there was excited talk all around. But a woman moved out from amongst them and stood in front of Rowan. She stared at him intently and Rowan's eyes met her's. Her aged face seemed to be joyful but her joy was tempered by a burden of worry. When she spoke, her voice caught Rowan by surprise. The old woman's voice did not seem to fit her aged features. Instead Rowan heard the voice of a much younger woman.

"There is a way to tell if this is truly the sword of the King," she said.

Rowan replied defensively, "This is the Sword of Acclimoss. We were told by a Keeper where it was and we found it with the help of Ilah."

The woman laughed. "Stories and tales of adventure are all very well, but there is a test. The test will prove if what you say is true and—"

Rowan interrupted her. "It is true!" he said abruptly, with a sense of annoyance growing in him.

The old woman looked at Rowan for a moment and then said, calmly, "If it is true then you will pass the test. If you lie, then our hope will be diminished but we will remain defiant. I feel that either way, something has already started that cannot be easily stopped. This is perhaps the time that the people of Anasaria say 'Enough' and even without the Sword and the Stones, we will take war to Ultamar and die in the attempt if necessary. For too long have we lived in fear and suffering. We will fight, and then we shall see if the strength of Anasaria is the match of the evil might of Ultamar."

Rowan looked at her uncertainly. He looked back to where Biren-So stood and saw the figure of Carlan approaching. The Abessairian came and stood beside Rowan.

"What is this test that you want to put the Swordbearer through?" asked Carlan, sternly.

There were rumblings of anger and disbelief amongst the crowd at the sight of the large soldier, his uniform still stained the dark hue of that of an

Ultamarian. The Anasarians seemed ready to erupt but the woman held her hand up. Her gaze was fixed on Carlan.

"Peace, comrades," she said. "Before you stands something we haven't seen for generations. This is a soldier of Abessair. Things are definitely changing, but we still must be cautious."

She looked directly into Carlan's eyes and said softly. "You have suffered for too long, soldier, but you have been kept for this. To help the power of Abessair return."

Carlan's face softened and a look of sadness passed across it.

The woman continued, "You must see that that power has not been seen since Darion left Anasaria. You and your comrades were seduced by the idea of the glory of the past that had gone. The Anasaria that the army of Abessair was created to protect, was not the same. But it has long been foretold that it would return. The power of Abessair is the power of good that still burns among the people. We have been subject to the brutality of Ultamar, but throughout the land, there is power that the Dark Lords do not understand."

A voice spoke stridently from behind Rowan. "We cannot be held up for too long. We must pursue the Artorans."

Duburinga stood there looking at the woman determinedly. The woman returned his gaze and looked at the Caramar intently.

"The warrior burns in you," said the woman, "and the power of stone flows from you, but you also understand wisdom. The claim needs to be tested if a challenge is to be made. The test will not take long and then the quest will continue."

Rowan spoke up, "What is this test, and who are you?"

"Well," said the woman, "my name is Crieven but, more importantly, I am part of a legacy that has been carried through my family for hundreds of years. We are followers of the one true King and his heirs. We bear allegiance to the line of King Darion."

"But, Darion was not—" began Rowan.

Crieven's face glowed with defiance and surety as she continued, "Darion's twin brother, Keridan, was not the first born. Something worked evil upon the fate of Anasaria. That evil still lives and we have guarded it over the generations to ensure that it cannot cause any more harm. Back down my line, when Bharain left Anasaria there became a belief among us that when the Sword of Acclimoss returned, evil would be put to the test and the Sword would prove itself. You must accompany me to prove that this is the true Sword and that our vigil has not been in vain."

Rowan was bewildered, and the woman's words left him confused, but the desire to prove himself welled up in him.

"Let us put the Sword to the test!" he said vehemently.

Duburinga beside Rowan, began to protest. "You cannot put Rowan in danger. We have vowed to protect him and we cannot allow him to be diverted from his mission."

"We are all in danger," said Crieven. "We have been in danger since the evil Lords took possession of Abessair. Rest assured that if his mission is to be fulfilled he will need to confront the past of Anasaria. The twin brothers, Keridan and Darion, were born near here, far from Abessair. We believe that the place that they were born, distorted the truth of their heritage and affected the course of the history of Abessair and Anasaria.

Come with me and I will tell you more. We do not have far to go and you will be back on the road and in pursuit of the Artorans before you know. Whatever time you lose, will be repaid by the knowledge of the truth of the past, and of your destiny."

Rowan looked at the woman intently, pondering, trying to make up his mind. He then looked at the two soldiers to his left, Carlan and Duburinga. One looked almost dazed and the other looked concerned. He turned to his right. There stood Arienga. She looked at him expectantly but her expression was hard to read. Rowan saw defiance but he also felt that behind her proud visage there was something else, perhaps anger. He thought briefly of his own anger at the thought of her talking to the young Quigling. He felt ashamed and looked into her eyes. He smiled at her awkwardly and then turned back to Crieven.

"I will come with you," he said.

The party headed out away from the village and travelled southwestwards. As they walked, Crieven told Rowan of the legend that had been passed down from generation to generation within her family, and of the history and nature of the place that they headed for…

⁕

Arionus, King of Anasaria, rode alongside the Queen, Tiranus. The Sword of Acclimoss hung from his hip. They rode through a peaceful and prosperous land. The power of good prevailed here. The Fortress of Abessair stood watch over Anasaria. The Twin Stones of Angil were safely ensconced in their tower, watched over by their faithful servants, the Priests of the Order of the Stones.

Mounted Abessairian soldiers, their uniforms shining white and silver in the afternoon sun, rode just ahead of Arionus and Tiranus, with many more following behind them. Their time in Seasview, the castle in the coastal hills that edged the Plain of the Winds, had sadly come to an end. The beginning of the storms of late summer presaged the passage through autumn to the snows of winter. And it was time to go home. Behind them, as they rode northwards towards Abessair, the sky began to darken.

They had hoped to make Fort Kirenk by nightfall but had been delayed by washed out river crossings and flooded fords. Their best hope now was one of the villages in the farmland near the crossroads with the road that ran eastwards towards Roaring Gorge, and onwards to Artora. The ominous clouds coming up from the ocean behind them, gave them a sense of urgency.

Arionus was worried. Tiranus was heavily pregnant. Arionus had suggested that she travel in one of the wagons that followed the entourage but Tiranus had insisted that she ride as usual, even if it meant riding side-saddle.

The afternoon sun was suddenly dimmed and then darkness seemed to grow all around them. The pursuing storm clouds caught the sun as it began to descend towards the west and then engulfed it. The wind was beginning to increase in intensity. General Carbin, who rode just ahead of the King, turned and addressed Arionus.

"The storm is coming in quickly," he shouted into the wind. "We will need to find shelter soon or we will be caught out in it."

Arionus looked towards Tiranus with concern on his face. He noticed that her usual calm, determined expression was tinged with pain.

"What is it Tira?" he said.

The Queen collected herself and said, "It is nothing to be concerned about but I feel that my time may be near."

Arionus paled slightly and then called to the General. "How far is the next village?"

Carbin answered, the wind snatching at his words, "It is still a reasonable distance; about an hour's journey."

"Send soldiers ahead," said Arionus. "Prepare somewhere to stop for the night and ensure that there is a healer at hand."

Carbin looked back at the King questioningly and then glanced at the Queen. Her pained expression hit home and the General launched into action, directing one of his Captains to marshal soldiers to ride ahead. Immediately a contingent had ridden off at a fast pace towards the main road. The General sent other riders ahead, and into the areas away from the road, to see if there were any healers living in the surrounding countryside.

They travelled on. Arionus becoming increasingly worried as his wife began to look more and more uncomfortable beside him. The wind was whipping at the trees that lined the roadside. The sky now was cloaked in clouds. The fierce wind occasionally brought stinging drops of rain. There was a gasping groan from beside Arionus.

"Alright," said Tiranus in a pained voice. "I don't think I should ride anymore. We have to stop soon."

"Carbin!" called Arionus. "We need to find shelter soon."

"There may be dwellings in the hills further ahead," the General called back, "but the village is still a way off, beyond the hills."

Arionus brought his horse to a standstill and dismounted. He turned and offered his hand to Tiranus and then helped her down from her horse. Tiranus stood there looking uncomfortable and now a bit worried. General Carbin signalled to soldiers behind them and Arionus turned and saw that one of the wagons had already been brought up from the rear. He looked back at Carbin who just shrugged.

"Just doing my job," said the General.

As they approached the hills, gusts of rain started to hit them more frequently. Arionus began to hear groans from the wagon behind him. Ahead, through the dim light, the sound of hooves was heard. A soldier came into view and rode up to them coming to a halt before the General.

"General," he said formally, "there is a woman ahead who claims to be a healer and says that she has a place to shelter."

General Carbin looked to the King. Another groan escaped from the wagon behind.

"Take us to her," said Arionus firmly.

In a copse of trees, not far from the road's edge, the woman stood hunched. Before her stood the King of Anasaria. Rain fell around them, filtering through the trees. Lightning flashed all around, as the dim light of the afternoon moved towards the blackness of night. Arionus looked at the woman intently.

"You are a healer?" he asked urgently.

"I am from a long line of healers," said the woman with a croak in her voice.

"My wife is in need of you," said the King. "She is about to give birth."

"There is a place nearby where it is dry," said the woman. "She will be safe there and I can help her."

The healer led them down into a small vale and towards a scar in the hillside. It was now difficult to see, but the Abessairians held guttering torches and lightning continuously bathed the area in flashes of light. As they neared the hillside they could see that there was a dark opening. The woman led them to the cave entrance and motioned for one of the soldiers bearing a torch to move forward.

They walked, crouching at times, through a passage. Tiranus was being carried on a bier by four Abessairians. The light of the torches suddenly lit a larger space as they came out into the interior of the cave. In the torchlight Arionus could see rough pillars and boulders that hid places where the light didn't reach. Further back in the cave, hidden by a ridge of rock that jutted from the floor, a faint blue glow could be seen. The floor was sand. At places around the walls there was the odd piece of furniture. In a nook there was a bed. Beside the bed were bundles of cloth and other equipment. Alongside sat a pot of steaming water. The woman beckoned for them to bring the queen over. Arionus helped her from the bier and onto the bed. Tiranus was now panting softly as she lay down.

The healer crouched down beside the queen and said softly. "Your babies will be here soon."

"Babies?" said Arionus in a startled voice.

"The queen carries two boys," said the woman. "I am here to make sure that they are delivered safely."

"It seems as if you knew that we were coming," said Arionus.

"The Stone knew and commanded me to be here," said the woman.

"Which Stone?" asked the King.

"The Eye Stone at the heart of this cave," replied the woman. "Now please leave me to my work."

"Of course," said Arionus. "What can we do to help?"

"There is nothing you need do. I have everything prepared," said the woman and a strange smile danced across her face.

Arionus stood behind the woman looking at his wife. The nook that the bed lay in was too narrow to allow him to be beside his wife, with the woman and her equipment blocking the way. He began to pace nervously as Tiranus's groans got fiercer. The King looked towards the end of the cave. From this spot deeper in the cave the blue light was much brighter and he could see it flickering more clearly.

He became mesmerised by the flickering blue light and felt drawn too it. He wandered closer to it. As his wife's cries grew more strident he felt that the blue light became fiercer. He saw that one of the soldiers was standing staring at the blue light. He moved past the ridge of rock in the cave floor, past the immobile soldier and looked directly into a large blue eye. The Stone was embedded in the rock of the cave wall. Although the eye was made of stone Arionus felt the intensity of its gaze. The blackness of the pupil seemed to swallow him up. Behind him he heard a desperate, intense cry from his wife. He tried to turn but felt the eye holding him.

He then heard the cry of a baby. As the cry hung in the air the Eye Stone burst into brilliant, blinding, blue light. Arionus felt himself bombarded by the stench of evil. The blue light continued to pour from the Stone. The King resisted the pull of the Stone and grasped the hilt of his sword. The Sword of Acclimoss flashed from its sheath and Arionus raised it, and then, lunging at the Stone, thrust it into the centre of the eye's pupil. There was a mental struggle as he was beset with malevolence.

In the midst of this turmoil, Arionus heard another baby's cry. The blue light seemed to gain in intensity momentarily but he thrust harder with his sword and suddenly something broke and the blue light diminished and shrank down to a dull blue glow.

Arionus pulled the end of his sword from the Stone. There was a hole in the dark centre of the Stone and flashes of gold could be seen where the sword had penetrated, Arionus sheathed his sword quickly and turned. He noticed that the soldier who had stood nearby, was now sprawled on the floor unconscious, or worse. He rushed back towards where Tiranus lay. The healer was kneeling at the foot of the bed swaddling the twins. Arionus moved up behind her and looked down at his sons. The woman placed one of the babies in Tiranus's arms.

"The first," she said quietly.

The woman then turned to the King and held out the other baby. At first she seemed to have a look of satisfaction on her face but a grimace of pain contorted her features. Her expression became one of bewilderment and confusion but she controlled herself, and said calmly, "Your two sons."

The woman looked into the eyes of the King and began to weep softly.

"I do not know how I came to be here," she said in a strained voice, "but it is well that I am here. You were in need of a healer."

Arionus looked down at the woman and then reached out his free hand to help her to her feet.

"What of the Stone?" he said, wearily.

The woman looked around in a panic.

"The Stone?" she asked, confused.

"The Eye Stone," said the King.

"I remember a blue eye," began the woman. "It came to me in my dreams. It frightened me but it was as if it was calling to me. I did not like it. The eye was evil."

"I have defeated the eye," said Arionus. "Whatever evil it sought to do is over. The Sword of Acclimoss was strong enough."

He moved past the woman and knelt down next to his wife. Tiranus's face was weary and bathed in sweat but she smiled up at him.

"Our sons," she said softly. "Keridan."

She motioned with her head towards the baby she cradled. Arionus placed the other baby on the other side of his wife.

"And Darion," she said.

The King kissed Tiranus on the forehead. He rose to his feet but stumbled a little. He felt so tired. He turned to General Carbin who waited nearby.

"Once this storm has passed we must return to Abessair," he said to the General. "Get things ready. This is no place for infants."

He then wandered over to the heart of the cave. The soldier still lay there but was alive and groaning. Another soldier knelt beside him. Arionus looked to where the Stone had glowed within the wall. The blue light could only be seen faintly but instead of the blackness in its centre, flashes of gold danced within the Stone. The King sat down and rested his back against the ridge of rock. "So tired," he thought. "I must rest."

⁘

Crieven looked at Rowan as she spoke. Rowan listened intently, fascinated by the tale.

"Arionus never recovered from that day," continued Crieven. "He became very ill, and before Keridan and Darion were a year old the King was dead. Tiranus ruled Anasaria until Keridan's sixteenth birthday, when the boy became King. Anasaria was never the same again. There developed a great rivalry between Keridan and Darion and a few years after Keridan's ascension to the throne Darion decided to leave Anasaria. The land fell on hard times; crops failed and things began to fall into decay. The Abessairian army held together for many years but after a few generations, even the loyal soldiers began to question their service.

Everything changed from the time of the events in that cave. My family have come to learn that evil was at work that night and that the twins were switched. The second born son was named Keridan and the eldest who was handed to the King second by the woman was named Darion. Our sorrow began then. We have tried to spread the news but none believed us and by the time of King Bharain, none seemed to care."

"How do you know all this?" asked Rowan.

"Well," said Crieven, "the woman in that cave was named Gariana. She was my ancestor. She was a healer, as were those that came before and after her. But she was bewitched by the Eye Stone. She later recalled that she came across the cave while seeking out healing Stones and medicinal plants. The Stone hypnotised her and made sure that she was ready to play a part in its evil intents. After the Stone was pierced by the Sword of Acclimoss the evil was drained out of it and instead it held some of the power of the Sword. It is our belief that the evil flowed into Arionus and while not able to defeat his mind destroyed his body. We have communed with the Stone over the centuries. It still retains some evil but the power of the Sword has blinded it and it struggles within itself. The Stone is in conflict between good and evil but when the power of good is dominant the one consistent thought is that one day it will meet the Sword of Acclimoss again and then it will know that balance will be restored."

With that Crieven held up her hand and pointed. Rowan saw that they had come to a halt in front of a cave mouth in the hillside. The sky above had now become darker. The wind blew fiercely from the southwest.

"Unlike Arionus you are here before the rain begins," said Crieven.

The interior of the cave was dim. The healer had lit a torch that made muted shadows dance around them. Duburinga lit another torch, and the brighter light showed the extent of the cave with its pillars and protrusions of rock sprouting from the sandy floor. Occasionally Rowan saw a flash of gold light from the back of the cave. Carlan stood beside Rowan, and Duburinga and Arienga stood just behind him. Biren-So accompanied Crieven as she began to lead them towards the place where the gold flashes emanated.

Rowan glanced to his right and saw a niche in the wall. He thought about the story that Crieven had told. Darion was born here. He followed the Healer and, as they walked forward, he saw the ridge in the floor of the cave which Crieven had described. She and Biren-So passed around it and then stopped. The flicker of gold lit Biren-So's face as he turned and beckoned for Rowan to come forward.

"The Stone is indeed in conflict," said the Quigling.

Rowan came alongside Biren-So and looked into the Stone. It was just as Crieven had described. The oval shaped Stone was embedded in the rock. Where it met the rock, there was a halo of dim blue light. In the centre of this halo was what looked like a whirlpool of flashing gold light.

Rowan stood transfixed and felt the whirlpool dragging at his thoughts. He thought he heard almost a cry for help from the Stone. He sensed a deep feeling of need. The whirlpool became his mind. There was the power of good, the power of a King, fighting, striving desperately to not be sucked down into a deep black hole, surrounded and trapped by an incessant, evil hatred. The memory of that night centuries ago felt like a piercing brightness; the flash of steel and the flow of power struggling with a sickening blackness. He was that blade. Rowan felt a strong hand grab at his arm. But it was not his arm. He was Arionus, King of Anasaria and the Sword of Acclimoss drove itself deep into the centre of the whirlpool.

Rowan tried to come back to reality but felt himself being sucked down into a place where no light could ever shine. A blackness so complete that he began to feel himself and his essence being drained. But the Sword was in his hands and he could feel its brightness in his mind. The Sword of Acclimoss stood like a beacon in a sea of black. He just needed to reach the light. He struggled as he felt the dark water pulling at him, trying to drown him. In his mind, he kept his eyes fixed on the brightness of the Sword. He drew up a well of determination from within and forced himself through the blackness. The Sword grew before him, and as he got closer, he saw that it was standing, thrust into a small island of rock, the brightness of the Sword bathing the island in a golden light.

As he struggled against the pull of the black water he felt solid ground beneath his feet. He planted his feet against the rocky bottom and strode up the shore of the island and stood facing the Sword of Acclimoss. He grasped the hilt of the Sword and began to pull it from the rock. As he did he saw that black water began to flow from where the blade pierced the rock. He felt faintly that the rock he stood on began to sink slightly.

Rowan stopped pulling at the Sword and instead thrust it deeper into the rock. He suddenly felt hands upon his, helping him to drive the Sword of Acclimoss deeper into the rock. As he began to look up, he could see that a pale shape stood on the opposite side of the Sword. He raised his head and before him stood, smiling but determined, a tall king. He was ghostly in appearance, glowing white. Rowan was transfixed. He felt the King's power; felt what he had driven into the centre of the Eye Stone.

The ghostly king looked deeply at Rowan and smiling broadly said, "Together."

The King pushed harder, driving the Sword deeper, and Rowan summoned up all his strength. He drove downwards with all his might. He strained and saw that the King was using all his energy as well. All of a sudden it was as if something had burst. A fountain of pale blue light burst from where the Sword pierced the rock. The pale figure of the King was blasted into the air. He smiled down as he rose and then his form began to dissipate.

Arionus said just one word before he completely disappeared, "Darion!"

Rowan stood at the top of a tower that stood tall above a large fortress.

The sun shone brightly as he looked out over a green and beautiful land bathed in golden light. The wind blew lightly from the east and he felt the power of far off mountains, and in his hands he held the twin children of those mountains. To the north he felt the blackness of a storm disappearing over the wall of mountains that protected the land. He heard the low distant grumble of thunder. He held firmly to the Twin Stones and felt their voices in his head. Then he noticed that his sword lay on the ground before him. He tried to grasp at the sword but the voices of the Stones sounded louder in his head.

"Are you alright? Rowan? Rowan? Are you alright?"

The scene of the land stretching out before him began to fade but the brightness of the sun still shone around him. He still groped for his sword but from out of the brightness a dark shape appeared. The shape was silhouetted by golden light. He tried to make out the shape and then a face emerged from the darkness. A worried face, a face he knew well, a face he…

"Rowan?" said Arienga. "Are you alright?"

"Arienga," said Rowan a little shakily.

He lay on the stone floor of the cave.

"Rowan," said Arienga with a sigh of relief.

"I'm sorry," said Rowan.

"What for?" said Arienga.

"I'm sorry about before," said Rowan. "It was stupid."

Arienga was confused, but then realised what he meant and said with a wry smile, "Yes, it was, but don't worry about that. I'm just thankful you're alive. Why did you attack the Stone suddenly like that? It was crazy… but you did something to it."

Rowan saw that the golden light still poured from behind Arienga.

"What happened?" he asked.

From his right a voice said, "It is done. The Sword of Acclimoss has returned to Anasaria. Just as Arionus did, you fought the Stone, but you finished what Arionus started."

Crieven stood there with a look of peace and wonderment on her face.

"He called me Darion," said Rowan remembering.

"Who did?" asked Arienga.

"The King," replied Rowan.

Crieven gasped. "You saw the King?"

"I think it was Arionus," said Rowan. "I felt like I was him at first."

Rowan then collected his thoughts and propped himself up on his elbow.

"But what happened to the Stone?" he asked.

A voice spoke in his head and he was reminded of the feeling of standing before the Sagenstone.

"Now I can see, and the other eyes can not see me," said the Stone.

Rowan looked past Arienga and saw that a golden eye peered out from the rock wall.

The voice spoke in his head again. "The King is waiting for you and you will meet him soon enough."

"Where is the King?" asked Rowan in his head. "And who is the King?"

"You will find out when he is ready," said the Eye Stone.

At that moment there was a tremor through the ground. Rowan felt the Stone cry out in anguish and then abruptly the golden light was extinguished leaving them in darkness apart from the guttering light of the torches behind them and the one in Crieven's hand.

"What was that?" asked Biren-So from beside Crieven.

"Evil has been used against the forces of good and against the very rock of the land," said the healer.

Carlan appeared beside Rowan looking down on him with concern and awe.

Duburinga growled impatiently from behind them. "You have had your test. Now we must give pursuit to the Artorans. Our comrades are in danger and the Stone slips from our grasp."

Rowan tried to get up, but felt like a great weight was on him. Arienga reached out and grasped his hand. Rowan took it gratefully. Arienga helped him to his feet and then steadied him as he swayed and then regained his balance.

"Let's get back to the horses," said Duburinga forcefully. "Now we give chase. The rock of this land calls out to us."

Duburinga strode back towards the cave entrance and Arienga followed, still supporting Rowan. Carlan walked beside them with Biren-So and Crieven following behind.

Arienga leant close to Rowan and whispered in his ear, "From now on, I'll only challenge you to fight me."

Rowan's heart skipped a beat and he wanted to reply, but instead just beamed tiredly at the Caramar warrior as she helped him across the cave, and through the entrance tunnel and out into the pouring rain.

They rode fast down the roadway, the thunder of hooves echoing all around them as the land rose up on either side. Rowan sat upon Arrow's back and held on to Arienga as she drove the horse to keep pace with Biren-So, Dooren-Ga and Duburinga riding ahead of them. Carlan stayed alongside them, with the other riders not too far behind.

Rowan had farewelled the healer as she stood in the small valley, surrounded by Anasarians from the village.

"The Sword has truly returned," Crieven had said joyously, and her face was aglow as she continued. "And now we know that it is the time to fight."

The rocky hillsides to either side grew steeper as they continued down the road, until eventually they were riding through a canyon. They rode through rain, and bursts of thunder and lightning. The road ahead took a sharp curve to the left and as they thundered around the bend, they saw ahead a deep gorge with a bridge vaulting across it. The three riders slowed. Arienga pulled up Arrow. The roadway was strewn with boulders just before where the entrance to the bridge lay. They could see people busily at work clearing the road. Beyond, across the bridge, a large wall of rubble blocked the road. They could see figures milling around the rubble, but Rowan noticed just ahead and to the left of the road a familiar armoured figure. The figure stood facing them, waiting as they approached and pulled up before him.

"Gorum," said Biren-So. "Where are the Artorans?"

Rowan looked at the Underdweller as Gorum, standing soaked, with water running down his face, turned towards the bridge. Rowan had a sudden fearful thought.

"Where is Bregal?" asked Rowan abruptly.

Gorum looked towards the rock wall at the left of the road. A large bundle lay there. A bundle that moved and spasmed. Beside the bundle a horse stood motionless its head drooping downwards. A horse that was immediately familiar to Rowan. Marron.

"He is here," said Gorum solemnly. "But he has been wounded by an evil force."

Rowan despite his weariness climbed down from Arrow's back and walking forward stood facing the Underdweller. Carlan dismounted and stood at Rowan's shoulder.

As the rest of their party caught up with them, Grengal rode towards them. A hooded figure leapt down from where they had been seated behind Grengal horse. She threw back her hood. There stood the healer, Crieven.

She stood before Gorum and asked anxiously, "Has anyone touched him?"

"I brought him here from the bridge," said Gorum.

The woman looked at Gorum and then said forcefully, "Look into my eyes, soldier."

Gorum looked straight at Crieven and held her gaze. The healer stared at him intently.

Finally, she said, "It is well. You don't seem infected, but your friend here," she looked towards the restless body of Bregal, "emanates the scourge of evil."

"What can we do?" asked Gorum desperately.

"You must continue the quest," said the healer. "I am here because this is where I am needed. I will tend your companion. There is nothing that you can do. This is beyond you and perhaps beyond me, but there is help nearby. Leave him to me."

"Can the Sword help?" asked Rowan.

"No, Rowan," said Crieven. "You are the wielder of the Sword but you are too drained of strength. My family has been trying to repay our debt to Anasaria since that fateful night so long ago. This is my chance to help. Go, continue on, and all my wishes and hopes go with you."

The Quiglings and Anasarians were creating a path over the mound of debris that blocked the road. The questers stood where the bridge met the road at the other side of the river. Behind them the river complained loudly as it fought its way between the steep rocky walls of the gorge. A tall Quigling stood on the side of the mound and called down to them.

"We have sent people ahead on foot to pursue the Artorans. We hope to be able to get horses across soon."

"Do you know which way they have gone?" Biren-So shouted up to the tall Quigling.

"They are heading out into the wild to the south of the road," replied the other Quigling.

Biren-So turned towards where Rowan sat behind Arienga.

"The country out there is treacherous lowlands crisscrossed by gullies and ridges," he said. "There are forests and woodlands but the land is full of bogs and marshes where the Trebian spreads out as it pushes towards the sea."

"Are there more Artorans there?" asked Rowan.

"It is still Anasaria and there are Anasarians living there away from the power of Ultamar. There is a strong force of resistance that has stood in defiance of the Dark Lords. My comrades also move amongst them and indeed further to the south near the coast we Quiglings have an outpost. It reminds us of the home that we lost long ago. Our home that now sits deep behind enemy lines, far to the east." He paused and then said, "But this land extends out to the walls of Artora. I have no doubt that they send personnel out into these lands, but our people are well hidden and well armed. Any Artoran scouts or spies that venture near would not return to Artora. It would take a Sorcerer to challenge them and they are not likely to go to that trouble."

Members of their party began to help clear a path over the rubble. Rowan was too tired and sore to be of any help. There was a guard post to the left of the bridge and Rowan now sat inside. The room was dirty but he was glad of a dry place to rest. The rain pounded down outside and the lightning flashed, accompanied by crashes of thunder. The Sword of Acclimoss lay beside him in its sheath, the hilt occasionally illuminated by the flashes of lightning through the windows and broken door. He felt like he was dozing as he stared at the Sword. A flash of lightning played across the hilt and it seemed that the images of the Stones at either end of the guard danced with light, and the light remained after the lightning and then faded. Rowan shook his head. He was falling asleep and imagining things.

Just then Arienga came through the door. She looked to where he sat in the dim light.

"Rowan, are you alright in here?" she asked. "We should be able to get through soon and we need to be ready."

Rowan pulled himself to his feet.

"I'm fine. I'm ready to go," he said confidently as he tried to stop himself standing unsteadily.

"Alright, hero," said Arienga, turning back towards the doorway. "Let's get going."

Arrow struggled up the path that had been cleared over the mound of rubble. Arienga led the horse, while Rowan rode. They came to the top of the mound and saw that the rock walls lined the road for a short way, and then the land opened out. The path down the other side of the mound was makeshift and Arienga had to navigate carefully, talking encouragingly to the horse as they went. After a while Arrow stood on the roadway and the rest of the party made their way down, leading their horses in turn, and gathered around them. Last to make his way down, was Gorum, leading his stubborn but resigned chariga.

Duburinga spoke briefly to Biren-So, and then he and Dooren-Ga quickly rode off to scout the road ahead. The rest of them mounted their horses and Gorum his chariga. Grengal and Charen-Ba accompanied them. The other Quiglings had returned to their troop. Arienga threw the reins over Arrow's head and climbed up in front of Rowan. Carlan waited resolutely beside them.

Biren-So then led them off down the roadway. The rain still fell and the dim light of late afternoon struggled to break through as they travelled down the road to where the steep walls at either side petered out. Lightning still flashed in the sky and thunder rumbled, but the worst of the rain seemed to have gone. They left the road and rode down a gentle forested slope. They followed where Duburinga had disappeared, down into the wilderness that fell away to the southeast, down to where the Artorans had escaped, leaving behind uncertainty, and the fear that the Stone of Angil would move beyond their grasp, into the land of the evil Sorcerers.

Rowan lay down. He felt tired and sore. The sky was dark now. The clouds had blotted out the setting sun. They had travelled through a small expanse of marsh and then into low hills covered with a sparse woodland. As they began to make camp, six riders rode up from behind, following their trail. Four of them Rowan recognised instantly and his heart rose. Boriega, Terrana, Jorunum and Kerian had arrived on horseback accompanied by two Quiglings. Rowan was introduced to the Quiglings but quickly forgot their names. He rested now, while the others secured the campsite and prepared food. Carlan sat against a tree nearby and settled down to eat while keeping a close eye on Rowan. Grengal sat across from Rowan. The young Quigling was watching Rowan with a look of disbelief, or awe, on his face.

Arienga walked over, bringing Rowan a bowl of stew, along with a bowl for herself.

"Don't get used to this," she said sitting down beside him.

She looked at Rowan with a slight smile but her expression still held concern. Rowan looked at her and smiled back.

"I wouldn't want to get used to it," he said. "Somehow you waiting on people, unless you were looking for an opportunity to kill them, doesn't seem right."

"Hey," said Arienga offended. "I'm nice to people all the time. I am trained to protect people, not to kill them." She paused and said seriously, "We shouldn't talk lightly about killing. The act is only one of need. Anyway," she said, leaning in conspiratorially, "if anyone needed to be killed, I wouldn't waste my time pretending I liked them."

"That's a relief," said Rowan sleepily.

Arienga almost retorted at the implication that she was saying she liked him.

"Just eat something before you fall asleep in your food," she said.

Arienga looked across to the other side of the clearing where Grengal sat watching Rowan.

"It looks like you have an admirer," she said softly to Rowan.

Before Rowan was able to respond, Boriega called out, "Arienga! You're on first watch!"

"Well, duty calls," said Arienga to Rowan, as she got to her feet.

She looked at him and said gently, "Get some sleep Rowan. I think you're going to need it."

She walked off, hurriedly spooning food into her mouth.

Rowan ate some more, but was having trouble chewing. Everything seemed like such an effort and the darkness was increasing. Flashes of lightning still flashed against his eyelids as they closed.

Suddenly he was wide awake. The sky to the north was rent by a bright light that flashed off towards the east. He scrambled out of his blankets as others around him all gathered to look to the sky.

"What is it?" he called out.

"I don't know," said Biren-So from nearby. "It is some show of power."

Abruptly the light ceased and the night returned. They milled about, concerned and questioning, but none of them had a clear idea what it meant.

"I fear that Ultamar awakes," said Carlan from behind Rowan.

"I feel that you are right, my friend," said Biren-So.

Duburinga emerged from the trees and appeared before them in the dwindling firelight.

He spoke decisively. "We must start early in the morning. We are getting too far away from where we need to be. Concern for the Stonebearer plays in my mind."

Rowan's heart caught in his throat. "Hyrn!" he thought desperately.

He looked around, but Arienga was nowhere to be seen. Carlan stepped forward from behind him and lay his hand on Rowan's shoulder. Rowan turned back towards him and in the dim light noticed that the rain had washed much of the dirt out of Carlan's uniform.

"We will unite the Sword and the Stones," said the Abessairian soldier. "I will make sure that you are safe, and Garan will protect your brother with his life."

"Hyrn must be safe," thought Rowan. "He was surrounded by elite warriors."

"We continue to do what we were assigned to do," said Duburinga. "We continue to pursue the Artorans to find if they carry the Stone."

"Once we confront the Artorans, whether they have the Stone or not, our path is clear," said Kerian. His uniform too, was cleaner.

The Abessairian continued. "War gathers around Ultamar and we must be of what assistance we can."

Rowan felt for the sword at his shoulder but it still lay on the ground beside where he had been sleeping.

He clenched his fists and said determinedly. "We continue to pursue Ivah."

He had to believe that they were pursuing the Stone otherwise this was just wasting time.

"Tomorrow," said Biren-So. "It is pointless moving in the dark. The land becomes marshy again beyond these hills. And the storm will have only made things worse. But I feel that the morning will be clear and the walls of Artora will be in plain sight."

'Tomorrow', thought Rowan as he settled back down to sleep. They pursued the Artorans and perhaps Ivah. The Stones had to be reunited. This was what he and Hyrn were asked to do by Devarnia. He hadn't thought about the Keeper for a while, or that day so long ago.

"Tomorrow," he said to himself.

He quickly fell asleep. His hand rested on the hilt of the sword of the Kings of Anasaria.

CHAPTER SIXTEEN

The Drarg Thwart

Careil rode at a steady pace along the old road towards the east. The dark mass of Castle Herardin disappeared behind him. He followed the tracks of riders among the dirt and detritus that covered the stonework of the roadway. He had seen no trace of the Ultamarians but kept a watchful eye out. He was tempted to ride faster but the condition of the road, and his need to seek any signs of the enemy, tempered his desire for haste. He could feel a storm brewing on the air, and sensed that rain was not far off. He caught a glimpse of lightning off to the south as he rode. Erras seemed impatient to move forward faster, as the storm approached. They had continued forward, Erras steadfast despite his impatience.

Then the great horse shuddered, and turning his head against the reins, veered away from the right hand side of the road snorting with alarm. Careil pulled Erras to a halt. He jumped down from the saddle and approached the horse's head patting his neck.

"What is it, Erras?" said Careil.

The horse snorted but calmed under the touch of the Rider. Erras shook his head and pushed at Careil. Careil rubbed the horse's neck and then, walking slowly back down the roadway towards the point where Erras had shied, drew his sword and held it out before him. Erras, almost as if ashamed, trailed slowly behind. Careil crept towards the trees that lined the roadway. Grass grew in thick tufts along the edge of the road and as Careil approached he heard a muffled groan. He froze. He crouched lower and moved stealthily towards the source of the groaning. Gently he pulled aside the thick grass with his left hand. His right hand still held tightly to his sword.

It took all his training and resolve to remain stoic at the sight before him. An Ultamarian soldier lay in the leaves and twigs at the edge of the trees. The soldier was badly injured. His arm lay at an awkward angle and deep wounds and gashes covered his upper body. The wounds on his body glowed with a malevolent purple light and gave off a sickly smell of corruption. The injured soldier groaned again and attempted to move, scrabbling at the ground.

Careil could see that there was a trail leading back into the forest where the Ultamarian had dragged himself along. Drops of purple fluid glowed along the trail. Careil scanned the forest but could see no signs of movement or hear any sounds, apart from that of the trees whispering and groaning in the wind from the approaching storm. Careil steeled himself and then rose to his feet. He held his sword downwards pointing towards the Ultamarian and approached the soldier cautiously, remembering Yarga's warning. Erras remained standing at the edge of the road. Careil bent down and picked up a small stick and tossed it at the Ultamarian. He spoke loudly and fiercely. "Where are the others?" he demanded.

The Ultamarian spasmed, startled, and then turned his head towards Careil, his eyes glassy but wide with fear. The eyes tried to focus on the figure standing there. The soldier's gaze was feverish and the eyes seemed to glow with the same purple light. He sneered and his expression was one of anger and fear. He tried to speak.

"Rebel scum," he managed, spitting the words out as blood and venom oozed from his mouth.

"Do you have the Stone?" asked Careil.

At this question the Ultamarian arched his back away from the ground as if stung. Careil watched him thoughtfully and then spoke stridently.

"You swore an oath to the throne of Anasaria and to Abessair," he said. "The power of the Stones of Angil still burns in you."

The Ultamarian soldier writhed on the ground as if in agony. His expression was tortured. His face showed pain and anger but his eyes looked as if he was about to weep.

"Ilah and Ivah hold the true power of Anasaria," said Careil. "Try to remember that you were a soldier of Abessair."

The spasms of the soldier lying on the ground became more violent. The purple light seemed to glow more brightly in his wounds and in his eyes.

"Where is Ivah?" asked Careil forcefully.

The soldier cried out in pain and his face contorted. He spat weakly towards Careil and a blob of purple sputum splattered onto the ground well away from where Careil stood. The Ultamarian spasmed again and then a look of immense sorrow flashed across his face. He looked imploringly at Careil.

"Kill me," he said desperately.

"Tell me where the others are and where the Stone is," demanded Careil.

"Bardan is…" the soldier began to speak, but a defiant malevolent look came to his face.

"Ultamar will triumph over you all!" he said with a harsh laugh that became a gurgling cough, as more purple bile ran from his mouth.

"Where is Bardan?" asked Careil, calmly. "The Stones of Angil need you to fulfil your oath."

The soldier roared with anger but it became a sharp groan of pain. He lay on the ground before Careil and began to weep.

He said mournfully, "They left me behind. We were going to see the Dark Lords together without anyone knowing… but they left me. We would have been…"

The soldier shrieked and then made as if to launch himself at Careil. But he collapsed back and began to sob again.

"When did Bardan decide that you were going straight to the Dark Lords?" Careil asked in a measured tone.

The Ultamarian's face contorted in anger and pain. "We all decided," he said proudly and defiantly. "Captain Bardan asked us, after the Artorans ran." He paused and then almost whispered, "We have the Stone."

He looked feverishly at Careil. "They cursed us for stealing the Stone as they fled."

The soldier laughed raspily and then coughed. Purple sputum oozed from his mouth.

He seemed to lose all energy, and then said weakly, "We were going to be great. The Dark Lords…"

He coughed again and then opened his eyes. They glowed a deep violet and shone with malevolence.

"Who are you?" he asked in a strangled voice.

The Ultamarian struggled to get up.

"Did you see Ivah?" asked Careil. "Did you see the Stone of Angil?"

The soldier's face contorted with anger. "Bardan looked upon it. He said we were not strong enough!"

As he spoke the Ultamarian suddenly launched himself to his feet. His wounds flared with bright, purple light. His eyes seemed like two beams of violet hatred. Careil, in one swift motion, swung his sword in a wide arc, all his force projected into the edge of his blade. The Ultamarian's head was lifted from his neck and as it rose into the air and his body slumped, sprays of purple liquid came flying through the air towards Careil. Instantly, Careil launched himself sideways away from the spray, still keeping his sword held out before him as its blade dripped with purple ooze. He brought himself to his feet and threw his sword to the ground. With a sense of panic he quickly checked himself over. He could find no traces of the purple fluid.

He looked down at the sword lying on the ground. Its blade glowed with violet light. As he watched, the metal began to dissolve. Careil looked around trying to find something that he could wipe the blade with but turned back and watched as it became apparent that his sword was beyond saving.

He stood looking around at the carnage. The Ultamarian's body lay slumped on the ground. The soldier's severed head lay to his left. The dead eyes stared up at Careil. The evil light was extinguished but he was heartened to see that his face was smiling. The Rider's hope was that, in the moment of death, the scars of Artora and the curse of Ultamar had been lifted and the soldier died an Abessairian.

The trail was not hard to follow. The soldier had dragged himself for a long distance and the marks of blood and the evil ooze were not hard to see. Erras trudged along behind Careil. The horse had been worried about following at first, with the stench of death and corruption all around, but had listened when Careil talked to him soothingly. They moved steadily down the hillside through forest that grew denser as they went. Ultamar appeared from time to time through the trees. There was a sense of danger in the air, and at one point, Careil felt something ominous. And then it started to rain.

The rain made it harder to see as the trees closed in around him. Careil felt the threat of danger and regretted the loss of his sword, even though he carried other weapons.

He travelled further down hill as the trail led him eastwards and inextricably towards Ultamar. The trail at times petered out, and it became clear that the Ultamarian had been upright and walking before falling down and crawling on again. At other times, rivulets of water ran down the hillside obliterating the trail. Little creeks and waterfalls appeared as the water flowed down the slope from above. Careil moved cautiously but determinedly until the trail suddenly seemed to disappear. He walked on for a little way but then retraced his steps.

The trail ended at a patch of small scraggly bushes that grew uncertainly beneath the darkness of the large trees. Careil lifted aside some foliage and saw that the marks led into the bushes. He tied Erras's reins loosely to a tree away from the trail. The Rider made sure to keep the horse away from the trail of purple venom. If Erras needed to, he could release himself and flee.

Careil inspected the tunnel that led into the bushes. He could see no obvious signs of the purple stain on the branches and leaves but he hesitated. He backed out of the bushes and stood and scanned the area. He could see that the bushes followed a crease in the hillside that led downwards. He made his way up and around the bushes to the right following the slope of a small ridge above the bushes. Erras snorted from behind him, irritated by the evil smell all about. Careil came down the ridge to where the bushes ended and the ground levelled out.

The ground had been disturbed as if by many footprints but the rain had washed away much of the evidence that anyone had been there. He saw marks that suggested that someone had dragged themselves up towards the bushes and he followed the trail until he came to where the bushes began. He could see that branches and leaves had been thrown over where the trail led into the shrubbery. He pulled aside these branches carefully and within the bushes he saw that a small bivouac had been made. There was a small enclosure within. A blanket lay on the ground. There was a small pot and a flask to one side. Then something caught Careil's eye. At the side of the bower, a sword lay in its sheath. It seemed that perhaps the Ultamarian had left it behind when he had dragged himself to where a trail of purple drops led up through the bushes, back to where Erras waited.

Careil crawled carefully in the gloom. Any traces of the venom glowed with purple light making them easy to discern. He knelt beside the sword. There seemed to be no traces of the evil ooze on the hilt of the sword. Then Careil remembered seeing the Ultamarian's arm twisted and broken by his side. His sword arm. He could not wield the sword or remove it. Someone else must have laid this sword here. But why? Careil wondered as he inspected the sword, still reluctant to touch it. Then it came to him. They left him here to die. This was his burial. A warrior's funeral with his weapon laid at his side.

The design on the hilt of the sword was not clear to Careil at first. The pommel had what looked like a crown embossed upon it. The grip was plain but each end of the guard ended in a circle with an oval embossed on it. The Twin Stones. This was an Abessairian sword. Why were Ultamarians…? But then he remembered Ferian's sword. His was just like this but larger. The Ultamarians fought with the weapons they had been given as soldiers of Abessair. It seemed like an evil twist of the Dark Lords to make their army fight with the weapons of the defeated enemy, but also the weapons of their true selves. Torment upon torment.

Anger flashed in Careil's mind. He reached out and grasped the sword. He turned, still crouching, and made his way out through the bushes back to where the trail had been hidden by the Ultamarians. Once he was clear of the bushes, he held the hilt of the sword in one hand and the sheath in the other. In one sweep he drew the sword and held it out before him. Lightning flashed in the sky and the blade of the sword shone momentarily.

"For Abessair," Careil said quietly, but forcefully.

He walked back up the ridge around the bushes and made his way to where Erras was. As he came into sight, the horse saw him with the sword held before him. Erras whinnied and nodded his head up and down.

"We've got some Ultamarians to hunt," said Careil.

Erras snorted as if with impatience. He pulled at the reins still tied to the tree and they came loose. The horse walked over to Careil. Careil sheathed the sword and Erras came up to him and pushed his head against the Rider. Careil threw the loose reins over the saddle and walked back down the ridge with Erras following loyally and resolutely behind him.

The Lake of Light glowed brilliantly before them as King Darlam led them through the outskirts of the City of the Vortex and onto the shore. The Ultamarian prisoners were surrounded by soldiers; Underdwellers, Abessairians and Caramar. Darlam stopped astride his chariga and looked out over the lake. They had come steadily and inexorably to this spot. He still did not know if this would work but the vision of the bright pink light flashing across the battlefield in the valley burned in his mind. There were patrols hunting for any Ultamarians that approached the Underrealm, but fighters had also been sent to attack the guard posts that led to Anasaria and they were charged with capturing as many Ultamarians alive as possible and bringing them here. He had put those fighter's lives in danger. Capturing the guard posts was an end in itself but he worried that he may have been hasty, in a misguided belief that this would work. He turned in his saddle.

"Drive the prisoners into the water!" he cried.

At the very least the Ultamarians would get a much needed wash, he thought.

With much pushing and shoving the Ultamarians were cajoled forwards toward the lake shore. Some were forced at the point of a sword. Captain Evlan, still bound but exhausted from struggling against his bonds, and the forced march, stood defiantly. Two Abessairian soldiers grasped an arm on either side and dragged the Captain towards the water.

Darlam watched as the Ultamarians entered the lake. They resisted, cursing and swearing. They were driven further into the lake and stood waist deep thrashing against the touch of the water. Darlam felt doubt and disappointment bearing down on him. It wasn't going to work. Then he felt something. A surge of power. The centre of the lake began to glow more brightly. The roof of the cavern was suddenly lit more intensely by the pink glow. The brightness moved slowly across the surface of the lake at first and then began to move more rapidly.

King Darlam held his breath as the bright glow approached the Ultamarians. Some of the Ultamarians saw the light moving towards them and tried to move away from it. Their companions were alerted and also moved to escape. A wall of armed soldiers with blades drawn blocked their way. The band of light hit the rearmost of the Ultamarians and then reached the rest. The Ultamarians thrashed about as the light hit them. Then the lake water rose in a wave of bright pink light and the evil soldiers were swamped and pushed under the water.

For a moment it appeared as if the Ultamarians had been drowned as they all seemed still, floating or crouching in the water. Then all of a sudden one of them leapt from the water with a whooping yell. The others all came alive and rose to stand in the water. Their uniforms and armour shone with a bright white light. They were all smiling, or laughing, or even weeping. Now, where almost fifty Ultamarians had been, stood an equal number of Abessairians. The King laughed out loud with relief and joy.

The newly freed Abessairians looked confusedly at each other and then joined in as their fellow Abessairians, soldiers of the Underrealm, and Caramar warriors, as well as the citizens of the City of the Vortex who had gathered to watch, all cried, "Desultamar!"

And the sound echoed loudly, and exuberantly off the walls of the Underrealm.

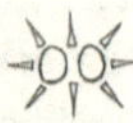

The ground had now levelled out as Careil followed the trail of the Ultamarians. Erras followed doggedly behind. At times the trail had been hard to follow as it moved over rocky ground or else was washed away by the torrential rain. Careil had retrieved his travel cloak from his pack to try to keep dry. Erras ignored the water that dripped from him. With the gloomy weather, the shadows of the damp sombre forest, and the pale glow of the sun sinking behind the mountains, it was beginning to become harder to see the signs of the passage of the Ultamarians.

Careil was beginning to come to the decision that it was best to stop before he lost the trail in the dim light, when he heard a sound from ahead. He turned to stop Erras but the horse had already halted, his head up and his ears pointed forwards towards the sound. Careil drew his newly acquired sword and then crouched low and moved cautiously through the forest. The trees fell away from the level ground they had been following. The trail led down a rock strewn slope and into the dimness of the forest below. Vague sounds came up the slope. The sounds of movement, and Careil thought that he could discern voices. He gestured to Erras to wait and watch, and then moved quietly down the slope, travelling side on to maintain his balance. Once he had made his way further down the slope, he stopped and listened.

He could definitely hear voices. He concentrated through the sound of the rain and wind and the occasional rumble of thunder. The voices were speaking harshly. They seemed to be arguing. He moved carefully down the slope from tree to tree, keeping himself hidden. The voices were clearer now. There was some sort of debate going on but it was difficult to hear what was being said. Careil moved a little further down the uneven ground and then stopped again.

They were talking about Bardan and the Stone. It was still hard to hear exactly what was being said, but Bardan obviously wasn't present. The Ultamarians were talking about their Captain and they didn't seem very happy. It sounded as if they were doubting Captain Bardan's leadership and his selfish guarding of the Stone.

But where had Bardan gone? Careil thought.

He stepped out from behind the tree where he was hiding and headed for one further down the slope. As he made his next sideways step down the slope, his foot caught against a rock and he stumbled. He threw his arm out to catch a low hanging branch. The branch took his weight momentarily and then, with a loud crack, it broke and Careil, his arms flailing, tumbled down the slope. As he gained momentum he brought his limbs in and balled himself up. He crashed down the slope being whipped by branches and bruised by stones. His sword flailed around and at one point dug into the ground vaulting him further down the slope. By sheer chance he avoided hitting any trees as he went. He reached the bottom of the slope and hit level ground and came to a halt.

He launched himself to his feet and despite the pain lifted his sword and stood poised; in the middle of a group of five Ultamarians.

The soldiers were all sitting around a clearing. A small fire burned, only dimly lighting the clearing. Lightning still flashed in the sky, breaking the darkness that grew as the night closed in. The Ultamarian's gear was lying in piles on the ground. They all stared at Careil with shock and amazement on their faces.

For a moment no-one moved.

Then one of the Ultamarians went for the sword lying on the ground at his feet. He grasped the hilt and drew his sword, as his fellow Ultamarians began to move. Careil leapt forward and before the sword wielder had a chance to lift his sword the Abessairian blade drove through his chest.

Careil leapt back, withdrawing his sword as he moved. The other four had all gained their feet and were reaching for their weapons as their compatriot slumped to the ground gasping. Careil swung around assessing his options, and then targeted the soldier closest to retrieving his weapon. As Careil closed, the Ultamarian had drawn his sword and, as Careil brought his sword down, the soldier blocked the blow with his blade. Careil jumped back and brought his sword up again, moving forward before the Ultamarian had time to regain his stance. The Rider's blade slashed at the Ultamarian, striking his face and leaving a bloody gash across his cheek and nose. Careil began to raise his sword again preparing to strike. The Ultamarian lunged at Careil from his semi-crouched position driving his blade before him. Careil leapt to his right as the blade grazed his ribs. The Ultamarian barrelled past him and then stumbled to the ground. To Careil's right another of the evilful soldiers launched an attack. Careil's attention diverted quickly from the soldier on the ground. He swung his sword swiftly to the left and it struck the sword hand of the attacking Ultamarian. The blade cut deeply into the hand, smashing it aside and sending the soldier's sword flying into the air. Careil brought the hilt of his sword up and flipping his grasp over drove the sword into the throat of the Ultamarian.

As the soldier fell to the ground, leaving blood dripping from Careil's blade, the mood in the clearing suddenly changed. A purple glare flared around them. All those in the clearing froze. Careil felt like he couldn't move. Out of the corner of his eye he saw a figure who seemed to glow in the darkness.

The figure of Captain Bardan stood there, a small stone chest bound with iron clutched to his chest. He looked dismissively at Careil. When he spoke his voice sent shudders down Careil's spine. The voice was harsh, angry and forceful.

"Gerlan! Get up and kill this rebel dog!" yelled the evil Captain.

He looked at the two soldiers lying on the ground then said to Gerlan's two remaining companions, "You two, with me!"

Careil stood upright in the middle of the clearing as the lightning flashed around him. He raised his sword and fixed his expression as the Ultamarian now stood defiantly a look of violent hatred on his face. Careil and the evil soldier both launched themselves at each other at the same instant. The bursts of light from the storm threw the clashing figures into stark relief against the darkness of the forest. The figure before Careil fell to the ground as the Rider dealt him a savage blow. Careil did not hesitate and drove his sword deep into the chest of the Ultamarian. He looked around and saw that the others had fled. Bardan had taken the small casket, and the other two, despite any misgivings, had followed obediently behind.

Careil knelt alongside the fallen Ultamarian and withdrew his blade. As he made to get up the Ultamarian grabbed at his leg. Careil prepared to strike again but the Ultamarian looked at him.

The dying soldier spoke to Careil raspingly but clearly. "An Abessairian blade used in the service of Anasaria." He coughed bloodily and then said, "To die like this and to remember the beauty of Abessair. Ah. The torment is finally over."

He looked at Careil and then his head dropped and he did not move again. His face was calm and peaceful. Careil sighed deeply. He looked up, as moonlight shone from above, peeping through, as broken sheets of cloud moved across the sky. Ahead and above he saw the dark towers of the fortress of Ultamar. It stood on the plateau that now loomed above him, occasionally silhouetted against the light of the moon.

All that Careil could feel was anger at those up in the fortress. The quest to free Anasaria burned in him and at that moment he thought of the two boys he had accompanied from Wesmere. He had abandoned them. He had left them both. He felt doubt at the choices he had made. But as he looked up at that edifice the moon was obscured again and the clearing was sunk into darkness. He rose to move towards where Bardan had fled.

Then a flash of lightning from the north lit the clearing. Out of the corner of his eye, a large dark shape loomed to his right. Ice went through Careil's body but he steeled himself quickly and began to raise his sword. The lightning flashed again and at the sight before him Careil laughed with relief.

There stood his ever faithful companion, Erras.

All King's Riders formed a special bond with their horses, but standing there in the clearing with death all around him, Careil felt how deeply he loved and relied on Erras. The horse approached him silently with his head down and leant against Careil's shoulder. Careil dropped his sword and threw his arms around Erras's neck. Erras nickered softly and then pushed at Careil and breaking free shook his head and snorted as if with impatience.

"Come on old friend," said Careil.

He bent and picked up his sword and began to walk towards the edge of the clearing. He stopped and looked down at the blade that gleamed dimly in the dark. He then looked back to where the bodies lay in the darkness. He stopped and lay his gear down and headed back. He took a little time to lay the bodies out. He then placed their swords atop them. He then straightened up and walked back to where Erras waited. The horse nodded his head and they both headed out of the clearing following Bardan and his two soldiers.

The forest had thinned out and the moon had been peering out more often as the storm disappeared to the north. Lightning still lit the sky from time to time. Careil had taken the opportunity to ride. His side hurt where the blade had cut through to his flesh and he was bruised from his fall. Riding was a relief and Erras seemed satisfied to be moving more quickly. As he rode, Careil suddenly heard the clash of steel ahead and the sounds of battle. He pulled Erras to a halt and leapt painfully down from the saddle. His sword was out as he moved towards the sound of fighting; the pain momentarily forgotten.

Between the trees he could see a purple glow amongst the black shapes of the trees. The glowing figure of Bardan could be seen fighting. It was more difficult to discern who he was fighting with. Careil crept closer to the edge of the small space among the trees. One of the Ultamarians half knelt on the ground clutching his upper arm. The other was attacking Bardan but the Captain was more than a match for him. Calculating the odds and with the desperate need to discover if Bardan held Ivah, Careil leapt out and joined the fray. He attacked Bardan as the Ultamarian parried a blow from the other soldier. Bardan swiftly blocked Careil's blow, and turning his attention back to the soldier before him, struck out, catching the other's throat with the tip of his sword.

As the soldier fell, Bardan screeched at the other Ultamarian still crouched on the ground, "Get up soldier! The Stone commands you!"

The soldier on the ground released his bleeding arm and leapt at Careil. Careil blocked the blow but was driven backwards, stumbling, but managing to stay on his feet.

And then he saw it. Against a tree, behind Bardan, the small casket lay on its side. What it held was still nestled inside.

It was not Ivah. A fist sized purple Stone glowed from inside the casket. Before he had a chance to look more closely the Ultamarian swung his sword at Careil. Careil blocked him again and thrust at the soldier's injured arm, driving his sword to where the bloody wound gaped. The pain made the soldier contort with agony and Careil smashed the flat of his sword blade against the head of the Ultamarian. The soldier collapsed to the ground unconscious.

Careil turned quickly towards where Bardan had been. The other soldier lay there dying on the ground. Beyond, Bardan was already escaping between the trees, heading eastward toward the plateau and the fortress of Ultamar. The casket no longer lay on the ground. Bardan was intent on delivering the Stone to the Dark Lords.

'Fool!' thought Careil. The Artorans had given Bardan and his men a Stone, but not the Stone they thought. This one was cursed. The evil bewitchment from the Stone was making the Ultamarian Captain believe that he was carrying Ivah. The evil intent of the Artoran Sorcerers became clear now to Careil. They meant to betray their alliance with Ultamar and bring their power directly to the Dark Lords. Careil watched the glowing figure until he could no longer be seen. He shrugged painfully. Who was he to stand between the forces of evil while they were attacking each other?

The Ultamarian soldier on the ground groaned as he gained consciousness. Careil let out a soft, sharp whistle. Erras came through the trees from just beyond the edge of the clearing. Careil walked over, opened one of his saddlebags and withdrew a bundle of rope. He walked back and knelt beside the Ultamarian, He took the rope and quickly bound the soldier's wrists and then ran the end of the rope down and bound his ankles. He stood and then took the long end of the rope that ran from his prisoner's wrists and tied it to Erras's saddle. He turned purposefully and walked over and picked up the sword of the dead Ultamarian and lay it alongside him. He rose and walked over to the bound Ultamarian. Light from the fading storm flashed to the north.

He knelt down and shook the man. The soldier groaned and his eyelids fluttered. He moved his arm as if to reach for his sword but realised that his hands were tied. He struggled against the ropes binding him. He fixed his gaze on Careil and his face was contorted in anger.

"Release me!" snarled the Ultamarian. "I must pursue the Stone. The Dark Lords will reward me when I bring them one of the two Stones."

At that moment the sky burst into brilliant light. A beam of light rent the sky from Careil's left and flashed above him. To his right a massive dark form was thrown into relief. A huge wall towered beyond the small clearing the trees growing right up against it. The dazzling beam of light hung in the air for a few more moments and then was abruptly extinguished. After the brightness all seemed pitch black in the forest but after a while Careil's eyes adjusted again to the light from the moon.

The Ultamarian was dazed and confused by the bright light.

He mumbled to himself incoherently and then said feverishly, "The Stone…the Stone."

"Bardan does not have Ivah," said Careil forcefully. "Your Artoran friends hold the Stone of Angil."

That thought cascaded in Careil's mind. 'Rowan'. The Artorans had the Stone and Rowan was in the party that pursued them. And he had to let Hyrn know, but where was he?

Suddenly a screeching horn sounded from high up above. Careil rose and walked over to Erras.

"Watch him," Careil said to the horse.

Careil walked through the trees and came to a space where the trees grew more sparsely. Before him loomed the wall. The Wall of Detradin, the Drarg Thwart, built by King Abess when Abessair was first constructed; a massive defensive wall to block assaults by Drarg forces from the east, into the forests of Anasaria.

He looked up at the wall in the moonlight. The stonework seemed smooth but as he came to the wall he placed his hand upon it and could feel that the surface was rough and weathered. The wall was made up of large stone blocks. The wall towered above him and stretched out of sight in both directions. As he stood there a clamour came from up above.

He heard the sound of riders clattering across the top of the wall. There was obviously a large number and they were riding fast travelling out of Ultamar northwards towards the old road and in the direction the beam of light had come from…and where Hyrn was! The clatter of hooves grew to a frenetic pace and then it seemed as if a roaring wind rushed above him. The sound filled Careil with a sense of dread. Panic grew in him. Did Hyrn have anything to do with the light? Maybe it was Ilah?

But he was too far away from them and had no way of getting back up to the road without retracing his path. That would be difficult through this terrain in the dark and the moon would begin to get lower in the sky and set behind the mountains before he could get anywhere near the road. He would have to wait until morning if he was to get back to where Hyrn should be.

Careil considered his situation. Hyrn had Caramar warriors, Abessairians and an Underdweller Ranger protecting him, and was guided by a Caramar Elder and the Priests. By now The Quiglings and Droom must have met up with them. And Hyrn had the Stone. They no longer had to worry about pursuing the Ultamarians…

But Hyrn did not know that. He needed to let Hyrn know. But how?

Careil turned around and quickly made his way back to where Erras and the Ultamarian were. The Ultamarian still lay on the ground. Erras stood watching him, the rope binding the Ultamarian stretched taut. As Careil approached, the Ultamarian struggled but Erras snorted and stamped his front hooves in warning. The Ultamarian groaned and lay still again. Erras turned his head and looked at Careil as he approached. Careil walked up to the horse and patted his neck.

"Any trouble?" asked Careil.

Erras stood proudly and defiantly and then shook his head slightly. Careil went to his saddlebags and drew out a small pouch. He took this to the base of a large tree and gathering up dry leaves took out a flint and struck it until he managed to get it to catch. He gathered more kindling and fed the flames until a small bright fire was burning. The light from the fire threw shadows around the small clearing. He crouched near the flame so that his face was brightly illuminated.

He then said in a clear loud voice, "Ilah! Ilah! The Ultamarians do not have Ivah. Your twin is being carried by the Artorans. Ilah! The Ultamarians do not have Ivah!"

He stood up and then stamped the fire out plunging the clearing back into darkness. That would have to do. He just hoped that the Stone would see and would let Hyrn know. He was too far away to do much else. Bardan would take the other Stone to Ultamar and maybe that would help them.

A sudden thought came to Careil. Bardan would want to take the Stone directly to the Dark Lords. That is what the Artorans had bewitched him into doing for them. He would not want to go up to the main road. The approaches to the fortress would be heavily guarded. There must be another way. He looked over at the Ultamarian who lay on the ground, at times still, and then squirming in pain from his injured arm. Careil walked over and crouched down alongside him.

He thought for a moment and then said, "Bardan is going to get all the glory. All your efforts will be forgotten."

Careil could just see in the dim moonlight that the Ultamarian had opened his eyes and was looking at him intently, a look of pain mixed with contempt on his face.

"You said he doesn't have the Stone," sneered the Ultamarian.

"Oh, he doesn't," said Careil matter of factly. "He has something that the Dark Lords will prize even more. He has the Stone of an Artoran Sorcerer. I'm sure the Dark Lords will realize what a powerful weapon they are being given. But Bardan must know that. That is why he has kept it from you. He wants all the glory for himself."

The Ultamarian thrashed around furiously against his bonds with anger and frustration; his pain temporarily forgotten.

"He said we would share the glory!" screeched the Ultamarian.

"Your Captain is only interested in himself," said Careil. "Why should he care about a common soldier? He was the one who commanded. It is he who should be rewarded."

"We were the ones who did the fighting," snarled the Ultamarian. "He just stood back and let our men be killed. Now he runs off back to Ultamar while I am left here with a…"

The soldier paused and then looked at Careil intently and said, "Who are you? Are you the ones that were pursuing us?"

Careil thought for a moment. He needed to be careful if he wanted the Ultamarian to help him.

"I am a traitor," he said calmly. "I betrayed my King and was pursuing the Stones but I have abandoned my friends and comrades. I am now only interested in Bardan. If you help me, we can get to him before he has a chance to reach the Dark Lords. If we both take the Stone to them surely they will look upon us with favour. Imagine the life we could have. There is a place for us beside the Dark Lords."

"Hah!" snorted the Ultamarian. "You have no love for Ultamar. The stench of you fills my nostrils. And you called to the other Stone. I could hear you. Is the other Stone of Angil here in this land?"

He stared at Careil suspiciously.

"You are from somewhere else," he said. "There is something going on, some sort of invasion."

Careil spoke truly but cryptically. "We come from the Underrealm. We were pursuing the Stone."

"And now your friends have heard that the Artorans have the Stone, they will try to claim it," said the Ultamarian with suspicion.

"If they follow it they will go to their deaths," said Careil savagely. "They will pursue the Artorans and they will die. But we, we can ensure that Ultamar triumphs and we also benefit. Ultamar will reign over Anasaria, and the Artorans will be next. Once the Dark Lords have the Stone of the Sorcerer they will be able to defeat them. Then imagine what rewards we will get for our part in that victory."

The Ultamarian soldier looked puzzled and then said, "Untie me. I am wounded and need help. I will show you where Bardan is going but if you try to betray me I will spend my last breath making sure you die a painful death."

Careil got to his feet and walked over to Erras and began to untie the rope attached to the saddle. Erras looked at him and snorted softly.

Careil spoke softly to the horse. "I will be on guard but if he tries anything you may trample him into the ground."

Erras relaxed at that, and Careil finished untying the rope and then pulled something from his pack. He went over to unbind the Ultamarian. His heart was beating fast in his chest. This whole idea was crazy but the opportunity to find a hidden way into Ultamar presented itself. He finished untying the Ultamarian and helped him to his feet. He took a small pot that he had placed on the ground and unsealed it. He scooped out some of the contents and smeared it on the bloody wound on the Ultamarian's arm. He then took a cloth and bandaged the wound.

All the while he kept thinking. "He is an Abessairian, but at the moment he is an Ultamarian."

He walked over and picked up the soldier's sword that lay on the ground. He walked back and replaced it in the sheath at the soldier's hip.

"I am Careil," he said to the Ultamarian.

The soldier looked at him warily but then responded, "My name is Hernan. I do not trust you Careil, but if you help me catch Bardan, then we will see."

It was as good as Careil could hope for at the moment. They made their way off through the trees, back towards the lower depths of Ultamar.

"Why do you carry a sword of Abessair?" snarled a voice from behind Careil as he led Erras through the trees. The Ultamarian, Hernan, was bitter and suspicious.

"I took it from your friend that you left to die in the bushes," said the Rider.

"Kirligan?" said Hernan. "What happened to him?"

"I cut his head off," replied Careil, solemnly.

"Did you touch him?" asked Hernan quickly.

"Only with my sword," said Careil. "Which is why I needed his sword."

"Those Artoran creeps," said Hernan. "They have no love for Ultamar. They poison us with their spells and curses."

"That is why we must help the Dark Lords defeat the Artorans," said Careil.

But he thought to himself. You are already cursed, but by Ultamar, not Artora.

An odour of something unpleasant began to waft through the trees towards them as they moved through the trees. It was almost indiscernible at first, but steadily grew into a persistent stench.

"What is that smell?" asked Careil.

Hernan laughed. "That is the smell of Ultamar that washes out of its sewers and drains. That smell means that we are not far from Sewer Town."

"Sewer Town?" said Careil.

"Yes," said Hernan.

"What is Sewer Town and why would anyone call a town that?" asked Careil.

"It isn't a town," growled Hernan. "And it is not officially called that. It doesn't really have a name. It has sprung up around the lower entrances to the dungeons and defences of Ultamar. It is a constant source of nuisance for us but it is where we get things made and fixed, and there is drink and other pleasures there. There are many Anasarian rats living there and they tend to look friendly, but we soldiers need to be careful that we don't get our throats slashed. There are plenty of rebel scum and traitors in the sewers."

"It sounds great," said Careil sarcastically. But he secretly thought to himself that it did sound promising.

Careil suggested to Hernan that they rest for the remainder of the night and then continue towards the town at daybreak. Hernan had been distrustful but his weariness made him acquiesce.

"It will be the first test of our alliance," said the Rider. "If you like you can stay up and watch me, but I am going to sleep."

The Rider looked at his horse. Erras peered at him but just snorted softly. Careil went to the horse's flank and pulled out two blankets from his packs. He threw one towards the Ultamarian.

"Here," he said.

The Ultmarian swatted the blanket aside.

"I don't need your stinking blanket," he snarled.

"Suit yourself," said Careil dismissively.

Careil settled down to sleep. He pulled his blanket over his face to try to block the smell that lay all around. He could hear the soft breathing of Erras near him. He had not unloaded his packs from Erras, but the war horse understood and rested. He thought about the situation he had found himself in. Both Rowan and Hyrn were beyond his reach. He had to trust that the warriors that accompanied them would protect them. He thought back to when they had left the farmhouse and he had told Meralie and Baraman that he would protect their sons. He felt a weight in his chest. So much had changed since then. He never imagined that this is where they would be. The three of them that had set out that morning, now separated from each other, in another land, and all facing dangers that they could not possibly have imagined.

As Careil watched, Hernan sat down against a tree. The Ultamarian looked straight ahead fiercely but his gaze wavered and his head began to nod forward. He jerked up and shook his head and straightened his back and stared forward again. Careil watched the soldier's head start to nod again, and then fell into sleep himself.

CHAPTER SEVENTEEN

The Water Stairs

Trion had led Ferian up into the small gully. The day had moved towards midday, and clouds were now beginning to obscure the blue of the sky. The young Priest was labouring with the weight of the General's sword on his back, along with his own pack. The General continued to urge the Priest on. Trion was finding it very frustrating that the Abessairian had a severe wound, and was old, but didn't seem to need to rest. He would gladly have lain down under a tree and had a nap, but General Ferian was driven. They approached the large stone that blocked the entrance to the underground labyrinth of Detrasarn.

Trion walked up to the stone and laid his hand against it. He began to chant softly. He continued for a while, but nothing happened. Ferian looked on bemusedly.

"Do you know what you're doing?" asked the General, impatiently.

Trion turned around frustrated. "I can't concentrate carrying all this stuff. He pulled his pack from his shoulders and dropped it on the ground. He then reached and pulled the sword harness over his head. He held it out as if he were about to drop it alongside his pack, but Ferian stepped forward and grasped the sheathed sword.

"I will hold that for you," said the General sternly.

"But, but," began Trion.

"You cannot just throw a sword of Abessair on the ground like that," said the General. "I will behave myself. Just get on with it."

Trion turned back to the large stone, placed his hand on it again, and began to chant. The rock began to hum and there was a slight grinding noise. Ferian swore he saw the stone move a little, and then nothing.

"Are you sure you know how to do this?" asked Ferian.

"I am a Priest," protested Trion. "I know all the pass keys. Just… with you watching. You're making me nervous."

Just then the large stone started to slide aside with a grinding sound.

"See," said Trion, turning to face the Abessairian. "I told you I knew the pass key."

The General looked past him and smirked, and when Trion turned around, he saw the figure of an elderly Priest standing there.

"Trion! So you have returned," said the Priest. "When will you learn your incantations properly? The protest in the stone cries for all to hear."

"Curion," said Trion breathlessly. "I was having trouble because of him."

The young Priest gestured towards Ferian timidly.

"General Ferian, I presume?" said Curion.

"Yes," said Ferian.

"Welcome," said Curion. "We have heard about your release from the power of Ultamar."

"So, it is true," said Trion. "But how do you know?"

"The Stone of Angil has been here," said the older Priest.

He didn't elaborate, as Trion stood open-mouthed, but instead turned to the Abessairian General.

"What can we help you with, General?" inquired Curion.

"Ah. Swans," said Neferelon.

They were seated around a large wooden table. They all sat on wooden chairs except the old Priest who still rested in an armchair.

He continued, "Swans have had a long association with Anasaria and Abessair. When the old kingdom was being established, the Anasarians came upon a wide valley in the mountains dominated by an immense lake. The surface of the lake reflected the sky above surrounded by the sides of the valley. In places the steep side of the valley plunged down into the water of the lake, and in other places, the lake lapped against meadows and forests. The lake itself was a spectacle to behold. All across the water spread a flotilla of swans. The whole valley seemed bright with the light of them.

The swans were not as they seemed, just swans. They were imbued with power that came from the lake. They had the ability of language and communicated in much the same way as do most sources of power. They spoke mind to mind. The King swore a pact with the swans that they would leave them in peace. In return the swans said that if Abessair was in danger they would come to its aid. We do not know if they are aware of our plight."

"A swan took the key to the Chamber of the Stones before the Dark Lords were able to enter," said Ferian.

"What?" gasped Neferelon.

"He has told me this tale," said Trion meekly. "I didn't know whether to believe him.”

“Your caution serves you well, Trion,” said Curion. “You are right to be cautious. But what of the key, General? Where did the swan go?”

“Up into the mountains, these mountains, I believe,” said Ferian. “Where is this lake?”

“It is high up, on the other side of this mountain,” said Neferelon. “There is a way up but it is only vaguely known to us now. No Anasarian has been that far into the mountains for centuries.”

“How far is it?” asked Ferian.

Neferelon considered. “It would take two or three days of hard travelling at the very least. The paths may be blocked, and they are sure to be in a state of disrepair, and potentially hazardous, so it would probably take much longer.”

“Is there no quicker way?” the General asked impatiently.

“That is the only way that I know of?” said Neferelon.

“What about the Water Stairs?” The question burst from Trion.

“Hush now, Trion,” said Curion. “Legends and stories are no use here.”

“There is a way through… and the Water Stairs are real!” said Trion, defiantly. “I have read about them and I think I know where they are.”

“Just as you knew how to find Neferelon, against our counsel and got yourself captured,” said Curion irately. “It is just as well for you that Herardin was liberated when it was.”

Trion seemed abashed, and looked down at the table in silence.

Curion looked at Ferian, “Trion’s head is full of fantasies and legends,” he said.

The General ignored the older Priest and instead looked directly at Trion.

“Tell me more about these Water Stairs,” he said.

They passed a doorway that led to a disused storeroom. The light of the torch flickered against the walls of the corridor as they walked. The corridor then took a sharp bend to the left, and abruptly ended. Trion, Ferian, Curion and Neferelon stood before a blank wall. Curion turned to Trion.

“Well?” said the older Priest.

“Listen!” said Trion, gesturing for quiet.

They stood and listened intently. As he concentrated, Ferian could just hear the faint sound of running water.

“Put your ear to the wall,” said Trion, moving over and placing his ear against the stone. Ferian did the same and then he could hear it more clearly; water roaring and splashing.

Curion said dismissively. “Yes. There are drains throughout the labyrinth of Detrasarn."

"Yes," said Trion, but I found in an old text mention of the way to the Water Stairs. They lie where the rushing water is heard and they described this alcove and then spoke of a hidden doorway, and something about using the strength of Anasaria. And I found this place just as described, but I don't know how to open the door."

"There is no door, Trion," said Curion.

Trion ignored him and went over to the left hand wall.

"I found this," he said.

He pointed to the wall and Ferian saw that there was a wide horizontal slot in the wall. In the middle of the slot there was a deep hole and at each end there were smaller, shallower holes.

"I've tried to open it," said Trion, "but nothing I've used has worked. But I've figured out what will."

He looked at Ferian. "When I handed you back your sword, you reminded me that it was a sword of Abessair."

"Yes?" said Ferian.

"The strength of Abessair. The sword of the Abessairian army," said Trion with triumph.

"I don't like the idea of using my sword blade as a key," said the General.

"Not the blade," said Trion. "I have spent many hours studying this."

"While you no doubt should have been carrying out your tasks and studying more useful things," interrupted Curion.

Trion hesitantly continued.

"General Ferian," said the young Priest. "I know that I have been disbelieving and suspicious of you, but I now realise that you truly are a soldier of Abessair and I believe that you are able to open this door with something every Abessarian soldier carries, an Abessairian sword."

He looked at Ferian almost pleadingly. "The hilt of your sword fits this lock. I am sure of it."

Ferian looked at the young Priest searchingly.

He held his gaze and then said, "Very well. If you are right we may have a quicker way through to the lake. If you are wrong and I lose my sword, you will need to find an Ultamarian and get me another one."

Trion gulped and said, "It will work. I just know it."

But in his mind he called on the Stones to help him.

Trion stood aside as Ferian moved forward. The General undid his sword belt and grasped the sword by the top of its sheath. He stood sideways to the side wall facing the blank wall ahead and held his sword horizontally as he lined up the hilt of the sword with the horizontal slot. He hesitated and then slowly pushed the pommel into the central hole and then as it disappeared, the guard of the sword, with the discs at either end bearing the images of the Twin Stones of Angil, slotted securely into the wall.

Ferian looked momentarily panicked as the stone of the wall clasped the sword hilt tightly but he was suddenly dazed as bright light shone down from above. There was the sound of stone grinding against stone, as locks moved within the end wall. A faint line grew into the outline of a door and then the door slid slowly aside, revealing a lit chamber within. A roaring, rushing sound burst out from within the doorway and the smell of fresh running water washed across them. Curion looked on with awe. Trion stood triumphantly.

Curion turned to the young Priest and said with approval, "Trion your studies have served you well. You have uncovered something that has not been seen for centuries."

Trion beamed.

"Does it lead up to the valley and the lake?" asked Ferian.

"That is what I have read," said Trion.

"That is what the stories say," said Curion. "But those stories are from long ago and mostly forgotten."

"I must leave at once," said Ferian. "I have all I need with me."

"You will need food," said Curion.

"I have food!" said Trion excitedly.

He brandished a pack that bulged slightly.

"Trion this is much too dangerous," said Curion. We will send one of the older Priests."

"But I know the way," said Trion, "and I have read about the traps and gates."

"Traps?" asked Ferian.

"The way is guarded, of course," said Trion, and hurriedly added, "but it was built by Anasarians so we should be able to pass. I have spent much time studying this."

"Yes, but at the very least you should have a more experienced Priest with you," said Curion.

"I will accompany Trion and Ferian," said Neferelon from beside them.

Curion looked shocked. "Neferelon, you are wounded and tired and … and"

"Old?" suggested Neferelon.

"You, you—" began Curion.

"Curion, I have waited all my life for a chance to see the Stones returned to Abessair," said the old Priest solemnly. "I have seen the light of Ilah and I am renewed. I must go. I feel it deep within me."

Curion looked a little sheepish. "You must go if you see fit," he said.

He turned to Trion. "Do you have enough food for three?"

"It is only a day's journey. We should have enough," said Trion.

"I have some stores," said Ferian, "and we will have plenty of water. It will suffice if there is food above."

"I am afraid you cannot rely on finding food in the mountains," said Curion. "I will arrange for food to be prepared quickly and that you have anything else you need."

"We must not delay too long," said Ferian impatiently.

"It will be done as quickly as possible," assured Curion.

Suddenly there was a shudder through the stone of the mountain. They stood and listened. They could hear the muffled sound of thunder from above but what they felt was not of the storm.

"What was that?" said Trion in a worried voice.

"Something evil," said Neferelon, "but far away."

They gathered together in the doorway, the sound of rushing water before them. Trion's pack bulged even more now, but at least he no longer had to carry the sword. Ferian carried a pack, and Neferelon had been given a smaller pack and a stout staff to help him on the climb. Other Priests had come to see them off and Curion stood before them.

"I wish you well," said Curion. "May the power of the Stones guide you on your way." He held a book in his hand and had it open. "I have looked hurriedly through texts in the library and found one you missed, Trion. I have read some of it. The valley is high above, over the other side of the ridge above us. The top of that ridge is steep and inaccessible and the lake lies hidden behind the ridge. The only other way is to go around the ridge to the west and then climb. This book says that the Anasarians built this stairway as a quicker route. This route passes under the ridge and directly into the valley near the lake's edge. It is a much shorter path but it is still treacherous and there is a storm passing over the mountains. The rain could feed the waters that run beside the stairs."

He closed the book and handed it to Trion.

"Take it Trion," he said. "Hopefully you have space in your pack. You can put it with the other book, the one that was already missing from the Library."

Trion gave a guilty smile, but said gratefully, "Thank you, Curion."

"Alright," said Ferian, "let's get going. The day is dragging on and we will need to rest before we reach the valley."

There was a chorus of farewells as the three passed through the doorway, turned to the left, and approached to where the stairs began heading up towards the north, lit by a dim light that faded into darkness above. Ferian stepped onto the first step and then hesitated. He turned to Trion.

"When do we come across the first trap?" he asked warily.

"Ummm," said Trion with a thoughtful expression. "Not until the stairs turn to the west."

"Onwards then," said Ferian.

The light at the bottom of the stairs began to fade as they climbed. The stairway was still lit by a dim glow from the rock walls. In places the walls were smooth where they had been worked and in other places the natural rock wall had been left. It seemed that this was a natural waterway that had been widened, and through which, the stairs and sluiceway had been hewn. The stairs were damp and in places wet and slippery. Ferian led the way and Neferelon climbed behind him, with Trion following behind the old Priest. At times there was debris on the stairs; the flotsam from old stormwater that had flooded the stairs. The sound of the water to their right became background noise but the sound of their footsteps was masked by the constant clamour.

Ferian could hear something though and as he listened he heard faintly "Two hundred and eighty-three, two hundred and eighty-four..."

He stopped and looked past Neferelon at Trion, as the two Priests also came to a halt in the dim light.

"What are you doing?" asked the General.

Trion looked sheepish and said, "I'm counting the steps."

"Why?" asked Ferian.

"I couldn't find anywhere where it said how many steps there were, so I thought I would count them," said Trion.

Ferian rolled his eyes and said gruffly, "Well, do it in your head."

With that they went on. The stairs were not steep but they continued for a long way straight up. The three were tiring as they climbed higher. At one point they halted. A tree branch blocked the stairway. Sticks and leaves had piled up behind it. Ferian bent down and grasped the branch and lifting it threw it toward the water flow, where it was swept downwards. He groaned slightly as the wound in his shoulder protested at the exertion. He dismissed the pain though, and kicking debris aside, continued to climb. The two Priests followed doggedly behind. As they climbed higher, they began to see above them that the light was brighter and gave off a green glow. As they approached the green light, they could see that there was an open area and a rock wall directly ahead.

"That must be where the stairs turn westward," said Neferelon. He spoke haltingly and with short breaths.

Ferian halted suddenly and turned back towards the Priests.

"Let's rest here and Trion can tell us about the trap ahead before we stumble into it," suggested the General.

"Oh," said Trion, hesitantly, as he removed his pack. "Well it is a little hard to decipher."

Ferian looked at him questioningly.

"I think I know what it means," continued Trion quickly.

"What does it say?" asked Neferelon, who now sat on a step and rested with his staff planted between his feet.

Trion spoke confidently. "It says that those who are healthy may pass and that those who can be healed will be healthy and that sickness, or decay, or something like that… cannot pass." He paused. "I think it means that nothing evil can get through."

"What if it means that people who are sick or wounded are not allowed through?" said Ferian, and as he spoke he unconsciously glanced at his shoulder and then something dawned on him.

"What if…?" he began.

The thought of all the interminable years spent doing the bidding of the Dark Lords crashed in his mind.

"What if it still thinks I am an Ultamarian?" asked Ferian finally.

The old Priest looked up at the General who towered above him.

"Your heart will tell them that you have been healed," said Neferelon. "You are an Abessairian soldier."

They approached the landing that was bathed in green light. Trion spoke. His voice quavered a little but he was steadfast.

"Let me go first," he said as he moved past Neferelon and stood behind Ferian.

"No!" said Neferelon. "If there is danger I should face it. You can continue without me but you will both be needed to find a way through."

But Trion was already bounding up the stairs, and leaping past Ferian he cleared the last few steps and stood on the landing.

At first nothing happened.

He stood bathed in the pale green light but with a sudden burst, bright green light surrounded him. He stood as if frozen while he appeared to be burning in green flames. Ferian made to run up the steps towards him but some force held him back. Trion was caught in an explosion of green light.

It looked as if he was trying to walk towards the source of the light but was being buffeted by a ferocious wind. Then the light abruptly ceased and became a green glow again. Ferian watched as Trion turned and began to ascend the stairway that led off to the left, and then disappeared from sight. Then the General began to continue up towards the landing.

A frail hand reached out and grasped his arm. He turned and looked into the face of the old Priest. Neferelon's face shone with wonder and determination.

"Can't you feel it General," he said. "It feels like being young again."

Ferian paused. He sensed the air, and the Priest was right. It was as if a spring afternoon had come into the tunnel. The Priest released his arm, and the General stood immobile as the Priest ascended the stairs until he stood on the landing, with the light shining upon him. Again bright green light flooded the tunnel. The light washed over the old Priest. Neferelon stood with a smile on his face, and as Ferian watched, the old man seemed to stand straighter and taller. Neferelon's face became serene and all the pain of age and injury drained away until he stood anew. He did not look at the Abessairian but, as Trion had, he turned and made his way up the stairs and out of sight.

Ferian collected himself. Doubt and the memories of his unforgivable deeds played in his mind. The light on the landing above him seemed to take on a dangerous and sickly hue. The air in the tunnel still smelled of life and health. He let out a sharp sigh, and then with determination on his face, walked up the steps. He paused on the last step and looked at the source of the light. A green gem was mounted in the wall on the right. Intricate carved patterns decorated the rockwall around where the Stone shone. The General lifted his left foot and stepped onto the landing.

He walked forward and turned to face the green Stone, its light surrounded him and filled his sight and senses. The events of his life flashed through his mind. The pain of some of those memories pierced his heart. He was a traitor and he had performed evil deeds. Then he remembered something that he had never been able to recall. A room that stank of evil, where an iridescent purple light burned into his brain and slowly but methodically removed his love of Abessair, and the oaths he had taken, from his heart.

He felt like screaming as the brutality of Ultamar, and his service to evil, coursed through him. He hated himself. At that moment he would have gladly driven a dagger through his own heart. He deserved it. He had betrayed his people, and murdered, and tortured. He began to weep as the pain and suffering he had inflicted assaulted him. He grasped at the air. He sensed the beauty of the Stone before him and he reached out to it.

"Please?" he pleaded. "Make it stop. I am sorry."

Nothing happened for a moment, but then suddenly bright green light burst into his vision. His mind was filled with a feeling so intense that it made him feel nauseous. His vision swirled and he felt as if he was going to faint. Then it felt as if the green light was washing through his body. He felt that all the darkness in his being began to be attacked. The battle between the light and the dark raged in him, and then he could feel the darkness being dissolved. He began to feel light-headed as the strength of the green light poured into him. The pain of the wound in his shoulder began to subside and he could feel that he was being healed. Then as it reached its peak, the light ceased and just the dim green light remained.

He stood there strong and whole, a General in the army of Abessair, finally free of the evil of Ultamar. He smiled, and straightening his pack and gripping the hilt of the sword at his hip, turned and made his way up the stairs, following where Trion and Neferelon had gone before.

The three of them continued up the stairs, Trion leading the way with Neferelon behind him, and trailing further behind them, General Ferian. They did not speak as they made their way up the stairs. They climbed steadfastly and with renewed strength and purpose. The exertion of the climb did not tax them. They were strong and their bodies were healed. The stairs curved back and forth as they climbed. The light from the rock walls filled their path with a soft glow. After a while the light began to brighten ahead. Trion halted and turned back towards Neferelon and Ferian. His face glowed with vitality.

"I think it is the next test," he said.

He sat down on a step, and laying his pack between his feet, reached in and drew out the old book. He opened it up and then flicked through the pages until he found the one he was looking for. He scanned the page and then read to himself. He paused, realising the other two were looking at him intently.

"Well?" asked Ferian.

"Well," began Trion, "it says that the…"

At that moment, there was a humming that filled the stairway. A sense of power passed through the rock for a few moments and then abruptly ceased.

"What was that?" asked Neferelon.

"I... I..." Trion stammered and then looked at the book.

"It doesn't say anything about that," he said bewildered.

"It is something else," said Ferian. "It came from the east but it is gone now. It did not have the sense of evil that we felt before."

There was silence between them as they pondered and then Neferelon spoke.

"What does the book say, Trion?" he asked quietly.

The young Priest looked back down at the book and read, "Only one who has drunk twice can open the door."

"There must be a door above," said Ferian. "But what does it mean to have drunk twice?"

"Maybe we have to drink the water twice?" suggested Trion.

"That seems too easy," said Ferian.

"Not if you didn't know," said Trion defensively.

"Well let's at least see what this door looks like," said Ferian.

They stood on the landing. On their left was a rockwall. To their right was the coursing water, flowing strongly and swiftly downwards. Ahead of them stood a blank stone door. Trion was bending down retrieving a wooden cup from his pack. He stood, then walked over to the right and then leaning out caught some of the water as it cascaded down the rock sluice. He raised the cup to his lips and then drank it. He finished swallowing and then bent and held the cup out and filled it and then drank again. He paused and then walked to the door. He stooped and put the cup on the stone floor of the landing. He placed both his hands, palms out, on the door.

His mind seemed to fill with white light.

As Ferian and Neferelon watched, Trion's face took on an expression of puzzlement and then pain and then suddenly there was a flash of light and the young Priest was blown back towards them. Ferian jumped forward and caught Trion and held him. Trion looked dazed and disorientated but his eyes were open and he looked up at the General.

"No," he said firmly.

They now sat on the top step with the door behind them and the water rushing to their left.

"It is late and we should be resting," said Ferian. "Although, I don't feel in the least tired."

"Neither do I," said Trion.

Neferelon spoke. "The green Stone that we passed was a powerful Halestone. It has healed us and refreshed us. I myself feel like I am young again."

Ferian looked at the Priest.

"The weight of evil has been lifted from me," said the General. "But all I can think of is my comrades. They have been under the yoke of Ultamar. How will they be cleansed?"

"When the Twin Stones are united, then they will be free," said Neferelon reassuringly. "That is what the Order have always believed since Abessair fell into evil. It is said that the army was weakened when Darion fled with Ilah. Rituals that had used the light and power of both Stones could only be fulfilled with the light of Ivah. It is written that those who were washed only with the light of…"

Neferelon leapt to his feet. He spoke half to himself. "It is an archaic expression, but…" He looked down at Ferian

"General?" he asked. "When you were sworn to the service of Abessair did you see Ivah?"

The General looked at the Priest with a puzzled expression on his face.

"Yes," he said. "King Bharain himself held Ivah, when I was sworn in with my fellow cadets, once we had completed our training and were worthy. The light of Ivah shone upon us."

"And you were bathed in the light of Ilah when it washed across the battlefield and freed you?" continued Neferelon breathlessly.

Trion jumped to his feet.

"You have drunk from both Stones," blurted the young Priest. "Of course. The soldiers of old Anasaria would have sworn allegiance in the presence of both Stones."

Ferian and Neferelon both looked at Trion. Ferian rose to his feet and then turned his gaze to Neferelon. The old Priest's expression was one of encouragement.

"I had enough trouble with the last trap," said Ferian.

"It makes sense," said Neferelon.

Ferian turned and faced the door. He approached and then turned and looked at each of the Priests in turn.

"Don't stand behind me," he said. "I don't think even the power of the Halestone has made you strong enough to catch me."

General Ferian turned back and faced the door. He straightened himself up and then stepped forward. He held his hands out and then looked in turn again at the two Priests who now stood to either side of him. Trion nodded vigorously and Neferelon bowed his head to him in assent. He turned back towards the door and hesitantly he moved his hands towards it. He placed his palms against the stone.

He felt something he had never felt before. The feeling filled him with awe. He stood rigid and transfixed. He understood the nature of the Stones that had each filled him with their power. And he understood that together the Stones were truly powerful. He felt a white power flow through his hands, and up his arms, and into his mind. He saw that what he witnessed was a sacred bond that was at the crux of an old and deep power that was the foundation of Abessair and the kingdom of Anasaria.

As he stood there, it seemed as if something flowed out of him through his hands. He wasn't sure if it was in his head or that the others could hear it, but a persistent hum grew, and then there was a resounding series of clicks and grindings, and the stone in front of him moved aside. A warm light grew around them as the door opened revealing a glowing stairway that led straight upwards, and then curved to the right until the stairs disappeared far above. Ferian shepherded the Priests through the doorway and the stone door slid closed behind them.

Neferelon grasped Ferian's arm and said to him, "You are truly a soldier of Abessair. There have been none like you in this place since Darion took Ilah."

As the stairway arced to the right, following the curve of the watercourse, the area opened out into a large glowing chamber. Ahead, the waterway curved further to the right and then back to the left. They could see that the stairs before them became a stone bridge that vaulted the water as it flowed through a narrow gorge below. On the far left wall of the cavern, the water poured out of a dark roughly hewn tunnel in the rock wall. The stairway continued beyond the other end of the bridge and disappeared into another tunnel, this one smoothly carved and forming an arch. Ferian led them forward.

"Wait!" shouted Trion. "There is something about a bridge."

He brought his pack down from his shoulder and then fumbled around in it until he pulled out the book again. He opened it and studied the pages as Ferian and Neferelon waited patiently.

"No, it's not the bridge," said Trion finally. "It says that there is a bridge and then a tunnel, but then it says that the faithful will be tested in the darkness."

Ferian looked at Trion and said, "How many more of these tests do we have to go through?"

"I think this is the last one," said Trion and then he continued a little hesitantly. "Although there is the Gate of Tears… or maybe Fears. I'm not sure … the writing is faded."

"Let me look, Trion," said Neferelon.

Trion handed the book to the old Priest. Neferelon took it and read the script. He gently turned back a page and continued to read, then turned back to the one Trion had been reading.

He studied the book for a few moments and then said, "Trion is right, the next test is surely in the tunnel. The text says that you will face your enemy and only one of you will continue on."

Neferelon paused and read on and then said, "I think that the Gate may be another test. The fact that it has a name means that it is significant. Whether it says 'tears' or 'fears', neither sound promising."

"Who goes first?" asked Ferian.

"I think it is my turn," replied Neferelon before Trion had a chance to volunteer.

As the three of them approached the bridge, the sound of the water rushing through the narrow channel grew louder. There was debris littered across the stone of the bridge where water had obviously risen in times gone by. As they stood and surveyed the path ahead they began to notice that the sound of the water began to grow louder still. A roaring sound appeared to be increasing from the black tunnel from where the water flowed.

Suddenly, Ferian grasped Trion's arm, and pushing at him, shouted, "Run! Across the bridge now!"

With the roaring noise feeding a growing panic in Trion, he didn't hesitate but raced up onto the bridge and jumped over an old tree branch that lay across his path. Ferian didn't ask any permission but grabbed Neferelon and hoisting him up over his shoulder broke into a run. As he stepped onto the stone of the bridge and began to run, the roar grew and he felt a blast of air buffeting them.

Then suddenly from the tunnel to the left burst a wall of water. Ferian sprinted up the arch of the bridge and vaulted the branch. His right foot hit the bridge and he sped over the top of the bridge's arch but as he did the wall of water rose alongside him ready to pounce as he approached the other side. He saw before him, Trion standing with his mouth wide in a cry of warning or despair.

"Catch him!" cried Ferian.

He grasped the Priest's waist with his big hands and thrust him through the air towards Trion. He saw the young Priest reach out with a startled and worried look on his face. Ferian watched as if time had slowed, as Neferelon flew through the air towards Trion, and then the water crashed into him lifting him off his feet and over the edge of the bridge.

Trion tumbled backwards as he threw his arms around Neferelon. He braced himself for impact but his fall was cushioned by the bulky pack on his back.

He rolled to his left cradling Neferelon who had already started to protest. "Let go of me! Let go of me!"

Trion released him, and they both got to their feet. Water from the torrent soaked the stone in front of them, but both their gazes were fixed on where water now gushed over the bridge.

"Ferian!" shouted Trion desperately.

He shucked the pack from his shoulders and dropped it on the ground. He walked towards the bridge. The water splashed around him more vigorously as he approached where it cascaded across the bridge and down the causeway. He approached the side of the bridge where Ferian had disappeared, and looked down to where the water swirled against the wall and then rushed down the stairs that they had ascended. The stairs would now be waterfalls, he thought. He stood there with despair and a deep sense of loss.

"Help me up!" said a voice at his feet.

The fingers of two large hands gripped the edge of the gorge. An arm and then a shoulder appeared, and then the other shoulder, and between them the exasperated and straining face of General Ferian, water still washing against him. His uniform glowed silver and white through the cascade.

"Grab my pack," he said desperately.

Trion knelt down and grasped the shoulder strap of Ferian's pack. He strained backwards pulling at the pack with all his strength. His knees started to slide towards the edge but the General was now pulling himself up on his elbows. With a sudden lunge Ferian threw himself forward and Trion let go of the straps as Ferian thumped beside him. Trion windmilled his arms as the edge loomed below him and then he caught his balance and pushed his weight sideways. He lay there panting. Beside him, Ferian groaned and then spat out a mouthful of water.

Ferian climbed gingerly to his feet and then reached out towards Trion. The uniform of the Abessairian General shone in the rocklight. Trion held out his hand and the General took it and helped him to his feet. They both quickly looked to where Neferelon lay prostrate on the ground staring up towards the stone ceiling. They moved towards him and over the roar of the water heard a strange sound.

The old Priest was laughing,

"I haven't felt anything like that in years," laughed Neferelon.

He stopped abruptly and then looked up at the other two. "Are you both alright?" he asked.

"We'll live," said Ferian brusquely. "I don't think that was the test though, just floodwater. The tunnel awaits."

"Yes," said Neferelon, climbing slowly to his feet. "Me first."

Neferelon walked between Ferian and Trion as they stood at either side of the tunnel entrance, and then plunged into darkness. There was no rocklight, and the torches that Ferian carried were wet and refusing to light.

"It shouldn't be too far," said Trion reassuringly.

Neferelon felt along the rock wall of the tunnel as the light of the chamber dwindled behind him. The tunnel curved and the light behind him disappeared, leaving complete blackness. He stumbled ahead for what seemed like ages and then he saw what he thought was a brief glimmer of light ahead. It disappeared, and he thought that it was just his mind playing tricks on him. But the light appeared again and then became a steady glow. The light seemed to be coming from where the tunnel bent back around again. The light grew in intensity as he moved forward.

A glowing figure came sauntering around the bend seemingly deep in thought and softly whistling tunelessly. It was a young man in Priest's robes that appeared too big for him. He almost bumped into Neferelon and then suddenly looked up and locked his gaze with the Priest. There was an instant sense of recognition for Neferelon but he couldn't quite remember where he knew this young man from.

Before he had a chance to collect his thoughts the young man snarled at him, "You old fool! What do you think you're doing?"

Neferelon was taken aback at this. It was disrespectful for a novice such as this to speak to him so rudely.

"Who are you?" Neferelon asked sharply.

The young man looked at Neferelon with contempt on his face.

"Who do you think you are?" he sneered. "What do you hope to gain old man? Do you think these people need an old, helpless, useless piece of baggage, like you?"

In a flash, it dawned on Neferelon who this angry young man was.

It was him. When he was young and hopeful, before the years spent waiting and hoping had led him to become desperate and foolhardy. He had attempted to try the old road to the west only to end up captured and tortured by Ultamarians.

"You may as well just lie down here and die," continued the figure. "All those things you hoped for, all the glory. That is just your stupid pride, and it has grown as you grew older. That desire in you to see the Stones back again is just you seeking glory. To live to see Abessair and to share in the victory. That is just your vanity old man. You do not care about Anasaria. Ever since you were me you have wanted only to be special. You attempt the stairs with your companions because you still seek glory. You still hope to prove that you are special. But you are nothing. You are old and useless, and you made the young and the strong drag you along with them. Hah! You can't even cross a bridge without being carried."

Neferelon stood dumbfounded. His head spun as thoughts of his life flashed through his mind. He had been proud and foolish as a young Priest. He believed that he would be the one that would find the Stones and free Anasaria. His studies of the Stones had filled his head, not with the peace of the Stones, but with the glory of old Anasaria and the strength of Abessair. He had pictured himself high in the Chamber of the Stones awash with the power of Ilah and Ivah, and in the favour of the King.

"You! The Keeper of the Stones!" screamed his young self. "You are a miserable old fool. What makes you think you are worthy of anything?"

Neferelon stifled a sob. He wasn't worthy. All that he had dreamed of was folly and he was just a worthless old man. But he had seen Ilah. He remembered the light of the Stone, the power that had flowed from it. He had lived to see it and the prophecy was coming true. The Twin Stones had returned along with the Sword of Acclimoss and he was filled with a sense of wonder, and he was content.

"You are right!" said Neferelon calmly. "I was a young fool and I became an old fool, but that glory I dreamed of, it no longer means anything. I have lived to see the Stones return and even if my path ends here, I die happy. You are no longer who I am. Evil corrupts your thoughts and evil will be defeated. I remember you, but you are just the folly of youth. You are a lesson learnt and you strengthen me by showing me what I no longer wish to be."

He leant forward towards the young Priest and whispered. "Be gone."

Neferelon stood defiantly with a smile on his face and looked at the young vision of himself. He peered into the clear eyes and the figure before him began to become less solid. The sneer on the fading face became a slight smile. The figure became transparent and misshapen until it became like a wisp of smoke and, as if a breeze washed over him, the smoke wafted around him and disappeared leaving him old but wise. Ahead he could see the faint glow of rocklight and he continued on up the passage, leaving the darkness behind.

Trion stepped into the dark passage. He walked slowly and carefully, feeling the rock wall of the tunnel to his right. He continued on until the blackness of the tunnel became complete. Something caught his foot, and he stumbled and fell to his knees thrusting his hands out to break his fall. He stopped there on his hands and knees and began to get up but as he raised his head he saw that a softly glowing figure stood looking down at him.

"Get up you stupid boy," said the figure of Curion sternly. "What are you doing down there? Looking for secrets? Follow me!"

The figure turned and moved off quickly and rounded a bend in the tunnel. Trion got quickly to his feet and followed the glow. As he rounded the bend the Priest passed through a doorway but before Trion reached the door it slammed shut leaving him in darkness, apart from a brief flicker of light that washed across the surface of the door, then all was black again.

He stared ahead to where the door lay and slowly reached out his hand. He placed his palm against the stone of the door and concentrated. He felt power within the stone; felt it keeping him out. He sensed that the door was questioning him. He tried to remember about incantations, and chants, and passwords, but it was all jumbled in his mind. He sensed something behind him and saw that a soft light flickered around him casting his shadow dimly on the door.

He turned around and three familiar figures stood glowing behind him. His fellow novices. They all began laughing at him and jeering. His hands dropped to his sides and he clenched them into fists.

One of the figures called out. "Trion, can't you remember even the simplest password? How do you expect to become a Priest?"

But he couldn't remember. He had never been able to remember. It didn't make any sense. He could feel the stone and he knew what was needed but he could never get it straight in his head. He could read though, and he loved it more than anything else. The script meticulously laid down on the page, sometimes by a hand that had withered into dust long ago, but it was almost as if you could hear the scribe's thoughts. But keys and passwords were chants and incantations that made no sense. They did not tell a story. They just needed to be learned and remembered until you understood how the power worked. It didn't make any sense to him. If the power was there, why did you have to learn confusing things? Couldn't you just understand the power?

The jeering behind him continued and he felt the familiar feeling of shame and embarrassment creep up his neck and into his face. They were right. How did he expect to become a proper Priest if he couldn't learn? … He could learn though. The things he read were clear in his mind. He just liked to read about the old kingdom and its secrets. They made sense. The people were steeped in the power of the Stones. Their service and their oaths bound them to the power.

"Come on, Trion," shouted one of the figures. "We're going to be late."

He felt pressure building in him. He couldn't concentrate properly. He felt his face flushing and his palms were sweating, but he steeled himself. He wiped his hands on his robes and then placed his palms back against the door. He began to try to decipher the answer to the door but instead he thought of the old kingdom and the power that was at its heart. It was all about duty and purity. The chants seemed harsh in comparison to that pure power. The people of the old kingdom knew how to speak to the stone and, he thought, so did the older Priests. And then he realised that the chants didn't matter, they were just a crude way of learning to communicate with the power in the stone.

He thought of how the words of the scholars and scribes leapt out of the page when he read. How they flowed into his mind and he tried to read the door as if its power was written on the stone. He let the words sink into him and he vaguely saw a story where characters were speaking. The story was incomplete though, but he just had to write the next piece to complete it. The words flowed from his thoughts and through his hands.

And with a click the door opened. A figure stood before him. It wasn't Curion, Instead Neferelon stood there. He quickly glanced behind him but there was no one there.

"Trion?" said Neferelon in a worried tone. "Are you alright? Where is General Ferian?"

"I'm fine," said Trion smiling. "The General will be coming soon, hopefully."

Ferian waited until Trion had disappeared and then stood for a while gathering his strength. Then he steeled himself and stepped into the darkness of the tunnel. He walked on resolutely as the dark surrounded him. As he continued on, he saw a faint violet light ahead, lighting the wall where the tunnel curved around. As he moved towards the light, it grew in intensity, and as it did, he began to feel ill. A sickly smell of decay filled his nostrils. The smell was familiar. He had smelt it countless times over the last two centuries and it had filled him with reverence. It became harder to move forward, but he drove himself on and he felt his body bowing under the weight.

He rounded the bend and the sickly light shone all around him. Ahead of him were seven figures. They were formed of darkness but their features were highlighted in iridescent purple light. The one closest to him held something in his hands. Something he had only seen once, two centuries ago. It was a Stone that gave off the same light as the figures. He felt himself being driven to his knees, felt his head bowing down before the figures. The Dark Lords were calling him back to their service. He crouched on the ground under the evil power that emanated from the Stone and the seven dark figures.

"Where have you been Ferian?" snarled the figure holding the Stone. "We have been waiting for your report."

Another of the Dark Lords spoke. "Did you think you could escape our power? We gave you that power, and you were able to do all that your heart desired."

Ferian felt fury grow in him. He struggled against the force that held him down. He managed to lift his head.

"No!" he shouted. "It wasn't what my heart desired. It was you. You corrupted me, made me your tool. I won't do it again."

"Look into the Stone, General," said the lead figure as he held it out before him.

Ferian felt his head being forced upwards. His gaze was being pulled towards the Stone. He strained the sinews of his neck to stop himself facing the Stone.

"Remember how it felt to be so powerful and free," said another voice.

Ferian did remember. He commanded armies and none stood before them. They were free to act as they wanted. He winced with the painful memories, but that was not him. That was these evil creatures.

Ferian wrenched his head aside and said forcefully. "I was not free. I was enchained. I lost my free will, and did only what I was told to."

Ferian thrust his hands against the ground and with an almighty effort launched himself to his feet. As he did his sword was already in his hand. He jumped forward and his sword arced through the air. The sword caught the lead figure just above the wrist of the hand holding the Stone. The Stone flew through the air. It crashed into the wall and fell to the floor. A dark claw-like hand was still gripping the Stone. In front of Ferian, purple fluid poured from the stump that the Dark Lord held out. The fluid poured towards the ground, and as it did, it turned into a purple mist. The light from the figures and the Stone on the floor also became misty and then tendrils of smoke wavered in the air and then disappeared.

The Dark Lords and the Stone were gone. The tunnel was dark without the purple light, but he moved forward, and as he continued on, he saw that there was a faint glow ahead. He rounded another bend in the tunnel and saw that rocklight lit the tunnel. Against the light of the rock walls further ahead he saw the silhouettes of two familiar figures.

CHAPTER EIGHTEEN

The Wisdom between the Moon

and the Sun

Hyrn crouched against the parapet wall. Wren cowered beside him. Infiron fumed in front of him.

"We will need to talk about this further, but for now we have to get away from here," said the Priest, sternly.

Hyrn was dazed and bewildered. The misshapen form of the statue stood before him.

He thought wildly. What had he done? And why had he done it? Hyrn felt as if he had been under someone else's control. Not a person, but… Ilah. Hyrn felt resentment growing inside him, but then he felt a familiar soothing feeling in his mind, but only weakly.

Not this time! He steeled himself against the power of the Stone. Ilah fought against Hyrn briefly and then her voice disappeared from his mind.

Hyrn rose to his feet and said haltingly to Infiron, "I don't know what happened. It was as if Ilah was controlling my mind. Her voice became the voice in my head."

Infiron's face moved between anger and fear and then contemplation and then took on a look of worry.

"The Stone spoke to you?" she asked finally.

"She speaks in my mind and sometimes it feels like she is in my mind," said Hyrn.

Infiron looked taken aback and gasped softly. "That is a power that the greatest of our Order were said to have. The Twin Stones are said to not speak as other Stones do. They are secretive and reticent."

Hyrn said, "Devarnia said not to use Ilah lightly, but she didn't mention to be careful of Ilah or that the Stone could lead us into danger."

"The Keepers, no doubt, know more about these things than we do," said Infiron, "but the Order of the Stones observed and protected the Stones when they were within the fortress of Abessair. The Stones mostly spoke out loud but only when they chose, and usually in times of need. They are one of the mysteries of the world."

Hyrn stood looking at the statue trying to fathom what had happened. The statue had spoken to him.

At that moment Harla leapt from the trapdoor.

"We have to get away from here!" she said urgently.

They all froze momentarily as the distant harsh sound of a horn echoed up from across the darkened land. Harla reached towards Hyrn but he was already moving towards the stairs. Wren sheepishly followed quickly behind. They made their way urgently through the chamber and then back down the spiral staircase. As they neared the bottom of the tower Hyrn could see that the rest of the party were packing up quickly. Hyrn and Wren made their way down and moved towards where their gear was. Yarga dashed over to Hyrn as Infiron stepped down from the stairs behind them.

"What happened?" asked Yarga worriedly.

"They awakened the tower," said Infiron, bluntly. "And by the sound of it they have alerted Ultamar to our presence."

"Hyrn?" said Yarga, shocked. "How could you do something so foolish?"

"I-I…" began Hyrn.

Suddenly Ilah burnt hotly and brightly inside his vest. Hyrn pulled the Stone out and the voice of Careil burst from within.

"The Ultamarians do not have Ivah!" said the familiar voice stridently.

Then the Stone went dead. Hyrn's heart leapt at the sound of the Rider's voice but then dread filled his mind.

"Ilah! Ilah!" said Hyrn desperately, but the Stone was dark and silent and did not respond.

Hyrn turned to Yarga and said frantically, "Careil?"

Yarga stood transfixed for a moment and then said, "Careil was free and safe enough to be able to contact Ilah. He is still able to carry out his duty to the quest. Don't worry Hyrn."

Hyrn still stood looking uneasy. The dark silent Stone was still clutched in his hand but behind him a commanding voice sounded, breaking him out of his malaise.

Harla had taken in what the Stone had said, but immediately checked that everyone was present, and then raised her voice and shouted. "We need to get moving now! Evil approaches and we need to get to safety."

Gebarana said, "Ultamar is far from here. It will take them some time to get here."

"There are always the Kragon," said the Priest, Drivian.

Wren gasped beside Hyrn and clutched at Hyrn's sleeve.

"We have to get out of here," said the young Anasarian.

Hyrn was bewildered.

"What are the Kragon?" he asked.

"They are horses, or they were horses," said Drivian. "The Dark Lords have used some evil power to corrupt them. They travel fast, too fast for normal horses and they will drive themselves to death if commanded."

The Priest paused, then said, "They do not move in a way that we understand. They are imbued with power, and it is as if they are only horses in form. They move like the wind and carry their riders along with them."

Infiron was already at the door, releasing the enchantment that held it closed. Harla was behind her, shepherding people forward. The door opened and Hyrn realised that he hadn't retrieved his gear. Turum appeared in front of him and thrust Hyrn's pack towards him and then passed Wren his sleeping roll. There was a sense of urgency and fear. Hyrn hurried behind Yarga as the rest of the party moved towards the door. Margana and Gebarana helped Drivian extinguish the last of the fire and the torches that guttered around the walls in the breeze from the open door. Drivian was the last to leave, extinguishing the final torch. He moved past Infiron. She closed the door and turned the key, locking the tower's defences.

Harla led them down and around the base of the tower and back along the hillside towards the southernmost of the towers. Already they felt that something was approaching. Harla moved towards the southern edge of the tower where there was thick vegetation. The road was in sight below them as they hid themselves amongst the grass and shrubs in the shadow of the tower. The tension was palpable as the clatter of hooves approached rapidly and then slowed as the riders approached.

Hyrn felt terror grow within him. Wren shrunk beside him as the evil force approached. Hyrn held his breath as up the roadway rode a large number of riders astride horses that glowed with a strange blue light. The riders rode towards the tower. A deepening sense of dread came over Hyrn. He felt exposed even though they were hidden in the darkness. He felt a sense of relief that they were not still within the main tower. The riders were gathered around the entrance. And then came the sound of pounding. The need to run grew in Hyrn, but Harla crouched facing them all, her face locked in determination and her hands extended in caution.

The incessant pounding continued, but then another sound could be heard. There was a thunder of hooves that came up from the direction of the old road. And then, in the dim light, could be discerned a large mass of riders. It almost seemed to Hyrn that they glowed with a pale golden light. And then an exultant cry came from the approaching horde and Hyrn's heart leapt within his chest.

"Desultamar!" came the battle cry. The riders rode proudly, and with swords raised and bows drawn, raced steadfastly towards where the Ultamarians stood.

The Ultamarian soldiers had begun to turn to face the oncoming riders but the narrow roadway restricted them from forming a wide front. The rebel force thundered at them and crashed violently into their midst and their battle cry roared out again. The sounds of battle were horrendous. The clash of steel, the fierce shouts of attack and the cries and screams of pain.

The battle raged below them.

Harla stood up slightly but still crouched and said quietly but forcefully. "We must go that way."

She pointed up towards the mountains that stood above where the old road led back to where they had earlier emerged from the ancient tunnels of Detrasarn. Hyrn didn't need any coaxing. As far as he was concerned the quicker that they could get away from the carnage below the better. They filed out with Turum leading the way. Harla held her position until the last of them had moved off. She then scanned the area taking in the continuing battle below. It was not clear from this distance and in the dim light who had the upper hand. The warrior in her itched to go and join the fight, but she shrugged to herself, and then turned and followed Gebarana.

They made their way up onto the mountainside.

Yarga spoke to Harla. "I think we need to sleep until daylight. It is too dangerous to continue on in the dark. And we don't know where we're going," he added.

Harla looked at the young Elder.

"You are getting much better at this," she said.

The sound of a subdued dawn chorus awoke Hyrn. He wondered for a moment where he was, but as he opened his eyes and looked out, he saw that the sun rose in the east and lit the expanse of Anasaria, throwing the dark form of Ultamar into relief. Beyond his feet, stood the Caramar and Turum, their chanting continuing, then ceasing. Hyrn noticed that Wren stood beside them. The Anasarian looked out to the east and then down to the forests of Anasaria where his home lay. He then turned back and noticed that Hyrn was awake. He walked back.

"There are riders coming this way," said Wren.

Hyrn was shocked and began to scrabble out of his blanket.

Wren laughed.

"They are on our side," he said.

Hyrn breathed a sigh of relief and then continued to extract himself from his bedding.

"How many are there?" asked Hyrn. "Is Careil with them?"

"Hold on, hold on," said Wren. "I don't know. But Harla returned before dawn to tell us that the battle went well and that they were following our trail."

Jarta-Den stood beside the armoured figure of Captain Droom. They both looked weary and spoke in subdued tones to the party gathered before them. Hyrn was glad to see the Underdweller soldier again. Droom generally carried an air of decisiveness and purpose but he seemed a little restrained as he spoke.

"We took our attack directly to the Ultamarians," said the Captain. "We outnumbered them and we were able to gain the advantage but many of our fighters were lost. Our intent was to keep these Ultamarians from finding the Stonebearer or taking any news back to Ultamar."

"The second task we failed," he said, despondently.

"What happened?" asked Yarga.

Jarta-Den answered. "A group of Ultamarians escaped us. Our mounts cannot hope to keep up with the Kragon. They will return to Ultamar and report to the Dark Lords."

"What of Herardin?" asked Harla.

"The relief garrison didn't manage to get there," replied Droom. "Well, some have now gone there," he added. "They will enjoy the hospitality of the new owners."

Infiron spoke. "We can take Hyrn and Ilah back to Detrasarn, back amongst the defences of the old kingdom."

Hyrn spoke up fiercely. "No! We cannot hide. The Anasarians will suffer while we wait safely. We came here to defeat Ultamar. We have already started. I don't want to hide. Plus we have to find Careil."

Jarta-Den looked at Hyrn and said, "The enemy is already aware that something is up. They will now release their strength."

The Quigling then spoke solemnly to Hyrn. "We picked up Careil's trail and we found a dead Ultamarian. His head was severed from his body and the whole area reeked of the evil of Artora. Careil has followed that evil down into the forest towards Ultamar."

"He contacted us," said Hyrn. "He must be alright."

"How did he contact you?" asked Droom.

"He spoke to Ilah," said Yarga. "The Ultamarians do not have the other Stone. It must be carried by the Artorans. As for Careil…well he only left that message. We do not know where he has gone."

Wren, standing beside Hyrn, spoke up boldly. "If Careil is heading towards Ultamar, and we want to find Careil and we want to attack Ultamar, maybe we should just follow Careil's trail. I would like to go there and free my father."

Everyone looked at Wren and then at each other.

Harla spoke first. "That seems like the best idea I have heard so far."

Wren tried to look serious and determined but his face broke into a smile. He then had almost a look of wonder on his face.

"Can we really free my father?" he said.

"We are here to free them all," said Hyrn. "Your father and all Anasaria."

They made their way back down to the old road. There were rebel soldiers on foot and some mounted, waiting for them at the roadside. Jarta-Den had gone ahead and now reported back to them. Some of the rebels came with him.

"Word has gotten out amongst the rebels posted nearby, and amongst the Anasarians living secluded in this area. The news of the Stone spreads out through our secret networks," said the Quigling. "All of the area between here and Herardin and back within sight of the causeway are under the control of our forces. They await someone to lead them forward. They are willing to storm the very gates of Ultamar!"

"What are the gates like?" asked Hyrn.

Garan spoke up. "The gates are magnificent!"

Everyone looked at him but he seemed in reverie. "The road leads up from the forest and crosses the gorge below where the Trebian crashes down from the valley beyond the wall. The roadway then passes through a stone canyon carved through the base of the plateau. The canyon walls are adorned with monuments, edifices, statues and sculptures right up to the gates. Beyond, a great chamber opens and a roadway leads up through the plateau to the beauty and power of Abessair."

Garan stopped as if surprised he had spoken.

"The gates are gateways to evil," growled a voice from behind Jarta-Den.

A middle-aged Anasarian rebel spoke. Others around him agreed. "Any who go in don't return," said another rebel.

Hyrn felt dread and uncertainty as they spoke.

"Is Careil heading to the gates?" he asked.

"Careil is heading down towards where the base of Detradin meets the plateau," said Jarta-Den.

"Is that safer?" asked Hyrn.

"There is evil there, and extreme danger," answered Jarta-Den. "The troops of Ultamar patrol the area heavily. There are entrances to the fortress, heavily guarded. But they are surrounded by warehouses, and workshops, and bars, and emporia, and places where evil mixes with greed. Anasarians work there, and trade, and live their lives. But amongst them there still burns the spirit of Abessair. There are many Anasarian rebels there. There are the local rebel group who are part of the underground that seeks to infiltrate Ultamar, but they are bolstered by people coming from outside, many seeking relatives arrested by Ultamarian soldiers. We have a network of people there."

"That is it," said Hyrn defiantly. "We go to the gates."

"What do you mean the gates?" said Wren. "I thought we were going to find your friend and to free my father?"

"We have to go to there," said Hyrn. "That is where Rowan will go. If there are good people where Careil is heading, he will find them."

He felt a lump in his throat but continued.

"Careil will do what needs to be done. He is really good at his job." Hyrn said, proudly.

A hesitant voice spoke up. "I am not sure about storming the gates," said Yarga.

"There will be no storming of gates," said Harla. "We must at least wait until we have sufficient strength of numbers."

"We have to go there," said Hyrn determinedly.

Harla looked at Hyrn and then looked towards Yarga.

The young Caramar Elder stood looking at Hyrn. His right hand was near his throat, clutching the crystal there.

Yarga turned to Harla. "We must follow the Stonebearer," he said.

Hyrn had turned away from the Elder and instead faced Wren.

"We have to do this for every Anasarian," he said. "Your father will be free."

He pointed around to the people milling around.

"This is it," he continued. "The beginning of the end of Ultamar."

Hyrn turned and raised his fist in the air. Wren, reluctantly at first and then defiantly also raised his fist. The two boys held their fists high.

They looked at each other and shouted. "Desultamar!"

The people around them and those beyond gathered along the road in either direction also raised their fists. The cry rang out again and it echoed along the mountainside. It almost felt as if a wave spread down and out across the forest below, and washed against the plateau where the dark forbidding shape of Ultamar stood.

In Hyrn's mind, the fortress seemed tossed like a ship in a violent sea and then it righted itself and stood as solid and unmoving as before.

"There's a storm coming," said Droom. "I can feel it. And it's going to get rough."

The troop of Abessairians marched through the Underrealm. They strove tirelessly. The quest to free Anasaria burned in them. Leading them was King Darlam. They had left the City of the Vortex far behind and now marched eastwards nearing the city at the gates. As they marched, they heard the sound of other people coming towards them out of the darkness ahead. Eventually the lights of torches could be seen and then a large number of people came into view. Some were riding and others on foot were marshalling the throng. As they grew closer, Darlam saw that there were a large number of Ultamarian prisoners, perhaps as many as two hundred. As they approached, one of the Underdweller soldiers rode up and greeted the King.

"We have captured large numbers of Ultamarians right up to the entrance to Anasaria," said the soldier. "The Anasarians in the mountains are helping now and if there are any more patrols around they will also be caught."

"You know what to do?" asked the King.

The soldier nodded.

"There are people to help at the Lake," said Darlam. "Once the Abessairians have been freed, all the spare force we have must move east. We go to Anasaria."

The soldier saluted and then rode back to lead the host. As the Ultamarians passed by, their faces showed anger, or fury, or defiance, or many just weariness, but they all looked at the Abessairians with confusion and awe on their faces.

One of the Abessairians shouted out with a laugh. "You just need to have a swim and then you'll feel much better. Then you can join us. We march to defeat Ultamar."

This sent a ripple of consternation and anger amongst the Ultamarians, but their escorts reasserted order. They continued to file past until they all eventually passed through and began to disappear down the roadway into the darkness, but towards the light that awaited them.

The path, long ago, had been well paved and level as it stepped down the mountainside and into the forest. Now, it was broken and uneven, and treacherous in places. There were ruins, and broken or weathered statues, and monuments along the way. The forest had encroached on what was once a major thoroughfare that led between Abessair and the defences of the old kingdom. They were joined by Droom and Jarta-Den. Drivian still accompanied them but Mergon had gone to Herardin with a rebel escort to give what help she could. Jarta-Den had brought supplies of fresh food, liberated from the well stocked storerooms and larders at Herardin.

"This will lead us down to meet the road beyond the Fort at the Trian Bridge," said Jarta-Den. "The rebels plan to marshal at Herardin and then march on the fort. They hope to take the fort or at least lay siege to it. Even without the troops that went west towards the Underrealm, there will be a sizeable Ultamarian force still stationed there. Our major danger, and theirs, will be if more troops come up from Forest Ford."

"Do we need to keep to the road?" asked Harla.

"It is difficult to move through the forest except by the road," said Jarta-Den. "The forest beyond is dense and ancient. There are old paths through the trees but they are overgrown and lead only deeper into the forest."

"We used to go into the deep forest along the old paths," whispered Wren to Hyrn. "That is on the other side though and we never went too far. It is like a different world there. Giant trees, and there are old ruins in some places; really old. My father said that they are from the old people that lived there before King Abess came."

"Who were they?" asked Hyrn softly.

"I don't know," replied Wren. "But they were gone a long time ago."

They sat hidden in the trees near the edge of the road and had a satisfying meal of cold meats, cheeses and fruit, while they waited for Harla, Gebarana and Turum to return from scouting the road. The three scouts had gone beyond a bend in the road, keeping to the trees at the road's edge moving swiftly and silently.

Infiron came over and sat beside Hyrn as he finished eating.

"Stonebearer," said the Priest. "I need to know what you did. How you awoke the statue. The Towers of Arkenegelon were built long ago when the old kingdom was established. It has been centuries since the old kingdom was at its height. We only have scant information concerning their purpose."

"I don't know what I did," said Hyrn. "I took the hook from amongst the treasures of Abessair in that room. I don't know why. Then something was driving me on to the Towers. That same something made me go up and wake up the statue. I think it was Ilah."

Infiron looked at Hyrn with a look of exasperation on her face.

"But why?" she said. "Why would Ilah want to alert Ultamar?"

"What do you think the Towers were for?" asked Hyrn.

"It was said that they were used to communicate with the Angilanians, and with Abessair as part of our defences, but we no longer know how," answered Infiron.

"The light went off into the distance, not to the fortress," said Hyrn.

"Mergon will look into the lore concerning the Towers," said Infiron. "It did seem to me that the light was beaming far to the east. It is possible that was how contact was maintained all those centuries ago."

"The statue spoke to me and asked who I was," said Hyrn.

"I wonder if there is some connection between Ilah and Ivah and Angilania that …?" Infiron trailed off and then said, "I must give this more thought."

By the time the scouting party returned, the others were finished eating and were ready to move out. Jarta-Den and Droom went first, leading their mounts, eager to get back to where they could ride. Yarga and Infiron followed them and Hyrn and Wren came behind, with the wary figure of Garan keeping a close eye on Hyrn. The rest of the party spread out to the sides and rear. They made their way out through the trees and onto the roadway. The paved road led in either direction in a great arc. Trees towered on either side, forming a canopy high above. They set off eastwards, towards Ultamar. All around them the forest was filled with a constant sighing and rushing as the wind buffeted the trees.

They had been travelling for an hour or so. Droom and Jarta-Den had ridden ahead and had disappeared around a bend. The two riders had been gone for a considerable time when they reappeared ahead and rode desperately towards them. As they approached, Harla moved from her position along the roadside to stand beside Yarga and Infiron.

Jarta-Den spoke fiercely. "There are a large number of Ultamarians coming. Word must have been sent to Forest Ford, or else these are troops from Ultamar itself. We cannot hope to confront them."

Harla looked around quickly. The terrain here was hilly and this part of the road cut through a spur of a hill. The ground rose on each side, the rocky slopes heavily forested. She looked further down the road.

"The terrain levels out ahead of us," said Harla. "I would advise that we move ahead quickly and then take to the trees and wait for the Ultamarians to move through."

Yarga spoke. "Harla's counsel should be heeded and quickly."

They were well within the trees when the first of the Ultamarians rode at speed up the roadway westwards towards the mountains. More riders soon followed and thundered past. It looked as if they would pass without incident, when one of the lead riders circled back skirting the roadside. He called to one of the officers and a group of a dozen or so riders came to a halt as the others rode on. The rider spoke insistently to the others just below where the questers hid quietly amidst the trees. Hyrn crouched beside Wren and watched the scene below and then his heart dropped into his stomach as the Ultamarian pointed into the forest and directly to where they were hidden.

Harla hissed urgently. "They have discovered our trail! We must move deeper into the forest!"

The trees grew denser as they made their way through the trees. They moved as quickly and as quietly as they could. They could hear the sound of the Ultamarians behind them and this drove them onwards.

Droom spoke as he led his chariga amongst the trees and through dense brush. "Let us just turn and fight," he said angrily.

Harla said calmly but directly, "I would love to take the fight to them but our duty is to the Stonebearer. Hyrn and Ilah must be protected at all costs."

"They're not going to give up," said Droom. "Now that they have found our trail they will continue to pursue us."

Harla considered this and then addressed Yarga. "Elder, I fear that Captain Droom is correct. We may well have to fight."

"Can we ambush them?" asked Yarga.

"Stealth is our best option," interjected Jarta-Den. "Send our best archers to pick them off. If we can reduce their numbers we can then hope to meet them in open battle."

"I will stay here with Hyrn," said Harla, "and Garan is charged to protect him. I would send Gebarana and Margana and I am sure that Turum would happily show his skills with the bow."

"I will go with them," said Jarta-Den. "Take my horse. If needed, he can carry Hyrn."

"I am not one for stealth," said Droom. "I will stay and protect here. I will be ready to fight if they come anywhere near the Stonebearer."

They continued to force their way through the dense trees. There were occasionally sounds of commotion from behind them. The ground dropped away slowly as they moved carefully but urgently through the forest. Hyrn was leading Jarta-Den's horse. Garan walked at his shoulder. Wren was just ahead of him, and Harla walked further ahead with Yarga, Infiron and Drivian. Droom took the rearmost position continually keeping an eye behind them to make sure that the Ultamarians were not bearing down on them.

Hyrn noticed that those ahead of him had stopped and that the light was brighter there. As he came through the trees he saw that the others stood on a green and overgrown path that led through the forest to the northeast. Harla was peering ahead and then signalled for them to move down the path and deeper into the forest.

"This leads us roughly towards the plateau," she said. "Hopefully we can make our way back to the road further along."

The path wound its way through the forest. Other paths could be seen leading away into the forest on either side. Occasionally there were overgrown and moss covered ruins visible between the trees. The air was still here and there was a sense that they were now deep in the forest, and that the path they travelled on had not felt the tread of feet for an immeasurable number of years. All around them they felt the age of the land bearing down on them. It filled them with a feeling of reverence and awe.

Droom turned his chariga around quickly as there was a sudden crash and a group of five Ultamarians broke from the trees and stood in the path behind them. The soldiers drew their swords. Droom's face broke into a grim smile as he drew his sword. Garan pushed Hyrn behind him and drew his sword, holding it out in front of himself. Harla sprinted back and took up a position beside Droom. The Ultamarians, seeing their quarry in plain sight, moved ready to attack. At that moment an arrow flew through the air and lodged in the side of one of the Ultamarians. Their leader shouted orders and the Ultamarians broke into a run towards Hyrn and the others.

Droom charged forward towards them. At that moment four figures moved out of the forest behind the Ultamarians and ran to pursue them. Droom reached them first. His sword scythed out catching their leader in the throat as his chariga crashed into them. Harla unleashed an arrow that hit one of the Ultamarians in the arm, knocking his sword from his grasp. Jarta-Den led the three others into the pack of Ultamarians from behind and there was fierce fighting as steel crashed and arms flailed. The fighting continued briefly, but before long the Ultamarians were lying dead surrounded by the six fighters. Although Hyrn saw with concern, that Jarta-Den was bleeding profusely from a wound in his upper arm.

Jarta-Den had propped himself against the trunk of a tree. Wren had retrieved bandages from his pack and was now handing them to Infiron. Infiron had applied ointment to the Quigling's wound and now, taking a bandage from Wren, began wrapping the nasty gash. Harla and the others had lain the bodies of the dead Ultamarians under a broad tree that grew amidst the ruins of ancient stonework.

As soon as Infiron had finished binding Jarta-Den's wound, she stood and spoke to Yarga. "We are safe for the time being but I am not sure that we will be able to find our way back to the road easily," she said.

Harla spoke. "For now our safest route is to follow this path. We are still heading towards Ultamar though we have been going downhill and the fortress is out of sight beyond the forest."

"We do not know where this path goes," said Droom.

"If we head back to the road we will need to travel uphill," said Harla. "Hopefully the terrain will level out when we get closer to Ultamar, and we can travel more easily through the forest and back to the road."

The path wound backwards and forward as the sun began to sink lower in the sky. They had still been heading roughly towards Ultamar but a ridge of land still separated them from where the road lay to the south. They passed a large stone archway that stood on the northern side of the road to their left. There were the remnants of a path through the arch that led into a dark channel that was thick with growth. They passed it by and kept travelling down the road. They had not left the arch far behind when the path they were on came to an abrupt halt at a rocky slope thick with trees and bushes. At the foot of the slope, large boulders were piled where the path ended. Steep forested hills thrust up all around them. There was no way through without a difficult and dangerous climb.

"What now?" asked Droom bluntly.

Harla looked about and spoke to Yarga. "We cannot go this way," she said. "An ancient landslide must have blocked this path. It looks as if the path continued where this hill now stands. There is no way of telling how far we would have to go to meet it on the other side."

"What about the arch?" suggested Hyrn. "There was a path. Maybe we can get through that way."

"It seemed to be blocked," said Harla, "and it leads north not east."

"I fear it is our only option," said Yarga. "It will start to get dark soon and we should at least try. If we are unable to get through, we can make camp until morning and then find another way."

The Caramar warriors, with Turum and Droom, were beyond the arch hacking at the undergrowth. Vines and shrubs blocked the path but their blades began to make progress as they disappeared into the dimness of the channel through which the path led. Droom was at the front, his great sword slashing at the foliage and his armour protecting him from scratches and cuts from the often thorny branches. The others waited on the path. Yarga stood staring up at the arch. There was lettering on it but the stonework was worn with age and the characters were difficult to make out. There were some symbols that were almost complete, and they seemed vaguely familiar. He thought about retrieving his book of lore from his pack but at that moment there was a cry from beyond the archway.

"There's a wall here!" boomed the voice of the Underdweller captain. "And it has a door in it!"

Harla stood beside Droom facing the large stone door. They had hacked away the vines covering it. Gebarana, Margana and Turum had worked their way back towards Hyrn and the others, widening the path through the undergrowth as they went. They led the rest of them down the path and they came up behind Droom and Harla.

The face of the stone door was blank. There was no sign of a handle or a lock. Yarga moved forward and stood beside Harla.

"There is no way to open the door that I can see, Elder," said Harla.

Yarga moved towards the door. Infiron moved past Harla behind him. Yarga stared at the door. He turned to Infiron, who now stood beside him.

"Is this of the old Kingdom of Anasaria?" he asked.

The Priest stared at the stonework and then said, "It is not like any stonework that I have seen. All of the ruins that we have seen since we left the road are older than Abessair."

"Infiron," said Yarga, "perhaps if you try to feel for power within the door?"

"I am a little apprehensive," said Infiron. "We do not know who built this."

But the Priest moved forwards and placed her hand on the door. She closed her eyes and stood as if listening intently. A glow flowed from her hand. The light brightened the faces of those gathered in the clearing in the growing dusk. Infiron let out a gasp and then quickly pulled her hand away from the door. She paused and collected herself.

"It is old and watchful," she said. "It is from long ago."

Yarga spoke. "There is old power within the Caramarhc," he said humbly.

The Elder passed his hand across his eyes as he said the name. He then stepped forward and placed his hand on the door. He stood concentrating and a dim red glow grew beneath his hand and became a bright red glare. It looked to Hyrn as if Yarga's hand was burning. Hyrn looked at the strain on Yarga's face. His mind leapt to helping him, with... Ilah.

He had pushed thoughts of the Stone out of his head since the Towers. He had concentrated on the goal of going to the gates of Ultamar and helping defeat the Dark Lords. The Stone had been quiet, the voice in his head gone. Although sometimes he wondered if his thoughts, his decisions, were his own. He had no wish to wake the Stone and ask her for help.

Yarga stood rigid. Then a bright red light seemed to pour from the Elder's throat. Harla stood beside Yarga, and Hyrn moved quickly forward to see what was happening. The look on Yarga's face was one of joy. The crystal around his neck hung horizontally in the air pointing at the door and straining against its chain. Red light poured from the tip of the Stone and then seemed to flow back into the crystal from the door. There was a grinding squeal, and dust and detritus fell all around, as the door opened before them.

Light came through the doorway as it opened wide. Yarga stepped through the doorway followed closely by Harla and Infiron. Hyrn moved through the doorway behind the Priest.

As Hyrn emerged a light wind blew against him. They stood on a platform on a hillside. Before them stretched a great green bowl. The golden light of sunset shone through the haze above the forest that stretched below them. All around was a circular wall of hills, their sides and tops covered with dense forest. The forest within the bowl was uneven and sparse in places. Hillocks and ridges covered in trees formed patterns at the bottom of the bowl. In the centre there was a space where there seemed to be no trees. The sun began to set beyond the mountains to the west and the golden light began to die.

Harla turned to those who had entered behind Hyrn.

"Torches!" called the Caramar warrior.

"They value wisdom," said Yarga.

They had made camp for the night alongside the stone pathway that wound its way downwards around the rim of the bowl. They had lit a fire and eaten a satisfying hot meal of stew and still reasonably fresh bread. The spoils of Herardin were greatly appreciated. They were secure and far from pursuit within this place. The door had closed behind them, as they left the platform and headed eastward along the path. Parts of the stonework of the path had been broken and loose and Droom had insisted they stop. It was difficult in full armour to lead his chariga forward and Jarta-Den had been forced to dismount despite his injury.

"They felt the power of the Sagenstone and allowed us to come in," continued the Elder.

"Let us in where?" asked Droom.

"They are the old ones," said Wren, from beside Hyrn.

"They are old," said Yarga, "but their power still lives in the stone."

Yarga paused, and the light of the fire glistened in eyes bright with wonder.

Finally, he said, "They were questioning me. Seeing if I was worthy."

"Are they still here?" asked Hyrn.

"They are long gone," said Yarga. "Yet they seem close, and there is something about this place that reminds me of…Well, I'm not sure quite what."

"Elder, is there danger here?" asked Harla. "We need to find a way out and towards Ultamar."

"Yes," said Yarga. "There is danger here and there is power, but it is directed at those who try to corrupt wisdom. The search for truth is at the heart of this place. They seek balance against corruption and deceit."

"Where did they go?" asked Hyrn.

"That's enough questions for tonight," said Yarga. "I am tired and I think we could all do with some sleep."

Harla looked at the Elder with admiration.

"I think that is a good idea," she said.

Jarta-Den spoke from where he lay just beyond the fire. "I do not know the power that resides here. My people have travelled far and gathered knowledge from many places. This power here is strong but it comes from somewhere distant."

The Quigling turned slightly, and grimaced with pain as he said, "But I for one could certainly do with some sleep."

The dawn chorus seemed to echo around the bowl as if there was an answering call from all around. The echo seemed to carry the power and mystery of this place. They all felt safe here, but there seemed to be something lurking below and all around. Something that was indefinable but ominous. Hyrn shivered as he stood looking out as the sun crept over the rim of the bowl. The land below was heavily forested, but it looked as if there were ruins amongst the trees. He felt a stirring beneath his vest but it was almost as if Ilah turned over and went back to sleep.

They ate a light breakfast and packed up quickly. Gebarana and Turum had reported back to tell them that the path only led downwards and to get to the other side they would need to go through the thick but broken forest below. They shouldered their packs or stowed them on Jarta-Den's horse and Droom's chariga. They made their way down the path as it wound its way through the trees. More ruins began to appear as they traversed the sometimes hazardous footing. These ruins became more prevalent as they continued on. Great structures began to appear with trees growing through them and vines and shrubs covering their stonework.

"It's a city," gasped Wren from beside Hyrn.

"A very old city," said Infiron in a mesmerised voice.

"Whose city?" asked Hyrn.

"I think," said Yarga, "that it is from before we have histories to tell. Although, there is power here that feels right, and good…and familiar," he added.

The sun had risen higher above the rim and sent shafts of sunlight down into the misty forest. They now travelled along the basin floor and through the ruins of a city. The city was green and overgrown. A pattern of streets stretched all around them, some lit by shafts of sunlight that led off into the gloom, and others dark and shrouded by towering trees. Apart from the breeze blowing through the trees, the occasional rustling in the undergrowth, or the call of a bird, there was no sound. The city was silent and empty. The road that they followed headed northwards. It was much wider and less overgrown than the streets that led off from either side. This was a road, and its destination seemed to be the heart of the city.

A young fawn leapt into the road before them. They halted and watched as an older deer came into the roadway and stood beside her young. The adult deer peered at them as if mystified, and then with a flick of her ears, herded her fawn into a side street thick with bushes and trees, and disappeared from view.

They continued on but still heard no sounds of habitation. As the sun rose higher it began to feel humid. The structures became higher as they neared the centre of the city. Great forested hills towered above, but up close, the shapes of buildings could be discerned. As they approached the city centre, a large forested mound appeared from between the trees. They made their way towards it and as it grew before them they could see that it was a monumental building; doorways, windows, pillars and archways could be made out, all drowning in a sea of forest.

Harla and Margana had gone ahead, and now waited for them to approach. The two mounted riders reached them first; Droom astride his chariga and Jarta-Den, riding determinedly despite his injury. As Hyrn stopped alongside Yarga, he saw that there was a road that ran around the base of the building, crossing the road they now stood on. Directly in front of them was a large arched doorway. An old conifer grew out from the base of the right-hand pillar of the arch. Some of the stones of the arch were cracked but they were held in place by a cage of thick vines. The alcove that led to the doorway was shaded by strands of creepers that hung down like a curtain. Where the road ended, the base of the doorway was blocked by a mound of rubble and dirt and mulch that had collected over the centuries.

Harla spoke to Yarga. "Elder, I counsel that warriors examine the area before we proceed."

Yarga nodded and Harla, Gebarana and Turum moved off towards the doorway. They climbed over the mound and passed under the leaning trunk of the tree and disappeared into the darkness of the alcove.

Harla soon reappeared, and making her way back said, "The door is broken and open. We will need torches. It is dark inside. We should post guards outside and the rest of us should make sure to stay together. I don't think anyone should go wandering off."

She looked directly at Hyrn and Wren as she said the last part.

One of the massive stone doors was open, but only partly. It was a bit of a tight passage, and within, broken stone and detritus made it difficult to get through. Droom and Jarta-Den had remained behind with their mounts and Gebarana had stayed behind to stand guard with them. They had left their packs outside, except for Yarga who had insisted that he carry his pack with him. Harla stood further down the passage, inside where it was clear of debris. She held her torch high as the party moved through and stood beside her. The corridor they were in was straight and wide. Grimy sculptures stood in places along the walls, cobwebs and curtains of thin tree roots hung from the ceiling, and the floor was thick with dust and scatterings of dead insects and in places the bones of small animals and birds. A heavy, musty smell of age and decay, hung in the air.

The passageway led to a large entrance hall that was cloaked in darkness at either side where the torchlight did not reach. In front of them towered a massive stone staircase. Like everything else the stairs were covered in dirt and grime. Harla paused facing the stairs and then turned her head and looked to Yarga, questioningly.

Yarga hesitated, staring up into the darkness.

"We go up. I think," he said.

At the stop of the stairs was a mezzanine that looked out over the dark foyer below and up into the dark unknown above. Across the landing directly in front of them were two large doors. Harla approached the doors and inspected them, then pushed at one with her hand. The door swung inwards easily. She tried the other and that opened as well but with a slight squeal of complaint. Harla held her torch in front of her. Margana and Turum walked beside her with their torches. The others followed the three through the doorway.

As they entered, Harla walked straight ahead while the other two fanned out to either side. Their torches revealed a large hall with a high vaulted ceiling. On either side there were doorways like the one they had just entered through. It was difficult to see the opposite end of the hall. In the centre of the space was a large monumental altar on a large square rostrum with steps all around. They approached and could see that there were some sort of ornamental sculptures atop the altar, although the shadows thrown up by the flickering torches made it difficult to discern what they were. Yarga moved to stand beside Harla and then gestured for her to move forwards. As the torchlight illuminated the altar they could see that the large stone block was carved with symbols.

Yarga, mesmerised, moved forward to study the symbols. He stared at several of them as he bent to examine them more closely, and absent-mindedly nodded his head. He then straightened up and shrugged his pack from his shoulders. He undid the drawstring of his pack and reached inside and drew out a bound tome. This was different to the one that Hyrn had previously seen him writing in.

Yarga put down his pack and, kneeling on the top step, opened the book.

"Harla more light if you please," he said.

The warrior brought her torch closer and Yarga studied the book closely. He flicked through the pages and then reaching a particular page read intently looking back and forth between the book and the symbols on the altar.

"Hah!" he said triumphantly. "I knew this writing was familiar. It is an old language written in an old script that only a few scholars now know."

"What does it say?" asked Hyrn.

"Just a moment. Just a moment," said Yarga as he continued comparing the writing in his book of lore with the inscription on the altar.

"It says something about knowledge," the Elder said concentrating. "And there are symbols for the sun and the moon."

He continued to inspect the writing.

"Ahhh. Of course," he said, and then laughed. "It is an old saying. It is a maxim we learn as novices. 'Seek wisdom between the sun and the moon.'"

"What does it mean?" asked Hyrn, puzzled.

"Well," said Yarga. "We were taught that it meant that the search for wisdom encompasses everything. Everything between the sun and the moon."

"But how is it here?" asked Harla. "If it is known to the Elders."

"I don't know," said Yarga. "I think I need to examine this a bit more closely."

The Elder stood up and approached the altar. Harla moved beside him holding the torch up to light the sculptures atop the altar. Hyrn and the others moved closer to get a look. On one side of the altar was a sculpture that looked like a crescent moon. At the other end was a representation of the sun with its flaming corona. Yarga looked at the sculpture in the centre. It resembled a mountain peak. As he looked at it, he suddenly gasped. Hyrn peered at the sculpture and a burst of recognition hit him. Yarga turned and looked at the others, thunderstruck.

"It is the Sagenstone, carved in stone," he whispered in a shocked voice. "How can this be?"

Yarga was seated on the top step of the rostrum, with his back to the altar. He still held the book in his hand but it was now closed. He was deep in thought and his face was creased with concentration. Drivian stood at the foot of the stairs facing Yarga.

"When was the Sagenstone discovered?" asked the Priest.

"The exact place in time is not recorded, but Caramar history extends beyond a thousand years. It is said that the first people woke up the mountains but they were pursued by evil creatures. They took refuge on Calaborn and in the hour of their need the Sagenstone was revealed to them. The power of the Stone awoke something in them and they fought the creatures and drove them from the mountain. It was declared that they had found the place they were looking for, where they could finally live in wisdom and peace."

Yarga paused and looked at Infiron. "What if this is where the first Caramar came from and they left to follow a quest to find the Sagenstone. But somehow, along the way, they forgot what it meant and were just looking for somewhere safe."

"What does it mean?" asked Hyrn. "And what about the sun and the moon?"

Harla looked at the Elder. "What about the Stone of the Sun? Those of us in the Eastern Watch, visit the Temple of the Sunrise and remember the legacy of the Stone. It is said that the Stone kept evil at bay, and when it was taken and we lost its protection, the Fortress of the Eastern Watch was built to protect against the forces of evil."

"But what of the moon?" asked Yarga.

The Elder became lost in silent thought and then said tentatively, "I do remember a story about the Temple and something that was said to have happened before the Stone of the Sun was taken. There was quarrel amongst the Priests of the Temple. It was said that some believed that they needed to seek the sunrise, and others believed in the legend of the Stone of the Moon. It was this disagreement that led to some of the Priests taking the Stone. It was said that other Priests set off on a quest to seek the Moon Stone but they disappeared in the west of the mountains and were never heard of again. Maybe what they believed was true; that there was both a Sun Stone and a Moon Stone. That would make some sense of this."

Yarga looked weary and lost but continued, "It is clear that the people who built this city sought the Sagenstone but I don't know what it all means. I wish that I could speak to the Council of Elders. I am only newly appointed. There are wiser heads among the Council than mine."

He clutched the crystal hanging around his neck. He knew that Elders could communicate via the Sagenstone, using the crystals that they wore, but he had not had any training in the use of his crystal. Aliana had not…"

Yarga's thoughts trailed off into sadness, but before despair could seep in, Harla placed her hand on his shoulder.

"You are an Elder," she said reassuringly, "and you have been assigned to the quest of the Stones and the Sword. You will get the chance to speak to the Council when we return home. For now, we have our duty to fulfil."

"You are right, Harla," said Yarga. "I am so glad that I have you here to help guide me."

Harla smiled at the young Elder.

"I am just a warrior," she said. "We follow the ways of the arts of vigilance and war. We look to the Elders for guidance."

Yarga nodded and then said hesitantly. "Yes, we must follow our quest. This city has stood here for perhaps thousands of years. Its truth can wait a little longer to be discovered."

Wren spoke up obstinately. "But where did the people that lived here all go?"

"I think," said Yarga, "they went to seek wisdom."

CHAPTER NINETEEN

The Watcher on the Mount

The three figures emerged from the dim tunnel into daylight. They passed beneath the teeth of stone that hung above. They had faced their fears and the gate was open to them. As they stood at the top of the Water Stairs, a vast lake spread before them dominating the valley. The lake was white with swans and light. The sky above was blue with just the trace of clouds above the wall of mountains to the north.

To the south, powerful events unfolded. A Stone of Angil moved towards an ancient city in the forest, and its twin moved eastwards pursued by the Sword of Acclimoss.

Voices of welcome and questioning filled their minds.

Trion moved forward. A compulsion came upon him and he acted without thinking.

He spoke in a strange, solemn tone; just one word. "Olum."

Four swans took to the air from amongst the vast flock. As Trion, Neferelon and Ferian looked up they saw the glint of gold flashing in the morning sun at the throat of the lead swan.

A large swan approached them and in their minds they heard a voice.

"The time has come and you are here." The swan looked at each of them in turn as it spoke. "You can no longer help against Ultamar but your purpose heralds the end of the war between good and evil. One or the other will triumph, or balance will be attained. You have come here to undertake a task that we cannot. You have passed the trials; the loyal soldier, the wise Priest, and the seeker of knowledge. Together you may be able to unlock something that is hidden to even the most powerful. Your path now lies beyond Anasaria to the north and east. The forces of evil gather and the fate of the world lies on the edge of doom. Come now and rest. Bask in the light of the lake and drink of the power that lies there. While this light remains to you, take what you can, for darkness and evil lie before you."

As Duburinga stood and faced the east, awaiting the sunrise, his mind was troubled. The light in the northern sky the night before was towards where the Stonebearer was. The thought left him uneasy. As he tried to clear his mind and prepare for the dawn, a vision came into his mind. A vision of Harla.

Then she seemed to speak to him. "The Ultamarians do not have Ivah. You must pursue the Artorans."

The message was conveyed to them all, after the sun had risen. Rowan felt a renewed sense of purpose. They now were sure that they pursued Ivah. As he finished packing up, he finally picked up the Sword of Acclimoss. He held the sheathed sword out at arm's length and studied it. He could feel its power and it seemed to flow into his hand. Arienga came up beside him and touched his shoulder.

"Ready to go?" she asked, looking intently at Rowan.

Rowan nodded, and said firmly, "Yes."

It was difficult to see anything. A deep fog had descended on them as they set off and had only worsened as they made their way down into the marshlands. The air was still, and there was only the sound of their passing, as they wound their way down along a muddy path. Small shrubs and reeds, and pools of water loomed out of the fog as they moved. Rowan led Arrow. Carlan followed immediately behind him. Arienga was off scouting northwards towards the road.

Ahead of Rowan, Grengal led his horse. There was not much conversation amongst them but Rowan spoke to the young Quigling.

"Grengal, why do you only have one name when all the other Quiglings have two?" he asked.

Grengal looked back briefly at Rowan but continued moving forward through the fog.

"Swordbearer," he began, Rowan flinched at this. "I have not defeated an enemy in combat."

Rowan thought about this for a moment and then asked. "Do you get to choose a second name after you defeat someone?"

"You don't get to choose," said Grengal. "And you don't have to just defeat them. You get the honorary part of your name when you fight to the death and win. Then you get a part of the name of the enemy that you have killed."

"How do you know their name?" asked Rowan.

"You ask them or, if not, you name them in the old language," replied Grengal.

He paused and then said, "The older Quiglings speak of how it is not a badge of honour, but a sign that death should be acknowledged, and that it is really evil we fight, not those we kill. We wear their name, or a word that describes how they fought."

"It must be hard," said Rowan, "living with the knowledge of such great evil. I grew up on a farm not knowing about any of this. There were stories about battles and wars but they were just about people fighting over castles or land, in the past, not a real war against evil."

Carlan spoke up from behind him. "There is evil everywhere, and even small battles have some sort of evil intent behind them."

The light grew around them as they continued on, and the fog grew lighter. The path they were on began to wind upwards for a while and the land around became drier. They came to an area of grass and trees where they stopped and rested and had something to eat from their packs. They then moved on, as the blue of the sky began to show through, and the lightly wooded landscape opened out around them.

Duburinga and Jorunum appeared on foot from out of the trees to their right. Their clothing was muddy and wet.

They approached them and Duburinga spoke. "We have picked up the trail of the Artorans. They are travelling to the south. This path here follows a ridge that runs west to east. The Artorans are on a ridge further south that runs in the same direction. The land between is treacherous and almost impassable. We cannot take horses through. Further east the two ridges converge. That is the point at which we can either intercept the Artorans or follow their trail."

"We must move quickly," said Biren-So. "But we also must prepare for battle."

"The Swordbearer must be protected," said Carlan.

"We can keep a guard around Rowan to the rear," suggested Kerian.

"No!" said Rowan forcefully.

Everybody looked at him.

Rowan continued more calmly. "The fact that this is the Sword of Acclimoss has been proven. The Sword of the King must fight for Anasaria. Otherwise why did it come here now? The Artorans have Ivah. The Sword must be used to recover the Stone."

"You are not ready," said Duburinga, sternly.

Rowan was about to say something, when a voice from behind him said, "He is ready to be tested in battle."

Arienga had returned. She looked at Duburinga apprehensively.

"I'm not suggesting that he can go against the enemy single-handedly," she continued determinedly, "but he is ready to fight and he wields the Sword well enough. But there is something else. It is the weapon itself, and its essence. He knows the Sword. He is in tune with it and he has already used it in a way that we don't understand."

"The Sword itself contains power," said Biren-So. "It is imbued with the power of the Twin Stones, but I do not know if Rowan is ready to wield it."

Gorum had a harsh grin on his face as he spoke. "Why do we keep debating whether Rowan should wield the Sword? He does, and he has drawn it in battle according to Bregal. This quest has been given to him for a reason. We must protect him, but we can protect him in the same way that fellow soldiers protect each other. Let's ride. I for one am eager to destroy those Artoran bastards."

He paused and then said angrily, "I owe them that for Bregal!"

High up on a sheer hillside he stood, his eyes fixed, ever staring. He looked out over the approaches to Artora, and beyond to the haze of the forests and rivers of Anasaria. The mountains of Anasaria lined the horizon, and in his right field of vision stood the dark shape of what was once Abessair. As he watched, over interminable days and years, the once shining fortress had become a dark and evil place. He saw all before him, and they knew. He could do nothing about it. His eyes were theirs. He tried to shift his vision and inwardly laughed. It was no use. He had tried almost every day for centuries. His feet were fixed, his body rigid. He just stood and stared at the land beyond and they used his eyes for their purposes.

He had been there since before the great battle, when King Eriallen rode to the walls of Artora. He had been amongst the soldiers that had besieged the approaches to Artora as the King, leading the rest of the Abessairian army, approached. He was captured and imprisoned up here to keep watch. He had seen it all for those eyes that lurked behind his. But it was no use to them. The host behind the King was too great, and they proved victorious. Yet none saw him high up on the mount. The Anasarian army went home in triumph, but he remained. None knew of him but those who used his eyes, the inner sanctum of the Sorcerers of Artora. It was they who had enslaved him and forced him to betray and spy on his people. To keep watch. They saw everything, and he could do nothing. He stood, resigned to his fate, and just watched.

He caught movement out of the corner of his eye, high in the sky to the north. Probably a flock of birds. They wheeled in endless circles over the plains and the river valley below, generation after generation. As the mass came more clearly into his arena of sight he saw that it was not a flock of birds but a single bird, a large white bird with a long slender neck. A swan, a very large one, veered in its flight and flew towards him.

His heart leapt. The swan neared him and pulled up in its flight, flapping its wings, and then settled on the ground at his feet. He could not move his head to look down at the bird. He was startled when, for the first time in many lifetimes, he heard a voice.

"I am here to fulfil the promise of my ancestors, to play our part in the restoration of Anasaria." The swan spoke to him, and the sound was joy without bounds to his ears.

The voice of the swan continued. "We have endured, concealed in our mountain haven, steadfast and unwavering, waiting to carry out this duty as foretold. It was prophesied that there was a man, a soldier, who was once bound to the Twin Stones of Angil. We knew not where we would find such a man, but it was foretold that there would come a time when we would be called, and then we would find the answer to the riddle.

You are the answer. The years that you have stood here looking out, have held you in readiness for this purpose. I have around my neck a key, the key to the Chamber of the Stones, atop the Tower of the Stones, in the Fortress of Abessair. The Stones are not there. They will return. Only one bound to the Twin Stones by their allegiance to the true King of Anasaria can enter that chamber now that it is locked. The power that protects the Stones' rightful place, was bound to an oath of service sworn to the King in the presence of Ilah and Ivah. It is only you that can open that door. It is you that will allow the Twin Stones to be placed back in their rightful position."

There was a pause and then the swan spoke again. "Bardewan of the army of Eriallen, I name you Doorwarden of the Chamber of the Stones."

With that the swan lifted itself from the ground, and beating its wings, hovered behind Bardewan's head out of his line of vision. She rose higher, and stretching her neck down, placed her beak upon his head. A golden key on a golden chain slid down the swan's neck and over the Watcher's head and around his neck. The key dangled at his back, chiming against his tarnished armour.

The swan then spoke one word. "Olum."

And he was free.

Suddenly, the presence that had sat behind his eyes for centuries, was gone. The swan then descended and came to rest at his feet. He looked downwards. He could move his head and his neck and then he felt that his whole body was free to move. And all that he could see, they could not. He laughed aloud, and the swan spoke again.

"The bond that I have put on you is stronger than the bond of their spell," she said as Bardewan sat down beside her. "You are now bound to your position and only the King can release you. When the time comes, you must fulfil your duty. I now go east, for I have another task to perform, but I hopefully shall return when I am needed. You must go to Abessair. There is a party moving towards the road that lies below us. They are pursuing three Artorans who have stolen Ivah. One of the party carries the Sword of Acclimoss. They are gaining on the Artorans, but the evil ones may elude them yet. Artora at least does not have eyes to see. But they may come here to find why their eyes have been blinded. I cannot help you. Time is pressing, and I am already weary. You must be steadfast, Bardewan."

Bardewan sat in a daze and watched as the swan rose into the air and swung eastwards. Three other shapes flew out of the west and joined her and they continued on swiftly and diminished into the distance. Bardewan smiled and then laughed out loud again. It felt good. Then he steeled himself. He pulled the chain around and felt the key in his hand. He had a sacred mission to perform, and he would see the power of Abessair return, even if it took all his strength.

Rowan rode with determination but with a knotted feeling in his stomach. Arienga rode Duburinga's horse just ahead of him. Duburinga was off scouting on foot away towards the other ridge. Rowan looked at Arienga as they rode, with a feeling of admiration, and gratitude, and something else he tried not to think about too much. Carlan rode beside him or dropped just behind, when the way was too narrow. The ridgetop was wide enough in places to allow them to ride fast, and at other times became rocky and treacherous. There were times when it became impassable and they were forced to head down the hillside, often along steep and narrow paths, until they could ascend to the ridgetop again. Midday had moved to afternoon as they rode. At times, the road to the north came into view. Each time it became visible it seemed to be growing closer. The ridge they were on, and that used by the Artorans, were converging towards where the road neared the approaches to Artora.

As the afternoon wore on Duburinga, Boriega and Jorunum returned. They reported that the Artorans were ahead of them and moving fast and would reach the convergence of the ridges before them. They would then be able to gain the road and possible escape. Biren-So urged them on, and they rode as hard as they could in the terrain. They reached a high point and could see that the ridgeline sloped down into an area of thick forest. The point where the ridges met was now not far ahead, down where their path disappeared into forest. There was no sign of the Artorans.

They continued quickly on, and after a while plunged into the forest. As they made their way through the trees, the ridge flattened out. The ground became a gentle slope and before long they came across the path that led down from the other ridge. The signs were clear. The Artorans had been through this area some time before, and were heading down to the road. But the party were now following their trail and they moved forward with determination and purpose. The Stone of Angil was before them and now was the time to play their part in the quest to reunite the Stones.

Apprehension grew in Rowan's mind as they rode onwards. He had heard Gorum's account of the encounter at the bridge, and the thought of confronting the Artoran Sorcerer loomed in his mind. He looked around at his companions. Their faces all seemed to bear the same expression; that of fierce resolve. The path widened as they grew closer to the road. The sun was beginning to sink to the west. The trees stretched around them blocking their view ahead. But as they rode at speed down the path they suddenly emerged into the open, and before them stretched the road.

They soon came to where the path met the road. The Artorans were nowhere in sight but the trained eyes in the party could see that they had headed eastward towards Artora. That way, the road led up a slight incline and rounded a bend through a wooded cleft. The setting sun illuminated their way.

"Now we give chase!" said Gorum forthrightly.

The party mounted up. Duburinga reclaimed his mount from Arienga and she rode with Boriega. Rowan felt a pang of disappointment but he clutched Arrow's reins. The party broke into a gallop and thundered down the road, the thrill of pursuit, and the prospect of battle driving them forward.

As Bardewan made his way down the hillside, he breathed in the air and revelled in the sunshine. He looked at everything around him with joy and a new found wonder. A small brook ran close to his path at one stage. He knelt and looked at his reflection in a place where it pooled. He hadn't changed as far as he remembered. His beard had grown no longer and his face seemed no older. He cupped water from the pool and splashed it on his face. He laughed at the feeling of the water and then felt that he was thirsty. He cupped more water and took a drink. He felt the cool water run down his throat. He laughed with amazement, and then coughed and spluttered as he inhaled some of the water. The sky above was blue in the afternoon sun. The nearby trees sighed in the slight breeze. He felt that he could just lie down here and bask in the wonder of his new life.

But no. He had his duty to perform.

He rose to his feet. He felt for the sword at his hip. He laughed. It had been taken from him centuries before, but his duty was making him remember what it felt like to be a soldier again. He had taken sacred oaths. He drew himself up and continued down the hill towards the road. The trees became denser and the undergrowth thicker as he drew closer to the low ground that led down to the road. He climbed down rocky embankments and pushed through bushes and branches. He became hot and sweaty and his hands and face were scratched in places and he felt bruises on his body. He revelled in the sensation, and joy and purpose drove him on.

As the sun grew lower in the sky, he moved through small, tree-covered gullies and dales, until finally he broke from amongst the trees, and the road appeared across a bare expanse of land. He made his way through this narrow stretch of land and then clambered down the side of a ditch near the road. The ditch was not overly wide but stormwater still lay deep along it. The opposite side that edged the road had steep stonework that reinforced the roadway. It was difficult to find a stable flat space to leap across the water. Bardewan climbed back up, and then walked along the edge of the ditch for a way, until he came to the broken trunk of a tree that leant out across the water.

He looked around and then headed away from the ditch and up a small slope. He turned back towards the ditch. Then, with a triumphant grin on his face, he launched himself at a run down the slope. He sped towards the broken tree and, as he grew close enough, leapt onto the sloping trunk and ran up its length. With an exuberant yell, Bardewan launched himself from the end of the stump. He windmilled through the air as he descended towards the rocky edge. The thought went through his mind that he wasn't going to make it and that he would cannon into the stonework.

"No!" He willed himself towards the other side.

"Just a bit more." he gritted.

He thrust his left leg out, and his foot made contact with the very lip of the stonework. As he felt the solid ground he threw himself into a roll. The ground was marshy from the recent rain running off the road. Bardewan cartwheeled across this ground and then rolled a few times and came to rest in the gravel at the side of the road. He lay there for a minute breathing heavily and looking up into the sky. He smiled as he lay there but then finally struggled to his feet and brushing himself off straightened his back and strode off westwards.

The land began to sink into twilight as he made his way down the road. It was becoming difficult to see clearly in the fading light. He rounded a bend. There was a crest ahead, and as he trudged up the slope, he became wearier and looked forward to going downhill. As he passed over the crest of the hill he could see that the road stretched down into a heavily forested area. The tall trees encroached upon the road's edge. The dimness beneath the trees made it even more difficult to see.

Bardewan thought that he caught a glimpse of something ahead. There was a dark mass that grew, and as it did it resolved into a group of people. Bardewan made his way towards them and then as an icy fear crept into his heart, he saw that there were three Artorans, and he felt a pain at the back of his head. The Artorans had already seen him and moved quickly towards him. Bardewan felt an itch to draw the sword that he no longer held but another force seemed to be driving him back into the frozen position he had held for centuries.

The Sorcerer cackled as he approached Bardewan. His harsh face was puzzled.

"Watcher? What are you doing away from your post?" he snarled.

Bardewan felt as if he couldn't move but said through gritted teeth, "I am not your Watcher anymore."

The Sorcerer laughed again and then spoke harshly. "I don't know how you broke your bonds but you will soon be back on your hillside."

Bardewan fumed, but the thought of how it felt to be free came to his mind and he smiled.

"You will have to kill me first," he said defiantly.

"That won't be necessary," said the Sorcerer, "and not nearly as enjoyable as watching you suffer."

Bardewan drew himself up. His new found sense of freedom and his sense of purpose filled him.

"You will suffer. Your days are numbered," he said. "Abessair will rise again and your oath will bind you, and then Artora will feel the might of the forces of good."

Bardewan was not sure why he said the last bit, but it seemed to make the

Artoran angry.

"The doom of Abessair will be complete," sneered the Sorcerer. "The might of Artora will do something that the crows of Ultamar could not."

He summoned the men behind him.

"Take this worm and bring him along," he said harshly. "Do not damage his eyes but feel free to damage anything else. If he is any trouble, cut off his fingers, then his hands. Make him suffer but do not kill him."

The shorter of the Artorans walked towards Bardewan with his blade out. Bardewan stood still as if compliant but as the Artoran drew close the Abessairian quickly moved to one side and launched a fist directly into the Artoran's face. The evil soldier sprawled on the ground. The Sorcerer signalled to the other Artoran.

"We may need to get a new Watcher," he said dismissively. "Kill him!"

The tall Artoran drew his sword and walked menancingly towards Bardewan. The Abessairian summed up his options. He dived towards where the other Artoran lay groaning on the ground, and scrabbled to get hold of the blade he had dropped. He grasped the handle and attempted to turn and climb to his feet, but a foot caught him in the back and he crashed into the dirt at the road's edge. The Artoran was quickly on him and loomed over him, his sword ready. Bardewan held the short sword out but it was no match for the large sword. The Artoran raised his sword up ready to strike a fatal blow.

He stopped suddenly, mid-strike, and looked quickly back down the road. And then Bardewan heard it, the sound of thundering hooves moving quickly towards them. Bardewan turned his head quickly from where he lay on the ground. He watched as the Artoran Sorcerer turned and faced back down the road. In the gathering twilight Bardewan could see the faint shape of riders approaching. All of a sudden the air lit up with a sickly purple light that drove a sharp spike behind Bardewan's eyes. Fear filled him. The purple light began to throb. The Artoran standing over him turned back and raised his sword but the Sorcerer turned. His face was contorted in strictures of rage and evil intent.

"Bragga!" he screeched. "Go! Head for the walls!"

The tall Artoran looked at Bardewan angrily and then turned on his heel and broke into a run down the road. As he quickly moved off, Bardewan saw that there was a chest strapped to his back. The Abessairian was suddenly struck with realisation.

He has Ivah!

Bardewan leapt to his feet. He looked back at the Sorcerer, but he was focussing all his evil intent on the approaching riders. Bardewan paused with the short sword in his hand and looked at the back of the Sorcerer. He desired to strike a blow but the light of the evil Stone held him back. Instead the Abessairian turned eastward and saw where the figure of the tall Artoran was quickly dwindling from view. Bardewan broke into a run, and he relished the feeling of his legs driving him forward, and felt his heart pumping in his chest, and he steeled himself. He must not let Ivah be taken to Artora.

The Artoran Sorcerer stood summoning the power in the Stone. Its evil light pulsed and the air throbbed as the power built. The Sorcerer's face was locked in a rictus of hate. The riders rode towards him, and he began to focus his aim upon them. As they streaked towards him a familiar sight met the Sorcerer's eyes. The strange armoured man on his even stranger horse. The rider led the others and stormed towards him. The Sorcerer laughed at the folly of this strange man and prepared himself to strike.

Gorum drove his chariga forward. The Artoran who had struck down Bregal loomed ahead of him. He had pulled ahead of the others determined to strike a blow, but suddenly it happened again. His chariga came to a grinding halt. The other riders thundered past him and to his shame and horror, he saw that drawing ahead was Rowan, the Sword of Acclimoss drawn and held high. Carlan and Duburinga strived to keep up with Rowan, but as they did, the Sorcerer held up the Stone, and thrusting it forward, unleashed a blast of purple light.

"No!" screamed Gorum.

Rowan, riding fast, saw the bolt of purple light shoot towards him. As he did, he raised the Sword of Acclimoss, but, now beside him, Carlan's horse crashed sideways into Arrow. The bolt of light flashed past, just missing Carlan, and blasted into the road sending a shower of rocks and dirt erupting into the air. Arienga, Boriega and Biren-So were close behind and swerved to avoid the blast. The others followed through a cloud of dust and debris.

Rowan glanced at his Abessairian protector beside him but then spurred Arrow on as he closed on the Sorcerer. He could see the intent on the Artoran's face as the Sorcerer began to prepare another strike. Rowan held the reins in his left hand and raised the sword in his right. He would get there first and his sword would… But the Artoran unleashed a blast of purple light again. His face grinned sickeningly. The light streaked directly towards Rowan.

All Rowan could do was strike at the bolt of light with his sword. The sword intercepted the path of the light and it struck the blade heavily. The flat of the blade flashed with golden light and the purple light was deflected back, but now flecked with gold. It smashed into the Sorcerer, lifting him off his feet. The Sorcerer flew backwards and crashed heavily into the surface of the road. The purple Stone was flung from his grasp, spinning through the air in a large arc. It cannoned into the road sending up purple sparks as it bounced a few times and rolled into the grass on the verge.

The riders all came to a halt and Rowan started to dismount, his sword at the ready. The rest of the party also dismounted. But at that moment an armoured Underdweller came galloping past, his chariga pulling up just before the Artoran. Gorum leapt from his saddle, his sword already drawn. He bounded quickly over to the Sorcerer and without hesitation drove his sword through the Artoran's heart. He looked down into the contorted evil face.

"That's for Bregal," he said grimly, through gritted teeth.

The Artoran looked at him with fury and incomprehension and struggled against the steel that pinned him to the road.

"Feel the power of the light in the dark," said the Underdweller, still gripping his sword tightly. And it seemed as if a pink light flashed briefly in the Sorcerer's eyes, and then the light went out and he lay still.

The party all stood momentarily dumbstruck, and then Rowan cried out. "The Stone!"

They all looked down the road, and saw in the fading distance, a figure running away from them down the road. Duburinga leapt into the saddle and the others mounted quickly. Rowan jumped onto Arrow's back and then he saw that Arienga stood beside the horse. Rowan reached his hand out, but she was already leaping up behind him. He urged Arrow forward and they broke off at a gallop towards the disappearing figure. Gorum still stood over the Artoran.

As they rode past, Biren-So spoke to Gorum with a tone of warning in his voice. "Do not touch the Stone!"

As they grew closer to the figure, in the fading light, they could see that he was running fast but beginning to tire. The man came into view and Rowan saw that it was not an Artoran but what seemed to be an Ultamarian, or an Abessairian. They drew alongside and checked their speed.

"Stop!" demanded Rowan.

Bardewan looked sideways and saw the Sword of Acclimoss grasped in the hand of a young man. He stopped running and came to a halt, puffing and panting. The riders stopped beside him.

"I haven't run like that for centuries," he said looking up at the sword holder.

Carlan rode forward and looked at the man standing there wearing the same uniform as him.

"Who are you?" he said.

"I am… Bardewan," he said, still trying to catch his breath. He looked at the strange gathering of people and the boy that wielded The Sword of Acclimoss.

"You are dressed as an Abessairian, or an Ultamarian," said Biren-So.

"I am an Abessairian soldier," said Bardewan. "I served in the Anasarian assault force in the army of King Eriallen."

There was a pause as those gathered tried to make sense of this.

"But… Eriallen was … he …" tried Rowan. "That was a long time before…"

"What do you mean?" he said, finally

"I have been under an Artoran spell since that time," said Bardewan wearily. "But a tall Artoran soldier is running up the road away from us, and I believe that he is carrying Ivah. We can tell stories later."

"How do you know about, Ivah?" asked Rowan hastily.

"A swan told me," replied Bardewan, and then said insistently, "but we should really focus on pursuing the Artoran."

Duburinga spoke urgently. "Bardewan, you can ride with me. We must give chase."

Boriega and Jorunum had already moved off, scouting ahead. The others mounted up and they rode up the road at speed while keeping their eyes alert in the fading light. Tall trees loomed on either side. They hadn't ridden far, when Jorunum and Boriega came to a halt ahead. They had quickly dismounted and were searching the ground at the road's edge. The rest of the party drew up alongside them.

"The Artoran left the road here, but he must be close," said Jorunum. "Unfortunately he is heading into the forest and it will be difficult to track him in this light."

"He is heading for Artora," said Bardewan from behind Duburinga.

He jumped down and looked into the trees and then continued. "Unless he means to go a long way around, he will have to return back to the road eventually. The trees soon disappear beyond here and the land descends into more open terrain. However, the foothills of the approaches to Artora are a bewildering barrier. The Gates are the only way through. Where the land opens up the terrain becomes marshes and lakes. They will force him to head back to the road, or turn south and skirt the lakes, and head back to the Gates, through the hills."

"Some of us must pursue on foot as best we can," said Duburinga. "The rest should ride up the road with the other horses and wait for us there. Hopefully we can trap him between us."

The old warrior climbed down from his horse and looked at his fellow

Caramar in turn. "Boriega, Terrana, ride ahead," he said. "Arienga with me. We give chase on foot."

He looked at Rowan. "Rowan, your choice lies with you. Others may go as they see fit, but I counsel that we try to split our numbers evenly and only those that have the energy give chase on foot."

He glanced at Bardewan.

"Ohhh, no," said Bardewan, "I'm going after him. I've been waiting for too long."

Arienga had already dismounted and Rowan was close behind.

"I must pursue Ivah," said Rowan.

Carlan stood beside Rowan.

"I go with Rowan," said the Abessairian.

The two groups assembled immediately and quickly moved off. Duburinga, Arienga, Rowan, Carlan, Bardewan, Biren-So, Jorunum, and Grengal moved on foot through the forest. Kerian led the others as they galloped off up the road, leading the six riderless horses.

It had become fully dark now. Duburinga and Jorunum were ahead of them seeking for any traces of the passage of the Artoran, Bragga. As their keen eyes adjusted to the darkness, they began to pick up signs of their quarry. The soldier had been moving through the trees and brush quickly and had not tried to be stealthy. His path crashed through low hanging branches and undergrowth. Even by starlight, his path was possible for trained eyes to follow. It was a slow and painstaking process but it was necessary to take their time so as not to lose the trail.

As time passed, the land began to slope downwards. They had come across a place where the Artoran must have rested but he had since moved on, perhaps aware that the pursuit was closing in on him. As they descended through the forest, the trees began to thin out. Duburinga held up his hand and they all stopped and listened. There was the unmistakable sound of someone moving ahead of them. The sound stopped and then continued again. They could hear that the Artoran was now moving north, back towards the road. In the east, the moon began to rise above the horizon, its light glittering through the branches of the trees and throwing a patchwork of shadows all around. They went as stealthily as they could and as the trees gave way to open ground, they saw that a marsh stretched before them, its pools reflecting the light of the rising moon. The rains had made this area impassable eastwards. The road would be the easiest way through.

Rivulets ran out from the edge of the forest down into the marsh, and the footprints of the Artoran were plain to see. There was a small ridge ahead where trees grew down close to the marsh and they saw at its peak the figure of the Artoran, before he quickly disappeared from sight. The sight of their quarry drove them on and they leapt a small creek and dashed up the side of the ridge. They stopped at the crest, and then, seeing the soldier moving out from the trees into the moonlight, without any signal or command, charged down the other side.

As they ran, Rowan's hand itched to draw his sword but they were wending their way between trees. As they broke into the open the Artoran was not too far ahead. Rowan reached up to his shoulder and drew the Sword of Acclimoss. Behind him ran Arienga. Her bow was drawn, an arrow notched. They briefly glanced at each other and Arienga gave Rowan a nod of encouragement and they both looked ahead resolutely.

The Artoran, Bragga, sensed the sounds of pursuit behind him and turning back saw the sight of armed enemies behind him. He turned quickly to his right and headed down towards the marshier ground. Here, closer to the road, the pools had given way to damp meadows but the ground was still boggy and Bragga had not gone too far when he was forced to turn and stand ready to fight. He felt the straps over his shoulders that held the casket, within which lay the Stone that he had been commanded to bear to Artora. His only option was to fight. He was strong, and the evil of Artora burned in him. Despite their numbers, he could stand against these worms.

And then he saw it. In their midst a sword glowed brightly. It did not light those around it but seemed to glow only in his mind. That glow filled him with hatred and the need for revenge, a revenge that would only be fulfilled when the Stone on his back had been delivered to the Sorcerers. Then their shameful oath would be destroyed forever. Fortified by hatred and malevolence, he drew his sword and stood ready to fight.

An arrow flew through the air towards him and he swatted it from the air and laughed. Another arrow imbedded itself in his upper arm but he ignored it. A large Quigling reached him first.

Biren-So brought his sword crashing down towards the Artoran. The evil soldier brought his sword up, and there was a clash of blades as he blocked the Quigling's attack. Duburinga loosed another arrow past Biren-So and it thudded into the Artoran's hip. Bragga staggered and Biren-So brought his sword up again. The Artoran deftly swung his sword underhanded and caught the Quigling in the midriff biting deeply into his flesh. Grengal was charging from behind, but at that moment the Artoran flinched in pain, and as he did a sword thrust through the air and was driven through his chest. All Bragga saw was a flash of golden light that filled him with pain as it drove through the air towards him, and then burned through him. The Artoran staggered back and fell away from the sword as he crashed into the ground.

He slumped on his side, and on his back an iron casket lay glinting dully in the moonlight.

Everyone came to a standstill. There seemed to be a moment of silence where everything paused, and then Biren-So collapsed to the ground with a groan. Grengal gasped and fell to his knees beside Biren-So. The elder Quigling drew in painful rasping gasps. Jorunum was beside him unloosening his pack and withdrawing medical supplies. Rowan looked down to his left at the Quigling but then looked up to where Duburinga stood over the body of the Artoran. Duburinga turned and looked back at Rowan.

"I think this is yours to do," he said.

Rowan paused. The bloody sword still hung in his grasp. He looked to his right. Arienga stood there beside him. She looked at him with a strange expression and then nodded. He turned back to where the Artoran lay, and then approached slowly. Arienga moved forward with him. As he drew alongside, he dropped to his knees where the casket lay still strapped to the Artoran. Arienga held out a short dagger. He placed his sword on the ground and then leant forward to cut the straps that bound the casket.

The Artoran suddenly turned towards Rowan with a screech of hatred, his face twisted in pain. In a blur of motion Arienga had grabbed the dagger from Rowan's hand and driven it into the throat of the Artoran. Rowan was frozen in shock as the Artoran collapsed back, but Arienga quickly cut the straps and the casket dropped to the ground. Arienga looked at Rowan but he still seemed in shock.

"Rowan!" she said sternly. "Take it!"

He shook his head and looked at her.

"Take it," she said more softly.

Rowan looked down from where he knelt and the casket lay on the ground just to his right. He reached out and grasped it. He held on tight to it and then stood up, the severed straps still dangling from it. He stood up and looked about him. He saw the party gathered around. Saw Biren-So lying wounded. He looked at Arienga as she stood and grasped his arm in support. He held the casket out in front of himself, and it dawned on him. This was it. Ivah… or else some sort of trick.

He looked at the casket. There was a lock on it but it had no keyhole. Bardewan approached Rowan. He examined the casket and the lock and then paused in thought.

"I think you will need the Artoran Stone to open the lock," said the Abessairian. "The Sorcerer would have made it so that only someone wielding the Stone could open it. He would not have trusted his soldiers."

"We have to go back," said Rowan desperately.

Duburinga looked around in the moonlight. "It is best that we head straight to the road through this open ground. We have been travelling back towards it and it is where the others will be expecting to meet us. We have been much delayed hopefully they are still waiting."

He turned to Arienga. "Arienga, stay here with Biren-So and tend to him. I will send Terrana with horses. Meet us back where Gorum is waiting."

Arienga looked momentarily crestfallen but concealed it quickly. Rowan had the urge to say that he would wait also, but his duty was with the Stone.

"I will stay here also," Grengal spoke from where he knelt beside his ailing comrade.

Rowan's heart jumped into his throat but Arienga grasped his arm.

"I will catch up with you back on the road, Rowan," she said reassuringly.

Rowan nodded and said, "Alright."

But something in him twisted at the thought of Arienga and Grengal left here together.

"We need to move," said Duburinga.

The riders were spread out along the flat open stretch of road within sight of each other. Boriega saw the group led by Duburinga first. They emerged out of the roadside ditch where they had crossed in a place where the water was shallow. He signalled to those riders closest and they signalled to the others. Soon all the riders were gathered around. Rowan moved toward where Terrana led Arrow.

"We began to be concerned," said Kerian. "Did you intercept the Artoran?"

"He is dead," said Duburinga bluntly. "We have what we believe is the Stone but we had a slow pursuit and Biren-So has been wounded."

"Terrana," Duburinga addressed the Caramar warrior. "Take Grengal and Biren-So's horses. Follow the tree line and before where a ridge of trees meets the marshes you will find the Quiglings with Arienga. Send Arienga back on Biren-So's horse. Biren-So is wounded. Arienga is tending him. You will need to follow us as best you can, but your first duty is to look after the wounded soldier."

"I will go with her," said Jorunum. "I can show her the way. We will meet you when we can."

One of the other Quiglings spoke. "I will also go with them."

Jorunum retrieved his horse and mounted up. He was given the reins of Grengal's horse and Terrana led Biren-So's. They made their way to the ditch and carefully rode down and disappeared from sight, and then after a brief moment, emerged on the other side. They spurred their horses on and faded off into the moonlit countryside.

The mounted company then made their way back down the roadway towards where they had encountered the Artoran Sorcerer. Rowan had secured the casket in front of his saddle. He rode determinedly but his mind still strayed back to where Arienga was waiting with Grengal. He turned back to the task at hand, and reassured himself that Arienga was just doing her job. As the road entered the forest, from within the shadows of the trees in the moonlight, Gorum came into view, riding his chariga. They pulled up in front of him.

"Have you reclaimed the Stone?" asked Gorum.

"We have it," said Rowan. "But we need the Artoran Stone to open the lock."

"I left the Stone where it lay," said Gorum.

Gorum joined them as they galloped down the road. As they approached the scene of the confrontation, they saw the body of the Sorcerer still lying in the roadway in the moonlight. They rode up and quickly realised that the other Artoran was gone. They stopped where the Artoran Stone had come to rest and saw with dismay that the evil Stone was no longer there.

CHAPTER TWENTY

The Sewers of Ultamar

Careil awoke suddenly to the sound of Erras whinnying warningly. He opened his eyes and blearily saw the figure of the Ultamarian disappearing through the trees. Careil awoke fully instantly, and threw off his blanket, as he got to his feet.

"Where are you going?" shouted Careil.

"Can't a man empty his bladder in peace?" growled Hernan.

Careil was rolling up his sleeping gear when Hernan reappeared.

"Well we didn't try to kill each other in our sleep," said Careil.

"Oh, I thought about it," said the Ultamarian. "But that horse of yours kept looking at me every time I moved. I should have just slept. My neck and back are sore. That tree is not very comfortable."

"Do you ever stop complaining?" asked Careil, but then added. "How is your arm?"

"It can swing a blade if needed," said Hernan threateningly. "Your wound does not look so good."

Careil looked down to the gash that showed through his torn clothing. He had been ignoring the pain. He had also neglected to clean it. He bent his head down and caught a whiff of corruption. He moved towards Erras to get some salve from his pack. Hernan was rummaging around in the bag that he carried and he withdrew a small vial.

"Here," he said, thrusting it towards Careil. "This will fix it."

"What is it?" asked Careil.

"It is some potion the Anasarians sell," said Hernan. "Ultamar has its own cures but some of those can make things worse. Those of us who know, can find Anasarians willing to sell us remedies."

Careil sensed from this that there was a degree of discontent in the soldiers of Ultamar. Obviously not everything about Ultamar appealed to them.

"Let me test it first," he said abruptly.

"How?" said the Ultamarian, indignantly.

Careil walked over and took the vial from Hernan's outstretched hand. He uncorked it and then turned and moved over to Erras. He held the vial out and Erras moved his head forward and sniffed at it. The horse snorted softly but didn't flinch at the smell. He looked at Careil steadily. Careil retrieved a cloth from his pack and poured some of the liquid onto it. The smell was pungent but refreshing. He then pulled up his jacket and vest.

The wound stood out as a bright red blaze across his side. He took the cloth and wiped the wound. There was an instant stinging burn as the liquid seeped into his flesh. The pain nearly caused him to pass out and he steadied himself against Erras. The worst of the stinging subsided leaving a burning pain. He removed his jacket and his vest and folded them up. He retrieved fresh clothing from his pack and placed the other back in the pack. He took out a bandage and wrapped it across the wound and around his chest a couple of times, then donned the clean clothes.

"We need to hurry up if we are to catch Bardan," said the Ultamarian impatiently.

Careil handed back the half-full vial to Hernan. He then finished packing his gear, stored it in his packs, and they made their way through the trees towards the plateau.

Careil had become used to the pervading smell overnight, but as they drew closer it steadily grew worse and began to invade his senses again. The ground around was marshy and criss-crossed by streams of black, evil smelling water. As they went on some of these streams became wider open sewers and Hernan led them to places where small wooden bridges had been thrown across. Paths wound through the trees. The sun was hidden behind the plateau but the sky above was clear. All around them though, there was a miasma of fogs and reek.

As they moved on they began to hear the sounds of voices and the clamour of people, and could smell smoke. The path they were on joined a wider path and before they knew it buildings started to appear. The buildings were dull and shabby, their walls blackened by years of damp and mould. Smoke filled the air, and as they drew nearer they could see people milling about going about their business. As they continued on, some of the people moved towards them. Careil tensed and felt for the reassurance of the sword at his side. But these people carried trays and held out objects towards them. The man that met them first was well dressed but his clothing was dirty and shabby. He held out a tray of what looked like frogs.

"Care for some breakfast, sirs," he said. "Only three Ults a piece."

"Get out our way," snarled Hernan.

"Come now, soldier," continued the man. "Surely you must be hungry."

Other people began to gather around them and all began to call out their wares. Hernan began to look annoyed.

"Get out of our way, you scum!" he roared putting his hand on the hilt of his sword.

The crowd fell back and the first man bowed.

"Yes, sir. Yes, sir," he said, as he retreated.

They made their way past the hawkers and as they moved on they heard a voice call out. "What about two Ults?"

Hernan turned and glared threateningly at the man who fell into silence. Careil noted that as they moved further on, the people behind them all just began talking casually amongst themselves. They must be used to being abused by Ultamarian soldiers. They didn't seem to take any notice of Careil's clothing or the fact that he led a large horse. Something struck Careil and he glanced back and saw that two men were following close to Erras. They seemed to be keeping a casual eye on the saddlebags. Careil looked to Erras but the horse had already begun to turn towards the men. Careil released the reins and Erras spun and faced the men snorting and stamping his front hooves. The men backed away and then quickly scrambled back to where their fellows waited. Erras turned back and Careil took up the reins again as he walked up and patted the horse's neck.

Hernan growled impatiently. "Come on. We're wasting time."

Through the fog and smoke, the steep walls of the plateau towered above them. The town followed a gentle slope up towards the foot of the plateau. At the base of the cliff, there were various dark openings; gates and drainage outlets from the labyrinth that led up into the fortress. Ultamar was now out of sight this close to the plateau. It was almost as if the town hid here out of the watchful gaze of the Dark Lords. The buildings grew haphazardly but close enough together that they supported each other. The streets were muddy and potted with rank puddles of water. There were darkened doorways, and crooked alleys, and in places stalls and carts laden with goods for sale. Some looked wholesome, and some unsavoury, and the prices seemed to vary accordingly. In some places multi-storey buildings teetered above the street, and from some of these soldiers wandered, unkempt and bleary-eyed. Careil eyed them warily, but Hernan just ignored them and kept heading through the town towards the plateau. As they grew closer to the wall, there was an area that seemed busier and more populated. There was raucous laughter and calling out, and the sounds of drunken revelry.

Careil looked at Hernan.

The Ultamarian sneered. "The Night Guard have finished their watch."

Careil was still surprised that no-one had challenged them as they made their way through the town.

"Don't you lot keep guards down here to keep an eye on things?" asked Careil.

"Sewer Town is not worth protecting," replied Hernan. "This is where we go to let off steam out of sight of the fortress. We occasionally send patrols through here, but the soldiers and the servants of the fortress need somewhere to get a drink and get things that they can't get while they're on duty."

"What do your Lords think of that?" asked Careil.

"Hah!" exclaimed Hernan. "Their Excellencies don't bother themselves about what happens down here, or in the depths of their dungeons. They just send scum and traitors down here to die or suffer."

"What about you?" continued Careil. "Do you come here after working in the fortress?"

The Ultamarian just stared momentarily at Careil.

"Shut up with your questions!" he spat. "You sound just like a filthy spy."

"Just making conversation," said Careil with a shrug.

The street they were on continued to steepen as it led up towards the cliff face. Careil could now see that a large iron portcullis blocked a wide archway that led into the darkness of the depths of Ultamar. But Hernan suddenly turned to one side and headed down a narrow side street that led down towards a small bridge. There were people around them but they seemed to ignore them as they moved through. Then there was a sharp whistle. Suddenly, all the people around them turned and blocked their path and then moved to hem them in. Careil looked quickly at Erras and signalled with his palm for the horse to be calm, but on guard. Erras dipped his head slightly in response.

The entrance to a dim alley stood to their right and the crowd swarming around them drove them through. Careil went through first leading Erras. The Rider looked back to where Hernan was. The Ultamarian had gripped his sword hilt but already a large gloved hand was smothering his mouth and a broad arm was around his throat.

They were in a small courtyard surrounded by rickety buildings. Dark windows looked down upon them. The courtyard carried the stench of the town but was relatively clean. Careil still held Erras's reins and there had been no attempt to take Erras or to assault Careil. Hernan on the other hand was a different matter. The Ultamarian had been stripped of his sword and pack and now stood gagged being restrained by two dirty, fierce-looking men. The large man who had taken Hernan prisoner, now walked over to Careil.

"Who are you?" demanded the man. "And why do you accompany this soldier? Where is he taking you?"

"Are you a Quigling?" asked Careil looking at the man's clothing.

"Hold on there," said the man. "You do not get to ask questions."

He looked Careil up and down and then glanced at Erras.

"Where do you come from?" asked the man. "You are much better equipped than most that come to Sewer Town, and your garb is unfamiliar."

"Who I am is a long story and I am reluctant to speak of it here," said Careil.

"What do you know of the Quiglings?" the man asked.

"I have heard of them," said Careil cagily. "I have heard that they treat their prisoners well."

The large man stood right in front of Careil, confronting him.

Careil leant forward and said softly. "Guran-Badur."

The man's eyes lit up at this.

"What did you say?" he demanded.

Careil looked the man directly in the face and said angrily, but with a wink and a slight dip of his head towards Hernan. "You can torture me but I will never tell you anything."

The man grasped Careil's arm but only applied slight pressure.

"We shall see!" he said, roughly. "You can come with me!"

They stood in a small room in one of the houses that lined the courtyard. The man had dragged Careil there with a feigned struggle. Two Ultamarians stood guarding the door.

"Alright," said the tall man. "How do you know the name 'Guran-Badur'?"

"I have met people who know of the name," said Careil but then continued urgently in a low voice. "But, I need to know that you are not an enemy."

"I am an enemy," said the man, quietly. "I am an enemy of those evil vultures that sit atop that fortress above."

"But you are accompanied by Ultamarians," said Careil softly.

"They have been assigned to help locate spies," said the Quigling. "He then whispered to Careil. They're obviously not very good at it, otherwise I'd be dead."

Careil took heart at this but was still hesitant as he continued in undertone. "What do you know of the Stones?"

"The Stones?" asked the man.

"Of Angil," said Careil.

"That is enough," said the man. "You need to tell me who you are and where you come from."

"You first," said Careil.

"Very well," said the man. "I am Karra-Bar. I am a Quigling. However, the knowledge won't do you any good, surrounded as you are."

"The Ultamarian needs to be guarded," said Careil. "And Captain Bardan came through here. We need to find out where he is or where he went."

"When did Bardan get here?" asked Karra-Bar.

"Sometime last night or this morning," replied Careil.

The Quigling was looking at him intently.

"Now you need to tell me who you are," he said.

The Rider straightened up and said confidently. "I am Careil, King's Rider of Wesmere, recently deserted and aiding a quest that seeks to free Anasaria!"

Karra-Bar reached out and grasped Careil by the shoulder. And then drove the Rider downwards. Careil resisted the pressure on his shoulder but the larger man had the upper hand. Careil was forced to his knees and then a fist smashed into his face.

Careil fell to the ground and the Rider heard the sneering voice of Karra-Bar say loudly, "I think their Lordships would like to talk to you."

Careil vaguely saw more figures in uniform entering the room and then felt another blow to his head.

"Erras!" he thought desperately.

And then blackness.

⁕

Erras reared within the courtyard slashing out with his front hooves. Darkly dressed men approached from behind and the war horse stood and then kicked out sending two of them flying through the air and knocking others over. In front of Erras, others moved forward warily trying to grasp the reins that hung over his saddle. With a great lunge, Erras launched himself forward. Dark figures were knocked aside. One still stood and grasped for the reins but the haunches of the big horse crashed into him sending him careering away. The alleyway that they had entered through, lay ahead. A large man stood defiantly for a moment but the sight of the big horse bearing down on him made him leap aside.

Erras galloped through the narrow alley and out into the lane. He made his way at speed back up towards the main street, and as he ran, people jumped aside. He turned into the street and then opened his stride. His sensitive nose took in the stench of the dirty town, but beyond that he could smell the forests of Anasaria. A group of soldiers had emerged from a tall building and one of them saw the horse and moved drunkenly to stop him. Erras bowled him aside and he crashed into his companions. The edge of the town drew nearer and the smell of the forest grew in his nose. A path opened out before him as people stepped back at the sight and sound of a large horse in full flight.

He saw ahead the edge of the town and the forest beyond and he thundered down the street. At that moment a small cart came out onto the street blocking his way. Erras gathered all his strength and as he raced towards the cart the great horse leapt into the air and sailed over the top of the cart and hit the road at a run. He flashed past the last of the buildings and quickly galloped up a path into the forest and out of sight. People moved into the street at the edge of town, staring up the roadway with bewildered expressions on their faces.

Careil's head hurt and other parts were beginning to develop bruises and cuts as he was dragged behind the houses and down into a gully. He was not sure how long he had been unconscious; possibly hours. His hands were bound tightly. His ankles were also tied but loosely enough that he was able to hobble. A putrid cloth had been tied around his mouth. They had not blindfolded him, so he could see where they were going. His tied ankles made him stumble down the side of the gully but he was dragged along between two large Ultamarians. The Quigling led the way down. All that Careil could think of was what was happening with Erras.

The smell in the gully was overpowering and Careil saw, as they descended, that the gully was a drainage ditch, a sewer, and the filth of Ultamar flowed along it. Closer to the bottom a path ran just above the edge of the dark flowing sludge. They followed it as it wound its way up towards the base of the plateau that towered above them. As they made their way around a bend in the path, Careil could see that the course of the sewer ran straight, leading them up towards a black tunnel in the rockface. It appeared even from this distance that the tunnel was barred, but Karra-Bar led them unwaveringly on.

As they grew closer Careil sensed that they were not alone, and soon soldiers began to appear around them. These soldiers were dirty and dishevelled. There was no speaking as the soldiers fell in beside them and followed the Quigling. The path led upwards until it reached a straight and level road that ended at the tunnel entrance.

A group of six soldiers stood guarding the path. At their head stood a large Ultamarian. He moved towards them, and then stopped, blocking their way.

"Where do you think you're going?" said the Ultamarian addressing Karra-Bar.

"Stand aside, Skelan," said Karra-Bar.

"You do not command here," said Skelan.

"I serve the Dark Lords," said the Quigling. "Move out of our way."

"Ah, you have a prisoner I see," said the soldier, Skelan, looking towards Careil. "Who is he?"

"Who he is, is none of your concern," said Karra-Bar threateningly. "Move your men out of our way."

"My, you certainly are an uppity piece of filth," sneered Skelan. "A traitor to your own people, but here you think you can command soldiers of Ultamar."

Karra-Bar drew his sword. Skelan quickly drew his, as did the men behind him and the soldiers on either side of them. The soldiers following Karra-Bar also drew their swords.

Careil started to have a bad feeling about this. Here he was surrounded by armed enemies and his feet and hands were bound. He looked desperately around. The path was bounded on the right by a high ridge of stone that ran down from the walls of the plateau. To his left the edge of the road sloped down towards the sewer. There was nowhere to go even if he could get free from his bonds.

The soldiers stood poised. To his right Careil saw one of the Ultamarian soldiers who had been escorting him raise his sword. To the side, one of Skelan's men stood. He also wielded a sword. Careil without giving himself time to think braced himself and then threw his weight against the soldier who stood alongside him. The soldier, caught off guard, stumbled towards the other soldier. That soldier, assuming he was being attacked, brought his sword down defensively. There was a clash, and then all hell broke loose.

As fighting broke out all around, Careil threw himself to the ground and then began crawling towards the edge of the road. An Ultamarian staggered back as he was attacked. He stumbled over Careil and careened over the edge of the road and rolled down and plunged into the filthy black water. He struggled in the water coughing and gagging but the black water swirled around him sweeping him downstream and dragging him under. His attacker saw Careil and made towards him but at that moment another Ultamarian swiped out with his blade catching the other across the upper arm. They faced each other and their blades clashed.

Careil quickly wriggled forward until he could peer over the lip of the road. Just below, was a narrow path that was overhung by the road embankment.

Careil tensed himself and then rolled over the edge. He dropped heavily onto the path and then managed to stop himself before he continued rolling down the slope towards the stinking black sludge below. He caught his breath and then began to crawl along the path as it followed the road upwards towards the tunnel. He suddenly felt a heavy weight crash into him and he looked to his left as a soldier bloodied and limp tumbled down and splashed into the sewage. Careil turned back and continued to crawl up the path. As he went he struggled against the ropes that bound his wrists. They were tied tightly and he was unable to loosen them even slightly. The sounds of battle raged above him as he continued to crawl. It was difficult to see how far this path went but he just kept crawling as fast as his bonds allowed. He was making progress and he sensed that the sounds of battle were behind him now. If only he could get far enough away, he could give himself enough time to try to get these ropes off.

His elbows and knees were getting bruised and sore as he struggled on. The ropes at his wrists were biting at his flesh as he moved. Further along, the path came to an abrupt halt where the ground dropped away. He pulled himself up to the edge. Below a broad stone sluice led down towards the sewer. On the right, water poured out of a culvert under the road and ran down the centre of the sluiceway. The water was clean and clear; rainwater washing down from the sheer cliffs above. The side of the sluice sloped down below him. He held his breath and then pushed himself over the edge. He slid slowly and then picked up speed before he crashed to the bottom of the channel. He slid forward and stopped at the edge of the flowing water. He pushed his head towards the water. He sniffed at it and then thrust his face into the water at its edge where the flow was slower. He lifted his face out of the water and shook his head. He then bent down and gulped some water. He lay there panting for a while and caught his breath.

His mind kept going back to Erras. The horse was trained to retreat to safety if he was separated from his Rider and was unable to help. He thought of the bond he had with Erras and something in him felt that the horse was safe. He gathered his strength and then looked towards where the culvert led under the road. The water was flowing swiftly but there was not a large volume of water pouring out. He got onto his knees and elbows and began to crawl towards the opening.

Behind him, there was a thump and then the sound of footsteps stomping towards him.

"Where do you think you're going?" said a harsh voice.

It was Skelan. Careil felt a boot slam into his ribs just beside where he had bandaged the gash in his side. He looked around and saw the legs of Skelan.

They went past and then Careil was wrenched to his knees by the ropes binding his wrists. He looked up into the cruel face of the Ultamarian. The evil soldier released his hands and stepped back and looked down at Careil with a sneer.

"Where are you from?" he asked.

Careil said nothing.

"I asked you a question!" shouted Skelan.

He lashed out with his foot and caught Careil in the side of the face. Careil sprawled backwards his knees straining and then fell sideways onto the wet stone.

"What did you tell the Quigling?" asked Skelan sharply.

Careil was silent as he tried to make sense of this situation. He thought desperately. Finally, he said, "I know about the swans."

Skelan looked down at him with a puzzled expression. Then understanding came over his face, soon replaced with a look of cunning.

The Ultamarian leapt up the sloping edge of the sluice until he was high enough to see back down the road. Satisfied he jumped back down. He went around to where Careil's feet were and drew his sword. Careil lay there expecting the blow to come and preparing to roll out of the way. Then he felt Skelan pulling at the rope on his ankles. No, not pulling, cutting. After a few moments Careil felt the ropes around his ankles loosen and then fall away. Careil pulled himself around and looked up at the Ultamarian.

"Get up," said Skelan, "and be prepared to move quickly. You are coming with me. If you try anything, if you try to run, I will start to cut pieces of you off. I'm sure the Dark Lords won't mind if you're a little damaged, with some nice, fresh, open wounds, when they start to ask you questions."

Careil rose gingerly to his feet. His ankles were sore but he was able to stand and walk. The Ultamarian held a sword pointed at him. He motioned for Careil to move back up to the road. Careil walked towards the edge of the sluice. He began to climb, but with his wrists still bound he was unbalanced and stumbled forward crashing into the stone. Skelan lashed out again, kicking Careil in the leg just below the knee.

"Get up!" snarled the Ulatamarian.

Careil got to his feet and then steadily and carefully climbed up the sloping stone until he was able to step onto the path and then up onto the road. Skelan followed close behind. Careil looked back down the road. Bodies were strewn everywhere. There was no sign of anyone still standing.

"Move! Fast!" demanded Skelan sharply. "Up towards the gate!"

The Ultamarian poked Careil with the tip of his sword, Careil turned and began to trot up the roadway. Skelan matched his stride and then pushed the tip of his sword into Careil's side.

"Faster!" he growled.

Careil broke into a jog and then opened his stride and began to run. The Ultamarian kept pace behind him. Careil's body was a mass of pain as he ran and he groaned silently as he pushed himself forward. They approached the tunnel entrance. Bars covered the entire tunnel entrance and the dark putrid water flowed between the bars and into the sewer below to their left. The road stopped at a gate in the bars. There were no guards. Careil slowed as they neared the gate and then stopped before it. Skelan stepped past him and produced a key from within his uniform. He placed the key into the lock and turned it. He pulled the gate and it swung outwards.

"In!" he barked at Careil.

The sun was moving towards evening behind him as Careil stepped through the gate and entered the labyrinth that formed the bowels of the fortress of Ultamar. The gate clanged shut and he heard Skelan locking the gate behind them.

"Get moving, scum," said the Ultamarian. "Straight ahead. If we meet anyone, keep your mouth shut."

The tunnel was dimly lit by braziers that burned at intervals along the walls. The smell of the sewer was strong in this confined space, but as they continued on, the tunnel and the sewer diverged, and the tunnel narrowed into a stone corridor that sloped upwards. They came to stairs and Skelan urged Careil forward. Careil's body protested as he mounted the stairs and began to climb. After a while, the stairs ended at a small landing. More stairs continued onwards, but on either side passageways led off into darkness. Ahead of them, Careil suddenly heard the sound of booted footsteps. They seemed to be coming down the stairs. Careil felt the tip of a sword at his ribs.

"Into the right passage," hissed Skelan.

They crossed the landing and entered the passage. Skelan pushed Careil against the wall amongst the shadows and clamped his hand painfully over Careil's mouth. They watched as a troop of seven soldiers travelled across the landing and down the stairs. The soldiers filed past and the last of them disappeared from sight. They waited as the footsteps faded and then Skelan released his grip on Careil and shoved him back towards the landing.

"Up the stairs," said Skelan.

"Friends of yours?" asked Careil.

"Shut your filthy mouth!" snarled the Ultamarian.

They moved up the stairs, and these ended at another landing from which three passages led off. Skelan pushed Careil towards the right hand passage, and they continued on. The passageway was straight for a while and then began to curve back around. It then straightened out, and they came to a place where passages led off to either side. Again Careil was pushed into the right hand tunnel. This ran straight for a while and then ended in an archway. Careil moved through the arch and they stood on a large landing. Open space yawned around them. A spiral staircase led down from the landing to the right, and upwards to their left. Dim light fell on the stairs from braziers that were spaced along the wall following the stairs. Each light lit only the area directly below so that it appeared as if there were islands floating in the air above and below bathed in pools of light.

Skelan pushed Careil to where the steps climbed up. The stairs had no rail, and below them was just black void.

"Climb," said Skelan.

They made their way steadily up the stairs. Careil's body screamed in protest. He was tired, and sore, and hungry. He concentrated on walking up the stairs. A fall could be dangerous, especially with his hands still bound. The darkness yawned beside him, falling away into who knew what depths. Careil's breath was labouring. He wasn't sure that he could keep this pace up for much longer. His ribs burned with pain and he felt a dampness oozing down his side. He looked down, and in the dim light he could see that there was a dark stain on his clothing.

He was bleeding.

He tried to focus, to think. How was he going to get out of this? He was tired and injured. His hands were bound. And an Ultamarian with a sword followed closely behind. His legs were free. He could run but there was no way he could outrun Skelan. He could turn and attack, but with Skelan armed, and his hands bound, he didn't like his chances of overpowering Skelan or avoiding plunging over the edge of the stairway into darkness.

Skelan spoke. "Tell me about the swans," he said.

"Why should I?" said Careil defiantly.

"I could just kill you right now," said Skelan coldly.

"Karra-Bar promised me payment," Careil lied.

"Funny," said Skelan, "but it didn't look like you were coming along willingly."

"He betrayed me," said Careil. "He said he would pay me, and then he took me prisoner and said that I would tell the Dark Lords whether I liked it or not, and that my payment would be to be put out of my misery after they had finished with me."

"That sounds like a reasonable deal," said Skelan. "But I can begin your torture here and now if you don't tell me what you know of the swans."

Careil had slowed his pace. Skelan's curiosity seemed to have made him forget his haste. Careil caught his breath and thought for a moment.

"They have the key," he said.

"Yes," said Skelan. "I know they have the key. Have you seen it?"

"No," replied Careil slowly, "I haven't seen the key, but I have seen the swans."

"Where are they?" asked Skelan, and Careil sensed the hunger in his voice.

"Up in the mountains," said Careil.

"Where?" demanded Skelan.

"To the south, beyond the Pass of Exile, near to the sea." Careil continued. "But there are Underdwellers in the mountains. They guard the secret to the Lake of the Swans."

"There?" questioned Skelan.

He pondered this for a while and then continued, "It would make sense. Those mountains are full of enemies and rebels."

There was silence for a while as Careil continued to plod up the stairs.

"Do you know where the key is?" asked Skelan suddenly.

Careil paused then said, "I think so."

He stopped and turned back towards the Ultamarian. The soldier raised his sword threateningly. His face tensed.

"I could take you there," said Careil.

Skelan paused at that and thought for a moment.

"Did you tell Karra-Bar anything about where the swans are?" he asked intensely, still pondering.

"No," said Careil. "He decided that this knowledge would be kept only for the Dark Lords. He seemed afraid."

"Hah!" said Skelan scornfully. "The Quigling is a coward and he is weak."

The Ultamarian looked at Careil thoughtfully. "Maybe you could take me there and I could get the key," he said and then continued almost to himself. "But it is far. It would take days. Unless we could..."

He turned his attention back to Careil. "Do you know how to ride?"

Careil almost laughed out loud but stifled it and said, "I have been taught to ride, yes. I'm not sure if I can ride like this." He held his bound hands out towards Skelan.

Skelan paused and looked up and down the stairs. He then held out his sword and played it across the ropes at Careil's wrist. The keen blade sliced throught the ropes. Careil shook his arms, and the severed ropes fell onto the stone steps between them. It felt so good to be able to use his hands again. He looked at the Ultamarian.

Skelan said brusquely, "Move up the stairs. There is a landing above." And then continued almost conspiratorially, "There has been a change of plan."

The Ultamarian thrust his sword towards Careil. "Hurry up and get moving!"

Careil sighed inwardly with relief. It didn't look like they were going to see the Dark Lords. He turned and headed doggedly up the stairs again. After climbing for a while, they came to another landing. An archway led off to their left. Careil looked back, and Skelan motioned with his head towards the arch. Careil walked through the arch. A tunnel disappeared into the darkness where the dim light from the stairway didn't penetrate. Careil paused. He could hear Skelan behind him scrabbling at the right hand wall. There was a striking noise and a spark of light and then a steady glow spread from behind him, casting his and Skelan's shadow onto the floor and walls of the passage. The light grew in intensity and Careil could see that the tunnel led in a straight line as far as the torchlight reached.

"Get moving," said Skelan. "We don't have much time."

They moved along the passageway for a while, the dim glow of the torch lighting the walls on either side. Suddenly, to their right, a dark alcove appeared.

"Stop," said Skelan.

Skelan came up to where Careil had stopped, and the torchlight revealed the small alcove. It led to a large wooden door with a small grate at head height. He pushed Careil forward and then moved just past him, and with a jangle withdrew a bunch of keys from his pocket. He fumbled for a second, looking back and forth between Careil and the keys. He finally found the one he was looking for and thrust it into the lock. He turned the key and there was a rasping noise as the lock released. He pulled the door and it creaked open. Skelan motioned Careil forward. Careil walked through the door into a gloom, only barely lit. A musty stench assaulted the Rider's senses and he turned back towards the Ultamarian.

Skelan slammed his open hand against Careil's throat and shoved him further beyond the door. Careil, in pain, stumbled, and then crashed into a stone floor littered with debris. The dim light around him disappeared, as he heard with alarm, the sound of the door slamming, and the key being turned in the lock. He tried to get up and managed to rise a little. He looked up at the grate as the light beyond faded until he was left in complete blackness. He collapsed back to the rough floor and breathed in the musty stench in despair, but his body just said 'rest here'.

He awoke and felt at first that he could not open his eyes. He realised that his eyes were open but all around him was absolute darkness. His body was a sea of pain. All his wounds combined with the pain of sleeping sprawled on a rough stone floor. He tried to calculate how long he had been sleeping but had no luck. There were bits of what felt like wood digging into him where he lay. He could see nothing even after his eyes should have adjusted to any light, just blackness.

He fumbled around and then remembered that he no longer had his pack. They had taken it from him. No. His pack was strapped to Erras's saddle. Take care of it, Erras. He stifled a groan of distress at the thought of Erras out there somewhere. He convinced himself that Erras knew his training and could usually take care of himself when threatened. But he still had no pack.

From where he lay on his back, he rolled himself onto his left side and then pushed himself onto his knees. He steadied himself as his head spun with the exertion and the flood of pain that wracked his body. Now upright, he attempted to look around. No glimpse of light could be seen. He crouched down and began to sweep his hands around as he moved slowly forward. On his left, he felt more pieces of wood; some broken piece of furniture. With his left hand he felt rough cloth and small sticks. No, straw he realised. It was an old mattress. He felt along the edge of the mattress and then his hand hit the wall in front of him. He then felt along the wall to the right and his hand came across what felt like something bundled in cloth. He moved his hand trying to determine what it was. As his hand moved up there was a round…

His hand recoiled. There was a body huddled in the corner. He had felt dry skin stretched over bone. The dank smell emanated from there.

Anger at the indignity of it steeled Careil and drove him to his feet. He stumbled and then steadied himself in the darkness. He felt anger at the fate of this person left here in the dark to die and rot. He turned round and faced in the direction he assumed the door was. He stepped carefully forward with his hand outstretched. He tested each footfall carefully to make sure he didn't stumble over anything. His right hand hit the wall at an angle. He straightened up and placed both hands on the wall and began moving them outwards. His right hand came in contact with the wooden door frame. He stepped carefully sideways until both hands were on the door and then systematically ran his hands over the wood. He came across the metal grate. He sensed a slight hint of fresher air. He made sure that he left no part of the door untouched. The door had no handle or lock on the inside and the grate was too fine to grasp. He thought that maybe he could break through the grate, but it would do no good, the window in the door was too small to be any use. He gave up resignedly.

He shuffled around and then with his foot began pushing aside the material littering the floor alongside the left hand wall. Once that area of floor was clear he sat down. The temperature in the cell was neither warm nor cold. He removed his jacket and rolled it into a bundle. He placed it in a roll and then gingerly lay down facing in the general direction of the door, with his head resting on his jacket. He was tired and he was sore and he was hungry and thirst burnt in his throat. He resigned himself to try and sleep.

He lay there contemplating his fate. His thoughts wandered to Hyrn and Rowan and Erras, and he drifted into a fitful and uncomfortable sleep. He awoke a couple of times, still unaware how much time had passed and then dozed again. Then finally out of sheer exhaustion, he fell into a deep sleep.

CHAPTER TWENTY ONE

The Darkness and Despair

It only took a short while for Duburinga and Boriega to find the trail of the Artoran soldier. They had followed it for a while and then returned and reported. It led north of the road into the trees, and through undulating ground that led down to the plains of Anasaria. There, farmland stretched north towards Ultamar and westwards towards the rough terrain along the edge of the gorge where the River Trebian cut through the landscape. The trail of the Artoran, though, turned sharply to the east, back towards Artora. Duburinga approached where Rowan stood next to Kerian.

"We cannot all pursue the Artoran quickly enough," said the Caramar warrior. "I counsel that Boriega and I go ahead on foot and slow him down. Ultimately our path lies west and north. Once we can open the lock, we need to head quickly back down to the road. Rowan, I believe that you, and the bulk of the party, should await us here and follow the road in the morning. Some will need to wait here for those with Biren-So if they haven't returned by then."

Rowan sensed that he was seeking his agreement instead of Kerian, or Gorum or the Quiglings, and he felt a little uncomfortable. He thought of Arienga, hopefully on her way back to join them, and then pushed that thought to the back of his mind. His path was clear to him.

Rowan said determinedly, "I will come with you on foot. No others need come."

Carlan spoke from beside him. "I will not leave your side, Swordbearer."

"I agree we should wait here until morning and then head westwards towards the bridge," said Kerian. "If you have still not rejoined us we will wait for you at the bridge."

The others agreed to this and began to set up camp for the remainder of the night.

The two Caramar moved swiftly down the sparsely forested hillside. The moon still shone brightly above them from a clear sky. Rowan jogged behind them with Carlan following closely. As he moved, the casket bounced on his shoulder where he had hastily strapped it. Rowan could see no trail but Duburinga and Boriega were unerring in their pursuit. After a while, Rowan began to tire. It had been a long day and it was now deep into the night. He continued on doggedly until, as they approached the crest of a rise, the two Caramar came to a halt. Duburinga motioned hurriedly behind for Rowan and Carlan to stop.

There was a sudden cry of pain, and simultaneously, a blast of purple light that threw the ridge top into sharp relief. Duburinga signalled for them all to stay and he then snuck close to the top of the ridge and moved to the right where a bush stood at the crest. Duburinga watched for a while. The evil light had dimmed. Duburinga signalled to Boriega to join him. The other Caramar warrior quickly moved up the hill in a crouch. Duburinga motioned to him to move left, and then gave a signal that Rowan thought from his training, meant to circle around.

Duburinga then motioned for Rowan to follow. As Rowan began to move up the slope Carlan loped past him keeping low but intent on shielding him from whatever lay ahead. Rowan, without bothering to protest, followed Carlan until they both stood just behind Duburinga.

Duburinga turned to them and whispered, "The enemy is just below. He attempts to wield the Stone but he is burned by it. At my signal, Boriega and I will attack. Draw your swords and be prepared to follow."

The seasoned warrior turned and looked directly at Rowan. He studied him for a moment.

"I trust the judgement of my warriors," he said. "Arienga reports that you are ready to fight. Now you may need to do so."

With that Duburinga turned back, gave a brief hoot and then leapt from behind the bushes. He sped over the crest and silently down the hill. Carlan moved next and Rowan followed. As Rowan crested the hill he saw below the bright light that emanated from the Stone. It lay unattended on the ground. He saw the shape of Duburinga momentarily block the light, but he could not see where the Artoran was.

Suddenly to one side, a figure burst out of the darkness and crashed into Carlan. The Abessairian did not have time to raise his sword. Below, Duburinga turned at the noise, but Rowan was closer. Carlan struggled as the figure grappled with him. The Sword of Acclimoss was in Rowan's hand and he leapt towards the wrestling figures. He hesitated as the two fighters rolled on the ground. Then with one decisive stroke, Rowan thrust the sword into the melee. There was a cry of pain.

With a disgusted yell, Carlan threw himself free of the Artoran. The Artoran struggled painfully. The Sword of Acclimoss pinned him to the ground through his left shoulder. Rowan looked quickly down the slope, to where Duburinga and Boriega stood over the Stone, their faces lit by the violet glow. The two Caramar warriors seemed to be transfixed.

"Don't touch it," shouted Rowan.

Carlan stood beside him looking down at the Artoran.

Rowan withdrew his sword and spoke beseechingly to Carlan. "Please bring him quickly."

The big Abessairian bent down to where the Artoran writhed on the ground and grasping him by the front of his tunic wrenched him to his feet. The Artoran cried out with pain and fear. Rowan had moved quickly down the hillside. Carlan dragged the Artoran behind Rowan to where the two Caramar warriors stood looking confused.

Rowan knelt down before the Stone. The Sword of Acclimoss was still in his hand.

He said to Carlan, "Bring him close."

The Abessairian yanked the evil soldier forward and then pushed him to his knees near to Rowan but pushed his bulk between the two of them. The Artoran panted with the pain of his wound and the touch of the Stone. Rowan removed the casket from where it was strapped over his shoulder. He placed it on the ground near the evil Stone. He then turned to the Artoran where he cowered on the other side of Carlan.

He raised his sword and held it out towards the evil soldier.

"Pick it up!" he commanded.

The Artoran mewled in pain, but he looked to where the casket lay on the ground beside the Stone and then up at Rowan and snarled, "I won't!"

Rowan brandished the Sword before the Artoran. The Artoran's face twisted in agony.

Rowan repeated more forcefully. "Pick it up!"

The Artoran collapsed towards the Stone and then he reached his hand out and grasped it. Rowan took up the casket and held it so that the lock faced towards the Artoran.

"Place the Stone against the lock," he demanded.

The Artoran soldier moved the Stone towards the lock as Rowan pushed the casket towards him. The Stone and the lock met and there was a blinding purple flash. They were all stunned momentarily, and then they saw that the Artoran was sprawled on the ground. The Stone lay on the ground beside him. Purple vapour rose from it, and as it did, the light from the Stone seemed to diminish.

The casket in Rowan's hands shuddered. The lock that held it closed seemed to melt and then it fell into shards and disappeared. The casket was now still. The clasp on its front was still closed. Rowan held the casket in one hand and then hesitantly grasped the clasp with the other. The thought of what they had come all this way to pursue filled his mind. He grasped the small tongue of iron and flipped it up. He then gripped the lid of the iron casket. Time seemed to stand still as he slowly opened it.

Inside the casket all was dark. Almost instantly, a bright light burst from within and they, and the surrounding area, were bathed in a brilliant white glow.

"Ilah! Where are you?"

The voice was deafening in its intensity. It cried out with loss.

"Ilah! I cannot see you." The voice of Ivah pierced the night.

Far away, beyond the hills and the river and through the forests of Anasaria, Ilah slept against Hyrn's chest, hidden within the power of the ancient city in the forest.

"Ivah! Ivah!" said Rowan desperately. "Can you see Hyrn?"

The Stone still glowed and then spoke. The voice that Rowan and Hyrn had heard back in Errasarn poured forth. "I cannot see your brother. He is hidden from me."

There was a pause and then Ivah spoke again. "We must head for Ultamar. The people of Anasaria are in grave danger. What the outcome will be is beyond my sight but that is where the fate of Anasaria will be decided."

With that the Stone went dark. Rowan stared at Ivah for a moment. He tossed the iron casket on the ground and then tucked the Stone inside his tunic.

"We must go," said Rowan urgently.

Duburinga was still recovering from his stupor but said, "Back to the road. We will join the others and then head north down the road."

"What about him?" asked Rowan, gesturing towards the Artoran.

"We cannot leave him here," said Carlan sternly. "He is treacherous."

"Bind him and bring him with us," said Duburinga to Boriega. "He may have information that is useful."

"He will betray us at the first opportunity," said Carlan.

Rowan stood looking thoughtfully as Boriega pulled rope from his pack and bound the Artoran's hands. The Artoran grimaced in pain as Boriega pulled him to his feet. Rowan moved forward and stood facing the Artoran. He pulled Ivah from his vest. He had no idea what Ivah was capable of but he thrust the Stone towards the Artoran's face.

"What is your name?" demanded Rowan.

The Artoran looked at Rowan painfully, his features contorted and then croaked. "Carak."

"Carak of Artora, your people swore an oath on this Stone and its twin," said Rowan. "They have returned and you must honour that oath. If you do not, you will be destroyed."

He held Ivah closer to the Artoran's face. The Artoran cowered away from the Stone.

Rowan spoke sharply. "You will help us, and if you do anything to hinder or betray us your death will be swift. Do you understand?"

The Artoran felt the power in Rowan's voice and nodded silently.

"Say it!" demanded Rowan.

"I will obey and do nothing to betray you," said the Artoran bitterly.

Rowan, satisfied, placed Ivah back in his vest and then said, "What about the Artoran Stone?"

"Get the Artoran to place it in the casket then close the latch," said Carlan. "It is too dangerous to leave lying here."

Rowan almost walked in a trance as they approached the road. In his stupor he saw a glowing light dancing ahead of him and then a friendly welcome face. Arienga walked from amongst the trees, accompanied by Terrana. Rowan's heart leapt at the sight of Arienga. She gave him a quick smile, and then looked puzzled as she noticed the Artoran being escorted by Boriega. She turned though and addressed Duburinga.

"We have made camp just beyond, away from the road," she said. "Biren-So is badly wounded but he still lives. He is fitful. We have tended to him and let him rest for now, but we will have to move him once he is stable. He needs the help of a healer."

The rest of the party were gathered at the campsite amongst the trees not far from the road. Everyone was exhausted and most were already asleep. A meal had been prepared earlier and Rowan ate without thinking. Weariness seemed to invade his whole body. There was a small cooking fire still burning and Rowan settled groggily down near it, with Carlan close by. Terrana and Gorum were on first watch. Arienga set down near to Rowan and he roused himself and told her briefly and haltingly what had happened. They did not talk for long though and Rowan was soon fast asleep.

He dreamt of a dark army; massive and evil. They marched in their thousands, row upon row. The faces of the soldiers were grim and full of evil hate. Beyond the mass of the army, seven tall figures stood glowing with evil light, driving their army before them. People stood watching the approaching army. They were unarmed, or held makeshift weapons. They looked weak and helpless but still they stood defiantly as the brutal army drew their swords and drove into them. Suddenly, a dark whirlwind approached. As it moved towards Rowan he started to feel sick. He awakened momentarily and started to stand. He felt hands reach out and catch him as he fell back down towards the ground.

And then he felt the dark cloud engulf him.

Hyrn felt apprehensive as he followed closely behind Yarga. He listened for the voice of Ilah but the Stone was silent. The light of torches illuminated their way through the darkness, flickering off the walls, and casting shadows all around. They had traversed the great hall and exited through the eastern doors. Margana had gone back to report to Gebarana, Droom and Jarta-Den, and to retrieve their packs. They were to meet back again on the eastern side of the citadel. Harla walked ahead of Yarga, leading them. The layout was different here and there was no landing overlooking an entrance. Instead they walked through corridors, and up and down steps, and past doorways and passageways that led away on either side. They eventually came to stairs that led to a small foyer. Opposite the bottom of the stairs across the foyer was a pair of doors.

"This must be the way out," said Harla.

To Yarga she said, "We may need your help to open the doors, Elder."

They approached the doors and Yarga stepped forward beside Harla. At that moment there was a shudder through the ground. Yarga stood dumbstruck and clasped the Stone at his throat.

"There is something here," he said with a pained expression. "Something horrible."

There was the faint noise of groaning from beneath their feet.

"What is it?" asked Wren.

His face was pale with fear.

"We need to get out of here," said Yarga, a hint of terror in his voice.

Harla placed her palms against the door and pushed. The doors did not yield.

"Elder?" she entreated.

Yarga approached the doors and felt the stone with his right hand. In his left he held the piece of the Sagenstone. His face became locked in concentration and the doors quivered. He grimaced with effort and sweat glistened on his forehead in the torchlight.

"I can't…!" he said in a strained voice.

Infiron stepped forward and placed her hand on the door beside Yarga's. Her expression quickly changed and the same intense look of concentration and pain came over her face. Together they challenged the defences of the door. The others looked around with fear and a growing sense of panic. The doors began to shudder and Yarga and Infiron's faces were locked in fierce concentration. Behind their backs they heard gasps and a strangled cry from Wren. Hyrn looked up to the top of the stairs that they had just descended.

A figure stood there in the dark where the torchlight didn't reach, but a shimmering light shone from it. The light moved between an iridescent blue and a brilliant violet. The air around them grew cold. The figure was silent, but stretched out his hand as if grasping towards them. Then as if floating the figure began to move slowly down the steps towards them.

Yarga and Infiron continued to desperately struggle with the door. Their breath was misting as the air became icy cold. The others were momentarily paralysed, but Harla moved forward, and the other fighters then took up defensive positions behind her. Hyrn stood back and Wren hid behind him. In front of Hyrn stood the bulk of Garan. The air grew colder and it felt as if it became charged with power. Hyrn felt as if his will and his strength was being sucked out of him.

All of a sudden Yarga charged forward. He spoke to Drivian.

"Help Infiron," he said and then turned to Hyrn. "Hyrn, I ask that you lend the power of Ilah to the Priests," he implored.

Yarga then moved quickly and stood beside Harla. He moved his left hand up and felt for the Stone he wore. Hyrn turned back towards the door and moved to where Drivian had joined Infiron. Wren followed closely. Garan backed up, still facing forward and maintaining his position between Hyrn and the approaching figure. Hyrn withdrew Ilah. The Stone was cold and dark.

"Ilah," whispered Hyrn. "We need your help."

The Stone began to glow but not with the usual white light. Instead the light that shone from Ilah was tinged with red.

Ilah spoke in Hyrn's head. "This is old and deep. The wisdom of the Sagenstone barely understands. Place me against the door."

Yarga stood defiantly, but terrified, beside Harla. As the figure descended the last of the stairs, it paused and seemed to draw on more reserves of power. The light it radiated grew in intensity. The party were bathed in the swirling blue and violet radiance. The figure appeared to be a man. It was not clear whether the man was old or young. He moved forward and they could see that his eyes burned with a purple light that was piercing and malevolent.

Harla challenged the man, her sword held firmly before her.

"Hold your position and state your purpose," she said commandingly.

The man's face broke into a ghastly smile.

"So you return," he said and his voice was cold and terrible.

Yarga said hesitantly. "Return?"

"I know who you are," said the glowing man. "My people, the little fools, searching for wisdom. There is only one true path to wisdom and in your folly you chose to ignore it. Instead you left it all to me."

"Left what?" said Yarga.

"The rest of yourselves. The lust for power. The strength to take what you need. The things that make you truly strong."

"It is not strength you speak of," said Yarga. "It is corruption."

"It is power you fool!" screamed the man. "You thought that you had trapped me, defeated me, but you are weak. You had the chance to kill me but you did not have the strength or the will. Instead you imprisoned me here. I waited over the centuries in my prison and my power grew. Now you come to free me, to let me out into the world."

Understanding grew in Yarga. The old legends of the Caramar. The flight from darkness. The search for wisdom.

"You are the Darkness," said Yarga.

"You wished to rid yourselves of evil," said the man sneeringly. "You sought to make yourselves pure so that you would be free to pursue wisdom. But I alone was willing to take it all. You poured your darkness into the Stone that you found in the depths."

He laughed. "And I took it and it filled me with a power that you can't imagine. And none could stand against me and yet I was tricked and imprisoned. But you all fled."

He looked directly at Yarga. "I am the Darkness. The dark of the nightmares that haunt your sleep."

Yarga spoke softly, but defiantly. It was clear now. "We found wisdom, and we found that we could not escape evil, but that it still lives in us, and in the world around us, and we recognise the truth of the existence of evil but follow the path of goodness, and it will overcome evil until there is balance in the world."

Hyrn held Ilah against the door and the reddish light poured into the door. The Stone also gave off flashes of white light that lit the faces of the Priests, Infiron and Drivian. Finally, the stone doors began to creak open and as they did a shaft of light poured through. There was a cry of evil triumph as the doors opened. Hyrn turned back towards where the others stood, facing the evil called the Darkness. Before the big Abessairian could stop him, Hyrn bounded past Garan and stood behind the two Caramar.

The Darkness had begun to move towards where Yarga and Harla stood. Harla wielded her sword defensively, but in a blinding flash red light burst from Ilah and it spread out and seemed to form a bubble that surrounded them all. The man continued to move forward but when he came into contact with the red light he recoiled as if burned. He tried again and screamed with pain. He then looked up to where the doors were now opened widely, and with a cry of anger and then triumph, he moved swiftly and fluidly and then became a cloud of blackness that rushed past them and through the doorway out into the open, his cry echoing all around and then fading as he disappeared from view.

They stood as if in shock and then Infiron moved towards the doorway but Harla moved swiftly past her followed closely by Turum. Hyrn began to move towards the door but Garan held his arm out to stop him and then moved ahead of him. Hyrn followed with Wren close behind. They came out into the bright sunlight of midday. Forested ruins stretched out eastwards towards the steep walls of the crater. The city seemed silent and then the sound of the wind moving through the trees came to them, and it seemed as if the ancient city had been holding its breath. They could no longer see the dark cloud, but to the north as the wind moved they sensed the evil presence fleeing and then vanishing into the distance.

They had allowed something evil to escape into the world.

Hyrn was surprised to see that Margana had not arrived from the western side of the citadel with the others. It seemed as if their journey through, towards the eastern entrance of the temple, had taken ages, but not a great deal of the day had gone since they had first entered. There seemed to be some trepidation amongst them but Harla rallied them to be prepared to continue on.

"The quest still lies ahead of us," she said stridently and then continued more somberly. "But doom gathers for good or ill. I can feel it on the air."

They rested on a low moss-covered stone wall that curved around where the road that circled the citadel met the main road heading east. They ate a little and talked less as they sat. Wren was restless though, and had got up and was wandering around looking at stone columns and structures and peering into hidden doors and overgrown alleys. Hyrn joined Wren, as they wondered at the power and beauty of the ancient city.

Before long the sound of hooves came to their ears and around the southern side of the citadel came Captain Droom riding his Chariga at a slow trot. Following him came Margana leading a horse carrying Jarta-Den. Behind them, bringing up the rear strode Gebarana. Harla came out to meet them and Margana gave a quick routine report. Harla's recounting of the events at the door had a greater impact.

Jarta-Den's condition seemed to have improved. He was speaking coherently, if still a little stiffly. They all took heart though and, gathering their belongings, they made their way eastward down the road. Droom led them, with Harla keeping pace beside the Underdweller Captain astride his chariga.

The eastern side of the city looked similar in layout and was equally overgrown with forest. However, as they continued further in the afternoon light, tall pines began to encroach upon the road. The forest here was thicker and the buildings were engulfed within. The tall trees threw dark shadows as they moved steadily onwards, winding their way between the trees, until they came to a point where the road led up the forested side of the crater to the south.

They began to climb and the road diminished to a stone pathway that in places had become twisted and bent. Great paving stones now lay at steep angles in places where tree roots thrust them aside. The path came to a junction where it met a wider way. They turned onto this wider path and started heading north, back to where they assumed there would be a gate leading to the east. The sun was getting lower in the sky ahead of them as they made their way slowly along the broken and overgrown pathway. A sense of purpose and determination filled them and they remained mostly silent as they struggled on.

A voice close to Hyrn said, "Do we know where we're going? We seem to be just following paths through the forest."

Hyrn looked around at Wren. The Anasarian looked tired.

"We have to trust Yarga and the Priests," said Hyrn. "And we have Harla and Captain Droom and the others. We will be alright."

Hyrn paused and then said, "But I get the feeling that we need to hurry up and get out of here and back into Anasaria."

"But we are in Anasaria," said Wren.

"I don't think this was ever part of Anasaria," said Hyrn. "It is from before and no Anasarian has ever been here."

"It is familiar to me," said Wren. "I was born near ruins in the forest like these."

The sky was beginning to redden when they came suddenly upon a wide place where the road ended. To their right, a short path led through a cutting between the trees and abruptly ended against the trunk of a massive conifer that soared into the sky above, catching the light of the setting sun. Harla moved forward and examined the tree. She skirted around where its girth met the edge of the cutting. She disappeared around the trunk and then quickly returned.

"There is a stone wall and the remains of an arch," she said. "If there is a doorway here it is completely blocked by this tree."

Above them the forested wall of the crater towered. If they could not pass through the wall the only way east was to climb the towering slope above. There was a council amongst the party. The greatest concern was how they were going to climb with the horses and Droom's chariga.

"We will need to scout the area and see if there is a way to easily traverse this slope," said Harla.

⸎

Rowan swam in dreams of violence and fear. All before him was a wasteland full of dark forces that battled with him. A pain burned in his chest. It filled him with a sense of loss and despair. He felt a shining, warm presence beside him and it filled him with strength and hope, but he continued to be battered by the dark and chill wind, and he felt the warm and comforting presence slip away from him, and he fell once more into darkness.

He awoke slowly and opened his eyes. Sunlight slanted through the trees and a breeze from the south ruffled their leaves. He lay wrapped in a blanket on soft leaf-covered ground. He looked up at the dappled and fluttering light that illuminated the trees above him. All of a sudden, silently and without warning, a dark shadow appeared above him. He tensed up and began to prepare to jump to his feet.

"Rowan. You're awake." Arienga's voice was full of relief.

Rowan focussed on the familiar face leaning over his, and tried to collect his voice and then said hoarsely, "Where…? How long…?"

Arienga replied. "It is the late afternoon, Rowan. You are not well."

Rowan tried to raise himself up onto his elbow saying. "I'm fine. Just a bit tired, but we have to go on."

Arienga spoke softly and quietly. "Everyone is worried about you Rowan, and Biren-So is still in a grave condition. We have stayed here and set a watch. Duburinga has counselled that we wait and regain our strength."

She looked down at Rowan and said, "A true warrior knows when to hold back and conserve their strength."

Rowan groaned, "No training now please, Arienga."

His eyelids fluttered and then he said sleepily. "I like the sound of that."

"The sound of what?" she asked, confused.

"Arienga," he replied dreamily, and then fell back into sleep.

CHAPTER TWENTY TWO

Ultamar Awakes

"Get up!" roared a voice that wrenched Careil out of sleep. Wakefulness was pain and discomfort. He felt a sudden cold cascade on his face. Water! He opened his mouth and captured as much of the water as he could. It poured off his face, washing dirt and dried blood with it. He didn't care. He gulped as much as he could before the flow ceased. The cell was lit by torchlight and the figure of Skelan stood over him, an upturned waterskin in one hand and a sword in his other. The Ultamarian lashed out his foot, striking Careil's leg.

"I said 'get up'!" Skelan shouted more forcefully. "The Dark Lords are preparing to amass an army. Something is making them anxious. They are not happy about something. There has been talk of spies within the borders and a rebellion brewing."

He looked hard at Careil. "I don't suppose you know anything about that?"

Careil said nothing and tried to keep his face as inexpressive as possible. The dirt and bruising helped, and Skelan continued.

"We stick to our objective. If we can get the key, then perhaps we will help the Dark Lords greatly. This is my chance. There is a staging area within the gates. There will be a lot of activity there where the army is marshalling. We have to go that way. Through the gates and along the road is the quickest way and we may even be able to find some swift mounts."

Careil thought that this all sounded a little risky but it still seemed preferable to facing the Dark Lords. He also noticed that Skelan had said 'my chance'. He got painfully to his feet. Skelan stepped back, his sword pointing at Careil. He motioned for Careil to move through the open door and back out into the passage. The tip of a sword directed him to the right. He moved off down the passage and Skelan followed behind him. The passage continued straight for a considerable distance and then came to a junction. To either side a passage led off into darkness.

"Right," growled Skelan.

Careil turned into the right hand passage, and as Skelan entered behind him, the light of the torch showed that the passage followed a gentle curve to the left. He walked on as they continued to follow the curve. Occasionally a dark doorway appeared to their left but the right hand wall remained blank. After a while the passage straightened out and as they followed it Careil began to hear muffled sounds. As they grew closer he could hear the sound of movement and voices. Ahead there was dim light. The light grew as they moved forwards and it seemed that shadows flickered.

Suddenly the light around them disappeared and only the light ahead was visible. Skelan had extinguished his torch.

The Ultamarian said in a hushed but harsh voice. "You are going to walk as if you are meant to be here. Do not speak to anyone. If we are challenged I will do the talking."

He paused and looked piercingly at Careil.

"Oh," he said, "and if you try anything I will gladly kill you. Now that I know where the swans are, although you may be useful, you are not indispensable."

Skelan waved his sword menacingly at Careil.

"Just remember that I have this in easy reach," he said.

Skelan then sheathed his sword and motioned for Careil to move. Careil turned and walked towards the dim light ahead. He flexed his hands and arms, trying to get rid of the stiffness. The light ahead grew and the sounds of activity increased as they moved. Eventually the passage ended at the intersection with a larger and well lit corridor. They came to a halt at the junction and Careil could see that the larger way sloped downwards forming a large ramp. Soldiers moved down the ramp. Some were in small formations and others were in groups. Sometimes lone soldiers hurried downwards. They all seemed to be of one mind. There was much chatter amongst the soldiers.

Careil listened as two soldiers passed by.

One of them said to the other. "I've heard that the Artorans are attacking our forts to the south."

"I heard that Angilanians have invaded from the north," said the other soldier. "Did you see that light the night before last?"

"I was on patrol down here," said the other, "but I heard it blasted the tops of the fortress towers."

"No," said the first soldier. "It …"

Careil could no longer hear the words, over the clamour, as the two soldiers moved further down the ramp. Skelan pushed him to one side and surveyed the scene. The soldiers passing by paid him little attention. There was a break in the procession and then a lone soldier came into view trying to fasten his sword belt as he hurried along.

Skelan stepped out of the passage and confronted the soldier. The soldier looked up, startled, but before he had a chance to react, Skelan struck him across the side of his head and then grabbed his arm as he collapsed. He quickly dragged him into the dark passage just before another troop of soldiers came into view. These soldiers marched in formation, the sound of their footfalls in unison. There was no talking amongst them as they marched resolutely forward, passing the entrance to the passage, and continued onwards down the ramp.

"Quickly," said Skelan, as he began to remove the soldier's uniform. "Take your clothes off."

As Careil got undressed he winced with pain. When he removed his tunic and vest he could see that they were soaked with blood. Skelan threw the breastplate at Careil's feet followed by the soldier's tunic. Skelan got to his feet holding the soldier's sword and sword-belt. He faced Careil as he began to don the soldier's tunic.

As Careil pulled it over his head Skelan held out the sword and said, "You are going to wear this, otherwise you will look out of place. If I see your hand move towards the hilt I will cut it off."

They waited in the darkness near the passage entrance. A large unruly group of soldiers moved past talking loudly. After they passed there was a break and Skelan pushed Careil out into the walkway. They both turned and strode down the ramp. Careil walked painfully but stoically downwards. They were just two Ultamarian soldiers off to join the assault forces of the Dark Lords.

The broad stone ramp led them down. Ahead of them the sound seemed to grow louder. As they descended Careil saw ahead that soldiers were turning right. They grew closer and he could now see that this passage joined another larger one. A larger mass of soldiers streamed past and those ahead of them joined the throng. They continued on, and as they passed the junction, Careil was pushed forward into the jostling stream of soldiers. The large ramp they were on skirted the side of a massive cavern. Down the centre of the floor of the cavern, far below to their left, a large roadway lay packed with soldiers. Careil followed its course with his eyes and saw that it ended against two massive stone gates that formed the far wall of the cavern. At the base of the gates an evil blue light flared amidst the purple glow of the cavern. The light threw into relief a seething mass of thousands of soldiers.

The soldiers ahead of them were slowing down, and Careil could see that there was a bottleneck below where the ramp they were on approached the road. Soon they were part of a noisy chaotic mass of soldiers shuffling slowly downwards. Men pressed in on either side of Careil. He was being pushed against the soldier ahead of him. Behind him he felt a sharp pain. Skelan had his dagger pressed into Careil's lower back.

Skelan leant forward and hissed, "I'm still right here."

As they slowly made their way downwards a smell caught Careil's senses. He breathed it in and his stomach began to growl. He could smell food cooking. Off to the right, just beyond the end of the ramp, Careil could see smoke and steam rising. Around were benches where men were sitting around … and eating. Careil's stomach gave another loud grumble. He turned his head back towards Skelan.

"I need to eat," he said. "I'm not going to be able to make it much further unless I get some food."

"I hear that," said the soldier alongside him. "I wonder what they're cooking us."

Skelan leant forwards. His dagger pressed harder into Careil's back.

"I think we should both have something to eat," he said in a low voice. "Just remember that I will be watching your every move, but also remember that you have no friends here. Each man here would gladly kill you."

"I just want food," said Careil and the thought filled his mind as they shuffled excrutiatingly slowly towards where the kitchens were.

They sat on a bench. To Careil's right an Ultamarian soldier sat eating a chunk of roasted meat. He looked to Careil as if he were too young to be a soldier but that same bitter look was on his face. The curse of Ultamar. On Careil's left sat Skelan. He also was biting at a chunk of meat. Careil held a bowl in his lap. It was empty. The thick stew that he was served was thick and satisfying even if it tasted a little strange. His stomach began to protest at the sudden gorging.

He said softly to Skelan, "Are there latrines here somewhere?"

Skelan looked at him, as he chewed a chunk of meat.

"If this is some sort of plot to try and escape," he said under his breath.

"No," said Careil. "I assure you."

"Very well," said Skelan.

Skelan finished the last chunk of meat and then tossed the bone on the floor. He got up. The soldier alongside Careil paid no attention as Careil also got to his feet.

"Back towards the ramp and over to the left," said the Ultamarian gruffly.

Careil made his way back towards the ramp pushing through soldiers moving towards the kitchens. Skelan followed closely behind. They moved further to the left to avoid the stream of soldiers coming from the ramped walkway. They were now close to the side of the cavern and Careil could see that there was a passage between the cavern wall and the base of the ramp. As they grew closer to the passage Careil began to smell the stench. Soldiers moved in and out of the passage and Careil could see that they were entering or leaving a dark archway in the left hand wall of the passage.

Skelan leant forward and said, "Just remember that you have no allies here except me. If you try to escape you will soon be exposed and these soldiers will tear you apart. I will be close."

As Careil made his way back out of the passage he could sense that Skelan was watching him.

He suddenly heard a hiss in his ear. "Good. You are smart enough to not try anything."

Skelan shoved Careil forward as if to emphasise his command of the situation. They walked out of the passage and back towards the kitchens. Skelan though, grabbed Careil's arm and pushed him to the left towards the walkway and over towards where blue light lit the great gates.

"Where are we going?" asked Careil, turning his head as they walked.

"Just keep your mouth shut," said Skelan with a note of menace in his voice.

The main body of the army was massed in front of the gates. Many of them were laid out trying to get some sleep, while others were thronging around the base of the gates where the blue light was brightest. Skelan drove Careil between the soldiers lying on the stone floor, and then into the throng near the gates. They pushed their way through. The soldiers around them were craning their necks, and Careil could hear a harsh commanding voice speaking. The strange blue light flickered between the figures before them and grew in intensity as they made their way towards the front. As they approached, Careil could see that the light was like a seething mass. The crowd at the front became more tightly packed but the insistent threat of Skelan drove Careil forward. Finally, they were within the front most rank of soldiers and the source of the light became apparent to Careil but the sight was almost beyond comprehension.

A tall General stood facing the soldiers. He bellowed at them, inciting them in preparation for battle. Behind him were cavalry. Soldiers were mounted on horses, but these were like no horses Careil had ever seen. They glowed with a vivid blue light that engulfed their riders so that they also shone. The light made the horses and their riders shimmer and it seemed to

Careil that whenever the horses moved they seemed to blur. A rider pushed his mount into a trot and the horse seemed to almost disappear and then reappear, suddenly further across the cavern.

Careil felt Skelan close behind him and turned to ask what they were but suddenly realisation dawned on him.

"Oh, no!" he said to Skelan, shaking his head.

Skelan pushed his dagger against the side of Careil's neck.

"Just do what I say," said Skelan. "You said you could ride. They are just horses."

Careil looked at him with a perplexed expression.

"They are Kragon," said Skelan. "They move very fast. They have been filled with the power of Our Lords."

Despite the pressure of the point of the blade near his throat Careil began to protest. "But how…?"

Abruptly the atmosphere in the immense chamber changed. It was as if reality became distorted. Careil suddenly felt ill. A palpable sense of evil pervaded the air around him. A fear he had never experienced before grew in the pit of his stomach. There was a commotion from behind. The sound of thousands of soldiers getting to their feet filled his ears. The soldiers around him all stared intently forward and came to attention. Careil felt the point of the dagger fall away from his neck. In an instant the hubbub died away and there was just an eerie silence.

Behind the General, seven figures now stood. Behind the figures the Kragon had instantly become still and stood in ordered rows. As one, the seven figures held up their hands. All around Careil, with a thundering crash, the soldiers, in unison, fell to one knee. For a moment Careil stood amidst a sea of genuflecting soldiers but a rough hand grabbed him and yanked him to his knees. There was silence again. The General, too, had turned and now knelt before the figures. The Dark Lords of Ultamar stood before their army.

A painful chorus of seven voices grated in Careil's ears. "Soldiers of Ultamar, it is time to show our true power. Those we despise are moving in open rebellion to our glorious reign. In their stupidity and confidence, they dare to defy the might of Ultamar. We will drive them into the dust. We will crush them so that they never again have the audacity to believe that they can threaten us."

As the Dark Lords spoke, the soldiers around Careil were silent but he felt the power build in their ranks. It was mesmerising. The voices seemed to be seeping into Careil's head and he felt himself being seduced by their authority. He struggled to think clearly. He felt as if they were speaking directly to him and bending him to their will.

The voices continued. "You will feast on the suffering of those who defy us, and you will take from them all that you desire. There are now no bounds. We no longer have need of these worms. All of them rebel against us. When the sun rises the glorious army of Ultamar rides forth. None can stand before them."

There was a pause then the voices screamed, "Kill them all."

The Dark Lords brought their hands down and then raised them up. The soldiers all around, with an almighty roar, leapt to their feet and raised their arms.

"Ultamar!" they all yelled, and the deafening sound echoed around the cavern like thunder.

Careil had barely got to his feet before he realised that the figures of the Dark Lords had disappeared as instantly as they had first appeared. Careil looked around at Skelan. The Ultamarian's face was locked in a paroxysm of wonder and adoration. Once the voices had stopped and the evil figures had gone, Careil had immediately regained his senses. The soldiers around him still seemed to be enthralled but ahead the General turned towards the gathered army.

"Rest now, soldiers of Ultamar!" thundered the General. "At the rising of the sun we go to war!"

The soldiers cheered and there seemed to be a relaxation of tension, but this was replaced by a sense of excitement and enthusiasm, and hatred. Just behind Careil, Skelan came to his senses and, shaking his head, immediately turned his attention back to his prisoner.

"Our chance will come soon," said Skelan. "I will be high in their favour when I bring them the key."

The Ultamarian's face still shone with wonder. Careil had been worried about what was going to happen to him. He was resigned to the fact that he probably wouldn't get out of Ultamar alive. Now, he was more concerned that this massive evil army, which stood all around him, was going to be unleashed into Anasaria. And Rowan and Hyrn were out there somewhere.

Skelan was now in control of himself. "Move towards the right of the gates," he said to Careil.

Careil looked over to the right of the gates. He could see that the Kragon and their riders had moved towards the wall of the cavern in that direction. In front of the gates there was a wide semicircular space elevated a step above the floor of the cavern with a broad central ramp. The massed soldiers were below this step, with only the Kragon and their riders and a few officers, including General Gardwan, atop it. As he watched, the riders began to dismount and lead the horses towards what Careil could now see was a large pen. The Kragon were taken through a gate and pushed into the enclosure. Careil tried to count them. It seemed there were around twenty or more, but their movement made him unsure. They coursed around the confines of their pen in a seething blur.

Careil suddenly realised what they were attempting. The Ultamarian soldier who walked right behind him, wanted them to steal two of these horses, and then somehow escape. There didn't seem to be any way out of the cavern apart from the gates and the ramps back up into the fortress.

Careil turned his head slightly back towards Skelan and asked quietly, "How are we going to get out?"

"Don't concern yourself with that at the moment," said Skelan bluntly. "We just need to get close enough to make a dash to where the Kragon are."

"How are we both going to get across that space without being seen?" asked Careil.

"Oh, we're not," said Skelan.

"But if we're seen?" protested Careil.

"No," said Skelan. "You misunderstand me. We're not both going to dash across the space."

He paused and said matter of factly, "Just you."

Careil began to protest under his breath.

Skelan ignored him and said, "Just remember that you are avoiding being tortured, at least for the time being."

Careil considered this and then definitely knew he wasn't getting out of this alive.

They made their way towards the very right hand edge of the step surrounding the platform. There were soldiers standing or lying all around them. Skelan grasped Careil's arm and turned him around to face behind them. Back through milling soldiers, beyond the kitchen, was the ramp they had come down. There were now only a few soldiers on the ramp although there were also some now camped around the base.

"That is our way out," said Skelan in a low growl. "Once we have the Kragon we ride up the ramp and back the way we came."

"But even if I manage to get the Kragon, the others will give chase," whispered Careil.

"We will be a long way away before they can mount up," said Skelan "They will not know which way we went. They don't know the lower reaches of Ultamar as I do. I am Sergeant of the Under Guard. I know hidden passages that lead to a way out where we can escape undetected."

Careil considered this. Given his options it sounded promising. He may get the chance to strike a blow. If he could at least sound the alarm and warn of the imminent invasion.

"What about all the soldiers in the way, leading up to the ramp?" asked Careil.

"Hah," said Skelan, dismissively." Nothing stands before a Kragon in full flight."

"I still need to get two Kragon," said Careil. "Even if I make it to their pen. I don't know how to ride them."

"They are just horses," said Skelan. "You just need to be able to make them stop in time."

The Ultamarian looked at Careil and said forcefully, "You need to grab one horse's reins and then mount another. Once you are atop one, ride here. You will be here instantly. Only spur the horse a little and concentrate all your mind on stopping here. I will mount immediately and then we ride as fast as we can."

"Simple," said Careil.

Skelan glared at him angrily.

The rock wall at the edge of the broad platform led around to where the Kragon were penned. The wall was rough, with buttresses of stone at its base. These buttresses cast shadows broken by well lit areas. Careil considered that he would need to use these shadows, and move across the lit spaces when there was nobody close, or looking in that direction. He calculated. Four short sprints including the one to the first buttress. The soldiers around them were the biggest threat on the first sprint. He looked back at Skelan.

"I need a diversion," he whispered.

Skelan studied his face for a moment and then said, "Very well, but just remember that I am your only hope of surviving the night. You have no friends here. All of these soldiers would love to uncover a spy and to be the one to give them to our Lords. You have no other way out. Wait until you hear a disturbance."

"What are you going to do?" asked Careil.

Skelan brought his hand up to Careil's side. It held his dagger and he pushed it into the Rider's wound. Careil gasped with pain.

"What makes you think you have the right to ask me questions?" Skelan growled. "Just get those horses and bring them back here."

Careil shrugged and said, "Alright, alright. I'm ready."

He sighed inwardly. He wasn't ready, but Skelan was right. The only way out of here was to follow the Ultamarian's plan.

Skelan shoved Careil towards the rock wall. He almost fell over a soldier lying on the ground. The soldier protested but rolled over and tried to get back to sleep. Careil walked over until he stood against the rockwall where the smooth step before him met the rough stone that towered above. The ground underfoot was ridged and uneven so thankfully no soldiers were trying to rest there. Careil stood on the toothed stone and looked along the rockwall that bordered the step. He looked at the jutting stone column of rock ahead of him and the dark shadow before it directly in front of him. To jump onto the step and run across the space would take only a few seconds but he would be in plain view. He steeled himself and waited.

Skelan stalked back towards the centre of the cavern. All around the soldiers still hummed with the fervour of being addressed by the Dark Lords and the prospect of serving them in battle. He had not gone too far when he stopped. He looked around and then saw what he wanted. A soldier was moving towards the centre of the stage, ahead of him. He grabbed the soldier next to him and shouted above the noise of the army. "That's him. He's the one that insulted our Lords."

He pushed the soldier forward and the soldier was momentarily confused but Skelan shouted, "Get him! He is a traitor!"

The soldier responded to command and began to chase the other soldier.

"Look!" shouted Skelan. "They're getting away. They have plans to attack the Dark Lords!"

He jostled and pushed at the soldiers around him. Others began to move forward. He reeled around and began to kick at soldiers lying on the ground.

"Get them you fools! Traitors!" he yelled.

More soldiers leapt to their feet and, confused, began to follow, rousing other soldiers as they moved. Satisfied, Skelan began to make his way back towards the wall as other soldiers awoke to the commotion and thinking that they were under attack or that they were about to march joined in.

Careil stood as suddenly soldiers began to get to their feet beside him and head away. There was a commotion towards the centre of the chamber. Careil looked quickly around. Skelan had done the job. A soldier just beyond where he stood was moving off. He glanced at Careil for a moment but followed the crowd. The thought of what he was about to do crashed into Careil's mind. He thought of Rowan and Hyrn and about why they were here. "Here goes," he said to himself.

The King's Rider gathered all his strength and leapt up the step and into the open space alongside the wall. To his left there were Ultamarian officers but their attention was diverted by the commotion amongst the soldiers below. He ran swiftly, despite his pain and weariness, and skidded into the darkness and came to a stop with his body pushed against the stone buttress.

He looked out from where he was hidden in shadow and surveyed the scene.

He saw that the Ultamarians were all concentrating on the disturbance, so he gathered himself and quickly darted around the base of the buttress and back out into the light. As he ran towards the shadow of the next buttress he glanced to his left and saw one of the officers starting to turn his head back towards him and he threw himself into a dive. He slid along the stone floor and with a crunch he collided with the stone of the next buttress.

He lay there panting with pain and exertion, but mentally sighed with relief. The dark shadow of the rock engulfed him. He lay alongside the jutting stone with his head pointing out towards the stone dais and his feet against the cavern wall. He raised his head and looking out he saw that the officer had turned back to where a fight was beginning to break out amongst the soldiers. He groaned, then lay flat on his stomach and inched forward so that he could peer around the point where the stone column ended. In order to do so he needed to move his head into the blue light that glowed beyond.

He cautiously moved forward checking for any attention from the Ultamarians who were in sight of him. His sanctuary was also his biggest problem. He could not see towards the gate unless he brought his head out into view of whatever lay behind. He now lay just at the edge of the shadow. He collected his thoughts and thought about what he had seen ahead. There was one more buttress before he needed to run towards where the Kragon were. From that shadow he would have a clear view of the gates and the dais, apart from the area directly alongside the wall where the pens ended. From memory there weren't any soldiers in that area but he may not have been able to see them behind the column of rock. He just hoped that, if there were, they weren't now between him and the next piece of shadowy sanctuary.

He took a deep breath and pulled himself forward into the light, watching for any movement. He inched past the edge of the rock and peered around. For a moment he thought he saw movement but realised that it was the light of the Kragon flickering as they moved about their pen. He moved a little further forward. He could not see around the prow of the column of stone but he was already exposed and he would have to take his chances. The area alongside the end of the pen was hidden by the last protuberance of rock. He needed to make it behind this rock. He could see a large part of the pen enclosing the Kragon and was momentarily transfixed by their movement. How could he hope to capture two of these creatures?

The words of Skelan came to him. "'They are just horses.'"

With all his strength he pulled himself up into a crouch and ran as quickly as he could towards the slab of darkness.

"Hey!" the voice boomed out from behind him.

He just kept moving and again threw his bruised and battered body into shadow. He spun around and quickly looked back to where the voice came from. With relief he saw that a group of brawling soldiers had sprawled onto the step. One of the officers was rushing towards them shouting for them to get off. As far as Careil could see, no-one had seen him yet. Now he only had to make one last dash, and steal the Kragon, and then… It was no use trying to think of more than one step at a time. He was exhausted and he would gladly have just lay there in the dark and closed his eyes and whatever happened to him, so be it. But the people of Anasaria and the members of the quest needed to be warned. He thought of Rowan and Hyrn and he thought of his faithful companion, Erras. He felt a lump in his throat and a sick feeling grew in him but he fought it and just concentrated on what needed to be done.

As he concentrated he heard a sound nearby. It was a muffled scraping noise. It sounded as if things were being moved around. He froze and listened intently, his heart beating faster. The sound was coming from around the other side of the rock. He couldn't quite make out what the noise was. He placed his ear against the ground and listened. There were some scrabbling noises and occasionally the sound of boots against stone. But it only seemed to be one pair of boots.

He lifted his head from the stone floor and rolled onto his back deeper into the shadow. He reached his hand down to the sword that lay alongside him. He felt the hilt of the sword and his fingers traced the symbols of Abessair and the Twin Stones. He then grasped the hilt of the sword and drew it from its sheath. He was careful to keep the blade within the confines of his dark hiding place. He tried to slow his breathing and control his mind. There was at least one soldier potentially standing in his way. He focussed on the sound from the other side of the rock. It was faint at first and then became louder. The footsteps were moving back and forth. Behind him he could hear that the commotion was dying down. He felt somehow as if the eyes of Skelan were boring into him. Careil could think of only one thing. With all his mind he sent all his thoughts to Erras. "Run Erras as far as you can. Find help."

He got up into a crouch and then launched himself forward and then skidded around the end of the buttress. He brought his sword up as the space opened up before him and he stood bathed in blue light. A soldier was walking towards him carrying a large wooden box. At the sight of Careil appearing in front of him wielding a sword, the Ultamarian froze. He looked puzzled and then angry.

He started to speak. "What are you doing here, soldier? You…"

Then he looked at Careil and looked right into his eyes. A look of shock and bewilderment came over his face. He dropped the box and reached for his sword. Before he had a chance to draw his weapon Careil had leapt across the space between them and slashed at his sword arm. The Ultamarian's sword clattered against the stone floor. Without thinking Careil stepped forward and grasped the soldier by the throat with his left hand and held his sword threateningly with his right. Pain wracked his body but desperation drove him on.

"Do you know the Kragon?" demanded Careil.

Fear now gripped the soldier as he stammered, "I-I-I j-just feed them."

Careil dragged the soldier closer to his face. "Listen closely and do as I say, or I will kill you."

The Kragon pens were lit in brilliant blue light. The Kragon had been housed for the night. Two soldiers approached with hay for the Kragon. A rider sat leaning against his pack a short distance away, but he was concentrating on polishing his boots. One of the soldiers moved ahead to open the gate. The other followed closely behind carrying his load awkwardly.

"Just as you would normally. Don't do anything stupid," hissed Careil, as the Ultamarian lifted the latch on the gate and walked though.

Careil closed the gate after himself, turning his head back swiftly to face the Ultamarian, but didn't latch it. He held his sword down low but it was still pointed towards the soldier in front of him. The soldier stood there like a dark shadow against the shimmering blue light in front of them. Within the light Careil saw horses wandering around restlessly or standing alertly. As some horses moved they blurred and became a smear in Careil's vision.

Careil spoke sternly. "Drop the hay and grab one of the horses."

The soldier turned to him quickly. "But...?" he squeaked.

"Just do it and then hand me the reins," said Careil fiercely.

The soldier looked behind Careil, then back to the Kragon and then down at the point of Careil's sword.

"You would be dead before you had moved towards me," said Careil. His voice was stern but if the Ultamarian had listened he would have heard the pain.

The Ultamarian looked back towards the horses and stood for a second in front of the blur. He thrust out his hand and withdrew it holding reins. He then walked back towards Careil leading a large glowing horse. He thrust the reins towards Careil.

The Rider said bluntly, "Another."

The soldier sighed and walked towards the front of the glowing light.

Careil meanwhile moved around behind the Kragon out of sight and stood beside its head.

"Just a horse," he muttered.

The horse stood proudly, as Careil spoke softly and calmly to it. Careil stroked the horse's neck and then patted it, still speaking in a soft voice. The horse snorted and then lightly scraped its front hoof. Careil spoke of running and breathing and the wind whistling past. He spoke of the joy of the world rushing past. Behind him the Ultamarian led another horse. Careil turned back to where the Ultamarian stood.

"Pass me the reins," he said quickly. "Once I mount, open the gate and stand out of the way."

The soldier resignedly handed the reins to Careil. He then began to move towards the gate. Careil spoke softly to the new horse. He then sheathed his sword and stepped up and quickly mounted the first horse. He switched the reins around in his hand so that he led the other horse with his left hand. He softly moved the horse towards the gate as it swung open before him. Before he knew it, he was moving through the gate and across the dais.

"Stop!" he said loudly.

A short distance away some soldiers turned around and with sudden realisation began to move towards him. The Kragon came to a halt close to the edge of the step. Careil flicked his head around looking for Skelan and then spun back to look at the soldiers coming towards him. Beyond them he could see other Ultamarians moving back towards the Kragon's pen. The gate had been closed behind him. He looked back to where the army were encamped in front of him, still searching for Skelan.

Suddenly there was a thump beside him. He turned quickly and there sat Skelan astride the other horse. Skelan moved forward towards Careil's Kragon.

"Follow," he said sharply.

He then immediately turned to Careil.

"Ride!" he shouted.

The soldiers on the dais were almost upon them. Careil hesitated no longer. He spurred his horse and they broke into an instant gallop that became a blurred tunnel. They seemed to slice through the cavern through the gathered soldiers, and flying over every obstacle, they shot up the ramp and up into the side ramp. They seemed to pause momentarily and then shot into a dark passage and then into a blurring dark maze.

They seemed to be travelling deeper and deeper down towards the lower levels, the air growing quickly danker. They suddenly came to a gut wrenching halt. They were in a dark passage but ahead of them was a violet haze more brilliant than the blue glow of the Kragon. They moved forward. Before them they saw a figure hunkered in the dark, glowing and holding something that glowed even brighter. At the appearance of the Kragon, the figure turned towards them, and then Careil recognised the face from the glade in the forest.

Captain Bardan.

The twisted figure of Bardan lay on the passage floor before them, propped up against the wall. The palpable presence of evil permeated the air. Skelan dismounted and then signalled to Careil to join him. Skelan had grasped Careil's horse's reins and his sword was in his hand. Careil also dismounted and the two approached the Ultamarian Captain.

Skelan spoke. "Captain Bardan? What are you doing here?"

The figure on the ground turned his head towards them and made as if to get up, but he just slumped back to the floor. Careil could see that he had a wound across his shoulder and upper chest. Purple fluid seeped from it.

"Why do you carry an Artoran Stone?" asked Skelan.

"No. No," said Bardan, trying again to rise. "It is the Angilanian Stone. The one the Dark Lords seek. I will bring it to them and then… then…"

He collapsed back down exhausted.

"It is an Artoran Stone," said Skelan bluntly. "And you are under an Artoran curse. Your wounds are oozing from their sorcery."

"No," rasped Bardan. "We defeated them. We stole the Stone."

Skelan looked down at Bardan with contempt.

"You can stay here and rot," said Skelan angrily. "We have no time for this."

A voice spoke suddenly from the tunnel beyond. "You have no time at all."

An arrow whooshed through the air and thudded into Skelan's chest. The Ultamarian grunted and then he groaned sharply as he fell backwards and crashed into the floor of the passage. Skelan gurgled and writhed on the floor as blood flowed from his chest.

Careil looked down at the Ultamarian for an instant, and then back to the shadows beyond the light of the Artoran Stone. A large figure emerged from the shadows. As he came into the light, Careil reached for his sword. It was the Quigling traitor, Karra-Bar. He still held a bow in his hand but he had not fitted another arrow to it.

"What are you doing here?" asked Careil angrily as he brandished his Abessairian blade.

"Looking for you," said Karra-Bar.

From the passage floor between them Bardan sneered, "The traitor and the spy."

"Shut up, you," said Karra-Bar sharply to the Ultamarian.

"Listen to me, Careil," said the Quigling. "My position here is perilous. I had hoped to use you to get back into Ultamar."

"You are a traitor to Anasaria and to your people," snarled Careil.

"No," said Karra-Bar quickly. "You do not understand. I am a Quigling. The power of Ultamar does not sway us. Those vultures above could never influence me, unless whatever they wield is used."

"I seem to have heard that before," said Careil. "Just before you punched me in the face."

"Careil, believe me," the Quigling implored. "I had to act quickly. I needed to use you to get into Ultamar to find out what is going on and find out something of their secret power. I had hoped that the Dark Lords would reveal it and that we could then strike against them together."

"That doesn't sound like a very well thought out plan," said Careil dryly.

"I said I had to act quickly." protested Karra-Bar. "We can still attack them, now that we have two Kragons."

"We?" said Careil indignantly. "I stole these Kragon."

"Yes," conceded the Quigling. "But I killed Skelan so rightfully I can claim his."

Careil looked at him for a moment and then said commandingly. "There's a change of plan. There is a massive army gathered inside the gates. They attack Anasaria at dawn. We need to put the warning out."

Karra-Bar considered this for a while, and then asked, "What about him?" turning to where Bardan lay.

But Bardan was gone.

"Where did he go?" asked Karra-Bar.

"I don't know," said Careil. "He didn't look too good, but Skelan was right. We don't have time for him."

"But if he escapes?" began Karra-Bar.

"I don't think he's going anywhere," said Careil. "We need to get out of here now and use these horses to rouse the Anasarians. If you are a true Quigling you will join me."

Karra-Bar led the way through the maze of passages that crisscrossed the bowels of the fortress. Their progress was more stuttering than when Skelan led the Kragon with his knowledge of the underways.

"Do you know where you're going?" asked Careil when they paused for a moment. "You may have killed our best way out of here."

"I came most of the way through in the dark," said the Quigling. "I didn't dare show any light in case Bardan knew that I was following him."

"How did you find Bardan?" asked Careil.

"At the fight on the path leading up to the gate," began Karra-Bar. "I slipped off and let the Ultamarians fight amongst themselves. It's one of their favourite pastimes. I went back into Sewer Town and pondered what you had said about Bardan. So I searched for signs of power. I am a Quigling, remember. It took me a while to pick up the trail. I had to scout your path. I finally found a trace of power. It did not lead into Sewer Town but out towards Detradin. It led me straight to a hidden entrance beside the wall and I followed the trail until I came upon Bardan and you."

"So you know where this entrance is?" said Careil bluntly. He still hadn't forgiven the Quigling for punching him in the head.

"Not far now," said Karra-Bar. Then he said, "Follow!" and the two Kragon and their riders sped off into the dark tunnels.

The moon had risen and the land was bathed in moonlight beyond to the western mountains, but the shadow of Ultamar cast the towering wall to their right and all around in darkness, as they emerged from the confines of the labyrinth of tunnels beneath Ultamar. Apart from the wind in the leaves of the trees that grew up to the wall, all was silent.

"Where do we go?" asked Careil. "We need to rouse the people."

"Back to my company's base of operations," said Karra-Bar. "It is around and beyond Sewer Town and then deeper in the forest. We should be there soon."

The now almost familiar blur of riding took Careil as Karra-Bar called his horse to follow. Forest flashed past them as the Kragon supernaturally avoided all the obstacles in their way. Or perhaps rode straight through them, thought Careil. They came to a sudden stop in a dimly moonlit glade. Thicker trees crowded around them but directly in front of them was a short path, surrounded by dense bushes, which led to a thicket where the path came to an abrupt end.

"This is it," said Karra-Bar.

He leapt down, and led his Kragon. Careil's mount followed at the same walking pace. Suddenly a horse leapt from the bushes ahead of them to the left and charged straight for them. It avoided Karra-Bar, as it came to a rapid halt in front of Careil's Kragon. The horse snorted in anger, and as Careil looked into the horse's eyes, he could tell that he was not happy, but his heart leapt at the sight.

"Erras!" yelled Careil.

He leapt down from the Kragon's back and dashing forward threw his arms around the horse's neck. Tears streamed down the Rider's face. In that moment, he felt that every happiness he had ever had, faded to insignificance. Erras stamped his hoof. Careil released his grasp and looked up at the great horse. Erras snorted and looked at the Kragon and then shook his head in disapproval. He then pushed his head at Careil in disgust.

"Hey, I'm sorry comrade," protested Careil. "But I was held prisoner. I had to escape somehow."

The horse looked at him disapprovingly and then nuzzled the Rider.

"I take it you two know each other," said Karra-Bar.

"Old friends," replied Careil.

"I will lead the Kragon," said Karra-Bar. "I'm sure I can get another rider for yours."

Karra-Bar continued along the path leading the two glowing horses. Careil and Erras stood facing each other. Then Careil continued forward and Erras turned and walked beside him as they followed the Quigling towards where the path ended.

"I think you came to the right place, Erras," said Careil.

Erras just nodded his head softly in agreement.

They were suddenly surrounded by armed men.

One of them called sharply, "Halt!"

"Peace, Ferek-So," said Karra-Bar.

"Karra-Bar!" said the Quigling. "You are back from…"

"Who is this?" he demanded, pointing to Careil standing tiredly beside Erras.

Karra-Bar ignored the question saying vehemently, "Ultamar Awakes. The Dark Lords are preparing to unleash the army that garrisons the fortress."

"There is more." interrupted Careil. "The Twin Stones of Angil and the Sword of Acclimoss have returned to Anasaria!"

Karra-Bar turned quickly to Careil, with a look of astonishment on his face,

"Who is this?" asked Ferek-So, addressing Karra-Bar in a puzzled voice.

"I'm not really sure," said Karra-Bar, shaking his head. "We really haven't had a chance to get to know each other."

The Quigling outpost was made up of tents and chambers of canvas within columns of tree trunks. The outer edge was surrounded by thick undergrowth and trees that grew closely together. The horses waited near the entrance in a small grassy space. Erras faced the two Kragon, looking disapprovingly and disappointedly at them.

Careil told as much of his story as he could in a short space of time, conscious of the fact that there was an army ready to be unleashed all around them… and Hyrn had been heading this way and Rowan was somewhere off towards Artora chasing Ivah. It was only a short time until Karra-Bar and Ferek-So were mounted on the Kragon, ready to ride far and wide to rouse the Anasarians, and the Quiglings amongst them. Careil had decided that he and Erras would go southwest towards where Hyrn should have been when he had tried to contact Ilah. He thought that this had perhaps been two days ago, but it was all very vague. He seemed to have lost a day when he was imprisoned in the dark cell. He shuddered at the thought. He was exhausted, sick, and sore, but desperation and hope drove him.

Careil would spread the message as he went. All gathered there agreed that the message, that the Twin Stones and the King's sword had returned, was their clarion call.

The two Kragon flashed past him in blurs of blue light as Careil rode off with Erras at a proud gallop that needed no evil curse, just heart, and courage, and a bond of shared duty and friendship. They rode off to call the Anasarian people to war, and to seek the members of the quest and the two boys Careil had pledged to protect.

CHAPTER TWENTY THREE

Anasaria Arises

War! War is upon us!" The voice wrenched Rowan from sleep. He felt a burning against his chest. It was Ivah. He pulled the Stone out and it shone brightly.

Ivah spoke again. "The gates of Ultamar are open and an army pours forth. The people of Anasaria are in peril. We must ride forth."

The sun had newly risen. Those of the party that had not been awake to greet the dawn were now rousing. Rowan looked around as he stood with Ivah in his hand. Arienga was nowhere to be seen. They ate quickly as they packed their gear and readied their horses. As they prepared, Gorum rode into view up the road from the west where he had been scouting the road, accompanied by one of the Quiglings. A short while later, Arienga and Terrana appeared from where the trees led up a slope towards a high ridge east of the road. Terrana spoke to Duburinga where he stood beside Kerian watching Gorum's approach.

"There is a clamour and much smoke out towards Ultamar," said the Caramar warrior. "Boriega and Jorunum still keep watch, but will return shortly."

"Ultamar has unleashed its forces, I fear," said Duburinga.

Gorum had come to a halt and he and the Quigling had dismounted.

"The road is clear down to the bridge," said the Underdweller. "But it will take us much of the day to make our way across and back through the forest that surrounds the approaches to Ultamar."

"We could ride northward across the plains," said Kerian, "but we will be in open view if the Ultamarians send soldiers this way."

"I'm not sure that Biren-So could survive the journey," said Terrana.

"There is another way." A voice spoke from behind them.

The Artoran, Carak, sat on the ground at the base of a tree, still bound to the trunk.

Everyone looked at him with mistrust.

The Artoran continued, "There is an old path that follows the river gorge and crosses the East Road and then continues beyond and comes out at the Plains Road near the castle at Forest Ford."

Rowan turned to face the Artoran. He still held Ivah in his hand and the Artoran shrunk back in fear at the sight of the Stone. But Ivah began to glow and spoke.

"He speaks the truth," said the Stone.

Just then, Boriega and Jorunum appeared.

"There are signal fires burning across the land," announced Jorunum. "The people of Anasaria are being called to war."

Rowan stood there. His body still felt weak, but something burned within him, and taking the Stone in his left hand he drew the Sword of Acclimoss with his right. He held it aloft.

"We ride to war!" he cried. "The people of Anasaria need our help."

Ivah began to glow as he spoke. "The time of Ultamar is drawing to a close," said the Stone.

All around the call went up.

"Desultamar!" they all roared.

They had ridden at speed down the road. As they approached the bridge, all was quiet. The mound of rubble had now been cleared to the extent that a steep-sided path ran through the middle. There was no-one about. The Quiglings and Anasarians who had been working to clear the rubble were now nowhere to be seen. Boriega came to a halt ahead of them. The Artoran, Carak was mounted before him.

"He says to head east towards the spires of rock that follow the line of the river," said the Caramar.

The party had to skirt back around the blasted hillside where the Sorcerer had brought down an avalanche of earth, stones, and broken trees. On the eastern flank of the scarred hill a small gully ran with a forested hill forming the other side. They were led up into this gully and it wove its way up until they came to a patch of thick forest where the two hills met. Carak signalled to the left and they passed into the forest. The path wove between thickly growing tall trees that cast dark shadows all around. The path wound steadily up the hillside.

They continued upwards until they came to a ridge. As they looked out beyond the ridge they could see that the land fell away down to the plains to the south and east of them. Ahead of them, to the north, lay a ridge of steep stony hills. This ridge fell away abruptly on its western flank where the gorge of the mighty Trebian River ran. The ridge they were on dropped steeply away below them. Carak pointed to the left and Boriega signalled that they were heading that way.

They travelled west along the ridge as it led towards the river gorge and then became steeper as it led to a sharp spine of stone that blocked the way. Carak spoke quietly to Boriega, and the Caramar turned his horse towards where a rocky forested slope plunged below them. He rode forward and the others followed as he skirted the top of the ridge still heading westwards towards the spine of rock. As they rode the path began to veer to the north and before long they had found themselves on a narrow ledge that led steeply down to the northwest.

It was treacherous going at first. The path was steep and rocky as they made their way down, guiding their horses carefully. After a while the path levelled out and widened and then slowly arced to the right. It then plunged down, heading northward, following the course of the river that was now hidden behind a steep wall of stony hills.

Yarga, Harla, Gebarana, Margana, Turum and Droom stood on the platform facing the east. A towering tree blocked the path as the sky above them lightened and they welcomed the dawn. Yarga, the thought of the sun burning before them in his mind, looked through the tree and through the immense stone wall, and out across the eastern plains of Anasaria. The tree shimmered in his mind, and he had a vision of just beyond, where an ancient stone doorway stood within a stone arch. He felt a thrumming at his throat and the tree for an instant disappeared.

The dawn chorus had finished and Yarga stood looking at the tree. His eyes moved up the trunk and he moved his head back slowly as his eyes continued upwards. The top of the massive tree stood pointing to the sky high above, still and silent. Yarga looked around quickly. The shorter trees all around them rustled in a gusty wind that blew from the southeast.

But the tall tree blocking their way was not affected by the wind at all.

Harla approached Yarga.

"We will scout the country further in the daylight, Elder," she said.

Yarga looked at Harla to give his assent and then suddenly turned back to the tree.

He gave a short laugh and then exclaimed, "The tree is not there."

Harla was preparing to move but turned back at Yarga's outburst.

"Elder," she said, "what is wrong? What are you saying? The tree is there.

We all see it. I have felt it with my own hands."

"Your mind felt it, and your mind sees it," said Yarga, triumphantly. "But it is the power of the door and the stone of the walls that surround the city."

Yarga, still staring at the tree, walked forward slowly and moved up the path. He held the crystal at his throat with his right hand and held his left out in front of him. He approached the tree, and as he drew near, the Stone at his throat glowed red. He came before the tree and thrust his left hand against it.

"Oww!" he cried sharply.

He withdrew his outstretched hand and shook it in pain. Harla dashed to his side.

"Elder!" she said worriedly.

"There's a tree there," he said.

"Yes, Elder," said Harla evenly.

"But it is not there," said Yarga defiantly.

"Elder, perhaps you need to rest," said Harla."We will go, and try to find a path out of here."

Yarga turned to the Caramar warrior. He felt a little unsure of himself. He paused and collected his thoughts. He still felt like a Novice as he faced the seasoned and experienced Warrior.

"I am sure of it, Harla," he said finally. "There is a way through. This is the only way out of here without returning the way we came."

Harla considered this then said, "Very well, Elder. How do we find a way through?"

"The power of wisdom," said Yarga

The path now led up into a region of rocky gullies. As Rowan rode, he looked to where Arienga rode just ahead of him. He took advantage of a place where the path opened out into the flat floor of a gully, and moved up beside her.

"Arienga," he said.

She turned to look at him.

"Yes, Rowan," she said.

"Arienga, will you help me?" he asked.

"Help you with what?" she asked in return.

"I don't know what I'm doing," Rowan said quietly. "I have the Sword, and now I have Ivah, but I don't know what I'm supposed to do."

"I think you do, Rowan," she said. "And I think you need my help, and that of all of us here."

"Arienga…" he began and then fell silent, unsure, and reluctant to say what he wanted to.

"Yes, Rowan?" Arienga asked intently.

"I need to talk to you. Not to you as a warrior, or my trainer. Just to you. Arienga."

Arienga spoke softly as she rode. "I am what I am Rowan. When you talk to me you talk to a Caramar warrior. It is who I am."

"I know," said Rowan. "But can you just forget your duty for a moment and think about just being…?"

He started thinking that he was getting himself into trouble. Then he pushed on.

"I think I am beginning to… to…" he began hesitantly, "…well, love you," he finished awkwardly.

Arienga turned her head quickly from where she had been watching the path. She looked at the Wesmerian boy riding beside her, and felt a warm smile grow on her face. She steeled herself despite the feelings that welled in her. She had to remain true to her calling, but she still felt the need to tell Rowan.

"Rowan, I…," she started, and then faltered.

At that moment, Boriega turned back and called. "There is a village ahead. Our friend suggests we follow a path that skirts the village further to the east."

Rowan spurred Arrow forwards and came up to where Kerian and Gorum had halted just behind Boriega's horse.

"No," said Rowan. "These are Anasarians. We are here for them. They must know. We ride on."

Rowan realised suddenly that he had begun to command people again without knowing he was doing it, but Gorum turned to Rowan and then faced forward.

"Let's ride on!" said the Underdweller loudly.

The village was silent. It was just a scattering of houses and a communal lodge, nestled in a small oval valley. The path became a wider street as they passed the outskirts. There was a smell of smoke in the air but they could see no villagers as they moved past closed doors.

"If you move any further, I will shoot!" A voice rang out across the street and the party came to a halt.

They looked around and then Duburinga pointed up towards the roof of the large building. A young girl stood there defiantly. She held a bow with an arrow ready to fire. The arrow pointed directly at Boriega. Boriega raised his hands.

"Who are you?" the girl called down to them.

Duburinga called up to her. "We come here in peace. We move towards Ultamar and to war."

"On whose side?" she asked.

Rowan jumped down from Arrow's back. He felt the soldiers bristling behind him but motioned for them to hold. He stepped towards the house. The girl swung her bow around and pointed the tip of the arrow at Rowan.

"Don't move!" she shouted.

Rowan stopped and looked up at the girl.

"I am Rowan," he said loudly. "The Sword of Acclimoss has returned and the Twin Stones are back in Anasaria."

He reached behind his shoulder towards the hilt of the sword but the girl yelled. "If you touch that sword you are dead."

Arienga moved her horse slowly towards Rowan until she was just behind him.

"Let me handle this," she said quietly to him.

Arienga rode further forward past Rowan. The girl moved her bow so that it now pointed at Arienga.

"Why are you left to defend the village?" asked Arienga. "Where are the other fighters?"

The girl paused and raised her sight from her aimed arrow. She looked at Arienga.

Arienga pushed the point. "Where have all the men gone?"

"They've gone to fight the Ultamarians without me," she said despondently. "The boys all went as well."

Arienga looked at her expectantly.

The girl continued defiantly, but with disappointment in her voice. "I could beat all those boys in a fight but they are allowed to go…"

Arienga interrupted. "We are going to war against Ultamar. Why don't you join us? Rowan here speaks truly. He does wield the Sword of Acclimoss and…"

The girl let her bow drop to her side and said, "But that means he must be the King."

Arienga started to interrupt her but the girl blurted out. "There was a rumour that has started to spread, that the King and his sword have returned to us."

Arienga looked at Rowan. He shrugged. Rowan drew the Sword and held it aloft.

"It is true!" cried the girl. "The King!"

She slid down the roof and grasping the edge dropped down onto the road. People started to move out from where they had been waiting behind closed doors. They were mostly older women and a few old men. The rest of them were children of various ages. None of the boys seemed older than twelve summers.

"The King!" the girl said.

There was a murmur and the people began to repeat the refrain. "The King!"

"No! I am not the King!" protested Rowan.

"You are close," said a voice in his head.

Rowan dismissed the thought and said, "We must ride forth. Anasaria is in peril. We seek to unite the Stones and destroy Ultamar."

People had begun to move to where Rowan stood, still holding the Sword.

An old woman cried. "The Sword goes to war!"

The voice in his head spoke again. "We must hurry."

They had asked amongst the villagers if they knew of a healer. An old man was brought forth. He walked in a slow crouch and had trouble seeing but he made his way directly towards where Biren-So had been laid down. Terrana and Arienga had cleaned his wound and bandaged it but the Quigling had become feverish.

"This wound stinks of more than rot," the old man croaked. "Carry him to my home and leave him with me. I will help him as I can. It will be good to be doing something useful against the enemy. I was never a fighter but I am glad I still live to see the coming of the Sword and the Stones."

They carried Biren-So into a wooden house. His fellow Quiglings, Dooren-Ga and Charen-Ba, helped to carry him. There was a sense of vitality as they went through the doorway. A soft yellow-green glow lit the front room.

"I don't have much power here but I hope it will suffice," said the old man.

They gave their thanks, and farewelled the old healer and their wounded comrade.

"Where are your parents?" asked Arienga.

The young girl who had introduced herself as Mielen, rode beside Arienga on an old bony horse. There was no-one to object to her leaving with them.

"My mother is dead," said Mielen. "My father has gone to fight. He refused to let me go. He said it was too dangerous for a girl."

"You defy him though," said Arienga.

"He thinks that I am not strong enough," said Mielen. "I think sometimes that he wishes that I was a boy."

Arienga shook her head. "Perhaps I could show him what girls are capable of," she threatened lightly.

"No," said Mielen. "He is a good man and he looks after me well, but he is afraid for me."

Mielen looked at Arienga. "Are you a soldier?" she asked. "You don't look like one."

"I am a Caramar warrior," said Arienga.

Mielen looked puzzled.

"We have come from far away. We are here to help free Anasaria and defeat the Dark Lords."

Mielen's eyes lit up. "Are you friends with the King?" she asked, motioning to where Rowan rode ahead of them.

"Yes," laughed Arienga. "I am friends with Rowan but I am not sure that he is the King."

"He is very handsome," said Mielen.

Arienga looked at the Anasarian and her eyes narrowed.

"How old are you?" she asked.

"I am almost fifteen," said Mielen.

"I may need to watch out for you," said Arienga softly.

As they made their way further, they came across other villages hidden in the hills and gullies, away from the eyes of Ultamar. People came to look, and amongst them there was the talk of war and the Sword of the King. Rowan felt that he should shout out to them as they passed that he was not the King. But there was hope in their eyes so he kept his mouth closed. From the surrounding hills, people came riding or marching, going off to war, so that as they continued on, a growing number of fighters joined them. At one point Rowan looked back and saw that their party had grown considerably and was now almost a small army. As they continued on, following the river, Rowan could hear the sound of their passing echoing through the surrounding hills.

Harla paced back and forth impatiently. The morning was wearing on. They had eaten, and everything was ready for the party to move on. Yarga had been in conversation with Infiron and Drivian regarding the tree that was apparently not real, but Harla was eager to move on. Her duty to the quest, and her belief in the virtues that she was sworn to serve, burned in her. The power of the Sagenstone and the spirit of the Caramarhc resided in her, and it emanated from the young Elder who sat on a stone wall and spoke of ancient lore. She looked at the Stonebearer where he stood before the tree, with the young Anasarian, Wren. There was power there too, but the power that burned in her called for action.

"Elder," she said stridently. "The day passes. We must decide what to do soon. I would gladly run straight through that tree and hurl myself through the door if it meant that we could move swiftly."

Yarga looked up to where Harla stood, and said, "Peace, Harla. Even if we passed through the tree, the door would still need to be opened…"

He suddenly stopped as if frozen for a moment and then said with a rush of understanding, "No! It wouldn't! It…! Of course!"

Harla looked at him puzzled, as he paused and then continued, "The tree is the door. We do not have to remove the tree. We have to open the door!"

Yarga stood before the tree. The two Priests, Infiron and Drivian, stood either side of him. He took a deep breath and placed his hand against the tree. He held the piece of the Sagenstone in his other hand and concentrated. He did not concentrate on the tree but instead threw his mind forward through the tree to the stone door beyond. Infiron and Drivian also placed their hands against the tree and thought of the door on the other side of the vast trunk.

Hyrn could hear a soft humming in the air like the buzz of a small insect. It grew until it sounded like an angry swarm. The three figures in front of him seemed to be locked to the tree and the sound seemed to make them vibrate. Yarga and the two Priests seemed to become almost transparent. Then something changed. The vibration seemed to move to the tree. The sound grew in intensity and the three figures seemed to become more solid as the tree itself seemed to become less solid, and fade. The sound had now reached an almost unbearable pitch. Suddenly, something seemed to break, and with a resounding crack and a rasp of stone on stone, the giant tree disappeared. Beyond where it had been, a stone door opened at the end of the path and a dark tunnel led beneath the towering walls.

They all stood there in disbelief, and then Harla darted forward and caught Yarga as he collapsed towards the ground. She dropped to her knees cradling the Elder. He opened his eyes and looked up at her.

"I'm alright, Harla," he said. "Just a little drained. The way is open. We should hurry and move on. Anasaria awaits."

They gathered their gear. Yarga and Harla headed through the dark doorway first, with the others following closely behind. Jarta-Den and

Droom, leading their mounts, brought up the rear. The tunnel was longer than the one they had traversed to enter the city, but daylight soon appeared ahead. They walked towards it. Yarga and Harla were just ahead of Hyrn as he emerged out of the darkness and into the light of day. Before them a stunning vista opened. The forest of Anasaria stretched ahead of them across to where the plateau rose, with the fortress of Ultamar standing stark against the sky.

As they emerged, they heard a resounding thud as the door closed behind them. Instantly a burst of power erupted amongst them. Hyrn was buffeted by a searing blast of heat. He wrenched Ilah from within his chest. Ilah glared with blinding light and the Stone's voice cried, "Ivah! Ivah!"

Riding beside Kerian, Rowan suddenly felt a burning in his chest. His first thought was that he had been pierced by an arrow. He clutched at his chest and then realised that it was Ivah. He withdrew the Stone. It burst with light and a sense of joy and relief flooded his mind.

"Ilah! I am here!" roared the Stone.

Rowan's thoughts went straight to his brother.

"Hyrn!" he shouted. "Are you there?"

Rowan tried to look into the Stone but its brightness dazzled his vision.

"Rowan!" said a voice. "Is that you?"

"I'm here, Hyrn," Rowan called. "Are you alright? Where are you?"

The party had halted and looked at Hyrn. They heard Rowan's voice and saw the look of relief on Hyrn's face.

"We are in the forest heading towards Ultamar," said Hyrn. "Where are you?"

"We are on the other side of the Trebian River heading towards Ultamar," said Rowan. "A war has started, Hyrn."

Beyond where Hyrn stood, Harla looked out over Anasaria.

"The smoke of war surrounds Ultamar," said the Caramar warrior solemnly.

They marched on. It was now past midday and they still had a long way to go. Gorum and Kerian rode as the vanguard, with Rowan just behind them. They no longer needed the Artoran to show them the way, and Boriega had dropped behind. A stocky Anasarian on a large horse moved up from amongst the ranks behind. He spoke out once he came alongside Rowan.

"I need to speak to you, whether you are the King or not, you carry the Sword and the Stone," he said.

Rowan looked at him expectantly and the Anasarian continued. "These hills continue on past the East Road but the path through them is difficult. I have come up from where my farm overlooks the plains. A large force of Ultamarians is heading out eastwards into the farmlands. They are coming from Forest Ford down the Plains Road beyond where these hills end and before the river drops down into the gorge. There the Trebian is wide and shallow and, before the Trian joins its course, the river flows less swiftly. That crossing will be heavily guarded. If we take the East Road we can cross the Trebian at the bridge below where the two rivers meet. The East Road meets the Coast Road which comes up from the south and leads northward towards Kirenk, and then continues on to Forest Ford. We can attack more easily from there."

"Of course." Kerian had been listening to the Anasarian. "Kirenk. If things have gone well, we can expect the fort to have been captured."

"There have been no Ultamarians coming from Kirenk for days," said the farmer.

"Even if the fort has been freed, we still need to get over the other river," said Rowan.

"Fort Kirenk is the way over the river," said Kerian. "It is built atop the bridge there."

They had agreed that following the East Road to the Coast Road, was the most strategic route. As the army wound through a rocky, heavily forested slope, the road suddenly appeared beneath them. Those leading them waited and watched for a while. There was no movement that they could see.

The paths that led down from the city in the forest looked much like those on the other side. Forest encroached on either side, growing amongst ancient ruins. As they moved down, the land began to flatten out and the horizon was blocked by the forest. Yet as they moved, the spectre of Ultamar appeared before them continually between the trees. They wound their way down the main path, but it suddenly came to a halt and branched off into two narrow overgrown paths. They took the right path back towards the road. In places they had to skirt around trees and undergrowth that blocked the path, but after a while the path became clearer and it seemed as if it was used regularly. As they continued on, the smell of smoke on the air became more pungent. The ruins now disappeared behind them as they continued on.

"Hey! I know this place!" said an excited voice beside Hyrn.

Wren was looking all about.

"My village is near here. I know the way back to the road from here," he said triumphantly.

They followed the path for a while. It diverged at one point and they followed Wren's directions and before long they came upon a collection of small houses. The village was deserted. There was no sound of movement. They travelled slowly between the houses. In Hyrn's head, the feeling of being surrounded grew. It didn't feel threatening but watchful. He felt that there were eyes around them.

Hyrn withdrew Ilah from her nest and held her aloft. "Desultamar!" he cried and the Stone flashed in his hand.

An old woman stepped out from a doorway ahead of them and out onto the road. She looked at them and then she gasped and said, "Wren? Is that you?"

"Skileen," said Wren. "Yes, it is me."

"We thought you were dead," said Skileen. "Running off like that. We thought you had gone to Ultamar."

"That's exactly where he was going," said Jarta-Den. "And no doubt he would have if we hadn't come across him."

"It is a strange coincidence," continued the woman. But Harla interrupted her musings.

"What is happening?" Harla asked the old woman. "There is war?"

"Aye," said Skileen. "Ultamar has unleashed its army. Many troops headed west and we believe that many have gone east but the main force is at Forest Ford. All that can be spared have gone to defend our land against the Ultamarians. News is that the west has already arisen. So we are preparing our defence in the lands surrounding the fortress. The road to Ultamar is heavily guarded."

Wren interrupted impatiently. "Skileen. The Twin Stones and the Sword of Acclimoss have returned."

"We know," said Skileen. She turned to Jarta-Den. "Two of your fellow Quiglings are riding across the land spreading the story of their return and alerting us that Ultamar were about to attack. They ride Kragon."

"Kragon?" said Jarta-Den incredulously. "How did they manage to capture Kragon?"

"They had the aid of another rider. This one is riding a horse too, though not a Kragon. He has been asking about a young man accompanied by a party of strangers, along with Quiglings, Priests and an Anasarian boy, called Wren. The Quiglings had heard this was where Wren was from, so they suggested he try here. That was the coincidence, because here you are."

"They've heard of me?" said Wren with wonder.

Hyrn smiled at this, but one thought leapt into his mind.

"Where is this rider?" he asked.

"Asleep," said Skileen. "He is injured and exhausted. I have done what I can to ease his pain but he needs rest."

"Where is he, and where is his horse?" asked Hyrn.

Hyrn looked around and noticed there were other people who had emerged from hiding. From amongst them a large horse trotted and moved quickly towards them.

"Erras!" yelled Hyrn.

He dashed forward and the horse stopped before him. He reached up and threw his arms around the horse's neck.

"Are you alright, Erras?" asked Hyrn. "Where is Careil?"

The horse snorted softly and then pushed at Hyrn. Hyrn moved and the horse turned and walked forward and on through the crowd. Those gathered murmured softly but excitedly. Hyrn realised that he still held Ilah in his hand. Erras halted in front of a doorway. Hyrn walked forward and hugged the horses's neck. Wren came up behind Hyrn, accompanied by the old woman, Skileen. She moved past them and opened the door and beckoned Hyrn to enter.

The room was small and some dim afternoon light came through a window. It took a moment for Hyrn's eyes to adjust. As they did, he saw that to one side a bed stood against the wall. There was a shape lying on the bed covered with a blanket. Hyrn walked over and saw the face of Careil nestled on a pillow. He slept, and Hyrn almost turned to leave him to his rest but suddenly Careil stirred and his eyes fluttered open.

"Hyrn," said Careil slowly. "Is it you, or is this just another dream."

"It's me," said Hyrn.

Careil's eyes widened and he looked intently at Hyrn. He made to rise and then groaned with pain. He reached out and grasped Hyrn's arm.

"Hyrn! Ultamar is sending out their troops!" said Careil, desperately. "Where is Rowan?"

A voice spoke in Hyrn's head and he repeated the words to Careil. "He is heading for Forest Ford with Ivah and the Sword. He is leading an army."

The bridge across the Trebian was longer and wider than the one that crossed the gorge further downriver. They had descended down the East Road into the river valley. The land was flatter here and heavily forested. The river was broad and moved more slowly before it plunged into the steep gorge to the south. The bridge was guarded by a small ragtag group of armed people. Anasarians accompanied by two Quiglings.

Rowan now led an army numbering in their hundreds. The guards at the bridge at first took up defensive positions, and then, realising that they were not being attacked by Ultamarians, set up a cheer. The army continued down to the bridge until they stood before the guards.

Someone further back behind Rowan called out. "Make way for the King."

Rowan cringed at this, but his only thoughts were of Hyrn and bringing the Stones together. Rowan raised his arm, and the people guarding the bridge moved aside, and he led the army through and onto the bridge. Carlan and Kerian rode either side of him, with Duburinga and Gorum just behind. Arienga was further back riding with Mielen. She watched Rowan ahead of her, as he led them over the bridge. She was not sure what was happening to him, but she had a sense of foreboding.

On the other side they were met by more defenders. One amongst them Rowan recognised, the Quigling, Herra-Yen.

"How did the attack on Kirenk go?" asked Kerian.

"We hold Kirenk," said Herra-Yen. "But troops from Ultamar are attempting to take the fort back. We will be glad of reinforcements."

He paused and then said, "How did your pursuit go?" and then he looked at those gathered before him and said, "Where is Biren-So?"

Dooren-Ga spoke up. He had moved forward to greet his fellow Quiglings. "He is badly wounded. He is with a healer."

Rowan answered his other question. "We have Ivah, and Ilah is heading to meet us."

Careil sat on the edge of the bed.

"You can't come with us," said Hyrn. "You are hurt."

"I must," said Careil. "I have to make sure that you and Rowan fulfil your quest and that I can get you safely home again."

Home. Hyrn hadn't thought about returning home for ages. The thought seemed distant and unreal. After all they had been through, the idea of the peaceful comfort of his home seemed to belong to a different world.

"If you don't get better you won't be able to take us home," said Hyrn.

"I can't let you go without me," said Careil determinedly. "I will not let you out of my sight again. We need to go and find Rowan."

They headed southwards towards the road through thick forest, following paths that wound and zigzagged between the trees. The ground rose steadily as they moved on and then levelled out. They came to a place where the path they were on petered out into an area of brush and undergrowth. Harla had been scouting ahead with Gebarana, and returned to report that the road was not too far ahead. They pushed their way through the low vegetation that crowded beneath the trees that verged the road. Eventually they came out onto the wide way that led towards Forest Ford and onwards to the gates of Ultamar. The road that led from Herardin met this road back down the road to the west. This was the West Road, and behind them it continued westwards to the crossroad and then climbed up to the Pass of Exile. The sun was starting to set, and its glow lit the underside of clouds that were starting to move in from the southeast. They set off down the road with Droom and Jarta-Den scouting ahead.

The two riders were soon out of sight beyond a crest in the road, while Harla and Gebarana scouted ahead on foot. Careil rode slowly alongside Hyrn and Wren with Garan close behind and Yarga, Infiron and Drivian following. Margana and Turum were to the rear keeping a watch behind them. They travelled easily down the well travelled road as the light grew dimmer.

After a while Droom and Jarta-Den rode back into sight. They came up the road quickly and stopped before the party. Far up the road from where the two riders had come the figures of Harla and Gebarana appeared and jogged back towards them.

Droom waited for the two Caramar to arrive and then spoke. "The road leads downwards in a great sweep where the forest leads down towards the river. There is a great castle there."

"It is the fortress of Forest Ford that guards the approaches to Ultamar, just below where this road meets the Detrian Road from the north, the Coast Road from the south, and the Plains Road from the east near where it crosses the shallows of the Trebian river," said Jarta-Den. "The Causeway Road then leads eastwards through the fortress and climbs up to the gates of Ultamar."

Droom continued, "It is difficult to gauge the situation from this distance. There is much smoke futher to the east and south."

"That's where Rowan is," said Hyrn looking southwards into the forest.

"It will be dark soon," said Harla. "I suggest that we get some rest. We have no hope of attacking the fortress in darkness, especially tired and hungry. The new light of day will help us to better assess our options."

It was moving from afternoon towards evening, as the army following Rowan approached Fort Kirenk up the Coast Road. The westering sun was beginning to peek under the clouds that blanketed the sky above them. The forest was thick all around them. The opposite side of the river was also heavily forested, where a steep rocky bank plunged into the river. They could see no sign of the Ultamarian army on the opposite bank, but they could hear the muted babble of an encampment beyond. The Ultamarians were preparing to assault the fortress guarding the river. As they neared Kirenk, people began to emerge from the forest around them; Anasarians, and a scattering of Quiglings, all preparing to defend the line of the river. They hailed the army as it marched through, and they marvelled at the young man who led them carrying the Sword of Acclimoss openly and, if the rumours were true, one of the Twin Stones. A throng of people, their faces glowing in the light of the setting sun, formed a guard of honour along the sides of the road. The gates of the fort stood before them but they halted.

An Anasarian man dashed out of the ranks. "Mielen!" he shouted. "What are you doing here?"

Seated behind Arienga, the Anasarian girl looked sheepish and a little embarrassed.

"Father," she said desperately. "I was just… I…I nearly shot the King!"

The man looked bewilderedly at his daughter. He tried to speak but Mielen jumped down from behind Arienga and rushed to embrace him.

"Father, don't be angry," she implored. "I have been riding with the King. They invited me to join them."

The man hugged his daughter, and then said sternly, and with finality, "You will now stay close to me."

Fort Kirenk was a massive block of black stone that straddled the river with a road passing beneath. At each end were two stout towers with wide walls spanning the bridge, and large gates guarding the road. A Quigling came out from the gates to meet them. He was accompanied by a tall broad Anasarian, and Rowan saw as they approached that it was the innkeeper Gerardien.

"We meet again," said Gerardien. "Well, you have certainly stirred up a hornet's nest."

Rowan began to object but the Quigling beside Gerardien said, "The Ultamarians are staying out of range of sling and arrow. We have archers stationed in the towers at the other side. We have been carrying stones up into the towers and there are Anasarians with slingshots aiding the archers. There are also many fighters holding the gates but we are too few to attack the numbers arrayed against us."

Gerardien then spoke. "We have received word that our forces are moving in from the northwest. We have had no word from the people of the plains apart from those that were able to move down the East Road and make it here before the Ultamarians blocked the roads. We know that there were rebels coming from the Detrian Road to the north. From the West Road we have heard little beyond the road to Herardin. There have been reports of Quiglings riding Kragon rousing the people around Ultamar. That is where the signal fires to rouse us all to war were first lit. They were also rumoured to have been heading east towards the Plains Road. Since then there has been no word from them."

Rowan's head spun with questions but Duburinga spoke from where he had come to stand beside him.

"We need to prepare for war," said the Caramar warrior bluntly. "Battle is preparing before us. Everything seems to be moving towards the road to Ultamar. We need to gather our strength. Dawn will be here quickly enough, and that is when we need to be ready to put forth a unified attack."

His mind sought that of Harla's and he felt her strength moving towards Ultamar.

Rowan sat propped against a stone wall. Night had descended and he and the members of the quest were preparing to sleep within the fort and await the dawn. Carlan sat against the opposite wall of the small stone room. The Artoran, Carak had been locked in a room at the base of the southwestern tower. Bardewan sat down next to Rowan.

Rowan looked at him and the young, but ancient, Abessairian looked back and then said earnestly.

"I served the King of Anasaria when we were at the height of our power. You don't believe that you are a king but the people gathering here believe that the King has returned. You must do what you feel is right, but I feel that you have something in you."

Rowan groaned inwardly, but in his mind he felt that sense of purpose driving him on.

"Thank you, Bardewan," he said. "I just want to do what we were asked to do."

"It is all that you need do," said Bardewan.

The Abessairian soldier rose to his feet and walked away. A figure walked by him coming towards Rowan. Rowan, although still troubled, smiled inwardly as Arienga sat down beside him.

"How are you, Rowan?" she asked.

Rowan looked at Arienga and sighed.

"I still don't know what I'm doing," he said. "Sometimes it feels as if it's not me doing things. And all around me there are people thinking that I am the King…but I can't be."

Arienga grasped Rowan's hand.

"Rowan," she said, "it doesn't matter. If that is what it takes for people to have hope, then that is a good thing. I am more concerned for you. We go into battle and you are putting yourself forward to lead an army."

She stopped and thought for a moment, and then looking directly at Rowan said, "Please promise me you won't do anything stupid."

Rowan began to protest but she continued, "Or at least promise me that I can ride at your side."

Rowan paused and then after a moment asked. "What does Duburinga say?"

"He wants me to look out for you," replied Arienga.

Rowan looked at the determined expression on her face and resignedly gave up all hope of protest.

Smiling tiredly, he asked. "Would it make any difference if I refused?"

"No," said Arienga.

CHAPTER TWENTY FOUR

The Battle of Forest Ford

The sky across Anasaria was blanketed by a thick layer of cloud. A cold breeze came from the south, carrying the hint of rain to come. The dawn light was muted and dismal, and those who rose to greet it, did so out of sheer hope and determination. Separated by an expanse of forest, two groups of Caramar and Underdwellers joined in a chorus that became almost a call for strength in the coming storm. Across what had now become the frontier of war, armies awoke and prepared to meet whatever fate awaited.

"Hyrn! Hyrn!"

He woke up suddenly, and opening his eyes, saw the face of Wren looking down at him. Hyrn had slept fitfully. The impending confrontation, and the restless stream of impatience from the Stone, had blurred his waking thoughts and troubled dreams. As dawn came closer, he had managed to fall into a deep sleep, until Wren had wrenched him from it. He almost cursed Wren out loud, but the look on the face of his friend was filled with hope, and, Hyrn thought, a trace of worry.

Hyrn looked around. The forest was dim and still full of shadows. Everyone was up. Even Careil was awake and eating sitting against a tree. Erras stood by Careil as if still unwilling to let him sneak off again. Hyrn threw off his blanket and climbed to his feet. He walked over to the Rider, with Wren in tow.

"How are you feeling, Careil?" asked Hyrn.

"I'm fine after a sleep," said Careil. "Infiron cleaned my wound with some of her balm and it is feeling a lot better."

The Rider looked up at the young Wesmerian.

"How about you, Hyrn?" he asked. "Are you ready? Things are getting serious. This is war and you are ill-equipped, as I fear we all are. We have too few numbers to attack the Ultamarians, and get you to Rowan."

"Maybe," said Hyrn. "But we have no choice. We need to find a way through to Forest Ford."

The army gathered on the darkened roadway of the bridge that passed beneath Kirenk. Rowan stood atop one of the towers. He was accompanied by Duburinga, Arienga, Kerian, Dooren-Ga and Gorum. Just behind them stood Carlan, ever alert to any danger to Rowan. As they looked out between the crenellations they beheld a grey, evil army forming up ready to attack. The army was large, but it was just a small part of the army amassed further up the road, beyond where it climbed over a ridge. The ridge before them sloped down eastwards towards the Trebian River and to their left rose westwards up in the direction of where the West Road came through the forest, where Hyrn was preparing to move off. From Kirenk the Coast Road climbed up over this ridge and led down towards where it met the junctions of the Detrian Road, Plains Road and West Road. There above, where the road led towards Ultamar, stood the castle that formed the outer defences of the approaches to the fortress, Forest Ford. It sat defiantly, watching over the roads and the river crossing.

The Anasarians who had retreated the previous day, as the Ultamarians advanced, and who were now gathered in Fort Kirenk, had reported that the army guarding Forest Ford was immense. Even with the strength they had gathered, they were outnumbered by the soldiers that assaulted Kirenk, and even if they managed to get through the besieging forces, they had little hope of making an impact on the vastly larger Ultamarian army beyond. A power seemed to emanate from the soldiers before Kirenk and beyond them there were flashes of blue light.

"They have Kragon," said Dooren-Ga. "They seem to be keeping them in reserve though."

"We must attack this force holding the road," said Duburinga. "If we have fighters moving in from the northwest we must create another front here."

"We must also hope that my comrades who went out towards the plains riding the Kragon are rousing the people there," said Dooren-Ga.

Suddenly there was a wall of rushing whistling noise. Rowan felt himself tackled to the ground by a large mass. There was the immediate sound of a rain of impacts, as arrows cascaded down upon them. There were cries as some of the defenders were hit. As Rowan lay on the ground against the turret wall, with Carlan hunched over him, he heard a grunt alongside them and saw a figure fall to the ground.

Rowan looked at the figure of Kerian pierced by two arrows lying bleeding and groaning in the grey light. The figure of Gorum stood to his right. He had not moved. Any arrows that had hit him had bounced off his armour. Rowan tried to look around but Carlan blocked his view. Where was Arienga?

"Ari—" he began.

"I'm right here Rowan near your feet," said Arienga. "Duburinga and Dooren-Ga are here too. Kerian has been hit."

"I know," said Rowan.

"Kerian!" he called to the prostrate figure just beyond him.

Kerian turned his head slowly and looked at Rowan glassily and then, with his last breath, wheezed, "Desultamaaar."

"The army is preparing to attack," said Duburinga. "We cannot stay trapped here. Our strength is useless if we do not use it."

"They have not reloaded," said Dooren-Ga. "Let us get down to the gate before any more arrows rain down."

"What about Kerian?" asked Rowan.

Carlan released Rowan and got to his knees. He looked upon the body of his fellow Abessairian.

"We will return for him, but his desire was clear," said Carlan, solemnly. "We go to free Anasaria and destroy the Dark Lords."

The road that ran through the heart of Kirenk and spanned the River Trian, was packed with an army. Behind them the gates were open, and more Anasarians and Quiglings could be seen massing on the southern bank. Rowan sat astride Arrow. The gates stood before him. Arienga and Carlan were mounted to either side of him, Arienga on his right and Carlan on his left. Duburinga was now mounted just beyond Arienga, and to Carlan's left was Dooren-Ga. Only one fighter was ahead of Rowan, Gorum, mounted on his hardy chariga.

Rowan looked about him. He took out Ivah and transferred the Stone to his left hand. With his right hand he reached up to his shoulder. He grasped the hilt of the Sword of Acclimoss and withdrew it from its sheath and held it high. He then raised the Stone of Angil. The Stone flashed and the blade of the Sword of Acclimoss flashed like a bright flame.

"Desultamar!" cried Rowan.

And all about him and from behind him, came the roar of many voices taking up the call to war. Before them a crack of light appeared as the gates were released. They swung open revealing the Ultamarian army gathered just beyond. As soon as the gates were fully opened, with a cry, Gorum launched himself forward and Rowan and the others followed, and they poured out of Kirenk like a swarm of angry wasps.

They moved determinedly up the road. Captain Droom and Jarta-Den again rode on ahead. The road steadily climbed upward towards a crest. After a while they saw that the road ahead passed through and over the top of the ridge in a long cutting ahead of them. The sloping walls of rock were crowned with tall trees. The tops of the trees moved in the wind that blew from the south. Hyrn heard the sound of the trees but then another sound reached his ears. At first he wasn't sure what it was but then a voice called out.

"Riders!" shouted Harla. "Into the trees!"

Fortunately, they had not yet reached the cutting, as they would have been trapped with nowhere to head. The party dispersed into the forest at either side of the road. Careil and Erras followed Hyrn and Wren as they were herded into the forest by Garan. Droom and Jarta-Den were still far ahead scouting the movements of the Ultamarian army. The sound of riders grew and it soon became apparent that it was a large force. The sound of many hooves echoed up the road and along the cutting ahead.

Hyrn peered out between the trees. He could only see slices of the road. Before long, as the sound grew, he saw riders flashing between trees as they drew close. The riders shone white and silver and bright with the sound of armour clanking. As the riders approached nearer to where they had left the road, one figure stood out clearly leading them. A figure in bright mail with a ringlet of silver crowning his head. The crown seemed out of place at first, but Hyrn recognised the figure. Without thinking, Hyrn burst through the trees and down to the road. Wren tried to restrain him and Garan was already leaping forward to move ahead of Hyrn.

The Abessairian relaxed with realisation, as Hyrn yelled, "King Darlam!"

The King of the Underdwellers brought his chariga to a quick halt and those behind him came to a cascading stop. Stretching back up the road was a phalanx of Abessairian soldiers, and armoured Underdwellers. Amongst them were Caramar riding an assortment of charigas and horses. Further back behind them was a horde of Anasarians riding a variety of horses, and carrying an assortment of weapons. More were following on foot further behind. Beside Darlam rode Captain Evlan, strong and proud, and cleansed of the stain of Ultamar.

They formed into a broad wedge as they moved towards the Ultamarians. Rowan had replaced Ivah under his shirt but the Sword was still in his hand. The Ultamarians who had been preparing an attack now took up defensive positions. The towers behind Rowan began to rain arrows and stones upon the evil army, and the Ultamarians answered with a barrage of arrows. Carlan rode across the front of Rowan and Arienga, as the arrows fell all around them. One glanced off of Carlan's breastplate and another was swatted from the air by Arienga as she wielded her short sword. The arrows had found their mark amongst the ranks of Anasarians. Gorum, heavily armoured, laughed in the face of the fusillade and led them all in a charge directly towards the enemy. Those mounted led the way, with fighters on foot running behind. Rowan brandished his sword and focussed on the path towards Forest Ford, and prepared to fight through to where Hyrn was heading.

The Ultamarians, in their pride and confidence in the Dark Lords, were not expecting such an onslaught. Highly trained warriors, Underdwellers, a bright and painful sword and a mass of the Anasarian worms angry, armed and in open revolt and defiance. And still from above stones and arrows rained down decimating those further back in their ranks. The anger and hatred from generations of subjection and oppression burst upon them, and their front ranks fell before the onslaught, as the rebels crashed into them. The sound was ghastly as weapons clashed, and bit, and smashed. From the rear of the Ultamarians a path opened out and blazes of blue light flashed towards them. Rowan was still surrounded by fighters. The charge had been slowed by the wall of Ultamarians. As the Kragon burst through towards them, Rowan let go of Arrow's reins and in an instant Ivah was in his hand bursting with white light.

The bright blue blurs of light seemed to suddenly freeze and become a handful of horses and their riders, suspended in mid flight as a soft white light poured upon them. The horses cried out and shook off the power that had been imprisoning them, and their riders became easy marks. The bows of the Caramar sang out, and others targeted the riders as the attackers drove a wedge deep into the heart of the Ultamarian soldiers. The Ultamarians, used to submission and fear from the Anasarians, were met with pent up fury and vengeful retaliation for countless years of suffering.

The ranks of the Ultamarians began to break up, and those behind, seeing their forward troops being slaughtered, broke into open retreat. The fighting continued as the Ultamarians who remained battled on, now fighting for their lives. Fighters from each side fell wounded and dying. Yells, and screams, and moans, filled the air. Rowan watched as Gorum hacked at any Ultamarian within reach of his sword. As the Underdweller confronted a tall

Ultamarian, Rowan saw another Ultamarian rushing towards Gorum from the side. Rowan spurred Arrow forward and the Sword of Acclimoss arced out catching the soldier in the side of the head and he crashed into the flank of Gorum's chariga and slumped to the ground. Gorum, momentarily distracted, was struck by the sword of the Ultamarian. The blow glanced off his breastplate and he turned and drove his sword under the raised arm, into the chest of his attacker.

The Ultamarians were now routed, and those further back were fleeing up the road and over the ridge. The fighting continued as pockets of Ultamarians still resisted. Many Ultamarians had been confounded by the light of Ivah but others, still driven by the power of the Dark Lords, battled on. Others, trapped now by the mass of fighters, fought for their lives. Some of those that were encircled threw down their arms and surrendered. These Ultamarians were taken prisoner by Anasarians and marched back to Kirenk to be thrown into cells. After a few more desperate skirmishes the battle was over and the approaches to Kirenk became quiet, apart from the groaning of the wounded and dying, and the sound of the wind in the trees.

Rowan sat astride Arrow, still surrounded by those who guarded him. He surveyed the scene and looked up at the Ultamarians fleeing over the ridge. He looked around at the people gathered there and saw that around him people were looking at him expectantly. He raised his sword tiredly, and a cheer went up.

"Gather your strength," he called. "We march on Ultamar!"

The ragtag army cheered again, but Rowan took in the sight of those who were wounded. He thought of Ivah and the hope of being able to heal them all.

"It is not in my power," said a voice in his head. "We must go on."

Rowan was momentarily puzzled by the sound of the voice in his head, but he drew himself up.

"Some must stay and tend the wounded," he said loudly. "The rest of us must continue to march. The strength of Ultamar still lies ahead. All those willing must be ready to fight again soon."

There was a momentary pause and then a voice just behind him, a defiant voice cried. "Desultamar!"

The call was taken up all around, in the face of what lay ahead.

Grengal sat astride his horse with his bloody sword raised. Dooren-Ga moved his horse towards him.

"You have killed, Grengal?" he asked.

"Yes," said Grengal quietly.

"Whom did you kill?" asked Dooren-Ga.

"I do not know but he fought with skill and with such hatred, that I was almost daunted," said Grengal.

"Ah," said Dooren-Ga thoughtfully and then continued. "You are now a Quigling soldier and know the reality of wielding death. I name you Grenga-Da."

Grenga-Da did not smile or rejoice. The look on his face was grim and resigned. He now understood what it meant to take a life, and he accepted his part in the war against evil with bitter determination.

"Thank you Dooren-Ga," he said, and then he looked ahead to where Rowan held his sword, calling them to war.

Rowan raised his hand to the Quigling soldier in acknowledgement, and then the stark reality of what lay all around hit him.

The Wesmerian farm boy looked around as if waking from a dream. People were suffering and people were preparing to fight again. He looked at Arienga and she met his gaze. She gave him a weary, but reassuring, smile. He was surrounded by warriors and trained soldiers. The last two days had been a blur. He had been ill and they had ridden hard and he had gathered an army but it felt like a dream. That he wasn't himself. That he was just….

It had started when he got the Stone. When he thought of Ivah now tucked inside his shirt, he suddenly felt reassured and comforted again.

"Wesmere is far behind you," said the voice in his head. "Abessair lies ahead."

"Yes," he thought. "We must move."

He looked at Arienga and she looked back at him calmly. The Caramar warrior kept her face stoic, but her eyes looked intently at Rowan, full of worry and concern.

The army formed up behind Gorum. Around them, some of their number tended to the wounded and collected the dead. The prisoners had been escorted back to Kirenk, and the archers now came out from the fort to join the army. Many of the Anasarians who stood ready to march carried the weapons of the Ultamarians. They now brandished the swords of Abessair. Scouts had gone ahead, Boriega, Terrana and Jorunum amongst them.

Rowan felt nervous despite his sense of purpose. Fear and determination battled in his head. He tried to shake it off; to think clearly, but his thoughts still felt foggy. He thought perhaps he was still ill, but he heard himself calling for the army to march forward.

And the Sword of Acclimoss was in his hand.

Hyrn now rode with Wren behind him. Horses had been commandeered to carry the members of the quest. Ahead of them, leading the battalion at a canter, rode King Darlam, and to his left rode Captain Droom. On his right rode Jarta-Den. They were flanked on either side by a guard of Abessairian and Underdweller soldiers. To either side of the two boys rode Garan and Captain Evlan guarding the Stonebearer. Careil rode Erras doggedly behind Hyrn, and behind him rode Yarga, Infiron, and Drivian. Around them, and ranked to the rear, rode Abessairians and Underdwellers distinguishable by their different mounts and garb. Hyrn glanced back and observed the procession of fighters, trained and untrained, marching towards the enemy. He felt within him the pull of the Stone, and felt Rowan still distant, but nearer. But it didn't quite feel like the Rowan he knew.

The ridge was heavily forested. On the flank of the ridge that plunged down to the river behind them, the trees and undergrowth were dense and impenetrable. The road ran like a scar as it disappeared over the crest of the ridge ahead of them. A break in the treeline over the ridge above marked where the road passed further on. They came across an escaping Ultamarian wounded and weary. Gorum paused and looked back. Rowan felt the need to speak but Duburinga spoke from his right.

"Take his weapon and bind him," said the Caramar. "We must not fall into the ways of the enemy."

They came upon more Ultamarians as they rode up the steep slope, and each time the course was clear. Some of the soldiers fought back fiercely as they were surrounded and restrained. They cursed as the army left them behind, bound and helpless. As the vanguard of the army moved over the crest, they saw that further ahead the ridge climbed higher and the road continued on. From the forests on either side, more Anasarians joined them from their defensive positions amongst the trees. The time for defence was over. They went to war.

They looked out through the forest where the road led down from the ridge. Beyond, looming ever closer, stood the fortress of Ultamar. Beneath them the forest petered out and they could see the towers of Forest Ford. The junction where the roads met before the castle was shrouded by a grey swarming mass. Only the passage of the river cut a swathe through the mass. There swarmed the army of Ultamar, a bastion before the approaches to the dark fortress above, marshalling and preparing to destroy all that defied their Lords.

Rowan and the vanguard waited as the troops on foot behind them came up to assemble, ready for a desperate and dangerous assault upon the evil wall that stood before them.

Hyrn felt a sense of danger grow within him as they passed a crest in the road. They could now see where it stretched out eastwards towards Ultamar. Their scouts came down from where the ridge climbed northwards, led by Harla and Turum. Others appeared out of the forest to the south, led by Gebarana and Margana. The scouting parties were bolstered now by the Caramar and Rangers that had come from the west with King Darlam. Those from the south reported that there was no clear approach to Forest Ford apart from the road which was still heavily defended. Those from the north had more heartening news. To the north there was the smoke of battle and the Ultamarians were retreating southwards back towards the road.

Jarta-Den spoke. "Our forces from Herardin and the old road must be mounting a defence through the forest and along the Detrian Road. The Ultamarians are being hemmed in but their numbers are vast and the road is heavily garrisoned."

Gebarana then reported. "Southwards the forest is thick and the ridge falls away steeply but there are Ultamarians retreating along the Coast Road. Something is driving them back but we cannot get through that way."

"Our path lies down the road," said Harla. She looked back through the ranks, ignoring the mounted soldiers, to where Yarga sat mounted upon a sturdy plough horse.

"What do you counsel, Elder?" she called.

Yarga rode forward past Hyrn and halted beside King Darlam.

"Harla, you have my support in this," he said. "I fear that my counsel fails in this time of war. One path is clear to me. The Stones are moving towards each other and I sense that the other Stone has been used in battle. We need to do what we can to bring the two Stones together."

Rowan felt the palpable tidal wave of anger and anticipation building around him and behind him. Before him, he felt an obdurate wall of hatred. Boriega and Jorunum had returned from where the ridge led eastwards towards the river.

"There is much commotion to the east," said Boriega. "The Ultamarians on that flank are moving off to the southeast beyond the ford."

Rowan considered this news but the strategy of war eluded him. All he could feel was the need to drive on. He looked about him at the warriors and soldiers.

"What should we do?" he asked.

"We attack the castle," said Duburinga. "The castle is the key to the defences of the fortress and this army stands between you and Hyrn."

Rowan thought of Hyrn and he felt his little brother's thought reaching out to him.

'We are coming, Rowan and we have an army behind us but there is a large force blocking the road.'

"We ride," said Rowan. "We need to draw the army away from the West Road. We need to give Hyrn a way through."

Gorum ahead of Rowan laughed harshly.

"We ride!" he bellowed.

Rowan turned Arrow about and faced the ranks of fighters behind him. They became quiet and Rowan felt the weight of their expectation and he almost wilted as they all turned to listen to him, but something within bolstered him, and his voice spoke.

"People of Anasaria. Your fate lies ahead of you," he said unfalteringly. "We go to war. The yoke of Ultamar is upon you, but now is the time for us to break that yoke. The Dark Lords will pay." He pointed at the dark fortress brooding atop its vast pedestal of rock. "Abessair will be free. The moment has come when centuries of pain will end. The Twin Stones must be reunited."

The army drew themselves up and he cried out, "Will you follow me?"

The roar of many voices assaulted him.

They shouted, "Yes!" Yes!" and, "The King! The King!" and then the cry of defiance, "Desultamar!"

Rowan felt sick. He wasn't ready for this. But he turned his horse back around and faced forward towards the evil army beneath them.

He drew his sword and called. "We ride to war!"

He and those around him urged their horses forward, with Gorum leading the charge again. And like an avalanche the army swept down the road, and from the surrounding hillsides, towards the waiting army.

As they rode, the Ultamarian army grew before them and became not an undifferentiated mass, but rank upon rank of individual soldiers. Rowan's heart was in his mouth.

"What am I doing?" he thought desperately.

They were preparing to assault a massive army, and despite their now considerable numbers, they were still well outnumbered. His eyes lifted. The trees began to thin out as they neared the bottom of the ridge and he looked ahead to the right and his heart was bolstered. The Ultamarians were under attack from the East. The people of the Eastern plains had been marshalled and were joining the fight.

Before him Gorum drew his great sword. From behind arrows began to shower the Ultamarian ranks. Answering swarms of arrows came from the Ultamarians but he ignored these as they passed over his head. He glanced quickly at Arienga riding beside him. The look on her face was fierce and intense. She looked at him quickly and nodded defiantly.

And then they careered into the front ranks of the Ultamarians. As the two forces collided, the noise was horrendous.

Ultamarian soldiers were massed on the West Road as it led down from the ridge and continued unerringly on towards Forest Ford. They waited, daring any of the rebel scum to approach. They were secure and confident in their might, and in the depth of their worship of the Dark Lords and the power of Ultamar. The sight that met their eyes was at first like a mirage. Uncertainty and disbelief filled them as the vision became clear. A large army marched before them. Amongst the gathered Ultamarian soldiers something about some of the approaching army pierced at their very being. Abessairians. But they were something else. Something from long ago. Just vague memories of a past that no longer existed.

The cry went up from the approaching army. That accursed rebel cry. Consternation grew in the Ultamarian ranks as they prepared to take up defensive positions. The attacking army swept down the road, fierce and determined. And then they were upon them and the Ultamarians fought for their lives, and for the glory of Ultamar.

Hyrn was cosseted amongst armoured fighters. Beside him the figure of Garan rode. The Abessairian did not attack the Ultamarians but held a defensive position beside Hyrn and Wren. Careil had moved up on the other side, his sword drawn. Evlan had moved forward to where Darlam, Droom and Jarta-Den led the offensive. The rest of their force poured relentlessly forward sweeping Hyrn, and those that protected him, along with them until they were an island in the midst of a seething sea of violence and noise. The anger of the Underdwellers, avenging centuries of assault, the lethal skill of the Caramar, the determination of the Abessairians, atoning for the evil they had performed, and the pent up fury of the Anasarians, drove them on, and the force that guarded the road broke before them. Behind Hyrn, amidst the relentless sound of battle, there came a chanting. He turned and saw Yarga clutching the crystal at his throat flanked by the two Priests. Their chanting felt like a shield surrounding them.

Hyrn felt like reaching in and retrieving Ilah to aid them but a familiar voice in his head said calmly, "Not yet."

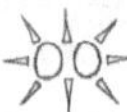

It was utter chaos. Rowan swung his sword at any Ultamarians that came near, but he was mostly surrounded by those that sought to protect him. As they broke through the forward ranks of the army, he saw ahead a mounted column moving towards him. At their head rode a tall, heavily-built Ultamarian. He had the power of command, and he drove his troops straight towards where Rowan was. Rowan did not pause to think. He tightened his grip on the Sword of Acclimoss and spurred Arrow forward, directly towards where General Gardwan led his elite troops to wipe out the heart of the treacherous resistance.

"Rowan! No!" cried out Arienga.

She urged her horse forward, but Carlan was already ahead of her, in pursuit of Rowan as he raced towards the Ultamarian General.

They pushed through the soldiers that were massed on the road, intent on just moving forward. Hyrn heard the sound of fighting all around him, but he was well protected. The Ultamarian soldiers guarding the road were not great in numbers. Their strength had been drawn off to the north to confront the mass of rebels that attacked their flank through the Forest of Evelar. Hyrn felt the fighting lessening as they passed through the ranks. The road opened out before them, and then further down he could see, surrounding Forest Ford, the main body of the army. The road ahead leading to the castle passed through the ranks of Ultamarians. He then felt a sudden dread. Rowan! He looked out to where there was commotion amongst the gathered army.

'Rowan! No!' The thought echoed in his head and he saw that the ranked army ahead was starting to flow southwards towards where they were coming under attack. The road was starting to become less heavily guarded. Then as the rebel army started to amass around him and behind him, Hyrn heard the voice of King Darlam booming out.

"Their forward scouts have seen us. They are aware of us," called out the King of the Underdwellers. "Now is the time! We must ride hard to Forest Ford!"

Hyrn pointed to the right to where a large mass of the Ultamarian army were converging and yelled desperately, "Over there! We need to go over there! Rowan is there!"

Darlam had turned his head and looked at Hyrn, and then out to where he was pointing. The road levelled out ahead to where the evil army waited. The trees gave way to an open swathe of land that separated the West Road and the Coast Road. The King took in the lay of the land and then turned and led them to the southeast, calling out in a voice that echoed out across the following army.

The reply came, loud and defiant. "Desultamar!"

Rowan approached the dark General at a gallop. Arrow, beneath him, did not baulk but carried him forward directly towards the column of soldiers. Carlan managed to catch up to Arrow's hindquarters and pushed forward to get alongside Rowan. Arienga was driving her horse on, desperately trying to reach Rowan. Behind them, other members of the quest were trying to fight their way towards where the Wesmerian boy rode unerringly towards the General. Gorum rode through a pack of soldiers swinging his sword wildly. Charen-Ba had swung his horse around at Arienga's cry. An Ultamarian lance pierced his body. Duburinga rode from Arienga's right, converging on where Rowan and Gardwan closed on each other. There were Caramar warriors on foot behind running to follow, beating down enemies as they went.

Rowan was oblivious to all this, and didn't see the cruel blow that hacked Boriega to the ground. His sword was raised and as the General loomed before him he swung it in an arc from left to right and with a resounding clang he met the sword of the Ultamarian. Gardwan's sword was knocked sideways. Rowan reined Arrow around, and slashed Acclimoss upwards to his left. He had moved too far though, and the tip of the sword clanked off the General's breastplate and slashed his chin. Gardwan's sword swung up from Rowan's right towards him, but an arrow lodged in the General's shoulder and the blow went astray.

As Rowan had turned his horse to attack Gardewan, Carlan had been pushed sideways towards the troops following the General. They confronted the Abessairian but Carlan hacked his way through them, desperate to get between Gardwan and Rowan. Gardwan ignored the arrow in his shoulder and turned back towards his attacker. Another arrow hit him but bounced off his breastplate. Only two more soldiers stood between Carlan and Rowan and he struck one down savagely. As Carlan began to prepare his next strike a sword was driven upwards into his throat and he let out a strangled, gurgling cry.

Rowan turned with horror as the Abessairian began to topple from his horse and the Ultamarian General's sword drove through his side in a searing, terrifying scream of pain. Beside him now, Arienga cried out in anguish and fury, and standing tall in her stirrups, she crashed into the General and drove her short sword into his neck and then withdrew it and instantly slashed back slicing a savage gash through his throat.

Gorum and Dooren-Ga and other members of the Quest were now fiercely attacking the rest of the General's guard, driving them back, away from where Rowan still sat astride Arrow. He had slumped forward in pain and Acclimoss now hung limply in his hand. Arienga leapt down from her horse. She let go of her sword and it fell to the ground. Rowan collapsed sideways from his saddle and Arienga caught him as he fell, a sob bursting from the warrior as she lowered him to the ground. She knelt and cradled his head on her lap. He looked up at her and his face was puzzled and he seemed to be searching her eyes for an answer to a painful question.

"Rowan," she moaned.

She looked around frantically.

"He needs a healer!" she shouted tearfully.

She looked down at Rowan and saw the pain on his face. She could see that his clothes were soaked with blood.

"Rowan? Why did you…" she began but she couldn't finish.

Rowan's mind swam with pain and he felt the Stone against his chest. He tried to speak but his mouth tasted like iron.

He wanted to tell Arienga to take the Stone but it cried out in his mind, "I cannot heal you. It is beyond my power."

Rowan's eyes fluttered but he opened them with effort and looked up into Arienga's eyes. He tried to speak but felt like he was drowning and his eyes felt heavy as he seemed to float away.

"Rowan! Rowan!" cried Arienga.

She saw his eyes becoming glazed and with deep sadness in her voice, said, "I love you too, Rowan."

His eyes flickered open, and a slight smile came to his bloodied mouth, but there was no strength left in him to reply, and he went into blackness.

The front ranks of the Ultamarian army were being driven back and the Anasarian army were now all around them as King Darlam drove the army from the West Road directly towards the thickest of the fighting. The two forces carrying the Twin Stones were now united on the southern front. Other rebels pushed in from the east and the north and west. The Ultamarians were finally hemmed in, and being pushed back towards Forest Ford.

Only one thought was in Hyrn's head and it screamed out, blocking everything else. 'Rowan!'

He could feel Rowan ahead but the feeling was one of pain. The Stone of Angil drove him forward as he felt the other Stone emanating alarm and despair. There was a throng of Anasarians gathered ahead and he saw the garb of Caramar warriors standing amongst them. There were wails and cries of sorrow and disbelief. Beyond, the battle raged with a great clamour.

Hyrn stopped and climbed quickly down from his horse. Wren dismounted behind him. Hyrn walked in a trance towards the backs of the people gathered. He felt numb. In his mind there was a keening that filled him with fear, but somewhere amongst it there was a sense of anticipation. He pushed his way between the people. Duburinga greeted him with concern in his voice, but Hyrn barely noticed. He moved past the front ranks of the crowd and came upon a circle of trampled grass surrounded by a sea of faces looking down at a sight that sent a flash of ice through his body.

Rowan lay covered in blood. Arienga knelt with Rowan's head on her lap, and she was crying. Hyrn's heart leapt into his throat, and he felt the world swirling around him as he tried to move forward. Careil had moved past Wren and had come up behind Hyrn without him noticing. He made to hold him back, but Hyrn shook him off, and stumbled forward and fell to his knees beside Rowan. He looked at Arienga searchingly but there was only despair in her eyes. Then he looked down at the lifeless face of his brother.

"Rowan!" he cried with despair.

He moved closer and grasped his brother's shoulder. He leaned down toward him and looked at his face. Rowan's eyes were half open but there was no life there.

"Ivah!" called a voice in his head.

He almost felt like screaming, "What about my brother? What are you going to do for him?"

There was a fierce compulsion upon him though. He looked down at

Rowan's bloody clothing and saw the shape of the Stone there. He, carefully, but unthinkingly, reached inside Rowan's tunic, and he felt the heat of the Stone. He grasped the hard mass and withdrew it. Ivah glowed slightly. He felt the desperate plea of Ilah to be free. He moved Ivah to his left hand and then, with his right, reached inside his vest and withdrew the other Stone.

The effect was immediate and cataclysmic.

A devastating blast of dazzling white light erupted out in a swiftly expanding circle. The ring of people gathered around Rowan were thrown off their feet as the wave of power burst out across the battlefield.

Hyrn felt a roaring in his ears and his eyes were filled with blinding light. He sensed Arienga still kneeling beside him supporting Rowan's head and felt Rowan lying there, unmoving. He looked at his hands. He could almost sense the shape of the Stones as he held them. He tried to look down at Rowan but could just see a formless shape. The sound of the Stones' voices cascaded through his mind. They were speaking to each other but he could not tell what they were saying. He ignored them and concentrated on the body of his brother.

His mind suddenly filled with the vision of a stone cottage, and a dying Caramar warrior lying on a bed. The shape in his right hand burst with a green light. The light shot downwards, and Hyrn could see that it was pouring from Ilah into Rowan's chest. The shape of Rowan's body shone green before him. The intense green light continued to stream into Rowan but it gradually seemed to falter.

Hyrn began to feel dizzy. The stream of green light began to flicker, but, with a sudden burst of intensity, the Stone in his left hand, Ivah, shot a bolt of white light into Ilah, followed by an unrelenting flow. The stream of green light gained in intensity until it became a roaring waterfall and Hyrn felt himself being drawn towards the edge until, unable to fight against it, he was sucked down and fell into the abyss below.

He came awake as if from a deep sleep. He was lying in soft grass. The sky that had been dark with cloud, was now blue and the sun shone down upon him. He wondered what had happened and then he smelt a familiar smell of flowers, and the buzz of insects came to his ears. This was like…

He leapt to his feet.

The meadow stretched out all around him. He turned his head and saw the line of dark forest at the edge of the meadow. His heart leapt. Over towards the forest, a familiar figure was walking. But the figure was walking away from him, heading for the forest. Hyrn sensed something dark and dangerous waiting in the eaves of the forest. They were not calling his name this time. They were calling Rowan. He stood momentarily transfixed as he saw that Rowan was striding onwards. In his raised and outstretched hand was the Sword of Acclimoss.

"Rowaaaan!" screamed Hyrn. "No! Come back!"

As Rowan continued doggedly on, Hyrn had already broken into a run. As he ran he felt his feet lifting off the ground and he again began to feel as if he was floating. A steely determination filled him, and defiantly he drove himself towards Rowan, and his feet hit the ground and he ran on.

As he grew closer to Rowan, he called out his name. Rowan didn't turn, but just kept moving towards the trees.

Hyrn reached him and called again loudly, "Rowan!"

He grasped Rowan's shoulder and tried to make him stop. Rowan strode on but glanced at Hyrn. His face was full of anger and his eyes burned with something that filled Hyrn with dread. Hyrn lost his grip but he would not be cowed.

He shouted directly at Rowan, "You cannot fight them, Rowan!"

He grabbed at his brother's shoulder and tried to wrench him around. Rowan stopped suddenly and Hyrn came to a halt. Rowan turned sharply and faced his brother. His sword was still raised in his right hand. His face seethed with anger and Hyrn thought for a moment that Rowan was going to strike him. But Rowan's face contorted with pain and his eyes were filled with bewilderment and he lowered his sword.

"Rowan," said Hyrn quietly amidst the soft sound of the meadow.

The darkness at the edge of the forest echoed him.

"Rowan! Rowan!" they called in their harsh voices.

Hyrn sensed that behind Rowan, dark shapes were beginning to move from the forest's edge towards them.

"Come on, Row," said Hyrn calmly. "Let's get away from here. Come on back. There's a lot of people waiting for you."

Rowan made as if to speak but his voice was just a guttural growl. He turned and looked back towards the forest and his face lit up with determination. He turned away from Hyrn and raised his sword again.

Hyrn caught Rowan's sleeve and said firmly. "Rowan, you cannot defeat this enemy. Now is not the time. It will always be waiting. You need to come back."

Hyrn pointed back towards where he had come from, and out the corner of his eye saw a shining light. He turned around fully and saw, atop a hill, a gleaming tower. Crowning the tower was a star of white light.

"Rowan, Rowan, look," said Hyrn with wonder, turning back towards Rowan.

The light washed over the two of them and the darkness of the forest seemed to be driven back.

"Rowan," called Hyrn desperately.

Rowan turned from where he stood and his face was filled with confusion. Hyrn pointed back towards the bright light and Rowan raised his head towards it.

"Look," said Hyrn again, and then smiling at Rowan continued. "Come on! Let's go!"

Rowan's face was bathed in the light, and the hint of a pained smile crossed his face.

"Hyrn?" said Rowan hoarsely.

Hyrn grabbed his brother's arm and pulled him towards the tower on the hill. Hyrn strode forward and felt Rowan following him. The burning star atop the tower filled his vision with light and he felt himself disappearing into it, with Rowan close behind.

CHAPTER TWENTY FIVE

Desultamar

Hyrn looked up from where he knelt beside Rowan, and tried to adjust his sight after the brightness of the blinding light. He turned to his left and saw the still kneeling figure of Arienga. As her face came into focus, she looked at Hyrn with a panicked expression. Hyrn looked back at her and then they both looked at Rowan.

Rowan spasmed slightly and then coughed painfully. He then turned his head and spat out a mouthful of dark blood and spittle. He looked up at Hyrn.

"What happened?" he asked hoarsely.

"You were…" Hyrn faltered. "I thought you were…"

But Arienga burst out, "Rowan, I thought you were dead."

He looked up from where his head lay in the Caramar warrior's lap.

"Arienga?" he asked. "What happened?" and then as if remembering something said, "Oh, yes. The battle…"

Arienga looked down at him and, with a note of fury in her voice, said, "What did I say to you about doing anything stupid?"

"I… I…." began Rowan.

He couldn't think of anything to say and then he remembered what Arienga had said to him before his wound had taken him. The look on Arienga's face told him that this was not the time to remind her of that.

"…Ummm? Not to?" he said finally.

Despite everything, Hyrn smiled at this. He then looked around. His vision had cleared. The Stones were still in his hands, but they were dark now. All about, figures were getting to their feet. He then noticed that the sounds of battle had disappeared. There was still much movement and noise about him though. Wren came up behind him, with Careil alongside.

"What was that?" asked Wren dazedly.

"I don't know," said Hyrn hesitantly. "The Stones healed him I think, and…"

"The Ultamarians," said Careil. "Look!"

Hyrn looked around and was filled with wonder and relief. Anasarians, Quiglings, and Abessairians in their thousands, were standing all around as far as Hyrn could see.

"We did it, I think, Row," said Hyrn.

Rowan looked up at his brother.

"We did, but you saved me," he said.

"It was the Stones," said Hyrn.

Rowan reached out and grabbed Hyrn's arm.

"You brought me back," he said. "I would have kept going."

Rowan paused and winced with pain.

"You would have missed all this," said Hyrn pointing all around, and then added seriously, "I couldn't let you go."

Arienga looked between the boys with a look of confusion on her face but did not speak. Rowan pulled himself up to a sitting position. Arienga released her hold on him but still looked at him with uncertainty and concern.

As Rowan sat up, he was buffeted by the sound of voices nearby, and soon all those around were joining in.

"The King lives! The King lives!" The cry went up.

Rowan looked wearily at Hyrn.

"Why do they think I'm the King," he said. "I can't be. It doesn't make sense. How could it even be possible? Even if somehow we were related to the Kings of Anasaria, surely we would know about it."

"Also," said Hyrn, "as he is still alive, that would make our father the King, and knowing Pa that doesn't seem likely."

"And as my brother wouldn't that make you a prince or something?" asked Rowan wildly.

Hyrn frowned at Rowan questioningly but had no answer.

Whether they spoke out loud or in their heads, Hyrn and Rowan heard the voices of the Twin Stones speaking together in a strange echoing harmony.

"The two of you are brothers," said Ivah and Ilah in unison, "but not by birth. Meralie and Baraman were not your birth parents, Rowan. You were brought to them as a baby, and left with them, and became their son. Hyrn was born when you were still young and you have been brothers since that day. An old woman carried you to the Fairbrow farm. Both of your parents were dead. You were the last survivor of the royal house of Errasarn. But you were also the heir to the throne of Anasaria. You are the direct descendant of Darion, the true King of Anasaria."

"No!" cried out Rowan. "This can't be! I am not a king! I barely know how to run a farm. All of this makes no sense."

A voice spoke from nearby. Rowan realised that he had been speaking out loud.

"Don't worry too much about the title," said Darlam. "Kingship can be thrust upon you, but being a true leader is a matter of character. Trust in yourself, Rowan."

Hyrn looked up at the King of the Underdwellers. Coming up behind him were two familiar soldiers; Droom, reunited with his lieutenant, Gorum. Beyond them he could see that vast numbers of people were gathered around. Rowan began to rise stiffly to his feet. As he did, Arienga and then Hyrn got to their feet. They stood warily beside him. Rowan stumbled a little, and then stood erect. He faced towards the castle ahead and up beyond to the road that led up to the gates in the wall of the plateau, and up to the dark fortress brooding above them.

But he dropped his gaze and looked around at the aftermath of battle. With despair he saw, past where dazed soldiers stood amongst the fallen, that on the ground lay the body of his protector and friend, Carlan. He dashed unsteadily towards the fallen Abessairian. Arienga, moving quickly behind him, reached out and gripped his arm to stop him from falling. He walked closer and crouched down beside Carlan and looked down on him. His neck was a bloody mess. The soldier's eyes blinked open. He looked up at Rowan with pain in his eyes.

Hyrn had come up behind Rowan holding the two Stones but they were dark and their voices were just a murmur in Hyrn's mind.

"Heal him," said Hyrn softly to the Stones.

"We do not have that power anymore," said the duet of voices in his head.

Carlan stared up at Rowan intently. Blood spilled from his mouth as he tried to speak.

He sputtered painfully, but said fervently, "Swordbearer I am proud to have served and to have protected you. You have helped me to pay for my sins, and to be a soldier of Abessair again."

Carlan paused and coughed up a gobbet of blood. His breathing became laboured but he said thickly as his strength faded, "My King. King Rowan."

"Carlan," said Rowan desperately.

Tears came to Rowan's eyes but he spoke steadily. "You saved my life more than once. I would not be here if not for you, and the quest would not have succeeded. You put yourself in danger because of my stupidity. You have more than paid for your sins and you will be remembered for the part you have played."

Carlan smiled weakly, and rattled, "The Stones burn in you."

His eyes closed slowly. The Abessairian soldier let out a soft sigh and then his body became still.

Rowan was filled with a burning sorrow, and a wave of anger swept through him. He leapt to his feet and cried out with fury, "Ultamar will pay! For Carlan and for every life they have destroyed!"

As he stood, there came a sudden crash as vast numbers of soldiers fell to their knees before him and all around. The Anasarians joined them. They were free, and before them stood their King. The Sword of Acclimoss had been drawn in battle. The Twin Stones were reunited. Only one thing still stood before them.

Rowan sensed it. The stark towers of Ultamar loomed in his thoughts, and into his mind came the vision of the towers bright white and glowing in the sunlight.

Now, above the black towers, dark clouds were gathering. Rowan detected a flicker of purple high up in the fortress and he felt an anger grow in him.

"Abessair will be freed," he called. "We must march on Ultamar!"

The mass that knelt before him rose to their feet. They roared out in many voices. There were cries of "Abessair," and numerous calls in praise of the King, but amongst it all came the familiar chant.

"Des-Ultamar! Des-Ultamar!"

This time the chant was not just defiant, but enraged. The massive army of Abessairians that had just been released from the service of Ultamar, for the first time took up the chant that until a short time ago had infuriated them. Joy was in their hearts but their voices were raised in wrath and the desire for vengeance

High above in the uppermost tower that dominated the massive fortress of Ultamar, the Dark Lords looked out and saw, and felt, that their army was gone, released from their hold. They had also felt the power of the blast of white light. They brooded in their tower and thought of their defences. Their power was strong yet.

And they still held the fortress.

An Abessairian soldier stood before Rowan. They had moved down towards the castle of Forest Ford. Rowan had remounted Arrow, despite the protests from Arienga and Hyrn, and the advice of Careil.

"By your leave," said the Anasarian. "I am Captain Durhan, stationed at Forest Ford. Reports have come in that the gates of Ultamar are closed. They…"

He paused and a look of anger came over his face but he went on. "They have closed the fortress's defences and they still have an army inside."

Rowan considered this and then said, "But surely they would be free."

Behind him a well known voice spoke.

"They are still under the power of Ultamar," said Hyrn. "The power of the Twin Stones did not reach beyond the walls of Ultamar and there is some power inside that the Stones cannot pierce."

Hyrn sat atop his horse beside Rowan and beside Hyrn was Bardewan. Rowan had relinquished the care of Ivah to the Doorwarden. All around Rowan were most of the reunited members of the quest.

Durhan continued. "We cannot hope to assault the walls of the fortress if it is secure."

King Darlam rode up from where the road passed between the towers of Forest Ford. Droom and Gorum rode alongside him, with a retinue of Underdweller soldiers following. But pulling ahead of them rode two Caramar warriors, Duburinga and Harla. They rode together, strong and resolute. Harla spoke first.

"They have locked down the approaches to Ultamar," she said.

Duburinga continued. "We cannot hope, even with this army that we could easily break through. The gate is secure."

"There is a way in though," Careil spoke from behind Rowan.

The Rider continued, "It is not a path for armies, though."

A council had been called. Rowan and the members of the quest had been welcomed into the castle at Forest Ford with heraldry and some excitement. There was a sense of accomplishment and anticipation. Emotions were tempered, though, by the loss of comrades. The newly released Abessairians were not as affected by the loss of their comrades. They instead mourned the deaths of those they had fought against. Their fellow soldiers had been freed from the curse of the Dark Lords and even those dead on the battlefield shone with the light of the Stones. Many Anasarians were dead and injured, and with them were Quiglings, Underdwellers and Caramar.

The loss of members of the quest hung heavily upon Rowan; Boriega, Charen-Ba, and hardest of all, Carlan. The Abessairian had been a stoic protector, but more than that, Rowan had come to treasure his friendship, and even his reprimands now seemed precious. The thought of that faithful service to the quest drove Rowan, more than anything else, to take responsibility for people's faith in him, and accept the challenge of kingship. The desire of those around him to defeat the evil of the Dark Lords drove doubt from his mind.

They sat in a large hall at a long wooden table. The room was dim, even with the light of torches that burned all around. The castle was dank and neglected but already soldiers were at work cleaning the filth of neglect, and freeing those imprisoned within the castle. Those released wondered at the change in their fortune, and the news of the Stones and the King passed among them.

Rowan felt overwhelmed by what had happened, and by the challenge of what lay ahead. He looked to his left where Hyrn sat. On his right sat Arienga. The warrior grasped his right hand beneath the table and gave it a squeeze. Rowan turned and looked at Arienga. She smiled at him and the look on her face steeled him.

Captain Durhan spoke. "Our two generals are not here to speak," he said. "Forgive me if I speak on behalf of the Abessairians in their absence. Gardwan is dead on the battlefield, released now from the evil of Ultamar. General Ferian has not been heard of in weeks."

He was interrupted by the voice of a Quigling fresh from the defence of Herardin and the attack on the northwestern flank.

"Ferian has gone in search of swans," said Cooren-Ba.

"Swans?" said Bardewan from further down the table.

"Yes," said Cooren-Ba. "He sought the key that I have since learned Bardewan now holds. I fear that his efforts were wasted and he would have been of more use here."

"His quest may not be fruitless," said Infiron. "Not all events and outcomes can be seen clearly."

Cooren-Ba nodded. "Perhaps," he said, and then continued. "There is also something else. The Drargs seem to have fled from Anasaria. Many have been seen heading northwards into the mountains. None have been sighted since."

"What does it mean?" asked Rowan.

Harla rose to her feet. "It is not something we can contend with at the moment. They are no longer a threat to us here. We cannot be distracted. We must fulfil the quest. We must attack the Dark Lords while they are unsure of themselves. We have no time to rest."

Durhan finally had a chance to continue. "Ultamar is strong but we hope to at least lay siege and perhaps attack the lesser gates."

Duburinga spoke. "We cannot hope to take the fortress by strength of arms. Even a long siege will not break down their defences. Our hope is in stealth. A small party must infiltrate the fortress. The Stones must be returned to their tower. We must attack tonight."

A voice spoke from beside Duburinga

"Whatever the evil is that the Dark Lords possess, I feel its power. I can feel the hate emanating from Ultamar."

The Caramar Elder, Yarga, had risen to his feet and spoke uneasily but with determination. To either side of him sat the Priests Infiron and Drivian.

"Only the power of the Stones is strong enough to challenge the evil of the Dark Lords," said Yarga.

He paused, and Infiron spoke. "Only by returning the Stones to their tower will Abessair be free."

As Rowan got to his feet, Arienga released his hand. He looked at those gathered around the table. He didn't know how to begin. He felt as if he was surrounded by people who were more competent, were highly trained, and knew what they were doing.

"Well...," said Rowan.

He looked at his brother beside him and prospects of war and destiny faded from his mind. The thought that they were not related seemed ridiculous. Something jumped in his stomach when he thought about it. He paused as something sad and painful began to burn in him.

But it was quickly extinguished when Hyrn said impatiently, "Well? What? Get on with it."

Despite all the faces watching him from around the table, Rowan leant down quickly, and before Hyrn had a chance to react, grasped him in a tight hug.

Hyrn protested and struggled against his brother. "Don't think you can harass me just because you supposedly have royal blood. You'd be milking all the cows for a year, if Ma and Pa knew that you'd been acting like such an idiot."

There were murmurs and uncertain smiles around the table. Rowan started to react to his little brother's bravado but instead he hugged him tighter.

"Well, you at least need to come with me," he said with a laugh. "I obviously need you to keep me under control."

"Wait," said Hyrn. "Where are we going?"

"To Ultamar of course," said Rowan, releasing his brother. "We have to finish this."

Hyrn looked up at him, confused momentarily, and a hint of fear washed through him, but then he shrugged with resignation.

"If that's where we have to go," he said.

The assault on Ultamar would begin soon. The Abessairian army, their ranks swelled with Anasarians, Quiglings, and lesser numbers of Underdwellers and Caramar warriors, prepared to attack the fortress. As far as could be reckoned, there were perhaps as many as five hundred Ultamarians still in the fortress, but the Dark Lords may have had hidden reserves. The Ultamarians stationed within the fortress tended to be small separate units. The size of the army that had gathered at the gates was the largest force that the Dark Lords had ever needed to amass. Much went on in the fortress that other units were unaware of. The Dark Lords did not seem to trust their soldiers.

To the north of the Detrian Road, the party with Rowan and Hyrn was already travelling towards Sewer Town, and beyond to the Wall of Detradin. Troops of soldiers marched behind, and mounted soldiers had already passed, on their way to the entrances where the sewers and drains of Ultamar emptied. The sky was dark in the late afternoon. The clouds above stretched beyond the western horizon, and the wall of the Anasarian mountains. There was little chance of any sight of the sunset, but they were filled with the hope of a sunrise and the dawning of a new day. Dark deeds lay before them.

Rowan and Hyrn rode side by side. Careil, astride Erras, rode directly behind them, with Bardewan beside him carrying Ivah. Wren rode with Hyrn again, and Garan rode resolutely beside them on their right, flanked by Gebarana. Wren was filled with wonder at the thought that he was practically a friend of the King, but his thoughts kept returning to a prisoner that could yet still live, imprisoned within the bowels of Ultamar. Arienga rode to Rowan's left. Harla and Duburinga were scouting ahead. Yarga rode behind Careil, accompanied by Infiron. Drivian had stayed behind to attend to the wounded. Terrana was amongst the wounded and had protested at being left behind but yielded to the wishes of Yarga, and the advice of Harla and Duburinga. Jarta-Den, and the newly initiated Grenga-Da, rode to the outside of the party. Gerardien rode with them representing, with Wren, the Anasarians. Turum and Margana formed the rearguard. Ahead of them all rode Captain Droom. Gorum had asked leave of King Darlam to seek out a wounded friend. The King of the Underdwellers was not with them, but was riding at the head of the army that rode up the road beyond Forest Ford and along the causeway that led to the great gates of Ultamar. Jorunum accompanied the King.

As they passed through the forest they began to catch the smell of Sewer Town, off to their right. The party tasked with entering the fortress had now been left by the rest of the soldiers. Eighteen they numbered as they headed onwards towards where the great wall met the plateau. The gloom of a sunless afternoon had now given way to darkness as night descended. Once the stench of the Ultamarian sewers had fallen behind them Droom called a halt. They were to have a quick meal while scouts went ahead to observe the approach to the wall.

Arienga had gone ahead with Margana and Turum to meet with Harla and Duburinga. Garan had promised her that he would not let Rowan get into any trouble. Rowan sat with Hyrn and Wren. Garan and Careil were keeping watch on them. The scouts would be some time, so they took the opportunity to rest. Hyrn had still not come to terms with the fact that his brother was a king. Rowan had not come to terms with the fact either. They talked to each other lightheartedly, two farm boys caught up in the midst of an adventure that had become an unimaginable course of fate. Wren joined in the conversation, mostly to ask a succession of questions.

The sound of hooves approached them through the forest from the east; two horses. They thought at first that it was two of the scouts returning. The horses came on at speed and came to a halt where Droom stood on watch with Jarta-Den. Hyrn could hear them talking through the trees, but didn't recognise the voices of the newcomers and couldn't make out what they were saying. Careil though, leapt to his feet and made his way towards where the talking continued.

Careil approached behind Droom and as he did he saw Karra-Bar. The Quigling leapt down from his horse, the Kragon now free of its curse. He moved forward to meet Careil.

"There is someone here that is eager to see you," said Karra-Bar.

Careil could not see the other rider past the bulk of Captain Droom astride his chariga. He moved forward and saw a mounted Abessairian. The stern faced man looking down at him did not look threatening but instead looked sheepish.

"Hernan!" called out Careil.

The Abessairian climbed down from his horse and approached the Rider hesitantly.

Careil stepped forward.

"You led us into a trap," he said, sternly.

"Only unknowingly. I swear," said Hernan. His voice was still gruff but his tone was now good natured.

"It is true," said Karra-Bar. "He was imprisoned by the Anasarian rebels that were amongst the crowd in the street in Sewer Town. He was as unaware of us, as you were. He was only intent on pursuing Bardan."

"I told them nothing about you," said Hernan. "I am true to my bond."

Careil stepped forward and embraced him.

"I'm glad I didn't kill you," said Careil, as the two broke apart and faced each other.

"You? … Kill me? I'm glad that I…" began Hernan, but he faltered.

He looked beyond Careil as a large shape appeared from among the trees. Hernan stepped back nervously. Careil turned and saw Erras come up beside him. Careil reached up and rested his hand on the horse's neck.

"What do you think, Erras?" asked Careil.

Hernan looked worried momentarily, but Erras nickered and nodded his head.

"I think he approves of you now," said Careil.

Hernan, with barely concealed relief, said, "He is one of the strangest horses I have ever seen. It is almost as if he understands what you are saying."

Careil looked at Erras and the horse looked in turn at him.

"Really?" said Careil, and patted Erras's neck.

He looked back to Hernan. "Come and have something to eat. We're not stopping for long."

The wall loomed before them. The clouds above them were occasionally lit with flashes of purple. However, there were now breaks in the cloud revealing patches of starry sky and the underside of the cloud was lit from where the moon rose, hidden behind the bulk of the plateau that towered over them. Hyrn looked back and saw that the glowing white cloud above and behind them seemed to be shaped like an outstretched hand. The fingers reached towards Ultamar grasping out as if to seize the fortress.

"The passageways are narrow within," said Karra-Bar.

"Horses can pass through," said Careil, quickly adding, "Oh, and charigas, at least up to the way that leads to the main passes."

They had come to a halt where the sheer rockface at the base of the plateau met the might of the wall of Detradin. They were surrounded by tall dark trees. Karra-Bar rode towards what appeared to Hyrn to be a buttress of the cliff. The Quigling approached the rock and then began to turn into a hidden opening. As he continued behind the rock, his horse suddenly reared. Karra-Bar hung on to the reins as the horse moved back away from the entrance. As Karra-Bar gained control, Droom rode forward towards the hidden entrance. His chariga baulked at first, but continued on, and he disappeared behind the outcrop of rock.

Others moved their horses forward but their mounts seemed reluctant to enter. Careil rode through on Erras. The great horse strode on, following unflinchingly where Droom had led. Rowan urged Arrow onwards but he felt the horse resisting. Harla and Duburinga had dismounted and were beginning to lead their mounts but they shied and baulked as they neared the rock wall. Arienga was having the same trouble just behind them. Rowan was ready to call out to Careil, when suddenly Droom burst out of the entrance, struggling to control his chariga. Rowan with panic looked back towards the rockface.

Erras trotted out with Careil riding casually, the horse and the Rider, calm and at ease. Erras swung his head around and snorted. Careil leant forward and patted the horse's neck.

"I don't think they're up for it, Erras," he said. "I don't blame them."

Careil spoke to them all. "Captain Bardan came this way with a cursed Artoran Stone and the power of Ultamar fills this place. The horse that was once a Kragon must still remember the evil within. We cannot take the horses and the charigas through. We have a great climb before us but we must do it on foot. Erras too will stay behind."

The horse's ears pricked up and he turned his head back towards Careil.

"I'll be back," said Careil. "You need to keep an eye on things here."

The horse snorted, as Careil leapt down and patted his friend's neck.

The passages were wide enough to walk two or three abreast. They had lighted torches to guide them in the darkness. The atmosphere within the underbelly of the fortress was oppressive. Hyrn felt the weight of the evil intent above and before them. Only the power of the Stones pushed it aside and formed a barrier around them. Careil and Karra-Bar walked ahead. Karra-Bar tried to follow the way that he had come before he met up with Careil and Skelan. Infiron had spoken to the Quigling and now moved ahead with him and Careil. The Priest followed the trace of evil power that Bardan had left in his wake. No sounds of any defenders reached their ears.

They came upon it suddenly. The body of an Ultamarian was illuminated by the torchlight. He lay on his back, his legs bent awkwardly beneath him. An arrow protruded from his blood-soaked chest.

"Skelan," said Careil. "But I wonder where Bardan got to? We didn't have time to pursue him. He was sorely wounded and corrupted by the evil Stone."

"If he lives, the power of the Artoran curse will be driving him on," said Infiron. "I would rather that we did not meet him down here."

They filed past the dead soldier. As Hyrn walked past followed by

Bardewan, the body on the passage floor began to change. A light seemed to pass over the prostrate form. The dull grey of the Ultamarian uniform was flushed out and it now glowed the white of the uniform of Abessair. The sight lifted the hearts of the party, amidst the pervasive feeling of evil that radiated through the rock about them. Wren paused and looked down at the transformed body. Following behind, Yarga placed his hand on Wren's shoulder.

"The power of the Stones returns," said the Elder. "The evil of Ultamar is being driven back. Take heart, Wren."

Wren moved on with Yarga behind. The young Anasarian followed the quest, but burning in his mind was the thought that his father may be somewhere within this dark labyrinth.

He stopped and turned back towards Yarga.

"What about the prisoners here?" he asked. "Can we help them?"

Yarga looked at Wren as they walked. He was not sure what to say. He knew that the boy was wondering about the fate of his father. Behind the Elder walked Margana. He thought for a moment and then said, "What do you think of a side quest, Margana?"

The warrior hesitated. She had heard Wren's words.

"Elder," she said. "Surely, we must follow Hyrn and Rowan."

"They have the Twin Stones," said Yarga. "Their path is clear. The wisdom of the Sagenstone may be better used in other ways. Infiron is better equipped to make use of the power of Abessair but the Sagenstone has a way of helping open locks."

"Elder, I will need to consult with …" began Margana.

"I think we should discuss it when we have a better idea of where we are going," said the stern voice of Duburinga from behind them.

Beyond where they had come upon the body of Skelan, the party's knowledge became reliant on Careil's glimpsed view of the path as he had flashed through the passages, astride a Kragon. The trail of Bardan had led off into a side passage that ended in a dead-end, and then stopped. The Ultamarian captain was nowhere to be seen and no further trace remained. A halt had been called while they pondered this, and the way forward, and gathered their strength. From time to time they heard distant echoes of voices and movement but none had come near to them yet.

Yarga had spoken to the others of his desire to accompany Wren to find his father. Hyrn was crestfallen at the idea that Wren would not be coming with them but this was tempered by relief that he would not be leading Wren towards the evil that waited above. Wren wanted to stay with Hyrn, but his duty was to his father and the other Anasarian prisoners. There was a short discussion amongst all of the group, and it was agreed that their numbers were too great for stealth without a clear path ahead of them, and that there were other tasks that they could undertake. Harla and Duburinga had deferred to the wisdom of the Caramar Elder. The torment of the prisoners of Ultamar was something that could not be ignored. There was still hope in the quest but if they failed, at least there was a chance that the prisoners could be freed.

Turum had volunteered to join Yarga, Wren and Margana. Gerardien had also agreed to join them and help free any Anasarians that were imprisoned. Grenga-Da accepted the duty on behalf of the Quiglings. Jarta-Den was torn between his duty to the quest and his loyalty to Wren. His knowledge of the ancient enemy was too important to the confrontation with the Dark Lords that loomed ahead.

Harla and Duburinga agreed that one other Caramar warrior should accompany them. Arienga held her breath.

"Gebarana, accompany Yarga," said Harla.

"Arienga, double your vigilance," said Duburinga.

Arienga nodded and steeled herself to take on the challenge.

So a party of seven set out to attempt to release the prisoners of Ultamar. Thirteen were to continue upwards.

Hyrn stood facing Wren and Yarga.

"Good luck," he said to Wren. "I hope you find your father."

"Be careful," said Wren. "Don't go wandering off."

"Don't worry," said a gruff voice beside Hyrn, "he won't."

Garan stood there. "Take care, Wren," he said. "I'll look after this one but make sure you don't get into any trouble."

As Wren nodded in agreement, Yarga spoke.

"Your path is clear, Hyrn," he said. "Seek the path that your destiny holds. Keep the power of good within you. The Sagenstone cannot teach you any more than you hold in your heart."

Ilah reached out from within Hyrn's vest, and Hyrn could feel power coursing through him and out into the red crystal at Yarga's throat.

They were travelling back and forth through the criss-crossing passages but they could sense that they were getting higher. Occasionally they had to halt and remain silent, as footfalls and voices seemed to come from somewhere close at hand. The intricate network of passages made it hard to be sure where the sound was coming from. It was clearly ahead of them and became more distinct as they moved deeper into the fortress's understories and higher up towards the fortress itself. They were also moving gradually eastwards towards where the central roadway led down to the great chamber at the gates. This was an area that they wanted to avoid, but Careil remembered that the way that Skelan had gone at first was towards the main thoroughfare.

They came to a place where the passage they were in came out to a landing. Stairs led downwards into darkness. A dark passage stood to their left opposite the stairway. Ahead of them another passage loomed. Careil looked around with recognition. This looked like the way that Skelan had led him as they headed up towards the fortress. They had come up a stairway to a landing identical to this. They may be on a different level now but if the passages followed the same pattern on each level, they should reach the staircase that formed a spiralling path upwards.

"Straight ahead," said Careil confidently. "And then we should meet a staircase that leads to a landing. Then we need to take the right hand passage."

Just then, there came the sound of multiple feet. The sound echoed down the dark passage to their left. Hyrn thought he caught the glimpse of the flicker of torchlight but the voices coming towards them were unmistakable.

"Quickly! Go back! Torches out!" hissed Harla.

The party were back in the passage and barely had time to extinguish their torches before they heard many pairs of feet crossing the landing and then heard the voices of the Ultamarian soldiers.

"Why do we have to come this way through this rat-infested place?" said one voice.

"It is the quickest way down to the dungeons," said another. "We have to make sure that our prisoners, or should I say hostages," he sniggered at this, "don't go getting any ideas."

Careil peered out from the shadows and tried to count the soldiers. There seemed to be about a dozen and they were moving down towards where the others were headed.

After the sound of the soldiers had faded, Hyrn said desperately. "They're going down to where Wren is. We have to help them."

"I will go!" The voice came from beside Careil. A spark flashed and a torch erupted into light. Captain Droom stood there.

"I am a Guardian of the Light in the Dark," said the tall Underdweller. "I know the darkness and am at home fighting underground."

"I will go too," said Karra-Bar. "I know more of the depths of Ultamar than the heights and am of more use there."

"I must go also," said Harla and turned to Duburinga. "Take the strength of the mountains with you. I must follow Yarga. He is young and despite him being an Elder, I fear for him."

Duburinga grasped Harla's forearm and she grasped his. They nodded silently and then they released their grasp. Harla turned quickly and she, Droom and Karra-Bar moved out onto the landing and down the stairway, their torch throwing a ring of light that soon disappeared into the darkness.

They came to an arch and there before them was the massive column of black space with a staircase spiralling around its outer wall. Hyrn stood on the landing in the spiral stairway. A well of darkness yawned below and continued above, beyond the light of their torches. It was in the heights where he felt that danger awaited.

"What is this place?" said Hyrn. "And why are there no soldiers?"

They had heard no soldiers close at hand since Harla, Droom and Karra-Bar had left them. The stairwell was deserted. They could still hear distant rumblings and clatterings but these seemed to be away from this shaft towards the centre of the plateau where the great roadway led down to the gates.

"This was deserted when I was here before," said Careil.

Hernan spoke from beside him. "There are a number of these shafts leading down from the fortress to the lower levels. In the time of Abessair these shafts were brightly lit. They were used as service corridors. There were great winches at the top of the shaft and they were used to move goods and people between the service roads below and Abessair above. The bottoms of the shafts have long been clogged and impassable. The winches stopped working many years ago and the shafts have since been used to dispose of garbage."

He paused and then said bitterly, "Not all that the Dark Lords dispose of is just garbage."

"The stain on Abessair will be removed," said Infiron. "Ultamar will fall."

"Their doom approaches," said Jarta-Den darkly.

"We go on," said Rowan beside him. "Upwards to the fortress."

They turned and headed up the stairs. Careil and Hernan led the way, followed by Infiron and Duburinga.

"Well we're going up there just as you wanted," said Careil to Hernan.

"This time we have nothing to bargain with," said Hernan.

"This time," replied Careil, "we have both Stones."

Rowan walked behind Infiron and Duburinga. Arienga was beside him positioning herself on the outer edge of the stairs. Hyrn smiled at this, remembering the journey from Gardarvon. Hyrn also walked closer to the wall with Garan guarding him from the drop below. Jarta-Den with Bardewan brought up the rear as they climbed ever upwards to where the Dark Lords and their servants waited.

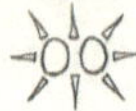

The circular room at the peak of the fortress glowed with a vivid blueish purple light. The air was thick and fetid. Malice and power emanated from the seven Dark Lords. The room pulsed with it, and the air shimmered with their anger.

Bright and painful power had been unleashed against them. Their army, apart from those that were within Ultamar, had been stolen. The seven hooded figures stood around the room. Only they occupied the evil chamber. The centre of the room was dominated by the large circular table. In its centre stood a Stone. It glowed and flickered with purple and blue light. Occasionally the flickering light revealed a skeletal face beneath a deep hood.

"There is something still out there," rasped Brevaliggen.

"But where is it, brother?" sneered Preskatchion.

"I can't find it," snarled the other. "It is obscured by a deep fog. But the sense of danger increases."

"They cannot get past the gates," said another of the Dark Lords, Kreskalan.

"We are safe here," said Brevaliggen. "The Stone of Erekslat is beyond all their power."

"The Stone is untested against the might of the Angilanians," croaked a figure that faced the window looking out to the south, where an army was gathering before the gates of the fortress.

Herazlion, most ancient of the Dark Lords, turned and faced the centre of the room. The light of the Stone shone under his hood and showed two lamplike eyes embedded in a skull held together with withered strips of flesh.

"But we do not yet know that the Stones of Angil are here," he said.

"You are too old, Herazlion," said Preskatchion. "Couldn't you feel that power on the battlefield? That was the strength of Angil."

"I know more of the enemy than a snivelling young coward like you," screeched the decrepit voice. "You left your comrades to die at Guran-Badur."

"Yes, but we took your worthless carcass with us," snapped Preskatchion. "And who was it that also stole the Stone?"

He threw back his hood and revealed a ghastly mis-shapen skull that in places writhed and pulsed with violet light. His eyes glowed.

"I believe it was your little lap-dog as I have told you time and time again," said Herazlion.

"You know that Gaskatch was just playing his part in my plan," said Preskatchion.

"Oh, little Gaskatch, eh? Gaskatchezon is a…" began Herazlion.

"Quiet!" roared a voice.

The tallest of the seven turned from where he was looking down upon the fortress that rose up beneath them.

"If they have the Stones their most obvious move will be to take the Tower of the Stones," said Carvilikon.

Down below, the scaffolding was empty around the tower that reached up towards them. Those who had continued in vain to try to demolish the tower, had gone off to war. It stood defiantly, and at its peak, the Chamber of the Stones lay, locked and inpenetrable.

"Send soldiers to the tower," said Carvilikon.

"The gate is more important, and we can give those who attack from below a lovely surprise," said Preskatchion, "and then nothing can assail us."

"The power of our Stone has poured into this fortress over the centuries. It will require us all to wield it effectively", said Kreskalon.

"We must defend the tower," said Carvilikon.

"Fine," said Preskatchion. "Soldiers will be sent to the Tower of the Stones."

He paused in concentration and his head pulsed with purple light as he silently issued orders to the Ultamarians that defended the fortress.

"None will be able to enter, anyway, once we're finished," said Preskatchion, finally.

"Those that are inside will suffer, too," said Kreskalon.

"Except us," said Preskatchion

There was laughter as the seven approached the table where the large Stone flashed and hummed.

As they climbed upwards they crossed more landings. The air seemed to become more oppressive and they began to sense that the stairway was turning more sharply. Soon the opposite wall could be seen, and they could see the stairway where it spiralled above them. As they moved higher, great ropes could be seen hanging down, and eventually they could see the great winch-housing at the top of the shaft, and the landing above. As they neared the top of the stairs a visible tremor went through the stone around them.

The party stood unsteadily as the stairs beneath their feet trembled. And then they felt it. A pulse of sickness filled the air around them. They felt the evil intent flowing through the fortress from above. They looked around with bewilderment. Infiron spoke.

"They are using the veins of power within the fortress," said the Priest. "They must have a powerful Stone. They are the veins by which Ilah and Ivah maintained the power of Abessair."

As the feeling of evil grew around them, Hyrn said shakily. "Don't they need to be in the Chamber of the Stones to do that?"

But the voice began in his head before Infiron had a chance to answer and Hyrn repeated it out loud.

"They have forged a path into the heart of Abessair," said Hyrn. "They are tapping into the base of the Tower of the Stones. It can only be stopped by destroying the Stone they wield or returning us, the Stones that is," corrected Hyrn, "to the Chamber of the Stones."

Hernan spoke. "We are now at the top of the plateau. This is where the fortress itself begins. We are directly below the fortress but to the west of the central entrance where the stairways to the towers divide. The path to the highest tower lies above. Gaining entrance to the Tower of the Stones will mean passing through the central mezzanine where the stairways lead off towards each tower. There is no other way into the tower. There will be guards, but we must hope that most troops are down below at the gates."

"We must confront the Dark Lords and take the evil Stone," said Jarta-Den. "I think it is as we have long feared. They hold the Stone of Erekslat. It was long thought lost or carried eastwards across the frontlines and to the forces of evil beyond. Obviously the lust for power led these scum to take the Stone for their own ends. It once stood at Guran-Badur before we took that city and freed our people. Guran-Badur was an outpost of the forces of evil, and the Stone of Erekslat stood at its centre. The Quiglings defeated the Badurians but some escaped. We thought at first that they had all fled east to join their forces. We left our devastated home and joined our forces with the Power in the East. We learned later of the plight of Anasaria and were sent to oppose them. It became clear to us that the Dark Lords were some of the Badurians who escaped."

"We need to decide now," said Duburinga. The expression on his face showed that he too suffered from the effects of the evil force. "We confront the Dark Lords, or we return the Stones, or we attempt both."

Rowan and Hyrn both spoke at the same time.

"We confront the Dark Lords," said Rowan.

"We must return the Stones," said Hyrn.

Duburinga looked at them both and then looked at the party gathered on the stairs.

"Arienga," he said, "the path to the Chamber of Stones requires stealth. Open battle will not avail you. Your skill with the bow serves that purpose. I will go upwards."

Rowan looked at Arienga but his face was steadfast. "I will go to confront the Dark Lords," he said. "Look after Hyrn, please Arienga. He's the only brother I've got."

"Wait a minute," said Careil. "Is this the best course of action? Wouldn't it be best if we stuck together?"

Jarta-Den spoke. "If we can distract the Dark Lords from the use of the Stone and prevent them from unleashing its power until the Twin Stones are returned, we at least have a chance of defeating them. If not, we and all those anywhere near the fortress are dead or lost anyway."

"Lost?" said Hyrn.

"Aye. Lost," said Garan from beside him. He placed his hand on Hyrn's shoulder. "Lost as I and Hernan here were." And he added, "I will stay with Hyrn."

Careil was torn. The thought that the two brothers would again be separated meant he had to make a decision.

Finally, he said. "I will go with Hyrn. Hernan, you will have to go and see them without me."

"I will lay my life down for the King, if necessary," said Hernan.

Despite the gravity of the situation Hyrn sniggered. "King." He shoved Rowan gently.

"Hyrn!" warned Rowan sharply but quietly. "Don't!"

"Sorry," said Hyrn and his guilty smile hid the growing dread he felt.

"My path lies above," said Jarta-Den. "I have an appointment long postponed."

In the end, Hyrn, Careil, Arienga, Garan and Bardewan were assigned to the quest to reach the Chamber of the Stones, and Rowan, Duburinga, Jarta-Den, Hernan and Infiron were to try and confront the Dark Lords. Infiron was torn between her loyalty to the Stones and her ability to discern the power of the locks of the fortress, and her instilled knowledge of the secret ways of Abessair. For the power of Abessair still waited within the stone of the fortress, hidden behind the corruption that infected it.

At the top of the stairs was a wide landing with two large doors. The doors opened without too much effort but with a grating noise as they swung open. The torchlight was lost in the large dark space beyond but a faint purple light glimmered on the walls of what appeared to be a warehouse. As they moved carefully around, collapsed and decaying shelving, pallets, crates and barrels appeared in the torchlight. Dark passages led off in several directions. The largest of these was closest to them, but prominent at each end were passages leading north and south.

"This one here leads up to the central tower," said Hernan pointing to the largest passage. "The other two large passages are part of the corridor that circles the castle and meets at the entrance foyer. The one on the right is the quickest way to the grand stairs that lead up to the mezzanine where the entrance to the Tower of the Stones lies."

Rowan hugged Hyrn tightly and then released him.

"Take it easy, Hyrn," he said.

"You too, Rowan," said Hyrn.

Both brothers wore determined expressions on their faces. Then Rowan punched Hyrn softly on the arm.

"I owe you that from when we separated last time," Rowan said.

Hyrn looked annoyed for a moment then shook his head with a brief smile.

Arienga walked up and stood beside Hyrn, facing Rowan. She glanced at Duburinga who stood watching. Despite Duburinga's stern look, she stepped forward and grabbed Rowan in an embrace and quickly kissed him on the cheek.

"Please take care and don't…"

"I won't," said Rowan as he put his arms around her and embraced her.

They broke apart and Arienga looked at him.

Her face became stoic and she said sternly, "Remember your training."

Rowan gave her a mock salute and she clenched her fist ready to punch him, but instead quickly turned away. Careil moved past her and faced Rowan.

"I'm not sure what to say to you, Rowan," he said. "Things have changed so much since we left the farm. Listen to the advice of those with you and keep your sword ready."

"I will, Careil," said Rowan. "You made your choice between the Sword and the Stones. They both could use your strength but I think Hyrn needs you more."

Careil smiled and embraced Rowan and then released him.

"You've grown," Careil said. "But I'll still be around to keep you in line if you play up."

The growing sense of evil around them hastened their parting, and the two groups moved off. Careil held aloft a torch and moved forward. Bardewan walked behind him, with Arienga and Garan flanking Hyrn as they moved southwards towards the great entrance hall.

Jarta-Den carried a torch into the broad passageway which led straight to a wide stairway. Infiron followed behind the Quigling, Rowan and Duburinga followed behind her, and Hernan kept watch behind.

As they departed, twin circles of light moved apart and disappeared down the two passages leaving the warehouse in darkness.

The Ultamarian was caught by surprise. His fellow soldiers had just disappeared around the corner ahead of him, when he was suddenly struck in the head, and he fell into blackness. Captain Droom crept down to where the Ultamarian lay at Harla's feet. He grabbed the limp body of the soldier and dragged him back up the passage and into a dark doorway. He stepped out and closed the door and slid the iron latch.

"We must remember that he is here," said Karra-Bar.

Just then there came a stifled shout from ahead of them at the end of the corridor. An Ultamarian soldier collapsed to the ground, his sword raised before him as he fell. Harla stood with a bloodied knife in her hand.

"We need to be more careful," said Harla, "and I need to maintain my vigilance. This one must have come back to look for his companion. I didn't hear him until he was about to attack. The others will soon notice that these two aren't behind them."

"I don't think we can sneak around any more," said Droom. "Yarga and the others cannot be too much farther ahead."

The three exchanged glances and then turned and moved quickly down the corridor. They turned the corner and then came to a stairway and passed downwards. The clinking of Droom's armour accompanied them as they went but they were now beyond worrying about stealth. The thought of those that needed their help below released them from caution.

The Stone at Yarga's throat pointed him in the direction they needed to go. Margana moved just ahead of him and Wren followed close behind. The others trailed after them. The whole place reeked. They had come across cells, but they were silent and stank of decay. Yarga began to guess that they did not bother with changing occupants, but just used new cells as prisoners were brought in. They had passed many cells and gone down several levels before they heard any movement. Margana held her hand up to bring them to a halt. Sure enough, there was a sound from a doorway to their right just ahead.

Yarga approached the door and laid his hand on it. The lock was mechanical and not a lock of power but Yarga felt the stone and iron and something within him focussed his mind and the lock clicked. He swung the door inwards. Margana brought the torch forward and its light illuminated the cell. An old woman lay on a cot swaddled in a dirty and ragged blanket. She groaned and then suddenly sat bolt upright.

"They're coming," she moaned.

Then she cried desperately, "They are here!"

Suddenly, all around them, a wave of evil power pulsed through the walls.

At that instant a troop of Ultamarians appeared from around the corner behind them. They turned, startled, and Gebarana and Turum moved quickly from their position at the rear, with swords raised to confront the evil soldiers.

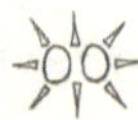

The first two Ultamarians they met were dead before they had a chance to cry out. Arienga retrieved her arrows as they passed by. The corridors had become more ornate as they grew closer to the entrance hall. They could hear the echoes of movement further on and they moved as fast as they were able to with stealth. They stayed close together. Careil led the way but Arienga moved just behind him and ahead of Hyrn, who walked guarded by Garan, with Bardewan, an Abessairian sword in his hand and Ivah within his uniform, protecting their rear. They had encountered no more soldiers, but as the entrance way grew nearer, the sound grew louder. They expected at any moment to meet enemies. Gradually they could see light ahead of them. They crept slowly to the end of the passageway, staying close to the wall.

The entrance hall to the fortress was immense. There was a wide straight central staircase with ornate columns at each side of the entrance to the stairs and intricately carved balustrades leading upwards. There were smaller curved staircases that led up to either side of the mezzanine. High above, tall windows faced east. Pale shafts of moonlight from the windows enhanced the lights of lanterns that beamed all around. The Dark Lords had not defiled the beauty of the work of the Anasarians. Even they had kept this impressive architecture intact as a way of awing those who entered.

Amidst the immensity, figures moved around. They were agitated, moving this way and that amongst the chaotic power that filled the fortress around them. Some moved downwards from various directions, but others were heading upwards but in one particular direction, up to the mezzanine and then into the lefthand archway that led up to one of the towers.

Careil whispered to Arienga, "That is our tower, I suspect."

Rowan felt a little queasy and fear built in his mind as they climbed higher. From above and before them Duburinga came out of the darkness and into the light of their torch.

"The main stairway to the tower meets these stairs at a landing not far above," said the Caramar. "There are guards there. There are torches burning above. We must extinguish ours and walk in darkness until we come to the light above."

Carefully they crept, feeling each step as they went. Rowan felt almost alone with the blackness all around. He began to imagine that there were lights bouncing in front of him. He attempted to feel in front of himself but realised that his sword was in hand and to either side of the hilt glowed two soft warm lights. The images of the Twin Stones glowed with the power of Ilah and Ivah. They were still with them, even as the actual Stones moved further away, along with his brother. Rowan renewed his grip on the Sword and readied himself for whatever was to come.

Light grew ahead of them as the stairway made a sweeping turn. They kept to the shadows as they approached the landing. Duburinga and Jarta-Den moved to the end of the wall of the stairway and peered out. Two guards stood at the other side of the landing where a large arch led towards the larger stairway that climbed up to the central tower. They could sense that the evil power grew stronger here. They watched and listened. The guards were silent and no other sound could be heard.

An arrow flew through the air and caught one of the guards in the throat. Another arrow followed but this glanced off the other guard's armoured shoulder, through the arch and into the stairwell beyond. Jarta-Den was already moving and his raised sword met that of the Ultamarian who had taken up a defensive stance. The Quigling drove the soldier backwards and then leaping sideways brought his sword around in an arc and sliced through the enemy's side. The Ultamarian grimaced but with the intensity of the evil curse that burned within him, snarled and brought his sword up.

The cursed soldier paused as a strange yet familiar light met his eyes. Rowan held Acclimoss and it shone with the power of Angil. The Ultamarian's mind spun. It was long ago but…He almost choked with the memory of a powerful splendour. He momentarily longed to serve that splendour as he crashed to his knees and fell forward.

He was bleeding profusely from the wound in his side but he managed to gasp, "The King of Anasaria," as he fell dying.

Rowan was again torn. This soldier was an Ultamarian but he had been an Abessairian. He remembered Kerian's words; that death was preferable to serving the Dark Lords and breaking their oath. Rowan was not comforted by the thought, and in his mind grew a determination to destroy those that made his people fight for evil.

'My people?' he thought, and then resolved, 'Yes. My people.'

The real enemy was clear, but they needed to get to them, and as the thrum of evil power grew, he knew that it needed to be soon. If the Dark Lords released their power, it could finish them all.

Duburinga moved forward towards the arch, and sliding through, looked up the stairway. He signalled silently for them all to follow.

As Gebarana attacked one of the two leading soldiers, Turum leapt to one side, and pushing himself off the wall, drove his sword down into the other Ultamarian's shoulder. The Underdweller landed on his feet behind where the wounded soldier was collapsing to the ground with a groan. As he brought his sword up he was faced by two Ultamarians, the one closest to him moved his sword swiftly, but with a flash of movement Margana was there, and the soldier fell. But the other Ultamarian thrust his sword out and even as Margana pivoted around and swiftly slashed at the evil soldier's throat, Turum felt a burning pain pierce through his stomach. It didn't feel right. He felt ill and then weary and all his strength seemed to flow towards the stone floor. As he fell, he heard the voice of his Captain invoking the Light in the Dark. That light shone in his mind but faded into dimness.

Droom crashed into the Ultamarians with his heavy sword slicing through them. Harla had already taken out two. But they watched Turum, Gebarana, and Margana's attack unfold even as they fought and saw Turum fall. Droom erupted in outrage and anger, calling out and fighting ferociously, as Harla moved to join the two Caramar. Gerardien stood alongside the cell door with his sword raised. Grenga-Da had pushed Wren behind him, and as an Ultamarian rushed towards him, the young Quigling killed again.

They stood breathlessly amongst the fallen. Margana crouched over the body of Turum as he lay on his side with a sword still lodged through his body. The stone was slick with his blood and the flickering torchlight reflected garishly where it pooled. Turum gazed up into Margana's eyes with a desperate look.

"I always wanted to see what was to the west," he gasped.

"Now…" he faltered.

"I am of the West," Margana said.

He smiled and let out a soft laugh, and she watched as death took him.

Arienga and Careil peered out to where the curved staircase closest to them led up to the left end of the mezzanine, opposite where the archway led to where they believed the Tower of the Stones stood. Soldiers moved on the stairs but most of the traffic was on the grand central staircase. To the side of the nearest staircase was a hallway that led to the lower level rooms. The light was muted there in the shadow of the stairs. They waited for a lull in the movement near them and then dashed across into the shadow. As they paused there, Arienga looked up to the mezzanine above where the stairs ended.

"We need to get up there," she whispered.

"We have to get past too many defenders to get up those stairs," said Careil.

"A diversion," said Hyrn.

"A disruption," said Bardewan.

The two moved against the wall of the stairway and each held a Stone. The Stones glowed dimly but as Hyrn and Bardewan in turn placed them against the wall, they burned brightly, but the light seemed not to pass beyond the five of them. There was a thrumming of power and the light of the Stones flowed into the wall.

There instantly came a change in the atmosphere around them. The pervading sense of evil dissipated and the movement of soldiers seemed to cease.

"Move now!" said Hyrn through gritted teeth.

Arienga crept quickly around to the end of the stone bannister and looked around in surprise. Some Ultamarian soldiers seemed frozen. Others lay on the floor, either still or convulsing.

"Let's go now," she called.

"It won't last," said Bardewan as he and Hyrn replaced the Stones and moved up with Garan and Careil shepherding them.

They dashed around and up onto the stairs. They needed to duck and weave between the Ultamarians. Some looked at them as they passed with fear or anger, or sometimes confusion. As they grew closer to the top of the staircase where it opened out onto the mezzanine, some of the evil soldiers began to move slowly and break out of the power holding them. Arienga leapt up the last of the stairs with the others close behind and they broke into a run across the marbled floor and towards the entrance to the Tower of the Stones.

A few soldiers stood before them and they were slowly coming back to awareness but still looked dazed. They moved past them and now only the two guards at the entrance blocked their way. These were now becoming aware of their surroundings and they realised that they were coming under attack. They fell with arrows in their chests. Arienga had already shouldered her bow and freeing her hands reached down and retrieved her arrows. She leapt the bodies, and Hyrn and Bardewan did the same. Careil and Garan came behind.

"Careil!" called Arienga.

Careil moved past Hyrn and Bardewan, as they entered a circular foyer, and moved towards a broad step that led to the beginning of a spiral stairway. Ultamarians stood on the step and they were dazedly drawing their swords. They came at them. Arienga hit one with an arrow. Her next shot went astray but she had already drawn her sword and sliced into the soldier closest to her, Careil felled one of the Ultamarians with a sweep of his sword. Garan moved to protect Hyrn. Bardewan had moved forward and his sword met that of an Ultamarian. The Ultamarian leapt back and brought his sword around and it struck Bardewan's breastplate and glanced off with a flash of light. The light seemed to flow through the Ultamarian's sword and into his hands. He fell to the ground moaning and Bardewan moved past him ready to continue to fight any Ultamarians still standing, but they lay all around. Just then, they heard from behind them the sound of approaching footsteps and angry shouts.

"Up the stairs now!" shouted Arienga.

Rowan sensed the evil power grow as they moved ever closer. The stairs had been deserted as they climbed quickly, but now they heard heavy footfalls coming towards them from above. Duburinga and Jarta-Den had moved quickly and silently forward. As they continued upwards, there was a change in the power around them. Something else pulsed through the rock. The evil intent lessened and they were filled with a sense of hope. As the Caramar warrior and the Quigling rounded the bend, two Ultamarian soldiers fell before them, writhing on the stairs.

"The Stones have been used," said Infiron.

"Hyrn!" said Rowan desperately.

"Not in battle," said Infiron. "They are challenging the evil Stone's hold on Abessair. Now is our best chance to make some ground closer to the chamber above."

Duburinga barked. "We must move now!"

The party leapt up the winding stairs as quickly as they were able. They climbed higher and higher. An Ultamarian soldier appeared before them standing in the lamplight still clutching a lance. At his feet lay another Ultamarian, his body still and his lance laying on the ground beside him. Behind them there was an opening to a landing. They dashed past the Ultamarians. Jarta-Den was the last to pass by the still standing soldier and as he did a hand reached out and grasped his left arm. The Quigling clenched his right fist and swung it into the jaw of the soldier, and the Ultamarian fell to the ground.

"We're going to be in trouble soon," called Jarta-Den.

"Hurry!" urged Duburinga.

Duburinga led the party up onto the landing. There was a large open circular room that filled the expanse of the tower. A circular ceiling was above them. On the opposite side of the room, the stairway continued. Several Ultamarians were coming to their senses within the room. Three stood between them and the stairway, and the others were close by. Duburinga was already moving and attacked the first Ultamarian as the soldier reached for his sword. Hernan moved past and drove his sword through the next. Duburinga had darted to his right and he then threw himself left and collided with the third. As the three Ultamarians collapsed, the party dashed across the room and up into the stairway. An Ultamarian came barrelling down the stairs towards them, still dazed. Duburinga deftly grasped the Ultamarian and using soldier's momentum flung him past. The soldier slid bumpily down the stairs. The others stepped aside as the helpless Ultamarian passed them. Another soldier appeared at the foot of the stairs and was met with his fellow Ultamarian cannoning into his stomach and throwing him backwards. They both sprawled at the base of the stairs.

The circular room that they now entered was richly furnished, though dilapidated and dimly lit. It was deserted. Directly above them they felt the source of the evil power strong and close at hand. They could hear movement above them and sounds coming from the stairs below. Hernan spoke.

"There is an antechamber above," said the Abessairian. "That is where the King's Company stood guard and where now the Dark Lords keep their elite guard. Above that is the Chamber of Vigil, as it was known. The Dark Lords do not name it, but it is from there they rule Anasaria."

They felt around them the evil power falter momentarily and in its place they sensed an anger.

"I think they know we're coming," said Jarta-Den.

"They sense the Sword of Acclimoss, I think," said Infiron. "But there is something else at work. It is almost as if Abessair knows that the Stones are returning and is resisting."

The five of them moved forward.

"Wait," said Hernan. "Are we going to try to storm through a heavily guarded room?"

"There is said to be another way up into the chamber," said Infiron.

She thought for a moment and then turned to Rowan.

"Rowan, quickly bring your sword," said the Priest. "There was said to be a secret stairway somewhere within the wall of the tower. Perhaps Acclimoss can find it."

Rowan hesitated. He could feel the power emanating from above, a little subdued, but still strong. He felt almost that the power from above was calling for help. He heard the rushing feet coming from below, and footsteps moving above. Jarta-Den had already moved back to the top of the stairs they had just exited. An Ultamarian charged up at him and then fell back, his throat gushing blood.

Rowan gripped the hilt of Acclimoss and followed Infiron towards the wall of the tower, near where Jarta-Den guarded the top of the stairs. Infiron told Rowan to hold the Sword downwards so that the hilt faced the wall. Rowan changed his grip and held the Sword, hilt out. The images of the Stones glowed softly but steadily in the shadowy room.

Harla moved from where she stood behind the form of Margana still kneeling beside the body of Turum. She looked beyond where Grenga-Da was wiping his sword, to where Wren stood terrified, an arrow held loosely in his small bow. Harla looked around with panic.

"Where is the Elder?" she asked desperately.

From the dark doorway behind Wren, where Gerardien stood, Harla caught the glimpse of a flicker of red and Yarga stepped out into the passageway.

The Elder faced the party. He then turned back to where an old woman in a ragged gown appeared.

"This is Milgan," said Yarga. "She is a Priest of the Order of the Stones."

"Hah hah," cried the woman. "I felt the Stones coming and I knew that they would help me."

She turned and looked down the passageway beyond.

"We do not have the Sword or the Stones though, and neither do those below. Nothing will protect them. We need to all get out as fast as we can. The clash between the Stones of Angil and that which lies above, will be too much to bear for the Anasarians kept here as prisoners."

They moved quickly. Harla spoke softly to Margana and the Caramar warrior climbed to her feet and moved forward. Droom stooped and pulled the Anasarian blade from Turum's body. He threw the sword aside and lifted his comrade and lay his body at the side of the passage.

"We will return for you unless other fate befalls," said Captain Droom. "If we can, you will return to the Underrealm. Your name will be remembered with honour."

The next level down was less quiet. They heard the sound of many people, fearful and desperate for release. They came down the stairs, Harla and Karra-Bar leading the way.

Without warning, a voice from behind them, to one side of the stairs, called out, "Oi? What are you all doing—?"

Harla moved so quickly that Karra-Bar was left looking into empty space. He turned his head and saw an Ultamarian, shabbily dressed and dirty, being dragged out of the shadows from beside the stairway. Harla's forearm was locked around his throat. He held a half eaten sausage in his hand and with his other reached for his sword which seemed to have disappeared. There was a jangle as Harla with her free hand held up an iron ring that held a large key.

Yarga came to the bottom of the stairs and Harla tossed the keyring to him.

"You may find this easier, Elder," she said, and then thumped the jailer on the back of the neck. He crumpled to the floor.

A pulse of power came through the rock and for a while the sickening feeling that flowed down through the plateau from the fortress above was diminished.

"The Stones return," said Milgan. "But we must hurry."

They followed as Yarga approached the first cell, and for a time, a sense of hope filled them. Wren's heart lifted and hope burned in him that his father was alive somewhere down here.

Hyrn felt the impatience in Ilah as he climbed. He looked sideways at Bardewan and the look that the Abessairian soldier gave him showed that Ivah was also impatient. As they rose higher in the tower, a sudden awareness came to Hyrn. At that moment the feeling of evil intent lessened. They had moved from the bulk of the fortress and were now in the tower proper. They now stood within the Tower of the Stones where it rose from the bulk of Abessair. He felt that pull beyond his conscious control and Ilah was in his hand. Beside him, Bardewan had retrieved Ivah and held the Stone up before him.

The Stones glowed softly and their light glanced off the walls. The party stood within a cocoon of light but tendrils flowed out into the walls. They moved upwards within the light of the Stones.

"The Ultamarians always talked of this tower with dread," said Garan. "The Dark Lords tried to destroy it, but they were unable to make any mark on it."

"There are soldiers above." The voice of Ilah flowed through Hyrn. "They are confused. They have not shaken off the curse of Ultamar but the power of Angil fills them with conflict."

"Let's keep moving," said Arienga.

Higher up the stairs they came across four soldiers. The four seemed to be jostling and fighting amongst themselves. As the Caramar warrior approached, one of them went for his sword. One of the others looked at the strangers coming up the stairs and blanched and then tried to restrain their comrade.

"No! No!" he cried. "Remember Abessair!"

"Filth!" screamed the other and, bursting past, he leapt at Arienga. By the time that the soldier arrived where Arienga stood, she had disappeared. She came at him from the side and drove her blade into the back of his neck. She withdrew her short sword and, as the Ultamarian fell to the ground, took up a defensive stance.

"Hold!" cried Careil. "Some of the Abessairians are showing themselves."

Hyrn spoke from beside him. "The Stones cannot keep this up. They need to conserve their strength for the battle above."

As Hyrn finished, the Stones went dark, leaving them bathed in the flickering light from the lamps that lit the spiralling stairs. Arienga and Careil were already shepherding them past the disoriented and confused soldiers. The party continued to move quickly up the stairs.

They reached the top, and a landing opened out before them. It swarmed with soldiers. All around them light pulsed through the walls and ceiling. A window stood to one side and they could see starlight twinkling beyond.

"We have to get through," said Careil, and then added to Arienga, "Try not to kill anyone unless you have to."

"That is always the way," said Arienga, impassively.

As the hilt of the Sword of Acclimoss passed over a particular place along the northern wall, something clicked. Hernan had moved back to help Jarta-Den against any attack from below. Duburinga called out in warning as the tramp of feet came down the stairs from above.

"Here!" called Infiron sharply.

A dark space had opened in the wall and Rowan stood in the entrance.

Duburinga moved forward and sliding past Rowan said, "Me first, Your Majesty."

Rowan was stunned by that, but more so by the wry smile on the face of the normally stern warrior as he moved past.

They were all in the stairway in a few moments. Hernan, coming in last, watched through the open doorway, as a throng of Ultamarian soldiers came stumbling down the stairs. Infiron signalled to Rowan, and quickly understanding, he pushed the sword hilt against the wall. Hernan saw the soldiers entering the room, but the door slid across before they were able to react. They were now in darkness apart from the glowing light that shone from Acclimoss, and the ghostly purple light that pulsed dully in the stone walls on either side of them. The stairway rose above them and also fell away below.

Duburinga had begun to move up the narrow step, but Hernan shushed them. There had been a sound below, he thought, down where the stairs led into darkness. They listened but they could hear nothing. They began to move up the stairs, relying on the opposing forces of the dim golden light from the Sword, and the dull malevolent purple glow from the walls. They had torches, but in this confined space they would have made it hard to breathe. The stairway was narrow as it wound steadily upwards. As they climbed, they could hear the clamour from the adjacent guardroom and they could feel the evil power growing closer.

Eventually, they moved past the noise from the Ultamarian guards who formed the last military defence of the Dark Lords. Above them, the stone stairway came to an abrupt halt at a stone ceiling. Duburinga was already inspecting the stone.

"It is a hatch," said the Caramar warrior. "It looks as if it slides."

The rest of the party moved up behind him. They stood and listened. At first they could hear nothing, then they heard a harsh voice shout something and then another voice. Duburinga reached up and felt the stone above. He pushed softly testing the stone. It didn't move. Rowan stood just behind the Caramar and he instinctively lifted up the hilt of Acclimoss. They heard a soft click. Duburinga tried the stone again and he felt it move with only a soft grating sound.

"Are we ready?" he whispered.

The others all nodded. Rowan had moved his grip on the Sword and now held it ready as Duburinga began to slide the stone slowly. At first there was nothing to see, and then a strip of bright purple light appeared and eventually opened out into a square of light above where the stairs ended. Duburinga continued sliding the stone until the opening was large enough for them to get through. He paused and looked behind at the party. The faces all looked at him expectantly.

"Well here goes," he said.

Duburinga leapt up the rest of the steps and out into the garishly bright chamber. Rowan moved up quickly behind him. Jarta-Den followed and stopped next to where Rowan stood behind Duburinga. Infiron and then Hernan came up behind.

The source of the garish light was clear. A large pulsing Stone stood in the middle of the large table in the centre of the room. Seven figures stood around the table, intent on the Stone. They had not noticed the intruders.

Rowan moved to stand beside Duburinga.

Suddenly one of the figures swung his hooded face around. Piercing eyes of violet shone within the hood. Jarta-Den loosed an arrow and it struck the figure in the chest. The figure staggered but then the arrow burst into flame; the fire purple and bright.

The Dark Lord laughed as the arrow turned to ash, and the rest of the evil figures looked away from the Stone and over to where enemies had entered their lair. The power of their gaze struck the five gathered at the secret entrance. Coldness and pain filled the air. The Dark Lords were surprised at the sudden appearance of intruders, but felt sure in their power within their stronghold. But then they sensed that some power lurked among the interlopers. The same power that had assaulted them, but not as strong.

Jarta-Den spat at them, "You escaped Guran-Badur but your time has come."

Preskatchion laughed. "A Quigling," he sneered. "And who else do we have?"

A voice sounded loud and strong. "The King of Anasaria!"

Rowan stood with the Sword of Acclimoss raised and pointed towards the Dark Lords.

A growing procession of prisoners followed behind as they checked each cell in turn. Some of those that were free were still healthy and they helped other prisoners that were unable to walk alone. Some prisoners were in too bad condition to walk at all and other more able Anasarians carried them bodily or on makeshift stretchers. Yarga moved steadfastly from side to side down the corridor opening each door in turn. Behind him bounced Wren desperately calling into each cell as they passed.

He called again. "Father! Father!" as the Elder opened another cell.

They peered into the cell but it was empty.

Then faintly from behind them came a voice. "Wren? Wren? Is that you?"

Yarga turned to move past Wren, but Wren had already bolted across the passage and had opened the small hatch in the opposite door. A desperate and amazed face peered through the hatch.

Yarga moving behind Wren said, "You will need to move out of the way Wren, if I am to unlock this door."

Wren moved quickly aside but waited impatiently as Yarga bent and placed the key in the door. Yarga turned the key and pushed the door inwards. He had to move quickly aside as a large man burst past. His clothes were dirty and ragged, he had bare blackened feet and his face was dirty and his hair and beard unkempt. He reached out and swept Wren up in a tight embrace.

"My boy. My boy," he cried. "I never thought I would see you again."

And the man then spoke hurriedly and excitedly. "How have you been living? How…" and he paused momentarily then rushed on. "I felt the power of something coming through the very ground. It broke up the evil of this place. But how did you get here? Thank the Stones you are still alive."

"It was the Stones," said Wren, still holding onto his father. "They are here. I have seen them." He paused and then continued with a note of wonder in his voice. "I held Ilah, Father."

Careil moved forwards to confront the Ultamarians ahead of him. Just then a loud knocking noise came from above and to their left. The Ultamarian directly in front of Careil, along with his fellow soldiers, turned towards the sound. Hyrn, amongst those gathered at the top of the stairs, looked upwards towards where the window was. A shape was silhouetted against the night sky. Moonlight lit the form of a large swan. It held itself against the outside of the tower with the flapping of its wings and tapped its beak against the window. The window was latched. The swan's desperate attempts to enter distracted them all.

Everyone seemed frozen momentarily, and then an arrow streaked above their heads and it flew high and straight and struck the latch. The window burst open, and a great swan came swooping through, followed by several others. Arienga stood with her bow still raised as the swans swooped into the room and began attacking the Ultamarians relentlessly. The soldiers swung around wildly trying to ward off this unexpected onslaught.

"Go! Now!" barked Careil.

Garan guided Hyrn, as Careil, Arienga, and Bardewan made their way through the throng, pushing Ultamarians aside and confronting any that stood in the way. Most of the Ultamarians were too intent on defending themselves against the storm of swans above but as the five made their way closer to the door, two large Ultamarians appeared in front of them, barring the way. The two glowed with a faint purple light. Their eyes were steadfast but pain gripped their faces. As Careil moved forward, brandishing his Abessairian sword, one of the Ultamarians raised his sword and swung it swiftly and there was a clash of steel as the two met. The Ultamarian took a step back and then thrust back against Careil, and the Rider was pushed to the side and stumbled to his knees. The Ultamarian brought his sword up to strike Careil, but as he did the blade of Arienga slashed out at his throat. He staggered and Arienga struck him again and he fell to the ground. As he fell, the Caramar warrior was already moving, and met the other Ultamarian guard. Her short blade blocked the thrust of his sword. An Abessairian sword slashed round catching the Ultamarian in the side of his head. Bardewan sheathed his sword as Arienga pushed the guard aside.

Hyrn came up behind Bardewan, shielded by Garan. An Ultamarian attacked from Hyrn's left but Garan's blade was already sweeping through the air. The Ultamarian collapsed just beside Hyrn. Arienga had moved to a defensive position behind them and Careil got to his feet and the two faced the melee. Bardewan moved to face the door and fumbled to remove the key from around his neck. An Ultamarian, wildly stepping back as a large swan battered his head and face, tripped backwards across the body of one of the guards and collided with Bardewan as he removed the key from around his neck.

The key on its chain was knocked from his hand and sailed through the air and amongst the chaos of the battle between the Ultamarians and the swans.

Rowan moved forward to face the Dark Lord closest to him. One of the others was calling towards the door opposite, alerting the guards. Duburinga sped forward and leapt up onto the table and bounded across jumping and landing next to the door. He grasped one of the long iron braziers and, tearing it from the wall, thrust it through the handle of the door. One of the Dark Lords moved to confront him but Duburinga was already out of reach and standing defensively.

Rowan continued to move towards the Dark Lord, but Hernan came up beside Rowan and moved past him with his sword raised to confront the evil figure.

"Ah!" said the Dark Lord, Carvilikon. "A deserter. Obviously you need to have another drink."

He pointed to the Stone behind him on the table and Hernan's gaze was diverted briefly, but that was enough.

The Stone called to him, "Remember your oath to Ultamar."

Hernan stood transfixed. He did not move. His mind was filled with the purple light.

"No!" shouted Infiron.

The Priest moved forward.

"Oh, good. A Priest," sneered Carvilikon.

Jarta-Den moved to Infiron's right, ready to protect her. The rest of the Dark Lords began to move towards where Rowan and the others stood. Duburinga was already in motion and he struck the figure facing Hernan. The Dark Lord threw out a hand and a blast of blue light sent the Caramar careening across the room and he crashed heavily into the wall and crumpled to the floor. Infiron reached out her hand and grasped Hernan's arm. Hernan flinched as if burnt by her touch. He turned round towards the Priest, his face a contorted mask.

"Kill her, soldier," said Carvilikon.

Hernan began to raise his sword. Infiron placed her hand against his arm.

"Fight it, Hernan," she said. "You have felt the power of Abessair."

"It has nothing of the power of Ultamar and the Stone of Erekslat," jeered the Dark Lord.

Suddenly Rowan leapt past Hernan and thrust the Sword of Acclimoss into the chest of Carvilikon. The Dark Lord screeched in pain but the power of the evil Stone burnt strongly in him. Mastering himself, he began to pull the sword from his body, driving Rowan backwards. He looked directly at

Rowan.

"King you say?" he rasped, mockingly. "You need to have a kingdom to be a king."

The Dark Lords closed around them. Hernan was frozen, in conflict between the two powers competing for his will, as he faced Infiron. Duburinga groaned from where he lay on the floor. Jarta-Den raised his sword.

Suddenly the atmosphere in the room changed. A new power seemed to be there and the light seemed to change. Something approached, from behind where Rowan stood.

Something powerful, yet evil.

They made their way up from where the dungeons of Ultamar lay, seeking a way out. Harla and Droom, with Karra-Bar led the rest of the party, with a long procession of Anasarians trailing behind. Some of the stronger Anasarians, not too long in Ultamar, now carried Abessairian swords or anything that could be used as a weapon. The old Priest, Milgan, urged them on. Wren with his father, Bertan, walked behind her and Yarga. Bertan's arm rested on Wren's shoulder, and sometimes it lay a little heavier as his father struggled on.

"There is a small gate above here," said the Quigling. "It is one of the passages to the delights of Sewer Town."

Waves of power came through the walls and floor. Evil power, sometimes strong and sometimes wavering.

"We must hurry," Milgan said desperately to Yarga.

"Come on, hurry!" Yarga called behind.

"Wait!" called Harla urgently.

They had come to the top of a stairway. A passage led off to either side. Karra-Bar had begun to lead them left, but Harla halted him. The Caramar listened intently despite the noise of the movement of the Anasarians following.

"There are soldiers ahead," she said.

"We have to move quickly," said Yarga, almost painfully.

"They won't know what hit them," said Droom to Harla.

The Caramar warrior looked at him and nodded in agreement.

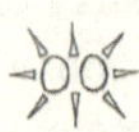

Bardewan leapt across a fallen Ultamarian. A swan tumbled through the air, broken and bloodied and collided with the wall. He dived along the ground amongst the scrabbling feet. He thought he glimpsed a flash of gold. A knee knocked the side of his head and dazed him momentarily. But he scrambled forward, on his hands and knees. As he placed his right hand a booted heel stepped back crushing his hand painfully. He could no longer see the key. The sound of fighting was all around and behind him he could hear Arienga and Careil clashing with the Ultamarians.

"Hurry!" called Hyrn desperately.

Then he saw it again, off to his right. A foot must have inadvertently kicked it away. He summoned all his strength and plunged through the sea of legs. He felt Ivah in his mind urging him. He slid along the stone floor with his hand outstretched. The tips of his searching fingers found the chain. He stretched his hand further and grasped it tightly. As he drew the hand back towards himself, a hand grabbed him from behind and dragged him backwards. He desperately held onto the chain holding the key as he was whisked through the struggling mass around him. He stumbled as he was brought to his feet and then he was bundled over fallen bodies until he stood in front of the door to the chamber.

Arienga released him and said sharply, "Hurry, Doorwarden! Open the door now!"

Behind Rowan the sense of evil grew.

A voice cried out, "My Lords. I have brought you the Stone."

There, beside the entrance to the secret stairway, stood a man. An Ultamarian, but he glowed with a sickly violet light. He looked around confusedly and unsteady on his feet.

Captain Bardan.

They had left the hatch open behind them. The Ultamarian had come up the stairway from far below where they had entered, and had fortuitously found the final barrier removed. They had opened the way for him. The chamber pulsed as the light of the Artoran Stone glared in his hand.

The Dark Lords were taken aback. Their power wavered behind them. The Stone of Erekslat pulsed and flickered. Hernan relaxed his sword. Rowan used the brief respite and pushed his sword deeper into the chest of Carvilikon.

"Fool!" screamed Preskatchion at Bardan. "Why have you brought that cursed Artoran Stone here?"

Bardan looked worried. "No! No, my Lords!" he wailed. "It is the Angilanian Stone that you desired. I have brought it to you. All by myself. I…I…"

He looked around uncertainly. He was tired and confused. There were strangers here and the Dark Lords looked angry. The Stone in his hand glowed with greater intensity.

Far away across Anasaria and beyond, past the sheer mountain walls of their realm, The High Sorcerers of Artora bent their will towards the Stone of Erekslat. Ultamar and Anasaria would be at their mercy. They strove to drive their power towards the Stone that lay in the top tower of Ultamar. The Dark Lords quavered at the power of their attack.

Bardan moved towards the Dark Lords. Evil power strove within the chamber. The light of the Stones fought against each other. The Artoran's pushed their will, and the light from the large Stone in the centre of the table began to fail. Rowan withdrew his sword and Carvilikon stumbled and fell to the floor. Bardan moved closer.

"Take it away! Away!" screamed Preskatchion.

"My Lords. My Lords," wept Bardan, as the distant Artorans felt their growing ascendancy over the Stone that was at the heart of the power of Ultamar.

The Dark Lords backed away from where Bardan approached. The power in the chamber grew to a sickening intensity. Jarta-Den grabbed Rowan's arm and urged him away, over to where Duburinga lay. Infiron followed, leading the dazed Hernan. They watched as Bardan approached the six Dark Lords still standing. The corrupted Ultamarian Captain looked at them pleadingly, but at a desperate signal from Preskatchion, the six gathered around the table again and bent their will on the Stone there.

The Artorans and the Dark Lords strove against each other. Bardan stumbled as he approached and fell to his knees but he still held the Stone out before him. The Artorans sought the veins of power that held the fortress and then there was an interruption to their will. The light from the Stone in Bardan's hand faltered. Something else was there. Some other power. They sought it out, but the will of the Dark Lords fought against them. The power in the chamber grew in intensity. Rowan held the Sword of Acclimoss out in front of himself as if to ward off the power, as they stood around the body of Duburinga. The keening figure of Bardan seemed to be almost burning with the light that engulfed him. Around the stone table, a webbed dome of purple light grew encompassing the six remaining Dark Lords and the figure of Bardan.

The Artorans pushed deeper, seeking the opposing power. And then they felt it. The power came from the other tower. The Twin Stones were there and close to the heart of the fortress's power. The Sorcerers desperately fought to gain the ascendancy and to send their power up into the Tower of the Stones. But the Dark Lords still battled against them.

Droom and Harla met the Ultamarians head on, before they even knew they were under attack. They seemed confused. The power of their Lords waxed and waned in the rock. At times they felt something else, some other power, like a distant memory, but their loyalty to the Dark Lords still held sway. There were about a dozen of them left. Others had gone down to the gate as the orders came to defend the fortress. They had not come back, and the soldiers there had waited, but all was quiet. And then suddenly they were overwhelmed by skilled fighters and a horde of angry Anasarians.

Karra-Bar led them down to the gate. It was open. At the entrance lay the bodies of Ultamarian soldiers. Cautiously Karra-Bar, Droom and Harla crept through the entrance. They were met with the stench and fumes of Sewer Town and they looked through the haze up and out to the east where the sky began to take on a few tinges of light. Around, all was quiet. The town seemed deserted.

Yarga came out behind them with Milgan.

"We have to get as far away as we can," said Yarga

"The others have escaped and moved beyond and into the forest," said Milgan.

They began shepherding the people through the gate. Harla and Droom helped move people through while Karra-Bar led the procession out through the laneways and streets of Sewer Town. High above them flashes of light showed hazy purple against the sky. Harla tried to hurry the Anasarians through. She became increasingly worried and then the last of them, those being carried on stretchers, were through. She and Droom then took up positions at the rear of the procession.

Yarga, walking ahead of Wren and his father, looked back. They were making their way as quickly as possible through the town. As he looked, Yarga saw that the pair had dropped behind and Bertan was leaning more heavily on Wren. Bertan stumbled and the pair came to a halt.

Yarga turned back to help them and as he did a large familiar horse came galloping out of a side street followed by a chariga and several other horses.

Wren looked up as the war horse came to a halt before him. "Erras!" he cried.

Erras approached Wren and pushed his head against the boy.

"Come on, Father," he said. "We can ride."

Bertan looked up confused and puzzled.

"How…?" but he failed to voice a question.

Wren helped his father up onto the horse and then he leapt up in front. Others in the procession, tired and ailing, were helped to mount and ride.

They quickened their pace as much as possible as they moved towards the outskirts of the town and on into the forest, following the trail of those that had already escaped. Off to the east, King Darlam had already ordered a general retreat, and gradually the lands around the plateau of Ultamar were evacuated.

Bardewan nervously tried to fit the key into the lock. His hands were bruised and covered in blood and grime, and the key was difficult to grip. He finally lined it up and the key slid into the lock. Bardewan felt power flow through the key and into his tired and sore body. He felt energised and he grasped the key tightly and turned the key in the lock. The power that surged through him seemed to be asking him a question and then as if satisfied, the door swung open. Bardewan removed the key and moved through the open doorway with Hyrn close behind him.

As they entered, the last bastion of the power of Abessair opened before them. The chamber glowed with glorious light. It was as if all the power that was Abessair had been drawn up and enclosed in this room. Garan followed behind and immediately Careil and Arienga backed into the room and slammed the door. Then they felt the tower wrench around them.

Careil sensed the pulse of power that had come from beneath their feet.

"I have felt that before," he said. "It is an Artoran Stone."

"Yes, I felt it too," said Arienga. "The power wielded by the Artoran Sorcerer."

In the minds of the two carrying the Stones came a shout that barely hid what sounded like suppressed fury, "The Oathbreakers! Return us!"

Bardewan was already leading Hyrn up towards the stepped podium in the centre of the room. Atop the podium stood two plinths, each was topped with a silver cup. Before Bardewan could reach the first step, the tower trembled and he stumbled and fell back against Hyrn.

Duburinga got groggily to his feet. Pain shot through his body as he stood. All around him, before his vision cleared, he could just see a blur of bright flashes of purple light. Slowly, the others gathered there came into focus around him. They were dark against the wall of evil power that filled the centre of the chamber. Rowan stood with the Sword of Acclimoss held out defensively. Hernan and Infiron stood beside him. Jarta-Den turned in amazement as Duburinga stood up.

"We have to get out of here," said Duburinga through clenched teeth.

Jarta-Den looked around. "Back into the stairway!" he shouted.

He gripped Duburinga's arm to help him but the Caramar said, "I am fine. Protect Rowan and Infiron."

Rowan was transfixed. Jarta-Den urged Infiron to move to follow Duburinga. He turned back to Rowan and then saw Carvilikon rise from where he lay outside the wall of power that coruscated behind him separating him from his evil companions. With anger the Dark Lord charged at Rowan. Jarta-Den was not quick enough to intervene. An Abessairian blade flashed through the air and drove through the chest of Carvilikon. The Dark Lord turned and confronted his attacker. Hernan stood with his sword still embedded in the evil flesh. Purple light pulsed through the blade as Carvilikon turned his anger upon the Abessairian.

Hernan shouted at his King, "Go! Go, now! Leave me. I will die here if I must, and strike a blow against these evil bastards. I have lived long in torment. Go!"

Jarta-Den had already grabbed Rowan's arm leading him to where Duburinga stood next to the open hatch, but Rowan struggled to help Hernan.

"We need the Sword!" said Jarta-Den sharply.

Rowan controlled himself and followed Jarta-Den across and into the top of the stairway. He looked back and saw Hernan struggling with the pulsing figure of the Dark Lord. The Abessairian was being driven to his knees but Jarta-Den pulled Rowan down into the stairway. Duburinga climbed down and slid the stone hatch across above them, trapping Hernan and blocking out the sickening light of the chamber. The battling evil powers still pulsed through the stone around them.

Bardewan rose to his knees and looked up at the raised platform and the pillars standing there waiting above. Past the podium, through the windows high in the chamber, he could see against the sky the top of the high tower pulsing evilly above. He turned back towards Hyrn and saw through the windows that looked east that the sky was lightening.

"Now, Hyrn!" he cried, reaching inside his uniform and grasping Ivah.

Hyrn had already risen to his feet holding Ilah. Within his head the sense of longing and desire was like a sharp pain. But burning more strongly was the feeling of a dam ready to burst. Hyrn followed quickly behind Bardewan as the Abessairian mounted the steps. Bardewan grasped Ivah and held the Stone out towards the furthest pillar as he approached. Hyrn moved just beside him to the closest pillar. Ilah was in his hand. The two Stones began to pulse and vibrate. The power within them built to a crescendo.

Strange lightning flashed above the fortress. Droom looked back, as shafts of purple light burst from cracks and openings in the plateau above. Eastwards at Forest Ford, marshalling the retreating army, King Darlam stood looking back at the power flashing and blasting from Ultamar.

In a dim stairway, enclosed in stone, the King of Anasaria, a Priest of the Order of the Stones, a warrior from the Caramarhc Mountains, and a refugee from the torment of Guran-Badur, huddled.

"Down the stairs," urged Duburinga.

"There is no time," Infiron said.

She turned to Rowan. "The power still exists here, Rowan. It is being corrupted, but it still waits. You are the King and you carry the Sword. Call Abessair."

Infiron gently grasped Rowan's shoulder. Jarta-Den supported the Priest and Duburinga held Rowan's arm as he placed the tip of his sword against the wall. He felt the hilt hum in his hand and he felt the blade vibrate as it interacted with the stone. There was power there. It was the power of the Stones but from long ago. He thought of his vision in the cave. King Arionus and his sword; this sword. He stepped back and the others stumbled a little but held on as he lifted his sword, the Sword of Acclimoss, above his head and then drove it with a blinding white flash into the stone wall.

Hyrn held Ilah out and towards the silver cup. His body froze. Something flowed up through his feet. Something that held him and fought against the will of Ilah. Hyrn saw that Bardewan was also struggling against the power. Ilah hummed angrily and dangerously and pulsed blindingly. Then almost as if a small relief valve was opened, a slice of the power of the Stones flowed into Hyrn and he reached out and he placed Ilah in her silver nest. Hyrn saw that Bardewan beside him had returned Ivah.

Then the battle for Abessair began.

The Chamber of the Stones erupted in bright white light. Hyrn felt the evil power wash out of him. And the explosion of power became a raging river, as the Twin Stones of Angil returned to take back Abessair. The Tower of the Stones was washed clean. The scaffolding that encircled the tower collapsed into wreckage and dust. The power struck the point at the base of the tower where the Artoran Stone and the Stone of Erekslat strived against each other and fought for control of the fortress. Ilah and Ivah, reunited, and in the heart of their home erupted in a torrent of devastating power. The forces of good and evil that battled sent deadly power coursing all around. Yet the power of the Twin Stones first sped up to the top of the Central Tower.

As Carvilikon was driven to the stone floor the six remaining Dark Lords strived to keep control of their fortress. They sat withered and almost incandescent in their struggle. Artoran Sorcerers fought against their power. But suddenly through the veins of power, and then through the very walls, coursed the power of the Twin Stones and the lifeblood of Abessair. In the centre of the King's Table sat an evil Stone and the evil power of usurpers and oath breakers flowed into it. The Dark Lords were blasted as the devastating power of the Twin Stones obliterated the Stone of Erekslat. The burning figures shattered into dust. A beam of light shot out and smashed into the Artoran Stone. Bardan crumpled in a burning heap.

Far away, as the dawn approached, the pinnacle of a black tower that stood within an arc of mountains like a tall dark splinter, erupted into a ball of blazing white light.

Then the power of the Stones reclaimed Abessair and drove out the power of Ultamar in an eruption of power that blasted through the walls, stairways, corridors, doorways and halls, and down through the passageways and shafts of the plateau. The filth and detritus that had clogged the arteries within the plateau met a cleansing tide. Like a fierce wind the power erupted. Swirling flashes of purple being driven before a white gale. The windows of the chamber atop the central tower shattered as an explosion of purple light and smoke blasted outwards in a huge churning ring. As it spread it lost its colour and then flared with a bright white light.

Below, and as far as they had been able to retreat, the enemies of the Dark Lords watched as the power of the Twin Stones fought for control of the fortress. Wind and dust blew around them as the explosive energy dissipated around them. The Tower of the Stones stood brightest first and then whiteness filled the central tower. They watched with awe and terror as the top of the central tower erupted. Then out from the base of the Tower of the Stones the brightness spread downwards, and across to the lesser towers. The shape of the fortress emerged above them. Everything went still, and everyone gathered seemed to be holding their breath.

And there stood Abessair, towering into the sky above, shining white atop the black rock of the plateau. At that moment the sun crested the eastern horizon, its orange glow brushing the towers of Abessair with a fiery light. Chanting started amongst those gathered around Forest Ford, and deep in the forest near Sewer Town. The Anasarians stood mesmerised and, as the chanting of the Caramar and Underdwellers came to an end, a roar went up from those gathered.

"Abessair! Abessair! Ultamar is destroyed!" and the sound seemed to bounce off the walls of the plateau.

In the Chamber of the Stones, Arienga chanted too, as the rays of sunlight burst through the high windows turning the domed ceiling orange above the brilliant white light that glowed all around. Then they all stood silent. They heard, as if the distant rumble of thunder, voices, thousands of them, shouting and cheering together.

Rowan heard a familiar sound from beside him. As the four stood enclosed in a ball of white light Duburinga greeted the dawn. The barrage of purple power that had buffeted their cocoon had disappeared. All around them they saw the walls glowing with a strong white light. Rowan gripped the sword and withdrew it from the wall, leaving a glowing wound. The ball of light disappeared from around them. The wound in the stone closed up.

They waited there momentarily, and then Jarta-Den said, "Ultamar is no more."

He stepped up and placed his hands against the stone above and slid it back. White light shone through tinged with orange. A soft wind buffeted them from above where the windows of the chamber had been shattered by the blast.

Rowan followed Jarta-Den up the stairs and into the chamber, with Duburinga close behind. Stone chairs and furniture stood scattered around. Anything that could burn had gone. The large stone table in the centre of the room still stood smothered in blackened ash but resolute. No traces of the Dark Lords or Bardan remained. Nor was there any sign of the body of Hernan.

As Rowan walked forward he saw the glitter of something on the floor to his left. It lay beneath the window that looked to the south and east. He walked over and saw an Abessairian sword lying there; Hernan's sword. He felt the wind that blew through the tall opening. As he approached the window he looked out. To his left below he could see the Tower of the Stones. Bright light shone from its windows. On the wind he could hear from far below, all around, the sound of cheering.

He stepped close to the lintel of the window. The wind buffeted his clothes and his hair. The fortress rose below him but he looked out over the land of Anasaria in the morning light. He raised his right hand. It clasped the Sword of Acclimoss. The Sword shone and flashed with the power of Abessair, and the light of the rising sun across Anasaria seemed to set the blade in flames. In the Chamber of the Stones, Hyrn looked up in wonder and saw the Sword flashing above. All around, far below, the people saw the light of the Sword of the King, like a beacon signalling the downfall of Ultamar, and they looked up and cheered, and rejoiced, and wept with joy.

Jarta-Den had opened the barricaded doorway, and the four of them departed the chamber. Rowan was eager to see Hyrn. As they made their way down the spiralling stairs, they came across the bodies of soldiers who had tried to flee the cataclysm above. They lay sprawling and contorted. They were now clad in white and silver and, despite the violence that had overcome them, their faces were serene. It was the same in the guardroom below, and beyond, as they continued down. Throughout Abessair, the Ultamarians lay dead, and in death, had been filled with the light of the Stones.

Outside the Tower of the Stones, Hyrn and the others were met with a different sight. On the landing dazed Abessairians were getting to their feet amongst the bodies of the wounded or dead, all now washed clean of the stain of Ultamar. The bodies of swans also lay amongst the fallen but other swans stood. One of the swans approached Hyrn. Bardewan stepped forward and stood beside Hyrn. The swan spoke in their minds.

"Our duty here is fulfilled and Ultamar has fallen as the prophecies foretold. Doorwarden, you have played your part, and all your years of torment have not been in vain. The swan looked to Hyrn. "Child of Light there is still much to do and the war against evil goes on. You may still have a part to play, if all comes to pass. Stay strong and prepare to fulfil your destiny."

Hyrn was confused by this but didn't ask for explanation. He instead said, "Thank you for your help. We wouldn't have been able to complete the quest without you."

"We came as needed and as promised," said the swan. "We must return to our home now. There are other tasks that await. Please take care of our fallen comrades."

Hyrn looked around, and then said solemnly, "We will."

"Farewell," said the swan. "General Ferian, and the Priests Trion and Neferelon, will be glad of the tidings we bear, but their path lies elsewhere."

"Wait," said Hyrn perplexedly. "Where are they?"

The swans did not wait though, and as if in silent agreement, they took to the air one by one. The air was full of the wind of their wings, and loose feathers floated and swirled all around as they flew in a line through the window and out westwards towards the mountains.

They watched them go, and then Arienga moved towards the top of the stairs. Bardewan had decided to fulfil his role as Doorwarden and now stepped back through the doorway to the chamber and locked the door. Garan looked around at the dozen or so soldiers who now stood around the landing. Some were wounded but he picked out two healthy looking ones.

"You two," he said, "stand here and guard this door. Two more of you," he pointed at two soldiers, "guard the stairs. The rest of you, follow us."

Arienga and Careil led them down the stairway.

Jarta-Den had dropped back to help Infiron. Rowan raced ahead down the stairway with Duburinga following behind. The Caramar, despite his pain, strode down the steps, sorely, but steadfastly behind. Dead soldiers lay on stairs as they passed. They reached the landing where they had entered the stairs. The dead guards still lay there but they hurried on downwards and eastwards towards the entrance to the fortress. Eventually, they came to a wide straight stairway that led down to two large doors. Eventually, breathlessly, they reached the bottom of the stairs and pushed through the doors. They opened onto the centre of the mezzanine that looked out over the entrance hall. There to their right, stood Hyrn, Garan, Careil and Arienga. They were accompanied by several Abessairians.

Rowan rushed forward and grasped Hyrn in a hug.

"We did it," said Hyrn in a muffled voice. "We actually did it."

"Yes, we did," said Rowan. He released Hyrn and then looked around at those gathered.

He looked back at Hyrn. "Remember when Devarnia spoke to us in Errasarn. I never thought…" he trailed off.

He looked around and then saw that Arienga was with Duburinga. She had been ready to report but saw that he was injured.

"Duburinga?" she said worriedly.

"I'm fine, I'm fine!" he insisted. "What do you have to report?"

"Well," replied Arienga with a smile. "We did it!"

"Alright," said Duburinga, resignedly, with a wince of pain. "You can give me a full report later."

Rowan looked beyond Hyrn to where Careil stood tiredly. The Rider smiled at Rowan. Rowan saw Garan there, and behind him more Abessairians were coming out of an entrance.

Hyrn looked back. "We found these still alive in the Tower of the Stones."

"Where is Bardewan?" asked Rowan. "Is he…? Did he…?"

"He is guarding the Stones," said Hyrn.

Rowan sighed with relief. Then he noticed that the Abessairians gathering were beginning to bow down before him.

"No. Stop that," said Rowan. "We need to get down to the gates and find out what has happened to the others."

Garan turned to the Abessairians that were gathered.

"Right!" he said. "I want soldiers down to open the main doors and then down to the gates, and clearing the way for the King. Others of you through there." He pointed down to the archway where they had entered earlier, and said, "Down to the dungeons and look for any survivors."

A weathered-looking sergeant drew his shoulders up, shook his head, and then began shouting at the soldiers as he organised them into two parties and sent them off on their missions.

They had made their way down to the great gates at the base of the plateau. They had come across more dead soldiers, but it seemed that the remaining Ultamarians that had still been within Ultamar, had mostly been pulled away for the defence of the Dark Lords, and up to guard the Chamber of the Stones. The massive gates were now wide open and the morning light flowed in. Soldiers had been sent to meet the approaching army. The huge space looked so different now from when Careil had seen it before. The vast chamber now glowed faintly white with the light of Abessair, buoyed by the sunlight shining through the gates. Careil walked down to look out of the great gates. The others all sat or lay there, and waited for the soldiers to report back. Rowan and Hyrn found a quiet place to sit and talk.

Arienga fussed over Duburinga where he lay resting, but she soon took the hint, that she should leave him alone, or maybe be given duties she did not want. She walked over and stood looking down at Rowan who sat resting against the wall with Hyrn beside him.

"Well done, Rowan," she said.

She paused, and then looked at him crossly and added, "Although, I heard that you attacked a powerful enemy with a thrust to the body, rather than using the weight of your sword in a cutting blow to the neck."

"I didn't have room," protested Rowan, "or time."

He fumbled for an explanation but Arienga cut him off.

"Get up, you idiot," she laughed, with a shake of her head.

Rowan got to his feet and stood facing Arienga. They looked at each other. Arienga glanced over to where Duburinga lay watching. The old warrior just rolled his eyes and shook his head slightly, but the slightest trace of a smile flashed across his face. Arienga looked back at Rowan as he stood there a little awkwardly. She moved close to him. He saw the intensity in her expression and he felt a prickling on his skin, and his stomach jumped a little. Her face was before him and her eyes looked deep into his, powerful, and scary, and beautiful, and when their lips met, he felt that everything else disappeared.

Trumpets sounded from beyond the gates. Rowan and Arienga broke apart. They both turned and faced the gateway. Rowan gripped Arienga's hand. King Darlam rode through the gates leading an army of Underdwellers,

Caramar, Quiglings and Abessairians, and behind them, from beyond the gates, came the cheering of thousands of Anasarians. Arienga pulled her hand gently from Rowan's.

"I think you should go down there," she said.

Rowan turned to her, and quickly kissed her cheek. Then with a smile, he straightened up and strode off towards the gates where Darlam was dismounting.

Hyrn came up beside Arienga. She looked down at Rowan's brother, a little embarrassedly. Hyrn looked at her with a reassuring smile.

"It's alright," he said. "He has always been a bit of an idiot."

King Darlam strode forward to meet Rowan. He removed his gauntlet and held out his hand and Rowan grasped it.

"I think you have shown that you are worthy of your title," said Darlam. "King Rowan."

Rowan shook his head. "But it couldn't be that simple."

"No," said Darlam. "There will have to be a ceremony and you will need to gain the approval of the people."

"How do I do that?" asked Rowan.

"Well," said Darlam, and a smile came to his face, "defeating the tyrants that have been enslaving them is a good beginning."

Darlam looked behind to where people were crowding around the gates of Abessair.

"I think you should go and see what they think," said the Underdweller.

"Show them the Sword," he suggested, as Rowan stepped forward and looked at the mass of people gathered.

Careil and Hyrn had come up behind Rowan.

Together, the three that had left the farm in Wesmere on an uncertain quest, now approached the mass of people gathered near the gates, and filling the canyon beyond. Ranks of soldiers and warriors cleared a path as the three walked towards the sunlight. As they approached the entrance where the crowds gathered, a figure moved out towards them and behind him he led a horse carrying a rider.

"Wren!" shouted Hyrn.

"I found him!" shouted back Wren. "My father!"

"And Erras, I see," said Careil, with a laugh.

The horse snorted as they approached. And behind them came Harla and Droom riding a chariga. Yarga rode behind them with Milgan. Others seemed to be missing but they saw Margana and Gebarana. From their left another figure came forth. A Priest.

As he approached, Drivian asked worriedly. "Where is Infiron?"

"She has gone up to the Chamber of the Stones," said Rowan.

"I ask your leave to join her," said Drivian.

"I think that is where you need to be," said Rowan.

Careil was helping Bertan down from Erras's back. Rowan strode forward towards the crowd with Hyrn beside him. Wren looked at his father and Bertan nodded in assent. Wren hurried behind the two brothers as they drew close to the gathered crowd. They stopped and Rowan looked at Hyrn.

"Do it," said Hyrn.

Rowan reached up to where the hilt of the Sword of Acclimoss protruded above his shoulder. He grasped the hilt of the Sword and paused with apprehension. Then with a sweep, he withdrew the Sword from its sheath. The blade glistened and flashed in the morning sun.

The sound that met their ears was deafening as the Anasarians cheered and roared.

"The King! The King! Long live Abessair!"

And Rowan roared in a voice that he never knew he possessed. "Ultamar is destroyed! Long live Anasaria!"

And the sound of the crowd rose in an uproarious tumult that reverberated around the cavern and shook the rock of the plateau, and the sound carried up to where the fortress of Abessair shone defiantly. Evil had been driven from the heart of their land, and their years of torment and struggle were over. Joy filled the hearts of all those there and not the least those soldiers that had sworn an oath to protect Anasaria, and had been cursed and broke their oath, but now were free.

They stood in the Chamber of the Stones.

Rowan, Hyrn, and Arienga.

They were taking some respite from the sad and wearying labours below, and the bewildering planning and preparation for the future of Anasaria and the reign of King Rowan. They had had a short sleep but with all that had happened and all that needed to be done, they did not feel like sleeping. Somehow, though, they felt energised.

Hyrn was continuing to bombard Rowan with questions about whether he knew how to be a king.

"Well, if you're King, then won't you need a Queen?" asked Hyrn and he motioned his head slightly towards Arienga just behind them.

Rowan flushed and felt like strangling his brother on the spot.

Hyrn tried to look innocent.

Red-faced Rowan looked around at Arienga. She appeared at first as if she had not heard what Hyrn had said. Then she looked casually at Rowan and he knew that she had. He gathered all his resolve.

"Well what do you think?" he asked, trying to sound nonchalant.

Then he added quickly. "I don't mean now. But in the future."

Arienga stared at him with a look of defiant indignation on her face.

"If you think I'm going to sit around idly while you play King, you can think again," she said.

Rowan's face began to take on a worried and confused look.

"Mind you," she continued. "You will need someone to keep you out of trouble."

She paused again.

"I'll only consider it if I get to make sure that you don't get killed," she said, then added, "or do anything stupid."

"I wouldn't have it any other way," said Rowan, and his weary face broke into a grin.

Hyrn stood facing the two of them, the light of the Twin Stones of Angil shining on his face.

"Good luck," he said.

Hyrn then turned to Arienga with a mischievous smile on his face, and said, "I meant with stopping him from doing anything stupid."

War Approaches

Curion looked down into the cell. He held out a torch.
"He seems unconscious, or…" he said to Mergon.
"He is free now, as all the Abessairians have been freed," said Mergon. "I hope that he lives."

The two Priests lowered the ladder into the cell below. Curion climbed down first followed by Mergon. They approached the supine body of the soldier. It was Mergon who first noticed it.

"He doesn't shine like the…," she began and then was cut short.

The body on the floor sprang to sudden life. In his hand, he held a bone sharpened to a blade. He plunged the blade into the chest of Curion and then leapt and struck Mergon in the face with a clenched fist. As Mergon fell, she momentarily saw Curion collapse to the ground, and saw the soldier dash towards the ladder. His uniform was still the dull brown of an Ultamarian. Her head met the floor, and before consciousness left her, she saw the Ultamarian climbing the ladder towards escape.

And the Mocker, an immense evil, wounded but driven in its purpose, moved determinedly eastwards, destroying anything that stood in its way. It sought a weapon of great power and evil. A weapon forged as if meant for its evil hand. The weapon was hidden, but the centuries of waiting and contemplation had developed a profound certainty of where it lay. As it surged forward, it sent out its evil intent, and an army began to converge in its wake.

The Mocker went to war.